HOMER'S *ILIAD* AND *ODYSSEY*

The Essential Books

HOMER'S *ILIAD* AND *ODYSSEY*

The Essential Books

Translation, Introduction, and Notes
by
Barry B. Powell

New York   Oxford
OXFORD UNIVERSITY PRESS

Oxford University Press is a department of the University of Oxford.

It furthers the University's objective of excellence in research,
scholarship, and education by publishing worldwide.

Oxford   New York
Auckland   Cape Town   Dar es Salaam   Hong Kong   Karachi
Kuala Lumpur   Madrid   Melbourne   Mexico City   Nairobi
New Delhi   Shanghai   Taipei   Toronto

With offices in
Argentina   Austria   Brazil   Chile   Czech Republic   France   Greece
Guatemala   Hungary   Italy   Japan   Poland   Portugal   Singapore
South Korea   Switzerland   Thailand   Turkey   Ukraine   Vietnam

Copyright © 2015 by Oxford University Press.

For titles covered by Section 112 of the US Higher Education
Opportunity Act, please visit www.oup.com/us/he for the
latest information about pricing and alternate formats.

Published in the United States of America by
Oxford University Press
198 Madison Avenue, New York, NY 10016
http://www.oup.com

Library of Congress Cataloging-in-Publication Data
Homer, author.
  [Works. Selections. English]
  Homer's Iliad and Odyssey : the essential books / translation, introduction,
and notes by Barry B. Powell.
    pages cm
  Includes bibliographical references and index.
  ISBN 978-0-19-939407-4 (pbk. : alk. paper) 1. Homer. Iliad. 2. Homer. Odyssey. I. Powell,
Barry B. II. Homer. Iliad. Selections. English. 2014. III. Homer. Odyssey. Selections.
English. 2014. IV. Title.
  PA4025.A15P69 2014
  883'.01--dc23
                                                            2014013435
Printing number: 9 8 7 6 5 4 3 2

Printed in the United States of America
on acid-free paper

To Grace and Spencer

Table of Contents

List of Maps and Figures

Maps

Figures

Acknowledgments

Working with the editorial and marketing team at Oxford University Press has been a huge pleasure. I want to thank John Challice, vice president and publisher; Patrick Lynch, editorial director; Cindy Sweeney, production editor; Lynn Luecken and Christi Sheehan, editorial assistants; Michele Laseau, design director; Eden Kram, marketing manager; and Alice Northover, publicity manager, for their insights and encouragement. I especially want to thank Charles Cavaliere, executive editor, who has now shepherded my *Iliad* and the *Odyssey* all the way through to publication. His unflagging support, attention to detail, and wise advice have made these translations fun. I also am grateful for the advice offered by the outside readers, including Marshall Johnston, Fresno Pacific University; John Lynch, Arizona State University–Barrett; Jacquie Scott Lynch, Arizona State University–Barrett; Margaret Svogun, Salve Regina University; and Walter Stewart, California Lutheran University.

About the Translator

BARRY B. POWELL has lived with the Homeric poems for fifty years and published widely on the topic. In *Homer and the Origin of the Greek Alphabet* (Cambridge, 1991) he advanced the radical thesis that the Greek alphabet was designed specifically to record the texts of Homer, a thesis that has gained gradual acceptance in the scholarly community and was the subject of a conference in Berlin in 2008. In 1997 he published (with Ian Morris) *A New Companion to Homer* (Brill), a standard scholarly companion. In 2004 he published *Homer* (Wiley-Blackwell, second edition, 2007), an overview of the scholarship on the poems and on the poems themselves, the single most widely read book on Homer. In 2009 he published a Greek edition of the poems, *Ilias, Odysseia* (Chester River Press), to accompany Alexander Pope's translation of the poems. He is the author of *Classical Myth*, now in its eighth edition (2014), widely used in college classrooms; *World Myth* (2012); and (with Ian Morris) *The Greeks: History, Culture, and Society* (second edition, 2009). He is the author of *Writing: Theory and History of the Technology of Civilization* (Wiley-Blackwell, 2011).

In 2013 Powell offered his new English translation of the *Iliad* and in 2014 of the *Odyssey*. Based on a thorough familiarity with the poems, the free verse translation, of which this is an abridgement, preserves the clarity and simplicity of the original language while recreating in English the original flavor of the oral-formulaic style.

Maps

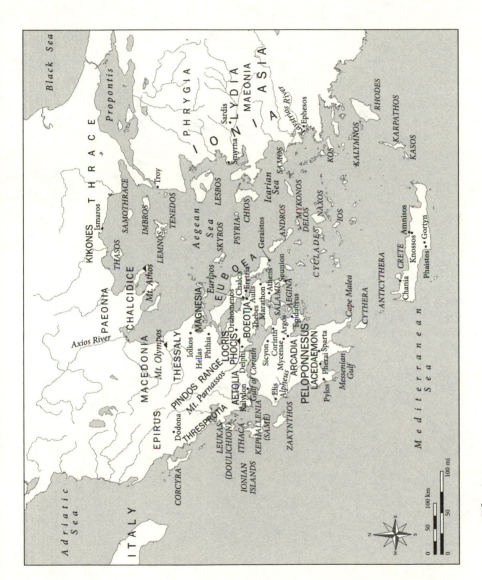

MAP 1   The Aegean

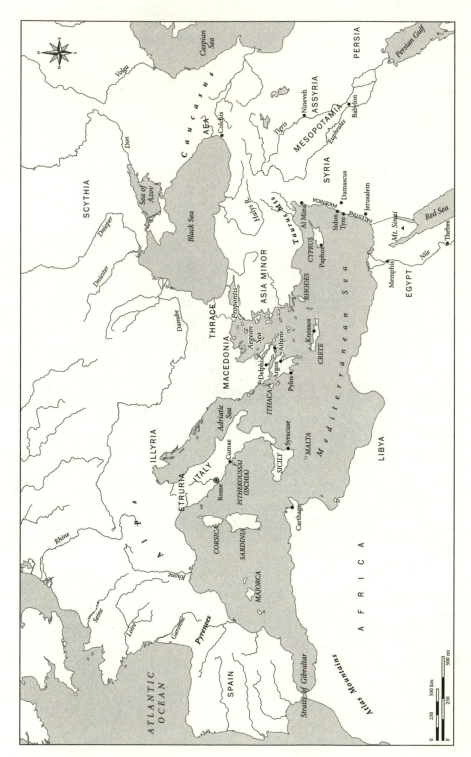

MAP 2   The Mediterranean

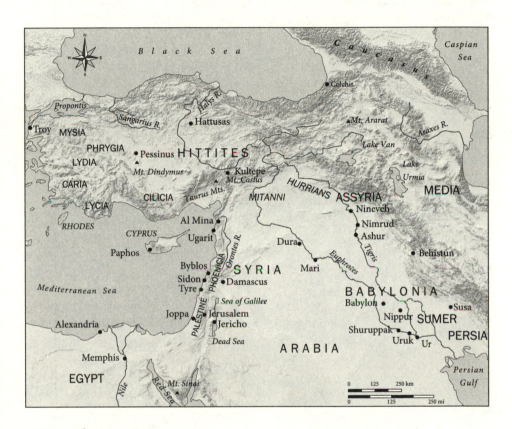

MAP 3 The Near East

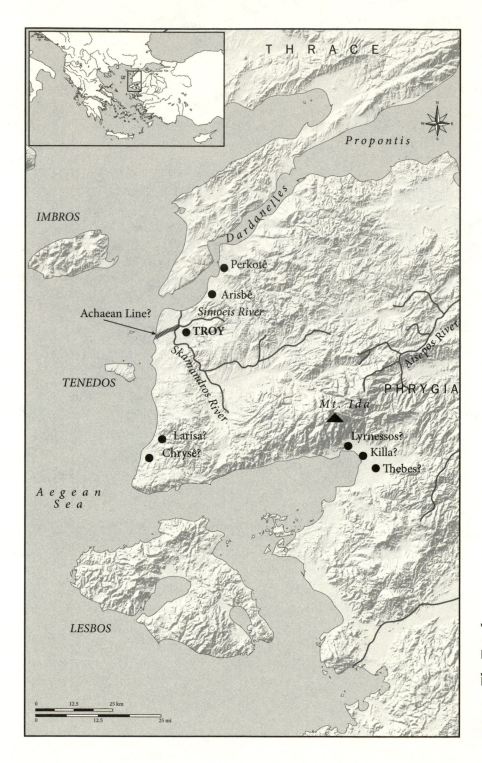

THRACE

Propontis

IMBROS

Dardanelles

● Perkotê

● Arisbê

Simoeis River

Achaean Line? → ● **TROY**

Skamandros River

Aïsepos River

PHRYGIA

TENEDOS

Mt. Ida

● Larisa?

● Chrysê?

● Lyrnessos?

● Killa?

● Thebes?

*A e g e a n
S e a*

LESBOS

MAP 4   **The Troad**

0   12.5   25 km

0   12.5   25 mi

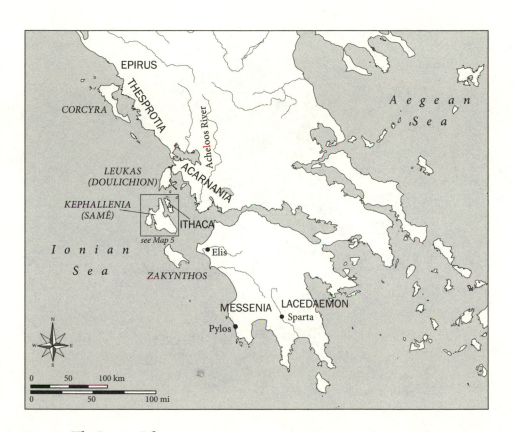

MAP 5   The Ionian Isles

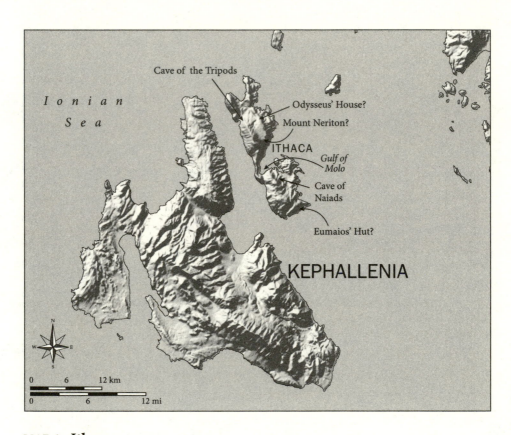

MAP 6 Ithaca

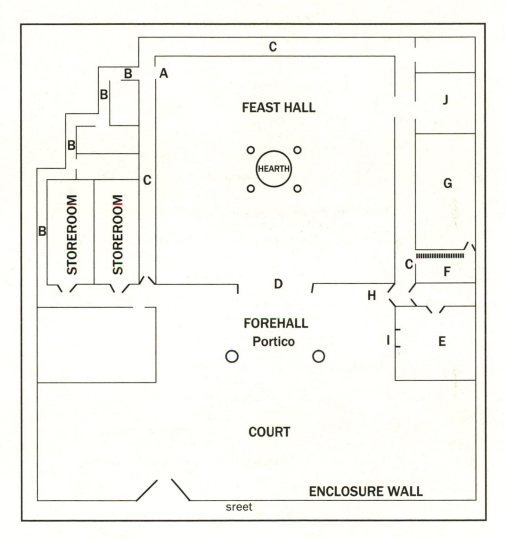

MAP 7   Odysseus' House

Homeric Timeline

c. 1200 BC	Fall of Troy
c. 800 BC	Dictation of the Homeric poems
	Invention of Greek alphabet
from 566 BC	Panathenaic festival
c. 450 BC	Herodotus
c. 200 BC	Alexandrian Vulgate
c. AD 950	Venetus A manuscript of the *Iliad* with marginal notations
c. AD 1000	Laurentianus manuscript of the *Odyssey*
c. AD 1500	First printed edition of the *Iliad* and the *Odyssey* in Italy
from 1598	Chapman's English translation of Homer
AD 1715–1726	Translation of the *Iliad* and the *Odyssey* by Alexander Pope
AD 1788	Publication of Venetus A by Villoison
AD 1795	Wolf's *Prolegomena ad Homerum*
AD 1871	Heinrich Schliemann digs at Troy
AD 1930	Milman Parry creates the oral-formulaic theory
AD 1991	Connection of invention of alphabet with recording of Homeric poems

Introduction

The *Iliad* and the *Odyssey* are the oldest documents in alphabetic writing in the world, the source of all Western culture. They appear mysteriously sometime around 800 BC when Greece was an impoverished, underpopulated backwater without monumental buildings or state institutions or other cultural forms. At this time Greece existed at the edge of the civilized world, the wealthy and highly advanced immense empires of the Near East and Egypt. Suddenly 28,000 lines of hexametric verse appear inscribed on expensive papyri, telling stories of moral complexity that have fascinated readers for nearly three thousand years. The Homeric poems are a mystery, but in the past hundred years we have begun to understand how this miracle of cultural transformation took place.

HOMER, *AOIDOI*, AND THE ALPHABET

FIGURE 0.1   The Walls of Troy. The translator standing before the walls of Troy, built c. 1200 BC.

In the Late Bronze Age, around 1200 BC, a great overseas campaign took place against the city of Troy (Fig. 0.1), located in northwestern Turkey near the entrance to the Dardanelles, the passageway to the Black Sea. We know absolutely nothing about this war, except that it did take place; we may have the names of its main participants. Its alleged events were the province of men called *aoidoi*, "singers," who sang songs about the Trojan War and the adventures men had while coming home after the city was taken. The *aoidoi*, themselves of mysterious origin, were entertainers in the houses of the Greek aristocracy—that is, men who owned enough land and enough slaves to build a house and to lord it over their neighbors.

The *aoidoi* sang their songs about the Trojan War and other wars to the accompaniment of a four-stringed lyre. They were skilled musicians. The *aoidoi* improvised their songs in a rhythmical verse that we can analyze from written examples into a six-beat line, with alternating long and short vowels (called dactylic hexameter), but the *aoidoi* would not themselves have been conscious of the structure of their verse. Rather, it was a kind of feeling that they absorbed from long exposure to older master singers, who had themselves learned it early in life. We cannot say where this technique of composing song comes from—its origins are lost in the mists of time. But the technique did exist and the *aoidoi* were masters of it.

A curious feature to this rhythmical language, learned by absorption, was the use of set phrases or formulas to assist in the formation of the metrical line. Instead of "Achilles," the singer would say "Achilles the fast runner"; instead of "Hector," it was "Hector of the flashing helmet"; instead of Odysseus, he would say "resourceful Odysseus." When the sun rose it was always "When dawn spread out her fingers of rose." The use of such set phrasing allowed the singer to compose without having to think of metrically correct words while giving capsule characterizations of Achilles, Hector, and Odysseus. It also allowed the poet to slow down the rate of the delivery of information while not slowing down the pace of his song, enhancing the singer's ability to hold the audience's attention.

Homer was such an *aoidoi*. He could neither read nor write, and in fact writing was unknown in his world. Homer was no doubt celebrated in his day as the greatest of the *aoidoi*, and evidently he inspired someone to alter a preexisting imported technology of writing to fashion a system capable of recording his verse. The preexisting technology was an entirely phonetic syllabary used in the Eastern Mediterranean that we call the West Semitic syllabary (or sometimes, quite wrongly, the "Phoenician alphabet"), invented perhaps around 1700 BC. East Semitic writing was the famous system called cuneiform ("wedge-shaped") writing, used in Mesopotamia from about 3200 BC. East Semitic cuneiform writing contained many nonphonetic elements (as did Egyptian hieroglyphics) and could not be pronounced from the evidence of the script alone. The entirely phonetic West Semitic writing could not be pronounced either, except by a native speaker with special training, because it consisted of signs that represented only the consonants. The trained scribe would have to provide the actual sound of the writing from his knowledge of the language as a native speaker.

Probably, West Semitic syllabic writing, used in the Hebrew Bible, was evolved as a system used in dictation and for this reason all its signs were phonetic—every sign had a sound attached to it (unlike cuneiform and hieroglyphic writing). Composition never took place on the page, but someone would dictate a poem or chronicle and another man, the scribe, recorded what was said. The Hebrew Bible seems to have been created in this fashion. Men who understood this form of writing were living in Greece in the late ninth and early eighth centuries BC, and we have found examples of West Semitic syllabic writing on Greek soil.

Evidently someone who spoke both Greek and a Semitic tongue, inspired by the greatness of Homer's performances, decided to write down his verse. Of course much of the song would be lost—its music and the emphases of a live performance—but still dictation was the regular way of making a text in the West Semitic system. Because of the differences in the Greek and Semitic languages, this man quickly discovered the inadequacy of a writing that recorded only consonantal values to encode a verse whose rhythms, and meaning, depended on the *alternation* of vowels and consonants. This man, whom we call the Adapter, therefore divided the West Semitic syllabic signs into two categories. One was pronounceable—the five vowels signs—and the other consisted of unpronounceable signs, what we call consonants. He invented the spelling rule that the unpronounceable signs must always be accompanied by one of the five pronounceable vowel signs. In this way he was able to render in symbolic form the approximate outline of the sounds of Homer's verse. The Adapter had just invented the Greek alphabet, the writing that appears on this page.

In attempting to fashion a system that could record the verse of Homer, the Adapter inadvertently created a technology of writing suitable for recording *any* human language. Unlike all preceding systems of writing, the alphabet is pronounceable by anybody, even if you do not know the language. The interior functioning of the alphabet, though its outer forms has many varieties, has not changed for nearly three thousand years. Today this writing is used in virtually every part of the world. It has changed human culture forever.

The Adapter seems to have encouraged the poet to make as long a version of his songs as possible. Modern studies of singers who work like the ancient Greek *aoidoi* show that their songs run about eight hundred lines, while the *Iliad* is around 16,000 lines and the *Odyssey* around 12,000 lines. However, the great pioneer in such studies, an American named Milman Parry (1902–1935) who worked with singers in Bosnia-Herzegovina in the 1930s, got his best singer to sing a song as long as the *Odyssey*. When dictating a song, the singer is freed from the pressure of a live audience, whose attention is limited, and in going slower he is able to contemplate all kinds of elaboration denied to him in a live performance. Apparently the Adapter, the man who invented the Greek alphabet and recorded Homer's songs, encouraged Homer to make them as long as possible. That is why the *Iliad* and *Odyssey* are unnaturally long.

This creates a problem for the modern reader, who can find such extension of themes to be tedious and even boring. I have prepared this abridged version of the complete poems so that the modern reader can grasp the *meaning* of the poems and not be distracted by their length and sometimes exasperating complexity. In this abridgement I have focused on the main thrust of the stories, on the principal events that drive the famous stories that Homer tells.

THE *ILIAD*

The *Iliad* is about *anger*, the first word in the poem. Anger is a valuable emotion for a warrior, enabling him to perform great deeds of valor on the field of battle. But when directed against one's fellow fighters, anger is a highly destructive emotion. The *Iliad* is a study in the destructive effects of anger.

Achilles is angry because after ten years of inconclusive warfare on the windy plain of Troy his military superior, Agamemnon, takes away a girl properly allotted to him in the division of the spoils. The girl is Achilles' "prize," an outward and visible sign of the honor due Achilles as a great fighter. Agamemnon takes away Achilles' prize because he is forced to give up his *own* prize, the girl allotted to *him*, a daughter of a priest of Apollo. When Agamemnon refuses to surrender her to the priest, the priest called on Apollo to send a plague to the Greek camp. Now the troops are dying of disease in addition to being worn down by the war. Agamemnon has no choice but to relinquish the girl, but in taking Achilles' prize as a substitute Agamemnon takes away Achilles' honor, what these fighters struggle for, the goal and purpose of their lives. Hence, the anger of Achilles.

Achilles is tempted to kill Agamemnon on the spot for his behavior, and would have done so except for the interference of Athena, who fears the expedition will collapse. So Achilles contains his anger, but only on Athena's promise that he will someday receive three times as many prizes, three times as much honor.

While Achilles nourishes his anger in his tent, the fighting proceeds. It is a chance for Homer to show the pluck and bravery of various heroes, including the Trojan Hector, the best fighter in Troy. In the meanwhile, Achilles has asked his mother to appeal to Zeus to turn the fighting against his own companions, the Greeks, so they will see how important he was to the campaign and regret that they let Agamemnon get away with taking Achilles' girl. This Zeus does. In despair at the military situation, Agamemnon sends a committee to Achilles to beg him to return. Achilles surprises all by spurning their request, saying that he does not need the prizes that Agamemnon now offers, or the fine opinion of others. "I get my honor from Zeus," he says, to the astonishment of his friends. In his refusal of the embassy Achilles rejects the moral basis of the Greek warrior. He rejects the heroic code, internalizing the basis for value: It is not the opinion of others that counts, but the sure knowledge of his own excellence.

The fighting resumes without Achilles. Soon the Trojans attack the protective wall and threaten to burn the ships. Patroklos, Achilles' companion in arms, comes to Achilles and begs that, if he will not return to the fight, at least Achilles should allow him to go in his place and turn back the Trojan threat. Achilles reluctantly agrees. Patroklos, wearing Achilles' armor, enters the battle. He kills important Trojans but consumed by blood-lust he forgets himself and is killed by Hector.

Achilles' anger against Agamemnon is now transformed into anger against Hector and the Trojans. He returns to the battle, kills many, and finally corners Hector. Achilles kills him before his parents' eyes, who watch from the towers. Achilles returns to the camp, dragging the body behind his chariot. Daily he abuses the corpse, as if such maltreatment will assuage his still burning anger. But it does not.

Thetis, Achilles' mother, tells him that he must give up the corpse. King Priam comes to the camp at night with a large ransom. In a touching scene, Achilles sees that Priam is like his own father, an old man who has lost everything in life, and he is about to lose even more. In viewing the humanity of Priam, in the resolution of the plot, Achilles at last gives up his anger, along with the corpse, and the poem ends. "And so they buried horse-taming Hector."

Commentators commonly refer to the tragedy of Achilles, because in tragedy the hero becomes progressively more isolated, until in death he is completely isolated. Even so, Achilles turns away from the heroic code that Agamemnon has shamelessly abused. He is still alive at the end of the *Iliad*, but he knows that he will die soon, a fate predicted to follow the death of Hector. All is gloom in this poem. All men are united in their suffering. All is from Zeus—the gods are behind everything that happens. In this world one can only do one's best, hoping for renown, hoping to be on people's tongues, who will one day say: "He was the best of the Achaeans." There is nothing more to tell.

THE *ODYSSEY*

The "comic" *Odyssey* follows the "tragic" *Iliad* and is an optimistic counterbalance to the earlier poem. It has a happy ending in which right triumphs, justice is restored, and the family is reunited. It is a folktale (unlike the *Iliad*) with a persistent moral: People blame their suffering on the gods (as in the *Iliad*), but really human suffering results from one's own evil behavior.

For example, as Zeus observes at the beginning of the poem, Aigisthos was warned not to sleep with his cousin Agamemnon's wife, Klytaimnestra, while the commander was at Troy, but he did so anyway. Then when Agamemnon returned from the war, Klytaimnestra and Aigisthos murdered him. For this they paid a terrible price: Agamemnon's son, raised abroad, returned and killed both Klytaimnestra and Aigisthos. The story is parallel to that of Odysseus, with one important exception: Penelope, Odysseus' wife, did not give in to sexual passion, unlike Klytaimnestra. When Odysseus returned from the war, he and his son worked together to kill Penelope's suitors, who hold the same position in the pattern as Aigisthos.

The story begins with Telemachos in Odysseus' house on Ithaca, besieged on every hand by the depredations of suitors who wish to marry his mother. Athena appears to him in disguise and recommends that he travel to Pylos and Sparta on the mainland to inquire after his father, but really so that he may leave his adolescence behind and grow into manhood. At Pylos the septuagenarian Nestor, the oldest fighter at Troy, receives Telemachos, and at Sparta he meets Menelaos and Helen, now settled into a grudging domesticity. He learns of Menelaos' adventures coming home, but nothing of his father.

Meanwhile Odysseus languishes on the island of Kalypso, "concealer," in the navel of the sea. He has been there for seven years after three years of wandering. We might say that Odysseus is in the land of the dead, across the trackless waters. Only the gods can bring him back to life. Hermes, the god who connects this world with the next, comes to him and tells Kalypso she must relinquish her captive. Odysseus sails away on a raft he has made. He gets into a terrible storm sent by his enemy Poseidon, for water is death. The raft breaks up and he is thrown naked, like a new-born babe, onto the island of Scheria, land of the Phaeacians, where he takes refuge in a womb-like cave of brush.

On the next day, the young princess of the island goes to the shore to wash her clothes in preparation for her wedding day. Odysseus appears before her naked—the sexual tension is high. Odysseus is like the suitor for whom Nausicaä is intended. There at the house of the king of Scheria, at a banquet, he tells the famous story of his wanderings. At first Odysseus and his men are marauders, attacking the Thracian coast, but with a disastrous result. From there they lose their way on the high seas and undergo a series of adventures in which the enemy is forgetfulness of home (the Lotus Eater), consumption by a death-demon who lives in a darkened cave (Polyphemos), the treacherous greed of his own men (the Wind-King), consumption by cannibal giants (the Laestrygonians, a doublet of Polyphemos), transformation into beasts (Kirkê), seduction by the power of song (Sirens), being swallowed whole (Skylla and Charybdis), and the hostility of the gods (the Cattle of the Sun).

These stories often turn on the folktale prohibition: Whatever you do, don't . . . So Odysseus' men were told not to open the bag of wind, and not to eat the Cattle of the Sun, but they did so anyway. The stories of Odysseus follow a pattern of endangerment, defeat of the enemy, then recognition. So Polyphemos eats several of his men, but when Odysseus escapes from the cave he shouts out, "I am Odysseus!" In the cave he was Nbdy. When Kirkê fails to enchant him, she cries out, "You must be Odysseus!" Odysseus is the folktale trickster who overcomes his enemy by stealth: He gives Polyphemos a false name that saves him; he resists Kirkê's charms through possessing the magic herb *moly*; he resists the Sirens by being tied to his mast, stuffing the ears of his shipmates with wax.

These stories depend on symbolism for their effects, and on the fact that they are all told at one remove from the poem's main narrative, at the banquet of the Phaeacians. But when Odysseus returns to Ithaca, he exercises many of the same tricks to overcome the 108 suitors who, like the dragon in folktale, consume his substance and sexually threaten his wife. He enters the palace in disguise, unrecognized. He tells many lying tales about his past. He strings the bow at the contest of the bow. He then is recognized as he casts aside his rags. Without mercy he destroys the enemy, marries the girl, and institutes a reign of peace and order.

HOMER THE MORAL GENIUS

In his two poems Homer gives us a picture of all of life: of its grim fatality, relieved only by the recognition that we are all together in our suffering; and of the triumph of good over evil in the slaughter of the rapacious and thoughtless suitors. It is a mature vision, not meant for young people, those too naïve to understand the ambiguities in the values by which they live; those too foolish to understand the need for restraint in sex and food. We can only be astonished at the modernity of these stories, coming from a frankly primitive world of a very long time ago. The perplexities and conundrums they present are very much alive today. Why do I live? What is valuable? What is the price of illegal behavior?

Good questions, then as now.

Selections from the *Iliad*

BOOK 1. *The Anger of Achilles*

The anger° sing, O goddess, of Achilles, the son of Peleus,
the destructive anger that brought ten thousand pains to the
Achaeans and sent many brave souls of fighting men to the house
of Hades and made their bodies a feast for dogs
and all kinds of birds. For such was the will of Zeus. 5

Sing the story from the time when Agamemnon, the son
of Atreus, and godlike Achilles first stood apart in contention.
Which god was it who set them to quarrel? Apollo, the son
of Leto and Zeus. Enraged at the king, Apollo sent an
evil plague through the camp, and the people died. 10
For the son of Atreus had not respected Chryses, a praying
man. Chryses had come to the swift ships of the Achaeans
to free his daughter. He brought boundless ransom, holding
in his hands wreaths of Apollo, who shoots from afar,
on a golden staff. He begged all the Achaeans, but above all 15
he begged the two sons of Atreus, the marshals of the people:°

"O you sons of Atreus, and all the other Achaeans,
whose shins are protected in bronze, may the gods who
have houses on Olympos let you sack the city of Priam!
May you also come again safely to your homes. But set free 20
my beloved daughter. Accept this ransom. Respect
the far-shooting son of Zeus, Apollo."

All the Achaeans
shouted out that, yes, they should respect the priest
and take the shining ransom. But the proposal was not
to the liking of Agamemnon, the son of Atreus. 25
Brusquely he sent the man away with a powerful word:
"Let me not find you near the hollow ships, either

---

1 *anger*: The Greek word is *mênis*, an archaic word used only of Achilles and the gods. It is the first word in the
poem and defines its theme.

16 *marshals of the people*: That is, Agamemnon and Menelaos, the leaders of the expedition.

hanging around or coming back later. Then your scepter
and wreath of the god will do you no good! I shall not
30 let her go! Old age will come upon her first in my
house in Argos, far from her homeland. She shall
scurry back and forth before my loom and she will
come every night to my bed. So don't rub me
the wrong way, if you hope to survive!"

                    So he spoke.
35 The old man was afraid and he obeyed Agamemnon's
command. He walked in silence along the resounding
sea. Going apart, the old man prayed to his lord
Apollo, whom Leto, whose hair is beautiful, bore:
"Hear me, you of the silver bow, who hover over
40 CHRYSÊ and holy KILLA, who rule with power
the island of TENEDOS°—lord of plague!° If I ever
roofed a house of yours so that you were pleased
or burned the fat thigh bones of bulls and goats,
then fulfill for me this desire: May the Danaäns° pay
45 for my tears with your arrows!"

                    So he spoke in prayer.
Phoibos° Apollo heard him, and he came from the top
of Olympos with anger in his heart. He had on his back a bow
and a closed quiver. The arrows clanged on his shoulder
as he sped along in his anger. He went like the night.

50   He sat then apart from the ships. He let fly an
arrow. Terrible was the twang of the silver bow. At first
he attacked the mules and the fleet hounds. Then he
let his swift arrows fall on the men, striking them
with piercing shafts. Ever burned thickly the pyres
55 of the dead.

---

41 ... *Tenedos*: See Maps I and IV: The first time that a place name on one of the seven maps appears in a Book,
the name will be in SMALL CAPS. "Chryses" is simply "the man from "Chrysê."

41 *lord of plague*: In the Greek, Chryses calls Apollo "Smintheus," seeming to mean "he of the mice," that is,
god of plague because that is what mice or rats bring (rats are "big mice" in modern Greek). Remains of a
temple to Apollo Smintheus have been found in the Troad. Apollo "shoots from afar" because his arrows are
the arrows of disease—invisible, mysterious, deadly.

44 *Danaäns*: Homer indifferently calls the invaders "Achaeans," "Danaäns," and "Argives," never "Greeks." The
first word should mean "the men of ACHAEA," perhaps a general name for Greece (though later a territory
located in the northwestern Peloponnesus); the second is a tribal name; the third should mean "the men
from the city of ARGOS" in the Peloponnesus.

46 *Phoibos*: An epithet of uncertain origin and meaning, though often interpreted as meaning *pure, radiant*.

For nine days he strafed the camp with his
arrows, but on the tenth Achilles called the people to assembly.
The goddess with white arms, Hera, had put the thought
in his mind, because she pitied the Danaäns when she saw
them dying.

      When they were all together and assembled,
Achilles, the fast runner, stood up and spoke: "Sons of Atreus,   60
I think we are going back home, beaten again, if we
escape death at all and war and disease do not together
destroy the Achaeans. So let us ask some seer or
holy man, a dream-explainer—dreams are from Zeus!—
who can tell us why Phoibos Apollo is angry.   65
Is it for some vow, or sacrifice? Maybe the god
can accept the scent of lambs, of goats that we kill,
perhaps he will come out to ward off this plague."
So speaking he took his seat.

      Kalchas arose, the son of
Thestor, by far the best of the bird-seers, who knows   70
what's what, what will happen, what has happened.
He had led the ships of the Achaeans to Ilion° by his seership,
which Phoibos Apollo had given him. He spoke to the troops,
wishing them well: "Achilles, you urge me, you whom Zeus
loves, to speak of the anger of Apollo, the king who strikes   75
from afar. Well, then I will tell you. But first you must
consider carefully. You must swear to me that you will
defend me in the assembly and with might of hand. For I'm
afraid of enraging the Argive who has the power here, whom
all the Achaeans obey. For a chief has more power against   80
someone who causes him anger, a man of lower rank.
Maybe he swallows his anger for a day, but ever
after he nourishes resentment in his heart, until he
brings it to fulfillment. Swear then, Achilles, that you will
protect me."   85

      The fast runner Achilles answered him:
"Have courage! Tell your prophecy, whatever you know.
By Apollo, dear to Zeus, to whom you yourself
pray when you reveal prophecies to the Danaäns—not so

---

72 *Ilion:* Another name for Troy.

long as I am alive, and look upon this earth, shall anyone
90   of all the Danaäns lay heavy hands upon you
beside the hollow ships, not even if you mean
Agamemnon, who claims to be best of the Achaeans."

The seeing-man, who had no fault, was encouraged,
and he spoke: "The god is not angry for a vow, or sacrifice,
95   but because of the priest whom Agamemnon dishonored
when he would not release the man's daughter. He would not take
the ransom. For this reason the far-shooter has caused these pains,
and he will go on doing so. He won't withdraw the hateful disease
from the Danaäns until Agamemnon gives up the girl with
100   the flashing eyes, without pay, without ransom, and until he leads
a holy sacrifice to Chrysê. Only then might we succeed in
persuading the god to stop."

So speaking, he sat down. The heroic
son of Atreus, Agamemnon whose rule is wide, then stood up,
deeply troubled by the words of Kalchas. His black heart
105   was filled with a tremendous rage, and his eyes shone
like blazing fire. First he addressed Kalchas, his eyes filled
with hate: "Prophet of evil, never have you said a word
pleasing to me! You only like prophecies of evil! Never have
you uttered a word of good, nor brought a good thing to pass.
110   And now you say in your 'prophecy' before the Danaäns that
the far-shooter causes us sorrow because I refused to take
the shining ransom for the daughter of Chryses! Because I prefer
to keep her in my house! In fact I like her better than Klytaimnestra,
my wedded wife. She is not inferior in beauty, in looks,
115   or in character, or in her skills in handwork. Nonetheless, I am willing
to let her go, if that is best. I'd rather that the folk prospered than
it perished. But you'd better get another prize for me. It's not right
that I alone of all the Argives be without a prize!
It is not right, for you see that my prize goes elsewhere."

120   Then answered him Achilles, the fast runner, like a god:
"Son of Atreus, most honored sir, most *greedy* of all!
How are the Achaeans, who are generous, going to give you a prize?
We have no wealth stacked in a warehouse, but everything
we've taken in our raids has been given out a long time ago.
125   We can't gather this stuff up again. Look—give up
the girl to the god. Then the Achaeans will give you three
or four times as much loot, if Zeus grants us to sack the high-walled
city of Troy."

King Agamemnon answered as follows:
"Don't, Achilles—though of good birth and 'like to a god'—
don't try to trick me with your mind! You will not get past me,   130
and you will not persuade me. Do you want to stand there,
yourself with a prize, while I sit without one? Do you order me
to give up this girl? If the great-hearted Achaeans will give me
a prize, fitting it to my heart, so that it will be of equal
value . . . but if not, I will *myself* take your own prize!   135
Or I will go to Ajax and take his, or I will go to Odysseus
and take his prize.° The man will be angry, no matter who.
But let us think this over at some later time. Come,
let us draw a black ship into the shining sea.
Let us get together appropriate rowers and load up   140
a sacrifice, and let us place Chryseïs° of the lovely cheeks
within. Let one man who knows what to do be the leader,
either Ajax, or Idomeneus, or brilliant Odysseus—or *you*,
son of Peleus, most ferocious of men. Then with our sacrifice
we might calm the far-shooter."   145

                    But Achilles, the fast runner,
glowered from beneath his brows and said: "Shameless fool!
Greedy, how now can your speech gladly persuade any
of the Achaeans either to go on an ambush or to fight
in the hand-to-hand? *I* at least did not come here to war
because of the Trojan spearmen. They have done nothing   150
to me. They have not taken my cattle, nor horses.
Not in Phthia° with its rich plowlands,
the nurse of men, have they laid waste the harvest.
For many are the shadowy mountains that lie between us,
and the echoing sea. No, we followed you—you dog   155
without shame!—that you might be happy, that you
might win honor from the Trojans for Menelaos —
and for yourself! Dog! You don't ever think about that,
do you? Are you troubled by that? You threaten yourself
to take *my* prize, for which I labored sorely?   160

---

137 *prize*: The Greek word is *geras*, which determines a warrior's *timê*, "honor," really "value." The woman, or
     geras, his "prize," is the external and visible testimony to *timê*, his "honor," without which life is not worth
     living.

141 *Chryseïs*: Chryseïs just means "daughter of Chryses," as Briseïs is "daughter of Briseus." Girls did not nec-
     essarily have their own names but were named after their father. *Chryses*, is the father; *Chrysê* is the place;
     Chryseïs is the daughter.

152 *Phthia*: Phthia (**thī**-a) is the homeland of Achilles in southern THESSALY, centering on the Spercheios River.
     See Map I.

The sons of the Achaeans gave her to me. I never
get a prize equal to yours, when the Achaeans take some
populous city of the Trojans, though I myself
bear the hard brunt of the fighting. When the spoils
165 are divided, your prize is always bigger. *I* get
some small, little darling thing and slouch off
to my ships, worn out with the war.
                              "All right, I'm off
to Phthia. I think it's better to head away in my beaked ships
than to hang around here and pile up endless wealth
170 for you, while I remain without honor!"

                              The king over men,
Agamemnon, then said in reply: "Go then, if that's what you
want to do. Don't stay on my account. There are plenty who
will honor me, and Zeus above all, whose wisdom is great.
You are most hateful to me of all the god-reared chieftains!
175 You ever love contention and war and battle. If you are strong,
that is because some god gave you the gift. Go home with
your ships and your companions. Rule over the Myrmidons!
I don't like you, I don't care if you are angry.
                              "But I tell you what
I'm going to do. Just as Phoibos Apollo takes away Chryseïs—
180 and I'll send her in a ship with an escort—even so
I will myself come and take the high-cheeked Briseïs,
your prize, that you might know how much stronger I am
than you, and so that any other may think twice
before saying that he is my equal and liken himself to me
185 to my face!"

        So he spoke. A great hurt arose inside
the son of Peleus, and his heart within his shaggy
breast was divided in two ways, either to draw his sharp
sword from his thigh, break up the assembly, then kill
the son of Atreus, or whether he should stop his anger,
190 bridle his tumult. While he pondered in his heart and in his spirit,
he drew out the great sword from its scabbard, but Athena came
from heaven—the goddess Hera of the white arms sent her
because she loved and cared for both men equally.

        Athena stood behind him and she seized the son of
195 Peleus by his light-colored hair. Only he could see her.

FIGURE 1.1   The anger of Achilles.   The seated Agamemnon holds the scepter of authority and sits on a throne, his lower body wrapped in a robe. Achilles, in "heroic nudity," pulls his sword from its scabbard ("heroic nudity" is an ancient artistic convention of unclear meaning, whereby heroes are shown without clothes). Athena, from behind, seizes Achilles by the hair. Roman mosaic, c. 1st century AD.

He was amazed. He turned around, and right away he recognized
Pallas Athena.° Her eyes shone with a terrible light. He spoke
to her with words that flew like arrows: "Why have you come,
daughter of Zeus who carries the goatskin fetish?°
200　To see the insolence of Agamemnon, son of Atreus?
But I will tell you this, and I think it shall come
to pass—through his insolence he will quickly lose his life!"

　　　Flashing-eyed Athena° answered him: "I have come
from heaven to stop your anger, if I can persuade you.
205　White-armed Hera sent me, because she loves
and cares for both of you. So come, let go
of this contention. Unhand your sword. Abuse him
with words. Tell him how things will be. For I promise you
that this will come to pass: You shall one day have
210　three times as many gifts because of this violence.
Hold back, trust us."

　　　　　Achilles, the fast runner, answered:
"What can I do but obey the two of you, goddess,
even though I am seething? It is better that way. The gods
listen to him who obeys." And he stayed his heavy
215　hand on the silver sword-hilt, and back into the scabbard
he thrust the great sword, not disobeying the word of Athena.
She went off to Olympos to the house of Zeus who carries
the goatskin fetish, to be with the other gods.

　　　But the son of Peleus again spoke violent words
220　to the son of Atreus. In no way had he abandoned his anger:
"Drunkard, dog-eyes, with a deer's heart—you don't arm with
your people and go out to war, nor dare in your heart to go on
an ambush with the best of the Achaeans. To you that is death!
Much better to take your ease in the broad camp of the Achaeans
225　and steal the gifts from whoever opposes you. Devourer

197　*Pallas Athena*: The "Pallas" is sometimes explained as from a Greek word meaning "to brandish," so the
　　meaning would be "[spear]-brandishing Athena." But probably it is preHellenic, not a Greek name.

199　*...fetish*: The Greek is *aegis*, which means "goatskin," maybe in origin either a shield, or a "medicine" bag
　　containing power objects. In Homer, the *aegis* is an object that offers divine protection or inspires terror.
　　In art somewhat later than Homer, the *aegis* has become a cloak with snake-head tassels and a Gorgon's
　　head in the center, worn more by Athena than Zeus. Apollo also occasionally carries the *aegis*.

203　*flashing-eyed Athena*: The Greek is *glaukôpis*, but it is hard to say whether it means "owl-eyed," "gray-eyed,"
　　or "flashing-eyed," the translation I have preferred.

of the people, 'king,' you rule worthless men. Otherwise
this would be your last act of insolence, O son of Atreus!

    "But I will tell you, and swear a great oath: By this scepter,
which will never grow leaves or shoots since first it left
its stump in the mountains. It won't again grow green. The bronze   230
has stripped its leaves and bark, and now the Achaeans
hold it when they judge, when they guard the laws given
by Zeus—this oath will be mighty among you! One day
the longing for Achilles will be great among the sons of the Achaeans!
But you will not be able to ward off evil, though your sorrow   235
is great, when many fall dead at the hands of man-killing Hector.
You will gnaw your hearts that when angry you did not honor
the best of the Achaeans!"

               So spoke the son of Peleus,
and he threw the scepter on the ground, fitted with nails
of gold. Then he sat down. But the son of Atreus on his side   240
still steamed with anger when Nestor stood up, whose voice
was sweet, the clear-voiced speaker of the men of Pylos,
from whose tongue flowed a sound sweeter than honey.
Two generations of mortals had passed away in his time,
men begotten and raised with him in sandy Pylos, but now   245
he was king in the third generation. He hoped to calm things
down: "Alas, I think a big sorrow has come to the land
of the Achaeans. If Priam and his sons and the other Trojans knew
about you two quarreling, they would greatly rejoice—you two,
best in counsel and best in battle! Listen—you are   250
both younger than I. When I was young, I mixed with men
more warlike than you. They never looked down upon me.
I have never seen such men since, nor shall I, men such as
Peirithoös and Dryas, the shepherd of the people, and Kaeneus
and Exadios and Polyphemos, like a god, and Theseus, the son   255
of Aegeus,° a likeness of the deathless ones. Most powerful of men
raised on the earth were these men. Most powerful they were.
They warred with the strong beasts° in the mountains and destroyed
them. I came from Pylos, far, far away, to mingle with
these men who had summoned me. I fought to the best of   260
my ability. I say that no one today who walks the earth

254–256 *Peirithoös . . . Aegeus:* The first names are princes of the Lapith tribe, who lived in Thessaly. Theseus, son
        of Aegeus, is from Athens. According to the story known elsewhere, at the wedding of Peirithoös the
        savage Centaurs tried to rape the bride and her attendants. A great war broke out in which Theseus, a
        friend of Peirithoös, took part.

258 *strong beasts:* It is not sure that Homer understood the Centaurs to be part horse, part man.

could have fought these men. They listened to my advice,
and believed it. So you believe it too. It is better that you do.
  "You, Agamemnon, though strong, do not take this girl,
265 but let it go—the sons of the Achaeans first gave her to him.
And you, son of Peleus, do not wish to contend head-on with a king.
A chief who bears the scepter holds a special honor,
one to whom Zeus has given glory. If you are a stronger
fighter, and your mother is a goddess, yet he is more powerful
270 because he rules more men. Son of Atreus, you stop your anger.
I beg you—let go your wrath at Achilles, who is like
a huge wall to the Achaeans in the midst of destructive war."

  King Agamemnon answered him as follows:
"You have spoken as is fit, old man, everything you say.
275 But this man wants to be over everyone. He wants
to be king over all, to rule every man, and to boss
everyone around. But there is someone who is not persuaded!
Just because the gods who live forever made him a spearman,
do they also egg him on to go around casting insults?"

280 But shining Achilles broke in and said: "Surely
I would be called a coward and of no account if I were
to yield to you in everything that you say. You may give others
your commands, but give no orders to me. I don't think
I will obey you. And I will tell you something else.
285 Think it over. I shall not come to blows over the girl,
neither with you nor with anyone else, the girl whom
you have and now take away. But of my other
possessions laid up beside my swift black ship,
you shall carry away not a thing against my will.
290 Go ahead and try it!—then these too will know.
Swiftly your black blood will run down my spear!"

  And so these two contended in savage words.
They stood up. The assembly dissolved beside the ships
of the Achaeans. The son of Peleus made his way
295 to the huts and his well-proportioned ships. He went with
Patroklos, the son of Menoitios, and his companions.

  But the son of Atreus dragged a swift ship to the sea.
He chose twenty oarsmen. He loaded a sacrifice for the god.
He placed high-cheeked Chryseïs in the boat.
300 Odysseus, the devious man, went along as leader.
They mounted the boat and sailed the watery paths.

Now the son of Atreus urged the people to purify
themselves. They purified themselves and threw the waters
they washed with into the sea. Then they sacrificed to Apollo
perfect bulls and goats beside the shore of the sea   305
that grows no crops. The scent spun, twisting in the smoke,
to heaven. And so they labored throughout the camp.

But Agamemnon forgot not the quarrel, when he
first threatened Achilles. He called to Talthybios and Eurybates,
his heralds and busy comrades in arms: "Go to the tent of   310
Achilles, son of Peleus. Take the high-cheeked Briseïs
by the hand and lead her here. If he won't give her,
I will myself go there with a large band of men and take her!
This will be shivery for him!"

                So speaking he sent
the two men forth, and he laid on a solemn command.   315
They walked in silence along the sea that grows no crops.
They came to the tents and ships of the Myrmidons. They found
him sitting beside his tent and black ship. Achilles
was not happy to see them. The heralds stood there terrified,
in awe of the king. They did not speak nor ask questions.   320

But Achilles knew in his heart, and he said the following:
"Greetings, heralds of Zeus and messengers of men.
Come closer. It's not your fault, but Agamemnon's, who sent
you forth on account of the girl Briseïs. But come,
Patroklos, of Zeus's line, bring out the girl. Give her   325
to them to take away. And may these two men
be witnesses before the gods and before all men who die,
and before that arrogant king—if ever in time to come
you need me to ward off a destructive fate from the troops . . .
The man is mad! He does not know how to   330
look before and after, so the Achaeans might fight
in safety beside the ships."

                So he spoke. Patroklos
obeyed his companion and brought high-cheeked Briseïs
from the tent and delivered her to the men. Again they walked
along the ships of the Achaeans, and the girl went, unwilling, with them.   335

But Achilles burst into tears, and he withdrew
apart from his companions. He sat on the shore beside
the gray sea. He stared over the huge deep.

FIGURE 1.2 The Taking of Briseïs. Achilles sits in a chair holding his spear while Patroklos, his back turned to the viewer, hands over Briseïs to Agamemnon's men. To the far left stands Talthybios with his herald's wand. Beside him is Odysseus in his skull-cap. The helmeted man beside Odysseus would be Big Ajax. Achilles' tutor Phoenix stands behind Achilles' chair. Other warriors stand in the background. Roman fresco, c. 1st century AD.

He raised his arms and prayed to his dear mother:
"Mother, because you bore me to a short life, Olympian   340
Zeus, who thunders on high, ought to have put honor
in my hands. But he has given me no honor at all. For the
son of Atreus, whose rule is wide, has dishonored me.
He has come and taken my girl."

               Thus he spoke, tears
streaming down his face. His reverend mother heard him   345
as she sat beside her aged father in the depths of the sea.
Swiftly she came forth like a mist from the gray sea. She sat
down before him, as he wept. She took him by the hand
and she spoke his name: "My son, why do you weep?
What sorrow has come to your heart? Tell me, don't hide it,   350
that we both may know."

               Then, groaning heavily spoke
Achilles, the fast runner: "You know! Why do I need
to tell the whole story when you already know? We went
to Thebes, the sacred city of Eëtion.° We burned it to the ground
and took everything. The sons of the Achaeans then divided the loot   355
among themselves. For the son of Atreus they chose
Chryseïs, whose cheeks are beautiful. Chryses then came
to the fast ships of the bronze-shirted Achaeans, a holy man,
a priest of Apollo the far-shooter. He wanted
to free his daughter, and he brought boundless ransom,   360
holding the wreaths of Apollo, the far-shooter,
around a golden staff. And he begged all the Achaeans, and
above all the two sons of Atreus, the leaders of the people.
All the Achaeans shouted we should respect the holy man
and accept the shining ransom. But Agamemnon, the son   365
of Atreus, did not like this, and he roughly sent the man
away, and lay on a strong word. Angry, the old man
went off. Apollo heard him as he prayed,
because he was dear to the god, and he sent an evil
shaft against the Argives. The people died like flies.   370
The missiles of the god fell everywhere through the broad
camp of the Achaeans. A knowing prophet explained
the doing of the god who strikes from a long way off.

---

354 *Thebes . . . Eëtion*: Not of course the Thebes in Greece or Egypt; see Map IV. Eëtion was king of the Thebes
    near Troy. Because Chryseïs was taken in Thebes and not in Chrysê, perhaps she was married to someone
    in Thebes, although she is from Chrysê. It is not clear why Thebes is "sacred," but cities often are, especially
    Troy.

Straightaway I was first to insist that we appease the god,
375 but anger seized the son of Atreus. He stood straight up
and lay down a threat, which now has come to pass.
The bright-eyed Achaeans are taking Chryseïs in a fast ship
to Chrysê, and they have gifts for the god. As for the other girl,
Briseïs, the heralds have taken her from my tent,
380 she whom the sons of the Achaeans gave to me.
        "But you, if you can, protect your son. Go to
Olympos and beg Zeus, if ever you have pleased him
in word or in something you've done. For I often heard
you boast in my father's halls that you alone
385 of the gods fended off disaster from the son of Kronos,
he of the dark clouds, when the other Olympians
wanted to tie him up—Hera and Poseidon
and Pallas Athena. But you went to him and set him
free from the bonds, having swiftly called
390 the hundred-hander whom gods call Briareos, but men call
Aigaion,° to high Olympos. He was stronger than his father Ouranos. He sat
down beside the son of Kronos, glorying in his power.
The blessed gods were frightened of him and did not bind Zeus.°
        "Remind him of this incident. Sit by his side.
395 Seize his knees—to see if he might help the Trojans
pen the Achaeans by the prows of their ships, their backs
to the sea. May they die like dogs! Thus may all share
in the wisdom of their chief, and Agamemnon, the wide ruler,
may know that he went insane when he dishonored
400 the best of the Achaeans!"

        Thetis answered him, pouring
down tears: "O my child, why ever did I bear you,
born to sorrow? I wish that you might have stayed
by the ships without weeping, without pain, since your life
is fated to be all too short. As it is, your fate is soon
405 upon you. You are more wretched than all men.
Therefore I bore you, in our halls, to an evil life.

        "I will make your request of Zeus, who delights
in the thunder. I will myself ascend Olympos, clad in snow,

---

391 *Aigaion:* The significance of alternate names for men and gods is unknown. It occurs several times
in the *Iliad.*

393 *... bind Zeus:* The story about Thetis saving Zeus from binding by Hera, Poseidon, and Athena is striking.
Her role in saving Zeus from a conspiracy shows her to be more powerful than we expect from merely being
the mother of Achilles.

to see if I can persuade him. You stay here, nursing
your anger, beside the swift ships. Don't fight any more.   410
Yesterday Zeus went to Ocean, to the Aethiopians who do
no wrong, to a feast, and all gods went with him. On the twelfth day
he will return to Olympos. Then I shall go to the bronze-tiled
house of Zeus. I will take him by the knees and I think I will
persuade him."   415

      So speaking, she went off. She left Achilles
there in his wrath on account of the slim-waisted woman,
whom Agamemnon took away by force, against his will.

  But Odysseus came to Chrysê with the sacrifice.
When they got inside the deep harbor, they folded up the sail
and placed it in the black ship. They quickly loosened   420
the ropes and let down the mast into the mast-holder. They rowed
to a good mooring. They threw out the anchor stones and bound
up the stern with cables. They went forth on the shore
of the sea, driving before them the sacrifice to Apollo,
who shoots from a long way off. Chryseïs got out   425
of the sea-going boat. Leading her to the altar, the clever
Odysseus placed her in the hands of her father and said:
"O Chryses, the king of men Agamemnon has sent me here
to give to you your child and to perform holy sacrifice
to Phoibos on behalf of the Danaäns, who would like to appease   430
the lord, who brings agonizing pain to the Argives."

  So saying he placed her in Chryses' arms. The father
received his dear child with joy. The men quickly set up
the sacrifice around the altar, made of dressed stone.
They washed their hands and took up the barley grains.   435
Chryses raised his hands on their behalf and prayed
in a loud voice: "Hear me, you of the silver bow,
who hover over Chrysê and sacred Killa and are king
with power over the island of Tenedos. You already
heard me when I prayed to you, and you gave me honor.   440
You mightily struck the Danaäns! So fulfill for me now
my new request: Let go from these Danaäns destructive
plague!"

  So he spoke in prayer. Phoibos Apollo
heard him. When they had prayed and sprinkled the barley,
they first drew back the heads of the cattle, then they cut   445

their throats. They skinned them out. They cut out the bones
of the thighs, hid them in two layers of fat, and placed
raw meat on top. The old man burned them
on splinters of wood. He poured out shining wine
450   on top. The young men beside him held out their forks
with five prongs. When he had burned the thigh bones
and they had tasted the guts, they cut up the rest
and spitted the pieces. They roasted the meat with care.
Then they drew it from the spits. When they were done
455   with their work and had prepared their meal, they ate.
Nor did their hearts lack for anything in the common feast.

When they had put aside their desire for drink and food,
the young men filled the mixing bowls to the brim
with wine. They poured libations from every cup,
460   then distributed the wine all around. They beseeched
the god with song, singing the Apollo-hymn,
the young men of the Achaeans, singing a hymn to him
who works from far away. And he was delighted
to hear them.

Then the sun went down and darkness came.
465   They slept by the sterns of the ships. When dawn came,
spreading her rose-colored fingers, they set out for the broad
camp of the Achaeans. Apollo who works from a long way
off sent them a favorable breeze. They raised
the mast and spread the white sail. The wind filled
470   the middle of the sail. The purple waves roared around
the keel of the ship as it went. She ran over the waves,
making her way forward. When they arrived at the broad camp
of the Achaeans, they dragged the black ship high on the sand
of the shore. They fitted long props beneath. The men
475   scattered to their tents and their ships.

But the god-reared
son of Peleus, Achilles, the fast runner, continued to nurse
his anger, sitting beside the fast ships. He never went
to the place of assembly, where men win glory, nor ever
to the war. He wasted away in his heart, remaining idle,
480   though he longed for the cry of war and the fight.

When twelve days had passed, all the gods, who live
forever, went in a band to Olympos, with Zeus in the lead.

Thetis did not forget the request of her son. She arose from
the wave of the sea. Early in morning she went up
to heaven and Olympos. She found the son of Kronos,   485
who sees things from far off, sitting apart from the others
on a steep peak of Olympos, which has many ridges. She sat
down near him and took hold of his knees with her left hand,
while with her right she gripped him beneath the chin.
Beseeching, she spoke to Zeus the king, the son of Kronos: 490

"Zeus, our father, if ever I have helped you among the
immortals either in word or in something I did,
fulfill for me this desire. Give honor to my son
who, more than others, is born to a quick death.
But as it is, now the king of men Agamemnon   495
has not given him honor. He has taken away his prize!
He holds it! But give him honor, O Olympian, counselor Zeus.
Give power to the Trojans until the Achaeans honor my son
and increase his honor!" So she spoke.

                            The cloud-gatherer
Zeus said nothing, but sat in silence for a long time.   500
As Thetis had clasped his knees, so now she held him
close, and asked again: "Make me this fast promise,
bow your head to it—or turn me away, you have nothing
to fear, so that I may know how of all the gods I have
the least honor . . ."   505

                            Zeus, who assembles the clouds,
was deeply disturbed. He said, "This is a bad
business. You will set me on to quarrel with Hera, who
will anger me with her words of reproach. Even as it is
she is always on my back among the deathless gods, saying
that in the battle I help the Trojans. So leave   510
now or she may notice something! Yes, I'll take care
of this. I'll bring it to pass. Here, let me bow
my head to you, so that you will believe me.
For this is the surest sign I give among the immortals—
I will never take it back. It is no illusion. It will always   515
come to pass, whatever I nod my head to."

Then the son of Kronos nodded with his brows,
dark like lapis lazuli, and his immortal locks fell all around
the head of the deathless king. Olympos shook.

520   After the two took counsel together in this fashion,
they departed, Thetis descending from shining Olympos
into the deep sea, and Zeus went to his house. All the
gods stood up from their seats when he entered. No one
dared to await his coming, but they all stood up.

525   So he sat there on his throne, but Hera
knew he'd made a deal with Thetis of the
silver ankles, the daughter of the Old One of the Sea.
She spoke to Zeus at once, the son of Kronos,
with mocking words: "Who, my clever fellow,
530 have you been making deals with? You just love that,
to stand apart from me and make judgments about things
that you have decided in secret. Nor do you ever
bother willingly to tell me what you have been up to."

The father of men and gods said the following:
535 "Hera, don't hope to know all my thoughts! It will be
the worse for you if you do, although I sleep with you.
What you should know, you will know, before all other gods
or men. But what I wish to devise apart from
the gods, don't ask about it. Make no inquiries!"

540   Hera, with eyes like a cow, the revered one,
then said to him, "O most dread son of Kronos!
What a thing you have said! In the past I have never asked
you about your affairs, nor made inquiry, but you
fancied anything you like. But now I greatly
545 fear in my heart that silver-ankled Thetis has led you
astray, the daughter of the Old One of the Sea.
She came this morning and sat beside you and gripped
your knees. I think you promised her that you would give
honor to Achilles, that you would destroy a multitude
550 beside the ships of the Achaeans."

Zeus, who assembles
the clouds, then replied, "You bitch! You have your ideas,
and nothing gets past you! Nonetheless, there is nothing you can do
about it. You will only drift further from my heart, which will
be the more shivery for you. If this is what I'm thinking,
555 I must like it. So shut up and sit down! Obey my word,
or all the gods in Olympos will do you no good as I close
in and lay upon you my powerful hands!"

So he spoke,
and the cow-eyed revered Hera took fright. In silence
she took her seat, curbing the impulse of her heart.

The Olympian gods in the house of Zeus were troubled   560
by what had happened, when Hephaistos, known for his craft,
said, bringing kindness to his dear mother Hera
of the white arms: "Surely this will be a nasty turn,
scarcely to be born, if the two of you quarrel like this
over men who die. You bring squabbling into the midst   565
of the gods. There will be no pleasure in the feast, when trouble
has the upper hand. I advise my mother, whom I know to be
sensible in her own right, to be kind to our dear father, so that
he does not tangle with her again and stir up trouble at the feast.

"Why, what if the Olympian, master of the lightning, wished to blast   570
us from our seats?! For his strength is much the greater.
So—please calm him with gentle words. Then the Olympian
will be kind to us."

So he spoke, and leaping up he placed
a two-handled cup in his mother's hand, and said to her:
"Courage, my mother. Hang on, though you are irritated,   575
or else I may see you beaten with my own eyes.
You are so dear to me, but, though grieving, you may be unable
to do anything about it. The Olympian is not someone
you want to go up against. Why, I remember the time
that I was eager to save you and he grabbed me by the foot   580
and threw me from the godly threshold. I fell all day.
When the sun was setting, I landed on the island of Lemnos,
barely alive. There, after my fall, the Sintian men
quickly cared for me."°

So he spoke, and white-armed
Hera smiled, and, smiling, she took in hand the cup   585
from her son. Then Hephaistos, moving from left to right,
poured out wine to all the gods, drawing sweet nectar
from the mixing bowl. An unquenchable laughter

---

584   . . . *cared for me*: For Lemnos, see Map I. The Sintians are the native inhabitants. The story about Hephaistos
being thrown from Heaven is told again (Book 18), with significant variation, the only time in the Homeric
corpus that a single myth is told twice.

arose among the blessed beings when they saw Hephaistos
590 puffing along through the palace.

                         So they dined all day
until the sun went down. They did not lack for anything
in the common feast, not the lovely lyre that Apollo
played, and the Muses sang in beautiful response.°
But when the bright light of the sun had disappeared,
595 they went to lie down, each to his own house,
where for each one the lame god, famous Hephaistos,
had made a palace with his cunning skill. Zeus,
the Olympian, the master of lightning, mounted his own bed.
There it was always his custom to rest, where sweet
600 sleep came to him. He went up and fell asleep,
and Hera of the golden throne beside him.

---

593 *response*: Apollo sings for the gods just as singers (*aoidoi*) like Homer sang for human courts. Hephaistos
is lame because real blacksmiths often were lame, and he is the bumbling butt of laughter. Yet he made the
shining houses in which the gods live, and they could not do without him. It is he who calms the quarrel
between his mother and father.

BOOK 2. *The Testing of the Troops*

The other gods and the chariot-charging men slept the whole
night through, but sweet sleep came not on Zeus. He wondered
in his heart how to honor Achilles and destroy many beside
the ships of the Achaeans. This seemed to him to be the best plan,
to send to Agamemnon, the son of Atreus, a destructive dream.   5

So he spoke to Dream words that sped like arrows:
"Go on, go, O Destructive Dream, to the fast ships of the
Achaeans. When you come to the tent of Agamemnon,
son of Atreus, tell him exactly what I tell to you:
Order him swiftly to arm the Achaeans with long hair,   10
for now he can take the city of Troy, with its broad roads.
The deathless gods, who live on Olympos, are no more
of two minds about this matter. Hera, with her begging,
has persuaded the gods to allow the destruction of Troy."

So he spoke. Dream went off at Zeus's   15
command. He soon arrived at the swift ships of the Achaeans.
He went to Agamemnon, son of Atreus. He found him
asleep in his tent, a godlike sleep upon him. He stood
over his head and, looking like Nestor, son of Neleus,
whom of all old men Agamemnon trusted the most,   20
he said, this dream from heaven:

            "You are sleeping, O son
of Atreus, wise tamer of horses. But you ought not,
a man of counsel, to sleep the whole night through, to whom
turn the people, you who have many troubles.
But listen. I come from Zeus. Although far away,   25
he cares greatly for you, and he pities you. He orders
you swiftly to arm the Achaeans with long hair,
for now you can take Troy, with its broad roads.
The deathless gods, who live on Olympos, are no more
of two minds about the matter. Hera, with her pleading,   30
has persuaded the gods to allow destruction to Troy.°

---

31 *destruction to Troy*: It is typical of oral style for messages to be repeated word for word.

Zeus has condemned the Trojans to destruction.
Now remember this, and do not forget it when honeyed
sleep lets you go."

        So speaking, Dream departed.
35 He left Agamemnon with a thought of things that would
never come to pass. For Agamemnon thought that on
that day he would take the city of Priam—what a fool!
He never knew what Zeus intended, how he was
going to cause, through grievous battle, pain
40 and agony among the Trojans and Danaäns alike.

    Agamemnon woke up. The divine voice sounded
all around him. He sat up straight on the edge of the bed.
He put on his soft shirt, a beautiful new one, then put
on his great cloak. Beneath his feet he bound
45 beautiful sandals, and over his shoulders he cast
his great sword with silver nails. He took up his scepter,
a family heirloom—deathless, lasting forever!—
and he walked along the ships of the Achaeans, clothed
in bronze.

      The divine Dawn went to tall Olympos
50 to proclaim to Zeus and the other deathless ones the light,
while Agamemnon ordered his clear-voiced heralds to call
to assembly the Achaeans with long hair. They called,
and the army gathered in haste.

[Lines 54–209 are omitted. Agamemnon tests the resolve of his men by suggesting
that they will never take Troy (contrary to the dream) and that they should all go home.
Humorously, they take him at his word and rush to the ships! Odysseus barely
restrains them and restores order, all except for the repulsive Thersites.]

210   Thus like a master did Odysseus range
through the army. And again they surged into the place
of gathering away from the ships and the huts, always chattering,
as when a wave of the resounding sea thunders
on the broad beach, and there is a roar from the deep.

215   The others sat down, all except brawling Thersites,
who went on scolding, whose mind was filled with disorderly
words to condemn the chiefs, all for nothing, and hardly in good form,
but whatever he thought would raise a laugh from
the Argives. He was the most disgusting man who went

to Troy. His legs were bowed, one shorter than the other,   220
and his shoulders curved inwards over his chest. His head
was pointy, and a scant tuft of hair grew on top.
Achilles hated him especially, but also Odysseus,
for Thersites constantly reviled these two men.

    At the moment, however, he attacked goodly Agamemnon   225
with sharp words, for the Achaeans were furious with
Agamemnon and blamed him in their hearts. In a loud voice
Thersites insulted him now: "O son of Atreus, what
is wrong? What do you lack? Your tents are filled, I think,
with bronze. You have fine women in your tents,   230
which we Achaeans gave to you as first pick whenever
we attacked some town. O—maybe you still lack gold,
which a horse-commanding Trojan has brought from Troy
as ransom for his son? Maybe I bound him and led him away,
or some other Achaean . . . or is it a pretty young thing   235
for you to bed, whom you will keep to yourself?
You've got no business as our leader to bring
us to pain, the sons of the Achaeans! Great gods,
miserable pathetic things, you are no men
but like the ladies of Achaea! Let us go home   240
in our ships and leave this man here in Troy
to ponder his prizes. Then he may know if we
are any good to him or not. He who dishonored
Achilles, a far greater man than he! For he took
that man's prize and he holds it. Achilles must know   245
no anger in his heart. He must have set it aside.
Otherwise, O son of Atreus, this would be
your last outrage!"

            So spoke Thersites, abusing
Agamemnon, the shepherd of the people. But Odysseus
quickly came up to him, and glowering beneath his   250
brows he put him in his place with a savage word:
"Be still, Thersites, fancy with words, clear-voiced
speaker—don't try and argue with the chiefs, alone
as you are! No one worse than you ever came to Troy
with the sons of Atreus. So don't go around with 'chief'   255
lightly on your lips, despising them, saying we should all
sail home. No one knows how this will all turn out,
or whether the sons of the Achaeans will return in victory
or defeat to our homes. You stand there insulting Agamemnon,
shepherd of the people, because the Danaän spearmen give   260

him many gifts! You rail on and on—but let me tell you
something, which surely will come to pass. If again
I find you playing the fool as you do now, then no
longer may my head sit on my shoulders, or I
265   be called the father of Telemachus, if I don't seize you
and strip off your clothes, your cloak and shirt that covers
your privates, and drive you wailing out of the assembly
to the fast ships in a rain of shaming blows!"

So he spoke, and with the staff he struck Thersites'
270   back and shoulders. Thersites bent over. A hot tear
rolled down his cheek. A bloody welt rose up
on his back beneath the golden scepter. He sat
down, deeply alarmed, in pain, with a helpless
look on his face. He wiped away a tear.

The Achaeans,
275   though they suffered, laughed merrily at his plight.
One would say, glancing at his neighbor, "Well, I think
that Odysseus has done a thousand good things in the council
and leading us in battle, but now he has done the best
thing of all among the Argives, who has shut up
280   this foul loud-mouth and stopped his prattle. I don't
think the proud spirit of Thersites will again urge him on
to speak ill of the chiefs with his insults!"

So spoke
one common man.

[Lines 283–444 are omitted. Odysseus and Nestor argue publicly for the
continuation of the war, and all agree that this is the best course.]

445   Thus Agamemnon immediately ordered the clear-voiced
heralds to summon to battle the Achaeans with their long hair.
They did summon them, and quickly the army assembled.
The chiefs around the son of Atreus, divinely nurtured,
ran through the crowd and organized them into gangs,
450   and among them went Athena with the flashing eye,
holding the goat-skin fetish, of exceeding value,
ageless, deathless. From it hung a hundred tassels
of solid gold, every one of them finely woven,
every tassel worth a hundred cattle. With it she raced
455   like lightning through the mass of the Achaeans,
urging them to go forth. She roused strength in the heart

of each man to fight and do battle without end. Instantly
war became sweeter to them than to sail away
in their hollow ships to the beloved land of their fathers.

Just as when a consuming fire ignites the endless   460
forest on a mountain top, and from a distance the gleam
is clear, even so the dazzling shining of the wonderful
bronze of the men as they came on reached heaven
through the sky. Even as the many tribes of winged birds,
of geese, or cranes, or long-necked swans in the meadow of Asia,   465
around the streams of the KAYSTRIOS,° flying this way and that,
thrilling in the power of flight, they settle with loud cry
ever onward, and the meadow resounds—even so
the many tribes poured forth from the ships and the tents
onto the plain of Skamandros.° And the earth resounded terribly   470
under the tramp of feet and the feet of their horses. They took
their stand in the meadow of flower-bound Skamandros, without
number, as many as there are leaves and flowers in their season.

Or as the many tribes of swarming flies that buzz
around the shepherds' yard in the season of spring,   475
when milk moistens the pails—so many of the Achaeans
with flowing hair took their stand in the face
of the Trojans, longing to tear them in pieces.

Even as when a goatherd easily picks out
his own goats scattered wide in the pasture, so did   480
the leaders organize the tribes on this side and that,
ready for battle, and among them King Agamemnon,
his eyes and head like Zeus who thrills to the thunderbolt,
his waist like Ares, his chest like Poseidon. Even as
a bull in the herd is by far the greatest of all—   485
for he stands out among the cattle as they gather together—
such did Zeus make the son of Atreus on that day,
outstanding among many, chief among the fighting men.

Tell me now, you Muses who have houses on Olympos—
for you are divine, you are at hand, you know everything while   490

465–466 *Asia . . . Kaystrios*: Asia vaguely designates an inland territory comprising part of LYDIA (Map III) and
further south. From this once restricted use the word has acquired its modern reference to a continent.
KAYSTRIOS (Map I) is a river that flows into the Aegean near EPHESOS.

470 *Skamandros*: One of the two rivers crossing the plain of Troy. See Map IV.

we hear only the sound about things.° We know nothing.
Who were the leaders of the Argives? Who were their captains?
I could never tell the masses, or name them all, not with
ten tongues and ten mouths and my voice unbroken and my heart
495 within made of bronze, if the Olympian Muses,
the daughters of Zeus who carries the goatskin fetish,
did not remind me of how many were those who went
beneath Ilion.

[Line 499–end of book are omitted. Homer lists the contingents of the Greeks
and the Trojans and their allies in the Catalog of Ships and the Catalog of Trojans.]

---

491 *sound about things*: Homer appeals to the Muses, who embody the oral tradition, at special junctures.
He perceives his power of song to come from outside him.

BOOK 3. *Helen on the Wall*

But when they were arranged, the opposing companies came
together with their leaders—the Trojans with a clang and a shout,
like birds when the clangor of the cranes fills the sky, when they flee
before the winter and the endless rain and with a clamorous
sound they fly to the streams of Ocean, bringing death   5
and destruction to the Pygmies.° Early in the morning
they bring the rough fight.

     But the Achaeans came
on in silence, breathing fury, eager in their hearts each
to help the other. As when South Wind lets down a mist
on the peaks of a mountain unfriendly to the shepherd,   10
for theft better than the night, and you can see
as far ahead as you can throw a stone, so did the dust
arise beneath their feet as on they came.

     Swiftly they
crossed the plain. When, advancing together, and the two armies
came near, Alexandros,° like a god, appeared wearing   15
a panther skin on his shoulders, and his curved bow,
and his sword. Shaking in his hands two spears° tipped
with bronze, he called out to all the best of the Argives
to meet him in dread combat. When Menelaos, whom Ares
loves, saw him coming forth from out of the crowd,   20
striding long, even as a lion rejoices when he chances
on a carcass when he is hungry, either finding a horned

---

6 *Pygmies*: The origin of this odd tale of the war between the cranes and the Pygmies is unknown, but it is
 sometimes thought to be an Egyptian folktale. It was a fairly popular subject in Greek art.

15 *Alexandros*: "defender of the city," is another name for Paris, about four times more common than "Paris."
 There seems to be no difference in meaning and the names are used indifferently, although the name Paris is
 not Greek and Alexandros certainly is Greek.

17 *two spears*: In hoplite warfare of the Classical Period, the fighter was armed with a single thrusting spear
 that he held at his side while marching in a line against the enemy. The spears of Paris are javelins, meant to
 be thrown, and he has two, one as back-up. This is usual for Homeric combat, although sometimes the poet
 seems to be thinking of combat with the single thrusting spear. Most Homeric combat revolves around
 single heroes fighting at the forefront, more a clash of heroes than one army against the next.

stag or a wild goat, and greedily the lion devours it
although fast dogs and brave young men assail him—
25 even so Menelaos rejoiced when he saw Alexandros,
like a god, with his own eyes. He thought that the criminal
was caught. On the instant he jumped from his chariot, fully
armed, to the ground.

But when Alexandros, like a god,
saw him among the foremost fighters, his heart collapsed,
30 and he shrank back into the crowd of his companions, avoiding death.
Just as when a man sees a snake in the wilds of the mountain,
and back he jumps, and his limbs tremble, and a whiteness
suffuses his cheeks, even so did godlike Alexandros
slip into the crowd of lordly Trojans, fearing the son of
35 Atreus.

When Hector saw him, he reproached
him with words that put Paris to shame: "Little
Paris, nice to look at, mad for women, seducer boy—
I wish you had never been born! I wish that you had died
unwed. That's what I wish. That would be better than
40 being an outrage, as you are, the object of everyone's
contempt. I think that the Achaeans, who wear their hair long,
would laugh aloud thinking that we have chosen as champion
someone just because he was good-looking, while in his heart
there was no strength or power. Was it in such a spirit
45 that you sailed across the sea in your sea-journeying ships, taking
with you your friends? You went to an alien people.
You brought back a beautiful woman from a faraway land.
She was the daughter of spear-bearing men, a sorrow
to your father, and to the city, and to the people. To your
50 enemies it was a joy, but to you a scandal. You don't want
to face off against Menelaos, beloved of Ares? You would
soon see what sort of man is he whose ripe wife you
possess! Your lyre will be worthless to you, and the gifts
of Aphrodite—your fancy hair and good looks when you
55 are mixed with the dust. The Trojans are meek—or long ago
you would have donned a shirt of stones for all the evil
you have done."

And godlike Alexandros answered him:
"Hector, yes, you reprove me rightly, you are not
out of order—but your heart is unyielding, like an ax driven
60 through a beam of wood by a man skilled in cutting

timber for a ship,° and it increases his power. Thus is
your mind in your chest never afraid. But please don't
throw in my face the splendid gifts of golden Aphrodite.
Not to be spurned are the wonderful gifts of the gods,
whatever they give, which you could never get just by wanting.   65
    "Anyway, if you want me to go to the war, let the Trojans
sit down and all the Achaeans too. Put me in the middle
along with Menelaos, dear to Ares, so that we can
fight over Helen and all the treasure. Whoever
is victorious, whoever proves the greater, may he take   70
all the treasure and take the woman home. Then
may all you others swear oaths of friendship, and seal it
with a sacrifice. Then may you live here in Troyland
with its deep soil, and let the others sail off
to Argos where they pasture horses, and Achaea,   75
land of beautiful women."

                    So he spoke, and Hector
was happy to hear his words. He went out in front
and held back the ranks of Trojans by grasping
his spear in the middle. They all sat down. The Achaeans,
with their long hair, fired their bows at him and tried   80
to hit him with their arrows, and they threw stones.

    But Agamemnon, the king of men, shouted
aloud: "Hold your fire, Argives, don't shoot,
you Achaean youth! Hector, whose helmet flashes,
is behaving as though he wants to say something."   85

    So he spoke, and they held back from battle
and immediately they fell silent. Hector spoke
between the armies: "Hear, O Trojans and Achaeans with your
fancy shin guards, the speech of Alexandros. On his account
this quarrel has arisen. He urges the other Trojans and all   90
the Achaeans to lay aside their beautiful armor on the rich earth.
He will come forth into the middle and so will Menelaos,
whom Ares loves. Then they will fight for Helen and
the treasure. Whoever is victorious, whoever proves
the greater, may he take the treasure and take the woman   95

---

61 *for a ship*: Similes are characteristic of Homer's style, but usually they are in the mouth of the narrator, not a
    speaker within the text. Hector's hard heart is like an ax in the hands of an expert carpenter.

home. Then let all the rest swear oaths of friendship,
and seal it with a sacrifice."

                  So he spoke, and everyone fell
into a deep silence. Menelaos, good at the war cry,
spoke to them: "Now listen to me. Above all the pain
100 has afflicted my *own* breast. I think that Argives
and Trojans should separate. You have suffered much evil
through the quarrel that Alexandros began.
For whichever of us death and fate is made,
let that man die! And may the rest of you
105 be parted as soon as possible.
              "So bring in two lambs,
one white, the other black, to Earth and to Sun. For Zeus
we will bring in another. Bring here the majesty of Priam
so that he might himself swear an oath sealed with a sacrifice.
Why, his sons are overbearing, faithless. That way no one
110 will go too far and violate the oaths of Zeus. I'm afraid
that the brains of the young are many times floating in air!
But in whatever an old man chooses to take part,
he looks ahead and he looks behind so that it works out
much the better for both parties concerned."

                       So he spoke.
115 And the Achaeans and the Trojans were glad, thinking that
they would soon cease from bitter war. They pulled up
their cars in the ranks, and out they leaped and took off
their armor. They placed it on the ground in close order,
and there was little space between. Hector sent
120 two heralds running to the city to bring back the lambs
and to summon Priam. Lord Agamemnon sent Talthybios
to the hollow ships, and he ordered him to bring a lamb.
Talthybios did not disobey the noble Agamemnon.

    But Iris came as messenger to Helen of the white arms
125 in the likeness of Alexandros' sister, the wife of the son
of Antenor whom the lordly Helikaon, son of Antenor,
had as wife—Laodikê, the most beautiful of the daughters
of Priam. Iris found Helen in her chamber weaving
a purple garment of double thickness on her large loom.
130 In it she embroidered the battles of the horse-taming Trojans
and the Achaeans with shirts of bronze, which they endured
on her account at the hands of Ares.

Standing nearby, Iris spoke,
the swift runner: "Come here, dear lady, so that you can see
the wonderful actions of the horse-taming Trojans and
the Achaeans who wear shirts of bronze. They who earlier 135
waged tearful war against each other on the plain, longing
for death-dealing war—now they are seated in silence.
War is ended. They are leaning on their shields. Their spears
are fixed in the ground. Alexandros and Menelaos, dear to Ares,
will fight with their long spears—for you!° You will be called 140
the wife of whoever is victorious."

So she spoke. The goddess placed
in Helen's heart the sweet desire for her former husband
and her city and her parents. Right away she wrapped herself
in brilliant linen and went forth from the chamber. She wept
a gentle tear. She did not go alone, but with her 145
went two servants, Aithra the daughter of Pittheus,°
and Klymenê, with cow-eyes. They came to the Scaean Gates.°
Priam and his advisors—Panthoös and Thymoïtes
and Lampos and Klytios and Hiketaon, of the stock of Ares,
and Oukalegon and Antenor, wise men both—they sat, 150
the elders of the people, at the Scaean Gates. Because
of old age they had ceased from war, but they were fine
speakers, like cicadas in the forest who sit on a tree and send forth
their voice graceful as a lily. Even so did the leaders of the
Trojans sit in the tower. 155

When they saw Helen
coming up the tower, softly they spoke to one another,
sending forth words like arrows: "It's no reproach
that Trojans and Achaeans with their fancy shin guards
should so long have suffered for such a woman!

---

140 *for you*: But the duel between Paris and Menelaos belongs to the opening days of the war, like much of the material Homer uses in order to give the illusion of the passage of time during which Achilles' anger is taking effect.

146 *Pittheus*: According to postHomeric accounts, Aithra the daughter of Pittheus, king of Troezen in the Peloponnesus, was the mother of Theseus, Athens' greatest hero. Theseus abducted Helen from Sparta when she was prepubescent and left her with his mother in Attica until she was old enough for sexual relations. But the Dioscuri, Helen's brothers from Sparta—Kastor and Polydeukes—saved the young girl while Theseus was in the underworld with his friend Peirithoös, king of the Lapiths; for Peirithoös wished to marry Persephone, queen of death! At this time the Dioscuri abducted Theseus' mother and made her Helen's slave, and she went with Helen to Troy. But Homer betrays no knowledge of these traditions.

147 *Scaean Gates*: "the left-hand gates," but to the left of what? Many fateful events in the war take place before these gates. Homer also refers three times to the "Dardanian Gates." Whether these are the same as the Scaean Gates is not clear.

FIGURE 3.1 Helen and Priam. The scene is not from the *Iliad* but inspired by it. Helen is inside—note the column on the left—and pours out wine into a special dish (phialê), from which Priam will pour a drink offering. The buxom Helen wears a gown covered by a fine cloak. She pulls the veil away from her face, perhaps to speak. Priam is an old man with a white beard who holds a staff in his left hand. Above him hangs from the wall a shield with a lion blazon and a sword. Interior of a red-figure Athenian wine cup, c. 460 BC.

Why, she resembles a deathless goddess, to look on her!   160
All the same, though she is beautiful, let her be gone
in the ships. Let her not be a curse to ourselves and to
our children who shall come."

          So they spoke, but Priam called
Helen over to him. "Come here, my dear, sit here
in front of me so that you can see your former husband   165
and your brothers-in-law and your friends . . .° It's not your fault,
my dear. It's the doing of the gods who have brought this tearful
war of the Achaeans to me. But tell me, who is that huge man,
this Achaean man so bold and so tall . . . Others are taller
but I've never seen such an imposing man, nor one so stately.   170
He looks a chieftain, all right."

          Helen answered him,
like a goddess among women: "I revere and am in awe of you,
dear father-in-law. Would that I had chosen foul death
instead of following your son, abandoning my bridal-chamber
and my family and my late-born daughter and my lovely companions   175
of girlhood. But that was not meant to be . . . So do I melt
away with weeping. But I will tell you, because you ask me.
This man is the son of Atreus, wide-ruling Agamemnon,
both a good chief and a powerful spearfighter. He was
my brother-in-law—slut that I am, if ever there was!"   180

   So she spoke. The old man was amazed, and he said:
"O happy son of Atreus, child of fortune, blessed
by heaven! I see that many are the youths of the Achaeans
who are your subjects. Once I went to PHRYGIA
covered in vines where I saw the multitudes of the Phrygians,   185
riding their horses with glancing eyes, the people of
Otreos and godlike Mygdon, who at that time were
camped on the banks of the SANGARIUS. Because I was
their ally, I was numbered among them on that day
when the Amazons came, the equals to men. But not so   190
many were they as the Achaeans with their glancing eyes."

   Next, seeing Odysseus, the old man asked:
"Well, tell me who is this other fellow, my dear child.

---

166   *your friends*: This famous scene is called the "View from the Wall." It too belongs to the early days of the
     war. Priam acts as if he had never before seen the leaders of the Achaean fighters.

He's shorter than Agamemnon, the son of Atreus, but
195 broader in shoulder and chest to judge by looking. He's put
his armor on the rich earth, but he himself, like the leading
sheep in a flock, goes through the ranks of the men
like a ram with thick fleece going through a large flock
of white lady sheep."

        Helen, sprung from Zeus,
200 answered: "This man is the son of Laertes, resourceful
Odysseus, who was raised in the land of Ithaca, a rugged place.
He knows every kind of trick and cunning device."

     Wise Antenor then answered her: "O my lady,
you have said that aright. He came here once, the shining
205 Odysseus, on an embassy on your account, with Menelaos,
dear to Ares. I received them in my halls and entertained them.
I got to know their nature and their clever tricks.
When they mingled with the Trojans, gathered together,
Menelaos' broad shoulders overtopped Odysseus,
210 but when they were seated, Odysseus seemed more
prepossessing.When they wove the web of speech and counsel
in the presence of all, Menelaos spoke fluently, not many
words but well put—a man of few words who didn't ramble.
He was the younger. But when many-minded Odysseus arose,
215 he stood stock still and looked down with fixed eyes.
He moved the scepter neither back nor forwards, but held it
motionless like a man without sense. He seemed like
a surly man, a fool. But when he let forth the powerful
voice from his chest, and his words fell like wintry
220 snowflakes, then might no other man equal Odysseus.
Then did we not so wonder at the way he looked."

     Old man Priam then asked: "Who is this other Achaean,
brazen and tall, standing out among the Argives
both for his height and his broad shoulders?"

225   Helen, who wore a long gown, answered him,
like a goddess among women: "This man is Ajax, a huge wall
for the Achaeans. Idomeneus stands right next to him
like a god among the Cretans, and the leaders of the Cretans
are gathered around him. Full often Menelaos, dear to Ares,
230 welcomed him in our house when he came from Crete.
But now I see all the other of the bright-eyed Achaeans,
whom I could easily recognize and name. But I cannot

see the leaders of the people, Kastor, a tamer of horses,
and Polydeukes, a fine boxer, my brothers, born of the same
mother. Either they did not follow from lovely Lacedaemon,   235
or they came here in sea-journeying ships but now they do
not want to enter in the battles of men, fearing
the words of shame and the insults set against me."

So she spoke, but the life-giving earth held them
in Lacedaemon, in their dear native land.°   240

*[Lines 241–322 are omitted. The sacrificial animals are brought onto the plain
and Priam and Agamemnon swear a trust-oath over them that whoever wins the duel,
Paris or Menelaos, will take Helen and the treasure.]*

The men sat down in ranks according
to where they had hitched their high stepping horses.
They set down their inlaid armor. Shining Alexandros put on   325
his gorgeous weaponry around his shoulders, the husband
of Helen with the lovely hair. First he placed the fine-looking
shin guards around his shins, fitted with silver anklets.
Next, he placed the breast-guard of his brother Lykaon
around his breast, and he fitted it to himself.°   330
He cast a sword with silver rivets around his shoulders,
a bronze one, and then a shield, big and tough.
On his powerful head he placed a well-crafted helmet
with a horse-hair crest. The crest was awesome as it
nodded down. He took up his sturdy spear, fitted   335
to his hand. Thus in the same way Menelaos, a man
of war, put on his own armor.

When they had armed themselves
on either side of the throng, they went forth, glaring dreadfully,
into the middle space between the Trojans and Achaeans.
Everyone was amazed when they saw them, both the horse-taming   340
Trojans and the Achaeans in their fancy shin guards. The men
stood near each other in the space marked off. They shook
their spears in anger. Alexandros threw his spear with
its long shadow, and he struck the shield of the son of Atreus,
perfectly round, but the bronze did not break through.   345

---

240 *land*: Kastor and Polydeukes had been killed on a cattle raid, according to later tradition. The brothers were
not known as the Dioscuri, "the sons of Zeus," protector of horseman and sailors, until the late 5th century BC.

330 *to himself*: As an archer, Paris has no breast-guard. Achilles later murders Paris' brother Lykaon in a
pathetic scene on the banks of the Skamandros River (Book 21).

FIGURE 3.2 The duel between Menelaos and Paris.   The figures are labeled. On the left, Helen stands behind Menelaos as he draws his sword and attacks Paris. Paris holds a spear in his right hand and runs away, but Artemis—with her emblem, the bow—not Aphrodite, stands behind Paris, perhaps because Artemis always favors Trojan affairs. The warriors are dressed as typical 5th century BC hoplites with breastplate and helmet, except that they do not have shin guards (greaves). Their shields have a strap for the arm and a handgrip, never found in Homer, where shields are suspended over the shoulder by a baldric (telamon), some shields as large as the whole body (see Figure 4.1). The artist is recreating the scene to include elements he remembers from Homer's story, but he is careless about details: Helen favored Menelaos; Paris ran away; the gods supported Paris. Red-figure Athenian wine cup found in Capua, Italy, c. 480 BC

The point of the spear was bent against the strong shield.
Then the son of Atreus, Menelaos, rushed on him
with his spear, praying to Zeus: "Zeus, king, allow me
to take revenge on the man who first wronged me, noble
Alexandros! Subdue him beneath my hands so that anyone   350
of those yet to be born may shudder to harm his host,
one who has extended friendship!"

               He spoke, and brandishing
his spear with its long shadow he threw, and he struck
the perfectly round shield of the son of Priam. The powerful
spear went through the light-reflecting shield and through   355
the ornately decorated breast-guard. The spear tore through the shirt
and slipped beside the flesh over the ribs. Paris bent away
and just escaped black death. The son of Atreus
then drew his sword with silver rivets and, raising
it high, brought it down on the ridge of Paris' helmet.   360
The sword broke in three or four pieces and fell from his hand.

   The son of Atreus groaned and looked into the broad heaven:
"Father Zeus, there is no god more harmful than you!
Here I thought that I'd take vengeance on Alexandros
for his wicked ways, but now the sword in my hand   365
is broken and my spear is flown from my hands, for nothing!
I did not hit him!"

             He spoke and rushing in he seized
Paris by the helmet, by its thick horsehair. Whirling him
around, he dragged him toward the Achaeans
with their fancy shin guards. The embroidered strap beneath   370
Paris' tender throat choked him, which stretched
tight beneath his chin to hold the helmet.

   And now would Menelaos have dragged Paris away,
and earned undying glory, if Aphrodite, the daughter of Zeus,
had not been quick to see? To Menelaos' harm, she broke   375
the strap made from a slaughtered ox. The helmet came away
in his powerful hand. He spun it around and threw
it into the crowd of Achaeans with fancy shin guards
and his trusted companions gathered it up. He sprang back,
eager to kill with his bronze spear,° but Aphrodite   380

---

380 *bronze spear*: It is not clear where he got this spear, since he seems to have begun with one spear, which he
    has already cast.

easily snatched Paris up. She covered him with a thick
mist and placed him down in his fragrant, sweet-smelling
chamber. She herself went to call Helen.

                                      She found her in
the high tower,° surrounded by Trojan women.
385 With her hand she took hold of Helen's fragrant gown
and she tugged at it, looking like a very old woman, a comber
of wool who had worked the beautiful wool when Helen
lived in Lacedaemon—and Helen loved her very much.

    In the likeness of this woman the divine Aphrodite spoke:
390 "Come with me! Alexandros calls you home. He's in
his chamber on the inlaid couch. He shimmers with beauty.
He is dressed in beautiful clothes. You would hardly say
that he came from warring with an enemy, but rather that he
was about to go to a dance, or that he sits there as if
395 he'd just come from a dance."

                                So she spoke, and she aroused
the spirit in Helen's breast, who recognized the exquisite
throat of the goddess and her lovely breast and her flashing
eyes. Helen was amazed and addressed her by name:
"Great lady, why do you want to fool me so? I suppose
400 you would now lead me farther, into the dense cities of Phrygia
or lovely MAEONIA,° if perhaps there is someone there
among mortal men who is dear to you. For as it is,
Menelaos has overcome the noble Alexandros and he wants
to lead me—hateful as I am!—home with him.
405 For this reason you have come here with your treacherous
thoughts. "But go to him—sit by his side. Give up the way
of the gods. Let your feet no longer carry you to Olympos,
but fuss over Paris and guard him until he either
makes you his wife—or more likely his concubine!
410 I will not go there. That would be a subject for reproach,
to bed with him now. All the Trojan women will blame me
after. This pain in my heart has no end!"

                              In anger the divine
Aphrodite answered: "Don't provoke me, you little hussy!

---

384 *high tower*: Helen has retired from the wall and gone to her chamber.

400–401 *Phrygia or lovely Maeonia*: See Map I.

I may abandon you in my anger. For I may hate you even
as now I love you fully. I may construct a destructive hate   415
shared by Trojans and Danaäns alike. °You would then suffer
a vicious fate!"

　　　　So she spoke, and Helen, of the line
of Zeus, was afraid. She went, covering herself
in a bright luminous cloak, in silence. The Trojan women did not
notice her. The goddess led the way. When they came   420
to the attractive house of Alexandros, the slaves quickly
turned to their duty while Helen went into the high-roofed
chamber, a goddess among women. Aphrodite, who loves
laughter, took a chair for her and placed it opposite
Alexandros. There Helen sat down, looking the other way,   425
the daughter of Zeus who carries the goatskin fetish.

　　She rebuked her husband with this word: "You've come
from the war. Would that you had perished there!
Overcome by a stronger man, who used to be my husband.
Once you boasted that you were stronger in hand and better   430
with the spear than Menelaos, dear to Ares. Well,
go then and call out Menelaos the war lover to fight
you again in the hand-to-hand! . . . but no, don't do that,
don't go up against Menelaos, don't be so foolish as to fight him,
or likely he will kill you with his spear . . ."   435

　　　　　　　　Paris answered her:
"Do not rebuke me with your rough words. For now
Menelaos has beaten me, with the help of Athena, but some
other time I will beat him. We have gods on our side too.
But come, dear, let us now make love, and lie down together . . .
for never has so much desire so enfolded my soul,   440
not when I first carried you from lovely Lacedaemon
and sailed away in my sea-journeying ships, and on a rocky
island I made love to you—as I long for you now in love
and delicious desire seizes me."

　　　　　　　　He spoke. He led her to
the bed, and his wife followed. And so the two of them   445
made love on the bed, whose mattress was made

416　*Trojans and Danaäns alike*: That is, a mutual hatred for Helen, when she might be killed by the Trojans as an
adulteress.

of cords. But the son of Atreus wandered through the crowd
like a wild animal, to see if he could see the godlike
Alexandros somewhere.° But no one of the famous Trojans
450   or their allies could show Alexandros to Menelaos, whom
Ares loves. Not for affection did they hide him, if someone
might have seen him, for they hated Paris like black death.

    The king of men, Agamemnon, spoke then: "Hear me
Trojans and Dardanians and allies! Victory seems to belong
455   to Menelaos, dear to Ares, and you must therefore give up
Helen and the treasure along with her, and you must pay a
suitable recompense, which those still not born will speak of."
So spoke the son of Atreus. And the Achaeans applauded.

---

449   *somewhere*: The scene is pure slapstick. Menelaos is looking everywhere for Paris who at that very moment
is having sex with Menelaos' wife, spirited away in a cloud from the plain of battle by the love-goddess!

BOOK 4. *Trojan Treachery*

The gods, seated beside Zeus, held assembly in the chamber
with the golden floor. The queenly Hebê° poured out
nectar among them. They drank to one another as they looked
out over the city of the Trojans.

Suddenly the son
of Kronos tried to provoke Hera with jeering words,   5
speaking slyly:° "Menelaos has two helpers in the
goddesses, Argive Hera and Alalkomenean Athena.°
They take pleasure in sitting apart and looking in on the action
while Aphrodite, who loves to laugh, always goes beside
prince Paris and pushes away fate. Why just now   10
she saved him when he thought he was going to die!
Anyway, Menelaos, dear to Ares, won the match.
Let us therefore consider how things will be. Shall
we rouse up wicked war and the horrible din of battle,
or shall we sponsor friendship between the two sides?   15
If this seems right, and a sweet thing to all, then
might the city of King Priam still exist, and Menelaos
might carry Helen of Argos home."

So Zeus spoke,
and Athena and Hera murmured among themselves.
They sat side by side, devising trouble for the Trojans.   20
Athena was silent and said nothing, though she was furious
with her father, and a wild rage had seized her, but Hera's
breast could not contain her anger and she said:
"Most august son of Kronos, what a word you have
spoken! You only want to make my labor useless and   25
without effect, and the sweat that I sweated, and the two
horses worn out with the effort of bringing the people

---

2 *Hebê*: "Youth," a child of Zeus and Hera and wife of Herakles after he ascended to Olympos.

6 *slyly*: Zeus needs to get the fighting going again so that he can fulfill his promise to Thetis.

7 *Alalkomenean Athena*: The epithet seems to mean "defender."

together to do evil to Priam and his sons° . . . Go ahead!
But the other gods are not going to like it."

Zeus, who assembles
30 the clouds, was angry with her, and he said: "Strange
woman, how has Priam and the sons of Priam done you
such harm that you relentlessly rage to destroy the well-founded
city of Ilion? Maybe if you went inside the gates and
the high walls and devoured Priam raw and the sons
35 of Priam and the other Trojans—maybe then you would
assuage your anger! But do what you wish. I don't
want this quarrel to be a cause of strife between the two
of us in times to come. And I'll tell you something else,
and you pay careful attention. When the day comes
40 that I am eager to destroy a city whose inhabitants
are dear to you, don't get in the way of my anger!
Let it go! For I agreed with you on this, but against
the will of my heart. For of all the cities inhabited
by mortal men beneath the sun and the starry heaven,
45 of those holy Ilion was most honored in my heart, and Priam
and the people of Priam with the strong ash spear. For my altar
never lacked in the equal feast,° or of the wine-offerings,
or of the scent of the burned flesh. We take it as our due."

Queenly Hera with cow eyes then answered:
50 "Well, there are three cities that are much the dearest to me—
Argos and Sparta and Mycenae, with its broad roads.
Go ahead, destroy them whenever they are hated by your heart.
I shall not stand before them, nor give them great importance.
Even if I begrudge it to you, and don't want
55 to allow you to go ahead with your destruction, I shall not succeed,
because you are much the stronger. Still, all my labor
should not be for nothing. For I am a god too.
I have the same begetting as you do. Clever Kronos
begot me as the most honored of his daughters.
60 I have my own status because I am the oldest
and because I am your wife, and you are king
of all the gods.

---

28 *sons*: Hera bases her complaint on the effort she and her horses expended in gathering the Achaean host,
    now threatened by Zeus's suggestion that the two sides make peace.

47 *equal feast*: In the "equal feast" everyone gets his fair share of the food.

"But let us yield one to the other,
I to you and you to me. The other deathless
gods will follow. You quickly dispatch Athena
into the terrible din of battle between Trojan and   65
Achaean. Let her contrive that the Trojans first begin
to harm the arrogant Achaeans against the terms
of the oath."

So she spoke, and the father of man and gods
did not disobey. Immediately he addressed Athena
with spoken words that went like arrows: "Quickly   70
go to the armies, into the midst of Trojans and
Achaeans, to attempt to contrive that the Trojans first
begin to harm the arrogant Achaeans against
the terms of the oath."

So speaking he stirred Athena
to act, who was eager before he even spoke.   75
She darted down from the peaks of Olympos, just as
when the son of Kronos who gives crooked advice sends
forth a star, a sign to sailors or to the broad host of
an army, a shining thing from which many sparks fly—
like that did Pallas Athena dart to the earth. She leaped   80
into the middle of them. An amazement fell on all,
both the horse-taming Trojans and the Achaeans with
fancy shin guards, when they saw. One would turn
to his neighbor and say, "O boy, there will again be hateful
war and the terrible din of battle . . . Or, Zeus   85
will set up a friendship between the two sides.
He after all dispenses battle among men." That's what
one of the Achaeans or Trojans would say.

Athena entered the crowd of Trojans in the likeness
of Laodokos, a son of Antenor,° strong in the spear-fight.   90
She sought out Pandaros, like a god. She found
the strong and noble son of Lykaon. He was standing there
surrounded by the powerful ranks of fighters with shields
who had followed him here from the waters of the AISEPOS.°

---

90 *Antenor*: One of the most prominent of the Trojan elders and adviser to Priam.

94 *Aisepos*: In the foothills of MOUNT IDA about seventy miles northeast of Troy: Map IV.

95   Standing close, she spoke words that went like arrows:
"Will you now be persuaded, wise son of Lykaon? Be daring—
let fly a swift arrow at Menelaos. You will then earn
the thanks of the Trojans and glory from them, and above all
from the chief Alexandros. You would then before others
100 earn splendid gifts from him, if he should see the warrior
Menelaos, son of Atreus, overcome by your shaft
and placed on the grievous fire. So come, shoot your
arrow at the glorious Menelaos. Make a vow to Apollo
the wolf-god,° famous for his bow, that you will perform
105 a magnificent sacrifice of yearling lambs once you
get home to the city of sacred ZELEIA."°

                  So spoke
Athena, and she persuaded his thoughtless mind.
Immediately he uncovered his polished bow made from
the horn of a full-grown wild goat that he himself
110 once had struck beneath its breast as it came from a rock.
Lying in ambush, he hit it in the chest. It fell
backwards into the rock. From its head grew horns
four feet long. These the hornworker fashioned and fitted
together. He smoothed the whole thing carefully and fitted
115 a tip of gold.°

      Pandaros placed the bow down well against
the ground, and he stretched it, bending the bow backwards.
His noble companions held their shields in front of him
so that the fighting sons of the Achaeans would not leap up
before he struck the warrior son of Atreus. He opened
120 the lid of the quiver. He took out a feathered arrow
that had never been shot, the support of black pain,
and quickly he fitted the terrible shaft to the string.
He prayed to Apollo, the wolf-god, famous for his bow,
that he would perform a magnificent sacrifice of yearling
125 lambs once he got home to the city of sacred Zeleia.
He drew the bow, gripping at the same time the notched arrow

---

104 *wolf-god*: The meaning of the Greek *lukegenes* is uncertain, either deriving from *lukos*, "wolf," or *Lycia*, a place
      near the Troad with which Pandaros is associated (not the better known Lycia in southern Asia Minor).

106 *Zeleia*: Northeast of Troy: Map IV.

115 *gold*: Homer seems to be describing a "composite bow" made from horn, wooden staves, and sinew. The
      horn is inlaid on the inside of the wooden staves and the sinew is laminated to the backside, making a
      weapon with considerably more power that if just made of wood. The tip is to catch a loop in the string
      attached to the other end of the bow. The mighty composite bow seems to have been invented in the second
      millennium BC by nomadic warriors and hunters on the plains of Asia.

FIGURE 4.1   Detail from the "lion-hunt" dagger from the shaft graves of Mycenae, c. 1600 BC, discovered by Heinrich Schliemann in the late nineteenth century.   Many scholars find remote echoes of this kind of fighting in Homeric accounts, preserved in the oral tradition. Here the shields are "like towers" and are carried by a strap around the neck, the *telamon*. On the far left a man wields a Cretan-style figure-of-eight shield, made of a convex frame covered by cowhides (but none survive). The man wears no armor. He carries the single thrusting spear. Next is a bowman without shield. In the middle the man's shield is rectangular-shaped. The man next to him uses his figure-of-eight cowhide shield as protection against the lion, which he threatens with a single spear. In front him lies the body of a companion, killed by the lion. The companion also carried a rectangu-lar tower-like shield. Gold, bronze, and niello, sixteenth century BC, from Tomb IV, Mycenae.

and the string made of ox sinew. He pulled the string
to his breast, the iron arrowhead° to the bow.
And when he had bent the great bow into a circle, the bow
130 twanged, the string cried aloud, the sharp arrow leaped,
longing to fly through the crowd.

But the blessed gods did not
forget you, my Menelaos!° Above all, the booty-bringing
daughter of Zeus, who stood before you and brushed aside
the piercing shaft. Athena brushed it away from the flesh
135 as when a mother brushes aside a fly from her child
when he lies in sweet sleep. She directed it to where the golden
clasps of the belt were fastened and the chest-protector doubled.
The bitter arrow fell on the clasped belt and was driven through
the fancy belt, and through the highly worked chest-protector
140 and the belly-protector too, which he wore as a screen and guard
for his flesh against any dart, a main line of defense.°
Yet even through this the arrow pierced. The dart scratched
the outermost flesh of the man. Immediately the dark blood
flowed from the wound. It was as if when a woman from MAEONIA
145 or CARIA stains ivory with Phoenician scarlet, to be a cheek-piece
for horses. It lies in a chamber, though many horsemen
pray that they can wear it. It lies there as a delight for the king,
both a decoration for his horse and a boast for the driver.
Like that, my Menelaos, were your handsome thighs stained
150 and your legs and the beautiful ankles beneath.

Agamemnon,
the king of men, shivered when he saw the black blood
run down from the wound. The warrior Menelaos shivered
too. But when he saw that the sinew and the barbs were outside
the flesh, then his breath-soul was gathered back into his breast.

155   With a heavy moan King Agamemnon spoke, holding
Menelaos by the hand, and his companions moaned too:
"Dear brother, it is your death I swore with the oath and sacrifice,
setting you out alone before the Achaeans to fight with

---

128 *arrowhead*: Ordinarily weapons in Homer are made of bronze, everyday implements of iron, but here the
arrowhead is iron.

132 *my Menelaos*: Homer sometimes addresses his characters directly, mostly Menelaos and Patroklos and, for
some reason, the swineherd Eumaios in the *Odyssey*, as if he felt a special sympathy for them.

141 *line of defense*: We cannot reconstruct exactly what Homer means by these pieces of armament.

the Trojans. Now the Trojans have shot you and trampled
down the trust-oaths! But not for nothing are Oath and the blood   160
of lambs and the drink offerings of unmixed wine, and handshakes
in which we place our trust. Even if at the moment the Olympian
does not bring it to fulfillment, in the end he does,°
and that man pays a heavy price not only with his own life
but with the lives of his wife and children too. For I know   165
this in my heart and soul: The day will come when sacred
Ilion will be destroyed and Priam and the people
of Priam with their fine ash spears. Zeus, Kronos'
son, from his high throne, dwelling in the upper air,
will himself shake the dark goatskin fetish over all,   170
furious because of this deception. Surely these things
will come to pass.
          "But O Menelaos, a terrible grief will
you bring, if you die and fill out the apportionment of life.
Most despised would I return to thirsty Argos.° For right away
the Achaeans will remember the land of their fathers, and we   175
would leave to Priam and the Trojans Argive Helen,
something to boast about. The earth will rot away your bones
as you lie in the land of Troy, your task unfinished.
And thus will one of the haughty Trojans say
as he leaps on the tomb of brave Menelaos: 'Thus did   180
Agamemnon fulfill his anger! He led an Achaean army
here to no purpose—he has gone home to his dear native land
with empty ships, leaving good Menelaos.' Thus he
will speak in times to come. On that day may the broad
earth open for me!"   185

          But red-haired Menelaos spoke
cheeringly to him: "Courage, don't panic the Achaeans.
The sharp arrow is not fixed in a mortal place. The belt stopped
it before it could penetrate through, and the flashing
kilt beneath and the belly-protector and chest-protector
that the copper workers made."   190

          King Agamemnon answered him:
"May that only be true, dear Menelaos! The doctor will have
a look. He'll apply a poultice that will stop the black pain."

---

163   *he does*: The first expression in Greek literature of the powerful dogma that Zeus punishes wrongdoing in
     the end.

174   *Argos*: Not the city of Argos, which belongs to Diomedes, but the reference is to the Peloponnesus in general.

Immediately he spoke to the godlike herald, Talthybios:
"Talthybios, call over Machaon right away, a son
195 of Asklepios,° the good doctor, so that he can have a look
at the warrior Menelaos, son of Atreus. Somebody
skilled in archery has shot him with an arrow, a Trojan
or a Lycian. Glory for him, but gloom for us."

                                        So he spoke,
and his herald obeyed him. He went through the army of bronze-shirted
200 Achaeans, looking everywhere for Machaon. He saw him standing
there in the midst of the powerful ranks of shield-bearers
who had followed him from Trikê,° which nourishes horses.
Standing near, he spoke words that went like arrows: "Get up,
son of Asklepios, King Agamemnon is calling for you to have a look
205 at the warrior Menelaos, captain of the Achaeans. Somebody
skilled in archery has shot him with an arrow, a Trojan
or Lycian. Glory for him, but gloom for us."

So he spoke, and he stirred up the spirit in Machaon.
He went through the crowding army of the Achaeans.
210 But when he arrived to where red-haired Menelaos was, wounded,
and around him gathered in a circle the head chieftains,
the godlike man stood in their midst and right away
he withdrew the arrow from the clasped belt. The sharp
barbs bent back as he withdrew the arrow. He loosed
215 the flashing belt and, underneath, the belly-protector
and the chest-protector which the workers in copper made.
But when he saw the wound where the sharp arrow had struck,
he sucked out the blood and with sure knowledge spread out
a healing poultice, which once the beneficent Cheiron° had given
220 to his father.

While they busied themselves around Menelaos,
good at the war cry, the ranks of the shield-bearing Trojans
came on. The Achaeans too put on their armor, watchful
of war. Then you would not have seen the godlike
Agamemnon asleep, or cowering, or not wanting to fight—
225 he wanted to enter the battle where glory is won!
But he let go his horses and chariot inlaid with bronze.

---

195 *Asklepios*: In Homer Asklepios and his sons appear to be ordinary mortals, but later Asklepios is of divine descent, the Greek god of medicine.

202 *Trikê*: In THESSALY.

219 *Cheiron*: Cheiron, "hand," was the "most just of the Centaurs," expert in medicine and one of Achilles' tutors.

His driver Eurymedon, son of Ptolemaios, son of Peiraios,
held the snorting animals to the side. Agamemnon gave out
a stern instruction to have them at hand whenever fatigue
should overcome him as gave orders through the multitude.   230

[Lines 231–416 are omitted. Agamemnon marshals his troops for the fight, addressing
each man personally. They go forth to the fight.]

      As when on a resounding beach
the swelling of the sea rises, wave after wave,
driven by West Wind— at first the sea forms a crest
out on the deep, then breaking on the land it makes   420
a huge sound like thunder as around the headlands,
swollen, it rears its head and spits out a foam of brine—
just so the battalions of Danaäns moved forward,
wave after wave, ceaselessly, to the war. Each captain
gave orders to his own men. All the rest went forward   425
in silence. You would not think that so great a people that
followed had any voice in their breasts, marching in silence
from fear of their commanders. Each man flashed the inlaid
armor that he wore.

      But the Trojans were like ewes in the court
of a rich man, who stand numberless waiting to be milked   430
of their white milk, bleating constantly when they hear the voice
of their lambs. Even so arose the clamor of the Trojans throughout
the broad army. For their speech was different, they did not speak
the same language, their tongues were mixed. They were a folk
summoned from different places. Ares urged them on,   435
but flashing-eyed Athena stood behind the Achaeans, and Terror
and Fear and Eris° that rages without end, the sister
and companion of man-killing Ares. At first she rears her head
just a little, but then she fixes her head against the sky
while her feet bestride the ground. And then she casts   440
dreadful strife in their midst, striding through the crowd,
increasing the groaning of men.

      When they had come
together into one place, they dashed together their shields,

---

437 *Eris*: "Strife," "Contention." According to later tradition, Eris was not invited to the Wedding of Thetis and
    Peleus, Achilles' parents, and so rolled a golden apple across the floor, saying it was for "the fairest." Paris
    was to decide among Hera, Athena, and Aphrodite in the famous Judgment of Paris, briefly alluded to in
    Book 24 of the *Iliad*. Paris chose Aphrodite, and Helen was his reward, so causing the Trojan War.

and spears, and the rage of men who wears shirts of bronze.
445 The bossed shields came together. A great din arose.
Then was heard the agony of the wounded and the boast
of victory as men killed and were killed, and the earth ran
with blood—as when rivers of winter run down from the mountains
from their great springs to a basin, and they join their mighty
450 flood in a deep gorge, and the shepherd hears the roar far off
in the mountains—even so did a cry go up and there was
work as the two sides came together.

[Lines 453–535 are omitted. Glorious scenes of war.]

Many others died around them. From that point on
no one might make light of the work of war, even should
he move through the crowd unscathed by arrow or the thrust
from the cutting bronze, and Pallas Athena should be leading
540 him on, holding his hand, protecting him from the rush
of missiles. Many were the Trojans and Achaeans who on
that day lay stretched out beside one another in the dust.

BOOK 5. *The Glory of Diomedes*

W ell then Pallas Athena gave to Diomedes, the son
of Tydeus, strength and boldness, that he might
stand out among all the Argives and that he might win
high praise. She kindled from his helmet and his shield
an unwearying fire, like the harvest star that shines   5
above all others when it has bathed in Ocean.° Just such
a flame did she enkindle from his head and his shoulders,
and she sent him into the thick of it where the most men
were encamped.

*[Lines 10–97 are omitted. Diomedes charges into the melee. He kills on every side, one
after another.]*

             But when Pandaros, the good
son of Lykaon, saw Diomedes raging across the plain and driving
the Trojan ranks before him, he stretched the curved bow   100
against the son of Tydeus. He hit him in the right shoulder
as he rushed onwards, on the plate of his bronze chest-protector.
The bitter arrow flew through the plate, it went straight
on its way, and the bronze chest-protector was drenched in blood.

       Then the glorious son of Lykaon boasted over him: 105
"Get up and go, you great-hearted Trojans, goaders
of horses! I have wounded the best of the Achaeans. I don't
think he can long endure the powerful shaft, if truly
the king, the son of Zeus, sent me forth when I came
from Lycia."° So he said in boast.   110

             But the sharp arrow
did not subdue Diomedes. Pulling back, he took his stand
beside his horses and his car. He spoke to Sthenelos, the son
of Kapaneus: "Come down, son of Kapaneus, from the car
and draw this arrow from my shoulder." So he spoke, and Sthenelos

---

6 *Ocean*: The harvest star is Sirius, called in Book 20 "Orion's dog." Ocean is the river that surrounds the
    earth. When Sirius is not visible, it is said to bathe in Ocean.

110 *...from Lycia*: The "king" is Apollo, archer-god and sponsor of such archers as Pandaros. This "Lycia" is
    northeast of Troy, not in the far southeast where the important fighter Sarpedon comes from, a son of Zeus.

115 jumped to the ground from the chariot. He stood beside him
and drew the sharp arrow all the way through the shoulder.
The blood spurted up through the supple shirt.

Then Diomedes,
good at the war cry, prayed: "Hear me, unwearied one,
the daughter of Zeus who carries the goatskin-fetish—
120 if ever with good thoughts you stood beside my dear
father in the fury of war, then now be kind to me,
Athena. Grant that I take my man, that he come
within the cast of my spear, whoever it was who hit
me on the sly and boasts of his blow. He doesn't
125 think I shall long behold the sunlight."

So he spoke
in prayer, and Athena heard him. She made his limbs
to be light, and his feet and hands too. Standing
near him she spoke words that went like arrows:
"Have the courage to go up against the Trojans now!
130 For in your breast I have placed the strength of your father
who never turned aside, such as had the horseman Tydeus,
wielder of the shield. I have removed the mist from your eyes
which lay upon them so you can recognize who
is a god and who a man. If any god comes here to make trial
135 of you, don't attack the deathless god—unless it is the daughter
of Zeus, Aphrodite, who comes into the war, then stab
her with the sharp bronze!"

So speaking, flashing-eyed Athena
went away. The son of Tydeus went back and tangled with
the foremost fighters. Although before he was eager to fight
140 the Trojans, now three times the rage came upon him, like a lion
that a shepherd guarding his wooly sheep in the field has wounded
as it leaped over the wall of the sheepfold, but he did not kill him.
He has roused its might and the shepherd gives up his defense
and lurks between the outbuildings, and the flock, having no
145 protection, tries to flee. But they are heaped in piles
next to each other while in his rage the lion leaps up
from the high-walled courtyard.° Even with such fury did
the powerful Diomedes tangle with the Trojans.

---

147 *courtyard*: Pandaros is like the shepherd who wounds the lion, then is overwhelmed by the enraged beast,
except the lion's strength is increased by the wounding, whereas Diomedes receives his strength from
Athena, not the wound that Pandaros has inflicted.

[Lines 149–170 omitted. Diomedes continues to ravage the Trojans.]

    Aeneas saw him throwing into chaos
the ranks of men. He went through the battle and the tumult
of spears looking for godlike Pandaros, to see
if he could find him somewhere. At last he found him,
blameless and strong, and Aeneas stood before him and spoke: 175
"Pandaros, where is your bow and your winged arrows
and your fame? No man here dares compete with you
in this, nor does any one in Lycia boast that he
is better than you. But come now, lifting your hands
to Zeus, fire an arrow at this man who is doing such   180
violence and ferocious harm to the Trojans. He has loosed
the knees of many noble young men. Maybe it is a god
angered with the Trojans because of some sacrifice.
The wrath of a god can be harsh."

               The fine son of Lykaon
then answered him: "Aeneas, good counselor to the Trojans   185
who wear shirts of bronze, this man looks like the valiant son
of Tydeus to me. I can tell from his shield and his helmet
with its crest, and his horses. Of course I can't tell
if it is a god. If this is the man I think, the valiant
Diomedes, it is not without some god's help that he rages,   190
but some one of the deathless ones who live on high Olympos
must stand near him, shoulders hidden in a cloud.
This god turned aside the sharp shaft as it made
its way to the mark. For I have already fired a shot. I hit him
in the right shoulder and the arrow went straight through   195
the plate of his bronze chest-protector. I thought that I had cast
him down to the house of Hades, but I did not subdue him.
   "It must be some angry god! I have no horses
and no car that I could mount, though in Lykaon's halls
there are eleven brand-new chariots, just made. Cloths   200
cover them. Beside each stands a yoke of horses
munching on white barley and wheat. The old spearman Lykaon
ordered me again and again before I set off to war
from the well-built house—he commanded me to mount
horse and car and to lead the Trojans° through the bitter   205
conflicts. But I wouldn't listen. It would have been better

---

205 *Trojans:* That is, his own people, the inhabitants on the slopes of Mount Ida southeast of Troy, who are
     called "Trojans."

if I had! I spared the horses. I was afraid that they
would lack feed in the midst of so many men
when they are used to eating their fill. So I left
them and came to Troy on foot, trusting to my bow,
which was to do me no good at all.
                                    "For already I have fired
at two captains, the son of Tydeus and the son of Atreus.
From both I drew true blood when I hit them,
but that only excited them the more. With bad luck I took
my curved bow from its peg on that day when I led
my Trojans to lovely Ilion, bearing pleasure to shining
Hector. If I return home and see with my own eyes the land
of my fathers and my wife and my high-roofed house,
may some utter stranger cut off my head if I do
not smash this bow with my hands and cast
it into the blazing fire! It is worthless to me,
like the wind!"

          Aeneas, a Trojan captain, answered:
"Don't talk like that. Things will be no different until
we go up against this Diomedes with horse and car
and take him on in our armor. So come, get in my car
that you might see what sort of horses are these
horses of Tros.° They know full well how to pursue
swiftly, and to retreat here and there over the plain.
They will carry us safely to the city, if Zeus again
grants glory to Diomedes, the son of Tydeus. But come,
take the whip and the shining reins. I will descend
from the car in order to fight him.° Or you can attack him,
and I will care for the horses."

          The good son of Lykaon
then answered: "Aeneas, you hold onto the reins yourself
and keep control of your own horses. They will better pull
the car made of bent rods when they recognize who is holding
the reins, if we have to flee from the son of Tydeus.
I am afraid that they may panic and run wild
and be unwilling to bear us out of the war

---

227   *Tros*: This divine breed of horses was begun by Aeneas' great-great-grandfather Tros, to whom Zeus gave
      horses in recompense for Zeus's snatching of Tros' beautiful son Ganymede to be his cupbearer.

232   *fight him*: That is, they will ride into the battle and Aeneas will dismount when they are close to Diomedes.
      Chariots in Homer are ordinarily used as transportation and not as fighting machines, no doubt reflecting
      actual practice in Greece in Homer's day. Chariots confer prestige and social power on their owners.

because they miss your voice, and I fear that the son   240
of Tydeus might then waylay and kill us both
and drive off the single-hoofed horses.° So must
you drive your car and control your horses. I'll take
Diomedes on with my sharp spear as he comes at me."

So speaking they mounted into the ornate car.   245
Eagerly they turned the swift horses against the son
of Tydeus. Sthenelos, the fine son of Kapaneus, saw them,
and at once he spoke to the good Diomedes with words
that flew like arrows: "Diomedes, son of Tydeus, dear
to my heart, I see two powerful men eager to fight you,   250
men with boundless strength. One is Pandaros, a straight
shot with the bow. He boasts of being the son of Lykaon.
The other is Aeneas, who boasts of being the son
of blameless Anchises, with Aphrodite for a mother.
But come, let us withdraw in the car. Don't rage in this   255
way among the frontline troops or you may lose
your life!"

Powerful Diomedes glowered beneath his
brows and said: "Don't speak of flight! I don't think you will
persuade me. It is not in my blood to fight by running
away, nor to squat, cringing. My strength is still steadfast ...°   260
I am not going to mount a car, but I will go against them
just as I am. Pallas Athena will not let me be afraid.
As for these two, their swift horses will not carry them back
from us again, even if one or the other gets away.
    "I'll tell you something else, and please pay attention to   265
what I say. If wise-counseling Athena gives me the glory of killing
both these men, then you hold back our swift horses
by wrapping their reins around the rail. And remember to rush
upon the horses of Aeneas and drive them from the Trojans to the
Achaeans with their fancy shin guards. For they are of the race   270
that Zeus, whose voice reaches far, gave to Tros as recompense
for his son Ganymede. They are the best horses beneath
the dawn or sun. The king of men Anchises° stole from this line
when, unknown to Laomedon, he had them cover some of his mares.

---

242 *single-hoofed*: Apparently to distinguish them from the cloven hoofs of cattle, sheep, and goats.

260 *steadfast*: Even though he has been wounded.

273 *Anchises*: Aeneas' father. Anchises was also descended from Tros through his mother Themistê, a daughter of
     Ilos (the son of Tros). The breed of horses was inherited by Laomedon, a son of Ilos and the father of Priam.

275 From these were born a stock of six in Anchises'
halls. Four of these he reared himself at the stall,
and he gave two to Aeneas, the deviser of rout.
If we can capture these horses, we will gain a handsome
reputation!"

So they spoke to one another. Just then
280 they came near, driving their swift horses. The good son
of Lykaon spoke to Diomedes first: "Son of lordly Tydeus,
stalwart and wise, I guess my sharp arrow did not
finish you off, the bitter shaft! Now I will try to hit you
with my spear, to see if I can take you down."

285 Pandaros spoke, balanced his long-shadowed spear,
and cast. He struck the son of Tydeus on his shield. The bronze
spear-point went straight through and reached the bronze
breast-plate. The good son of Lykaon shouted aloud over him:
"Got you, right through the belly! You won't last long!
290 You've given me great glory!"

Without fear powerful Diomedes
answered: "But you missed the mark! You did not hit me!
I don't think that you two will be done before one or the other
will glut Ares with his blood, the warrior-god who carries
the shield."

So speaking, Diomedes cast. Athena
295 guided the missile onto Pandaros' nose next to the eye
and it pierced his white teeth. The unyielding bronze cut the tongue
off at the root and the point came out beside the lower part
of the chin. Pandaros tumbled from the car. His armor
clanged about him—bright, flashing!—and the swift-footed
300 horses turned aside. His breath-soul and his strength
were loosened.

Aeneas jumped down with shield and long spear,
fearing that Achaeans would snatch the corpse from him.
He hovered over Pandaros like a lion trusting in its might.
He held his spear and shield before him, well-balanced
305 and round, impatient to kill whoever should come
against him. He screamed terribly.

The son of Tydeus
picked up a boulder in his hand, a mighty deed,

a stone that two men might carry such as mortals
are today. But he easily hefted it by himself.
With it he struck Aeneas on the hip where the thigh   310
bone rotates on the hip bone—they call it the "cup."
The stone smashed the cup, and it smashed the two tendons.
The jagged stone peeled away the skin. Then the warrior
fell on his knees and he stayed there. He rested
with his thick hand on the earth. Black night enclosed his eyes.   315

And now Aeneas, the king of men, would have died
if the daughter of Zeus, Aphrodite, had not caught sight
of him—his mother, who bore him to Anchises when he was
herding cattle. Around her beloved son Aphrodite placed
her pale forearms. She covered him with a fold   320
of her shining dress spread before him as a protection,
in case any Danaän with swift horses should throw the bronze
into his chest and take away his breath-soul.
She then carried her beloved son out of the war.

But the son of Kapaneus, Sthenelos, did not forget   325
the agreements he had made with Diomedes, good at the war cry.
He held back his own single-hoofed horses from the fray,
lashing their reins to the rail. He ran up to the horses
of Aeneas with beautiful manes and drove them out
from the Trojans to the Achaeans with fancy shin guards.   330
He gave them to Deïpylos to drive to the hollow ships,
his dear companion, whom he honored above all his age-mates
because they were likeminded. Then Sthenelos mounted
his own car and took the flashing reins. Swiftly
he drove the horses with strong hooves, eagerly seeking   335
the son of Tydeus. But Diomedes had gone in pursuit
of Kypris° with his pitiless bronze, recognizing that she
was a god without strength, not one of those who dominate
in the war of men—no Pallas Athena, nor city-sacking Enyo.°

When he came upon her, pursuing through the immense   340
crowd, he thrust with his sharp spear as he leaped upon her.
The son of great-souled Tydeus pierced the skin on her
delicate hand. Immediately the spear went into the flesh,

---

337 *Kypris*: Another name for Aphrodite because she was born on Cyprus and had a shrine at Paphos on
     Cyprus. For unknown reasons she is called "Kypris" five times in this book, and never again in the *Iliad*.

339 *Enyo*: A war-god, by this time identified with Ares; also called *Enyalios*.

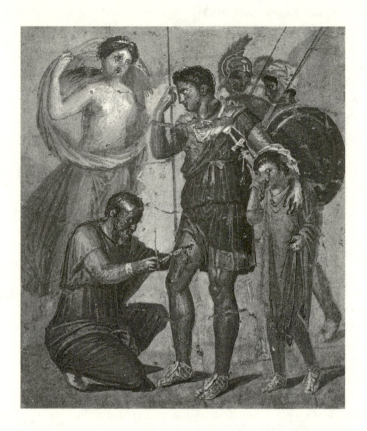

FIGURE 5.1   Aeneas wounded.   The bare-breasted Aphrodite stands to the left, her cloak around her head in a gesture typical of Roman gods. The physician Machaon cuts the missile from Aeneas' leg, who stands stoically holding his spear, his sword at his side, dressed in a breastplate. The boy would be his son, Ascanius (or Iulus), famous from Vergil's *Aeneid* (c. 19 BC). Other Trojan warriors stand in the background. Fresco from Pompeii, 1st century AD.

passing through the deathless clothes that the Graces°
themselves had made, injuring the wrist above   345
the palm. Immortal blood flowed from the goddess,
ichor, which flows in the veins of the blessed gods.
For gods do not eat bread or drink the shining wine.
Thus they are without blood and are called deathless.

    With a loud cry Aphrodite let her son Aeneas   350
fall from her. Phoibos Apollo took Aeneas in his arms,
from a dark cloud, so that no one of the Danaäns
with their fast horses might throw the bronze into his chest
and kill him.

       Over her Diomedes, good at the war cry,
shouted aloud: "Get out of here, daughter of Zeus,   355
leave this battle and the war! Isn't it enough that you deceive
strengthless women? If you are going to enter into battle,
I think you will shudder soon even to hear the word,
even should you hear it at a distance!"

        So he spoke,
and she left, beside herself and much distressed.   360
Wind-footed Iris took her and brought her out
of the throng, wracked with pain. Her beautiful skin
turned black. She found mad Ares on the left of the battle,
sitting down. He had leaned his spear against a cloud
and his swift horses were there.   365

       Falling on her knees, Aphrodite
fervently begged her dear brother for his horses with head-pieces°
of gold: "My beloved brother, save me! Give me your horses
to go to Olympos and the seat of the deathless ones. I am much
pained because of a wound that a mortal man has given me,
the son of Tydeus, who now would fight even with father Zeus."   370

    So she spoke, and Ares gave her the horses
with golden head-pieces. She got in the car, much distraught
at heart. Iris got in beside her and took the reins
in her hands. She lashed the horses to drive them on.
The two sped onward. Quickly they arrived at steep   375
Olympos, the seat of the gods. There wind-footed Iris

---

344   *Graces*: Goddesses of feminine charm who often accompany Aphrodite.

366   *head-pieces*: A decoration that fell over the horse's brow.

stayed the horses and set them free from the car
and cast before them immortal food.

                          But divine
Aphrodite threw herself on the knees of her mother Dionê,°
380 who held her daughter close and stroked her with her hand.
Then Dionê said: "Dear child, who of the heavenly ones
has foolishly done this to you, as if you were doing something
evil in full view?"

                 Laughter-loving Aphrodite answered her:
"The bold Diomedes, the son of Tydeus, has wounded me,
385 because I rescued my own beloved son from the war,
Aeneas, who of all people is by far the most dear to me.
The dread battle is no longer between Trojans and Achaeans,
but now the Danaäns fight against the deathless ones!"

        Then Dionê, the great goddess, answered her:
390 "Endure, my child, and hold up for all your suffering. Many
of those who live on Olympos, in bringing dire pain
to one another, have suffered from men. Ares suffered
when mighty Otos and Ephialtes, the sons of Aloeus,
bound him in powerful bonds.° He lay tied up in a bronze
395 jar for thirteen months. And Ares, insatiate for war,
would have died if his very beautiful step-mother
Eëriboia° had not told Hermes. He stole away Ares,
already much worn down, for the harsh bonds had overcome him.
Hera suffered when Herakles, the powerful son of Amphitryon,
400 wounded her in the right breast with a three-barbed arrow.
Incurable pain overcame her. Monstrous Hades
too suffered the sharp arrow when that same man,
Herakles, the son of Zeus, the cloud-gatherer, hit Hades

---

379 *Dionê*: But according to the account in Hesiod, a contemporary of Homer, Aphrodite was born from
the foam that gathered around the severed genitals of her father, Ouranos (*Theogony* 188ff.). "Dionê" is
the feminine form of Zeus, "Mrs. Zeus." She, not Hera, was the consort of Zeus at the oracular shrine of
Dodona in northwest Greece, referred to in the *Odyssey*. Presumably Dionê is a consort of Zeus before the
Greeks came into the Balkans bringing Zeus with them, when Hera, a local mother goddess, became the
consort of the male storm-god. The Mesopotamian god of the sky Anu had as consort a female counterpart,
Antu, simply the feminine form of his name.

394 *powerful bonds*: Iphimedeia was married to Aloeus, but she bore to Poseidon twin sons. They were called
the Aloads and were of monstrous size, over fifty feet tall at age nine. In addition to their attack on Ares,
they threatened to pile Mount Ossa on Olympos, then Mount Pelion on Ossa so as to reach heaven and
attack the gods. Apollo killed them before they reached maturity.

397 *Eëriboia*: Eëriboia was the granddaughter of Hermes (her father was Hermes' son, one Eurymachos) and
the second wife of Aloeus, hence the stepmother of the monstrous Aloads Otos and Ephialtes.

in Pylos among the dead and gave him over to pain.°   405
Hades went to the house of Zeus and to high Olympos,
lamenting in his heart and pierced with pains, for the arrow
had fixed in his strong shoulder and distressed his spirit.
Paieon° applied a pain-killing poultice and healed him—
for he was not made to die. Scoundrel, doer of violence!
Herakles cared not if he did evil! With his arrows he caused pain   410
to the gods who possess Olympos.
                "Now flashing-eyed Athena
has set this man upon you—the fool! Diomedes
knows not in his heart that he who goes up against
the gods does not last. His children do not call him
'papa' as they hover about his knees when he returns   415
from the war and the dread battleground. For all that
Diomedes is mighty, let him take care that he not go up
against someone stronger than you, or for sure the wise
Aigialeia, daughter of Adrestus, will wake from sleep.
She will rouse with her wailing all those in her house,   420
crying for her wedded husband, the best of the Achaeans—
even she, the strong wife of Diomedes, tamer of horses."
Dionê spoke and with both her hands she wiped away
the *ichor*. The arm was healed and the pains were lessened.

    When Athena and Hera saw Aphrodite, they thought   425
to irritate Zeus, the son of Kronos, with mocking words.
The flashing-eyed goddess Athena began to speak among them:
"Father Zeus, I wonder if what I will say will make you angry?
It seems to me that Kypris has been urging someone of the Achaean
women to follow after the Trojans,° whom she now loves so much . . .   430
and while stroking a certain one of the Achaean women,
who wear fine gowns, she has scratched her delicate hand
against a golden brooch!"

            So Athena spoke. The father
of men and gods smiled. He called to golden
Aphrodite and said: "The works of war are not   435
for you, my child. Follow after the lovely works

---

404   *to pain*: It is unknown why or under what circumstances Herakles shot Hera in the breast. His wounding
      of Hades is equally obscure as well as the mention of Pylos (which could mean "in the gate" instead of the
      settlement at Pylos—the gate of the realm of Hades?).

408   *Paieon*: A healing god known from the syllabic Linear B tablets; he appears only in this book and in *Odyssey* 4.
      Paieon or Paian eventually became a title of Apollo as healer. A *paieon* (*paean*) is a song to Apollo.

430   . . . *Trojans*: That is, Helen.

of marriage. Let all these other things be the concern
of swift Ares and Athena."°

             And so they conversed with one
another. Diomedes good at the war cry leaped on Aeneas,
440   realizing that Apollo himself held his two arms
over Aeneas. But Diomedes had no regard
for the great god. He was eager to kill Aeneas
and to strip off his famous armor. Three times he leaped
on him, desiring to kill him; three times Apollo
445   beat back his shining shield. But when for a fourth time
Diomedes rushed on him like a god, Apollo,
who works from a long way off, said, shouting
terribly: "Only think, son of Tydeus, and withdraw!
Don't wish to be like the gods. The races of immortal
450   gods and men who walk the earth are not the same."

    So he spoke. The son of Tydeus withdrew a little
backward, avoiding the anger of Apollo, who strikes from afar.
Apollo set Aeneas apart from the crowd in sacred
Pergamos, where his temple was built. Leto and Artemis,
455   who showers arrows, healed him in the great sanctuary,
and they glorified him. But Apollo of the silver bow made
an image of Aeneas, just like Aeneas himself and wearing
the same armor. Around that image the Trojans and the
good Achaeans struck their shields made of bull's hide
460   that protected their breasts, both rounded shields and long ones
with feathers attached.°

             Then Phoibos Apollo spoke to
mad Ares: "Ares, Ares, murderer of men, blood-stained
stormer of walls—will you not go into the battle
and withdraw this man, Tydeus' son, who now
465   would fight even with Father Zeus? First in a close fight
he wounded Kypris on the hand at the wrist, and then he
leaped on me as if he were a god!"

---

438 *Athena*: This passage was to spawn a whole genre of ancient poetry, especially Roman, where the lover
     insists that his battlefield is the bed, not the field of war. The wounding of Aphrodite may enhance
     Diomedes' prowess, but it is humorous in showing off Aphrodite's weakness against a mortal's violence.
     In spite of Dionê's warning, Diomedes comes to no harm through his attack on the gods. In fact nothing is
     known of the death of Diomedes.

461 *with feathers attached*: The meaning of the Greek is not clear.

So speaking he sat down
at the top of Pergamos while deadly Ares went among
the ranks of the Trojans and urged them on.

*[Lines 470–714 are omitted. The Trojans counterattack, alarming Hera and Athena,
who scheme to stop Ares' assistance to the Trojans.]*

Now the goddess white-armed Hera saw what was happening,   715
how the Argives were being destroyed in the terrible combat.
Right away she spoke words to Athena that went like arrows:
"Alas, O daughter of Zeus who carries the goatskin fetish!
Unwearied one, I think that we spoke to no purpose when we
promised Menelaos that he would sail home after sacking   720
Ilion, if we permit this ruinous Ares to rage in this way.
But come let us two think of savage valor!"

So Hera spoke, and the flashing-eyed Athena, divine,
did not disobey her, but went back and forth harnessing
her horses with head-pieces of gold. Hebê quickly   725
fitted the curved wheels to either side of the car.
The wheels were made of bronze with eight spokes,
and the axle was made of iron. The rim was imperishable
gold and on top of it were fitted tires of bronze, a marvel
to see. The hubs were made of silver, spinning   730
around on either side. The body was woven
of gold and silver strips. Two rails ran around it.
The pole was made of silver and from its tip
she bound a beautiful golden yoke and cast
on the yoke handsome breast-collars. Beneath the yoke   735
Hera led horses with lightning feet, eager
for strife and the cry of war.

But Athena, the daughter
of Zeus, let her soft embroidered gown fall
to her father's floor. She herself had made it
with her own hands. She put on the shirt of Zeus   740
who gathers the clouds. She armed herself for tearful war.
Around her shoulders she cast the tasseled goatskin
fetish, an object of terror, crowned by Rout, where
inside is Eris, inside is Valor, inside is icy
Attack, and inside is the head of the dreadful   745
monster, the Gorgon, hideous and awful, a wonder
of Zeus who carries the goatskin fetish. On her head
Athena placed a helmet with ridges on either side and four

golden plates, fitted with foot soldiers of a hundred cities.°
750 She stepped into the flaming chariot. She took up the spear—
heavy, large, powerful!—with which she overcomes
the ranks of men, of warriors with whom she is angry,
she of the mighty father.

               Swiftly Hera touched
the horses with the lash. The gates of heaven
755 groaned open. The Horai° keep them, to whom are
entrusted the great heaven and Olympos, whether to throw
open the thick cloud or whether to shut it up. There
through the gates they drove their horses, tolerant
of the goad.

             They found the son of Kronos sitting apart
760 from the other gods on the topmost peak of Olympos,
which has many ridges. Staying the horses,
the white-armed goddess Hera questioned
the exalted son of Kronos, Zeus: "Zeus, father,
don't you resent Ares for his violent acts?
765 He has destroyed so great and good an army
of the Achaeans, recklessly and not according to the right
order of things, to my sorrow. In the meanwhile, Kypris
and Apollo of the silver bow, free from care, take delight
in having sent down this mad man without respect for any law.
770 Zeus, father, will you be angry if I give Ares a good cuffing
and chase him out of the battle?"

               Zeus the cloud-gatherer
answered: "Well then, rouse up Athena, the gatherer of loot.
It's her habit most to bring Ares close to evil pains."

      So he spoke, and the white-armed goddess
775 Hera did not disobey. She applied the lash.
The two horses, not unwilling, flew between
the earth and starry heaven. As far as a man
can see into the misty distance, sitting on a place
of outlook and looking over the sea dark as wine,
780 just so far did the high-whinnying horses leap in a
single bound. But when they came to Troy and the two
flowing rivers, where the Simoeis and the Skamandros

---

749 *hundred cities*: Apparently emphasizing the helmet's enormous size, but the Greek is obscure.

755 *Horai*: The "hours" or "seasons," a personification of time, here as the gatekeepers of heaven.

join their streams, there white-armed Hera stayed
the horses, loosing them from her car, and she
poured about them a thick mist. Simoeis sent up   785
ambrosia° for them to graze on.

                 The two goddesses
went like nervous pigeons in their walk, anxious
to help the Argive men. But when they came
to where the most and best men stood, crouched
around powerful Diomedes tamer of horses, like   790
lions who eat raw flesh, or wild boars, hardly
weaklings, there white-armed Hera stood
and shouted in the likeness of greathearted Stentor,°
whose voice was like bronze, so loud it was like fifty men
shouting: "Shame on you Argives, a bitter reproach,   795
good only to look at! So long as Achilles came into
the battle, the Trojans did not come forth before
the Dardanian Gate. They feared his powerful spear.
But now they fight near the hollow ships far from the city."

   So speaking she excited the strength and spirits of every man.   800
The flashing-eyed goddess Athena leaped to the side
of Tydeus' son. She found Diomedes beside his horses and his car,
cooling the wound he had received from the arrow of Pandaros.
The sweat poured beneath the strap of his round shield.
He was bothered by it and his arm grew tired. He raised up   805
the strap and wiped away the dark blood.

                 The goddess lay
hold of the yoke of his horses and said: "Surely Tydeus
begot a son little like himself! Tydeus was short
in stature, but a fighter. Once I would not let him
fight or shine forth, when he went alone as a messenger   810
to Thebes among the many Kadmeians. I urged
him to dine, to be cheerful in the halls, but having his strong
spirit, as of old, he challenged the youths of the Kadmeians
and he easily defeated them. I was such a helper to him.
As for you, I stand at your side and protect you and I am   815
glad to urge you to fight against the Trojans. But either

---

786 *ambrosia*: The word means "immortal," a special food of the gods, but with many other uses, here said to
     grow on the banks of the Simoeis and to feed the divine horses!

793 *Stentor*: Although later proverbial (someone speaks in a "stentorian voice"), this character only appears
     here in Homer.

too many assaults have drenched your limbs in weariness
or a spiritless fear possesses you. You are no son of Tydeus,
the wise son of Oeneus!"

                    The mighty Diomedes
820 answered her in this way: "I know who you are,
goddess, daughter of Zeus who carries the goatskin fetish.
And so I will happily tell you my thoughts and I will
not conceal it. No spiritless fear possesses me, nor any
unwillingness to engage. But I am always mindful
825 of the instructions that you laid upon me. I am not to fight
face to face with the blessed gods, unless the daughter
of Zeus, Aphrodite, should come into the battle—
her I should wound with the sharp bronze. For this reason
I have withdrawn from the fighting and urged the other Argives
830 to gather. For I see that Ares is lording it over the battlefield."°

      Then the flashing-eyed goddess Athena answered him:
"My Diomedes, son of Tydeus, the darling of my heart,
don't be afraid of Ares nor any other of the deathless ones,
so powerful a helper to you am I going to be.
835 So come, turn your single-hoofed horses right away
against Ares. Fight him in the hand-to-hand.
Have no respect for great mad Ares—this raving one,
this evil made to order, this good for nothing! Just now
he was telling me and Hera that he was going to fight against
840 the Trojans and give aid to the Argives, but as it is
he's mingling with the Trojans, and the others are forgotten."

      So speaking, she drew back Sthenelos with her hand
and shoved him from his car to the ground. Speedily he jumped!
She got in the car next to good Diomedes, a goddess
845 anxious for battle. The great axle, made of oak, groaned
beneath the burden, for it carried a goddess and the best
of men. Pallas Athena took up the lash and the reins
and right away she headed the horses toward Ares.

      He was just then stripping the armor from the huge Periphas,
850 by far the best of the Aetolians, the fine son of Ochesios.
Ares, dripping with blood, was stripping the corpse,
but Athena put on the cap of Hades so that powerful
Ares could not see her.

---

830 *battlefield:* But we have just been told that Diomedes withdrew from the fighting in order to cool his wound!

When the murderous Ares saw
the good Diomedes, he let huge Periphas lie where he was,
where Ares had killed him, setting free his breath-soul,   855
and he headed straight for Diomedes, the tamer of horses.
When they came near, advancing against one another,
first Ares drove over the yoke and the reins of Diomedes'
horses, eager with his bronze spear to take away
the other's life. But the flashing-eyed goddess Athena   860
caught his spear in her hand and thrust it above the car,
making it fly away in vain. Next Diomedes, good at
the war cry, thrust at Ares with his bronze spear. Pallas
Athena sent it into his lower belly near the buckle
of the belly-protector. Diomedes wounded him and cut   865
the beautiful skin, then he pulled out the spear.

Brazen Ares bellowed as much as nine thousand
or ten thousand men yell in battle when they join
in the contendings of Ares. A trembling took hold of
the Achaeans and Trojans, they were afraid, so loudly   870
did Ares roar, insatiate of war. Even as when a black
air appears from the clouds after a heat wave,
when a blustery wind arises—even so the brazen
Ares appeared to Diomedes, son of Tydeus,
as he went together with the clouds into the broad sky.°   875

Soon he arrived at the seat of the gods, steep Olympos,
and he sat down next to Zeus, the son of Kronos,
pained at heart. He showed him the immortal blood
running down out of the wound, and with a wailing
he spoke words that went like arrows: "Zeus, father,   880
doesn't it anger you to see these violent acts?
Always we gods suffer shivery things from the desire
of one another, whenever we show favor to men.
We are all at war with you! You gave birth to that insane
and destructive daughter, always concerned with evil acts.   885
All the gods who are in Olympos obey you
and are subject to you. But you pay no attention to her,
whether in word or in deed, but you encourage her—
because you yourself begot this destroying child.
Now she has set Diomedes, high of heart,   890

---

875   sky: Ares' rising into heaven is compared to a tornado which is black in color and after descending rises
      rapidly into the sky. The scene of the wounding of Ares is more slapstick. The gods behave like clownish
      humans, provoking a laugh in Homer's all-male audience of men who were themselves warriors.

the son of Tydeus, to rage against the deathless gods.
First he wounded Kypris in the close fight on the hand
near the wrist, but then, like a god, he raged against
me myself! Luckily I was able to run away.

895 Otherwise I would have suffered pains there for a long time
amidst the vile heaps of the dead, or I would have been alive,
but without strength from the blows of the bronze."°

Zeus answered him, glowering beneath his brows:
"Ares, don't sit beside me and whine, you good for nothing.
900 You are most hated to me of the gods who inhabit
Olympos! Always dear to you are strife and wars
and battles. You have the mind of your mother
Hera, intolerable, unyielding. I can scarcely control
her with words. Therefore I think that you
905 are suffering these things because of her suggestions.
Nonetheless I will not let you continue to endure
these agonies. You are of my blood. Your mother bore
you to me. If you were born of any other god, destructive
as you are, then long before now you would be lower
910 than the Ouraniones!"°

Zeus spoke and he asked Paieon
to heal Ares. Paieon spread a poultice over the wound
and healed him, for surely Ares was not made to be mortal.
Even as the juice of the wild fig quickly makes to grow
thick the white milk that is liquid, but soon curdles as a man
915 stirs it, even so swiftly did he heal mad Ares.
Hebê bathed him and placed lovely clothes upon him.
He sat beside Zeus, the son of Kronos, exulting
in his glory.

Back to the house of great Zeus went
Argive Hera and Alalkomenian Athena, having put
920 an end to man-killing Ares' murderous rampage.

---

897 *bronze*: The rather stupid Ares seems impossibly confused in what he fears might have happened to him.

910 *Ouraniones*: The "heavenly gods," not here the Olympians but Kronos and the other Titans, the children of
Ouranos whom Zeus imprisoned in underworld Tartaros, according to the story told in Hesiod's *Theogony*.

BOOK 6. *Diomedes and Glaukos; and, Hector and Andromachê Say Goodbye*

[Lines 1–101 are omitted. The battle surges back and forth, but the Greeks push back. The Trojan Helenos, a brother of Hector, persuades Hector to go into the city to ask the women to offer a prayer to Athena. But first Hector rallies the Trojans.]

Immediately Hector leaped from the car to the ground in his armor,
and shaking his two sharp spears he went everywhere
throughout the army urging them to fight. He stirred
up the terrible din of battle. And so they rallied   105
and took their stand facing the Achaeans. The Argives
gave ground, they stopped the slaughter. They thought that one
of the deathless ones had come from the starry heaven
to assist the Trojans. That's why the Trojans rallied.

Hector called out to the Trojans, shouting aloud: 110
"High-hearted Trojans, and allies famed from afar,
be men, my friends! Remember your mad valor!
I must go into the city and tell the aged advisors
and our wives that they should pray to the gods
and promise sacrifice."   115

So speaking, Hector of the flashing
helmet went off. The dark skin of his bossed
shield at either end struck his ankles and his neck,
the rim that ran around the outside.°

Glaukos,° the offspring
of Hippolochos, and Tydeus' son came together in the space
between the two armies, eager to fight. When they came   120
near to one another, Diomedes, good at the war cry,

---

118 *outside:* Homer seems to be talking about a Mycenaean "figure of eight" shield, or a "tower" shield
     (see Figure 4.1), remembered in the oral tradition, not the smaller round "buckler" shields that most
     Homeric warriors carry. The "boss," a knob or protuberance at the center of the shield, belongs to the
     buckler type, so he has confused the two shields. The body shield, suspended by a strap or *telamon* around
     the shoulder, went out of use probably around 1200 BC.

119 *Glaukos:* Earlier mentioned only as Sarpedon's second-in-command (in Book 2).

was first to speak: "Who are you, mighty one among
mortal men? I never saw you in the battle where men win glory
until this day.° But now you come out much ahead of the others
in your boldness, and you challenge my long-shadowed spear.
They are the children of wretched men who face my power.
If you are one of the deathless ones come down from the sky,
well, I would not fight with the heavenly gods.°
No, strong Lykourgos, the son of Dryas, did not last long,
he who contended with the deathless gods. He drove down
over holy Mount Nysa° the nurses of raging Dionysos.
All together they let their wands° fall to the ground, struck
by the ox-goad of man-killing Lykourgos. Dionysos fled
and was submerged under the wave of the sea. Thetis
received him, terrified, in her lap. For a commanding fear
had seized Dionysos from the threats of Lykourgos. The gods,
who live in ease, were then supremely angry with Lykourgos,
and the son of Kronos made Lykourgos blind. He didn't
last long after that, for all the gods hated him.°

No more do I want to fight with the blessed gods.
But if you are a man who eats the fruit of the field, come closer
so that you might more quickly arrive at the bounds
of death."

The glorious son of Hippolochos answered
him in this way: "Son of Tydeus, great of heart, why
do you ask about my lineage? As are the generations of leaves,
so are the generations of men. Some leaves the wind
blows to the ground, but the forest burgeons and puts forth
new leaves, when the season of spring comes. So it is
with the generations of men—one grows while the other withers
away. But if you really want to hear about these things,
so you will know my background—and many know it—

---

124   *until this day*: Unlikely, unless Diomedes is insulting Glaukos.

128   *heavenly gods*: Diomedes does not mention that he has just fought against Aphrodite and Ares!

131   *Mount Nysa*: There were many mountains with this name in the ancient world, but probably here is meant a
        mountain in Thrace because Thetis lived in an underwater cave between the islands of SAMOTHRACE and
        IMBROS near THRACE (*Il.* Book 24).

132   *wands*: These would be the *thyrsi* of the Maenads, the ecstatic followers of Dionysos. *Thrysi* were phallic
        implements, sticks entwined with ivy and surmounted by a pine cone.

139   *hated him*: The myth of Lykourgos is the oldest of the many myths of resistance to the god Dionysus,
        (whom Homer mentions only three times), so popular later, especially in Euripides' celebrated play the
        Bacchae (405 BC).

there is a city called Ephyra° in a corner of Argos,
which nourishes horses. That was the home of Sisyphos,°
the most clever of all men, Sisyphos, son of Aiolos.
He had a son whose name was Glaukos,° and Glaukos   155
was father to the good Bellerophon. To him the gods gave beauty
and a lovely manliness. But King Proitos devised evil things
in his heart, and because Proitos was far the stronger he drove
Bellerophon from the land of the Argives—Zeus made them
subject to his scepter. Now the fair Anteia   160
went mad for Bellerophon, longing to mingle in secret love,
but she could not persuade the wise-hearted Bellerophon,
who always wanted to do what was right. She lied to Proitos,
the king, saying: "Either die yourself, Proitos,
or kill Bellerophon, who wanted to mingle with me   165
in love against my will."°

        So she spoke. The king was angered
to hear this word. He was reluctant to kill Bellerophon,
for he had respect in his heart,° so he sent him to LYCIA.°
Proitos gave Bellerophon ruinous signs scratched
on a folded tablet, many and deadly.° Proitos told Bellerophon   170
to show these to his wife's father, so that he might be killed.
He went to Lycia under the blameless escort of the gods.
When he came to Lycia and the river XANTHOS, the king
of wide Lycia honored him with a ready heart.
For nine days the king entertained Bellerophon. He sacrificed   175
nine cattle. But when the tenth Dawn came, whose fingers

---

152   *Ephyra*: An old name for Corinth, where Bellerophon tamed Pegasos.

153   *Sisyphos*: Punished in the underworld in the *Odyssey* (Book 12) for his many crimes by being compelled to roll a boulder up a hill, which would roll back just as he neared the top.

155   *Glaukos*: The namesake and grandfather of the Glaukos who fought on the plain of Troy.

166   *against my will*: This is the folktale type called "Potiphar's wife" after the biblical story, c. 500 BC, of the Pharaoh's general Potiphar whose wife tried to seduce Joseph. It is the oldest recorded folktale in the world, appearing in the much earlier Egyptian "Story of the Two Brothers" from about 1200 BC. The Greeks liked the story too, the subject of Euripides' *Hippolytos* (c. 428 BC) in which the Theseus' wife falls in love with Hippolytos, propositions him, then kills herself when she is turned down.

168   *respect in his heart*: That is, respect for the conventions of *xenia*, "guest-friendship," the unwritten rules that govern hospitality: You do not kill a guest, and a guest does not sleep with his host's wife. The Trojan War was caused by Paris' taking Helen, a violation of *xenia*.

168   *Lycia*: In southwest Asia Minor: See Map III.

170   *deadly*: The only reference to writing in Homer. Tablets, recessed and coated on the inner side with wax, were common in the ancient East (but not Egypt); one survives from a shipwreck c. 1400 BC. We cannot say what Homer means by *sêmata lugra*, "ruinous signs," but he does not refer to alphabetic writing, which is never called *sêmata*, "signs." Homer has heard of writing but does not know what it is exactly. The signs here are "deadly" because they mean "kill the bearer" or the like.

FIGURE 6.1   Bellerophon, riding Pegasos, prepares to stab the Chimaira.   The Chimaira ("she-goat") was a monster with a snake's tale, a goat's head growing from its back, and a lion's body. The monster is perhaps an invention of the Hittites, strong in central Anatolia around 1400–1180 BC, and later in northern Syria around 900 BC. Pegasos sprang from the blood of the Gorgon when Perseus cut off her head, along with a mysterious Chrysaör, "he of the golden sword" (Apollo has this epithet in Book 5 of the *Iliad*). From the rim of an Athenian red-figure epinetron (thigh-protector used by a woman when weaving), c. 425–420 BC.

are of rose, then the king questioned Bellerophon. He asked
to see the tokens from his daughter's husband, Proitos.
When he had received the evil tokens of his daughter's husband,
first he ordered Bellerophon to kill the invincible Chimaira.　　　　　180
She was of divine lineage, not of the race of men,
in the front a lion, in the back a snake, and in the middle
a she-goat. She breathed the terrible strength of shining fire.
He killed her, trusting in the portents of the gods.° Second
he fought against the stalwart Solymi.° He said this was　　　　　185
the hardest fight of men he ever entered. Third, he killed
the Amazons, the equals of men. When he came back,
the king wove another clever deceit. He set an ambush,
choosing from broad Lycia the best men. They never
came back home, for the blameless Bellerophon killed　　　　　190
them all.

　　　"But when the king saw that Bellerophon
was the noble offspring of a god, he kept him there
and he gave him his daughter.° The king gave Bellerophon
half of all his royal honor, and the Lycians cut him
out a territory better than all, a beautiful orchard　　　　　195
land and plowland, just for Bellerophon. The daughter
bore three children to wise Bellerophon: Isandros
and Hippolochos and Laodameia. Zeus the counselor
slept with Laodameia, who bore Sarpedon,
like a god, armed in bronze.° But when even Bellerophon　　　　　200
came to be hated of all the gods, he wandered
alone over the Aleian plain,° devouring his own soul,
avoiding the paths of men. Ares, insatiate of war,
killed Isandros, his son, as he warred against the glorious
Solymi. Artemis, whose reins are golden, grew　　　　　205
angry with Bellerophon's daughter and killed her.
Hippolochos fathered me, and from him do I say
I have come into being. He sent me to Troy
and he laid on to me a strict order: always to excel

184　*portents of the gods*: Such monsters of mixed type are otherwise unknown in Homer (except perhaps the
　　　Centaurs). Homer curiously suppresses any mention of Pegasos.

185　*Solymi*: A Lycian tribe.

193　...*daughter*: So that Bellerophon is now the brother-in-law of Anteia, the woman who slandered him!

200　...*bronze*: Therefore Glaukos is the nephew of Sarpedon, because Glaukos' father is Hippolochos who is
　　　brother to Laodameia, the mother of Sarpedon. Sarpedon is a son of Zeus and one of Troy's strongest allies.
　　　Patroklos kills him in Book 16.

202　*Aleian plain*: The "plain of wandering," a mythical place perhaps invented for this story. According to other tradi-
　　　tions, Bellerophon offended the gods when he attempted to fly to heaven on Pegasos. He fell off and was killed.

210 and to be superior to the others, and not to put to shame
the race of our fathers, who were by far the noblest
in Ephyra and in broad Lycia. Such is my background,
my bloodline, from which I am sprung."

                              So he spoke, and Diomedes,
good at the war cry, rejoiced. He planted his spear in the
215 much-nourishing earth. With gentle words he spoke to the shepherd
of the people: "Glaukos, you are a guest-friend of my father's
from long since! For Oeneus° once hosted the blameless
Bellerophon in his halls, entertaining him for twenty days.
They gave beautiful friendship-tokens to one another.
220 Oeneus gave a belt shining with scarlet, Bellerophon
a golden double cup which I left in my house when I came here.
I do not remember Tydeus, since he left when I was just
a boy, when the army of Achaeans was destroyed at Thebes.
So now I am a dear guest-friend to you when you
225 are in the midst of Argos, and you will be mine
when I arrive to the land of that people. Let us avoid
one another's spears even in the thick of battle. For there
are many Trojans for me to kill, and their far-famed
allies too, whomever a god will give me and my feet
230 to overtake. There are many Achaeans for you to kill,
whomever you can. Let us now exchange armor
with one another so that these other men might know
that we are guest-friends 205 from the days of our fathers."

    So speaking, leaping from the chariots, they took each
235 other's hands and gave each other assurances. Then Zeus,
the son of Kronos, took away the good sense of Glaukos,
who exchanged with Diomedes, the son of Tydeus, golden
armor for bronze, the worth of a hundred oxen as against nine!°

    When Hector came to the Scaean Gates and the oak tree,°
240 the wives and daughters of the Trojans ran up to him, asking
about their sons and brothers and relatives and their husbands.

---

217 *Oeneus*: "wine-man" is the grandfather of Diomedes, father of Tydeus, and king of KALYDON in the southwestern portion of mainland Greece.

238 *against nine*: No commentator, ancient or modern, has explained this bizarre incident. In Book 8 Hector tells *his horses* that Nestor has a shield of gold, but otherwise golden armor is unknown. Nothing is said about the armor when the conversation begins, and it is hardly practical. Evidently the conventions of folktale, with its exaggerated, improbable, and miraculous developments has for some reason influenced Homer's narrative, creating a break in the narrative as Hector goes into the city.

239 *oak tree*: A landmark on the battlefield near the Scaean Gates, first mentioned in Book 5 and several times later.

He urged them to pray to the gods, all of them and in order.
But sorrow was fixed on many.

When Hector came to the beautiful
house of Priam built with dressed stone porches—
in it were fifty chambers of polished stone built near 245
one another, where the sons of Priam slept with their wedded
wives, and on the other side, just opposite inside the courtyard,
were twelve chambers of the daughters of Priam, roofed
in dressed stone built near one another, where the sons-in-law
of Priam slept with their chaste wives°—there his bountiful 250
mother came toward him accompanied by Laodikê, the most
beautiful of her daughters, and she clasped him by hand and spoke
to him and said his name: "My child, why have
you left the fierce battle and come here? Surely the sons
of the Achaeans—a curse on their name!—are wearing you down 255
fighting around our city. Your heart has impelled you to come
here to raise up your hands to Zeus from the summit
of the city? But let me pour for you some honey-sweet wine.
First pour out some of it to Zeus and the other gods,
then you yourself might have its benefit, if you will drink. 260
Wine increases the great strength in a tired man,
and you have been exhausted defending your companions."

Then great Hector, whose helmet sparkled, said:
"Dear mother, do not bring me honey-sweet wine,
or you may sap the strength in my limbs and I 265
may forget my valor. And I am reluctant to pour
out flaming wine to Zeus with unwashed hands,
nor is it right to pray to Zeus of the dark cloud
spattered with blood and gore. But you go gather
together the older women. Take offerings to be burned 270
to the temple of Athena who gathers the spoil. Select
the robe that seems most precious and largest in the house,
one that you value above the others, and place it
on the knees of the goddess with the lovely hair.
Promise that you will sacrifice in her temple twelve cattle, 275
one-year old, that have never been goaded, if she
will pity the city and the wives of the Trojans and the little
children, in hope that she will hold off from sacred Ilion
the son of Tydeus, that wild spearman, the powerful

---

250   ... *wives*: We cannot really get a picture of the layout of the palace from this description, and it is hard
to see how twelve chambers can face fifty in a courtyard.

280 deviser of rout. So go to the temple of Athena
who gathers the spoil while I go to see Paris
and call him out, if he is willing to listen to me.
May the earth swallow him where he stands! The Olympian
has raised him to be a pain to the Trojans and to big-hearted
285 Priam and his sons. If I should see that man going down
to the house of Hades, I would think that my heart
had forgotten its joyless sorrow!"

So he spoke, and she,
going toward the hall, called out to her attendants.
They gathered together the older women throughout the city.
290 She herself went down into the fragrant storage-chamber
where were the finely wrought robes of Sidonian women,
which godlike Alexandros himself had brought from Sidon
when he sailed over the broad sea, on the trip when he abducted
well-born Helen.° Hekabê took one of them as a gift
295 to Athena, the most elaborately embroidered and largest,
and it shone like a star. It lay at the bottom of the pile.
Then she went her way and the many elderly ladies
hurried after.

When they came to the temple of Athena
at the top of the city, Theano of the beautiful cheeks,
300 daughter of Kisseus, the wife of horse-taming Antenor,
opened the doors for them. The Trojans had made her
the priestess of Athena. With a cry they all raised their hands
to Athena. Theano took up the robe and placed it
on the knees of Athena who has fine tresses. With vows
305 she prayed to the daughter of great Zeus: "Reverend Athena,
guardian of this city, divine goddess, break the spear
of Diomedes and cause that he fall down on his face in front
of the Scaean Gates so that we may sacrifice in your temple
twelve cattle, one-year old, that have never been goaded,
310 if you will take pity on the city and the wives of the Trojans
and the little children." So she spoke in prayer, but Pallas
Athena rejected the request.°

---

294 *Helen*: Evidently Paris was blown off course in returning to Troy and, improbably, ended up in PHOENICIA on the
coast of the eastern Mediterranean in modern-day Lebanon. SIDON was the most important of the Phoenician
ports. The Sidonians made a precious purple cloth. The purple dye, the most valuable in the ancient world, was
made from a shellfish that grew there in abundance. Probably *Phoinikes* means in Greek the "red-handed ones,"
named from the dye. These coastal-dwelling Semitic-speakers never described themselves as "Phoenicians."

312 *request*: It is odd that the Trojans should pray to Athena when she is resolutely on the Achaean side. The
Trojans must not see it this way.

Hector went to the beautiful
house of Alexandros, which he himself had built with
the best builders in deep-soiled Troy, who made
for him the chamber and the house and the hall   315
close to Priam and Hector at the top of the city.°
There Hector came, the beloved of Zeus, and in
his hand he held the spear sixteen feet long. Before him
blazed the bronze point of the spear, and around it ran
a ferrule of gold.   320

                Hector found Paris in the chamber
polishing his beautiful armor, his shield and chest-protector,
and handling his curved bow. Argive Helen sat among
the women attendants and gave orders to her maids
about the famed handicraft.

                When he saw him, Hector
rebuked Paris with shaming words: "What has come over you?   325
It is not right that you nourish this anger in your heart.°
The people perish in their fight around the city and
the high wall. It is on *your* account that the din and war burn
about the city. *You* would quarrel with anyone you saw
holding back in the hateful war, so get up or soon   330
you will see the city ablaze with consuming fire."

   Godlike Alexandros then answered him: "Hector,
you reprove me rightfully, and not without good reason.
I will tell you then: Please consider what I say,
and hear me out. It is not so much because of anger   335
or indignation against the Trojans that I sit in my chamber.
Rather, I want to give myself over to sorrow. Even now
my wife has tried to turn my mind with gentle words, urging
me to go to the battle, and this seems to me too
to be better. Why, victory shifts from man to man!   340
But come now, just wait. I'll put on my armor of war. Or go,
and I will come after. And I do believe I'll overtake you!"
So he spoke, but Hector of the sparkling helmet
said nothing.

---

316 *city*: Homer appears to describe a late Bronze Age settlement, such as Mycenae or Athens or Troy itself.
     Iron Age settlements, by contrast, never had monumental secular structures.

326 *heart*: Hector must mean Paris' anger at the Trojans for wanting to hand him over to the Achaeans when
     the duel with Menelaos ended as it did.

Then Helen addressed Hector with

345 honeyed words: "My brother—brother to a scheming, icy bitch!—
I wish that on the day my mother first bore me an evil
wind had come along and carried me away to the mountains
or beneath the wave of the loud-resounding sea, where
the wave could snatch me away before any of these things

350 happened. But since the gods have made such horrible
things come to pass, I wish that I could be the wife
of a better man, one that could feel the hostility of others
and their many insults. This man here—his mind
is not stable, nor will it ever be. Someday he will

355 reap the fruit, I think! But come now, come in,
sit on this stool, my brother, for the trouble falls
most on your spirit because of me—a bitch!—
and on account of the madness of Alexandros. Zeus
has placed a dark fate on us so we might be the subject

360 of song for men who come later."°

Great Hector, whose helmet
sparkles, answered her then: "Don't make me sit, Helen,
though you love me. You won't persuade me. Already
my spirit urges me to defend the Trojans, who want me
back among them. But you rouse this man to get going

365 by himself so that he overtakes me while I am still
in the city. Now I am going to go to my house to see
the servants and my dear wife and my little baby.
For I do not know if I will again return, or whether the gods
will kill me at the hands of the Achaeans."

So speaking, Hector

370 of the sparkling helmet went off. Quickly he arrived
at his house, a lovely place to live. He did not find
white-armed Andromachê in the halls, but she stood even then
by the wall with her child and her maid with the nice gown,
moaning and filled with sorrow.

Hector, when he saw

375 that his beloved wife was not within, stopped on the threshold
as he went out, and he spoke to the women servants:
"Come now, women, tell me straight out: Where has
white-armed Andromachê gone from the hall? Has she gone
to the house of one of my sisters or one of my brother's wives,

---

360 *come later*: As here, in Homer's *Iliad*.

whose robes are fine, or has she gone to the house of Athena,   380
where the other Trojan women with woven tresses are beseeching
the dread goddess?"

Then a harried servant said:
"Hector, because you strongly enjoin us to tell the truth,
she has not gone to the house of your sisters or of your
brothers' wives, who wear nice robes, nor to the house   385
of Athena where the other Trojan women, with fine tresses,
beseech the dread goddess, but she has gone to the great tower
of Ilion. She heard that the Trojans are hard pressed,
that the power of the Achaeans is great. She went to the wall
in haste, like a mad woman. With her a nurse carries the child."   390

So spoke the woman maid. Hector hastened from
the house, back the same way through the well-built streets.
When he came to the Scaean Gates, passing through the great city
from which he was about to go forth onto the plain,
there his wife with the generous dowry came running to him,   395
Andromachê, the daughter of great-hearted Eëtion, who had lived
beneath wooded Plakos, in THEBES under Plakos, ruling over the men
of Cilicia.° It was Eëtion's daughter that bronze-harnessed
Hector had to wife. She met him then, and with her
came a maid holding the tender-hearted boy, just a little baby,   400
like to a beautiful star, the beloved son of Hector.
Hector called him Skamandrios, but the others Astyanax,
because Hector alone protected Ilion.°

Hector smiled
when he glanced at his son in silence. Andromachê stood
beside him weeping. She clasped his hand and spoke   405
and called him by name: "My darling, your strength will destroy you,
nor do you take pity on your speechless babe and luckless me,
who will soon be a widow. For quickly the Achaeans will rush

---

398 *Cilicia:* Eëtion is Andromachê's father and mentioned several times. His name is nonGreek. Achilles sacked
     nearby LYRNESSOS when he captured Briseïs, and THEBES, when he captured Chryseïs after killing Eëtion
     and his seven sons (Map IV). Andromachê had earlier married Hector and at the time was safe in Troy. In
     the loot taken from Thebes is Achilles' lyre, which he plays in Book 9, and Achilles' horse Pedasos. Plakos
     seems to be a southern spur of MOUNT IDA. These "Cilicians" are distinct from the Cilicians in Southeast
     Asia Minor—unless they migrated here from there. Just so, Pandaros' "Lycians" lived in the Troad and are
     not the Lycians from southwest Asia Minor.

403 *. . . protected Ilion:* Skamandrios is the main river of the Troad; the child must be named after the river. He is
     called Skamandrios only here; elsewhere he is always Astyanax, "defender of the city," named for his
     father's role. Odysseus will throw Astyanax from the tower after the sack of Troy, as Homer's audience knew.

upon you and kill you. For me it would be better to go
410 under the earth if I lose you. Never will there be
comfort for me when you have met your fate, but only sorrow.
I have no father and no reverend mother. My father
Achilles killed when he sacked the city of the Cilicians,
high-gated Thebes. He killed Eëtion, but he did
415 not despoil him, for in his heart he respected him.
He burned Eëtion in his fancy armor, and he heaped
up a tomb. The nymphs of the mountains planted elm trees
all around it, the daughters of Zeus who carries the goatskin
fetish. I had seven brothers in my halls who went
420 into the house of Hades all in a single day.
The good Achilles, the fast runner, killed them all
as they tended their lumbering cattle and white-fleeced sheep.
As for my mother, who was queen in wooded Plakos,
they brought her here with the other possessions. Quickly
425 Achilles took abundant ransom for her and let her go,
but Artemis the archer shot her down in the house of her father.
    "But Hector, you are my father and my reverend mother
and my brother. You are my strong husband. So come, have pity
and stay here at the tower so that you do not make your son an orphan
430 and your wife a widow. Station your army near the fig tree,°
where the approach to the city is easiest and the wall is vulnerable.
Three times the best fighters have come here and tested the wall,
those who follow the two Ajaxes° and famous Idomeneus
and the two sons of Atreus and the brave son of Tydeus.
435 Some prophet told them about it, or their own spirit urges them
on and encourages them."

                    Great Hector, whose helmet sparkled,
then answered: "Yes, I worry about this, woman,
but I feel a terrible shame before the Trojans and the Trojan
women with their trailing robes, if like a coward I skulk
440 apart from the war. Nor does my spirit permit it,
for I have learned always to be valiant and to fight with the foremost
fighters of the Trojans, winning fine fame for my father
and for myself. For I know this well in my heart and in my soul:
The day will come when sacred Ilion will be destroyed

---

430 *fig tree*: The fig tree, like the oak tree, is one of the fixed points on the Trojan plain, apparently near the walls, but not near the Scaean Gates as was the oak.

433 *two Ajaxes*: Ajax the son of Telamon (Big Ajax) and Ajax the son of Oïleus (Little Ajax) are unrelated but often fight together.

and Priam and the people of Priam with his good spear of ash.   445
But not so much does the grief of the Trojans in times
to come trouble me, nor of Hekabê herself, nor of King Priam,
nor of my brothers, who though many and brave shall fall
in the dust at the hands of hostile men, as does
your grief when one of the bronze-shirted Achaeans shall lead   450
you away in tears, taking away your day of freedom.
Then in Argos you will work your loom at another's
command, and you will carry water from Messeïs or Hypereia,°
much unwilling, but a powerful necessity will compel you.
And someone will say who sees you weeping: 'This   455
is the wife of Hector, the best of the horse-taming Trojans
in war, in the days when they fought around Ilion.'
So will they say. To you will come fresh grief
in your lack of a man to ward off the day of slavery.
But let the heaped-up earth hide me, dead,   460
before I hear your cry as they drag you away."°

So speaking, shining Hector reached out his arms
to his son, but his son shrank back, crying, into the bosom
of the fair-belted nurse, amazed at the sight of his father,
and fearful of the bronze and the horsehair crest, seeing   465
it nodding terribly from the top of his father's helmet.
The father laughed, and his august mother did too. Shining
Hector at once took the helmet from his head and he placed
it gleaming on the ground. He kissed his dear son
and held him in his arms, and he spoke in prayer to Zeus   470
and the other gods: "Zeus and you other gods,
grant that this my son, like me, may prove to be outstanding
among the Trojans, and great in strength, and that he might
rule Ilion with power. Then someday one might say
that he is much better than his father, when he returns   475
from war. May he possess the blood-stained spoils of a gallant
man he has killed, and may he gladden the heart of his mother."

So speaking he placed his son in the arms of his dear wife.
She took him into her fragrant bosom, laughing through her tears.

---

453 *Messeïs or Hypereia*: Messeïs, "middle spring," and Hypereia, "upper spring," are generic names that cannot
be located specifically. According to postHomeric tradition, after the sack of Troy Andromachê became, first,
the wife of Neoptolemos, the son of Achilles; then after Neoptolemos was murdered at Delphi, she became
the wife of Helenos, Hector's brother, who survived the war and migrated to northwest mainland Greece.

461 . . . *away*: Hector emphasizes the work at the loom and the fetching of water, a slave's duties, and omits the
violent rape that awaits the women of the city.

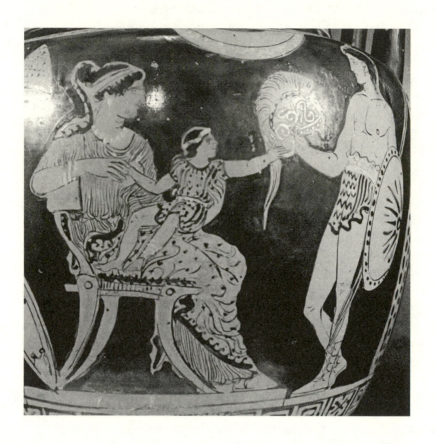

FIGURE 6.2   Hector bids farewell to Andromachê and Astyanax.   The boy stretches to touch his father's helmet. A beardless Hector, naked from the waist up, holds in his left hand a spear and shield. From a south Italian red-figure wine-mixing bowl, c. 370–360 BC.

Seeing her, her husband was moved with pity. He stroked her 480
with his hand and spoke to her: "My darling Andromachê,
I beg you, don't grieve too much for me in your heart.
No man will cast me into the house of Hades beyond
my fate. I don't think that any man can escape his fate,
neither a coward nor a brave man, when once he is born. 485
Go home now and busy yourself with your own tasks,
the loom and the distaff,° and urge your attendants to do
their work. War is for men, for all men but especially for me,
of those who live in Ilion."

So speaking shining Hector
took up his helmet with the horsehair crest. His dear 490
wife went off home, continually turning around,
weeping warm tears. Soon she came to the well-peopled
house of man-killing Hector. She found there her many
attendants. She roused among them all a wailing. They
lamented Hector while still alive, in his own house, 495
for they did not think that he would again return from war,
fleeing the strength and the hands of the Achaeans.

Paris did not stay long in his high house. He put on
his glorious armor, worked in bronze. He hurried
then through the city, trusting in his fleet feet, as when 500
a horse confined to a stable has fed his fill of barley
at the feeding trough, then breaks his bonds and runs
stamping across the plain exulting—for he is accustomed
to bathe in the fair-flowing river. He holds his head high,
and his mane streams around his shoulders. Trusting 505
in his splendor, his legs easily bear him to the haunts
and pastures of mares—even so Paris the son of Priam
came down from the summit of Pergamos brilliant in his armor,
like the blazing sun, laughing out loud, and swiftly
his feet bore him on. 510

Quickly he overtook his brother
Hector just as he was about to turn from the place
where he conversed with his wife. Godlike Alexandros
was the first to speak, saying: "My friend, surely

---

487   *distaff*: A distaff was a stick held beneath the arm, pressed to the woman's side, that held a mass of unspun
wool at its tip. From this mass the woolworker spun the thread. In genealogy, a family's "distaff side" is the
female ancestry.

my lingering holds you back when you wish to rush out,
515 nor have I come in due order as you commanded."

    Hector of the flashing helmet answered him:
"You're an odd fellow! No one who is of sound mind
could disrespect the work you do in battle, for you
are brave. But you willfully hold back and do not care.
520 My heart is grieved in my breast when I hear shameful words
about you from the Trojans, who because of you labor much.
    "But let us go. We will make all this right in the time
to come, if Zeus will allow us to set up a bowl of freedom
to the heavenly gods that live forever, once we have driven
525 from Troy the Achaeans with their fancy shin guards."

*[Book 7 is omitted. Hector returns with Paris to the fight. Hector offers to fight a duel with
any Greek. Big Ajax agrees and they fight to a draw. The two sides then agree to a truce so
that they can bury their dead. The Greeks build a defensive wall and dig a ditch in front of
their camp (in the tenth year of the war!).]*

BOOK 8. *Zeus Fulfills His Promise*

Dawn in her saffron robe spread out over all
the earth. Zeus, who delights in the thunder, called
an assembly on the highest peak of Olympos, which has
many ridges. He himself held forth, and all the gods
listened: "Hear me, all you gods and goddesses, 5
so that I may say what the spirit in my chest recommends.
None of you female gods, nor any of you male gods,
are to attempt to circumvent my word! I want you all
to agree, so that I may accomplish these things as soon
as possible. 10
     "If I catch any of you wanting to go to help
the Trojans or the Danaäns, he'll not come back to Olympos
without getting smacked around! Or I'll grab him and throw him
into murky Tartaros far, far away, where is the deepest
gulf beneath the earth, where the gates are made of iron
and the threshold is bronze, as far beneath Hades as the heaven 15
is from the earth—then you'll know how far I am the strongest
of all the gods! Go on—try it! So that you all
may know. Hang a golden chain from the heaven,
then all you gods and goddesses grab hold and tug.
You could not drag Zeus the counselor, the highest, 20
out of heaven to the ground, no matter how hard you try.
But if I wanted with a ready heart to drag you all up,
then I would do so, and bring up the earth and sea too.
And then I would tie the rope around a spur of Olympos,
so that everything should hang in the air. By so much 25
am I above the gods and men."

          So he spoke, and all
the rest fell into silence, amazed at his word, for he had
spoken with great power. At last flashing-eyed Athena
spoke: "O our father, son of Kronos, highest of all lords,
we all know very well that your power is unyielding, but still 30
we pity the Danaän spearmen, who will perish fulfilling
an evil fate. Nonetheless let us stay out of the war,
just as you command. We will give the Argives some advice
that will profit them, so that all do not perish from your wrath."

35   Smiling upon her, Zeus, who gathers the clouds,
said: "Be of good cheer, my daughter, Tritogeneia.°
I'm not really serious . . . I want to be kind to you!"

      So speaking, he ordered his horses with bronze hoofs,
very fast, to be harnessed beneath his car, their golden manes
40   flowing. He donned his golden clothes and took up his golden
finely crafted whip. He stepped up into his car. He touched
the horses with the whip to rouse them. And not unwilling
they flew off between the earth and the starry heaven. They came
to Gargaros° on Ida with its many fountains, the mother
45   of wild beasts, where is Zeus's sanctuary and its smoky
altar. There the father of men and gods stationed
his swift horses. He set them free from the car,
and he cast a thick mist around them.° He himself sat
on the peak, rejoicing in his glory. He could see the city
50   of the Trojans from where he sat, and the ships of the Achaeans.

      The long-haired Achaeans took a hasty dinner throughout
the huts. Afterwards they put on their armor. The Trojans,
on their side, put on their armor, too, in all parts of the city,
but there were fewer of them. Nonetheless, they were
55   eager to fight in the battle, compelled by necessity,
for they fought on behalf of their children and wives.

                            The Trojans
opened the gates. Their army rushed forth, the foot soldiers
and the charioteers. A huge clamor arose. When they had come
together into one place, they thrust together their shields
60   and spears in the rage of men who wear shirts of bronze.
The bossed shields came together. A great din arose.
The agony of the wounded and the boast of victory were heard
as men killed and were killed, and the bountiful earth
ran with blood.

      So long as it was dawn and the sacred
65   day still waxed, for so long the missiles of either side
struck home, and the warriors fell. When Helios
reached the middle of the sky, then the father lifted

---

36   *Tritogeneia*: A mysterious epithet of Athena.

44   *Gargaros*: The highest peak of Mount Ida.

48   *around them*: To conceal the horses.

FIGURE 8.1 Zeus and his emblem, the eagle.   The picture fills the inner portion (the tondo) of this wine cup. Zeus sits on a throne dressed in an elaborately embroidered cloak. His hair is long and braided and his beard full. Black-figure wine cup from Sparta, c. 550 BC.

on high the golden scales. He placed on it two fates
of bitter death, one for the Trojans, tamers of horses,
70   the other for the Achaeans, who wear shirts of bronze. He held
the balance in the center. Down dropped the day of doom
for the Achaeans. The fates of the Achaeans was settled
on the much-nourishing earth, but those of the Trojans rose up
to wide heaven.

        Zeus threw down a great bolt of thunder—
75   he sent a blazing flash into the midst of the Achaeans!

[*Lines 76–452 are omitted. Although the battle goes back and forth, with Zeus's help the
Trojans finally get the edge, which distresses the goddesses Hera and Athena. They arm
themselves and prepare to enter the fight when Zeus stops them. They take their places on
Olympos.*]

                                            And Zeus said:
"Why are you so upset, Athena and Hera? Are you tired out
455   through destroying the Trojans, against whom you hold a bitter
hatred, in the battle where men win glory? In any event,
such are my strength and my irresistible hands, I could not
be turned aside by all the gods in Olympos. As for you two,
a shaking took hold of your glorious limbs before you even
460   glimpsed the war and the horrendous deeds of war. I will
tell you this, and I think it has already come to pass:
You would not have returned upon your car back to Olympos
when blasted by thunder, where is the seat of the gods!"

        Thus Zeus spoke, and Athena and Hera murmured.
465   Despite sitting near him, they still devised evil for the Trojans.
Athena fell silent and would say nothing, so furious was she
with her father Zeus. A wild anger had taken hold of her.
Hera, too, could not contain her anger, and she said: "O most
dreaded son of Kronos, what words you say! Now we begin
470   to understand that your strength is immense. Nevertheless we feel
sorry for the Danaän spearmen who perish, accomplishing an evil
fate. But we will have done with the war, if you order it.
We shall give to the Argives some advice, in hope
to help them, so that not all die, thanks to your wrath."

475   Zeus, who assembles the clouds, then answered her:
"And at dawn you will see the most mighty son of Kronos
destroying, if you wish, O revered Hera with the cow eyes,
a far greater portion of the army of the Achaean spearmen!

For the powerful Hector will not cease from the war before things
are made right with Achilles the fast runner beside the ships,   480
on that day when they fight at the sterns of the ships
over the dead Patroklos. For it is so ordained.° Nor do I give
a fig for your anger, even should you go to the lowest bounds
of earth and sea, where Iapetos and Kronos sit and take
no joy in the rays of Helios Hyperion, nor of the breezes,   485
and deep Tartaros is all around.° Not if you go
there in your wandering do I care about your anger,
for there is no greater bitch than you!"°

               So he spoke,
and white-armed Hera did not answer him.
The bright light of the sun fell into Ocean, dragging   490
with it black night over the rich plowland. The Trojans
were unwilling to see the sun set, but to the Achaeans
the dark night was welcome, yes, three-times prayed for.
Glorious Hector called an assembly of the Trojans,
leading them away from the ships to the banks of the swirling   495
Xanthos, in a clean space where there were no corpses.
They dismounted from their cars to the ground to hear the word
of Hector, who was dear to Zeus. In his hand he held
the sixteen-foot spear, which before him gleamed with its bronze tip.
Around it ran a ferrule of gold.   500

               Leaning on this, Hector
spoke to the Trojans: "Hear me, Trojans and Dardanians
and allies! I thought to destroy the ships and all
the Achaeans now and then to go back to windy Ilion.
But before I could, darkness came on, which has saved
the Argives more than anything, and their ships on the shore.   505
Nevertheless, let us obey the dark night and make ready
our dinner. Let us unyoke the horses with beautiful manes
and give them fodder. Bring oxen and sheep from the city quickly.

---

482 *ordained*: Because that is the story that Homer inherited, according to which Troy did fall, and not even
     the gods can change that. Zeus is powerless before Fate, though he claims that he could overrule Fate if he
     wished (he never does). Homer here summarizes the story of the *Iliad*—the wrath of Achilles that results
     in the deaths of Patroklos and Hector—to remind his listeners and himself of where he is going.

486 *around*: Zeus imagines Hera going to Tartaros—the roots of earth, sea, and sky— where Zeus imprisoned
     the Titans, represented by the Titan Iapetos (the biblical Japeth), the father of Prometheus, and the Titan
     Kronos, the father of Zeus himself. "Helios Hyperion" means the "sun who goes across." After Homer,
     Hyperion was said to be an independent Titan, the father of Helios.

488 *than you*: Zeus's exaggerated resentment of his wife parodies the monogamous woes of the warrior elite
     that made up Homer's audience. The origins of monogamy are not clear, but in the ancient world only
     Greeks and Romans were monogamous.

Bring honey-sweet wine and bread from the halls. Gather
510 cords of wood so that all night long, until the light
of dawn, we might burn many fires, and the light will reach
to heaven so that the long-haired Achaeans do not hurry to flee,
even during the night, over the broad back of the sea. Let them not
board their ships at their ease and without trouble, but let
515 many of them contemplate some weapon, struck by an arrow
or sharp spear as they leap onto a ship. This shall be a lesson
to anyone who thinks he can bring dread war against the Trojans!
    "Let heralds, dear to Zeus, go through the city and announce
that the young children and old men with white hair should camp
520 on the walls built by the gods.° And may the women, every one
of them, build great fires in their halls, but let them always be wary
of an ambush coming into the city while the army is outside.
    "May it be so, O great-hearted Trojans, as I say.
This is my advice, which is sound and good. At dawn
525 I will speak again to the horse-taming Trojans. I hope
by praying to Zeus and to the other gods we shall drive out
of here these dogs borne by the Fates, those whom the Fates bore
on their black ships. For this night we will take care of ourselves,
but in the morning at break of dawn let us arm ourselves
530 and make dread battle at the hollow ships. I will know
if the son of Tydeus, strong Diomedes, will push me
back from the ships against the wall, or whether I will overcome
him in the fight and carry away his bloody armor. Tomorrow
he will come to know his valor and if he will await my spear.
535 Many of his companions will fall around him too
as tomorrow's sun rises. I wish that I were deathless
and ageless for all my days, and that I were honored as Athena
and Apollo, so surely as now this day brings evil
to the Argives!"°

        So Hector spoke, and the Trojans gave assent.
540 They loosed the sweating horses from beneath their yokes.
They tethered them with thongs, each man standing near his own car.
They brought cattle and sheep from the city, quickly, and honey-sweet
wine, and bread from the halls, and they gathered much wood.
The winds bore the smoke from the plain into the heaven.

---

520 *built by the gods*: They camp on the walls in anticipation of the great fight to come at dawn. Poseidon and
Apollo built the walls for Laomedon.

539 *Argives*: That is, as surely as he would like to live forever, and be honored as a god, just as surely will the
Achaeans be defeated.

Thus the Trojans with high hearts stayed all night long along   545
the bridges of war. The fires burned in their multitudes.

 As when in the heaven stars around the brilliant moon
appear shining, when the air is breathless, and easily seen
are the mountains and the high headlands and the forests
and clearings, and from heaven breaks open the infinite air,   550
and all the stars are clear, delighting the heart of the shepherd—
just so many, between the ships and the waters of Xanthos,
did the fires of the Trojans appear before the face of Ilion.

 A thousand fires burned on the plain, and next to each
sat fifty men in the glow from the blazing fire.   555
Their horses, eating white barley and wheat, stood next
to the chariots and waited for Dawn on her beautiful chair.

BOOK 9. *The Embassy to Achilles*

[Lines 1–173 are omitted. Agamemnon sends Odysseus, Big Ajax, and Phoenix—Achilles' tutor—to beg Achilles to return to the battle. Agamemnon offers rich prizes if Achilles will agree.]

The two men° walked along
175   the shore of the turbulent sea, praying hard to the shaker
of the earth, that they might persuade Achilles, the grandson
of Aiakos. They came to the huts and the swift ships
of the Myrmidons.° They found him refreshing his spirit
in the bright and beautiful sound of the lyre, wonderfully made.
180   The bridge on it was silver, loot from the time when he burned
the town of Eëtion.° With it now he refreshed his spirit
as he sang of the famous deeds of men.° Patroklos sat
opposite him, all alone, silent, waiting until the grandson
of Aiakos should finish his singing.

　　　　　　　　　The two men came up,
185   and Odysseus stood before Achilles, who, amazed,
leaped from his seat, holding the lyre. Patroklos, too,
rose when he saw them. Achilles, the fast runner,
spoke, greeting the two men: "Welcome! Some sorry
need must bring you here. But you come as friends!—
190   of all the Achaeans you are most dear to me,
though I am very angry."

　　　　　　　　　So speaking, he led
them to his tent, and he invited them to sit on chairs

---

174   *two men:* Suddenly Homer switches into the dual number (Greek has a dual form, in addition to the singular and plural), but he has just said that five men (or three, not counting the heralds) have been chosen for the embassy. Apparently in an earlier oral version only Ajax and Odysseus were on the embassy, but Homer has added Phoinix (and the heralds), who has a special role to play, without adjusting his diction.

178   *Myrmidons:* We cannot get a clear picture of the Achaean shelters. The Greek word *klisia* means either "tent" or "hut," and I translate it both ways. The *klisia* must be covered with cloths or skins, but sometimes, as in the description of Achilles' *klisia* in Book 24, it is a very elaborate nearly permanent structure with a heavy bolted gate. There must be a smoke-hole in the center for the hearth. Here the embassy simply walks in without ceremony.

181   *Eëtion:* The king of Asiatic THEBES, where Chryseïs was captured.

182   *deeds of men:* Achilles is behaving like an *aoidos,* an "oral-singer," in celebrating the "deeds of men." But otherwise in Homer *aoidoi* are always professionals, not amateurs. This is the only example in Homer of a *private* singer.

covered in purple cloths.° He spoke at once
to Patroklos, who stood nearby: "Son of Menoitios,
bring out the big bowl, mix in it stronger wine,   195
and give each man a cup. These men who have come
beneath my roof are most dear."°

              Patroklos obeyed
his comrade. He placed a chopping block in the glare
of the fire. On it he laid the back of a sheep and a fat
goat and the backbone of a big porker, brimming   200
with fat. Automedon gripped the meat while Achilles
sliced it. He cut small pieces and threaded them on spits.
The son of Menoitios, a man like a god, stoked up
the fire. When the fire had burned, and the flame had abated,
Patroklos scattered the coals and placed the spits   205
upon them. He sprinkled delicious salt on the flesh,
supporting the spits by means of andirons. When the meat
was cooked, he stacked it on platters. Patroklos took
bread and set it out on a table in lovely baskets,
while Achilles served the meal.   210

              Achilles sat down
opposite godlike Odysseus, who sat against the wall.
He urged his companion Patroklos to make the gods
an offering. Patroklos cast pieces of meat into the fire.
Then they ate the succulent meal before them.

   When they had satisfied desire for drink   215
and food, Ajax nodded to Phoinix. Odysseus noticed
and, filling his cup with wine, he toasted Achilles:
"Hail to you Achilles! There is no lack of the abundant feast,
either in the tent of Agamemnon, son of Atreus,
nor here either, where there is fine fare aplenty.   220
But now this succulent feast is not our concern.
God-nurtured Achilles, we are terribly afraid . . . We see
complete disaster looming before us. We doubt

---

193 *cloths*: Homeric heroes sit to eat, either on a stool or armless chair. Not until around 600 BC was the custom
of lying on a couch and dining from a central table imported from the East, as in the Last Supper. The
purple color indicates that the clothes are of Phoenician origin and of the highest quality.

197 *most dear*: Ordinarily wine was diluted one part wine to three parts water. Apparently wine was too heavy
to be drunk without dilution, or the Greeks simply had a taste for a wine punch, of which huge quantities
were drunk to judge by pottery from the classical period. There are no servants in Achilles' hut, but Patroklos and Automedon, the second and third in command, help out. Every man serves himself as equals in
this most elaborately described non-sacrificial meal in Homer.

FIGURE 9.1 The embassy to Achilles. Achilles sits on a chair covered by a goat skin, his head wrapped in a cloak of mourning, his hand to his head in grief. He holds a gnarled staff. Opposite sits Odysseus, with his characteristic rimmed hat on his back, holding two javelins. Behind Odysseus stands the aged Phoenix with a staff similar to Achilles', and on the right Patroklos looks on, leaning on his staff. Ajax does not appear. Red-figure vase, c. 480 BC, by Kleophrades.

that we can save our well-benched ships. We fear
they will be destroyed if you do not don your mantle   225
of power. For the Trojans, intrepid in their hearts, have set
up camp outside the wall near the ships, along with
their allies of wide renown. Their campfires burn
all along the battleline. Nor do they think they will go on
holding back, but soon they will fall on our dark ships.   230
Zeus, the son of Kronos, sends lightning on their right.
Hector, exulting, rages like a mad man, trusting
in Zeus. Nor does he care about men or gods. A mighty
insanity has taken hold of him. He prays for dawn.
He boasts he will cut the ensigns from our ships'   235
sterns and that he will set them afire, and destroy the Achaeans
confused from the smoke that consumes the hulls. And I
greatly fear in my heart that the gods will bring this
to pass—that it will be our fate to die on the windy
plain of Troy, far from Argos rich in herds.   240
    "But come Achilles, we implore you to save the sons
of the Achaeans even at this late hour, cowering as they are
at the war-din of the Trojans. You'll be sorry if you don't,
nor will you find a remedy for the harm once done.
No, think now how you might ward off that evil day   245
for the Danaäns! Did not your father Peleus say to you,
on that day when he sent you from Phthia to Agamemnon,
'O my son, Athena and Hera will give you strength
if you restrain your heart rampant in your breast.
Moderation is best. Keep aloof from strife that only brings   250
evil. In this way the Argives will honor you the more,
both the young and the old.' Thus your father advised you.
Do not forget his words. Let it go—give up your bitter
anger. Agamemnon will reward you richly, if only you
cast aside your wrath.   255
                    "Now hear me out!—I will tell
you what Agamemnon has for you in his tent—
seven unfired tripods, ten talents of gold,
twenty shining cauldrons, twelve powerful horses—
winners who have taken prizes through their speed.
Never will you lack for booty, nor want for precious   260
gold, when you have the prizes Agamemnon has won
through his horses' swiftness of foot.
                        "He will give you seven
women of Lesbos—women of surpassing beauty and skilled with
their hands—whom you yourself once captured when you
sacked that well-built city. These he shall give you, along   265

with the woman he took from you, the daughter of Briseus.
And Agamemnon shall swear an oath: Never did
he enter her bed, nor mix with her in love, as is
the custom among men and women.
                                    "All these things
270 are immediately available. And if the gods shall grant that
we sack the high city of Priam, then you can load your ship
with all the gold and bronze you want at the division
of the spoils. And take twenty Trojan women, those
who are most beautiful, after Argive Helen.
275   "And if we return to Achaean Argos, the rich land,
he will make you his son. He will honor you like Orestes,
his darling, whom he raises in the midst of abundance. He has
three daughters in his well-built hall, Chrysothemis
and Laodikê and Iphianassa. Of these you may take as wife
280 whichever you want—no bride-price necessary!—and lead her
to the house of Peleus. He will give you a dowry too,
so much as no man ever gave: seven towns
densely populated, Kardamylê, Enopê, and grassy Hirê,
and holy Pherai, and Antheia rich in meadows,
285 and beautiful Aipeia and vine-girt Pedasos, all of them
close by the sea on the edge of sandy Pylos.
The men who dwell within them are rich in sheep
and rich in cattle. They will shower you with many gifts
as if you were a god. They will gladly obey
290 your scepter-given commands. All this he will bring
to pass, if only you give over this rage of yours.
    "But if your hatred for the son of Atreus, and all
his gifts, is too great, at least take pity on the Achaeans
ravaged throughout, men who will honor you
295 as if you were a god. For now you might
attain great glory in their eyes. Now is the time
you might put to death Hector, who comes in close,
thinking only of his destructive rage. He thinks
there is no one of the Danaäns, whom the black ships
300 have carried here, who is equal to himself."

                                    In answer
Achilles the fast runner spoke to him: "Wise Odysseus,
son of Laertes, god-nourished, I must speak to you directly,
just as I see it, and how I think it will come to pass,
so that you might not sit there, and me here, wasting
305 our time in idle talk: I hate that man like

the gates of Hades' house who conceals one thing
in his heart, but says another. I will say to you
how matters seem to me.

            "I don't think Agamemnon, the son
of Atreus, can persuade me, nor any other of the Danaäns.
For there is no thanks for endlessly fighting the enemy.   310
The same lot comes to him who holds back as to him
who fights eagerly. In like honor are the shirker
and the brave. Death is the same reward for the man
who does much and for him who does nothing. It is
of no advantage to me that I have suffered pains   315
in my heart, ever risking my life in these contendings.
Like a bird who brings tidbits to her chicks, whatever
she can find, but goes herself without, so have I spent
many sleepless nights and bloody days passed
fighting with men on account of their wives. I laid   320
waste twelve cities from my black ships, and eleven
by land, throughout the Troad. From these I captured
a huge quantity of fine booty. Always I would
give the spoil to Agamemnon, son of Atreus. And he,
hanging back by the ships, took it all, apportioning   325
a small amount, but keeping most for himself.
So he gave some prize to the chiefs and the big men—
they have their prizes. But from me alone of the Achaeans
he took my bedmate, dear to my heart. Well, let him
lie beside her and take his pleasure!   330
            "But why,
I ask, must Argives fight against the Trojans?
Why has the son of Atreus gathered an army
and brought them here? Was it not for the sake of
fair-haired Helen? I suppose of all men the sons of Atreus
alone love their wives? No, every good and sensible   335
man loves and cherishes his wife, even as I loved
that woman with all my heart, though she was a captive
of my spear. As matters stand, Agamemnon has taken
my prize out of my arms. Surely he has deceived me.
He will not persuade me—I know him too well.   340
He shall not persuade me! So Odysseus,
I think he should take counsel how with you
and all the other captains he might ward off
the consuming fire. Why, he has accomplished so much
without me! He has built a wall, and he has dug a ditch   345
along it, wide and grand! He has fixed stakes within it!

Even so, he cannot stop the force of Hector, killer of men.
So long as I fought among the Achaeans, Hector
never roused the battle-cry away from the walls,
350 but ventured only as far as the Scaean Gates
and the oak tree. There once he awaited me alone,
and scarcely did he escape my attack.

                     "But as it is,
because I will not war against shining Hector, tomorrow,
after sacrifice to Zeus and the other gods, and heaping high
355 my ships, you will see me at the crack of dawn launch
forth on the salt sea—that is if you even care—
sailing on the Hellespont teeming with fish and my men
eagerly rowing. And if the mighty Shaker of Earth
grants us a fair voyage, on the third day we'll arrive in the rich
360 plowland of Phthia. There I have much wealth that I left behind
when I came here. I will add to it much more,
gold and ruddy bronze and lovely women and gray iron—
loot that I gained by lot, though King Agamemnon,
the son of Atreus, has seized with violence the prize
365 that once he gave me. You tell him everything, openly
in order that the other Achaeans may be angry
if he hopes by deceit to rob any other of the Danaäns,
clothed as he is in shame. For never would he dare
to look me in the face, that dog!

                     "No, I shall
370 give him no advice, nor shall I do anything on his behalf.
For he has deceived me, and done me harm. No, never
again will he trick me with words. I am through with that.
May he go in comfort straight to hell! Zeus,
I suppose, has taken away his wits. I despise
375 his gifts! He isn't worth a hair! Not if he gave me ten times
as much, or twenty times as much as he possesses—
even if he acquired still more. Not if he offered me
as much as Orchomenos holds, or Egyptian Thebes—
where the greatest wealth is stored in their houses—a city
380 of one hundred gates through each of which two hundred men
sally forth with their horses and cars.° Not if he gave me
as many things as there are sands by the sea or dust in the road—

---

381   ... *cars:* Orchomenos in northern Boeotia was just a village c. 800, Homer's day, but in the Bronze Age it
      was a great power, to judge by its ruins. Homer has heard something about the great capital of the Egyptian
      New Kingdom, c. 1600–1150, for some reason called Thebes in Greek (its Egyptian names were quite dis-
      similar). What Achilles thinks are gates in walls are really pylons in the amazing temples built there on both
      sides of the Nile—but hardly big enough for one hundred cars! Still today the ruins of these temples are as-
      tounding. The East, and Egypt, was a dim place for Homer, about which he has only distorted information.

not even then would Agamemnon persuade my heart—before
he has paid the full price for the anguish that torments my heart!

 "As for Agamemnon's daughter, I would not   385
marry her, not if she rivaled Aphrodite the golden in beauty,
or equaled flashing-eyed Athena in craft. No, I will
not marry her! Let her choose some other Achaean,
one of the same class, one of a higher station than I.
For if the gods will save me, and I come home,   390
Peleus will find me a wife. There are many daughters
of the Achaeans throughout Hellas and Phthia, daughters
of the chiefs who guard the towns. From these I shall choose
a wife and make her my own, if I wish. Many times
my proud heart urged me to marry a suitable helpmate,   395
to rejoice in the riches that old Peleus acquired.

 "Not worth a life is all the wealth that they say
Ilion once possessed, that well-peopled city, in the time
of peace before the coming of the sons of the Achaeans.
No, nor the wealth that the stone threshold of Phoibos Apollo,   400
the archer, contains in rocky Pytho.° You can always
take cattle by rapine, and stout sheep, and you can acquire
tripods in the same way, and chestnut mares. But the life
of a man does not come again. It cannot be captured
or taken once it has passed the barrier of the teeth.   405

 "My mother Thetis, the goddess with silver feet,
says that a twofold fate carries me toward my
death. If I remain and fight to take the city
of the Trojans, then my homecoming is no more, but
my fame will be forever. If I return to my home   410
in the land of my fathers, there will be no glorious renown,
yet I will live long, and the doom of death will not
soon find me.

  "And I strongly advise you others also
to sail to your homes. You can no more hope for steep Ilion.
Zeus, whose voice is heard from afar, holds his   415
hands in protection over her, and her people are emboldened.
Go now and tell the chiefs of the Achaeans what
I have said. For that is the burden of old men, so that
they may concoct some other plan, a better one—
some way to save the ships and the host of the Achaeans   420
beside the hollow ships. The plan they have
devised will not work, so long as I stand apart
in my anger.

---

401 *Pytho:* That is, in DELPHI, north of the GULF OF CORINTH.

"But let Phoinix remain here and take his rest,
so that he may follow me to my beloved native land,
425 tomorrow, if he wants. But I will not force him to go."

Thus Achilles spoke. They all fell into silence, numbed
by his words. For he had rejected them utterly. At last old man
Phoinix the horse-driver spoke, bursting into tears—because he feared
for the ships of the Achaeans: "If you are really thinking about
430 going home, excellent Achilles, nor are you at all willing
to help us ward off consuming fire from our swift ships
because an anger has settled on your heart—how can I, my dear child,
be left here without you, alone? It was to you that the horseman,
old man Peleus, sent me on that day when he sent you
435 forth from Phthia to Agamemnon, still a child, knowing nothing
of the horrors of war, nor of assemblies where men show
themselves to be excellent. For this reason he sent me along
to teach you everything—how to be a speaker of words and a doer
of deeds.° For this reason, my child, I would not want
440 to be left apart from you, not even if a god should
stand by me personally and promise to wipe away
old age and replace it with glowing youth, such as
I had when first I left Hellas° where the women are beautiful.
      "I fled a quarrel with my father Amyntor, son of Ormenos,
445 who grew angry because of the whore with the beautiful hair. My father
loved her, but he dishonored his bed-mate, my mother, who constantly
asked me, clasping my knees, to sleep with the woman
so that she might come to despise the old man. And I did that.
My father knew at once and called down many curses
450 on my head, and he called on the hateful Erinyes,° that never
should my dear grandson take a seat on his knees.
      "The gods fulfilled his curses, Zeus who lives beneath
the ground and the dread Persephonê.° So then I contemplated
how I might kill my father with the sharp sword. But one
455 of the deathless ones stopped my anger, reminding me of

---

439 *of deeds*: In the popular postHomeric tradition it was Cheiron, the one wise centaur, who taught Achilles all
these things. Many pictures survive of Cheiron educating the young Achilles (see Figure 11.2).

443 *Hellas*: A small territory in Thessaly under the political control of Amyntor, Phoinix's father. Peleus con-
trols nearby Phthia, though it unclear what is meant by "Phthia," whether it is a town or a territory. Later
"Hellas" came to designate all of Greece.

450 *Erinyes*: The Erinyes ("avengers") are underworld spirits who are the guardians of oaths and curses: the
"Furies." If an oath is violated, they persecute the person who violates it; when invoked in a curse, they
attack someone else, as here. They are associated with Fate because they also guarantee the natural order of
things. They punish such violations of the natural order as killing one's parents.

453 *... Persephonê*: Hades and his wife.

what people would say, and of the insults of men—the Achaeans
would call me the murderer of my father! Then my heart
could no longer be stayed to remain at all in the halls
of my angry father. My fellows and relatives, surrounding me,
begged me to stay there in his halls, and they sacrificed   460
many good sheep and crooked-horned shuffling cattle,
and many swine rich with fat were stretched to be singed
over the flame of Hephaistos.° And much wine
was drunk from the jugs of old Oeneus. For nine nights
they watched over me. Taking turns they held guard,   465
nor did their fires ever go out, one burning
beneath the portico of the well-fenced court, the other
on the porch in front of the doors of my chamber.
But when the tenth dark night came on, I broke
the well-fitted doors of the chamber and easily leaped   470
over the wall around the court, avoiding the guards
and the slave women. I then fled afar through spacious Hellas.
 "I came to PHTHIA with its deep soil, the mother
of sheep, to Peleus the king. He happily received me,
and he loved me as a father loves his only son,   475
the heir to his many possessions. He made me rich
and he gave me to rule over many people. I lived
in the furthermost part of Phthia, presiding over
the Dolopians. I made you such as you are, like to the gods,
Achilles, loving you from my heart. And you would never go   480
to the feast with another, nor take meat in the halls before
I set you on my knees and fed you with a tasty morsel
cut for you, and then given you wine. Often you
wet the shirt on my breast, blubbering out the wine
in your sorry helplessness. So I have suffered much   485
and labored hard, realizing that the gods would never
grant me an offspring. I made you my child, godlike Achilles,
so that you could protect me from shameful ruin.
           "But Achilles,
now you should control your mighty spirit, not have a heart
without pity. Even the gods can be persuaded, whose worth   490
and honor and strength is greater. Men turn their anger
aside by beseeching with incense and gentle prayers, and pouring
out wine and the smell of sacrifice when one has crossed
the line and made a mistake. *Prayers* are the daughters
of great Zeus—lame, wrinkled, and with eyes askance. Prayers   495

---

463 *Hephaistos*: Apparently they sacrificed to the Erinyes, to drive them away, but their intentions are unclear.

make it their concern to follow after *Blindness*. But *Blindness*
is strong and fast-moving so that she outruns them all, and goes
before *Prayers* over all the earth, bringing harm to mankind.
But *Prayers* come afterward, trying to heal. Whoever
500 respects the daughters of Zeus when they come near,
Prayers will help him. They hear him when he asks for something.
But whoever denies and strongly refuses *Prayers*, they go
and they pray to Zeus the son of Kronos that *Blindness* may follow
him and cause him to fall and to pay the full price.°
505   "Achilles, you should see that honor attend these
daughters of Zeus, who like to bend the minds of upright men.
If the son of Atreus were not bearing gifts and naming others
to come later, but remained furiously angry, I would not
counsel you to cast aside your anger and come to the defense
510 of the Argives, even though they are in much need.
But as it is he gives you many things right away
and promises others later. He has sent forth the best
men to beseech you, choosing them from throughout the army,
who are those men dearest to you. Do not scorn them,
515 nor their coming here.
                 "Before, no one could blame you
for being angry. And so we have heard of the famous deeds
of warriors of a time long ago, when a ferocious anger would
come upon them: They could still be won by gifts, turned aside
by words. I have in mind a deed from the olden days, how it was,
520 not something recent. I will tell it to you who are all my friends.
    "The Kuretes and the Aetolians, steadfast in war, were fighting
around KALYDON and slaughtering one another, the Aetolians
defending lovely Kalydon, the Kuretes eager to destroy it
by war.° For golden-throned Artemis had sent an
525 affliction against them, angry because Oeneus had
failed to offer to her the first fruits of his burgeoning
orchard.° While the other gods dined on great sacrifices, to the
daughter of Zeus alone he did not offer sacrifice, either because

---

504   *price*: A rare Homeric allegory. *Prayers* are the daughters of Zeus, that is, they are of divine origin, but they
      are old and slow. *Blindness* (*atê*) is much swifter, for example overtaking Agamemnon and causing him to
      take the girl Briseïs. But *Prayers* eventually come along to make things whole, for example the embassy's
      supplication. So Achilles should accept the *Prayers* and take what is offered. If not, then *Prayers* will see to it
      that *Blindness/Disaster* (*atê* means both) will overtake *him*.

524   *. . . by war*: The name Kuretes means simply "young warriors." The tribe is known only from this story. Their
      capital was at Pleuron about ten miles west of the town of Kalydon, which is in southwest mainland Greece
      (see Map I).

527   *orchard*: Oeneus, "wine-man," was an early king of Kalydon. The famous Kalydonian Boar Hunt took place
      during his reign, two or three generations before the Trojan War. According to the Catalog of Ships, all the
      sons of Oeneus are now dead and Thoas leads the Aetolian contingent.

FIGURE 9.2 Kastor and Polydeukes (probably), the brothers of Helen, attack the Kalydonian Boar during the famous Kalydonian Boar Hunt, one bearded, the other not (hence younger). The spear of one of the brothers has penetrated the boar and blood pours out. Birds fly around their knees. The fish beneath the ground-line indicate a lake or stream. Black-figure Spartan cup, c. 555 BC.

he forgot or thought it not important.° *Blindness* struck him
530   deep in his heart. She became angry, the archer-goddess,
begotten of Zeus, and sent forth a fierce wild boar
with white tusks, who did much harm, wasting the orchard
land of Oeneus. Many a tall tree did he tear up and throw
to the ground, roots and all, and the blossoms of apples.
535   Meleager, the son of Oeneus, killed the boar after he had
gathered hunters and hounds from many cities. The boar
was not to be overcome by a few men. He was huge
and he sent many men to an unhappy pyre.
                                   "But around
the head and shaggy skin of the pig there arose a great clamor
540   and shouting between the Kuretes and the great-hearted Aetolians.°
So long as Meleager, dear to Ares, fought, so long it went badly
for the Kuretes, nor were they able to remain outside the wall,
although they were very many. But when anger came
to Meleager, which also swells in the breasts of other
545   sensible men—anger against his own mother
Althaia—then he stayed in bed with his beautiful wife
Kleopatra of the beautiful ankles, the daughter of Marpessa.
Marpessa's father was Euenos. Her husband was Idas,
one of the strongest men on the earth at that time.
550   Idas even raised his bow against Phoibos Apollo because
of Marpessa, the girl with the beautiful ankles.° Marpessa's
father Euenos and her mother called Marpessa
'Alkyonê' because her mother, suffering the fate
of the sorrowing Halcyon bird, wept when Apollo,
555   who works from a long ways off, snatched away her daughter.°

---

529   *not important*: In ancient Greek religion intention counts for nothing, the act for everything.

540   *Aetolians*: According to later reports about the Kalydonian Boar Hunt, the huntress Atalanta, whom
Homer does not mention, drew first blood, then Meleager killed the boar. When Meleager gave the skin
as a trophy to Atalanta, a fight broke out between the Kalydonians and the neighboring Kuretes, who did
not think a woman should have the skin. During the war Meleager killed his mother's brothers, who were
Kuretes. In revenge she burned up a firebrand that contained Meleager's soul, and so he died. Homer may
know this account, but he shapes his narrative to the dramatic needs of the *Iliad*.

551   *beautiful ankles*: According to later sources, when Idas carried off Marpessa Apollo pursued them. Idas
drew his bow against the god to protect Marpessa from the god's advances. Zeus forced Marpessa to
choose; she chose Idas over Apollo. Idas and his brother Lynkeus were important in heroic myth: They
journeyed on the Argo and were killed in a cattle raid by Helen's brothers.

555   *daughter*: "Alkyonê" is Greek for kingfisher, which in reality has no voice, but in myth sings a calming
dirge for her dead mate. Once Alkyonê was human, but in her grief for her dead husband was changed into
a mourning kingfisher ("Halcyon Days" are those days when the bird sings its calming song). In this very
obscure reference Homer implies that Apollo was somehow successful in possessing Marpessa, giving rise
to her nickname "Alkyonê": Marpessa's mother suffered the same sorrow for her daughter as Alkyonê felt
for her dead husband.

"Meleager lay by Kleopatra's side, nursing a bitter anger
because of the curses of his enraged mother,
who prayed ardently to the gods, grieving over her dead
brother. Althaia pounded the rich earth, crying out to Hades
and to terrible Persephonê. She knelt down and wet the folds   560
of her gown with tears, begging that they bring death to her son.
The Erinys that walks in darkness, with the brittle heart,
heard her from Erebos.° Soon there came the noise of the Kuretes
at the gates and the thud of walls being battered. The Aetolian elders
begged Meleager. They sent their best priests of the gods,   565
who promised a great gift if Meleager would come out.
Where the fattest plain of lovely Kalydon lies, there
they urged him to pick a splendid district fifty acres big,
the half of it wine country, the other half to be clear plowland,
cut from the plain. The old man Oeneus, Meleager's father,   570
the horse-driver, begged him again and again—standing
on the threshold of his high-roofed chamber, shaking the joined
doors, supplicating his son. And his sisters and revered mother°
begged Meleager too. He only denied them the more.
    "Meleager's companions were most true and dear to him—   575
but even so, they could not persuade his heart
before the chamber was under attack. The Kuretes
were on the walls and the great city was going up in flames.
Only then did Kleopatra, Meleager's nicely-belted wife,
beg him, wailing, describing to him all the horrible things   580
that happen to people when a city is taken: Men murdered,
fire consumes the city, men lead away little children
and low-girdled women. His spirit was stirred when
he heard about these evil things. He got up to go.
Meleager put on his shining armor.   585
                                "And so he warded off
the evil day for the Aetolians, giving in to his spirit.
To Meleager thereafter they did not give the gifts,
many and dear, but still he warded off the evil.
Don't think like that! Don't let some spirit turn you
in that direction! It is a harder thing to do to ward off fire   590
once the ships are burning. But come—while there are still
gifts to be had. The Achaeans will honor you like a god.
If you enter without gifts the battle that destroys men,

---

563 *Erebos*: The realm of darkness, the underworld. The Erinys (now singular) is the agent of Hades and
     Persephonê. Because the Erinys heard, Meleager's death is certain. A primitive social structure seems to
     underlie this story in which a mother's emotional obligation to her brothers is stronger than it is to her son.

573 *revered mother*: Who has just cursed him to his certain death!

you will not enjoy an equivalent honor, even if you win
595 the war."

Achilles the fast runner answered him:
"Phoinix, dear fellow, old man nurtured of Zeus, you see I have
no need of this honor! I think that I am honored in the allotment
of Zeus, which will sustain me beside the beaked ships so long
as there is breath in my lungs and my legs still move.
600 "I will tell you something else, and please lay it to heart. Do not
confuse my spirit with your weeping and wailing, as you do the pleasure
of the warrior son of Atreus. You should not love him so that you are
hated by me, who loves you. It is a better thing that you trouble those
who trouble me. Be a captain like me. Share half of my honor.
605 This embassy will carry my message. You stay here on a soft bed.
At the break of dawn we will give thought, whether we will
go home or remain."

As he spoke he silently signed to Patroklos
with his brows to charge him to spread a thick bed for Phoinix,
so that the others might quickly leave the hut. But Ajax,
610 the godlike son of Telamon, spoke: "Zeus-born, son of
Laertes, resourceful Odysseus, let us leave. I don't think
we are going to accomplish our purpose. We must quickly
announce our message to the Danaäns, not a welcome one,
for I imagine that they anxiously await it. Achilles has let
615 his great heart in his breast go wild—cruel man!—and he cares
nothing for the love of his companions, nor how we honored
him beside the ships above all others—a pitiless man!
"You know, if a brother is killed, or a child, a man
will take a penalty-payment for the dead. And the killer stays there
620 in his own land once he's paid that high price. The heart
and the proud spirit of the kinsman are restrained by receiving
the penalty-payment. But you!° —the gods have put a stubborn
and evil spirit in your breast on account of a single girl.
We offer you seven girls, and those by far the best, and other
625 things beside. Have a generous heart. Respect your hall!°
Under your roof we have come, from the mass of the Danaäns.
We want to be dearest and beloved above all the other Achaeans."°

---

622 *you*: Ajax now addresses Achilles directly.

625 *hall*: As guests in Achilles' house, the embassy is entitled to friendliness and respect.

627 *Achaeans*: In a society where behavior is controlled by honor, disputes must be resolved by preserving the honor of both parties. The aggrieved party should accept recompense. If he does not, he dishonors the other party and brings censure on himself. But in his anger Achilles rejects this whole system, making him a man alone.

Answering him, Achilles the fast runner said:
"Zeus-born Ajax, son of Telamon, captain of the people,
everything you say seems to me to be spoken   630
in accord with my own mind. But my heart seethes
with anger whenever I think of that—how the son of Atreus
treated me with indignity among the Argives as if
I were some kind of man in flight and without status!
        "But you return and give this message: I will not think   635
of bloody war before good Hector the son of wise Priam
comes to the tents and ships of the Myrmidons,
killing Argives, and he sets fire to the ships.
Around my hut and black ship I think that Hector
will be stopped, eager though he is for battle."   640

        So he spoke. Each of them took up a two-handled
cup and poured out an offering, then they returned back
along the line of ships, Odysseus leading the group.

        But Patroklos ordered his companions and female slaves
to spread a thick bed for Phoinix as soon as possible.   645
Obeying him, the female slaves spread the bed
as ordered—fleeces and a rug and a linen sheet.
There the old man lay down and awaited the bright dawn.
But Achilles slept in the innermost part of his well-built hut.
Beside him lay a woman whom he had taken from Lesbos,   650
Diomedê of the lovely cheeks, the daughter of Phorbas.
Patroklos slept on the other side. Beside him slept the nicely
belted Iphis, whom Achilles had given him when he took
Skyros, the steep city of Euneos.°

[Lines 655 to end omitted. The embassy reports their failure to Agamemnon and the assembled captains. Diomedes urges that they fight on anyway, and they agree. Book 10 is omitted in which Odysseus and Diomedes go on a daring night raid against the Trojans. The next morning the fighting resumes.]

---

654 *Euneos:* Evidently unconnected with Euneos, the father of Marpessa. Nothing otherwise is known of this
     raid on the island of SKYROS east of EUBOEA, where according to later tradition Achilles was raised in the
     harem of the king dressed as a girl, until Odysseus unmasked him and recruited him for the war.

BOOK 11. *The Glory of Agamemnon and the Wounding of the Captains*

Dawn arose from the bed of noble Tithonos° to bring
light to the deathless ones and to mortals. Zeus sent
Strife to the swift ships of the Achaeans, bitter Strife,
having in her hands a portent of war.° She took her stand
5 at the huge-hulled black ship of Odysseus, which held
a middle position in the line of ships so that a shout
was heard at either end, both to the huts of Ajax,
son of Telamon, and to the huts of Achilles. These men
had drawn up their ships at opposite ends of the row, trusting
10 in their valor and the strength of their hands. Taking
her stand there the goddess shouted a great and awesome
cry, the shrill cry of war, and she placed great strength
in the heart of every Achaean to fight and make war
unceasingly so that war seemed sweeter to them than
15 to return in their hollow ships to the land of their fathers.

The son of Atreus shouted too and urged
the Argives to buckle on their armor. He himself put on
his gleaming bronze. First he placed the shin-guards
around his shins, beautiful and fitted with silver
20 ankle-pieces. Second, he placed a chest-protector around
his chest, the one Kinyras once gave to him as a guest-gift.
A rumor had reached Cyprus° that Achaeans were about
to launch a naval expedition against Troy. Therefore
he gave Agamemnon the chest-protector to do pleasure
25 to that king. There were ten bands on it of dark lapis lazuli,

---

1 *Tithonos*: A child of Laomedon and half brother to Priam. The goddess Dawn snatched him away to be her
lover. According to postHomeric tradition, he was father to Memnon, the last great hero killed by Achilles.
Dawn obtained immortality for him, but forgot to ask for eternal youth: Tithonos shriveled up with age
and became a cicada. This dawn marks the fifth since Book 2 and the twenty-fifth since the beginning of the
Iliad. This day will be the longest in the poem: The sun does not set until Book 18.

4 *portent of war*: Strife is not really a goddess, but a personification. We cannot know what the portent was.

22 *Cyprus*: The only time that the island of Cyprus is mentioned in the *Iliad*. Kinyras was in later tradition the
father of Myrrha and, by an incestuous union with her, the father of Adonis.

twelve of gold, and twenty of tin. Lapis lazuli
snakes wound their way toward the neck, three
on each side, like the rainbows that the son of Kronos
has fixed in the clouds, a portent to mortal men.° He cast
a sword about his shoulders, whose golden studs   30
glimmered, and around the sword was a silver scabbard
fitted with golden chains. He took up his mighty
shield, that shelters a man on both sides, highly decorated,
beautiful. Round about it were ten circles of bronze,
and inside twenty white tin bosses, and one big one   35
in the center of dark lapis lazuli. And thereon
Gorgo, horrid to look upon, was set as a crown,
glaring terribly, and around her Terror and Rout.°
There was a silver strap. On it was worked
a snake of lapis lazuli. It had three heads   40
growing from a single neck, turned in different
directions. He placed on his head a helmet with doubled
crest of horsehair divided into four parts,°
the crest nodding terrifyingly above. He took up
two sharp strong spears tipped with bronze,   45
bronze that shined far away into the heaven.

    Athena and Hera thundered to show honor
to the chief of Mycenae, rich in gold.° Then every man
ordered his driver to hold his horse in good order
there at the ditch, while they themselves, arrayed   50
in their armor, advanced on foot. An unquenchable cry
went up before the dawn. Far sooner than the charioteers
the infantry arranged themselves along the trench, and after
a little space followed the charioteers.° Among them the son
of Kronos raised up an evil din, and from the heaven   55

---

29 *mortal men:* We cannot form a picture of the chest-protector because we do not know in what direction the
    "bands" are arranged, nor what is their pattern.

38 *Rout:* Probably the "circles of bronze" are concentric. Gorgo must appear beneath the central boss, but it is
    hard to reconcile "was set as a crown" with the twenty small bosses and the one large central boss; nor is it
    clear how Terror and Rout were represented.

43 *parts:* It is obscure how this helmet worked, but in any event the horsehair crest of a Homeric helmet was not
    stiff, as on later classical helmets, but a kind of plume that nodded and terrified one's opponent.

48 *rich in gold:* In fact Mycenae was rich in gold during the Bronze Age, when this epithet must have begun, to
    judge by the spectacular archaeological finds there (for example Figure 4.1). Agamemnon's entry into
    battle needs a divine accompaniment, but Zeus at the moment is on the side of the Trojans. Agamemnon
    must be satisfied with a rumble from the goddesses on Olympos.

54 *charioteers:* The Achaeans must be assembled on the outer side of the ditch, toward Troy, though it is not said
    how they crossed the ditch. The foot soldiers are at the front of the line, the charioteers follow behind them;
    then comes the ditch, then a space, then the Achaean wall.

FIGURE 11.1   Winged Gorgo, as the "Mistress of Animals," holding a goose in either hand.
The position of her legs indicates that she is in motion. The Mistress of Animals was an ancient Near
Eastern artistic motif invoking the power of nature to be fecund. The scary face always has large
eyes, snaky hair, pig's tusks, and a lolling tongue. From Kameiros, Rhodes, c. 600 BC, excavated by
Auguste Salzmann and Sir Alfred Biliotti, photo by Marie-Lan Nguyen.

he rained down dew dripping with blood. For he was about
to send the heads of many strong men down to Hades.

The Trojans for their part, on the other side, on the rising
ground of the plain, assembled around great Hector
and blameless Polydamas° and Aeneas, honored by the Trojans   60
like a god, and the three sons of Antenor—Polybos and the good
Agenor and the young Akamas, like to the deathless ones.°

Hector carried his perfectly round shield among
the foremost, even as a star full of menace appears out
of the clouds, shining, then sinks again behind the shadowy   65
clouds, so did Hector appear now among the foremost,
now among the hindmost, giving orders. All in bronze
he showed forth like the lightning of Zeus the father, who carries
the goatskin fetish.

Even as reapers face one another
across a field of wheat or barley and drive a swathe   70
so that the handfuls fall thick and fast, even so the Trojans
and the Achaeans leaped on one another and killed, nor
did either side take thought of ruinous flight.° The battle
had equal heads.° Like wolves they raged. Strife, who
causes many groans, rejoiced at the sight. She alone   75
of all the gods was among the fighters. The other gods
were not with her, but took their ease at peace
in their halls, where for each was built a beautiful
house in the folds of Olympos. All the gods
heaped blame on the son of Kronos, him of the dark clouds,   80
because he wished to glorify the Trojans. But Zeus
certainly did not care at all what they thought.
He sat alone, turned aside from them, apart, exulting
in his glory, looking down on the city of the Trojans

---

60 *Polydamas*: Son of the Trojan elder Panthoös, he is an important figure who soon becomes Hector's stron-
    gest advisor.

62 *to the deathless ones*: Polybos is otherwise unknown, but Antenor is mentioned thirteen times in the *Iliad*.
    Akamas is in the Trojan catalog, leads troops in Book 12, and is killed in Book 16. Antenor is of Priam's gen-
    eration; he loses seven sons in the war.

73 *ruinous flight*: The simile is slightly confused. Because each army cuts down the other, Homer must combine
    the notion of reaping with that of two opposing sides. He pictures two teams of reapers working at opposite
    ends of a field and moving toward each other to be like the Trojans and Achaeans moving toward each other.
    But at the same time the crop, which is cut down, must also represent the Trojans for the Achaeans and the
    Achaeans for the Trojans.

74 *equal heads:* That is, neither side had the advantage.

85 and the ships of the Achaeans, on the flashing of the bronze,
on the killers and the killed.

So long as it was morning and the
sacred day progressed, just so long the weapons from both
sides struck home and the warriors fell. But when the time
came that a woodcutter prepares his meal in the valleys
90 of a mountain, when he has worn out his arms with the cutting
of tall trees, and weariness comes over his soul, and desire for
sweet food takes hold of his heart, just so the Danaäns broke
the Trojan battalions through their valor, calling to their fellows
along the lines.

Among them Agamemnon rushed forward
95 first, and he took down a man named Bianora, the shepherd
of the people, and afterward he killed his comrade Oïleus,
the driver of horses.° Oïleus had leaped down from his car
and faced Agamemnon. As Oïleus rushed at him
Agamemnon struck him with his sharp spear on the forehead
100 and the helmet heavy with bronze did not stop the spear.
It went through helmet and through bone and splattered
the brains within.° Thus Agamemnon overcame
the furiously charging Oïleus.

And the king of men
Agamemnon left the bodies there, gleaming with their shining
105 breasts after he had stripped away their shirts. He went
on to kill Isos and Antiphos, two sons of Priam, one a bastard
and the other legitimate, both riding in a single car.
The bastard Isos was the driver and the most famous Antiphos
stood by his side. These two men Achilles once bound with
110 willow branches when he caught them as they herded their sheep
in the valleys of Ida, and he let them go after taking ransom.

The son of Atreus, wide-ruling Agamemnon, hit Isos
with his spear above the nipple on the chest, and he struck
Antiphos by the ear with his sword. He cast Antiphos from the car.
115 Working quickly Agamemnon stripped the beautiful armor

---

97 ... *driver of horses*: Oïleus (also the name of Little Ajax's father) and Bianor are stock names like the names
of Agamemnon's many victims that follow. Of the about 340 Trojans and their allies named in the *Iliad*,
two-thirds have Greek names.

102 *within*: Though Agamemnon took two throwing spears when he armed (line 45), he now fights with a single
thrusting spear.

from the two men, whom he knew. He had seen them when
they were by the swift ships when Achilles, the fast runner,
had brought them from Ida. Even as a lion easily
crushes the speechless young of a swift deer,
coming into its lair, seizing them in its powerful   120
teeth and taking away their tender life—the mother,
even if she happens to be near, can do nothing.
On herself, too, comes a dread trembling and she runs
swiftly through the thick underbrush and through
the woods, moving fast, sweating, under attack by the powerful   125
beast—even so could no one of the Trojans ward off
destruction from Isos and Antiphos, but they were themselves
driven in flight before the Argives.°

                Then Agamemnon took Peisander
and Hippolochos, a holdout in the fight, sons of wise
Antimachos, who more than the others opposed giving Helen   130
back to Menelaos because Antimachos hoped to receive
gold and more shining gifts from Alexandros—
Agamemnon took them down as they rode together
in a car, trying to gain control of their swift horses.
The shining reins had slipped from their hands and   135
the two horses were running wild. The son of Atreus
leaped upon them like a lion. They begged him from the car:
"Please, take us alive, son of Atreus! Take a worthy
ransom—there is much treasure in the house of Antimachos,
bronze and gold and well-worked iron that our father would   140
give you as boundless ransom if he learned that we were alive
at the ships of the Achaeans."

                So weeping the two men addressed
Agamemnon with such honeyed words. They heard
an unhoneyed reply: "If you are really the two sons of wise
Antimachos, who, when Menelaos came with godlike Odysseus   145
on an embassy, urged in public assembly that Menelaos
be killed on the spot and not permitted to return to the Achaeans—
then accept repayment for your father's vile behavior!"

      Agamemnon spoke and threw Peisander down from the car,
striking him in the chest with his spear. Peisander was hurled   150

---

128   ...*Argives*: Isos and Antiphos are like the young of the deer crushed by the attacking lion, Agamemnon.
It is unclear whether Homer ever saw a lion, though it is one of his favorite animals in similes; he may
depend on earlier Eastern descriptions. Probably there were no lions in Greece in Homer's day. In Homer,
lions never roar, as they often do in life.

backward onto the earth. Then Hippolochos jumped down
and Agamemnon killed him on the ground. He cut off his arms
and head and rolled him through the throng like a wooden mortar.°

Then he let them be. There, where most of the battalions
155 were being driven in rout, he leaped in and with him went
others of the Achaeans with fancy shin guards. Foot soldiers
killed foot soldiers as they fled, compelled by necessity, and drivers
killed drivers.° Beneath them dust arose from the plain,
driven by the thundering feet of the horses. Everywhere
160 was havoc made with the bronze. And King Agamemnon,
killing as he went, followed after his troops, commanding
the Argives. As when consuming fire falls upon a wild
wood, and everywhere a whirling wind carries it
and the thickets crumble as they are assailed by the onrush
165 of the fire—just so tumbled the heads of the Trojans
under attack by the son of Atreus, Agamemnon,
as they fled. Many long-necked horses rattled
empty cars across the bridges of battle,° lacking their
drivers. Those drivers lay on the earth, more beloved
170 of buzzards than their own wives.

Zeus had removed
Hector from the rain of weapons and the dust and the killing
of men and the blood and the din of war. But the son
of Atreus followed after, calling fiercely to the Danaäns.
Past the tomb of ancient Ilos, the son of Dardanos,
175 the Trojans rushed, over the middle of the plain beside
the fig tree, longing for the city. Screaming ever followed
the son of Atreus. His invincible hands were drenched in gore.
And when the Achaeans came to the Scaean Gates
and the oak tree, there the two sides took their stand
180 and awaited each other.

But some Trojans were still being driven
across the middle of the plain like cattle that a lion
has put to flight, coming on them in the dead of night.
The lion has scattered all of them, but on one

---

153 *mortar*: Heads get cut off elsewhere, but only here are the arms cut off too, and the body rolled like a
column of wood!

158 *drivers*: We cannot be sure what Homer meant by this because, in general, fighting is never done from chariots. In individual encounters charioteers never kill charioteers in the *Iliad*.

168 *bridges of battle*: The word "bridges" is of uncertain meaning, but the phrase is formulaic for "battlefield."

is fixed a terrible death. He breaks her neck,
first seizing her in his powerful teeth, then he gulps   185
down all the blood and guts—even so the son of Atreus,
King Agamemnon, pursued the Trojans, always killing
the ones who fell behind as they fled before him.

   Many fell from their cars on their faces
and on their backs beneath the hands of the son of Atreus.   190
All around and before him he raged with the spear. But when
he was about to come under the city and the steep wall,
then the father of men and gods came down from the sky
and took his seat on the peaks of Ida that has many
fountains. He held a thunderbolt in his hands.   195

*[Lines 196–621 are omitted. Zeus sends a message to Hector that he should keep away
from Agamemnon until he is wounded, but that then Hector should attack. Agamemnon
is wounded. Hector leads the Trojans against the Greeks, who fall back. Odysseus and
Diomedes are wounded too, as well as the physician Machaon. From his camp Achilles
sees the wounded Machaon withdrawing from the battle in Nestor's chariot.]*

And so they fought like blazing fire.
The mares of Neleus, drenched in sweat, carried Nestor
from the battle along with Machaon, shepherd
of the people. Achilles, the fast runner, noticed then   625
while standing by the stern of his hollow-hulled ship,
watching the rough going and fearful rout. Directly he spoke
to Patroklos, his comrade, calling to him from beside the ship.
Patroklos heard and came forth from the tent, like to Ares—
and this was the beginning of evil for him.   630

                     The valiant son
of Menoitios answered Achilles first: "Why do you call,
Achilles? What do you need of me?"

                     Achilles, the fast runner, replied:
"Good son of Menoitios, most beloved to my heart, I think
that now the Achaeans will be standing about my knees
in prayer. An unbearable necessity has come upon them!°   635
But go now, Patroklos, dear to Zeus, ask Nestor who is
the wounded man that he carries from the war. From here

---

635   *upon them*: These words seem to ignore the embassy of Book 9, as if the Achaeans had never attempted to ap-
      pease Achilles, but for the story to move ahead Achilles needs to send Patroklos to Nestor's tent. At the same
      time Homer wants to return our attention to Achilles and his plight. Here Achilles expresses anew his anger
      with the Achaeans and how sorry they will be because he is not in the fight. This anger has never abated.

he looks like Machaon, the son of Asklepios, but I did not see
the man's eyes. For the horses ran past me, quickly pressing on."

640   So he spoke. Patroklos obeyed his comrade. He ran along
the huts and ships of the Achaeans. When Nestor and Machaon
arrived at Nestor's hut, they got down from the car onto
the bounteous earth. Eurymedon, Nestor's aide, undid
the old man's horses from the car. They dried the sweat
645   of their shirts in the breeze, standing by the shore of the sea.
Then they went into the hut and sat on chairs. Hekamedê
made a restorative drink for them. The old man had taken her
from TENEDOS when Achilles sacked it, the daughter of
great-hearted Arsinoös. The Achaeans chose her for him
650   because in giving counsel she was the best of all. First she
drew up a beautiful table with feet of lapis lazuli, highly
polished, and on it she placed a bronze bowl, and with it
an onion as relish for drink,° and pale honey, and a
meal of sacred barley, and a very beautiful cup that the
655   old man had brought from home, studded with rivets
of gold. It had four handles and around each two doves
were feeding, and two supports were beneath. Another
man could scarcely have lifted it from the table
when it was full, but old man Nestor raised it easily.°
660   In it the woman, like to the goddesses, mixed a refreshing
drink of Pramnian wine,° and over it she grated goat's
cheese with a bronze grater. Then she sprinkled on
some white barley and urged them to drink, when she
had made ready the drink. The two men drank it and put
665   aside their parching thirst. Then Nestor and Machaon
delighted one another by telling tales.

Looking up
they saw Patroklos standing at the doors, a man
like a god. When Nestor saw him the old man leaped up
from his shining chair. He took him by the hand and led
670   him in and urged him to have a seat. Patroklos
from his side refused and said: "I won't sit, old man,
nourished of Zeus, nor can you persuade me. Revered

---

653   *for drink*: One of the very few time that vegetables are mentioned in the *Iliad*. The heroes are meat-eaters
and avoid fish and vegetables.

659   *raised it easily*: A cup coming close to this description from the sixteenth century BC was found in the
fourth shaft grave at Mycenae, excavated and named by Heinrich Schliemann in 1876.

661   *Pramnian wine*: No place known as Pramnos or the like has been identified.

—to be feared!—is the man who sent me to find out who
is this man that you bring wounded from the battle. I see now
that it is Machaon, shepherd of the people. Now I must   675
return to Achilles and tell him what I've learned. I think
you know, old man, nourished of Zeus, what kind
of dread man he is. He is quick to blame one in whom
there is no blame."

        Then Gerenian Nestor, the horseman,
answered him: "Well, why does Achilles suddenly   680
have pity on the sons of the Achaeans, with all those wounded
by missiles? Does he not know the suffering spread
through the camp? For the captains are lying among
the ships, shot by arrows and cut by spears. The powerful
Diomedes, son of Tydeus, is wounded by an arrow. Odysseus,   685
famed with the spear, has a spear wound, and Agamemnon too.
Even Eurypylos has been hit in the thigh with an arrow.
This man Machaon is still one more that I have brought out
of the battle, struck by an arrow from the string. But Achilles,
though he is brave, does not care for the Danaäns or take pity   690
on them. Will he wait until the swift ships near the sea
are set aflame with devouring fire in spite of the Argives,
and we are all killed in a row?
                "My strength is not
what once it was when my limbs were supple. Would
that I were young and my strength were as when a quarrel   695
broke out with the Eleians and ourselves over some stolen cattle—
then I killed Itymon, the noble son of Hypeirochos, who
lived in ELIS,° when I was driving off booty seized
in reprisal. He was defending his cows and got hit among
the foremost by a spear thrown from my hand—   700
he fell, and the country folk around him fled in terror.
We took booty aplenty from the plain—fifty herds of cows,
as many flocks of sheep, as many herds of pigs, as many
herds of roving goats, and one hundred-fifty
tawny horses, all mares, and there were many with foals   705
at the teat. We drove them toward Neleian Pylos during
the night, toward the city.° Neleus rejoiced

---

698   *Elis*: The tribe of Eleians, famous from classical times, is mentioned only here in the *Iliad*, as is Itymon, son
      of Hypereichos. A few lines later the *Eleians* are called *Epeians*, a more general term to refer to inhabitants
      of the northwestern Peloponnesus in the heroic age.

707   *toward the city*: Elis is north of Pylos in the northwest Peloponnesus. Some have thought that another Pylos
      is meant because Nestor's Pylos, in the southwest Peloponnesus, is one hundred miles away, hardly reach-
      able in one night. But Homer is vague about the geography of the western Peloponnesus.

in his heart when he learned that I had been successful
in going to war, though still a youth.

[Lines 710–784 are omitted. Nestor, in the longest speech in the Iliad, *tells of his martial exploits as a young man. Nestor goes on to give advice to Patroklos about the situation, saying:]*

785   "In those days I was with men, if ever there were men!
But Achilles should know we have need of his valor, else
he will certainly have much to weep about when
everybody is dead. Remember what Menoitios told
you on that day when he sent you forth to Agamemnon
790 from Phthia—Odysseus and I were there in the halls
at the time and we heard what he said. We came to the well-built
house of Peleus as we were gathering the people
throughout Achaea with its rich soil. That's when
we found the warrior Menoitios° in the house and you,
795 Patroklos, and with you, Achilles. Old man Peleus, the driver
of horses, was burning the fat thigh pieces of a bull
to Zeus who delights in the thunder in the enclosure of the court.
He held a golden cup, pouring out an offering
of flaming wine over the glowing flesh of sacrifice.
800 You and Achilles were busy with the flesh of the bull
when we stood in the doorway. Achilles, amazed,
jumped up and led us in, taking us by the hand
and urging us to sit down. He gave us excellent
entertainment, as is the custom in greeting strangers.
805   "When we had partaken of food and drink, I began
to speak, urging you, Patroklos, to follow along.
You were quite eager, and Peleus and Menoitios lay
on you many commands. Peleus, the old man,
commanded Achilles, his child, to always be the best,
810 to be better than all others. To you, Menoitios,
the son of Aktor, commanded: 'My child, in birth
Achilles is higher than you, but you are the older.
In strength he is superior, but you must tell him
the truth, explain all things and give him guideposts.
815 He will be persuaded to his benefit.' So commanded the
old man—you have forgotten!

---

794 *Menoitios:* Conveniently for the story, Menoitios, the father of Patroklos, is now living at Phthia, but his former home is never clear. Later sources gave it as Locris (in eastern mainland Greece) or even that he was a brother of Peleus.

            "Even now you can say so
to wise Achilles, in hopes he will be persuaded. Who knows
if, with the help of some spirit, you might rouse his heart
with your persuasive speech? Advice from a comrade
is always good. If Achilles is avoiding some oracle in his heart,   820
and his revered mother has reported something to him from Zeus,
then he can send you forth, and with you the people
of the Myrmidons may follow. Then you may become a light
to the Danaäns. And let him give you his beautiful armor
to wear into the war, so the Trojans may mistake you for him   825
and withdraw from the battle. The warlike sons of the Achaeans
can get their breath. They are much worn down. It is hard
to catch your breath during war. Easily might you,
who are not tired, drive back men exhausted by battle
towards the city, away from the ships and huts."   830

    So Nestor spoke, and he stirred the spirit
in the breast of Patroklos, who broke and ran along the ships
towards the hut of Achilles, grandson of Aiakos.
But when Patroklos, as he ran along, got to the ships
of godlike Odysseus, to the very center place of assembly   835
where they gave out the rules,° and where there were
altars built to the gods—there he ran into Eurypylos,
the Zeus-begotten son of Euaimon, wounded in the thigh
with an arrow and limping from the battle. Sweat ran like rain
from his shoulders and head, and from his vicious wound   840
black blood was gushing. But his mind was steady.

    When Patroklos saw Eurypylos, the bold son of Menoitios
took pity and, wailing, he spoke to him words that went like arrows:
"Ah, wretched leaders and rulers of the Danaäns, it seems
you were destined to glut the swift dogs of Troy with your white fat,   845
far from your friends and the land of your fathers. But come,
tell me this, Eurypylos, nourished of Zeus and a fighting man:
Will the Achaeans still hold back the giant Hector, or will they perish,
overcome by his spear?"

                The wounded Eurypylos answered:
"No longer, Patroklos nourished of Zeus, will there be   850
a defense for the Achaeans, but they will die among
the black ships. All those who once were the best fighters

---

836   ...*rules*: Because Odysseus' ships were parked in the center of the line. The assembly was at the center of the line.

FIGURE 11.2 Achilles and Cheiron. In spite of Phoenix's claims in Book 9 to have educated Achilles, in the usual version, referred to by Eurypylos, Cheiron the Centaur taught him. Cheiron was the one learned and civilized Centaur in a wild race of savages. Cheiron taught Achilles the arts of a gentleman: to play the lyre and recite poetry, to hunt, and to heal. Here in this Roman fresco from Herculaneum in Italy, Cheiron, bearded and wearing an ivy wreath, holds a plectrum and shows the young Achilles how to play something on the lyre. The Romans loved mythical tales and painted them on their walls as decoration, usually set in a painted frame. This fresco was preserved when Herculaneum was destroyed by the eruption of Mount Vesuvius in AD 79.

now lie among the ships wounded by arrow or spear
at the hands of the Trojans, whose strength grows ever stronger.
But save me!—carry me to my black ship. Cut out the arrow   855
from my thigh. Cleanse the dark blood with warm water
and put soothing ointments on it, as they say that you learned
from Achilles, whom Cheiron, the most learned of the
Centaurs, instructed. As for the physicians Podaleirios
and Machaon—Machaon, I've heard, lies wounded among the ships,   860
needing a physician himself, and Podaleirios on the plain
holds out against the Trojans in the sharp contendings."

  The bold son of Menoitios then answered: "How has
all this come to pass? What are we going to do, Eurypylos,
fighting man? I will go to wise Achilles to tell him what Gerenian   865
Nestor, the guardian of the Achaeans, has advised. But even so
I will give you a hand, because you are in distress."

  Patroklos spoke and, grasping Eurypylos beneath the chest,
brought him to his tent. When his aide saw him, he spread out
some cow hides. There, stretching him out, Patroklos cut the sharp   870
piercing arrow from his thigh, and he washed the dark blood
from him with warm water. On it he placed a bitter
painkilling root, rubbing it in his hand, removing every pain.
The wound closed and the blood ceased to flow.

BOOK 12. *Attack on the Wall*

And so Patroklos, the bold son of Menoitios tended
to the wounded Eurypylos. The Argives and the Trojans
fought on in crowds. The Danaäns had dug a great ditch
and built a wide wall behind it to protect their swift ships
5 and abundant booty. But it would not hold—because they did
not offer glorious sacrifice to the gods! Because it was built
against the will of the deathless gods, it did not last long.
While Hector was alive and Achilles was enraged and the city
of King Priam remained intact, for so long the great wall
10 of the Achaeans stayed in place. But when the bravest of the Trojan
captains had died, and of the Argives many perished, though many
survived, and when the city of Priam was destroyed in the tenth year
and the Argives had gone back to the land of their fathers in their ships,
then Poseidon and Apollo contrived to sweep away the wall,
15 rousing the strength of all the rivers that flow forth from Ida
to the sea—Rhesos and Heptaporos and Karesis and Rhodios
and Granikos and the shining AISEPOS and SKAMANDROS and SIMOEIS°—
along which many shields of ox-hide and many helmets had fallen
in the dust, and the race of men who were half gods. Of all
20 these rivers, Phoibos Apollo turned the mouths together,
and for nine days they poured against the wall. Zeus rained
constantly, so that the wall would quickly disappear into the sea.
The shaker of earth, holding his trident in his hands,° led the way.
He swept away on the waves all the foundations of beams and stone
25 that the Achaeans had laid with such trouble. He made smooth the shore
along the powerful flow of the HELLESPONT. He covered the great
beach with sand, sweeping away the wall. He returned the rivers
to flow in their channels, where previously they made the beautiful water
to flow. So were Poseidon and Apollo to arrange things after the war.

30   But for now war and the din of war blazed around
the well-built wall, and the beams of the towers rang

---

17 *Simoeis*: Rhesos and Heptaporos and Karesos and Rhodios and Granikos are mentioned only here in the
Iliad. The first four rivers are unidentified; the Granikos and Aisepos flowed well to the east of the Troad.
Only the Skamandros and Simoeis actually flow across the Trojan plain (Map I).

23 *in his hands*: This the only place in the *Iliad* where Poseidon has his characteristic emblem, the trident, with
which he is always shown in art.

as they were struck. The Argives, overwhelmed by the whip
of Zeus, were penned-in beside their hollow ships. They were held
in check, terrified by Hector, the mighty master of rout.
He raged as before, like a whirlwind.   35

*[Lines 36–219 are omitted. Hector now leads the Trojans across the ditch to attack the
defensive wall protecting the ships.]*

                        Hector led the way forward.   220
The others followed with a tremendous shout. And Zeus
who delights in the thunderbolt roused from the mountains of Ida
a blast of wind that carried dust straight against the ships.
He enchanted the minds of the Achaeans, gave glory to the Trojans
and to Hector. Trusting to the portents° and to their own strength,   225
they attempted to smash the great wall of the Achaeans. They tore
down the tops of the fortifications. They dragged down the battlements
and pried out the supporting beams that the Achaeans had placed
in the earth to be buttresses for the wall.° They tried to drag out
the beams, in hopes of smashing the wall of the Achaeans.   230

   But the Danaäns did not even now withdraw from the path,
but closing up the battlements with the hides of bulls they threw rocks
down from there onto the Trojans coming under the wall. The two
Ajaxes ranged everywhere along the wall, stirring up the men,
encouraging the might of the Achaeans. To some they spoke   235
honeyed words, but to others, when they saw them pulling
back from the fight, they reproached with harsh words:
"Friends of the Argives! Those of you who are superior
in the fight, those who are of middling quality, and those
who are lesser—for in war not all men are equal—now   240
there is work for everyone, I think you know that! So don't
turn back to the ships now that you have been encouraged.
Throw yourselves forward and urge each other on in hopes
that Zeus of the lightning bolt may grant us to push back
this assault and drive the Trojans toward their city."   245

   Thus the two Ajaxes stirred battle against the Achaeans with their shouting.
As snowflakes fall thickly on a winter's day, when Zeus

---

225 *portents*: Presumably an earlier portent of an eagle devouring a snake.

229 *for the wall*: We cannot form a clear picture of how the Achaean wall was constructed. The word translated
     "tops" in "tops of the fortifications" is in fact of unknown meaning. Ordinarily in ancient warfare siege lad-
     ders would be placed against a defensive wall, but the Trojans do not use them.

the counselor is stirred to let snow fall, showing forth to men
his shafts and, lulling the winds, he pours forth constantly
250 until he covers the peaks of the high mountains and the high
headlands, and fields overgrown with lotus and the rich
plowlands of men, and the snow is poured over the harbors
and the shores of the gray sea, though the pelting wave
keeps off the snow, even so are all things wrapped
255 in snow from above, when the storm of Zeus falls heavily.
Like that the stones fell thickly on either side, some on
the Trojans and some from the Trojans onto the Achaeans as they
cast at one another. And a clanging din arose over the entire wall.

Even so the Trojans and noble Hector would never
260 have broken the gates of the wall and the long bolt if Zeus
the counselor had not stirred his son Sarpedon against
the Argives, like a lion against cattle with curled horns.
And then Sarpedon held his shield before him, perfectly round,
beautiful, worked in bronze that a smith had hammered out.
265 The bronze-smith had attached ox-hides stitched within
with thick golden pins, continuously around the inside.
Holding the shield before him, Sarpedon brandished two spears
and went like a lion raised in the mountains, who for long
has been without meat, and his proud spirit urges him to attack
270 the flocks, to go against a sturdy household. Even if he finds
herdsmen there with dogs and spears guarding the flocks,
he is not inclined to flee the fold without a fight, but leaps
into the flock and seizes one—or, like a champion
he is struck by a spear from a swift hand. Just so his spirit
275 urged godlike Sarpedon to leap onto the wall and to smash
the battlements.

And he exclaimed loudly to Glaukos, the son
of Hippolochos: "Glaukos, why are we honored above all
with the best seats, best cuts of meat, and with fat cups
in LYCIA? And why do all regard us as gods and we dwell
280 in large districts along the banks of the XANTHOS,° a fine tract
of orchard and wheat-bearing plowland? Therefore we must now
take our stand among the foremost of the Lycians, and face
this blazing battle, so that some one of the heavy-armed Lycians
might say: 'Not without fame do these men rule Lycia,
285 our kings. They eat fat sheep and drink choice wine,

---

280 *Xanthos*: The greatest of the rivers of Lycia (Map III), whose valley forms the heart of the country.
Considerable ruins survive from the classical city, including a tomb from which Figure 12 is taken.

sweet as honey, true—but their valor is unmatched,
and they fight among the foremost Lycians.' Yes,
my friend, if escaped from battle it were possible for the two
of us never to grow old and never to die, I would not myself
fight among the foremost, nor would I send you into the fight   290
where men win glory. But as it is, the fates of death
stand over us, ten thousand of them—no man can flee or escape
from them—so let us go forward and give glory to another,
or to ourselves."

       So Sarpedon spoke. Glaukos did not turn aside
or disobey. The two of them went straight on, leading   295
the large contingent of Lycians. Seeing them, the son of Peteos,
Menestheus,° shivered. For they brought devastation to his part
of the wall. Menestheus looked along the wall of the Achaeans,
hoping to see any of the captains who might ward off destruction
from him and his companions. He saw the two Ajaxes   300
standing there, ever lustful for war, and Teucer, who had just come
from his tent nearby. But it was impossible to make himself heard,
so great was the clamor, the din from the shields being struck
and the helmets with horsehair plumes. The clanging of the
closed gates reached the sky. The Trojans stood without and attempted   305
with great violence to force the gates and to burst inside.

  Quickly, Menestheus sent the herald Thoötes° to Ajax:
"Go, good Thoötes, run and call Ajax, rather, call both Ajaxes—
that would be best, for hideous destruction will soon
befall us. The captains of the Lycians lean heavily upon us,   310
they who earlier raged in furious battle. But if labor
and quarrel have arisen for the Ajaxes where they are—
at least beg Telamonian Ajax to come alone, and may Teucer,
the great bowman, follow with him."

          So he spoke, and the herald
Thoötes, hearing him, obeyed, and set off running by the wall   315
of the Achaeans who wear shirts of bronze. Arriving, he stood
near the two Ajaxes, and promptly said: "You two Ajaxes,
leaders of the Achaeans who wear shirts of bronze: Menestheus,
the beloved son of god-nourished Peteos, urges you
to come at once so that if only for a brief time you may face   320
this labor of war—both of you! That would be far the best case,

---

297 *Menestheus*: The leader of the Athenian contingent. His performance is typically ineffectual.

307 *Thoötes*: "Swift," a "speaking name."

FIGURE 12   Trojan and Greek warriors fighting hand to hand.   They are dressed as hoplites. The warrior on the left spears the other fighter in the chest. Frieze on the tomb of a Lycian prince, c. 380 BC, the Heroön of Goelbasi-Trysa, Lycia, Turkey.

else steep destruction will likely befall us. The captains
of the Lycians weigh heavily upon us, they who earlier raged
in furious battle. But if labor and quarrel has arisen
for you here, let at least Telamonian Ajax come alone,   325
and may Teucer, the great bowman, follow with him."

So he spoke, nor did Telamonian Ajax decline.
But immediately he spoke to Little Ajax, the son of Oïleus,
words that flew like arrows: "Ajax, son of Oïleus, the two
of you— you and strong Lykomedes—stay here and urge   330
the Danaäns to fight to the utmost. But I will go away
with Thoötes and face up to the war. I will come back
here quickly, once we have achieved a good defense."

So speaking Telamonian Ajax went off and with him
went Teucer, his brother from the same father, and with them   335
Pandion, who carried Teucer's° bent bow. When going along
the inside of the wall they came to the part defended by great-souled
Menestheus—they came to men hard pressed!—the powerful
leaders and rulers of the Lycians were astride the battlements
like a dark whirlwind. Thus they clashed together in battle   340
and the din of war arose.

Ajax, the son of Telamon,
was first to kill his man, Epikles, a great-hearted
companion of Sarpedon, hitting him with a sharp rock
that lay, huge, on top of the wall near the battlement.
No man could lift it easily with both hands, no matter   345
how young, such as men are today. But he raised
it high, threw it and smashed the helmet with four ridges.
Thus Big Ajax crushed all the bones of Epikles' head,
who fell like a diver from the high wall, and his breath-soul
left his bones.   350

And Teucer hit Glaukos, the son
of Hippolochos, with an arrow from the high wall as Glaukos
rushed on Teucer. He saw where Glaukos' arm
was exposed, and he put Glaukos out of the fight.

Glaukos covertly leaped back from the wall so that no one
of the Achaeans might notice he was hit and so boast over him.   355

---

336 *Teucer*: In Book 8 Teucer was wounded by Hector and taken back to his tent, but no reference is made to
     this earlier injury.

Distress settled over Sarpedon immediately when he saw
that Glaukos was missing.° All the same he did not forget
the battle, for he stabbed Alkmaon, son of Thestor,
hitting him with his spear. He then pulled it out.
360   Alkmaon, being pulled with it, fell on his face, and his armor,
inlaid with bronze, rang around him. Then Sarpedon seized
the battlement in his strong hands and pulled. The whole
length of it gave way. The wall above was exposed—
he had made a path for many. But Ajax and Teucer
365   acted together against him. Teucer hit Sarpedon with an arrow
on the shining strap of the protective shield that guarded
his chest. But Zeus warded death from his son, so he was not
overcome on the sterns of the ships. Ajax leaped on him
and stabbed at his shield, but the spear did not go through.
370   Ajax pushed him back as Sarpedon rushed on.
Ajax withdrew a little from the battlement, but he did not
wholly withdraw, for his spirit hoped to win glory.

    Wheeling around, Sarpedon called out to the godlike
Lycians: "O Lycians, why have you backed away from
375   your furious valor? It is hard for me alone, though I am strong,
to break down the wall and make a path to the ships.
But let us attack together. The job is better done when many
people do the work."

                    So he spoke. The Lycians, fearing
the reproach of their king, pushed harder around their advisor
380   and king. The Argives from their side strengthened the battalions
inside the wall—the task before them was great. The powerful Lycians
were unable to break the wall and make a path to the ships, but the
Danaän spearmen could not drive the Lycians from the wall
when once they closed on it. Even as when two men argue
385   about boundary-stones in a field held in common, having measuring
sticks in their hands and in a narrow space disagree about the equal
division, even so little did the battlements keep them apart.°
And above them they struck the ox-hide shields of one another,
well-rounded, like fluttering targets. The relentless bronze wounded
390   many in the flesh, both when they exposed their backs, turning
while they fought, and sometimes hit straight through their shields.

---

357   *was missing*: Glaukos survives the *Iliad*, but in post-Homeric tradition Ajax or Agamemnon finally killed
him. The kings of Lycia traced their descent from Glaukos.

387   *apart*: Two men are arguing over a small amount of common ground; they are no further apart than the
breadth of the battlements.

Everywhere the walls and the battlements were splattered
with the blood of men fighting on either side, blood from Trojans
and Achaeans alike. But the Trojans could not make the Achaeans
flee. The Achaeans held their ground, as a woman, an honest weaver   395
for hire, who holds the balance, makes equal the wool
and the weight in the scale so that she might earn a paltry
reward for her children—even so the battle and war was
stretched equally, until Zeus gave the glory of victory to Hector,
son of Priam—the first to leap within the wall of the Achaeans.   400

He roared a piercing shout, calling to the Trojans:
"Rise up, you horse-taming Trojans! Smash the wall of the
Argives. Cast glorious destroying fire into their ships!"
Thus Hector bellowed, urging them on. All the Trojans heard.
They charged the wall straight-on in a massed formation.   405
They climbed to the top of the wall carrying their sharp
spears while Hector picked up and carried a stone found
near the gate, thick at the bottom but sharp at the top, so large
that two men, the best of the people, could not easily
have muscled it from the ground onto a cart, such as men   410
are today. But Hector swung it up easily all by himself.
Zeus, the son of clever Kronos, made it light
for him. As when a shepherd readily lifts the fleece
of a ram all by himself, taking it in one hand,
with little trouble doing so, even so Hector raised the stone   415
and carried it straight against the doors that closed
the tightly fitted and powerful gates—double gates,
and high, and two crossbars coming from opposite directions
held them, and a single bolt fastened them.°

                              Hector went up close
to the gates, and taking a firm stand he threw the stone   420
at the middle of the gates, spreading apart his feet so that
his throw would have maximum power. He broke
both pivots° away and the stone fell inside of its own weight.
The gates on either side groaned. The bars did not hold.
The doors were smashed apart on this side and that   425
under the onrush of the stone. Glorious Hector leaped

---

419 *fastened them*: Hector carries his two spears in one hand and with the other he picks up the rock, which he
     then uses as a kind of battering ram.

423 *pivots*: Ancient doors did not have hinges as we think of them, but were attached by pegs at the inside top
     and the inside bottom that rotated in holes in the threshold and the lintel. Hector does not burst open the
     gates, but smashes them from their seating in the masonry.

inside, his face aglow like the sudden night. He shone
with the terrible bronze that he wore around his flesh,
and he held two spears. No one who met him could have
430   held him back once he leaped within, unless he were a god.
His eyes burned like fire. He whirled around in the crowd.
He called out to the Trojans to come over the wall
and they obeyed his urging. Some came over the wall,
others poured in through the strong gates. The Danaäns were
435   driven in rout through the hollow ships. An endless tumult arose.

BOOK 13. *The Battle at the Ships*

When Zeus had brought the Trojans and Hector to the ships,
he left them there to endure their pain and endless sorrow.
But he averted his shining eyes, looking far away
to the land of the horse-riding Thracians and that of the Mysians
who fight in close, and of the noble Mare-milkers who live   5
from milk, and of the Abioi, the most just of men.° For he did
not expect in his heart any of the deathless ones to come
to the aid of the Trojans or the Danaäns.

                         But Poseidon, the king,
the shaker of the earth, was not blind to developments.
He sat on the top of the highest peak of SAMOTHRACE,   10
marveling at the war and the skirmishes. From there all IDA
was clear, and he could see the city of Priam and the ships
of the Achaeans.° There he came out of the sea, because
he took pity on the Achaeans, beset by the Trojans. And he was
very angry with Zeus. He came straight down from the rugged   15
mountain, moving resolutely on his immortal feet; the high
mountains and the woods shook beneath Poseidon as he went.
Three times he strode out, and on the fourth pace he reached
his goal of Aigai,° where his famous house of gold
and stone was built for him in the depths of the water,   20
deathless forever. When he got there he readied the two
bronze-hooved horses with flowing golden manes, swift of flight,
beneath the chariot. Then he himself wrapped gold
about his flesh. He gripped the whip, nicely made
of gold, then mounted his car and set out to drive   25
over the waves. Dolphins leaped beneath him from
hidden places—they knew their king! The sea parted

---

6   ... *of men*: Zeus is looking north, across the PROPONTIS first to Thrace, then beyond to the Mysians (in modern Bulgaria), somehow related to the Mysians who lived in Anatolia east of Troy (MAP IV); then to the Mare-milkers, no doubt across the Danube in Scythia, where Herodotus describes tribes that live on milk; and finally to the Abioi, a mythical pacific tribe beyond the Mare-milkers.

13 *Achaeans*: The island of IMBROS intervenes between TROY and SAMOTHRACE (see MAPS II and III), but Samothrace's highest mountain peak is visible over Imbros. This detail seems to prove that Homer had visited the site of Troy.

19 *Aigai*: Variously identified, but here probably a headland on the coast of ASIA MINOR opposite the southeast corner of LESBOS.

FIGURE 13.1   Poseidon in his chariot rides across the waves, a scene inspired by Homer's description.   He holds his trident in his left hand and points in the direction he wants to go. He is heavily bearded and crowned and wears a scarf across his right arm. The chariot is drawn by four horses with dolphin tails. Roman mosaic, AD 2nd century, from a Roman villa in Sousse, Tunisia.

joyfully before him. The horses sped swiftly on,
and the bronze axle beneath was not dampened.
The prancing horses brought him to the ships of the Achaeans.   30

There is a broad cave in the depths of the deep water,
midway between TENEDOS and rugged IMBROS, where Poseidon,
the shaker of the earth, stationed his horses, uncoupling
them from his car and setting before them food to eat.
Around their feet he placed golden hobbles, unbreakable,   35
never to be loosened, that they might remain there until their king
returned. Then he went off to the camp of the Achaeans.

The Trojans, ever eager for battle, gathered like flames
or storm clouds. They followed Hector, son of Priam, shouting loudly
and crying out. They believed they would take the ships of the Achaeans,   40
killing all their best men. But Poseidon, the holder and shaker
of the earth, roused-up the Argives, coming from the deep sea
in the likeness of Kalchas—with his shape and untiring voice.

He spoke first to the two Ajaxes, both already
eager to fight: "You two Ajaxes, you are the ones to save   45
the army of the Achaeans, remembering your valor and giving
no thought to icy rout! I do not fear the mighty hands of the Trojans
in some other part of the fight, but here where they have climbed
the high wall in a mass—the Achaeans, who wear fancy shin guards,
will hold them! But right here I am terribly anxious that some   50
calamity will happen—here where that mad-dog Hector,
like a flame, is in the lead—he who *says* he is a son of Zeus.
So I trust that some god puts it into your hearts to make
a strong stand here and move others to do the same.
The two of you can push Hector back from the swift-sailing   55
ships, despite his eagerness, even if the Olympian himself
drives him on!"

Then the holder of the earth, the shaker
of the earth, struck the two Ajaxes with his rod and filled
them with powerful strength. He made their limbs light,
their feet and their hands fast and strong. Then, like a hawk   60
swift of wing, who hovering over a steep high rock
speeds forth over the plain to pursue another bird—
even so Poseidon, shaker of the earth, set off the fly, darting
away from them.

[Lines 65–781 are omitted. In this way, Poseidon rallies the Greeks. The Cretan captain Idomeneus distinguishes himself in a display of glory. Bitter fighting follows on both sides. A son of Ares, the Trojan Askalaphos, is killed.]

They went like a blast of savage wind that rushes down
upon the earth, accompanied by the thunder of father Zeus,
and with a wondrous howl mixes with the salt sea,
785   and in its track are many bubbling waves of the turbulent sea,
arched, specked with white, some in the front, some following—
even so the Trojans, packed tightly together, some in the front,
some following, all glittering with bronze, followed their leaders.

Hector, son of Priam, was in the lead, like man-destroying
790   Ares. He held his shield before him, equal on all sides,
made of thick ox-hide with added bronze. His shining helmet
shimmered around his temples. Everywhere on this side
and that he strode forward and made trial of the battalions,
to see if they would give way as he advanced under cover of his shield.
795   But he could confound no hearts in the breasts of the Achaeans.

Ajax was the first to call him out, not mincing words:
"Hey tough guy, come closer! Do you really believe
you can make the Argives fearful? We are in no way ignorant
of battle, only by the evil stroke of Zeus were we Achaeans
800   beaten down. Doubtless you have great hopes to destroy
our ships, but we have hands and the will to defend them!
It's much more likely that your own well-peopled city will fall
and be laid waste by our hands. And I think the time
is near when, fleeing, you will pray to father Zeus and the other
805   deathless ones that your horses with fine coats be swifter
than falcons—those horses that carry you through the dust
over the plain to the city!"

Even as he spoke a bird
flew across his right hand, a high-flying eagle. The army
of the Achaeans cried aloud, cheered by the omen.° But glorious
810   Hector answered thus: "Ajax, you are a rash speaker,
a bully—so you say! As I would like to be the son
of Zeus who carries the goatskin fetish, and my mother
be the revered Hera, and as I would like to be honored as Athena
and Apollo, so may this day bear a great evil for all the Argives!
815   And you too shall die. Stick around and my long spear

---

809   *omen:* Bird omens always come true in the *Iliad.*

will feast on your lily-white skin. Yes, and you will glut
the dogs and birds of the Trojans with your fat and your flesh
when you fall amid the ships of the Achaeans."

         So Hector spoke
and led the way forward. The Trojans followed after him
with a wondrous din, and the people behind shouted assent.   820
And the Argives shouted from the other side, their valor
not misplaced. And so they withstood the best of the Trojans
as they came rushing on. And the clamor of both sides
traveled to the upper air and the eye-rays of Zeus.

BOOK 14. *Zeus Deceived*

[Lines 1–149 are omitted. The wounded Agamemnon, Odysseus, and Diomedes have withdrawn to the camp. Nestor converses with them. Poseidon, disguised as a mortal, continues to assist the Greeks.]

Now Hera, whose throne is golden,
    saw Poseidon as she stood on a peak of Olympos. Right away
she recognized him busying himself with the battle
in which men win glory—her own brother and her husband's
brother—and she rejoiced in her heart. Then she saw Zeus sitting
155 on the topmost peak of Ida with its many fountains, and he
seemed hateful to her in her heart. Then cow-eyed revered
Hera pondered how she might charm the mind of the bearer
of the goatskin fetish. In her heart this seemed the best plan—
to go to Ida after making herself alluring, to see
160 if Zeus might desire to embrace her flesh and lie
by her side in love so that she might pour out harmless
gentle sleep over his eyes and quell his wily mind.

    She entered her chamber, which her son Hephaistos had
made for her. He had fitted thick doors into the doorposts with
165 a secret bolt that no other god could open. She went inside
and closed the shining doors. First of all she cleansed
her lovely skin with ambrosia° and washed away
every defilement. She anointed herself with a rich oil,
ambrosial, sweet, with a lovely fragrance. If this
170 were shaken in the house of Zeus with its bronze threshold,
the scent would reach to the earth and the wide heaven alike.
With this she anointed her beautiful skin. She combed
her hair and with her hands plaited her bright tresses,
beautiful and ambrosial, that fell from her imperishable head.
175 She put about her an ambrosial robe that Athena had scraped
into a finished product,° and placed on it many beautiful

---

167 *ambrosia*: Meaning "an immortal substance," it is the food of the gods, as *nectar* is their drink. Ambrosia prevents death and decay and is used to embalm the dead. The immortals also use ambrosia to cleanse their skin, as mortals use olive oil. This amusing scene parodies the arming of a warrior as he prepares to go out on to a glorious display on the field of battle.

176 *finished product*: The cloth was scraped either to make it smooth or to provide a nap.

embroideries. This she pinned around her breast with golden
pins. She bound a belt fitted with a hundred tassels
about her waist. In her pierced ears she placed earrings
with three drops shaped like mulberries. A great grace   180
shone from them. Then the bright goddess covered her head
with a kerchief over all—sparkling, brand-new, white
like the sun. She bound beautiful sandals beneath her shining feet.

When she had decked out her body with every adornment,
she went forth from the chamber and called Aphrodite apart   185
from the other gods, and she spoke to her these words:
"Will you obey me, my child, and do what I am about to request?
Or will you refuse me because you hold anger in your heart
because I give aid to the Danaäns and you to the Trojans?"

Then Aphrodite, the daughter of Zeus, answered her: 190
"Hera, august goddess, daughter of great Kronos, say
what you are thinking. My heart urges me to accomplish it,
if I can accomplish it and in fact it can be done."

The revered Hera answered her, with crafty thought:
"Give me now love and desire, by which you overcome   195
all the deathless ones and mortal men too. For I am about
to visit the limits of the much-nourishing earth, and Okeanos,
the origin of the gods, and mother Tethys, who nourished
and reared me in their home. They received me from Rhea when
far-thundering Zeus shoved Kronos down beneath the earth   200
and the murmuring sea.° I am going to pay them a visit, and I hope
to resolve their quarreling without respite. For a long time
they have held aloof from the marriage bed and from lovemaking,
because anger has invaded their hearts. If by my words I might
persuade the hearts of these two, and bring them back   205
to be joined in lovemaking, then I might forever be cherished
and thus be honored by them."

                    Aphrodite, who loves laughter,
then answered her: "It is not right that I deny you, for you sleep
in the arms of Zeus, who is the greatest of us all." So speaking,

---

201   *murmuring sea*: Homer refers to a different cosmogony from that familiar in Hesiod's *Theogony*, where first
came Chaos; then Earth; then the offspring of Earth and Ocean, the Titans; then the Olympians, who
under Zeus's leadership overthrew the Titans under Kronos' leadership, a victory to which Hera refers.
Evidently Homer has heard the Mesopotamian story wherein the first gods were Apsu (Ocean, the fresh
water) and Tiamat (Tethys, the salt water) so that all the world descends from these primordial waters. It is
not clear why Rhea, Hera's mother and Kronos' consort, gave Hera to Ocean and Tethys to be raised.

210 she unfastened from her breasts an ornate decorated strap
in which all kinds of spells° were fashioned. In it
were lovemaking, and desire, and the murmuring of sweet
nothings that steal the wits of even the wise. Aphrodite
placed it in Hera's hands and spoke and addressed her:
215 "There, place this embroidered strap against your breasts.
In it are all things fashioned. And I do not think
that you will return without accomplishing the goal
that you have in mind."

So she spoke, and the revered Hera,
with eyes like a cow, smiled, and then smiling she placed
220 the gift against her breasts. Aphrodite, the daughter of Zeus,
went to her house while Hera darted down and left
the peak of OLYMPOS. She stepped on Pieria and lovely
Emathia, and sped to the topmost peaks of the snowy
mountains of the Thracian horsemen. Her feet did not touch
225 the ground. Then from ATHOS she stepped onto the swelling
sea and came to LEMNOS, the city of the godlike
Thoas.° There she met Sleep, the brother of Death.

She took him by the hand and addressed him: "Sleep,
lord of all the gods and all men, if ever you hearkened
230 to my word, obey me now, and I will owe you thanks
for all my days. Put the shining eyes of Zeus
to sleep beneath his brows right after I lie with him
in love. I will give you the gift of a beautiful imperishable
throne made of gold. Hephaistos, my own son, the god
235 with crippled feet, will fashion it with skill, and he will place
a footstool under it for your feet. You will be able
to rest your shining feet upon it at the banquet."

Sweet Sleep then answered her: "Hera, august goddess,
daughter of great Kronos, another of the gods that last
240 forever I might easily put to sleep, even the streams of the river
Ocean, who is the origin of them all. But I would

---

211 *kinds of spells*: The amulet is not a belt, but perhaps a strap that went over one shoulder, between the breasts, and under the other arm, to judge from artistic representations of nude Eastern fertility goddesses.

227 *. . . godlike Thoas*: Pieria is a district of southern MACEDONIA, north of Mt. Olympos. Emathia, "sandy," is the coast of Macedonia. THRACE is here rather west of where it is usually located. The peak of Mt. ATHOS reaches to over 6,600 feet (since medieval times the site of famous monasteries). The grandson of Thoas ("swifty"), Euneos ("good with ships"), traded with the Achaeans in wine, metals, hides, Phoenician handiwork, and slaves (according to a passage in Book 23). Euneos was the son of Jason, the Argonaut, and Hypsipylê, the daughter of Thoas.

not come near the son of Kronos, nor lull him to sleep,
unless he himself urged me. For I remember another time
one of your commands pricked me on—that day
when Herakles, that mighty son of Zeus, sailed   245
from Ilion after he sacked the city of the Trojans. For I put
to sleep the mind of Zeus who carries the goatskin fetish,
pouring sweetly my potion about him while you devised
evil in your heart. You raised up the blasts of savage
winds over the sea, and then you carried Herakles   250
to the well-peopled island of Kos, far from his loved ones.
When Zeus woke up he was more than angry and tossed the gods
all around his house—but it was me he sought above all.
And he would have thrown me from the sky into the sea,
to be seen no more, if Night, the tamer of gods   255
and men, had not saved me. I came to her in flight,
and he left off a little, though he was angry. For he feared
that he might do something displeasing to swift Night.°
And now, again, you urge me to do something else
that is impossible!"   260

     The revered Hera with cow eyes then answered
him: "Sleep, why do you ponder these matters in your heart?
Do you think that far-thundering Zeus will help the Trojans
just as he became angry on account of his own son
Herakles? Come—I will give you one of the youthful
Graces to marry and to be called your wife."   265

       So she spoke.
Sleep was glad for her words and answered: "Come now,
swear to me by the inviolable water of Styx. With one hand
lay hold of the bountiful earth and with the other the shining
sea, so that one and all they may be witnesses between
the two of us—I mean the gods who are below with Kronos—   270
that truly you will give me one of the younger Graces—
Pasithea, whom I myself have longed for all my days."°

---

258 *swift Night*: Sleep refers to Herakles' earlier sack of Troy, already mentioned in Book 5. Hera was the
     implacable persecutor of Herakles, presumably because he was fathered by Zeus on a mortal woman. Sleep
     never says why the island of Kos, off the southwest coast of Asia Minor, was a dangerous place,
     or what happened to Herakles there.

272 *all my days*: An oath sworn by the underworld river Styx ("hateful") cannot be broken. The "gods below"
     with Kronos are the Titans, imprisoned there after their war with the Olympians, a story told in Hesiod's
     Theogony. The Graces (*Charites*), usually three in number, were the embodiment of feminine charm.
     Pasithea means "all-divine."

FIGURE 14.1 The wedding of Zeus and Hera on a metope (a square sculpture on a frieze) from the gigantic temple to Hera (the so-called temple E) at Selinus, at the southwestern tip of Sicily, c. 540 BC. Selinus ("parsley") was the westernmost of the Greek cities in Sicily, destroyed by the Carthaginians in 409 BC. A half-naked Zeus, sitting on a rock, clasps the hand of Hera. One of her breasts is exposed as Hera removes her head covering in a traditional gesture of sexual submission.

So he spoke, and white-armed Hera did not refuse.
She swore just as he asked, and she called on all the gods
below in Tartaros, who are called the Titans.° When she had sworn   275
and completed the oath, the two of them left the cities
of LEMNOS and IMBROS and, clothed in a mist, sped swiftly
on their way. They came to IDA, the mother of wild animals,
with its many fountains, then to Lekton, where they left
the sea. The two of them went over the dry land   280
and the tops of the trees shook beneath their feet. There Sleep
waited out of sight of Zeus, hidden in a high fir tree,
the highest on Ida, which reached through the mists into the sky.
There he perched, in the form of a shrill-voiced mountain bird
which the gods call Chalkis, but men call Kymindis,° hidden   285
by the dense needles of fir trees.

                Hera quickly advanced
to Gargaros, the highest peak of lofty Ida. Zeus
the cloud-gatherer saw her. He saw her and lust overran
his wise heart, just as when first they lay together
in love, going to the couch without the knowledge   290
of their parents.

             He stood before her and spoke, addressing her:
"Hera, with what desire have you come here from Olympos?
Your horses are not at hand, nor your chariot for you to mount."

   With crafty mind the revered Hera answered:
"I have come to visit the limits of the much-nourishing earth,   295
and Okeanos, the origin of the gods, and mother Tethys,
who nourished and reared me in their home. I am going
to pay them a visit, and I hope to resolve this endless
quarreling of theirs. For a long time they have held aloof
from the marriage bed and from lovemaking, because anger has   300
taken their hearts. My horses stand at the foot of Ida
with its many fountains. They will carry me over the solid
land and the watery sea. But now it is on your
account that I have come down here from Olympos, so that

---

275   *the Titans*: This is the only time that Homer mentions the Titans by name. Tartaros, a word of unknown
       meaning, is the deepest part of the underworld.

285   *Kymindis*: The Kymindis was a kind of large owl. Gods seem to have a more elevated speech than men, but
       otherwise in myth Chalkis was the mortal woman after whom the famous city of CHALCIS on the island of
       Euboea was named.

305 you will not become angry with me afterwards, if I go
without saying anything to the house of deep-flowing Ocean."

Zeus the cloud-gatherer then answered her: "Hera,
you can always go there later, but for now let the two
of us take delight, going to bed and making love.
310 For never yet has the desire for goddess or mortal woman
so poured itself about me and overmastered my heart
in my breast—no, not when I lusted after the wife of Ixion,
who bore Peirithoös, a counselor equal to the gods.
Nor when I desired Danaë of the delicate ankles,
315 the daughter of Akrisios who bore Perseus, preeminent above
all men. Nor when I longed for the far-famed daughter
of Phoinix, who bore Minos and godlike Rhadamanthys. Not even
when I fell in love with Semelê, nor Alkmenê in Thebes,
who gave birth to strong-minded Herakles as her son; and Semelê
320 bore Dionysos, a joy to mortals. Nor when I loved queen Demeter,
who has beautiful tresses. Not even when I loved famous Leto—
nor even yourself! as now I long for you and sweetest desire
possesses me."°

The revered Hera answered him with crafty
words: "Most dread son of Kronos, what words you've spoken!
325 If you want to make love on the peaks of Ida, where everything
is out in open, how would it be if some one of the gods,
whose race is forever, should peep at us as we sleep and then
go tell all the gods? Then I could not rise up from the bed
and go to your house—it would be too shameful! But if you want
330 and it is your desire, there is always your chamber, which your dear

---

323 *...possesses me*: This hilarious scene is predicated on the *hieros gamos*, "sacred marriage," when sexual intercourse took place between someone impersonating the storm god and someone impersonating the mother
goddess, a fertility ritual prominent in the temples of the Near East and, probably, in Corinth and on the
island of Cythera south of the Peloponnesus (where Aphrodite, the "Cytherean," was said to be born). But
Homer has changed this catalog of women into a delightful parody sure to amuse his all-male audience:
a husband trying to seduce his wife by listing all the women with whom he has betrayed her! Ixion was
himself a notorious rapist who lusted after Hera, then ejaculated his semen into a cloud that had her form
and so begot the Centaurs, who raped the women at Peirithoös' wedding. Zeus came to Ixion's wife as a
stallion and begot Peirithoös ("very swift"); later Peirithoös tried to rape Persephone but was entrapped
in the lower world. Zeus came to Danaë as a shower of gold that fell into her prison chamber. The daughter
of Phoinix is Europa, whom Zeus carried to Crete from Phoenicia in the form of a bull and there possessed her. Minos became king of CRETE and Rhadamanthys a judge in the underworld. Zeus appeared to
Semelê while pregnant in the form that he appeared to Hera—a thunderbolt!—and burned her to a crisp;
Dionysos was brought to term by being sewn into Zeus's thigh. Zeus appeared to Alkmenê disguised as her
husband, but her husband impregnated her on the same night so that she gave birth to one son fathered by
Zeus, Herakles, and another son fathered by her husband. Zeus begot Persephonê on Demeter. Hera drove
Leto all over the earth before she gave birth to Apollo and Artemis on the Aegean island of DELOS.

son Hephaistos made for you, and fitted with strong doors
to the door-posts. Let us go and lie down there, since the couch
is your pleasure."

The cloud-gatherer Zeus then answered her:
"Hera, have no fear that the gods or men will see! I will wrap
a cloud about us, a golden cloud. Not even Helios° could see   335
through it, he whose sight is the keenest for seeing things."

He spoke and the son of Kronos clasped his wife in his arms.
Beneath them the shining earth made the luxuriant grass
to grow, and lotus covered with dew, and crocus, and thick
and tender hyacinth that bore them up from the ground.   340
The two lay there and were covered in a cloud—beautiful, golden!—
from which fell drops of dew. And so the father slept peacefully
on the peak of Gargaros, overcome by sleep and love.
Thus he held his wife in his arms.

*[Lines 345 to the end of the book are omitted. While Zeus sleeps, thanks to Hera's wiles,
the Greeks rally and overwhelm the Trojans. Big Ajax even knocks out Hector with a
big stone.]*

---

335 *Helios*: Ordinarily the sun-god Helios sees all things.

BOOK 15. *Trojan Counterattack*

But when in flight the Trojans had crossed back through the stakes
and the ditch, and many were overcome at the hands of the
Danaäns, then they were stopped and halted beside their cars,
pale white from fear—terrified. And Zeus awoke on the peaks
5 of Ida beside Hera of the golden throne. He sprang up, stood,
and saw the Trojans and the Achaeans contending, and the Trojans
being routed—the Argives were driving them out from the rear,
and among them was Poseidon the king. Zeus saw Hector
lying on the plain, and around him sat his companions. Hector
10 was gasping for breath, distraught in mind, vomiting blood,
for it was not the weakest of the Achaeans who had struck him!

Seeing Hector, the father of men and gods felt pity,
and looking out from beneath his brows he said this
to Hera: "Well Hera—impossible to deal with!— your evil
15 trickery has put Hector out of the battle. And you have driven
the Trojans in rout. I think that again you should be the first
to profit from your troublesome scheming—to be whipped for it!
Or do you not remember when I hung you up on high,
fastening two anvils to your feet, and around your wrists
20 I threw an unbreakable golden bond? And you hung in the air
and clouds. Then throughout high Olympos the gods were plenty
angry, but they could not come near and set you free.
Whomever I caught, I laid my hands upon him and threw him
from the threshold until he fell to the earth, all strength gone!
25 Even so, endless pain did not release my heart for godlike
Herakles, whom you, in league with blasts of North Wind,
sent across the barren sea, devising evil as you carried him
to well-peopled Kos. I saved him then and brought him again
to horse-pasturing Argos, after he had suffered many pains.
30 Let me remind you of these things so you might give up your
deceptions and see whether your lovemaking and the couch
are really of any use to you. You tricked me into it, coming
forth from among the gods!"

So he spoke, and cow-eyed revered Hera
shivered. Addressing him, she spoke words that went like arrows:

"May Earth be my witness, and the broad Sky above, and the water   35
of Styx that flows, which is the greatest and most solemn oath
among the blessed gods—and by your own holy head I swear,
and by the couch of the two of us by which I would truly never
forswear myself: Not by my will does Poseidon, the earth-shaker,
work harm to the Trojans and Hector, nor give aid to the Achaeans.   40
It is his own heart that urges and drives Poseidon. He has taken
pity on the Achaeans, seeing them worn down beside the ships.
But I would counsel even him to walk in the path where you,
O lord of the dark cloud, do lead."

                    So she spoke, and the father
of men and gods smiled, and in answer he spoke words   45
that went like arrows: "Well then, O cow-eyed revered Hera,
if you wish to sit among the deathless ones with thoughts
like mine, then I think that Poseidon would quickly reorder
his mind to follow your heart and mine, even if he doesn't like it.

[Lines 50–205 are omitted. Poseidon is called away from the battle. Zeus sends Apollo to heal Hector.]

                    Then Zeus, who gathers the clouds,
spoke to Apollo:° "Go now, dear Phoibos, to Hector,
armed in bronze. Already the holder of the earth, the shaker
of the earth, has gone into the bright sea, evading our
dangerous anger. Else the other gods would have learned   210
of our quarrel, those who are beneath the earth in the company
of Kronos.° This was a much better outcome both for me and for him,
that, although angry, he has yielded to my hands. Otherwise
there would have been a clammy outcome! But take the tasseled
goatskin fetish in your hands, and shake it over the Achaean   215
fighters. Put them to flight! May glorious Hector be your care,
O you who strike from a long way off. For a spell,
excite his power so that the Achaeans flee to their ships
and to the HELLESPONT. From that point on I will contrive both word
and deed to see that the Achaeans have respite from the battle."   220

     So he spoke, and Apollo obeyed his father. He went down
from the mountains of Ida like a swift hawk, the speediest
of winged creatures, the killer of pigeons. He found
the son of wise Priam, the good Hector, sitting up—

---

207   *to Apollo:* Apollo is appropriate for this task because he is on the side of the Trojans and he is a healing god.

212   *in the company of Kronos:* The Titans.

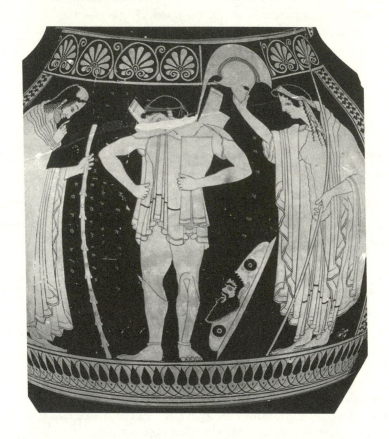

FIGURE 15.1   Hector arms for battle.   Priam stands to the left and Hekabê to the right. Hector has already donned his shin guards and now pulls a breastplate around his middle over a shirt. His mother, represented as a young woman, holds out his helmet with her right hand and with her left holds his spear. Hector's shield, decorated with the head of a satyr, leans against Hekabê's leg. The aged Priam, with balding head, supports himself with a knobby staff and instructs his son. The characters' names are inscribed. Attic red-figure water-jug, c. 510 BC.

he was no longer lying down, for he had recently begun   225
to recover his strength. He recognized his companions around him.
His gasping and sweating had stopped, for the will of Zeus,
who carries the goatskin fetish, had revived him. Standing
nearby, Apollo, who works from afar, spoke to him: "Hector,
son of Priam, why do you sit apart from the others   230
in a faint? Is something amiss?"

                Hector, whose helmet
flashes, his strength spent, said: "Which god are you,
most powerful one, who speaks to me face to face?
Do you not know that at the sterns of the Achaean ships,
as I wreaked havoc on his companions, that Ajax, good   235
at the war cry, hit me in the chest with a stone and put a stop
to my furious valor? Surely, I thought on this day that I had
died and gone to the house of Hades, that I had breathed
forth my life."

            Apollo the far-shooter, the king,
answered him: "Have courage! So mighty a helper has   240
the son of Kronos sent forth from Ida to stand by your side
and to aid you: I am Phoibos Apollo who carries a golden
sword—I who have saved you before, both you yourself
and the steep city. But come now, order your many charioteers
to drive their swift horses against the hollow ships. I will go   245
before and smooth the way clear for the horses, and I will turn
around the Achaean fighting men."

              So speaking, he breathed
great power into the shepherd of the people. Even as when
a horse confined to his stall, well fed at the grain crib,
breaks his bonds and runs galloping over the plain, exulting,   250
he who is accustomed to bathe in the fair-flowing river,
holding his head high, and around his shoulders his mane flows
and in his splendor he trusts his nimble knees to carry him
to the haunts and pastures of mares°—even so Hector moved
his feet and his knees, urging on his horses when he heard   255
the voice of the god. Or as when dogs and hunters pursue a horned
stag or wild goat, but he is saved by a sheer rock or a shadowy
thicket, for it was not fated that they catch him—and then at their

---

254 *of mares*: The same simile appears in Book 6 of Paris returning from Helen's boudoir to the plain to fight.
     There are about 180 similes in Homer; eight of them are repeats (seven in the *Iliad*). Similes often precede
     battle scenes, as does this one.

shouting a bearded lion shows himself the way and quickly
260 he turns back the hunters, although they are avid—even so,
the Danaäns for awhile followed on in a crowd, thrusting with their
swords and their two-edged spears. But when they saw Hector
going up and down the battalions of men, they took fright,
and the spirits of the men sank to their feet.

[Lines 265–632 are omitted. Under Hector's leadership the Trojans attack the ships.]

Now the Trojans were in the midst of the ships, but the ends
of the ships that were first drawn up confined them. The Argives rushed
635 at the Trojans, but gave way and of necessity pulled back from
the outermost ships. They made their stand in a crowd among the huts,
nor were they scattered throughout the camp. Shame held them—
and fear. They called to one another without cease.

Gerenian Nestor,
the guardian of the Achaeans, sought to rouse each man in the name
640 of his parents, beseeching them: "O my friends, be men and place
in your hearts shame before other men, and remember,
every one of you, your children, your wives, your possessions
and your parents, whether they are alive or dead. In their name
I earnestly beg you, even though they are not present here—
645 make your stand! Do not turn away in panic!"

So speaking,
he encouraged the strength and the heart of every man. Athena
pushed away from their eyes the bedeviling cloud of mist. A great light
appeared to them from both sides—from the side of their ships
and from that of the terrifying war. And they all saw Hector,
650 good at the war cry, and his companions, both they who stood
at the back and did not fight, and they who contended
beside the swift ships.

But it no longer pleased the heart
of great-hearted Ajax to stand where the other sons
of the Achaeans stood in the rear and did not fight.
655 And so he trod up and down the half-decks of the ships,°
taking long strides, and he wielded a great pike for sea-fighting
in his hands, a pike joined with glue and pegs, thirty-two

---

655 *of the ships:* Homeric ships had two half-decks, one at the prow and one at the stern; the steersman worked
from the stern's half-deck. The center was open with benches for the rowers and a large beam across the
center gave the hull strength and supported the mast, when it was raised.

feet in length.° As when a man, highly skilled in riding tricks,
harnesses together four horses selected from many,
and he races from the plain toward the great city along a public   660
highway as many men and women gaze at him,
as ever with sure step he leaps from one horse to another
and they fly along—even so Ajax ranged over the decks
of the swift ships, taking long strides, and his voice went up
to the sky. Shouting terribly, he commanded the Danaäns   665
to defend the ships and the huts.

                    Hector did not wait
among the crowd of the thickly mailed Trojans, but as a tawny
eagle leaps on a flock of winged birds feeding along a river's bank,
of geese or cranes or long-necked swans—even so Hector
went straight toward a dark-prowed ship, rushing right at it.   670
From behind Zeus pushed him on with his great hand,
and Hector roused his army along with him. Again the piercing
battle blazed beside the ships. You might think that unwearied
and fresh they went against one another in war, so furiously
did they fight. These were their thoughts as they fought: 675
the Achaeans believed that they would not escape from the peril,
but that they would perish, and the heart of every Trojan hoped
to set fire to the ships and to kill all the Achaean warriors.
These were their thoughts as they stood against one another.

    Hector then seized the stern of a sea-faring ship—   680
beautiful, fast on the salt sea, that had carried Protesilaos° to Troy,
but did not bear him back to the land of his fathers. Around his ship
the Achaeans and Trojans fought one another in the hand-to-hand.
No longer did they await the whizzing bow-shots of arrows
and javelins, but standing close to one another, all of one mind,   685
they fought with keen battle-axes and hatchets, great swords
and two-edged spears. Many beautiful swords fastened
with dark thongs at the hilt fell to the ground,
some from their hands, others from the shoulders of the men
as they fought there. The black earth ran with blood.   690

    Hector had seized the stern of a ship, and he did not let go
but held onto the carved stern-post° as he commanded the Trojans:

---

658   *in length*: Perhaps epic exaggeration, but the Macedonians in classical times used spears as long as twenty-
      two feet.

681   *Protesilaos*: The first man to die at Troy.

692   *stern-post*: Evidently a kind of curved horn fixed to the stern, to judge from pictures on pottery.

"Bring fire! Together in a mass raise the war cry! Now Zeus
has given us a day as repayment for all—let us take
695   the ships that came here against the will of the gods
and brought us so much pain through the cowardice of the elders
who held me back and restrained the people when I wanted
to fight at the sterns of the ships.° But if loud-thundering Zeus
baffled our wits then, now he himself urges us on and gives
700   the command."

            So he spoke, and they rushed still harder
at the Argives. Ajax could take it no longer. Oppressed
by missiles he backed off a little, thinking he would die there
on the seven-foot bench—he abandoned the half-deck of
the well-balanced ship.° There he took his stand, watching,
705   and he ever warded off the Trojans from the ships,
who carried fire. Shouting ever terribly, he commanded the Danaäns: "My friends,
Danaän warriors, followers of Ares—be men, be men
my friends! Remember your furious valor! Or do we think
that there are other helpers at our backs, or a stronger wall
710   that will ward off destruction from our men? There is no city nearby
fenced with walls by which we can defend ourselves—no,
we have no other people who will turn the tide of battle.
We are sitting in the plain of the thickly mailed Trojans, far
from our native land, with nothing as support save the sea.
715   Therefore the light of deliverance is in our hands,
not in wavering in the fight!"

            So Ajax spoke and kept driving
furiously with his sharp spear. He awaited the man who
would bring blazing fire to the hollow ships, doing the
pleasure of Hector's bidding. Ajax waited, hoping to pierce
720   Hector with his long spear. And he did kill twelve
Trojan warriors in the hand-to-hand before the ships.

---

698   *of the ships*: Hector's tendency to self-delusion is clear here: In fact the gods *did* will the Achaean expedition, because Paris had violated *xenia*, protected by Zeus, by taking Helen; and the Trojan elders did not
through cowardice prevent Hector and his men from fighting, but through fear of Achilles' prowess.

704   *well-balanced ship*: The "seven-foot bench" is the wide cross beam in the center of the ship that gave the ship
stability and supported the mast. Ajax seems to retreat from the half-deck at the stern to the central bench,
though the description is not clear.

BOOK 16. *The Glory of Patroklos*

A s they fought around the well-benched ships, Patroklos
came up to Achilles the shepherd of the people.° Tears
poured down his cheeks, like the dark water of a spring
that pours its black waters over a high cliff. When Achilles
saw him, godlike Achilles the fast runner felt pity   5
and he spoke words that flew like arrows: "Why do you weep,
Patroklos? You are like a little girl, a babe who runs
to her mother and begs to be picked up, clutching her gown,
holding the mother back from her work. Crying
she stares upward, begging to be lifted—you are like   10
that little girl, pouring forth your tender tears.
Do you have something to say to the Myrmidons, or to me
myself? Or have you heard some private news from Phthia?
Surely your father Menoitios, the son of Aktor,
is still alive, they say, and Peleus too, the son   15
of Aiakos, among the Myrmidons. Certainly
we would grieve to hear that either had died!
Or are you sad because of the Argives, who die beside
the hollow ships on account of their own arrogant act?
Say it, don't hide it, so that we both may know."   20

   You groaned deeply then, Patroklos the horseman,
and said: "O Achilles, son of Peleus, by far the best of
the Achaeans, do not be angry! For so great an anguish has
come to the Achaeans. Those who before were best in the
contendings, all of them now lie wounded among the ships,   25
pierced by missiles. The great Diomedes, son of Tydeus,
is wounded. Odysseus too, famed for his work with the
spear. And Eurypylos is shot with an arrow in the thigh.
The doctors, learned in drugs, are working to heal them.

---

2   *shepherd of the people*: In Book 11 Achilles sent Patroklos to ask about the wounded Machaon, but Patroklos'
    errand was interrupted when he met Nestor (he never gets to Machaon), who asks him to try to persuade
    Achilles to return to the fight, or at least to allow Patroklos to fight in Achilles' place. This will give the Achae-
    ans a break. Patroklos starts back to Achilles' hut, but stops on the way to help the wounded Eurypylos. He
    does not leave Eurypylos' hut until Book 15. Now at the opening of Book 16, he finally returns to Achilles.

30   "But you, Achilles, are impossible! I hope that no such
anger ever lays hold on me such as you nourish—a rashness
that only destroys! How shall anyone yet to be born
ever have benefit of you if you will not ward from the Argives
a terrible fate? You are pitiless. I don't think that Peleus
35   the horseman was your father, or Thetis your mother.
The gray sea bore you and the steep cliffs! For your mind
is unbending.

               "But if in your mind you are avoiding some
oracle, and your reverend mother has told you something she heard
from Zeus, at least quickly send *me* forth, and with me
40   the host of the Myrmidons, so that I might be a light
of salvation for the Danaäns. Let me wear your armor—
perhaps if I look like you, the Trojans will pull back from
the war and the sons of the Achaeans can catch their breath,
worn out as they are. For the breathing space in battle is brief.
45   Easily, I think, we who are fresh may drive back
toward the city men worn out by the battle cry, and so away
from the ships and the huts."

                         So he spoke in supplication.
The fool! For in truth he prayed for his own dark death
and fate.

          Deeply moved, Achilles the fast runner, said:
50   "Patroklos, who are like a god, what words you have spoken!
I take no heed of any oracle that I know of, nor has
my reverend mother said anything to me that she learned
from Zeus. But this terrible grief lies on my heart
and soul—when a man aims to steal from his equal
55   and take from him his prize, because he is greater in power.
This is a horrendous grief to me. I have suffered
pain in my heart! The girl that the sons of the Achaeans
chose for me as prize, whom I myself captured
when I sacked a well-walled city—the very girl
60   King Agamemnon, the son of Atreus, has taken from my
hands, as if I were some mere wanderer without rights!
     "All the same, we will let that pass—it is something
that happened. It was never my intention to nurse an unending
anger in my heart. I thought I would hold onto my anger
65   only until the war cry and battle should reach my own ships . . .

"But go ahead—you can dress in my glorious armor
and lead the war-loving Myrmidons to battle, if in truth the dark
cloud of the Trojans has powerfully shrouded the ships,
and only the shore of the sea supports the others,
and the Argives have a scant dab of land still left,   70
and the whole city of the Trojans has come without fear
against them—for the Trojans do not see the face of my helmet
glinting before them. Or they would soon fill the channels
with the bodies of the dead as they flee—if only Agamemnon
were well disposed toward me!   75

            "As it is, the Trojans have
surrounded the camp with battle. For the spear in the hands
of Diomedes, son of Tydeus, does not rage to ward off
destruction . . . Nor have I yet heard the voice of the son
of Atreus, as he bellows from his loathed maw. No,
it is the voice of man-killing Hector that breaks about me   80
as he urges on the Trojans, who with their din possess
the whole of the plain, overwhelming the Achaeans in battle.
    "But even so, Patroklos . . . go, fall upon them with power.
Ward off destruction from the ships, so that they do not burn
the ships with blazing fire and take away our homecoming.   85
Only listen! Let me place in your mind the sum of my counsel,
that you might win for me great honor and glory
among all the Danaäns, who then will return that most
beautiful woman along with wonderful gifts.°

    "Once you have driven the Trojans from the ships,   90
come back. If the loud-thundering husband of Hera grants
you success, do not desire to fight without me against
the war-loving Trojans. You will make my honor less.
And do not exult in war and the contendings in killing the Trojans.
Do not lead on to Ilion! I fear that one of the Olympians,   95
who never die, may enter the fight. For Apollo,
who works from afar, loves them very much. Come back,
then, once you have shown a light of salvation
among the ships. Let the others fight on the plain.

---

89 *wonderful gifts*: Critics have complained that in Book 9 the Achaeans made this very offer to Achilles. But
    although Achilles then rejected Agamemnon's attempt to buy him off, he remains angry and anxious to
    receive restitution.

FIGURE 16.1 Achilles binding Patroklos' wounds.   The younger beardless Achilles wraps a bandage around the arm of his older bearded friend. Achilles is in full armor, but without shin guards. Patroklos, who looks away in pain and squats on a shield decorated with a tripod (?), carries a quiver and bow on his back. He wears a felt cap. An arrow lies parallel to his calf. There is no such scene in the *Iliad*, but the painting was inspired by the intimacy of the two men and modeled on the scene where Patroklos binds the wounds of Eurypylos. Red-figure drinking cup (kylix), from Vulci, Italy, c. 500 BC, by Sosias.

"How I wish that father Zeus and Athena and Apollo   100
would allow not *one* of the Trojans to escape, of all
there are, and not one man of the Argives either,
but that just the two of us might escape death, that alone
we might loose the sacred veil of the city!" So
the two spoke to one another in this fashion.   105

But Ajax no longer held his ground, overcome
by missiles. The mind of Zeus and the mighty Trojans wore him
down with their constant firing. His shining helmet
rang incessantly around his temples as it was struck,
hit constantly on the handsome cheek pieces. His left shoulder   110
grew weary from holding the gleaming shield, but still
the Trojans could not drive it back upon him with their steady
fusillade. Ever tormented by heavy breathing, sweat poured
everywhere from his limbs in abundance, nor could Ajax
get a chance to catch his breath. Everywhere evil   115
piled on evil.

Tell me now, Muses who live
on Olympos, how fire first fell on the ships of the Achaeans!

Hector closed in on Ajax and with his great sword
struck his spear of ash just behind the socket.
He cut it clean away so that Ajax, son of Telamon,   120
now wielded a useless shaft. The spear's bronze point
spun away and clanged on the ground. Ajax saw
in his daring heart the doing of gods and he shivered,
seeing how Zeus, who thunders on high, had brought
to nothing Ajax' counsels of war, and how   125
he willed a Trojan victory.

Ajax withdrew
from the hail of arrows as the Trojans cast consuming
fire into the ship. Quickly an unquenchable flame
engulfed it. Thus fire took hold of the ship's stern,
but Achilles, striking both his thighs, addressed Patroklos: 130
"Rise up now Patroklos, master of horses. I see the rush
of consuming fire in the fleet. May they not take the ships
and prevent our escape! Quick, put on my armor. I will
assemble our companions."

So he spoke. Patroklos put on
the gleaming bronze. First he bound the beautiful shin guards   135

to his calves, fitted with silver fasteners. Second,
he placed around his chest the breastplate of the swift-footed
grandson of Aiakos,° handsomely made, decorated with stars.
Around his shoulders he slung the sword of bronze with silver
140 studs, then he took up the large and powerful shield,
and on his mighty head he set the helmet, well made,
with a crest of horsehair. Its plume nodded terribly
from on high. He took two strong spears that perfectly
fitted his grasp. But he did not take the spear of the grandson
145 of Aiakos—heavy, great, powerful! No other of the Achaeans
could wield this spear. Achilles, son of Peleus, alone
could wield it. Cheiron from the peak of Pelion had given
it to his father to be used for the killing of heroes.

    Achilles ordered Automedon,° the breaker of ranks,
150 quickly to yoke the horses. Patroklos honored him
most after Achilles, trusting him to await his call
in the midst of battle. Automedon led the swift horses
Xanthos and Balios, who ran like the breath of the wind,
beneath the yoke. The Harpy Podargê had born them
155 to Zephyr, West Wind, as she grazed in the meadow beside
the stream of Ocean.° In the traces he placed the fine horse
Pedasos, whom Achilles had captured when he sacked the city
of Eëtion, a mortal stallion following deathless horses.°

    But Achilles went through the huts and urged all
160 the Myrmidons to arm. And they ran out like flesh-eating wolves
in whose hearts is an unspeakable rage—wolves who have killed
a horned stag in the mountains and who dine upon him,
and their cheeks are red with blood, and in a pack they course
to the black waters of a dark spring. With their thin tongues

---

138 *grandson of Aiakos*: Achilles.

149 *Automedon*: First mentioned in Book 9, he is third in command among the Myrmidons. He serves as Patroklos' driver, as Patroklos was Achilles' driver.

156 . . . *of Ocean*: Xanthos is "red" and Balios is "patches." Podargê is either "white-foot" or "swift-foot." The
Harpies, "snatchers," were personified storm winds, perhaps originally spirits of Death, but here Podargê
takes on the form of a horse. It was widely believed in antiquity that the wind could impregnate mares in
sexual heat. With both parents being winds, Achilles' horses were the fastest at Troy.

158 *deathless horses*: Trace horses are rare in Homer, where most chariots are pulled by two horses yoked together. Trace horses seem to be attached to a hook on the yoke by means of a strap, but their function is
unclear. Only trace horses are ever killed in the fighting. Pedasos was taken in the same raid on which
Achilles captured Chryseïs.

they lap the surface of the water, all the while vomiting   165
blood and gore, and their hearts in their breasts are unflinching,
and their bellies are gorged—even so did the leaders
and rulers of the Myrmidons swarm forth around Patroklos,
the companion of the grandson of Aiakos the fast runner.
And among them stood warlike Achilles, urging on the horses   170
and the men in their armor.

             Fifty fast ships did Achilles,
beloved of Zeus, lead to Troy, and in each fifty
men rowed, his companions. He appointed five men
whom he trusted as leaders, to give commands, but he
himself ruled all, great in his power. Menesthios°   175
of the flashing corselet led one band, son of the
heaven-fed river Spercheios. The daughter of Peleus,
lovely Polydora,° bore him to untiring Spercheios, bedding
down with the god, but in name Menesthios was the son
of Boros, the son of Perieres, who wedded Polydora in a public   180
rite after Boros gave wedding gifts beyond counting.

   Warlike Eudoros led the second band. His mother
was unmarried, Polymelê the daughter of Phylas fair
in the dance. Powerful Argeïphontes° fell in love
with her when he saw her among the singers on the dance floor   185
of Artemis of the golden arrows and the echoing chase.
Hermes the Deliverer promptly went to her upper chamber
and slept with her in secret, and she gave him the noble son
Eudoros, superior in running and war. When the goddess
of childbirth Eileithyia had brought him forth into the light   190
and he saw the rays of the sun, Echekles, strong
and powerful, the son of Aktor, led Polymelê to his house,
after giving countless wedding gifts. The old man Phylas
raised Eudoros, nursing him and cherishing him as if
he were his own son.°   195

---

175 *Menesthios*: In the following catalog of Myrmidon leaders, the names seem to be made up—they do not
     reappear in the narrative—except for old man Phoinix, Achilles' tutor.

178 *Polydora*: Hence Achilles' half-sister (by another woman, not Thetis).

184 *Argeïphontes*: "Killer of the monster Argos," an epithet of Hermes.

195 *his own son*: Because Polymelê abandoned Eudoros when she married Echekles. His maternal grandfather,
     Phylas, then raised him.

Peisander led the third band,
the warlike son of Maimalos. He stood out among
all the Myrmidons for his spear-fighting, second only
to Patroklos, the companion of the son of Peleus, in his fighting
skills. Phoinix, the old horseman, led the fourth band,
200 and the fifth was commanded by Alkimedon, son of Laërkes.

When Achilles had organized them all in companies with
their leaders, he lay upon them a powerful command: "Myrmidons,
do not forget the threats that you made against the Trojans
as you waited beside the fast ships, all during the time of my anger.
205 And then you criticized me, saying, 'Cruel son of Peleus,
surely your mother suckled you on bile, pitiless one,
who hold your unwilling companions back beside the ships.
Let us sail home in our seafaring ships, because an evil anger
has fallen on his heart.' Often you would gather together
210 and make such criticism. But now the great work of war,
which before you so desired, is set before you. So let every
man go to the fight against the Trojans with a brave heart."

So speaking he roused up the strength and the spirit
in each man. They closed up their ranks when they heard
215 their king. As when a man builds a wall of close-set stones
for a high-roofed house that will resist the blasts of the winds,
even so they set side by side their helmets and their bossed
shields. Shield leaned against shield, helmet against helmet,
man against man. The horse-hair crests attached to the bright
220 shield-plates touched each other as the men nodded their heads,
so close to one another did they stand. In front of all, two men
put on their armor, Patroklos and Automedon, being
of a single mind—to fight in the forefront of the Myrmidons.

But Achilles went off to his hut, and he opened the lid
225 of a chest—beautiful, ornate—that silver-footed Thetis
had placed in his ship to carry with him, after filling it with shirts
and cloaks that keep away the wind, and woolen rugs.
He kept a well-made cup there, nor did any other man
drink from it the flaming wine, nor did he pour from it
230 an offering to any other god than father Zeus.
Achilles took it from the chest. He first purified it
with sulfur, then he washed it in beautiful streams of water.
Then he washed his hands and poured out the flaming wine.

Standing in the middle of the court, he prayed to Zeus.°
He poured out wine, looking to the sky and Zeus   235
who delights in the thunder was aware of him: "Zeus
the king, lord of Dodona, Pelasgian, you who live
far away, ruler of wintery Dodona—around you
live the Selloi, your diviners, who sleep on the ground
with unwashed feet.° Surely in earlier times   240
you heard my word when I prayed, and you honored me:
You punished the army of the Achaeans. So fulfill for me
now my desire. I myself remain now amidst the gathering
of the ships, but I send forth my companion with my many
Myrmidons to fight. O Zeus who thunders from afar,   245
grant him glory! Make brave his heart in his breast, so that
even Hector will know whether my companion knows
how to fight alone, or whether his hands rage invincibly
only when I have entered the toil of Ares.

        "But when he has driven
the battle and war cry away from the ships, may he   250
return unscathed then to the swift ships, with all his armor
and his companions who fight in close."

        So he spoke in prayer,
and Zeus the counselor heard him. The father gave him one half
his wish, but the other he refused. He granted that Patroklos
push back the war and the battle from the ships, but he denied   255
that he return safe from the battle.

        Once he had poured out a
drink-offering and prayed to Zeus the father, Achilles

---

234   ...*to Zeus*: Achilles' hut is imagined to have an open courtyard with an altar to Zeus Herkeios, "Zeus of the
     Courtyard," the guardian of the home to whom the hero prays. Such altars were typical of Greek houses
     throughout antiquity.

240 *unwashed feet*: Achilles prays to the Zeus of DODONA, far west from PHTHIA across the PINDOS range in
     a remote mountainous part of EPIRUS, where there was an ancient shrine to Zeus. Dodona is twelve miles
     southwest of the modern city of Yaninna. Homer derives Peleus' family from here. The Pelasgians were a
     prehistoric tribe who did not speak Greek, attesting to the shrine's antiquity. The unwashed feet of the Selloi
     and their practice of sleeping on the ground are probably ritual taboos. At first Zeus was thought to indwell
     the sacred oak itself, which had the power of speech, then the Selloi were the interpreters of the sounds made
     by the wind in the tree. In classical time the Selloi were replaced by women. Some read "Helloi" instead of
     "Selloi," and Aristotle said that the *Hellenes* originated from here before migrating to Hellas near Phthia.
     Dodona was also the home of the tribe of the Graikoi, from whom the Romans, just across the Adriatic Sea,
     took the name "Greeks" to refer to the inhabitants of the southern Balkan peninsula—the name we use today.

went back into his hut, and he put the cup back into the chest.
He came forth and stood outside his hut. For he desired
260 in his heart to behold the dread contendings of Trojan
and Achaean.

They who were arrayed with great-hearted
Patroklos rushed out in high spirits against the Trojans. At once
they poured forth like wasps on the roadside that boys habitually
torment, always teasing them in their houses on the road, the foolish
265 young children, and they make a common evil for many.
And if some wayfaring man stirs up the wasps by accident,
they all fly out in the bravery of their hearts to defend
their children—with a heart and spirit like this the Myrmidons
poured from the ships, and an unquenchable cry arose.

270 Patroklos gave a loud shout, calling out to his companions:
"Myrmidons, companions of Achilles, the son of Peleus!
Be men, my friends! Remember your furious valor that
we might show honor to the son of Peleus, who is by far
the best of the Argives—himself and his followers who fight
275 in close—so that the son of Atreus, wide-ruling Agamemnon,
may know his blindness, who showed no honor to the best
of the Achaeans!"

So speaking, he roused up the strength
and the spirit of each man, and they fell upon the Trojans in a mass.
Around them the ships rang terribly from the shouting
280 of the Achaeans. When the Trojans saw the powerful son
of Menoitios, himself and his aide° shining in their armor,
the heart in every man was stirred, and the battalions were shaken,
thinking that among the ships the swift-footed son of Peleus
had cast aside his anger and chosen teamwork.
285 Each Trojan looked to where he might flee total destruction.

Patroklos threw his shining spear straight into the midst
of them, where men thronged the closest, beside the stern
of the ship of great-hearted Protesilaos. He hit Pyraichmes,
who led the chariot-fighting Paeonians from Amydon,
290 from the wide-flowing AXIOS RIVER.° He hit him in the
right shoulder. Pyraichmes fell on his back in the dust, groaning,

---

281 *his aide*: Automedon.

290 *Axios river*: Pyraichmes means "fire-spear," appropriate to the action. The location of Amydon on the
AXIOS river in northern Macedonia (Map I) is unknown.

and his companion Paeonians were driven in rout. Patroklos
drove them all in rout when he killed their leader,
who was the best in the fight. He drove them from the ships.
He extinguished the blazing fire. The ship was left   295
there half-burned as the Trojans fled with a wondrous roar
as the Danaäns poured forth from the hollow ships. An
unquenchable cry ensued. Just as when Zeus who gathers
the lightning moves a thick cloud from the highest peak
of a great mountain, and all the mountain toplands and the high   300
headlands and the valleys are revealed as the infinite air breaks
out from heaven, so the Danaäns drove back the destructive fire
from the ships and gained a brief breathing space. But there was
no end to the war.° For the Trojans did not yet run headlong
from the black ships before the war-loving Achaeans—they still   305
held their ground and backed off from the ships only when
hard pressed.

       Then among the captains man killed man
as the fighting was scattered. First Patroklos, the powerful
son of Menoitios, hit the thigh of Areïlykos with his sharp
spear just as Areïlykos turned around, and he drove the bronze   310
straight through. The spear broke the bone, and Areïlykos fell
on his face on the earth.

               Then the martial Menelaos stabbed Thoas
where his chest was exposed by his shield. He loosed his limbs.
Meges, the son of Phyleus, watched the Trojan Amphiklos
as he rushed at him, but Meges was quicker and hit him on top   315
of his leg, where a man's muscle is thickest. The tendons were
cut by the point of the spear and darkness fell over his eyes.

    Then of the sons of Nestor, one, Antilochos,
stabbed Atymnios with his sharp spear and he drove
the bronze spear through his side. Atymnios fell forward.   320
But Maris, his brother, standing nearby, rushed on Antilochos
with his spear, enraged because of his brother, and he took a stand
in front of the dead body. But godlike Thrasymedes, another
son of Nestor, as too quick for him, and before
his enemy could thrust he stabbed at Maris. He did not miss   325
but hit him in the shoulder. The point of the spear sliced off
the base of the arm from its muscles and completely broke

---

304   ... to the war: As the sudden light breaks through the clouds during a storm, so did the Achaeans suddenly
     gain the advantage over the Trojans, but the storm is not yet over.

the bone. Maris fell to the ground with a thud and darkness
closed over his eyes. Thus the two brothers, conquered
330 by two brothers, went to Erebos, the noble companions
of Sarpedon—the spearman sons of Amisodaros, the man
who raised up the raging Chimaira, an evil to men.°

Ajax the son of Oïleus leaped on Kleoboulos and took him
alive as he tripped in the melée. But he loosed
335 his strength by hitting him in the neck with his hilted sword.
The whole sword was warmed by his blood, and the
powerful fate of dark death covered Kleoboulos' eyes.

Boeotian Peneleös and the Trojan Lykon ran right up
on one another, for with their spears they had missed—
340 the two men cast their spears in vain! So then they ran against
one another with their swords. Lykon smashed down on the plate
of Peneleös' helmet with its plume of horsehair, but the sword
was shattered at the hilt. Peneleös slashed Lykon on the neck,
beneath the ear, and the whole blade went in so that only
345 skin held his head on. It hung to one side as Lykon's
limbs were loosened.

Then the Cretan captain Meriones
overtook Akamas with swift strides and hit him in the right
shoulder as he was mounting his car. Akamas fell from the car,
and a mist came over his eyes. Meriones' companion
350 Idomeneus stabbed Erymas in the mouth with his pitiless
bronze.° The bronze spear went straight through
and came out beneath his brain, splitting the white bones.
Erymas' teeth came flying out and both his eyes
filled with blood. He gaped, spewing blood through his mouth
355 and nostrils, and the black cloud of death came down over him.

And so each of these men, leaders of the Danaäns,
killed his man. As ravening wolves assail sheep or kids,

---

332 *... to men*: A Greek also has the name Areïlykos in Book 14. Thoas is a common name, also borne by a
Greek in Books 13 and 17. This is the only time that two brothers, the sons of Nestor—Antilochos and
Thrasymedes—kill two other brothers, the sons of Amisodaros, Amphiklos and Atymnios. Erebos, "dark-
ness," is the daughter of Night, and refers to the subterranean gloom where the dead dwell. Nothing else is
known about Amisodaros' rearing of the Chimaira, the three-bodied fire-breathing monster that lived in
Lycia, killed by Bellerophon (Figure 6.1).

351 *... pitiless bronze*: Kleoboulos is otherwise unknown. Earlier in the fighting, Peneleos, from Boeotia, had
missed Akamas, the son of Antenor, but beheaded another Trojan. Here the Cretan archer Meriones kills
Akamas, and Peneleos beheads the unknown Lykon. Another Erymas dies later in this book!

selecting them from a flock who are scattered over a mountain
through the carelessness of a shepherd, and seeing the flock
the wolves quickly snatch them up, for the flock knows no valor—   360
even so the Danaäns assailed the Trojans, who thought only
of shrieking flight, forgetful of their zealous valor.

      And Big Ajax wished to throw his spear at Hector,
clothed in bronze, but Hector, through his knowledge of war,
hid his broad shoulders beneath his shield of bull's hide,   365
watching the whizzing of arrows and hearing the thud of spears.
Truly, he knew that the tide of victory was turning,
but he nonetheless held his ground and sought to save
his trusting comrades. As when from Olympos a cloud
comes into the heavens after clear weather when Zeus   370
spreads out a squall, even so did the cry of the rout
come from the ships,° nor did Trojans cross the ditch
again in good order. Hector's swift horses bore him away
in full armor, but he left his Trojan troops behind,
for the ditch held them back against their will.° In the trench   375
they had dug, many swift horses who drew chariots
broke the poles behind their yokes and abandoned the cars
of their riders.

            Patroklos followed close in, calling
violently to the Danaäns, urging on evil to the Trojans
who filled all the ways with cries of rout, for their ranks   380
were broken. On high a storm of dust spread up to beneath
the clouds, and the single-hoofed horses strained to go back
to the city, away from the ships and the tents. Patroklos,
wherever he saw the Trojans most huddled together
in rout, there he went, screaming. And the men kept falling   385
from their cars—headlong beneath the axles, and their chariots
fell over, rattling. Straight over the ditch leaped his swift horses,
immortal, that the gods had given to Peleus as a glorious gift—
flying ever onwards, his heart urged him to go up against Hector.
He wanted to strike him down, but Hector's swift horses   390
carried him safely away.

            As when a storm weighs down
the whole black earth on the harvest day, when Zeus

---

372 *from the ships*: The cloud starts on Zeus's mountain top, then moves off it as Zeus builds the storm, just as
     the Trojans are moved off from the ships.

375 *their will*: Evidently Hector escapes, while the other Trojans are caught in the ditch.

pours down the rattling rain because he rages against men
who by violence give false judgments in the assembly,
395 driving out justice without regard for the vengeance
of the gods, and all the rivers rise in flood, and the torrents
gouge ravines into many hillsides, and down to the dark sea
the rivers rush with a mighty roar headlong from the mountains
and they ruin the fields of men—even so mighty
400 was the crash of the Trojan mares as they raced away.

When Patroklos had cut off the foremost battalions, he hemmed them in
by turning back toward the ships. Nor would he allow them to enter
the city, though they desired to, but in the space between the
ships and the river and high wall of the city he rushed
405 upon them, killing as he went, taking revenge for many.

First of all he struck Pronoös with his bright spear
on his chest where the flesh was exposed, next to his shield,
and he loosed his limbs. Pronoös fell with a thud. Next
he rushed on Thestor, son of Enops, as he cowered
410 in his highly polished car, his wits distraught with terror,
and the reins had slipped from his hands. Patroklos came up
close and hit him with his spear in the right jaw. The spear
went through the teeth and with the spear Patroklos
dragged Thestor over the chariot rail, as when a man
415 sitting on a projecting cliff hauls in a sacred fish°
out of the sea to the land with a line and a gleaming
bronze hook—even so he dragged him, gaping,
with his shining spear. He released him face down.
Thestor's breath-soul left him as he fell.

420 Then Patroklos hit Erylaos with a rock as Erylaos
rushed on him. He hit him full on the head.°
The head split in two inside the heavy helmet. Erylaos fell prone
on the earth, and death that dissolves the breath-soul was poured
all around him. Then one after another he brought down
425 to the nourishing earth Erymas and Amphoteros and Epaltes
and Tlepolemos, son of Damastor, and Echios and Pyris
and Ipheus and Euippos and Polymelos, son of Argeas.°

---

415 *sacred fish*: No one has ever explained what Homer means by "sacred fish."

421 *on the head*: Patroklos must now be on the ground to pick up a rock: Homer takes it for granted that his
audience understands how Patroklos mounts and dismounts his chariot as the need arises.

427 *... Argeas*: All these victims' names are Greek. Most are unknown. Erymas is reused from earlier in the
book, and Echios, "snake," from Book 15. Epaltes means "owl."

When Sarpedon saw his companions, who wore their
shirts unbelted, fallen at the hands of Patroklos, the son
of Menoitios, he called aloud, scolding the godlike Lycians: 430
"Shame, O Lycians! Where are you running to?
Now sharpen up! I will myself take on this man so that I
might know who is wielding this power here and doing
so many evils to the Trojans.° For he has loosed the knees
of many fine men."   435

　　　　　　He spoke and leaped from his chariot
in full armor. Patroklos from the other side saw him jump
from the car, and just as vultures with bent claws and curved
beaks fight on the top of a high peak, scolding terribly,
even so did they rush on one another, shrieking. The son
of wily Kronos took pity when he saw them, and he spoke   440
to Hera, his sister and wife: "Woe, woe, that Sarpedon,
the dearest of men to me, is fated to die at the hands
of Patroklos, son of Menoitios!° My heart is divided
in two ways as I consider whether to snatch him alive
myself from the tearful battle and place him in the rich   445
land of Lycia, or whether I should kill him
at the hands of the son of Menoitios."

　　　　　　　　　Then the cow-eyed
revered Hera answered: "Most dread son of Kronos,
what words you have spoken! You want to relieve from
painful death a mortal man long ago doomed by fate? Do it!   450
But all the other gods will disapprove. And I will tell you
something else, and you best give it careful consideration:
If you send forth Sarpedon still alive to his own home,
consider then whether another of the gods will wish
also to send his own dear son out of the ferocious   455
contendings. For there are many offspring of the deathless
ones fighting around the great city of Priam,° and you
will instill a dread anger among them. But if he
is so dear to you, and your heart grieves for him—
well, let him be killed at the hands of Patroklos, son of   460

434　*to the Trojans*: Sarpedon knows only that the man is not Achilles, not that this is Patroklos: Homer makes surpris-
　　　ingly little use of the dramatic device of Patroklos being mistaken for Achilles because he wears Achilles' armor.

443　*son of Menoitios*: The Lycian leader Sarpedon is second only to Hector in prowess. Fate is stronger even
　　　than Zeus, whose power is thus limited.

457　*city of Priam*: In fact not so many sons of the gods fight at Troy: Sarpedon and Aeneas on the Trojan side;
　　　and Achilles, Menesthios, Eudoros, Askalaphos, Ialmenos, Podaleirios, and Machaon on the Achaean side.

Menoitios. But when his breath-soul and life have left him,
then send Death and sweet Sleep to carry him off until
they come to the land of broad Lycia, where his brothers
and relatives will bury him in a tomb and set up a marker.
465　For that is the reward of mortals."

　　　　　　　　　　　　　　So she spoke, and the father
of men and gods did not disobey. He poured out a bloody
rain to the earth in honor of his dear son, whom Patroklos
was about to kill in deep-soiled Troy, far from the land
of his fathers.

　　　　　When the two men had come close
470　to one another, Patroklos cast at famous Thrasydemos,
the gallant aide to Prince Sarpedon. He hit him
in his lower belly and loosed his limbs. Then Sarpedon,
throwing at him next, missed Patroklos with
his bright spear, but he killed the trace-horse Pedasos,
475　hitting the horse with his spear in the right shoulder.
Pedasos whinnied aloud and breathed out his life
as he fell down in the dust and his spirit flew from him.
The other two horses reared in opposite directions. The yoke
creaked and the reins were tangled as the trace horse
480　died in the dust. But for this Automedon, famed for his spear,
found a solution. Drawing his stout sword from beside
his thigh, he leaped down and cut away the trace horse,
and that work was not in vain. The other two horses straightened
and strained at the reins.

　　　　　　　　　Then the two fighters again
485　came together in strife that consumes the soul. Sarpedon
missed his shot with his bright spear. The point
of the spear went over Patroklos' left shoulder and did not
hit him, and Patroklos then rushed on with the bronze.
His missile did not leave his hand in vain. He got Sarpedon
490　there where the lungs shut-in around the throbbing heart.
Sarpedon fell, as when some oak falls or a poplar
or a tall pine that carpenters cut in the mountains with
their sharpened axes to be a beam for a ship—even so
before his horses and his car he lay stretched out, groaning
495　and grasping at the bloody dust.

　　　　　　　　　Just as a lion goes
into a herd and kills a tawny great-hearted bull

among the cows that shamble as they walk, and the bull
perishes moaning in the jaws of the lion, even so the leader
of the shield-bearing Lycians raged as he lay dying at the hands
of Patroklos, and he called out to his dear companion: 500
"Dear Glaukos, a warrior among men, now you must be
the spearman and the bold fighter! Now let evil war be your desire,
and you must be swift! First go up and down the ranks
and urge the leaders of the Lycians to fight for Sarpedon,
then yourself fight for me with the bronze. If the Achaeans   505
take my armor now that I have fallen in the gathering
of the ships, I will on every day in time to come be a shame
and a reproach to you. Hold your ground with power
and urge on all the people."

     So speaking, the end that is death
covered his eyes and nostrils. Patroklos set his foot   510
on Sarpedon's chest and drew the spear out of the flesh.
Sarpedon's lungs came with it. At one moment he drew out
the point of the spear and with it the breath-soul.
The Myrmidons held Sarpedon's snorting horses who longed
to flee, no longer connected to the chariot of their master.°   515

[Lines 516–645 are omitted. Trojans and Greeks battle over the corpse of Sarpedon.]

 No longer could even a clever man have seen good Sarpedon,
because he was wrapped in missiles and blood and dust
from his head all the way to the bottom of his feet. They crowded
around the corpse as when flies swarm in a farmstead
around the full milk pails in the season of spring, when   650
milk drenches the vessels—even so they crowded
around Sarpedon's corpse. Nor did Zeus ever turn his shining
eyes away from the savage contendings, but he gazed steadily
at the men and pondered much in his heart about the killing
of Patroklos. He wondered whether there in the savage fight   655
over godlike Sarpedon glorious Hector should kill Patroklos
with the bronze and strip away the armor from his shoulders,
or whether he should increase the labor of war for still more men.
As he thus pondered, this seemed to him to be the better course—
that the valiant aide to Achilles, the son of Peleus, should   660
again drive the Trojans and the heavily armed Hector
toward the city, and take the lives of many.

---

515 *their master*: In fact the horses are still attached to the chariot—a slip.

FIGURE 16.2   Sleep and Death carry away Sarpedon in the presence of Hermes and two unknown warriors, Leodamas and Hippolytos, who look on from either side.   The names are inscribed. Sleep, to the left, and Death, to the right, are winged, but otherwise fully armed mature warriors. The naked Sarpedon, stripped of his armor, is pierced by three wounds, one to his throat, one to his belly, and one on his thigh. The messenger-god Hermes, in charge of all transportation, wears a traveler's cap with broad brim and carries his wand, the caduceus. His feet are winged. One of the most celebrated of ancient paintings, the Euphronios wine-mixing bowl was a possession of the Metropolitan Museum in New York City between 1972 and 2008, when it was repatriated to Italy. It is now in the Villa Giulia in Rome. Athenian red-figure wine-mixing bowl, c. 515 BC, found in Cerveteri, Italy, signed by Euxitheos (potter) and Euphronios (painter).

In Hector first
of all he implanted the coward's spirit: Mounting his chariot,
Hector turned in flight, and he called to the other Trojans
to flee. For he recognized a turning of the sacred scales   665
of Zeus. The brave Lycians did not wait then but they
fled, all of them, when they saw their leader pierced
in the heart, lying in the assembly of the dead with many
fallen on top of him, for the son of Kronos strained taut
the cords of war.   670

From the shoulders of Sarpedon they stripped
the armor—bronze, shining!—and they carried it to the hollow
ships. The brave son of Menoitios gave it to his companions
to carry. And then Zeus who gathers the clouds spoke to Apollo:
"Come now, dear Phoibos, cleanse Sarpedon of the dark blood
when you have removed him from the shower of arrows, and carry   675
him far away and bathe him in the streams of the river. Anoint him
with ambrosia, and put around him immortal clothing. Send him
to be borne by swift conveyers, the twins Sleep and Death,
who will quickly place him in the rich land of broad Lycia,
where his brothers and relatives will bury him in a tomb and set up a   680
grave stone. For that is the reward for mortals."

So he spoke,
and Apollo obeyed his father. He went down from the mountains
of Ida to the dread din of battle, and immediately he raised up
Sarpedon from the storm of arrows. He carried him far away
and washed him in the streams of the river. He anointed him with   685
ambrosia and put around him immortal clothing. Then he sent him
to be borne by swift conveyers, the twins Sleep and Death,
who quickly set him down in the rich land of broad Lycia.

But Patroklos with a call to his horses and to Automedon
went after the Trojans and the Lycians—but he was blind, blind,   690
the fool! If he had obeyed the word of the son of Peleus,
he would have avoided the dire fate of black death. But the intent
of Zeus is always stronger than that of men. He drives even
brave men to rout and easily takes away victory when he
himself rouses men to fight. And it was Zeus who then put   695
spirit into the breast of Patroklos!

[Lines 697–731 are omitted Patroklos continues his rampage, but now Hector rallies and
prepares to take him on.]

Hector let the other Danaäns go
and did not try to kill them, but he drove his strong-hooved
horses against Patroklos, who from his side leaped
735 to the ground from his car, holding his spear in his left hand.
With his other hand he picked up a rock, shining, jagged—
his hand covered it completely. He planted his feet firmly
and threw it. Patroklos did not back off from his enemy, nor did he hurl
in vain, but he hit Hector's charioteer Kebriones, bastard son
740 of the famous Priam, right on the forehead with the sharp stone
as Kebriones held the reins of the horses. The stone smashed
both his brows together, and the bone did not withstand the blow.
His eyes fell to the ground in the dust right there before his feet.
Like a diver he sailed from the well-made car, and his breath-soul
745 left his bones.

Mocking him, O horseman Patroklos,
you said: "Ha, hey, here is a nimble man! How lightly he dives!
If he should ride on the fishy sea, he would satisfy many by
diving for oysters, leaping from the ship even in a storm—
considering how he now dives onto the plain from his car!
750 Well now, there are plenty of divers among the Trojans."

So speaking, he made for the warrior Kebriones, swooping
on him like a lion that in laying waste a farmstead has taken
a blow on its chest, and his own bravery brings him to ruin—
even so, O Patroklos, did you leap eagerly on Kebriones.

755 And against him Hector leaped to the ground from his car.
The two of them grappled like lions who fight on the peaks
of a mountain over a dead deer, both hungry, both with high heart—
even so the two masters of the war-cry fought over Kebriones.
Patroklos, the son of Menoitios, and glorious Hector
760 tried to slash each other's flesh with the pitiless bronze.
Hector took hold of the head of the corpse and would not let go.
Patroklos pulled at the foot, and other Trojans and Danaäns
joined the dread contending.

As East Wind and South Wind
strive with one another to shake a deep wood in the valley
765 of a mountain—a wood of oak and ash and smooth-barked
dogwood that dash their long branches against one another
with a wondrous sound amid a crashing of broken branches—
even so the Trojans and Achaeans leaped upon one another
and cut each other to pieces. Nor did either side think of ruinous

flight. Many sharp spears were fixed around Kebriones   770
and arrows flew from many bowstrings, and many large stones
smashed against the shields of the men as they fought around Kebriones,
where he lay great in his greatness, in the whirl of the dust, forgetful
of his horsemanship.

       Now for so long as Helios straddled mid-heaven,
for so long missiles hit men on both sides, and the people fell.   775
But when Helios turned to the time for the unyoking of oxen,
then the Achaeans were stronger than what was fated to be.°
Out from the range of arrows they carried the warrior Kebriones,
out of the battle-din of the Trojans, and they stripped the armor
from his shoulders. And then Patroklos, intending evil, fell on   780
the Trojans. Three times he rushed on them, the equal to swift Ares,
screaming terribly, and three times he killed nine men. But when
for the fourth time he charged, like a god, then, O Patroklos,
came the end of your life. For Phoibos met you in the dread
conflict, an awesome power.   785

       Patroklos did not see Phoibos
as he came through the melée: Hidden in a thick cloud Apollo
met him. Apollo stood behind him and struck him in the back
between his broad shoulders with the flat of his hand, and his eyes
went spinning. Phoibos Apollo then knocked the helmet
from Patroklos' head, and it rolled ringing beneath the feet   790
of the horses—the helmet with its fitted crest and plumes,
all befouled with blood and dust! It was not allowed before
that this helmet with horse-hair plume be befouled with dust,
for it protected the head of a godlike man and his handsome
forehead—Achilles! But then Zeus gave it to Hector   795
to wear on his head. And now destruction was coming on Hector.

And the long-shadowed spear that Patroklos held in his hands
was wholly broken—heavy, large, strong, with a bronze tip.
And from his shoulders the tasseled shield with its shield-strap fell
to the ground. And Apollo, the son of Zeus, the king, loosed   800
the breastplate.

       Now blindness seized Patroklos' mind,
his shining limbs were loosed beneath him, and he stood
in a daze. Then Euphorbos, the son of Panthoös, a Dardanian,

---

777 *fated to be*: This is the only time in Homer that something happens "beyond what is fated," emphasizing the
    extraordinary nature of Patroklos' achievements.

cast at him with his sharp spear from close range and hit him
805 in the middle of the back between the shoulders—Euphorbos
who surpassed all his agemates in throwing the spear and
in horsemanship and in swiftness of foot. He had
already thrown twenty men from their cars, coming
recently with his chariot to learn the art of war. He first cast
810 his spear at you, O horseman Patroklos, but he did not kill you.°

Euphorbos pulled his ashen spear from Patroklos' flesh
then ran back to mix-in with the crowd. He did not come again
at Patroklos, now naked in the fight. Patroklos, overcome
by the blow of the god and by the spear, withdrew back into
815 the throng of his companions, avoiding death. When Hector
saw great-hearted Patroklos withdraw, wounded by the sharp bronze,
he came close to him through the ranks, and he stabbed him with his spear
in the lower part of the belly. He drove through the bronze.
Patroklos fell with a thudding sound, greatly paining the Achaeans.

820 As when a lion conquers an untiring boar in fight, struggling with
high hearts over a small spring on the peaks of a mountain
that they both want to drink from—the boar pants hard but the lion
overcomes him with his strength—even so did Hector, son of Priam,
take away the life of the brave son of Menoitios, who had
825 killed many, standing near him and striking him with his spear.

Boasting, Hector spoke words that went like arrows:
"Patroklos, you said that you would sack our city and take away
the day of freedom from our Trojan women, and drive them
in your ships to the land of your fathers—fool! In front of them
830 the swift horses of Hector stride out to fight. And I myself
am preeminent among the war-loving Trojans, I who can keep them
from the day of slavery. But you—vultures will devour you here, poor wretch!
Achilles for all his excellence did you no good. He no doubt
gave you much advice as you went forth and he remained behind.
835 'Don't return to the hollow ships, Patroklos, master of horsemen,
before you have torn the bloody breastplate from around the chest
of man-killing Hector!' Thus, I imagine, he spoke to you,
and he persuaded you in your folly."

---

810   . . . *not kill you*: Patroklos' death is strange. Probably in an early form of the story, the armor was magical,
invulnerable, and so could only be removed by a god. The scene is perhaps modeled on the death of Achilles
told in some other epic. Euphorbos, of whom we have never heard, is a stand-in for Paris, who killed
Achilles at the Scaean Gates in alliance with Apollo. Like Paris, he is a noble herdsman, good at the games,
handsome, and an enemy of Menelaos, who kills him in Book 17.

Patroklos, the horseman,
you spoke back to Hector, all strength gone: "You make a great
boast now, O Hector. Zeus the son of Kronos has given you victory,   840
and Apollo, who easily overcame me—for they took my armor
from my shoulders. But if twenty men such as you had faced me,
all would have perished here, conquered by my spear.
But ruinous fate and the son of Leto has killed me,
and of men, Euphorbos. You are only the third in my killing.   845
But I will tell you something, and you best lay it to heart:
Your own life is not long, but death already stands close beside you
and powerful fate, that you be killed by the hands of Achilles,
the blameless grandson of Aiakos."°

                    So he spoke, and then death
covered him, and his breath-soul fled to the house of Hades,   850
lamenting its fate, leaving behind manliness and youth.

    Even though he was dead, glorious Hector spoke to him:
"Patroklos, why do you prophesy for me my sheer destruction?
Who knows whether Achilles, the son of Thetis with pretty hair,
might first be hit by my spear and lose *his* life?"   855

    So speaking he put his heel on the corpse and pulled out his bronze
from the wound, and he pushed Patroklos backwards from the spear.
At once he went after Automedon with his spear, the godlike
aide of Achilles the fast runner, for Hector wanted to strike him.
But the swift immortal horses, which the gods had given   860
to Peleus as splendid gifts, bore Automedon away.

[Book 17 is omitted. The fighting over the corpse of Patroklos is desperate. Antilochos, the
son of Nestor, goes to tell Achilles that Patroklos has been killed.]

---

849 *of Aiakos*: Dying men are thought to have prophetic powers.

BOOK 18. *The Shield of Achilles*

And so they fought like blazing fire, and Antilochos,
a fast runner, came as a messenger to Achilles. He found him
in front of his ships with pointed bows and sterns.
Achilles feared in his heart that what had actually happened
5   would come to pass.

            Sorely troubled, Achilles spoke
to his own great spirit: "But why are the Achaeans with their
long hair again gathering in confusion around the ships,
driven in rout from the plain? I only hope that the gods
have not made terrible suffering for me, as once my mother
10 predicted. She said that while I was yet alive the best
of the Myrmidons would leave the light of the sun at the hands
of the Trojans. I fear that the strong son of Menoitios is dead—
the fool! I told him to come back to the ships when he had pushed
away consuming fire from the ships. And not to take on Hector!"

15 While he pondered thus in his heart and spirit, the son
of brave Nestor came up close. Pouring down hot tears,
Antilochos spoke the sad message: "O son of Peleus, lover
of war, you are about to hear a sad tale, which ought never
to have happened. Patroklos is struck down, and they war
20 around his naked corpse. And Hector of the flashing helmet
has taken his armor."

            So he spoke, and a dark cloud
of pain covered Achilles. With both his hands he took up
the grimy dust and poured it over his head, wrecking
his pretty face, and black ashes° fell on his scented shirt.
25 He lay outstretched in the dirt, great in his greatness,
and with his hands he tore at his hair and disfigured it.
The slave girls that Achilles and Patroklos had taken as booty
cried aloud in anguish of heart, and they ran outside
to the battle-hardened Achilles, and all of them struck their breasts
30 with their hands, and the limbs of each were loosened beneath them.

---

24 *black ashes*: From the hearth fire.

Opposite them Antilochos wailed, pouring down tears.
Antilochos held Achilles' hands as Achilles moaned
in his noble heart, and Antilochos feared that he would cut
his throat with a knife.°

    As Achilles groaned terribly,
his revered mother heard him, sitting in the depths   35
of the sea beside her aged father. She then let out
a shrill cry, and the goddesses gathered around her,
all the daughters of Nereus who were in the deep sea.
Glaukê and Thaleia and Kymodokê were there, and Nesaiê
and Speio and Thoê and cow-eyed Heliê and Kymothoê   40
and Aktaiê and Limnoreia and Melitê and Iaira and Amphithoê
and Agavê and Doto and Proto and Pherousa and Dynamenê
and Dexamenê and Amphinomê and Kallianeira and Doris
and Panopê and the very famous Galatea and Nemertes and Apseudes
and Kallianassa. And there Klymenê came and Ianeira and Ianassa 45
and Maira and Oreithyia and Amatheia with the lovely hair,
and other Nereids who were in the deep sea.°

         The bright cave
was filled with them and they all beat their breasts, and Thetis
led in the wailing: "Listen, my sister Nereids, so that all of you
may know and hear the sorrow that is in my heart. I am wretched. 50
I am miserable in having borne the best of men. After I gave birth
to a son blameless and strong, the finest of warriors—he shot up
like a sapling, and I nourished him like a tree in a rich
orchard plot. Then I sent him forth in the beaked ships
to fight at Troy. But I shall never receive him again   55
coming home to the house of Peleus.° While he lives and sees
the light of the sun, he has sorrow, and I am not able to go

---

34 *a knife*: At this point Antilochos drops from the scene.

47 *in the deep sea*: Such lists of sea-deities are common in early oral poetry, and many of these same names
appear in Hesiod's *Theogony*. Homer's catalog contains thirty-three names (but he adds that there were
other Nereids): *Glauke* "blue" is an epithet of the sea; *Thaleia* "blooming" is the name of one of the Muses
and one of the Graces; *Kymodokê* is "calmer of the sea"; *Nesaiê* "island girl"; *Speio*, "cave" in the sea; *Thoê*
"swift" (as of waves); *Heliê* "of the salt sea"; *Kymothoê* "swift wave"; *Aktaiê* "of the shore"; *Limnoreia*, perhaps
"harbor protector"; *Melitê* "sweet as honey"; *Iaira* "swift"; *Amphithoê* "very swift"; *Agavê* "wondrous"; *Doto*
"giver"; *Proto*, perhaps "provider"; *Pherousa*, perhaps "she who carries ships along"; *Dynamenê* "enabler";
Dexamenê, perhaps "protector"; *Amphinomê* "rich in pasture land"; *Kallianeira* "handsome"; *Doris* "giver";
Panopê "all-seeing"; *Galatea* "milk-white," referring to the foam of the sea; *Nemertes* "infallible" and
Apseudes "truthful" are qualities of Nereus, the old man of the sea, a prophet; *Kallianassa* "beautiful queen";
Klymenê "famous"; *Ianeira* and *Ianassa* both mean "strong"; *Maira* "sparkler"; *Oreithyia* "mountain-rushing,"
perhaps of the wind rushing from a mountain down to the sea; *Amatheia* "sandy."

56 *house of Peleus*: According to the story current later, Thetis abandoned Peleus shortly after Achilles' birth,
but here Thetis speaks as if she and Peleus were still married.

to him and help . . . I will go all the same, so that I might see my dear
son and hear what sorrow has come to him while he stayed
60 apart from the war."

    So speaking, she left the cave. The Nereids
went with her, pouring down tears, and around them the waves
of the sea broke. When they came to Troy with its rich soil,
they stepped out onto the beach, one after another, to where
the ships of the Myrmidons were packed in close around swift Achilles.

65   Standing beside him as he groaned deeply, and crying shrilly,
she took hold of the head of her son. In pitying tones
she spoke words that went like arrows: "Why do you weep, my son?
What sorrow has come to you? Tell me, don't hide it!
Zeus has fulfilled your wish, what you earlier prayed for
70 and raised your hands—that the sons of the Achaeans be huddled
at the sterns of the ships, longing for you, and that they should suffer
disastrous things."

    Then Achilles the fast runner spoke, groaning deeply:
"My mother, yes, the Olympian has fulfilled my wish. But what
pleasure is this to me when my dear companion has died—
75 Patroklos, whom I honored above all my other companions,
like myself. I have done him in. Hector killed him and has taken
my beautiful armor, huge in size, a wonder to behold.
The gods gave it as a glorious gift to Peleus on that day
when they placed you in bed with a mortal man. I wish that you
80 had stayed where you were, with your deathless friends of the sea,
and that Peleus had taken a mortal wife!
                                        "But as it is—
now you too will have ten thousand pains in your heart because
of your dead son, whom you will never receive at home again.
But my heart no longer wants to live and remain among men—
85 unless Hector first, stabbed by my spear, gives up *his* life
in revenge for making Patroklos, the son of Menoitios, his spoil!"

    Then Thetis answered him, pouring down tears: "Then
you are doomed to a quick death, my son, if you do what you say.
For your death will follow soon after the death of Hector."
90   Greatly moved, Achilles the fast runner said: "Then may I die
soon. For I was of no use in warding off death from my companion.
He has perished far from the land of his fathers, and he needed me
to ward off ruin from him. So, seeing that I am never going
home to the land of my fathers, and when Patroklos was alive

FIGURE 18.1   Thetis consoles Achilles for the death of Patroklos.   She has pulled a cloak over her head in a sign of mourning. Achilles, lying on a couch before which stands a table filled with food, holds his hand to his forehead in a sign of grief. In this representation Thetis has already brought Achilles new armor from Hephaistos, which hangs on the wall. The shield is decorated with a gorgon's head. Shin guards hang nearby. To the right of the couch is old man Phoinix and to the left Odysseus—unlike in Homer's description—and Nereids (?) stand on either side. The names of all figures (except the Nereids) are written out. Corinthian wine jug, c. 620 BC.

95 I was no light of deliverance to him, nor to his other comrades,
the many who perished at the hands of the good Hector.
And here I sit beside the ships, a useless burden on the land,
I who in war am such as none other of the Achaeans who wear
shirts of bronze!—though in the conference others are better.
100   I wish that strife would perish from among gods and humans,
and anger that drives a man mad, though he is wise.
Much sweeter is anger than honey. It drips down into the hearts
of men and it swells there like smoke ... even so the king of men,
Agamemnon, angered me. But let all that go, though it makes
105 us sad. We must overcome the spirit in our own breasts.
We have to! And now I will go out to find the killer of the man
I loved—Hector.

As for my own fate, I will accept it, because
Zeus and the other deathless gods wish to bring it about.
Not even mighty Herakles, who was the dearest of all
110 to Zeus the king, the son of Kronos, escaped fate.
But fate overcame Herakles and the terrible anger of Hera. Even so—
if a like fate is really fashioned for me—I will be brought low
when I am dead ... But for now I will seize noble fame.
I will set many of the women of Troy, and of the deep-bosomed
115 Dardanians, to wail as they wipe away with both hands the thick tears
from their tender cheeks! May they see that for a long time
I have held back from the war. So don't try to keep me from going
to war, though you love me. You will not persuade me."

Then silver-footed Thetis, the goddess, answered him:
120 "Yes my child, as you have said, in truth it's not a bad thing to ward
off sheer destruction from your friends when they are hard pressed.
But your beautiful armor is held by the Trojans—bronze, glimmering.
Hector of the sparkling helmet has it. He wears it on his shoulders,
exulting. But I do not think he will glory in your armor
125 long—for his death is very near. But do not enter into
the moil of war before your own eyes see me coming
here again. In the morning I will return as the sun comes up,
bringing beautiful armor from Hephaistos the king."

So she spoke and turned away from her son. And, turning,
130 she spoke to her sisters: "Go down now into the broad bosom
of the waters to visit the old man of the sea, in the house of our father.
Tell him everything. I am off to high Olympos, to the house of Hephaistos,
the famous craftsman, to see if he is willing to give my son glorious,
shining armor."

So she spoke, and the Nereids plunged immediately
beneath the surge of the sea. Thetis, whose feet are silvery,   135
went off to Olympos so that she might bring glorious armor
to her son. While her feet bore her to Olympos, the Achaeans fled
with a fearful shouting, driven by man-killer Hector, as they
came to the ships and to the HELLESPONT. Nor were the Achaeans
with their fine shin guards able to drag away the body   140
of Patroklos from the flying weapons.° For they were again
overtaken by the Trojans and their horses, with Hector, son
of Priam, in fighting glory like a flame. Three times brilliant Hector
seized the corpse from behind the feet, anxious to drag it off,
as he called mightily to the Trojans. Three times did the two Ajaxes,   145
putting on the mantle of furious valor, hurl him back from the corpse.
But Hector, trusting always in his valor, would again charge at them
in the tumult of battle, then he would stand and howl aloud. And in no
way did he retreat, even a little. Just as when shepherds in the fields
cannot drive away a tawny lion from a carcass when the lion is hungry,   150
even so the two Ajaxes could not frighten away the armored
Hector, son of Priam, from the corpse.

           And Hector would have dragged
off the corpse and won undying renown, if the swift-footed Iris,
sent from Olympos, had not come running to the son of Peleus
as a messenger: He should arm himself! She came unbeknownst   155
to all the other gods: Hera sent her forth. Standing near,
Iris spoke these words that went like arrows: "Rise up,
son of Peleus, most fear-inspiring of all men. Defend Patroklos!
On his account have the dread contendings arisen before the ships.
Men kill men! The one side wants to defend the dead body,   160
the other side—the Trojans—wants to take it to windy Ilion,
and above all brilliant Hector wants to drag it off. He wants
to cut off his head from the tender neck and to fix it onto a stake.
So get up! Don't lie around! Be enraged that Patroklos
became a plaything for the dogs of Troy. Shame on you   165
if his body is mutilated!"

           The godlike Achilles, swift of foot,
then answered: "Iris, goddess, who of the gods sent you here
as a messenger?"

---

141 *flying weapons:* Earlier, Meriones and Menelaos were carrying off Patroklos' body, but this effort seems now
    to have failed.

The swift-footed quick Iris answered him:
"Hera sent me, the illustrious wife of Zeus. The high-throned son
170 of Kronos knows nothing about it, nor do the other gods
who dwell on snowy Olympos."

Achilles, the fast runner, then
answered her: "But how am I to go into the melée? They have
my armor! My mother forbade me to prepare for the fight before
I see her coming with my own eyes. She vowed to bring beautiful
175 armor from Hephaistos. I know of no other man whose glorious armor
I might wear, except for the shield of Ajax, son of Telamon.
But I think he is mixed in with the forefighters who rage
with their spears around the dead Patroklos."

Then Iris,
swift as the wind, said: "We know well that the Trojans have
180 your armor. Nonetheless, go to the trench as you are and show
yourself to the Trojans—perhaps you will put a fright into them
and they will pull back from the war, and the warlike sons of the
Achaeans will catch their breath. For the Achaeans are worn out.
It is hard to catch your breath in the midst of war."

So speaking,
185 Iris went off, swift of foot. Achilles, dear to Zeus, stood up.
Around his strong shoulders Athena threw the tasseled
goatskin fetish, and around his head the goddess made
a golden cloud—now a blazing flame burned from the man.

As when smoke goes up from a city and reaches the heavens
190 from afar, from an island that the enemy has surrounded—all day
long the besieged have fought a savage battle from the city, but when
the sun goes down, beacon fires burst forth close by one another,
and high above shines the glare, visible to all who live nearby,
so that the dwellers around may come in their ships and avert
195 destruction—even such a brilliance went from the head of Achilles,
to the heavens.

He went from the wall to the trench and took his stand
there. He did not mingle with the Achaeans. He respected his mother's
firm command. Standing there, he shouted, and Pallas Athena
added her own voice from afar. He created an unspeakable
200 confusion in the Trojans! As when the trumpet sounds its clear voice

in the midst of a murderous enemy who have invested a city,°
even so clear was the voice of the grandson of Aiakos.

When the Trojans heard the brazen voice of the grandson
of Aiakos, the spirit was crushed in the heart of each man. All at once
the horses with lovely manes turned their cars backwards— 205
they foresaw evil things. The charioteers were struck with terror
when they saw the unstinting fire burning above the head
of the great-hearted son of Peleus. The flashing-eyed goddess
Athena made the fire burn. Godlike Achilles shouted
three times over the trench—three times the Trojans 210
and their far-famed allies were stunned. Twelve of their best
men died right there, tangled in their cars and fallen
on their spears, as the Achaeans happily pulled out
Patroklos from the rain of arrows. They placed him on a bier.
His beloved comrades stood about it and wept. 215

In their midst
Achilles the fast runner followed, pouring down hot tears
when he saw his beloved comrade lying on the bier, mangled
by the sharp bronze. He had sent Patroklos forth with his horses
and chariot into the war, but he did not receive him returning.

The revered Hera with the cow eyes sent the tireless 220
sun to the shores of Ocean, although he did not want to go.
But the sun went down, and the godlike Achaeans eased
from the bitter strife and the evil war.

*[Line 224 to end of book are omitted. The Trojans meet in assembly. Hector rejects advice
that they pull back into the city—he wants to keep the troops out on the plain. The Greeks
mourn for Patroklos. Thetis goes to the house of Hephaistos to get new armor for Achilles
because Hector has taken the armor that Achilles lent to Patroklos. He makes a great
shield that has illustrations from Homer's world—two cities, a legal dispute, an attack on
one city, farmers, and dancers.]*

---

201   *a city*: It is not clear whether the trumpet has sounded to signal an attack or to rally the defenders.

BOOK 19. *Achilles Prepares for Battle*

Dawn with her robe of saffron rose from the streams
of Ocean to bring light to the deathless ones and to mortals.
And Thetis came to the ships bearing the gifts of the god.
She found her son lying down, clinging to Patroklos,
5   wailing shrilly. Around him his companions wept.

The goddess stood beside him and she took
his hand and she called his name: "My son, we must let
this man lie, though we grieve much, seeing he has been killed
beyond mending by the will of the gods. Now you must take
10   this exquisite sturdy armor, such as no man ever wore
on his shoulders."

So speaking the goddess set down the armor
in front of Achilles—it rang in its terrible splendor. Dread took
hold of all the Myrmidons, and not one dared to look,
as they shrank back in fear. But when Achilles saw the armor,
15   anger gripped him even more strongly, and his eyes blazed
forth beneath his lids as if they were flames. He exulted,
holding the glorious gifts of the god in his hands.

But when he had taken delight in his heart, looking
at the exquisitely wrought objects, right away he addressed
20   his mother with words that went like arrows: "My mother,
the arms that the god has given are just as the works
of the deathless ones should be, and nothing that a mortal man
could fashion. Now I will arm myself. But I am so afraid that
flies will come down into the wounds of the brave son of Menoitios,
25   rent by the bronze, and beget maggots, and defile the corpse,
for the life in him is gone, and all his flesh will rot."

Silver-footed Thetis, the goddess, answered him:
"My child, don't let these things be a trouble to you in your heart.
I shall surely ward off from him the savage tribes of flies,
30   who devour men killed in battle. Even if he should lie there
for a whole year, his flesh will remain always fresh, or even
better than it is now is. But you call the fighting men of the Achaeans

FIGURE 19.1   Achilles receiving arms from Thetis.   Thetis hands her son, in heroic nudity and carrying a spear, a wreath of victory. With her other hand, she gives him a shield. Behind her a Nereid named Lomaia ("bather"?), not named by Homer, carries a breastplate and what seems a jug for oil. Behind her an unnamed Nereid carries the plumed helmet and the shin guards. To the left, an armed Odysseus keeps guard (not in Homer). The figures are labeled. Detail of an Attic black-figure hydria, c. 550 BC.

to an assembly and give up your anger at Agamemnon,
shepherd of the people. Then arm yourself quickly for the war,
35 and resume your valor."

So speaking, Thetis instilled
in Achilles unvanquished courage, and on Patroklos she let seep
through his nostrils ambrosia and a red nectar so that his flesh
would remain incorruptible.° Then the godlike Achilles strode along
the shore of the sea, roaring a terrible cry, and so roused the fighting
40 men of the Achaeans. And those who remained in the gathering
of the ships—the pilots and the steersmen and those who provided
food beside the ships—these men too came to the assembly,
because Achilles had returned, he who had too long absented himself
from the grievous war. Two followers of Ares came limping along,
45 the stalwart son of Tydeus, Diomedes, and godlike Odysseus,
leaning on their spears. For painful wounds still afflicted them.
They went and they sat down in front of the assembly. Last of all
came wounded Agamemnon, the king of men. For Koön,
the son of Antenor, had cut him in the savage contendings
50 with his bronze-tipped spear.°

When all the Achaeans were
gathered together, Achilles the fast runner stood up and spoke
before them: "Son of Atreus, was this, then, the better course
for you and me—that we two raged in spirit-devouring strife
on account of a *girl*? I wish that amid the ships Artemis
55 had killed her with an arrow on that day when I took her from
the loot after I sacked LYRNESSOS!° Then so many of the Achaeans
would not have bitten the vast earth with their teeth
at the hands of the enemy because of the fierceness of my anger.
This is better for Hector and for the Trojans. I suspect
60 that the Achaeans will long remember the disharmony
between us.

"But let us leave all these things as past and done,
though we are full of grief. Of necessity we must tame
the spirit in our breasts. So here and now I renounce my anger.
There is no need for constant, unending anger. Come, let us
65 rouse the Achaeans who wear their hair long to battle, so that

---

38 *incorruptible*: Homer seems to refer to some kind of embalming. In Egyptian embalming, the brains were
removed through the nostrils and various preservative resins poured in, but no such technique is known
from Greece.

50 *spear*: Diomedes, Odysseus, and Agamemnon were all wounded in Book 11, but on the day after this they
are well enough to participate in the funeral games of Patroklos (Book 23).

56 *Lyrnessos*: The account of its sacking is in Book 2.

I may go against the Trojans and put them to the test, to see
if they still are willing to spend the night beside the ships.
But I think that many of them will be happy to bend their knees
in rest—whoever escapes from our savage war and my spear!"

Thus he spoke, and the Achaeans with their fancy shin guards   70
rejoiced that the great-hearted son of Peleus had given up his anger.

[Lines 72–252 are omitted. Agamemnon and Achilles are reconciled. Achilles agrees to
accept Agamemnon's gifts.]

The assembly quickly dissolved.
They scattered, each man to his own ship, while the great-hearted
Myrmidons busied themselves with the gifts, bearing them to the ship   255
of godlike Achilles. And they placed them in his hut and made the women
sit down and then the noble aides drove the horses into the herd.

Then Briseïs, like golden Aphrodite, when she saw Patroklos
torn by the sharp bronze, threw herself about him and shrieked
aloud, and with her hands she tore at her breasts and her tender skin   260
and her beautiful face. With a wail she spoke, a girl like the goddesses:
"O Patroklos, most dear to my sad heart, I left you alive
when I went from the tent, but now when I return, I find you dead,
leader of the people. So to me evil ever follows evil.
I saw my husband, to whom my father and revered mother gave me,   265
torn by the sharp bronze before our city, and my three brothers,
whom my mother bore, beloved—all of them met their day
of doom. But you would not let me weep, when swift Achilles
killed my husband and sacked the city of godlike Mynes,° but you
said you would make me the wedded wife of godlike Achilles,   270
and that he would carry me to Phthia in his ships, and make me
a marriage feast among the Myrmidons. So, dead, I bewail you
without end, for you were always kind to me."

So she spoke,
wailing, and the women too mourned, ostensibly for Patroklos,
but each one really bemoaned her own sorrows. Around Achilles   275
the elders of the Achaeans were gathered, begging him to eat.
In his sorrow he refused: "I beseech you, if I can persuade
any of my dear companions, do not urge me to satisfy
my heart with food or drink, for a dread pain has fallen

---

269 *Mynes:* The king of Lyrnessos, assumed by later commentators to be Briseïs' husband; but nothing in
Homer suggests this.

280 upon me. I will hold out until the sun goes down.
I will endure even as I am."

　　　　　　　　So speaking, he sent
the other chieftains from him, but the two sons of Atreus
remained, and godlike Odysseus and Nestor and old-time
Phoinix, the driver of horses, seeking to comfort him
285 in his terrible sorrow. But his heart would not be comforted
before he had entered the mouth of bloody war.

　　Thinking about the matter, he breathed a deep sigh,
and said: "Yes Patroklos, in the old days you were accustomed
to prepare a hasty pleasant meal in my tent, wretched one, most
290 beloved of my companions, when the Achaeans scrambled to carry
tearful war against the horse-taming Trojans. But now you
lie mangled, and my heart will have nothing of drink and food,
though they are at hand, from desire for you. I could suffer
nothing more awful, not if I should learn of the death
295 of my own father, who now in Phthia sheds tender tears
for lack of a son like me, while I make war against the Trojans
in a foreign country because of the detested Helen—not though
it were for my own son who is reared for me in SKYROS,
if in fact godlike Neoptolemos still lives.° Before, the heart
300 in my breast hoped that I alone would perish far from Argos,
the nurturer of horses, here in Troy, and that you would return
to Phthia, so that you could take my son in your swift black
ship from Skyros and show him all my things, my possessions—
my slaves, and my great house with the high roof. For by now
305 I think that Peleus is dead and gone, or if he still lives,
that he is now sorely pressed by hateful old age, and by ever
waiting to hear bitter tidings of me—when he shall hear
that I am dead!"

　　　　　　So, moaning, he spoke, and the old men
groaned with him, each remembering what he had left in his own
310 house. As they grieved, the son of Kronos took pity on seeing them,
and quickly he spoke to Athena words that went like arrows:

---

299 *still lives*: The only mention of Achilles' son in the poem. Later tradition reported how Odysseus went to
Skyros after Achilles' death and took Neoptolemos back to Troy, where he gave him his father's armor.
During the sack of Troy, Neoptolemos killed Priam on the altar of Zeus. Achilles fathered Neoptolemos
on one of the daughters of the king of Skyros when as a young man he was hidden in the women's
quarters dressed as a girl. Thetis placed Achilles there, fearing he might one day go to Troy and die on
the windy plain.

"My child, surely you have altogether abandoned your man—
is there no longer a care in your heart for Achilles? There
he sits in front of his ships with upright horns, bewailing
his dear companion. The others have gone to their meal,   315
but he will not eat, he fasts. But go and drip nectar
and lovely ambrosia into his breast so that the pangs
of hunger do not come to him."

                So speaking he urged
on Athena, who was already alarmed. She darted down
to him from heaven, through the sky like a long-winged   320
falcon with shrill voice. While the Achaeans speedily armed
themselves throughout the camp, she poured nectar and lovely
ambrosia into Achilles' breast so that the painful pangs
of hunger did not seep into his limbs.

                She herself went then
to the well-built house of her powerful father, while the   325
Achaeans burst forth from the swift ships. As when thick
chill snowflakes fly down from Zeus beneath the blast
of North Wind engendered in the bright air, even so the splendid
shining helmets issued forth from the ships, and the bossed
shields and the breastplates with massive pieces of metal,   330
and the spears made of ash wood. Their gleam reached the sky.
All the earth around laughed from the flashing bronze.
A din went up from beneath the feet of the men.

   In their midst, godlike Achilles armed himself for battle.
There was a gnashing of teeth, and his two eyes showed like   335
the gleam of a fire. Into his heart an unbearable pain descended.
And so raging against the Trojans, he put on the gifts
that the god Hephaistos had labored so to make. First,
he strapped on the shin guards around his legs—beautiful,
fitted with silver ankle straps. Second, he placed   340
the breastplate around his chest. Around his shoulder
he set the silver studded sword of bronze. Then he took up
his great sturdy shield, and its sheen gleamed like
the moon. As when the flash of a burning fire appears
to sailors over the sea, fire which blazes high on the mountains   345
in the corral of a lonely farm—but much unwilling the storm
winds carry the sailors over the fishy deep far from
their friends—even so the gleaming of the shield of Achilles,
beautiful, skillfully made, reached the heaven. He lifted
the strong helmet and placed it on his head and it shone   350

like a star with its crest of horsehair. And around it waved
the golden plumes that Hephaistos set thick around the crest.

Then godlike Achilles made test of his armor, to see
that it fitted him well, that his glorious limbs were free to move
355 within it. Achilles felt as though he wore wings, and the armor
lifted him, the shepherd of the people. He drew forth his
father's spear from the spear case, heavy, huge, strong.
None other of the Achaeans could brandish it, but Achilles
alone knew how to wield it—the Pelian spear of ash
360 that Cheiron had given his father from the peak of Pelion
to be the death of warriors.

Automedon and Alkimos busied
themselves with yoking the horses. Around them they placed
the beautiful harness-straps. They put bits in the horses' jaws
and drew the reins back toward the jointed car. Automedon
365 grasped in his hand the bright well-fitted lash and he
leaped onto the car. Achilles mounted behind him,
adorned for the fight, shining in his armor like bright
Hyperion.° He cried aloud a terrible cry to the horses
of his father: "Xanthos and Balios, far-famed offspring
370 of Podargê!° Think how better to save your driver
and bring him back into the throng of the Danaäns when
we have had enough of war. You must not leave your
driver there, dead, as you did Patroklos!"

Then beneath the yoke
nimble Xanthos, swift of foot, spoke to him, as suddenly
375 Xanthos bowed his head, and all his mane streamed from beneath
the yoke-pad next to the yoke and touched the ground,
and then white-armed goddess Hera gave him a voice:
"Yes, for *this* time we will save you, mighty Achilles, but close
by is the day of doom. We will not be the cause, but a great
380 god and powerful Fate will be. It was not through our slowness
or laxity that the Trojans stripped the armor from the shoulders
of Patroklos, but the best of the gods, whom Leto of the fair
tresses bore, killed him among the vanguard and gave glory

---

368 *Hyperion*: The sun, a Titan.

370 *Podargê*: A Harpy. Achilles' horses Xanthos ("red") and Balios ("patches") were begotten by the West Wind
(Zephyros) on Podargê ("swift-foot"), according to *Iliad* Book 16. Two of Hector's horses also have the
names Xanthos and Podargos (Book 8).

to Hector.° As far as we are concerned, we might run as fast
as the West Wind, which men say is the swiftest of all the winds.   385
But you yourself are fated to die by the strength
of a god and a man."°

       When he had so spoken, the Erinyes°
stopped his voice. Then, groaning deeply, Achilles the fast runner
said: "Xanthos, why do you foretell my death? There is no need.
I know well, of myself, that it is my fate to perish here, far from   390
my beloved father and my mother. Nonetheless I will not cease
until I have given the Trojans their fill of war." He spoke,
and with a cry he drove his single-hoofed horses into the forefront.

---

384   ... *to Hector*: This is the first time that Achilles has heard of Apollo's role in the death of Patroklos. Achilles
      had warned Patroklos of the danger of Apollo in Book 16.

387   *of god and a man*: In Book 22 Hector reveals that the god and man who will kill Achilles are Apollo and Paris.

387   *Erinyes*: This is the only time in Homer that the Erinyes function as guardians of the natural order.
      Probably Homer is thinking of their more usual function as the punishers of those who violated the rights
      of the gods (as in the breaking of oaths) and the rights of older family members, extended here to cover
      maintaining the normal rules of behavior.

And so around you, O son of Peleus, insatiate of battle,
the Achaeans armed themselves beside the beaked ships,
and over against them the Trojans did the same on the rising
ground of the plain. Zeus ordered Themis to call to assembly
5 the gods from the top of Olympos with its many ridges.
She went all around and ordered the gods to come
to the house of Zeus. There was no river that did not come,
except Ocean, nor any nymph, of those who dwell in the beautiful
woods and the springs of the rivers and the grassy meadows.
10 Coming to the house of the cloud-gatherer Zeus, they sat down
within the polished colonnades that Hephaistos had made for his father
Zeus with his matchless skill.

                    And so they were gathered
within the house of Zeus, nor did the shaker of the earth
fail to listen to the goddess, but he came to the assembly
15 from the sea. He sat down in the middle and he questioned
the purpose of Zeus: "Why, O lord of the white lightning,
have you called the gods to assembly? Do you have some
thoughts about the Trojans and the Achaeans? For now
is the time their battle is beginning."

                    Answering him, Zeus who
20 gathers the clouds said: "You know, O shaker of the earth,
the purpose in my heart for which I have called you together.
These men are a concern of mine, even though they are about
to die. Well, I will remain here sitting in a fold of Olympos,
from where I will look down with pleasure. But you others go forth
25 until you come amid the Trojans and the Achaeans, and bear
aid to this side or that, however you are inclined. For if
Achilles will fight alone against the Trojans, they will not
withstand the son of Peleus, the fast runner, even for
a little. Even before they trembled in looking upon him,
30 but now that he is enraged because of his friend's death, I fear
that he might smash the wall beyond what is fated to be."

So spoke the son of Kronos, and he roused up war that is not
to be turned aside. And the gods went each their way into the war,
being divided in their minds. Hera went to the gathering of the ships,

FIGURE 20.1 Achilles. Beardless because of his youth, the warrior is labeled ACHILLES. Dressed in a diaphanous shirt beneath a breastplate decorated with a Gorgon's head, he stands looking off pensively to his left. In his left hand he holds a long spear over his shoulder, his right hand propped on his hip. A cloak is draped over his left arm and a sword in a scabbard hangs from a strap that crosses his chest and rests at his side. He has no helmet, shield, or shin guards. On the other side a female, probably Briseïs, holds the vessels for a drink-offering. Athenian red figure water jar by the Achilles Painter, c. 450 BC.

35 and Pallas Athena and Poseidon, who embraces the earth,
   and the helper Hermes who surpasses all in the cleverness
   of his mind. Together with them Hephaistos went, exulting
   in his power, halting, though beneath him his slender legs moved
   quickly. But Ares, whose helmet flashed, went to the Trojans,
40 and with him Phoibos, whose locks are unshorn, and Artemis,
   who pours forth arrows, and Leto and the river Xanthos,
   and laughter-loving Aphrodite.

                          So long as the gods were apart
   from the mortal men, the Achaeans triumphed mightily because
   Achilles had come forth, he who had kept apart from
45 the contendings for such a long time. An awesome trembling
   came to the limbs of every Trojan in their terror when they saw
   the son of Peleus, the fast runner, blazing in his armor,
   the likeness of man-destroying Ares. But when the Olympians
   came into the crowd of men, up stood mighty Strife,
50 the rouser of the people, and Athena shouted aloud. Standing
   now beside the ditch outside the wall, now on the loud-sounding
   shore, she would give her brash cry. On the other side, Ares
   cried like a dark whirlwind, summoning the Trojans
   with shrill tones from the topmost citadel, now speeding toward
55 Pleasant Hill° that rises beside the Simoeis.

                          Thus the blessed
   gods urged on the two sides to clash in battle, and among
   them made deadly war break forth. The father of men
   and gods thundered terribly from on high, but from below
   Poseidon caused the huge earth and the steep peaks of the mountains
60 to quake. All the foothills of Ida with its many fountains
   were shaken, and all her peaks, likewise Troy and the ships
   of the Achaeans. Hades, the king of the dead, was terrified
   from below, and in fear he leaped from his throne and cried out,
   fearing that Poseidon the shaker of the earth might cleave
65 the earth above his head, and his house be opened to mortals
   and to the deathless ones—a dreadful moldy place
   that the very gods do loathe. So great a din arose . . .

[Line 68 to end of the book are omitted. Achilles searches for Hector. He duels with Aeneas and
nearly kills him, but Poseidon saves Aeneas (who will go on to found the Roman race). Achilles
rages over the plain, killing 14 Trojans one after the other. Hector avoids Achilles, but when Achilles
kills Polydoros, one of Hector's brothers, he takes his stand against him. He would have perished
but Apollo intervenes to save Hector—this time.]

---

55 *Pleasant Hill:* In the Greek, *Kallikolonê*, mentioned only once again later in this book when the proTrojan
    gods assemble there.

BOOK 21. *Achilles, Lord of Death*

And when the Trojans came to the ford of the easy flowing river,
the whirling Xanthos, the child of deathless Zeus, there
Achilles cut them in half, and the one troop he drove
to the plain toward the city where the Achaeans had fled
in rout only the day before, when brave Hector was raging.   5
Some fled away in rout there, and Hera spread out
a deep mist as they went, to hinder them. And the other half
Achilles penned up in the deep-flowing river with its silvery
eddies. Those fell in the water with a great racket,
and the descending steep streams resounded, and the high banks   10
boomed all around. They thrashed every which way in uproar,
whirled about in the eddies, as when, beneath the surge
of a fire, locusts take wing to flee to a river as the
relentless fire sears them with its sudden oncoming,
and they shrink down beneath the water—even so before   15
Achilles' onslaught the sounding stream of the deep-eddying
Xanthos was filled with a confusion of horses and men.

    Then Zeus-begotten Achilles left his spear there on the bank,
leaning against a tamarisk bush, and like a ghost he leaped in,
having only his sword. He had stored wicked deeds in his heart,   20
and turning now here, now there, he stabbed and he struck,
and a horrible groaning rose as the Trojans were cut down
by the sword, and the water ran red with blood. As when fish
flee before a voracious dolphin and fill the crannies of a harbor
with good anchorage in their terror, for the dolphin greedily   25
devours every one he can catch, even so the Trojans
cowered in the streams of the dread river beneath
the steep banks.

    When Achilles' arms grew tired
from killing, he chose twelve youths from the river, alive,
as blood-price for the dead Patroklos, son of Menoitios.   30
He hauled them forth, dazed like fawns, and he bound
their hands behind them with well-cut thongs that they
themselves wore around their stoutly woven shirts. He gave

them to his companions to drag away to the hollow ships.°
35 Then he leaped back in again, eager to kill.

He came upon Lykaon, a son of Dardanian Priam
trying to flee from the river—Lykaon, whom he had once
taken on a night raid, quite to Lykaon's surprise, catching
him in his father's orchard. Lykaon was cutting young
40 shoots of wild fig with the sharp bronze to serve as the rims
of a chariot. Achilles came on him like an unexpected evil,
and then he sold him into well-built LEMNOS, taking him
there in his ships. The son of Jason gave Achilles
a price for him.° From there a guest-friend paid a high sum
45 for him, Eëtion of Imbros. And Eëtion sent Lykaon
to shining ARISBÊ, from where he escaped and returned
to his father's house.° Escaped from Lemnos, he enjoyed himself
with his friends for eleven days. But on the twelfth day a god
cast him again into the hands of Achilles, who would send him
50 to the house of Hades, where he had no desire to go.

When godlike Achilles, the fast runner, saw Lykaon
naked without helmet or shield, nor did he have a spear because
he had thrown these things to the ground as his sweat oppressed him
when he fled from the river, and weariness overcame his knees
55 beneath him—then, Achilles spoke to his own large-hearted spirit:
"Well now, I think I see a great wonder with my eyes!
Truly the great-hearted Trojans that I have killed will rise up again
beneath the murky darkness! Look, this man has come back
after fleeing his day of doom, although he was sold into holy Lemnos.
60 The deep of the gray sea that holds back many against their
will has not held him. But now he will taste the point
of my spear so that I may see whether in like manner he will
come back from *there* too, or whether the life-giving earth,
which holds down even strong men, will hold him down too."

65 Thus Achilles pondered as he took his stand. But Lykaon
came close to him, bewildered, eager to grasp his knees,
for Lykaon wanted very much in his heart to escape

---

34 *to the hollow ships*: This is the only time in the *Iliad* that prisoners are taken. Probably the "well-cut thongs"
    are belts that the men wore.

44 *price for him*: According to Book 23, Euneos, son of Jason and Hypsipylê, gave as payment for Lykaon a
    valuable mixing-bowl of Phoenician manufacture. Arisbê is on the Hellespont (Map IV).

47 *father's house*: Eëtion has the same name as the father of Hector's wife, Andromachê. Living in Arisbê on the
    HELLESPONT (Map IV), this Eëtion was evidently a guest-friend of the house of Priam.

evil fate and black death. The good Achilles raised his long
spear high, ready to stab him, but Lykaon ran beneath
it, and stooping down he took hold of Achilles' knees.   70
The spear went over his back and was fixed in the ground,
though eager to be glutted with a man's flesh.

                      But Lykaon
with one hand beseeched Achilles, holding Achilles' knees,
while with the other he grasped the sharp spear and would not let go.
Speaking words that went like arrows he addressed Achilles: 75
"I beg of you, O Achilles, respect me and take pity! In your eyes,
O Zeus-nurtured one, I am already a holy suppliant,
for at your table I first tasted of the grain of Demeter on that
day when you captured me in the well-ordered orchard,
and you sold me far away, taking me from my father and my   80
friends, into the sacred island of Lemnos. And I brought you
the value of a hundred oxen. But now I have bought my freedom
by paying three times as much.° This is the twelfth morning
since I have come back to Ilion, and I have suffered very much.

   "And now deadly fate has again placed me in your hands.   85
Surely I am hated by Father Zeus, who has again given me
to you. My mother bore me to a short life, Laothoê,
the daughter of aging Altes—Altes who is king over
the war-loving Leleges, who hold steep Pedasos on the Satnioeis
river. Priam had Altes' daughter as a wife, and many other   90
women too. The two of us were born from Laothoê, and you
will butcher us both! For you killed godlike Polydoros
among the soldiers who fight in the forefront when you hit him
with your sharp spear.° But right here, now, an evil will come
on me too, for I do not think I will escape your hands. A spirit   95
has brought me close to you. But I will tell you something,
and you lay it to heart: Do not kill me! I do not come
from the same belly as Hector, who killed your friend,
kind and strong!"

     So spoke the bold son of Priam,
begging Achilles with words, but the voice Lykaon   100
heard was unlike honey: "Fool! Don't promise *me*
your ransom or hope to persuade me. Before Patroklos

---

83   *as much*: Apparently Lykaon had to pay Eëtion back the price of his freedom even though Eëtion was a
      guest-friend in the house of Priam. And a fancy Phoenician bowl must be worth a hundred oxen!

94   *sharp spear*: Achilles killed Polydoros in Book 20.

met his day of destiny, I was more inclined to have
mercy on the Trojans, and many whom I took captive
105 I sold for ransom overseas. But now of all the Trojans
no one whom the god has placed in my hand before Ilion
will escape death—and above all not the sons of Priam!
So, my friend, you die too. Why are you sad? Patroklos
died, he who was much better than you. Don't you see
110 how I am more handsome than you, and taller? I come
from a good father, and my mother was a goddess.
But dread fate and death hangs on me too, whether it will beat
dawn, at dusk, or at noon, when someone will give
my spirit to Ares by a cast of the spear or an arrow
115 flying from the string."

     So he spoke, then he loosed the knees
and the strong heart of the man. Lykaon threw away his
spear as he went down and spread his arms wide, both of them.
Achilles drew his sharp sword and cut him on the collarbone
beside the neck, and then he buried the double-edged sword
120 in his neck. Lykaon fell flat on the earth, and he lay there stretched
out as the black blood flowed from him and wet the ground.

  Achilles picked him up by the foot and threw him in the river
to be carried away, and he went on boasting, speaking
words that went like arrows: "Lie there now with the fishes,
125 who will gladly lick the blood from your wound without a care for you.
Nor will your mother get to weep over you and lay you out
on your bed, but Skamandros will bear you spinning to the broad
breast of the sea. Many a fish, as it leaps amid the waves,
will dart up beneath the black ruffling of the water to eat
130 your white fat, rash Lykaon.

     "So die Trojans! while I come
to the city of sacred Ilion—you in flight and I plundering
the rear! The broad-flowing river with its silver swirls will be
of no use to you, to whom you sacrificed many bulls and cast
single-hoofed horses alive into its eddies. In this way you will
135 perish by an evil fate, until all of you pay the price for the death
of Patroklos and the sorrow of the Achaeans whom you killed
at the swift ships when I was away!"

     So he spoke, and the river grew
still more angry in his heart, and he pondered in his spirit how he should
put a stop to Achilles and ward off destruction from the Trojans.

In the meanwhile the son of Peleus with his long-shadowing   140
spear leaped on Asteropaios, eager to kill him, the son of Pelegon
whom the broad-flowing AXIOS begot on Periboia, the eldest
daughter of Akessamenos—the deep-eddying Axios had
intercourse with Periboia. Well, Achilles rushed on Asteropaios
as he stepped out of the river, awaiting Achilles. Asteropaios   145
had two spears, and Xanthos had placed courage in his breast,
angry because of all the young men killed in the battle,
whom Achilles had cut in pieces along the bank,
without pity.

     When the two warriors had advanced
in close against each other, then first of all Achilles   150
the fast runner addressed Asteropaios: "Who are you
among men, and where do you come from, you who dare
to stand against me? You are the children of wretched men
who stand against my power!"

          The fine son of Pelegon
answered Achilles: "O great-hearted son of Peleus, why do you   155
ask about my lineage? I am from PAEONIA, with its
rich soil, far away, leading the Paeonians with their long
spears. This is now the eleventh dawn since I have come
to Troy. As for my lineage, I am a descendant of the Axios,
the most beautiful water of those that go on the earth,   160
who begot Pelegon famous for his spear. They say that
I am his son. Now let us fight, most glorious Achilles!"

    So he spoke in a threatening manner. The good Achilles,
the son of Peleus, then raised high his ashen spear, but the warrior
Asteropaios hurled with both spears at once, for he was ambidextrous.   165
The one spear struck Achilles' shield, but did not break through,
for the gold layer, a gift of the god, held it.° But with the other
he grazed the right forearm of Achilles, and the black blood
flowed.° Then the spear went beyond and stuck in the earth,
longing to be glutted on flesh.   170

         Then Achilles let loose
his straight-flying spear of ash at Asteropaios, eager to kill.
But he missed him and hit the high bank, and the ashen spear

---

167 *held it*: Now the gold layer seems to be on the top!

169 *black blood flowed*: This is the only time that Achilles is wounded in the *Iliad*.

was fixed half its length in the bank. Then the son of Peleus drew
his sharp sword from his thigh and leaped furiously on
175   Asteropaios, who tried but could not withdraw Achilles'
spear from the river bank with his powerful hand. Three
times he made it quiver as he eagerly tried to pull it out,
three times he gave up the effort. For a fourth time he tried
to bend and break the ashen spear of the grandson of Aiakos,
180   but before that Achilles moved in close and took his life
with his sword. He stuck him in the stomach beside the navel
and out poured all his guts to the ground. Darkness covered the eyes
of Asteropaios as he struggled to breathe.

                       Achilles leaped
on his breast and stripped him of his armor° and, boasting, said:
185   "Lie there then. It is a hard thing to fight against the children
of the mighty son of Kronos, even for one begotten of a river.
You say that you are begotten of the race of the wide-flowing river,
but I claim to be of the line of great Zeus! A man begot me
who was king over the plentiful Myrmidons—Peleus, the son
190   of Aiakos. And Aiakos was a son of Zeus. Even as Zeus
is stronger than rivers that gurgle their way to the sea,
so stronger is the seed of Zeus than the seed of a river.
And look, there is a river right beside you, a great river,
if it can do you any good. You ought not to go up against
195   Zeus the son of Kronos. Even King ACHELOÖS° does not think
he is equal to him, nor is the great power of deep-flowing
Ocean, from whom all the rivers flow and every sea and all
the fountains and the deep wells. Even he fears the lightning
of great Zeus and the ferocious thunder that he smashes
200   down from heaven."

                So he spoke, and out of the bank
he pulled his bronze spear, and he left Asteropaios there
lying on the sand after he had taken away his life, and the dark
water lapped around him. The eels and the fishes finished
off Asteropaios, tearing away the fat from his kidneys,

---

184   *his armor*: In Book 23 Achilles will offer the breastplate and sword of Asteropaios as prizes in the funeral
      games for Patroklos.

195   *Acheloös*: The longest river in Greece, in northwest Greece (another Acheloös river, in Lydia, is mentioned
      in Book 24).

plucking it away as Achilles went his way among the Paeonians,   205
masters of the chariot, who fled along the banks of the swirling
river, because they saw their best man killed in the savage
contendings at the hands of the son of Peleus and his sword.

[Lines 209–523 are omitted. The river Xanthos, resenting the piles of corpses in his waters,
rises against Achilles and nearly drowns him, but Hephaistos, at Hera's instigation, opposes
Xanthos with fire. Xanthos relents. The gods, in comic relief, battle with each other. Achilles
advances to the walls of Troy.]

                                                            Old man Priam stood
on the heaven-built wall and from there watched the monstrous
Achilles. The Trojans were being driven in headlong rout   525
before him. There was no help! With a groan he descended
from the wall and then he called out to his glorious gatekeepers
along the wall: "Hold open the gates wide so that the army
can come into the city, chased in rout. For Achilles is here,
and he is driving them on. Now there will be ghastly destruction.   530
But when our troops have found respite, gathered tightly behind
the walls, then shut the closely fitted doors again. For I am afraid
that this ravaging, this destroying man will leap inside the wall!"
So he spoke, and they undid the gates and thrust back the bars.
Then the gates, thrown wide open, offered the light of deliverance. 535

    And Apollo leaped forth so that he could stave off ruin
from the Trojans as they fled straight for the city and the high wall,
burning with thirst and covered with dust from the plain.
Achilles stayed on them ferociously with his spear, for a wild
madness had seized his heart and he longed to capture glory.   540
Then the sons of the Achaeans would have taken high-gated
Troy, if Phoibos Apollo had not roused up the good
Agenor, son of Antenor, blameless and strong. He filled
his heart with courage and himself stood by his side
so that he could ward off the heavy hands of death.   545
Apollo leaned against the oak, hidden in a thick mist.

    When Antenor saw Achilles, the sacker of cities,
he stopped, and many were his dark thoughts as held
his ground. Moved deeply, he spoke to his own great-hearted
spirit: "What should I do now? If I flee before mighty Achilles,   550
there where the others are driven in rout, he will take me
anyway, and he will butcher me in my cowardice. But if I let
these men be driven before Achilles the son of Peleus,

I can flee on my feet away from the wall to the Ileïon plain°
until I arrive at the valleys of Ida where I can hide in the
thickets. When the sun sets I can wash myself in the river,
ridding myself of the sweat, and then return to Ilion.
But why does my spirit ponder these things? Let him not
see me as I turn away from the city toward the plain
and overtake me, coming after me on his swift feet.
Then there will be no way to avoid death and the fates,
for he is more powerful than all other men.

"And if I go

to meet him in front of the city? Well, that man's flesh
too can be torn by the sharp bronze! There is but one life
in him! Men say that he is mortal . . . It is Zeus, the son of Kronos,
who gives him glory!"

So speaking, Agenor pulled himself
together and awaited Achilles, his brave heart now stirred up
to fight—to do battle. Even as a leopard goes forth
from a deep thicket in full view of a hunter and he is not afraid,
he does not flee when he hears the baying of the hounds.
And even if the hunter gets in first and stabs the leopard
or hits him with an arrow, even pierced through with the spear
he does not give up his attack before the leopard grapples
with the hunter or is killed—even so the good Agenor,
son of brave Antenor, was not going to flee before
he put Achilles to the test.

He held his shield before him,
well balanced on every side, and he aimed with his spear, and he
cried aloud: "I suppose you hope in your heart, O excellent
Achilles, on this day to sack the city of the brave Trojans—fool!
Many are the pains that shall be borne on her account. There are
many brave men within her, ready to defend Ilion under the eyes
of our dear parents and wives and children. You will meet
your doom here, although you are a bold fighter and dreaded in war!"

He spoke and cast his sharp spear from his heavy hand,
and he hit Achilles on the shin beneath the knee. He did not miss!
The shin guard of newly wrought tin clanged terribly and back

---

554 *Ileïon plain*: Referred to only here. Apparently the plain "of Ilos" is meant, an early king of Troy whose tomb
is referred to earlier.

leaped the bronze from the man it had struck. But it did not
penetrate, for the gift of the god stayed it.

       Then the son
of Peleus rushed on godlike Agenor, but Apollo did not
allow him to win glory. He snatched Agenor away   590
and hid him in a thick mist. He sent him out of the war
to go his way in peace. Then by craft he kept the son
of Peleus away from the Trojan army. Taking on the exact
likeness of Agenor, Apollo who works from afar stood before
Achilles' feet, and Achilles rushed on him in pursuit.   595
While Achilles pursued Apollo over the wheat-bearing plain,
turning him toward the deep-eddying river of the Skamandros,
Apollo running just a little ahead, for Apollo beguiled Achilles
with this trick, making him think that he could at any time overtake him.

 Meanwhile the other Trojans, fleeing in rout, came in a glad 600
crowd toward the city, and the city was filled with the throng
of them. Nor did they dare any longer to await one another
outside the city and the wall, and to learn who had fled
and who had been killed in the fight. With haste they poured
into the city—whoever was saved by the swiftness of his feet. 605

BOOK 22. *The Killing of Hector*

So throughout the city, huddled like fawns, they cooled off
their sweat and they drank and quenched their thirst, leaning against
the beautiful battlements. But then the Achaeans came close
to the wall, propping their shields on their shoulders,° and
5 a dreadful fate bound Hector to remain where he was, there
in front of Ilion and the Scaean Gates.

                                        And then Phoibos
Apollo spoke to Achilles the son of Peleus: "Why, O son
of Peleus, do you pursue me on your swift feet when you are
but a mortal and I a deathless god? Haven't you yet recognized
10 that I am a god? And still you rage incessantly. Are you indifferent
to all the trouble you went through, routing the Trojans,
and now they are safe inside the city while you are stuck out here!
You will never kill me—I am immortal!"

                                        With a flash of deep
anger the fast runner Achilles said: "You have fooled me,
15 you most destructive of gods, you who shoot from afar!
You have turned me away from the wall. Otherwise, many Trojans
would have bitten the earth with their teeth before they got
into Troy. As it is you have robbed me of great glory,
while you have saved them easily. You had no fear that
20 I would take revenge for your actions in the future. For truly
I *would* take revenge upon you, if it were in my power!"
So speaking, Achilles went off toward the city with grand ambition,
running like a race horse, a prize-winner who pulls a chariot,
who easily runs full-out over the plain—even so Achilles
25 swiftly moved his feet and his knees.

                                        Then old man Priam
first saw him as he sped all-gleaming over the plain, like the star
that appears at harvest time, when its rays shine in the midst
of many stars in the murk of the night, the star called the dog

---

4 *shoulders*: Apparently holding out their shields horizontally and propping one end on their shoulders, to
create a protection against missiles thrown from the walls.

of Orion.° It is most brilliant, but a sign of evil, bringing
much fever to wretched mortals—just so, the bronze shone   30
around Achilles' chest as he ran. The old man groaned,
and he beat his head with his hands, raising them up high,
and moaning mightily he called out, begging, to his dear son,
who stood motionless before the gates, eager to do battle with
Achilles. The old man spoke pitiful words, stretching out his arms: 35
"Hector, do not wait for this man, my dear son, alone
without others, or you may quickly meet your doom,
killed by this son of Peleus! He is much more powerful—
a cruel man! I wish that the gods loved him just as I do.
Then the dogs and vultures would quickly devour him as he lay   40
unburied, and this terrible sorrow would leave my breast.
For he has taken away many of my noble sons,
killing them or selling them off to islands that lie far away.
And now I do not see two of my sons—Lykaon and Polydoros,
whom Laothoê, princess among women bore me—gathered   45
into the city of the Trojans. But if they are still alive and in the
Achaean camp, then we will ransom them for bronze and gold.
We have it! For the famous old man Altes gave away much riches
at the wedding of his daughter. If they are dead and in the house
of Hades, there will be agony in my heart and in that of their mother,   50
she who bore them.° But there will be less suffering to others
if you do not also die, Hector, overcome by Achilles!

   "So come inside the wall, my son, so that you might save
the Trojan men and women, and so that you do not give
abundant glory to the son of Peleus, and you yourself lose your life.   55
Take pity on me, who yet can feel! O how wretched
I am, how ill-fated I am! I whom the father, the son
of Kronos, will destroy in a pitiful fate at the threshold
of old age. I who have seen many evils—the death of my sons,
my daughters hauled away, treasure-chambers looted,   60
little children thrown to the earth in the horrid war, my sons'
wives taken away at the hands of the deadly Achaeans.
And now, *now* the savage dogs will rip me to pieces at the doors
of my own house after someone has taken the life from my limbs
with a blow, or a cast from some sharp bronze. And my   65
own dogs, those that I raised in my own halls at my table—

---

29   *of Orion*: Sirius, the brightest of the fixed stars, called the dog-star. It appears at the same time as the rising
     of the sun in July, and henceforth until mid-September it brings excessive heat in Greece and Asia Minor.
     These are the "dog days," when the dog-star is in the ascendant. Throughout antiquity the rising of the dog
     star was considered to bring disease and pestilence.

51   *bore them*: They are, of course, dead.

after drinking my blood in the madness of their hearts, they will
then lie down in the forecourt!

               "Certainly, all looks good when
a young man dies in war, slashed by the sharp bronze, and there he lies—
70   everything is lovely that shows, though he is dead. But when dogs
put to shame a gray head and a gray beard and the shameful parts°
of a dead old man—this is the most pitiful thing for wretched mortals."

   So spoke the old man and with his hands he plucked
the gray hairs from his head. Still, he did not persuade Hector.
75   Then his mother Hekabê, standing beside Priam, wailed and shed tears,
exposing her chest, and with one hand she held her breasts
and poured forth tears, speaking words that went like arrows:
"Hector, my child, honor these breasts. Take pity on me!
If ever I gave you suck to ease your pain—remember these,
80   my son, and ward off that savage man from within the wall.
Do not stand forth to face him, stubborn boy! If he kills you,
I shall never bewail you on your bier, my dear child, whom I bore
from my own body. Nor will your wife, with her rich dowry.
But far away, beside the ships, the swift dogs will devour you!"

85   Thus importuning, they spoke to their son, begging him.
But they could not persuade Hector. He awaited Achilles
as he came ever closer in his might. As a serpent in the mountains
waits in his hole for a man to come along after eating
noxious herbs,° and a terrible rage has gone into him,
90   and he glares ferociously as he coils about in his hole,
even so Hector in his voracious might did not retreat
but leaned his shining shield against the projecting wall.

   Grieving, Hector spoke to his great-hearted spirit:
"O no! If I go through the gate and behind the walls, Poulydamas
95   will be the first to criticize me. For he encouraged me to lead
the Trojans to the city during this deadly night, when godlike Achilles
rose up.° But I wouldn't listen. It would have been a lot better if I had!
And now, after I have destroyed many through my own stupidity,
I am ashamed before the Trojans and the Trojan women with
100 their fine robes. I fear that someone, some lower-class type, will say,

---

71   *shameful parts*: In general Homeric decorum prevents all reference to the genitals, except here and in Book 2
     when Odysseus threatens to expose Thersites' private parts. Also, decorum prevents any reference to excre-
     tion or urination.

89   *noxious herbs*: Evidently snakes were thought to acquire their poison through the food they ate.

97   *rose up*: Poulydamas urged retreat behind the city wall in Book 18, advice rejected by Hector.

'Hector, trusting in his own strength, has destroyed the army!'
They will say that. It would be much better for me to meet
Achilles in the hand-to-hand, then return home after killing
him, or myself perish in glory for the land of my fathers.

"Or what if I set my bossed shield aside and my powerful   105
helmet, and lean my spear against the wall and myself go up
to dogged Achilles and promise that we will give up Helen
and with her all the treasure that Alexandros took to Troy
in the hollow ships for the sons of Atreus to take away—
the beginning of this dread conflict! And in addition, what if   110
we were to divest ourselves of half of all the things that the city
contains? I will take from the Trojans an oath sworn by the elders
on behalf of the Trojan people that they will not conceal *anything*,
but will divide in half all the wealth that our lovely city holds within.°

"But why am I having this conversation with myself?   115
I must not go to him! He will not pity me nor have any regard.
He will kill me right there, all unarmed, as if I were a woman,
once I have taken off my armor. There is no way, as if from
an oak or a rock, I may exchange pleasantries with him,
such as when a young girl chats with a youth —a young girl!   120
a youth!° Better to fight this out, the sooner the better.
Then we will know to which man Zeus the Olympian gives glory."

So he pondered as he waited. But Achilles was already
upon him, like Enyalios, warrior of the waving helmet, brandishing
over his right shoulder his terrifying spear of Pelian ash.   125
Around him the bronze flashed like the flames of a blazing fire
or the rays of the sun as it rises.

                    A trembling came over Hector
when he saw Achilles, and he did not dare to stay there
any longer, but he left the gates behind him and ran in fear.
The son of Peleus rushed after him, trusting in his powerful feet.   130
As a falcon in the mountains, the fastest of all birds swoops down
on a trembling dove who flees before him, but he darts in right
on top of her, crying shrilly, close, for his falcon spirit urges him on
to devour the dove—even so Achilles in his fury sped straight on.

---

114   *within*: This same proposal was made by the besieged city on the Shield of Achilles in Book 18.

121   *a youth*: Hector seems to fix on the pastoral scene of peaceful flirtation by repeating these words. In spite of
      speculation ancient and modern, no one has been able to explain what is meant by "from an oak or a rock,"
      a figure that occurs only here in the *Iliad*. In any event, Hector realizes that he will be unable to chat in a
      friendly way with Achilles.

135   Hector fled in terror beneath the wall of the Trojans,
swiftly plying his limbs. He ran beneath the place of watching,°
past the wind-tossed fig—always out from under the walls,
along the wagon track. He ran to the two fair-flowing
fountains where the two springs of the eddying Skamandros rise.
140 One flows with warm water, and around it much smoke rises,
as if from a blazing fire. The other flows cold even in the summer,
like hail, or cold snow or ice formed from water.
There, close to the springs are broad-flowing washing-tanks—
beautiful stone tubs—where the lovely Trojan women
145 and their daughters used to wash their shining clothes in the old
days of peace, before the coming of the sons of the Achaeans.°

    They ran past that place, one fleeing, the other close behind.
A man of worth fled in front, and behind him a man far greater
in strength swiftly pursued. It was not for a sacrificial beast
150 or for a bull's hide, which are prizes in a foot-race, that they competed,
but they ran for the very life of Hector, tamer of horses.
As when single-hoofed prize-winning horses turn swiftly around
the turning-posts, a great prize is at stake, a tripod or a woman
in games celebrated for a dead man—even so three times
155 they ran around the city of Priam on their fast feet.°

    And all the gods looked on. The father of men and gods
was first to speak: "Look now, I see with my own eyes an esteemed
man pursued around the wall. My heart goes out to Hector,
who has burned the thigh-bones of many oxen on the crests of Ida
160 with its many ridges,° and at other times made sacrifice in the upper
parts of the city. And now godlike Achilles is chasing Hector
around the city of Priam on his quick feet. But come, contemplate
and decide, my fellow gods, whether we will save Hector
from death, or whether we will deliver him to destruction at the hands
165 of Achilles, the son of Peleus, although he is a fine man."

    Bluegray-eyed Athena then answered him: "O father
of the white lightning, gatherer of the dark clouds, what words

---

136   *place of watching*: Not clear where this would be, but the fig is near the city walls (Book 6).

146   *of the Achaeans*: No such springs have ever been found in the vicinity of the ruins of Troy, but Homer wants
      to emphasize the contrast between the days of peace and the time of war.

155   *fast feet*: In fact you cannot run around Troy, located on a headland that projects into the plain.

160   *many ridges*: In Book 8 Zeus has a precinct on Gargaros, a peak of Ida.

you have spoken! Again you want to pull back from evil death
a mortal man who has long ago been doomed by fate?
Well, go ahead and try it. But none of the other gods will agree."   170

   Zeus the cloud-gatherer then said in reply: "Ease up,
Tritogeneia, my dear daughter, I am not so set on what
I have been saying. I want you to be pleased—do whatever
is your pleasure. Don't hold back!"

                              So speaking, he urged on Athena,
who was clearly anxious. She went dashing from the peaks   175
of Olympos while swift Achilles was unrelenting in pursuit of Hector.
As when a dog has rousted the fawn of a deer from its lair and chases
it through valleys and woods, and although the fawn evades it
for a while, hiding in a thicket, still the hound tracks him
out, running ever on until he finds him—even so Hector   180
could not escape the son of Peleus, the fast runner.

   As often as Hector rushed toward the Dardanian Gates
to gain shelter beneath the well-built walls, in hopes
that the Trojans could defend him with missiles from above,
so often Achilles would anticipate his movements and move   185
in front and turn him back, toward the plain, while he himself
sped on beside the city's walls. As in a dream where you
cannot snare someone fleeing from you—the one cannot evade
and the other cannot capture—even so Achilles could not
overtake Hector with his fleetness, nor could Hector get away.   190

   How could Hector then have escaped from the fates
of death were it not that Apollo came close to him
for the last time, to rouse his strength and quicken his knees?
Godlike Achilles nodded with his head to his followers—
he did not want anyone shooting deadly arrows or javelins   195
at Hector so that someone else might gain the glory
with a cast and he lose out.

                        When Achilles and Hector
came for a fourth time to the springs, then the father lifted
the golden scales. He placed in the pans two fates of bitter death,
the one for Achilles, the other for Hector, tamer of horses.   200
Zeus took the scales by the balance and held it up.
Down plunged the fateful day for Hector. He went toward
the house of Hades, and Phoibos Apollo deserted him.

Flashing-eyed Athena then came up to the son of Peleus.
205　She stood near him and spoke words that went like arrows:
"Now I hope that the two of us, O glorious Achilles, beloved
of Zeus, will be able to carry off to the ships great glory
for the Achaeans, once we have killed war-crazed Hector
in the hand-to-hand. Now he can no longer escape us,
210　not even if Apollo, who works from a long way off,
should suffer a great deal, thrashing around before father Zeus
who carries the goatskin fetish! Take your stand now—
catch your breath, while I will go and persuade that man
over there to fight in the hand-to-hand."

　　　　　　　　　　　　　So spoke Athena,
215　and Achilles obeyed, glad in his heart, and he stood leaning
on the ashen spear with barbs of bronze. Athena left him
and went up to the majestic Hector in the likeness of Deïphobos°
both in shape and familiar voice. Standing next to him
she spoke words that went like arrows: "My dear brother,
220　surely Achilles is doing you awful harm, pursuing you
with his swift feet around the city of Troy. But come,
let us take our stand, and staying here let us repel his attack."

　　　　And big Hector, whose helmet flashed, said to her:
"Deïphobos, of all the brothers whom Hekabê and Priam bore,
225　you were in the past always to me the most beloved.
And now I think that I will honor you still more in my heart,
because you have dared to come out from the wall on my account
when you saw me, while the others remained within."

　　　　Then the goddess flashing-eyed Athena said to him:
230　"My dear brother, truly my father and my revered mother,
and our comrades about me, begged me in turn—pleaded mightily—
that I stay. For they all tremble before Achilles. But my head
was troubled with bitter grief. Now let us charge straight at him
and fight, and let there be no sparing our use of the spears,
235　so that we might learn whether he will kill us and carry away
the bloody armor to the hollow ships, or whether you will kill
him with your spear."

　　　　　　　　　　So speaking, and with such cunning
Athena led him on. When they came near Achilles, as each

217　*Deïphobos*: Hector's brother, first mentioned in Book 12. He has a strong presence in Book 13, where he is wounded
　　by Meriones, Idomeneus' aide. According to the *Odyssey*, Deïphobos took up with Helen after Paris' death.

advanced against the other, Hector, whose helmet flashed,
spoke first, saying to Achilles: "I will flee from you 240
no more, O son of Peleus, as before I ran three times
around the great and shining city of Priam, when I did
not dare to await you as you came on. But now
my heart urges me to take my stand against you,
to see if I will kill you or you kill me. And let us take 245
the gods to witness—they will be the best witnesses
and guardians of our covenant! For I will do nothing unseemly
to you, if Zeus grant me to outlast you and I take your life.
After I have taken the famous armor of Achilles, I will give back
your dead body to the Achaeans. And you do the same . . ." 250

    Then Achilles, the fast runner, glaring angrily from beneath
his brows, said: "Hector, you are mad! Don't talk to me of covenants!
As there are no trusted oaths between lions and men, nor do
wolves have a friendly heart toward lambs but always they
think evil toward one another—even so there is no way 255
that you and I can be friends. Nor will there be oaths
between us before one or the other shall fall and glut
Ares with blood, the warrior with a tough hide shield.
So think now of all your fancy valor. Now you must be
a spearman and a bold fighter. There is no more escape. 260
Pallas Athena will kill you by my spear. Now you
will pay full price for the sorrow of my companions
whom you killed, raging with your spear!"

                            Thus Achilles spoke,
and brandishing his long-shadowing spear he cast. But the bold
Hector saw it coming and ducked, crouching in anticipation. 265
So the bronze spear flew over him and stuck fixed in the earth.
But up leaped Pallas Athena and gave it back to Achilles,
unseen by Hector, shepherd of the people.

                            Then Hector spoke
to the blameless son of Peleus: "You missed! Nor have you
learned from Zeus—O Achilles like to the gods!—of my fate, 270
though surely you thought so. But you have been glib of tongue
and a thug with words so that you frightened me out of my power.
You made me forget my valor. But you shall not spear me
in the back as I flee. Drive your spear straight through my breast
as I charge upon you, if any god grants it! Or avoid *my* spear of bronze— 275
may you take it entirely in your flesh . . . This war would be lighter
for the Trojans, if you were dead, for you are our greatest evil."

Hector spoke, and brandishing his long-shadowing
spear he cast it, and it hit in the middle of the shield of the son
280   of Peleus—he did not miss. But the spear glanced far away
from the shield. Hector raged that his missile had flown in vain
from his hand, then he stood abashed, for he did not have another
ashen spear. He called aloud for Deïphobos of the white shield,
requesting another long spear. But Deïphobos was nowhere near.

285   Hector then knew in his heart, and he spoke: "I understand.
The gods have called me to my death. I thought that Deïphobos
the warrior was nearby, but he is behind the walls. Athena has
deceived me. Now wretched death is near, not far away. I cannot
avoid it. In the olden times Zeus was more friendly to me,
290   and the son of Zeus, Apollo who shoots from a long ways off.
He who in times before stood by me with a steady heart.
But now my doom has come upon me. Let me not die without
a struggle, without fame, but having done something great,
something for those in later times to remember."°

So speaking
295   Hector drew his sharp sword, large and powerful, which hung
at his side, and pulling himself together he swooped like a
high-flying eagle that goes over the plain and through
the dark clouds to seize a tender sheep or a cowering hare—
even so Hector swooped, brandishing his sharp sword.
300   Achilles rushed to meet him. He filled his heart with wild
strength, and he protected his chest by holding the sturdy
finely crafted shield before him. As he ran he tossed the crest
of his shining four-plated helmet. All around it waved
the beautiful plumes of gold that Hephaistos had set thick as the crest.

305   As the evening star, the most beautiful star in the sky,
goes forth among all the other stars in the gloom of night,
just so the sharp spear that Achilles balanced in his right hand
gleamed as he looked at the fair flesh of majestic Hector,
looking to find the place that was most open to a thrust.
310   Now, bronze armor covered up all the rest of Hector's flesh,
the beautiful armor that he had plundered from the body
of Patroklos when he killed him. But there was an opening
where the collarbone joined the neck with the shoulders,
the gullet where the destruction of life comes most quickly.

---

294   *to remember*: The gods are behind it all: Athena, Zeus, Apollo, Fate. But the fame that will last forever
depends on the warrior's personal effort.

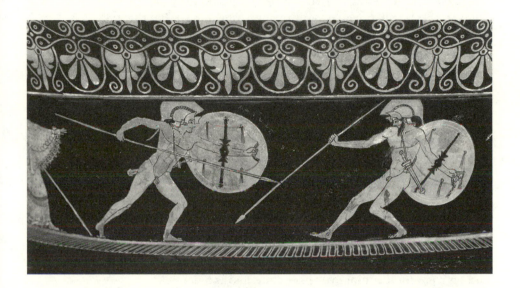

FIGURE 22.1 **Achilles kills Hector (the figures are labeled).** The illustration does not follow Homer's account very well. Both men are in "heroic nudity." A beardless Achilles attacks from the left, wearing shin guards, a helmet, and carrying a hoplite shield, sword, and spear. The bearded Hector is similarly armed (but without shin guards). He has already been wounded in the left thigh and in the chest, and is about to go down. Blood flows from the wounds. Athena stands behind Achilles. Red-figure Athenian wine-mixing bowl by the Berlin Painter, c. 490–460 BC. Found at Cerveteri, Lazio, Italy.

315 Achilles drove in his spear right there as he rushed on Hector,
and the point of the spear went straight through the tender neck.
But the bronze-heavy ash did not cut the windpipe, so that
Hector was able to speak and make answer to his enemy.

Thus Hector fell in the dust. And then Achilles gloated
320 over him: "Hector, you probably thought that you could despoil
Patroklos and stay safe. You had no thought of me, who remained
a long way off—you fool! Far from Patroklos a far greater helper
was left behind at the ships—me! I, who have just killed you!
Dogs and birds will eat you now, in an unseemly manner. But the
325 Achaeans will bury Patroklos."

Hector, whose helmet flashed, spoke
as his strength drained away: "I beg you by your life and your knees
and your parents—do not give me to be devoured by the dogs
beside the ships! My father and my mother will give you much bronze
and a large quantity of gold as gifts if you give back my body to be taken home
330 so that the Trojans and the wives of the Trojans can give me my due
of fire when I am dead."

Achilles, the fast runner, said to him,
looking with anger from beneath his brows: "Don't beg me,
you dog, by my knees or by my parents. As much as I wish
that my anger and my spirit would drive me on to cut up your flesh
335 and eat it raw for the things you have done, just as much
I know that no one will save the dogs from your skull—
not though your parents should come here and offer ten times
as much, or twenty times, and promise still more. Not if Dardanian
Priam should promise to weigh out your body in gold. Not even so
340 will your revered mother place you on a bier to bewail
her dear son. But dogs and birds will devour you completely!"

Then, dying, Hector whose helmet flashed answered:
"I know you too well. I knew this would be—that I could not persuade
you. The heart in your breast is of iron. Only think of this—
345 that I will become the anger of the gods on that day when Paris
and Phoibos Apollo kill you at the Scaean Gates,° though you
are great."

---

346 *Scaean Gates*: Hector foretells the death of Achilles as Patroklos foretold the death of Hector. Achilles will
die by an arrow fired by Paris, guided by Apollo, according to the usual account.

Thus he spoke. Then death covered him over, and his
breath-soul flew out of his limbs and went to the house of Hades,
bewailing her fate,° leaving behind manliness and youth.
Godlike Achilles addressed him, though he was dead: 350
"Die then! I will meet my own fate whenever Zeus and
the other deathless gods want to bring it about."

                                                    So he spoke
and he pulled his bronze spear from the corpse. He laid it aside
and stripped Patroklos' bloody armor from Hector's shoulders.
The other sons of the Achaeans ran up to admire the physique   355
and the wonderful handsomeness of Hector. And they all dipped
in their weapons, those who went near. And so one would say,
turning to his neighbor: "Yes, Hector seems more gentle to the
touch, now, than when he burned the ships with deadly fire!"

Thus someone would speak and plunge his weapon in the corpse,   360
standing nearby. When the good Achilles, the fast runner,
had finished stripping the corpse, he stood up among the Achaeans
and spoke words that went like arrows: "My dear leaders
and rulers of the Argives—because the gods have given it to us
to overcome this man who has done more harm than all the other   365
Trojans combined, let us stand in our might in front of the city,
fully armed, to find out what are the Trojans' intentions—
whether they will leave their high city now that their man is dead,
or whether they are eager to remain even though Hector is gone.

"But why does my heart have this conversation with itself?   370
Patroklos still lies dead at the ships—unwept and unburied.
I will never forget him, not so long as I am among the living
and my limbs still function. Even if in the house of Hades
men forget their dead, even there I will not forget my dear
companion. Anyway, let the Achaean youth sing our song   375
of victory and return to the hollow ships. We will bring
Hector there. We have won great glory. We have killed
the gallant Hector, to whom the Trojans prayed throughout
their city as if he were a god."

                              So he spoke, contemplating how he
would treat Hector shamefully. He pierced the tendons of both feet   380
from behind, from the heel to the ankle, and made fast ox-hide
thongs, which he tied to the back of his chariot. He let Hector's head

---

349 *her fate*: "breath-soul" is feminine in Greek.

drag on the ground. Then he mounted his chariot and loaded
the famous armor. He snapped the whip and drove away,
385 and his two horses gladly sped onward. The dust rose up
from Hector's head as he was dragged, and his dark hair
spread out on either side, and all in the dust lay the head that
before was so charming. But now Zeus had given him to the enemy,
to be treated shamefully in the land of his fathers. And all of
390 his hair was befouled by the dust.

                                His mother tore at her own hair
and she flung her shining headscarf far away—she wailed
aloud when she saw her son. His father piteously bewailed
him too, and the people fell into a howling and shrieking throughout
the city. It was as if all of Ilion with its beetling brows burned utterly
395 with fire.

        The people could scarcely hold back the old man
torn by grief who wanted to go outside the Dardanian Gates.
He prayed to everyone, rolling around in the filth, and he called
each man by name: "Hold off my friends, though you are distressed,
and let me go alone outside the city, to the ships of the Achaeans.
400 I will beseech this wicked man, this doer of evil, if perhaps
he will take shame before his fellows and have pity for my old age.
He has a father like me too—Peleus, who begot him and raised him
to be a curse to the Trojans. He has made sorrow for me above all
other men, so many are my sons that he killed in their prime.

405   But of all those I do not rue any so much, though I am rent
with sorrow, as for this one—Hector. Grief for him
will carry me into the house of Hades. How I wish that he had
died in my arms! Then we'd have had our fill of lamentation—
his mother who bore him to her sorrow, and I myself."

410   So Priam spoke, weeping, and the citizens cried too.
Among the Trojan women Hekabê led the loud lament:
"My child, how wretched I am. How will I live in my bitter
anguish with you dead? You who night and day were
my boast throughout the city—a help to all the Trojan men
415 and the Trojan women in the town. They greeted you as a god.
You were a great glory to them while you were alive.
Now death and fate has come upon you."

                                So she spoke, wailing.
But Hector's wife Andromachê had not yet heard, for no truthful

messenger had come to her to announce that her husband
remained outside the gates. She was weaving in a corner   420
of her high room, weaving a double cloth, purple in color.
Andromachê was weaving-in a design of multicolored flowers.
She called out through the house to her handmaids with lovely hair
to set a great tripod on a fire so there would be a hot bath for Hector
when he came home from the battle—poor woman. She did   425
not yet know that flashing-eyed Athena had killed him at the hands
of Achilles, far from any warm bath.

               Then Andromachê heard
the shrieking and shouting from the wall. Her limbs spun around
and the weaving comb fell from her hand to the earth.
She spoke to her handmaids with the lovely hair: "Come here,   430
the two of you—follow me so that we can see what has happened.
I heard the voice of my husband's mother, and from my breast
my heart leaps into my mouth, and beneath me my knees are numb.
Some evil is close by for the children of Priam. Would such word
be far from my ear, but I fear terribly that stalwart Achilles   435
has cut off Hector alone from the city and pursues him
over the plain—that he has put an end to the reckless manhood
that possessed him. For Hector would never remain in the mass
of men, but always ran ahead, yielding to no one in his power."

  So speaking Andromachê rushed out of the hall like a mad woman,   440
with throbbing heart. Her handmaids went with her, and when
they came to the wall and the crowd of men, she stood gazing
over the wall, and she saw Hector dragged before the city.
The swift horses dragged him without pity toward the hollow ships
of the Achaeans.   445

            Dark night covered her eyes. Andromachê fell backward
and gasped out her breath-soul. She threw the shining bonds
far from her head—the frontlet and the cap, and the woven band
and the headscarf° that golden Aphrodite had given her on that day
when Hector, whose helmet flashed, led her from the house of Eëtion
after Hector had given countless bridal gifts. Around about her   450
came Hector's sisters and the wives of Hector's brothers
and they bore her up, distraught unto death, in their midst.

---

448 *frontlet . . . headscarf*: The first three items are named only in Homer and it is not clear what they are; but the
      fourth word means "headscarf" (*krêdemnon*). The "headscarf" was the symbol of Andromachê's married state.

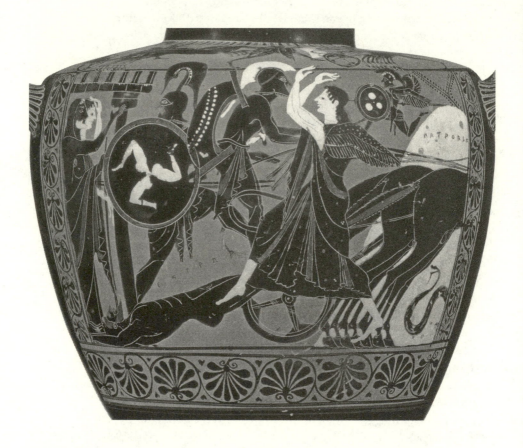

FIGURE 22.2 **Achilles drags Hector's body behind his chariot.** As Achilles (labeled) steps onto the chariot behind his charioteer, he looks behind at Priam and Andromachê lamenting from the wall. His shield bears a triskelis ("three-legged") design. Iris appears (she is white) to ask him not to treat Hector in this fashion. Behind the horses is the tomb of Patroklos, his breath-soul (psychê) hovering above represented as a miniature warrior. Patroklos' name is inscribed on the tomb. Notice the serpent at the bottom of the tomb: The beneficent spirits of the dead were thought to live as friendly snakes in tombs ("good spirit," agathos daimon). Black-figure wine-mixing pot, c. 510 BC.

When Andromachê caught her breath and her spirit was
gathered in her breast, she spoke to the Trojan women with
a deep moan: "Hector, I am wretched. We were born to a single fate,   455
the two of us—you in the house of Priam in Troy, I in THEBES
beneath Plakos covered in woods, in the house of Eëtion that
nourished me when I was little, an unlucky father to a
cruel-fated child. I wish I had never been born! But now you go
beneath the depths of earth to the house of Hades. You have   460
left me in dreadful sorrow, a widow in my halls. And our child
is still a mere babe, that you fathered and I bore—we who
are doomed to a wretched fate! You will be of no use to him,
Hector, now that you are dead. Nor he to you. If he escapes
the tearful war of the Achaeans, still there will be nothing   465
but labor and sorrow ahead for him. Others will take
his fields. The day of orphanhood cuts off a child completely
from those his own age. He bows down his head, his cheeks
are covered with tears. He goes in need to the companions
of his father, plucking one by the cloak, another by the shirt,   470
and of them who are touched by pity one holds out his cup
for a moment. The child wets his lips, but he does not wet
the roof of his mouth.° And one whose father and mother
still live pushes him from the feast, striking him with his hands
and reproving him with insulting words: 'Get away from here!   475
You have no father to dine with us!' Then in tears the boy
comes back to his widowed mother . . .

                    "O Astyanax! Before
he ate only marrow and the rich fat of sheep, sitting on his
father's knees. And when sleep came on him and he left off
his childish play, he would sleep on his couch in the arms   480
of his nurse. In a soft bed, his heart filled with happy thoughts.
But now he will suffer much sorrow because he has lost his dear father—
Astyanax, whom the Trojans called by that name because you alone
saved their gates and their high walls.° Now by the beaked ships,
far from your parents, wriggling maggots will eat you after   485
the dogs have had their fill, as you lie naked . . . All the while
that finely woven and lovely garments made by the hands of women
lie in your halls. But I will burn all these things in the blazing fire.
They are no longer of use to you. You shall not lie in them.
I'll do it as an honor to you from the men and women of Troy."   490
So she spoke through her tears, and all the women lamented too.

---

473   *of his mouth*: That is, he receives only crumbs, but never enough to satisfy his hunger.

484   *their high walls*: The name Astyanax means "king of the city," that is, its defender.

BOOK 23. *The Funeral of Patroklos*

Thus the Trojans lamented throughout the city. And when the Achaeans came to the ships and the Hellespont, some of them scattered to their own ships, but Achilles would not allow the Myrmidons to scatter. He spoke to his war-loving
5 companions: "My Myrmidons, with your swift chariots, my faithful companions—let us not unharness our single-hoofed horses from the cars, but with horses and chariots let us draw near Patroklos and bewail him. For such rite is due the dead. And when we've had our fill of unbridled lamentation,
10 then let us unhitch all our cars and eat a meal, all of us."

So he spoke, and all together they raised their sorrowful wail, and Achilles was their leader. Three times they drove their horses with fine manes around the dead body, keening. Among them Thetis stirred the desire for weeping. The sands were moistened,
15 the armor of the men was wet with their tears. They grieved for their mighty deviser of rout.

Among them the son of Peleus began the sad lament, placing his man-destroying hands on the chest of his companion. "Greetings, Patroklos, even in the house of Hades. I am bringing to fulfillment
20 all that I promised earlier—that I would bring Hector here and give him to the dogs to eat raw, and that I would cut the throats of twelve glorious sons of the Trojans on your funeral pyre, in my anger at your death."

He spoke and thought about how he could treat the valiant Hector in a cruel way, stretching him
25 out on his face in front of the bier of the son of Menoitios. As for the Myrmidons, all of them doffed their armor of shining bronze and unhitched their horses. They sat down beside the ship of Achilles, the fast runner, as he prepared for them a fitting funeral feast. Many sleek bulls bellowed
30 around the iron knife as their throats were cut, and many sheep and bleating goats. And many swine with white tusks, dripping with fat, were stretched over the flame of Hephaistos

to singe away the hair. There was so much blood streaming
around the corpse that you could easily dip in a cup.

But first the chiefs of the Achaeans took their chief,   35
the swift-footed son of Peleus, to the good Agamemnon.
They had considerable trouble persuading him to go, so distraught
was Achilles on account of his companion. When they came up
to the tent of Agamemnon, they immediately sent out the clear-voiced
heralds to set a great tripod on the fire, in hopes that they   40
might persuade the son of Peleus to wash off the bloody gore.

But he absolutely refused, and swore a great oath: "No,
by Zeus, who is the highest and best of the gods—it is not right
that cleansing water be used on my head before I have placed
Patroklos on the pyre and built a mound for him, and cut   45
my hair. Never again will such a pain come to my heart
for as long as I will live.

                        But for now let us yield to
the hated banquet. In the morning, King Agamemnon,
rouse your men to gather wood to prepare everything required
for a dead man when he is about to go into the murky gloom.   50
Let the untiring fire consume him quickly and remove him
from our sight. Then the people can return to their tasks."

So he spoke, and they heard him and obeyed. Eagerly each
man prepared his meal and they ate, nor did anyone lack a thing
in the equal feast. When they had put the desire for drink and food   55
from themselves, each man went to his tent to lie down.
But the son of Peleus lay on the shore of the much-resounding
sea in the midst of the many Myrmidons, groaning deeply
in an open space where the waves dashed against the shore.

When gentle sleep came upon him, pouring all around him   60
and loosing all cares from his spirit—for his glorious limbs were tired
from harrying Hector as far as windy Ilion—then there came
to him the breath-soul of wretched Patroklos, exactly like him
in size and beautiful eyes and voice, and he wore his usual clothing.°

He stood over Achilles' head and spoke thus to him: 65
"You sleep! Have you forgotten about me, Achilles? You were never

---

64 *clothing*: This is the only time in Homer that the vision of a ghost is described.

thoughtless of me in life, only in death. Bury me as soon as possible
so that I may pass inside the gates of Hades. The breath-souls
keep me far away, the phantoms of men whose labor is finished,
70 and they will not let me join them beyond the river, but vainly
I wander through the house of Hades with its wide gates.

    "And give me your hand, I beg you, for no more shall I come
back from the house of Hades when once you have given me
my fill of fire. No more, alive, will we talk things over,
75 sitting apart from our companions, for a hateful fate
has opened its maw for me, the fate that was my lot from birth.
And it is your fate too, O Achilles, who are like the gods,
to be killed beneath the wall of the wealthy Trojans. And I
will tell you something else, and I urge you to listen well:
80 Do not bury my bones separate from yours, O Achilles,
but let them be together, even as we were raised in your house.
Menoitios brought me, while still a little fellow, out of Opoeis
to your country on account of a dreadful homicide,
on the day when I killed the son of Amphidamas.° I was foolish,
85 I did not want to kill him but I became angry over a game of dice.
The horseman Peleus then took me into his house and reared me
very kindly, and he made me your aide. Therefore, let a single
chest contain our bones, the one of gold with two handles that
your mother gave you."

            Achilles, the fast runner, answered him:
90 "Why, dear fellow, have you come here to give me orders
about these matters? You know that I will accomplish these things.
I will do as you ask. But come, stand near me . . . let us throw
our arms about one another and for a little while take our fill
of sad lament."

            So speaking Achilles reached out his hands
95 but he could not clasp Patroklos. The breath-soul went beneath
the earth like smoke, gibbering faintly. Startled, Achilles stood up
and clapped his hands together, and he spoke a wailing word:
"Look, even in the house of Hades the breath-soul and the
phantom are something, although there is no mind there.
100 For all night long the breath-soul of miserable Patroklos
stood over me, wailing and weeping, and he gave me orders

---

84 . . . *Amphidamas*: Opoeis was the principal town of Locris, a territory south of Phthia. Hesiod sang
    at the funeral games of an Amphidamas, but there seems to be no connection with this Amphidamas.
    Exile because of homicide is common in the Homeric poems, occurring about seven times, but it is odd that
    Patroklos killed someone when he was just "a little fellow."

about each thing, and was wondrously like himself." So Achilles
spoke, and in all his Myrmidon cohort he roused a feeling of sorrow.

Dawn with its fingers of rose appeared to them as they wept
around the wretched corpse. And then King Agamemnon   105
sent forth mules and men from all sides out of the huts
to gather wood. A noble man, Meriones, the aide of brave
Idomeneus, oversaw the proceedings. They took up wood-cutting
axes in their hands and well-woven ropes and went forth.

The mules went before them. They went upwards, downwards,   110
sideways, and at a slant, and when they came to the mountain
valley of Ida with its many springs, the men set out at once
to fell the tallest oaks with their long-edged bronze—
and the trees fell with a great roar. Then they split the trunks
in half and bound the logs to the mules. The mules   115
tore up the earth with their feet as they dragged the logs
to the plain through the thick underbrush. All the wood-cutters
carried logs, for thus did Meriones command them, the aide
of brave Idomeneus. They cast them down on the shore
one by one where Achilles planned to heap up a great mound   120
for Patroklos, and for himself. And when on all sides
they had put down the huge amount of wood, they sat down
and waited in a group.

Achilles at once ordered the war-loving
Myrmidons to arm themselves with their bronze and each
one to yoke the horses to his car. They got up and put on   125
their armor, and the fighting men and the charioteers
mounted their cars. The men in their chariots went in front,
and after followed a cloud of foot soldiers, countless in number.
His comrades carried Patroklos in their midst. They clothed
his entire body with snippets they cut from their hair.°   130
Behind them Achilles held Patroklos' head in grief,
for he was sending his dear companion to the house of Hades.

When they came to the place that Achilles had designated,
they set down the corpse and quickly heaped up the huge supply
of wood. Then good Achilles, the fast runner, had got another idea.   135
He stood apart from the fire and cut a lock of his golden hair,
which he grew as a rich growth, a dedication to the Spercheios River.

---

130 *from their hair*: They seem to be cutting off snippets of their hair as they walk along in the procession.

Groaning, he spoke, looking over the wine-dark sea:
"Spercheios,° it was in vain that my father Peleus promised you
140 that when I returned to the land of my fathers I would cut
this lock of hair for you and make a sacrifice, and on the same spot
sacrifice fifty uncastrated rams, there, at the springs
where your precinct and your fragrant altar are. So promised
the old man, but you did not fulfill that wish for him.
145 Because I shall never return to the land of my fathers I want
to give this lock to the warrior Patroklos to carry with him."
So speaking, he placed the lock in the hands of his dear
companion, and this roused in all the Myrmidons a great
desire to weep.

And then the light of the sun would have gone
150 down as they wept, if Achilles had not gone up to Agamemnon
and said: "O son of Atreus, it is correct that the people of Achaea
should have their fill of lamenting. But because they have special
regard for your words, please now disperse them from the pyre
and urge them to make their meal ready. We will take care of all that
155 is required to grieve for the dead. Only let the captains remain here."

When the king of men Agamemnon heard this, he at once
scattered the army through the well-balanced ships, but those
who were dearest to the dead man remained and heaped up
the wood. They made a pyre a hundred feet square. Hearts aching,
160 they placed the dead man on the top of the pyre. They skinned
and dressed-out many strong sheep in front of the pyre,
and sleek cattle with a shambling walk. Great-hearted Achilles
collected the fat from all of them and covered the dead body
with the fat from head to foot. Then he flung the skinned
165 bodies on top. He placed two-handled carrying jars filled
with honey and oil against the bier. Swiftly he threw
four horses with long necks upon the pyre, groaning deeply.
Achilles the chieftain had nine dogs that fed beneath
his table. He cut the throats of two of these and cast
170 them on the pyre. He then killed twelve noble sons
of the great-hearted Trojans, slashing them with bronze.
For he was determined to do despicable things. He tossed
the iron might of fire on the pyre, giving it free range.

He groaned then, and called his companion by name:
175 "Greetings, O Patroklos, even in the house of Hades. For I am

---

139 *Spercheios*: The main river in Phthia, Achilles' homeland.

FIGURE 23.1 **The funeral of Patroklos.** Here Achilles prepares to cut the throat of a beardless Trojan youth. Achilles stands in "heroic nudity," but wears a cloak, in front of the pyre. A label across the bottom reads "tomb of Patroklos." Achilles grips the Trojan victim by the hair, the man's hands tied behind his back. Behind Achilles, to the far left, is the next Trojan in line, wearing a Phrygian cap. On top of the pyre and in front of it is stacked Patroklos' armor that Achilles has taken from Hector, once his own armor: two breastplates (for some reason), a helmet, a shield, and two shin guards. To the right, a fully clothed Agamemnon, holding a scepter, pours out a libation from a phialê, a kind of offering dish. A jug of wine or honey stands beside the pyre at Agamemnon's feet as in Homer's description. Red-figure south-Italian wine-mixing vase from Canosa, c. 340–320 BC.

bringing to completion all the things that I promised earlier.
Twelve sons of the great-hearted Trojans—the fire will devour them
along with you! But I will not give up Hector the son of Priam
to be devoured by fire, rather by dogs!"

           So he spoke, threatening,
180 but the dogs did not molest the corpse of Hector. Aphrodite,
the daughter of Zeus, kept the dogs from Hector day
and night, and she anointed his body with a rose-scented
oil, ambrosial, so that when Achilles dragged him by his chariot
Hector's skin would not be torn. And Phoibos Apollo
185 cast a dark cloud around him, drawing it from the heaven
to the plain. And he covered the place where Hector's body lay
so that the power of the sun might not too soon shrivel the flesh
around Hector's ligaments and limbs.

           But the pyre of the dead
Patroklos would not burn. Then Achilles swift of foot
190 had another thought. He stood apart from the pyre and prayed
to the two winds, North Wind and West Wind, and he
promised beautiful sacrificial offerings. He prayed heartily,
pouring out liquor from a golden cup, that they come
so that the corpses might burn as fast as possible and the
195 wood might quickly be kindled. Iris swiftly heard his prayers
and went off as a messenger to the winds.

           The winds were feasting
at banquet all together in the house of the tempestuous West Wind.
Iris stopped running and stood on the stone threshold. As soon
as their eyes saw her, the winds leaped up, and each called
200 her to himself. But she would not sit down and she said:
"I cannot sit. I must go back to the streams of Ocean, to the land
of the Aethiopians, where they are making great sacrifices
to the deathless ones, so that I too may partake of the sacred feast.
But Achilles prays that North Wind and noisy West Wind
205 come, and he promises beautiful sacrificial offerings
so that you might rouse the fire to burn where lies Patroklos,
whom all the Achaeans bemoan."

           So speaking, Iris went off,
and the two winds arose with a wondrous ruckus, driving
the clouds in rout before them. Quickly they came to the sea,
210 and they blew upon it, and a wave swelled-up beneath
their strident blast. The two winds came to Troy with its rich soil,

and they fell on the pyre, and the fire cried out a loud
and wondrous cry. All night long the winds beat together
on the flames of the fire, blowing shrilly. And all night
long swift Achilles, taking a two-handled cup, poured wine   215
that he took from a golden bowl to the ground, and the ground grew wet
as he mourned for the breath-soul of wretched Patroklos.
As a father weeps over the bones of his newly wed son
as he burns them, the son who in death brought sore pain
to his parents, even so Achilles wept, scrambling around the pyre,   220
groaning deeply.

              At the hour when the morning star goes forth
announcing new light over the earth, and after it Dawn comes
in her robe of saffron and spreads over the sea, so the flames
of the pyre grew faint, and then it ceased. The winds went
back again, returning to their home over the Thracian sea,   225
which surged and roared with swollen flood.

                            Then the son
of Peleus withdrew from the pyre to one side and he lay down,
exhausted, and sweet sleep came over him. But those who
were with the son of Atreus gathered in a crowd and their noise
and the uproar of them as they came near woke him up.   230
Then Achilles sat up straight and spoke to them, saying:
"Son of Atreus and you other captains of the Achaeans—
first extinguish all the fire with flaming wine, wherever
the fire is still strong. Then let us gather together the bones
of Patroklos, son of Menoitios. It will be easy to tell them from others   235
because they lie in the middle of the pyre, whereas the other corpses
were burned at the edge, where you'll find mixed bones of horse
and man. Then let us place the bones in a golden dish
wrapped in double layers of fat until the time when I myself
will be bidden to the house of Hades. I do not ask you to labor   240
to build a large tumulus, only one that is appropriate.
You Achaeans can build it high and wide later, you who
will remain behind, after me, in the ships with many benches."

      So he spoke, and they obeyed the swift-footed son of Peleus.
First they extinguished the fire with flaming wine, as far   245
as the flame had reached, and the ash had settled deep. Weeping
for their gentle comrade, they gathered up the white bones
into a golden dish and wrapped them in a double layer of fat.
Then they placed them in the hut, covering the bones with
a linen cloth. Then they drew the circle of the mound and set up   250

around the circumference of the pyre a base of stones. They piled
on a mound of earth. After piling up the grave, they went away.

But Achilles called his people together and had them sit down
where they were, in a broad assembly, and he brought prizes out
255 of his ships—cauldrons and tripods and horses and mules
and many head of cattle, and women with slender waists,
and gray iron.

[Line 258 to the end of the book are omitted. Achilles hosts funeral games in Patroklos'
honor.]

BOOK 24. *The Ransom of Hector*

[Lines 1–454 are omitted. Achilles drags Hector's body around the tomb of Patroklos every morning, but Apollo preserves its pristine appearance. Apollo persuades the other gods to order the release of Hector's body. Thetis goes to Achilles and he agrees. The messenger goddess Iris goes to Priam and he prepares a generous ransom. With Hermes' help, Priam in company with his herald Idaios crosses at night into the Achaean camp. Then:]

Hermes went off toward high Olympos. 455
Priam leaped from the chariot to the ground. He left Idaios
there to hold the horses and the mules. Then the old man
went straight toward the house where Achilles dear to Zeus
was accustomed to sit. He found him there, and his companions,
who sat apart. Only two, the warriors Automedon and Alkimos 460
of the breed of Ares, busily waited on him. Achilles
had just finished his meal, eating and drinking. The table
still stood by his side. The aides did not notice great Priam
as he came in. Standing nearby, he took Achilles' knees
in his hands, and Priam kissed the terrible man-killing 465
hands that had taken so many of his sons. As when a painful
madness takes hold of a man and he kills someone
in his homeland, then comes to another people, to the house
of a rich man, and wonder takes hold of those who see him—
even so Achilles was amazed when he saw godlike Priam. 470
And the others were amazed too and glanced at one another.

Making supplication, Priam spoke to Achilles:
"Remember your own father, O Achilles like to the gods!
He is old like I am, on the wretched threshold of old age.
Probably those who live around him are wearing him down, 475
and there is no one to ward off ruin and disaster.
But at least he rejoices in his heart when he hears that you
are alive, and he hopes every day that he will see his dear
son returning from Troy. But I have received an evil fate,
because I fathered many sons who were the best in broad 480
Troy, but of them I do not think that any remain.
I had fifty sons when the sons of the Achaeans came, nineteen

FIGURE 24.1 **King Priam begs Achilles for the body of Hector.** The old man, leaning on his staff, approaches from the left. Behind him slaves carry the ransom. Achilles lies on his inlaid couch, holding a knife with which he has been cutting up the meat served on the table in front of the dining couch; strips of meat hang down over the side of the table, and he holds a strip in his left hand. He has not yet noticed Priam's presence and he turns over his shoulder to call out to a slave boy to pour wine from a jug he holds. His shield (with Gorgon's head), helmet, shin guards, and sword hang from the wall. Beneath the couch lies Hector, his body pierced by many wounds. This is the most commonly represented scene from the *Iliad* in all Greek art. Red-figure Athenian drinking cup. c. 480 BC.

from one woman, the others from women in the palace.°
Though they were many, the fury of Ares has driven
most of them to their knees. And he who was left   485
to me, who by himself protected the city and those within it—
you have just killed him as he struggled to defend his homeland:
Hector! On his account I have come to the ships of the Achaeans
to ransom him from you. I bring boundless ransom.
So respect the gods, Achilles, and take pity on me,   490
remembering your own father. For I am far more to be pitied
than he—I who did what no man on earth has ever dared
to do: to stretch the hands of my son's killer to my mouth."

     So Priam spoke, and he stirred in Achilles a great urge
to weep for his own father. Taking Priam by the hand   495
he gently pushed the old man away. And so the two men
thought of those who had died. Priam wept copiously for Hector
the killer of men, as he groveled before the feet of Achilles.
And Achilles cried for his own father and now, again, for Patroklos.
Their wailing filled the hut.   500

                    But when valiant Achilles
had his fill of wailing, and the desire for it had departed
from his heart and limbs, immediately he rose from his seat.
He raised up the old man with his hand, taking pity on his white
head and his white beard, and he spoke words that went like arrows:
"Yes, you wretched man, truly you have suffered many evils   505
in your heart. How did you dare to come alone to the ships
of the Achaeans beneath the eyes of the man who killed your many
fine sons? Your heart must be iron! But come, sit on a chair.
We will let our sufferings lie quiet in our hearts, though burdened
by them. There is nothing to be gained from cold lament.   510

     "For so have the gods spun the thread for wretched
mortals—to live in pain, while they are without care.
Two jars of gifts that he gives are set into the floor of Zeus,
one of evils, the other of good things. To whomever
Zeus who delights in the thunder gives a mixed portion,   515
that man receives now evil, now good. But to the man
to whom he gives only pain, he has made him to be roughly
treated, and ravening hunger drives him over the shining
earth. He walks dishonored by gods and by men.

---

483   *palace*: Of Priam's fifty sons, twenty-two are mentioned by name in the *Iliad*. Two died before the poem
      begins, eleven die during the course of the poem, and the remaining nine are named earlier in this book.

520 "So the gods gave to Peleus wonderful gifts
from birth. He exceeded all men in wealth and riches,
and he ruled over the Myrmidons, and the gods gave him
a goddess for a wife, although he is mortal. But to him
the god also gave evil, because in his halls there is no
525 offspring who will one day rule. He fathered a single child,
doomed to an early death. And I will not tend him
when he grows old, for I sit here in Troy very far
from my homeland, bringing misery to you and your children.

"And yet, old man, we hear that in earlier times
530 you were rich—all the territory between Lesbos out to sea,
the seat of Makar,° and inland to Phrygia, and to the boundless
Hellespont. They say that you, old man, surpassed in wealth
and in the number of your sons all those that lived in these lands.
But from the time that the dwellers in heaven brought you
535 this curse, there is always fighting around your city, and the
killing of men. Bear up! Don't be complaining forever in your heart.
It is no use to bemoan your son, for he will never live again,
no matter what you do."

Then the old man godlike
Priam answered him: "Please don't ask me to sit on a chair,
540 O Achilles, fostered by Zeus, so long as Hector lies among
the ships without the proper care due to the dead. But release
him quickly so that I may see him with my own eyes. Take
the abundant ransom that I have brought you. May you enjoy
these things, and may you come to the land of your fathers,
545 for from the first you have let me remain alive and behold
the light of the sun."

Then looking angrily from beneath his brows
Achilles the fast runner spoke: "Don't you rile me, old man!
I fully intend to let you have Hector. My mother came to me
as a messenger from Zeus, she who bore me, the daughter
550 of the Old Man of the Sea. And I know full well in my heart,
O Priam, nor does it escape me, that some god has led
you to the swift ships of the Achaeans. For no mortal would
dare come to the camp, no, not even one very young. And he
would not escape the notice of the guards, nor would he easily
555 open the bolts of our gates. Therefore, do not stir more of wrath
in me, or perhaps I will *not* spare you within the huts, old man—

---

531 *Makar*: A legendary colonist of Lesbos, also called Makaria after him.

even though you are a suppliant—and so transgress the commands
of Zeus."

　　　Thus Achilles spoke, and the old man was afraid,
and did what he said. Then the son of Peleus sprang forth from
the house like a lion, and he was not alone, for with him   560
followed two of his aides, the warriors Automedon and Alkimos,
whom he honored above all his companions after the dead
Patroklos. They unharnessed the horses and the mules
from the yoke, and they led in the herald, the crier of the old man,
and they set him on a chair. They took down from the well-polished   565
car the boundless ransom for Hector's head. They left two cloaks
and a finely woven shirt so that Achilles could wrap the corpse
and free him to be taken home. Then Achilles summoned
two slave girls to wash the body and anoint it, moving it
to the side so that Priam could not see his son and in his grief   570
be unable to restrain his anger if he saw him, and Achilles'
own heart be then roused to anger so that he killed Priam
against the strict command of Zeus.

　　　　　　　When the slave girls
had washed the body and anointed it with olive oil, they put
a beautiful cloak and a shirt around him. Achilles himself   575
raised Hector up and placed him on a bier. Together with
his aides, Achilles then lifted him into the polished wagon.

　　　And then Achilles groaned and called out to his companion
by name: "Don't be angry, Patroklos, if you learn, though you are
in the house of Hades, that I have given up the valiant Hector   580
to his dear father. He brought a proper ransom, and I will
give you as many as is fitting of the things he brought."

　　　So he spoke, and then glorious Achilles went back into his hut.
He sat on the inlaid chair on the opposite wall from which
he had arisen, and he spoke to Priam: "Your son is given back,   585
old man, just as you requested. He lies on a bier. At dawn
you will see him when you take him from here. Now let us
think of food.

　　　　　　"Even Niobê with the lovely hair
thought of food. Twelve were her children who perished
in her halls, six daughters and six lusty sons. Apollo killed   590
the boys with his silver bow, for he was angry at Niobê,
and Artemis, who rejoices in arrows, killed the girls.

For Niobê had matched herself with their mother, Leto
with the lovely cheeks. Niobê said that Leto had borne
595 two children, but she herself had given birth to many. And so,
Apollo and Artemis, though they were only two, killed all
of Niobê's children. For nine days they lay in their gore, and
there was no one to bury them, for the son of Kronos had turned
the people into stones. But on the tenth day the heavenly gods
600 buried them, and Niobê bethought herself of food, for she was
wasting away with her weeping.

                    "Now somewhere amid
the rocks, in the lonely mountains on Sipylos, where they say
the beds of goddesses are, the divine nymphs who dance
around the Acheloös river—there, although she is a stone,
605 she broods over her agonies sent by the gods.°
                             "So come,
good old man, let us also think of food. Then you can bewail
your dear son, when you have carried him to Ilion. He will
cost you many tears."

                So Achilles spoke. Then he
sprang up and slaughtered a white sheep. His companions
610 flayed it and prepared it in accordance with custom.
They cut it up and skillfully threaded the pieces on spits.
They roasted them carefully, then drew them all off.
Automedon took up bread and set it around the table
in beautiful baskets, while Achilles shared out the meat.
615 Then they put out their hands to take the good things set out
before them.

       When they had put the desire for drink and food from
themselves, then Priam the son of Dardanos wondered at Achilles—
how tall he was and of what bearing. For he was like the gods
to look on. And Achilles wondered at Priam, the son of
620 Dardanos, beholding his fine face and hearing his words.

       When they had had their fill looking at each other,
then the old man Priam like a god spoke first. "Let me now

---

605   *by the gods*: The origins of the story must come from a rock image carved on Mount Sipylos, in LYDIA, northeast
of SMYRNA, the water on its face likened to the tears of Niobê (a daughter of Tantalos). Such an image has been
discovered: It is a Hittite carving of a mother goddess, probably Cybele, c. 1300 BC. The famous river Acheloös
is in AETOLIA in southwest mainland Greece, but evidently there was another river of this name in Lydia.

to bed as soon as possible, O Zeus-nourished one, so that
we might lie down and be renewed in sweet sleep.
For sleep has not yet fallen upon my eyes and beneath their lids from   625
the time that my son lost his life at your hands. Always,
I have been crying and nursing my ten thousand pains,
rolling through excrement in the closed spaces of the court.
But now I have tasted food and let flaming wine pass down
my throat. Before, I ate nothing."   630

                              He spoke, and Achilles ordered
his companions and his slave girls to set up a bed in the portico
and to spread out beautiful purple blankets, and on top to place
coverlets, and to place on top of all woolen cloaks for clothing.
The girls went outside the hut holding torches in their hands,
and in haste they quickly spread two beds.   635

                              Achilles, the fast runner,
now spoke mockingly° to Priam: "You sleep outside, dear
old man, in case some counselor of the Achaeans comes in.
They are always sitting down and taking counsel, as is only right.
But if someone should see you through the swift black night,
he might at once tell Agamemnon shepherd of the people   640
and then there would be delay in ransoming the corpse.

"But come now, and tell me truly, how many days
will you need to bury valiant Hector properly? For so long
I will myself hold back from the fight and I will restrain the others."
The old man Priam like a god then answered him: "If you really   645
want me to accomplish the burial of valiant Hector, then you
should do this, and it would please me greatly, O Achilles.
You know how we are pent-up in the city—it is far to bring wood
from the mountains, and the Trojans are very afraid. But we
would mourn his body for nine days in the halls, and on the tenth   650
we would bury him and the people would feast. On the eleventh day
we will make a tumulus for him. On the twelfth day we will fight
again, if we must."

                    Then brave Achilles, the fast runner,
said to him: "It will be as you say, old man Priam. I will suspend
the war for as long as you say."   655

---

636 *mockingly:* Perhaps because Achilles suspects that Priam will use sleeping outside under the portico as an
      opportunity to return to Troy, as in fact he does.

So speaking he took hold of the old
man's right hand by the wrist,° so that he would not be
afraid. Then they lay down to sleep in the forecourt of the house,
the herald and Priam, with hearts of wisdom in their breasts.
But Achilles slept in the innermost part of his well-built hut,
660 and beside him lay Briseïs of the beautiful cheeks.

      The other gods and men, the masters of chariots,
slept all the night long, overcome by gentle sleep.
But sleep did not come over Hermes the helper as he pondered in his mind
how he would guide King Priam forth from the ships, unseen
665 by the holy keepers of the gates.° Hermes stood over
Priam's head and spoke: "O old man, you must have
no thought of anything evil, if you still sleep in the midst
of the enemy simply because Achilles has spared you.
So you have ransomed your son, and you gave a high price.
670 But your remaining sons would pay three times as much
to have you back alive if Agamemnon, the son of Atreus,
should know that you are here, and all the Achaeans knew it too."

      So he spoke and then the old man was seized by fear.
He roused his herald. Hermes yoked the horses and the mules
675 for them, and swiftly Hermes drove them through the camp—
no one recognized them! But when they came to the ford
of the fair-flowing river, of the whirling Xanthos that deathless
Zeus had fathered, Hermes went off to high Olympos.
Saffron-robed dawn was spreading out over all the earth as they
680 drove the horses to the city, and the mules carried the corpse.
Nor did any other man or fine-belted woman recognize them,
except Kassandra, like golden Aphrodite, who had gone up to
Pergamos and saw her dear father standing in the car, and
the herald, the city-crier.°

                  Seeing Hector lying in the bier drawn by
685 mules, she cried out shrilly and called throughout the entire city:
"Trojan men and women, come and see Hector, if you ever rejoiced
when he returned alive from the battle, a great joy to the city
and to all the people!"

---

656 *by the wrist*: A gesture of reassurance.
665 *holy keepers of the gates*: "holy" because of the seriousness of their role.
684 *the city-crier*: Pergamos is the highest point of the city. Kassandra is mentioned only once elsewhere.
      Homer says nothing specific about Kassandra's prophetic powers, an important part of the later tradition,
      although her role as the crier of sad news may imply such powers.

So she spoke, and no man or woman
stayed in the city. An unbearable sorrow came over all, and they
gathered around Priam at the gates as he brought in the corpse.   690
First of all Hector's dear wife and his revered mother threw
themselves on the light-running wagon and tore their hair,
holding Hector's head, while the throng stood around and wept.
And they would have spent all day until the sun went down
weeping and wailing for Hector in front of the gate, if the old   695
man had not stood up in the car and spoken to the people:
"Make a way for the mules to pass through! Later you can have
your fill of lament, when I have brought him to the house."
So he spoke, and they stood aside and allowed the wagon
to come through. When they came to his famous house, they placed   700
Hector on a corded bed, and beside them they set singers, leaders
of the lament, who began the song of mourning. They chanted it,
and the women made lament.

                       Among them white-armed Andromachê
led the dirge for Hector, the killer of men, holding his head
in her hands: "O my husband, you have perished at a young age,   705
and left me a widow in our halls. Our child is still an infant,
whom we bore, you and I, doomed to a wretched fate. But I don't think
he will arrive at manhood—before that this city shall be utterly
destroyed. For you who watched over the city have perished—
you, who guarded it and kept safe its noble wives and little   710
children. Soon they will be carried away in the hollow ships,
and I among them. You, my child, will follow along with me
to a place where you will perform degrading tasks, working
for some ungentle master—or one of the Achaeans in his anger
will take you by the arm and throw you from the walls   715
to a savage death—someone whose brother Hector killed,
or his father, or his son.° For full many of the Achaeans have bitten
the vast earth with their teeth at the hands of Hector. Your father
was not gentle in the bitter war. And so the people wail for him
throughout the city, and you have made grief and unspeakable   720
sorrow for your parents, Hector. Savage pain is left for me
above all. You did not reach out your hands as you lay dying
on a bed, nor did you say to me some words full of meaning
that I might remember while weeping for you day and night."

---

717   *his son*: According to later tradition, Andromachê becomes the captive and concubine of Neoptolemos, the
     son of Achilles. Astyanax, the son of Hector and Andromachê, is thrown from the towers.

725 So she spoke, wailing, and the other women wailed too.
Among them Hekabê began her sobbing complaint: "Hector,
much the dearest to my heart of all my children . . . while
you were alive you were dear to the gods. And they still
care for you, although you are snared in the fate of death.
730 Achilles, the fast runner, sold others of my sons whom
he captured beyond the untiring sea, to SAMOTHRACE and IMBROS
and misty LEMNOS. When he took your breath-soul with
his long-edged bronze, he used often to drag you around the tomb
of his companion Patroklos, whom you killed. But he could not
735 raise him up. Now you are as fresh as new-morning dew and lie
out in my halls like one freshly killed—like one whom Apollo
of the silver bow has come upon and killed with his gentle arrows."

So she spoke, weeping, and she roused endless wailing.
Then Helen, third among the women, began her lament:
740 "Hector, much the dearest to my heart of all my brothers-in-law,
for my husband is godlike Alexandros who brought me to Troy—
would that I had perished before! It is already the twentieth
year since I went forth from there and abandoned the land
of my fathers. But I never heard an evil or unkind word
745 from you. And if some other of my brothers-in-law, or sisters-in-law,
or brother's wives with elegant dresses would reprove me
in my halls, or your mother—but your father was always
as gentle as if he had been my own father—you would restrain
them with your speech, and hold them back through your good
750 nature and your gentle words. And so I lament you, and I lament
my luckless self, with grief in my heart. For no longer
is there anyone in Troy so gentle to me and such a friend.
Everyone abhors me!"

So she spoke, weeping, and the huge
throng moaned. And now old man Priam spoke to the people:
755 "Bring wood to the city, my Trojans. Have no fear of a cunning
ambush. When Achilles sent me off from the black ships,
he promised he would do us no harm until the twelfth day
has come."

So he spoke, and they yoked oxen and mules
to wagons, and quickly they gathered in front of the city.
760 For nine days they gathered a boundless supply of wood.
But when the tenth Dawn, who sends light for mortals, arose,
they carried out the brave Hector, pouring down tears.
They placed him on top of the pyre, and they cast in fire.

As soon as Dawn with her fingers of rose appeared, the people
gathered around the pyre of the Hector. When they   765
were gathered and assembled in a group, they first extinguished
the fire with flaming wine—all of it, as deep as the vast strength
of the fire had penetrated. Thereafter his brothers and companions
gathered the white bones in sorrow. Hot tears ran down their
cheeks. They took the bones and placed them in a golden chest,   770
covering them with delicate purple cloths. Then they placed
the chest in a hollow grave, and over the grave stacked great
thick stones. Quickly they built up a barrow, and all around it
they placed watchmen, in case the Achaeans with their fancy
shin guards should set on them before the end of the truce.   775
After they heaped up the barrow, they went back to the city.
Gathered together, they dined on a splendid meal
in the house of Zeus-nourished Priam, the king. In this way
they held the funeral for Hector, tamer of horses.

Selections from the *Odyssey*

Sing to me of the resourceful man, O Muse, who wandered
far after he had sacked the sacred city of Troy. He saw
the cities of many men and he learned their minds.
He suffered many pains on the sea in his spirit, seeking
to save his life and the homecoming of his companions.   5
But even so he could not save his companions, though he wanted to,
for they perished of their own folly—the fools! They ate
the cattle of Helios Hyperion,° who took from them the day
of their return. Of these matters, beginning where you want,
O daughter of Zeus, tell to us.   10

                  Now all the rest
were at home, as many as had escaped dread destruction,
fleeing from the war and the sea. Odysseus alone
a queenly nymph, Kalypso,° a shining one among the goddesses,
held back in her hollow caves, desiring that he become
her husband. But when, as the seasons rolled by, the year came   15
in which the gods had spun the threads of destiny
that Odysseus return home to ITHACA, not even then
was he free of his trials, even among his own friends.

    All the gods pitied him, except for Poseidon.
Poseidon stayed in an unending rage at godlike Odysseus   20
until he reached his own land. But he had gone off
to the Aethiopians° who live faraway—the Aethiopians
who live split into two groups, the most remote of men—
some where Hyperion sets, and some where he rises.
There Poseidon received a sacrifice of bulls and rams,   25
sitting there and rejoicing in the feast.

               The other gods
were seated in the halls of Zeus on Olympos. Among them

---

8 *Helios Hyperion*: In other poets Hyperion, "going over," is a Titan, the father of Helios, but Homer uses
     Hyperion as an epithet of the sun-god.

13 *Kalypso*: "concealer," evidently Homer's invention.

22 *Aethiopians*: "burnt-faced," usually taken to refer to Africans living in a never-never land at the edge of the world.

the father of men and gods began to speak, for in his heart
he was thinking of bold Aigisthos, whom far-famed Orestes,
30   the son of Agamemnon, had killed. Thinking of him,
he spoke these words to the deathless ones: "Only consider,
how mortals blame the gods! They say that from us
comes all evil, but men suffer pains beyond what is fated
through their own folly! See how Aigisthos pursued
35   the wedded wife of the son of Atreus, and then he killed
Agamemnon when he came home, though he well knew
the end. For we spoke to him beforehand, sending Hermes,
the keen-sighted Argeïphontes,° to say that he should not kill
Agamemnon and he should not pursue Agamemnon's wife.
40   For vengeance would come from Orestes to the son of Atreus,
once Orestes came of age and wanted to reclaim his family land.
So spoke Hermes, but for all his good intent he did not persuade
Aigisthos' mind. And now he has paid the price in full."

     Then the goddess, flashing-eyed Athena, answered him:
45   "O father of us all, son of Kronos, highest of all the lords,
surely that man has fittingly been destroyed. May whoever
else does such things perish as well! But my heart
is torn for the wise Odysseus, that unfortunate man,
who far from his friends suffers pain on an island surrounded
50   by water, where is the very navel of the sea. It is a wooded
island, and a goddess lives there, the daughter of evil-minded
Atlas, who knows the depths of every sea, and himself
holds the pillars that keep the earth and the sky apart.
Kalypso holds back that wretched, sorrowful man.
55   Ever with soft and wheedling words she enchants him,
so that he forgets about Ithaca. Odysseus, wishing to see
the smoke leaping up from his own land, longs to die. But your
heart pays no attention to it, Olympian! Did not Odysseus
offer you abundant sacrifice beside the ships in broad Troy?
60   Why do you hate him so, O Zeus?"°

                    Zeus who gathers the clouds
then answered her: "My child, what a word has escaped the barrier
of your teeth! How could I forget about godlike Odysseus,

---

38   *Argeïphontes*: An ancient and obscure epithet of Hermes, usually taken to mean "killer of the monster
Argos," but explicable in other ways as well.

60   *... O Zeus*: The Greek for "hate" is *ôdusaô*, punning on Odysseus' name. In fact the etymology of *Odysseus* is
unknown; it is probably preGreek. In many later sources it is written *Olysseus*, giving rise to the Latin *Ulysses*.

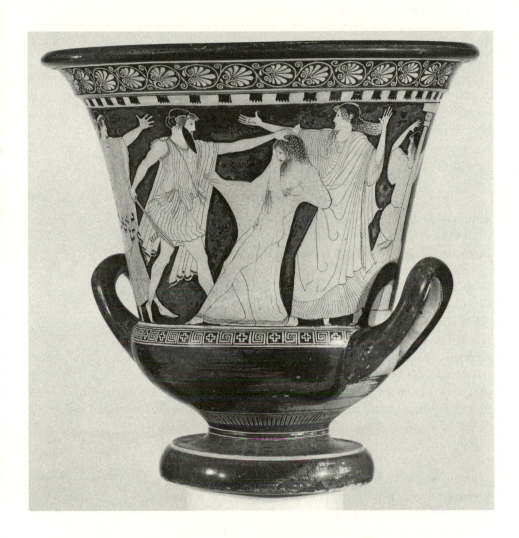

FIGURE 1 Aigisthos kills Agamemnon. Aigisthos holds Agamemnon, covered by a diaphanous robe, by the hair while he stabs him with a sword. Apparently this illustration is inspired by the tradition followed in Aeschylus' *Agamemnon*, where the king is caught in a web before being killed. Klytaimnestra stands behind Aigisthos, urging him on, while Agamemnon's daughter attempts to stop the murder (she is called Elektra in Aeschylus' play). A handmaid flees to the far right. Athenian red-figure wine-mixing bowl, c. 500–450 BC.

who is superior to all mortals in wisdom, who more than any other
has sacrificed to the deathless goes who hold the broad heaven?
65 But Poseidon who holds the earth is perpetually angry with him
because of the Cyclops,° whose eye he blinded—godlike
Polyphemos, whose strength is greatest among all the Cyclopes.
The nymph Thoösa bore him, the daughter of Phorkys°
who rules over the restless sea, having mingled with Poseidon
70 in the hollow caves. From that time Poseidon, the earth-shaker,
does not kill Odysseus, but he leads him to wander from
his native land. But come, let us all take thought of his homecoming,
how he will get there. Poseidon will abandon his anger!
He will not be able to go against all the deathless ones alone,
75 against their will."

        Then flashing-eyed Athena, the goddess,
answered him: "O our father, the son of Kronos, highest
of all the lords, if it be the pleasure of all the blessed gods
that wise Odysseus return to his home, then let us send Hermes
Argeïphontes, the messenger, to the island of Ogygia, so that
80 he may present our sure counsel to Kalypso with the lovely tresses,
that Odysseus, the steady at heart, need now return home.
And I will journey to Ithaca in order that I may the more
arouse his son and stir strength in his heart to call the Achaeans
with their long hair into an assembly, and give notice to all the suitors,
85 who devour his flocks of sheep and his cattle with twisted horns,
that walk with shambling gait. I will send him to SPARTA and to sandy
Pylos to learn about the homecoming of his father, if perhaps
he might hear something, and so that might earn a noble fame
among men."

        So she spoke, and she bound beneath her feet
90 her beautiful sandals—immortal, golden!—that bore her
over the water and the limitless land together with the breath
of the wind. She took up her powerful spear, whose point
was of sharp bronze, heavy and huge and strong,
with which she overcomes the ranks of warriors when she is angry
95 with them, the daughter of a mighty father. She descended
in a rush from the peaks of Olympos and took her stand
in the land of Ithaca in the forecourt of Odysseus, on the threshold

---

66 *Cyclops*: "round-eye," though Homer never says that Cyclops has but a single eye.

68 *Phorkys*: Probably a preGreek sea deity, like Proteus or Nereus.

of the court. She held the bronze spear in her hand, taking on
the appearance of a stranger, Mentes, leader of the Taphians.°

There she found the proud suitors. They were taking their pleasure,   100
playing board games in front of the doors, sitting on the skins
of cattle that they themselves had slaughtered. Heralds°
and busy assistants mixed wine with water for them
in large bowls, and others wiped the tables with porous sponges
and set them up,° while others set out meats to eat in abundance.   105

Godlike Telemachos° was by far the first to notice
her as he sat among the suitors, sad at heart, his noble
father in his mind, wondering if perhaps he might come
and scatter the suitors through the house and win honor
and rule over his own household. Thinking such things,   110
sitting among the suitors, he saw Athena, and he went straight
to the outer door, thinking in his spirit that it was a shameful thing
that a stranger be allowed to remain for long before the doors.

Standing near, he clasped her right hand and took the bronze
spear from her. Addressing her, he spoke words that went   115
like arrows: "Greetings, stranger! You will be treated kindly
in our house, and once you have tasted food, you will tell us
what you need!"

So speaking he led the way, and Pallas Athena°
followed. When they came inside the high-roofed house,
Telemachos carried the spear and placed it against a high column   120
in a well-polished spear rack where were many other spears
belonging to the steadfast Odysseus. He led her in and sat her
on a chair, spreading a linen cloth beneath—beautiful,
elaborately-decorated—and below was a footstool for her feet.
Beside it he placed an inlaid chair, apart from the others,   125
so that the stranger might not be put-off by the racket and fail

---

99 *Taphians*: Elsewhere in the *Odyssey* the Taphians are pirates and slave traders, living in some distant com-
    munity. *Mentes* means "advisor," like the later *Mentor*, the disguised Athena who accompanies Telemachos
    on his travels.

102 *heralds*: Heralds were free-born, but of a lower social class than the aristocratic suitors whom they serve,
    performing all kinds of subordinate functions.

105 *set them up*: In Homer's world tables are not permanent furniture but are set up on folding legs when eating,
    a little like "TV tables."

106 *Telemachos*: "far-fighter," presumably named from his father's excellence as an archer.

118 *Pallas Athena*: The meaning of *Pallas* is unknown, but is often interpreted as "brandishing" (from Greek *pallô*).

to enjoy his meal, despite the company of insolent men.
Also, he wished to ask him about his absent father.

130   A slave girl brought water for their hands in a beautiful
golden vessel, and she set up a polished table beside them.
The modest attendant brought out bread and placed it before them,
and many delicacies, giving freely from her store. A carver
lifted up and set down beside them platters with all kinds
of meats, and set before them golden cups, while a herald
135 went back and forth pouring out wine.

   In came the proud suitors, and they sat down in a row
on the seats and chairs, and the heralds poured out water for
their hands, and women slaves heaped bread by them in baskets,
and young men filled the wine-mixing bowls with drink.
140 The suitors put forth their hands to the good cheer lying before them,
and when they had exhausted their desire for drink and food,
their hearts turned toward other things, to song and dance.
For such things are the proper accompaniment of the feast.
A herald placed the very beautiful lyre in the hands of Phemios,°
145 who was required to sing to the suitors. And he thrummed the strings
as a prelude to song.

         But Telemachos spoke to flashing-eyed Athena,
leaning his head in near so that the others would not hear:
"Dear stranger, will you be angry for what I say? These gatherings
are their sole concern, the lyre and epic song, especially,
150 and they devour without penalty the substance of another—
of a man whose white bones rot in the rain, lying on the land,
or a wave of the sea rolls them about. If they ever saw him
return to Ithaca, every man of them would soon pray
to be swifter of foot, not richer in gold or cloth!

155   "But as it is, my father has died a wretched death,
nor is there any comfort for us, even if perhaps some one
of the men who live on the earth were to say that he would
come. The day of his return is gone.

             "But come, tell me
and say it truly—who are you among men, and where
160 do you come from? Where is your city and your parents?
On what kind of ship did you arrive? How did sailors

---

144 *Phemios*: "the man rich in tales," a speaking name, as are the names of many minor characters in Homer.

bring you to Ithaca? Who did they say that they were?
For I don't think that you came here on foot! Tell me this truly,
so that I may know—whether this is the first time that you
have come here, or whether you are a guest-friend° of my father.   165
For many were the men who came to our house. He was
widely traveled among men."

        The goddess, flashing-eyed Athena,
answered him: "I will truthfully tell you all. I am Mentes,
the son of wise Anchialos, and I rule over the Taphians,
lovers of the oar. Now, as you see, I have come with a ship   170
and my companions, sailing on the wine-dark sea to men
of foreign speech, to Temesa after copper, and I bring
shining iron. My ship is beached far from the city in a field,
near the harbor of Rheithron beneath wooded Neion.° We say
that we are guest-friends of one another from a long ways back,   175
even as our fathers were. If you want, go to the old warrior
Laërtes, and ask him. They say that he no longer comes
to the city, but that he suffers pains far away in a field
attended by an old woman as his servant, who places before him
food and drink when fatigue has taken hold of his limbs   180
as he creeps along the hill of his vineyard. Now I have come.

  "They said that your father was among his people,
but now I see that the gods prevent
his return. But godlike Odysseus has not yet perished
from this earth! He is still alive, held back on an island in the broad   185
sea surrounded by water. Savage men confine him,
wild men who hold him all unwillingly.

        "But now I will
utter a prophecy that the deathless ones put into my mind,
and I think it will come to pass, though I am no prophet
nor one wise in the flight of birds. He will not be absent   190
much longer from his father's land, not even if iron chains
should hold him! He will figure out how to return, for he is
a resourceful man.

---

165   *guest-friend*: A guest-friend (*xeinos*) is someone from outside the community who has exchanged gifts
      (*xeineïa*) to establish a lasting association of friendship and support (*xeinia*). *Xeinia* is inherited, it passes from
      one generation to the next. Much of the *Odyssey* is concerned with *xeinia*, its observation and crass violation.

174   ...*Neion*: *Temesa* is probably a port on the west coast of southern Italy; *Rheithron* and *Neion* are unknown.

"But come tell me this and say it truly,
if, being so tall, you are the son of Odysseus himself?
195 In your head and your beautiful eyes you seem amazingly like him,
for we often communed together before he went off to Troy,
where others too, the best of the Argives, went in their hollow ships.
Since that day I have not seen Odysseus, nor has he seen me."

Then the shrewd Telemachos answered her: "I will tell you
200 the whole truth, stranger. My mother says that I am
his child, but I'm not so sure. No man ever knows
for sure who his own parents are. Would that I was the son
of some favored man who grew old among his own possessions!
As it is, they say that I am the son of the most ill-fated
205 of mortal men—since you ask."

Then the goddess, flashing-eyed Athena,
answered him: "But surely the gods have made your lineage
famous for the times to come, seeing that Penelope°
has borne you such as you are! But come, tell me this,
and speak truly—what is this feast, what is this crowd?
210 What is your need of it? Is this a drinking-party, or a wedding?
Obviously this is no potluck. These men appear to act insolently,
partying with arrogance throughout your house. It's enough
to make a man of sense ooze anger if he came among them,
seeing these shameful acts."

Then the shrewd Telemachos
215 answered her: "Stranger, because you ask me these things
and inquire so, you should know that this house once was rich
and fine, so long as that man was among his people. But now
the evil-devising gods have wished otherwise. They have made
that man invisible above all men. I would not grieve so much for his death
220 if he had fallen among his companions in the land of the Trojans,
or in the arms of his friends—once he had reeled up the thread of war.°
All the Achaeans would then have made a tomb for him,
and he would have won great fame for his son, too, in the days
to come. But as it is, the storm-winds have snatched him away,
225 without report. He is gone from sight and out of hearing, and has left
me only pain and weeping. And I do not weep and wail
for him alone, because the gods have devised other pains for me.

---

207 *Penelope*: Seemingly from a Greek word meaning "duck." In Chinese and Russian folklore ducks are
        famous for their marital fidelity, but there is no trace of this tradition in Greece.

221 *thread of war*: The metaphor depends on weaving. You wind up the ball of thread once the task is completed.

All the leading men who rule over those islands—
DOULICHION and SAMÊ and wooded ZAKYNTHOS° and they
who lord it over rocky Ithaca—all of them are suitors   230
to my mother, and they ravage the household. She neither refuses
the hateful marriage nor can she get rid of them once and for all.
And they consume my substance. Before long they will bring me to ruin!"

    Pallas Athena indignantly answered him: "Yes, surely
you are in need of absent Odysseus, who would surely   235
lay hands on these shameless suitors. Would that he were here now,
standing before the outer doors of his house with his helmet
and shield and two spears, just as when I first saw him
in my house, drinking and taking his pleasure when he had come
from Ephyra and the house of Ilos, the son of Mermeros.°   240
Odysseus went there on a swift ship to get a man-killing poison
so that he might dip his bronze arrows in it, but Ilos would not give
it to him. He feared the anger of the gods who never die.
My father gave the poison to him, because he loved him very much.
Would that Odysseus appeared with such strength in the midst   245
of these suitors, I say! They would find a bitter and abrupt
end to their courtship!

                    "All of this rests on the knees
of the gods, whether or not he will return and take revenge
in his halls. But I urge you to consider how you can drive the suitors
from your halls. Come now, give me your ear, and listen   250
to my words . . . Tomorrow call the Achaean warriors
to an assembly and speak out your word to all, and may the gods
be your witness. As to the suitors, urge them to scatter each
to his own house. As to your mother, if she is minded to marry,
let her go back to the house of her powerful father. There they   255
will prepare a wedding and make ready the abundant gifts,
as much as is appropriate to go with a beloved daughter.

    "As for you, I will give you some good advice, if you will listen:
Fit out a ship with twenty oarsmen, the best you can find.

---

229 *Zakynthos:* Samê is probably KEPHALLENIA, where there is still a town called Samê. In the Catalog of
     Ships in the *Iliad*, Doulichion is not in Odysseus' realm, but is ruled by one Meges. Probably Zakynthos is
     the modern LEUKAS. See MAP V.

240 *. . . Mermeros:* Many places were named Ephyra, but this Ephyra seems to be in Thresprotia (it is not
     Corinth, as in the Iliadic story of Bellerophon, *Il.* Book 6). Ilos is a nonentity not mentioned elsewhere. His
     father Mermeros was a son of Jason and Medea.

260 Go and find out about your father who has long been away,
if some mortal will tell you. Or you may hear a voice from Zeus,
which most often brings news to men. Go first to PYLOS
and inquire of godlike Nestor, and from there go to Sparta
to blonde-haired Menelaos. He was last of the Achaeans
265 who wear shirts of bronze to return to his house. If you hear
that your father is alive and coming home, then, though
you are hard-pressed, you can hold out for a year. If you hear
that he is dead and no longer among the living, then return to your
native land and heap up a mound and make appropriate funeral
270 offerings, as many as is fitting, and give your mother to a husband.°
And when you have accomplished these things and done them,
then take counsel in your heart and mind how you will kill
the suitors in your halls, either by a trick or openly. It is not right
that you act as a child, for you are no longer a youth! Have you not
275 heard what fame godlike Orestes won among all men when he killed
the father's killer, the treacherous Aigisthos, who killed
his famous father? And you, my friend—for I see
that you are handsome and tall—be valiant so that many
of those who will live after will speak well of you.

280   "But now I will go down to my swift ship and to my
companions, who I think are impatient waiting for me. But you
give heed to my words, and pay them careful attention."

     Then the shrewd Telemachos answered her: "Stranger, truly
you have said these things with a friendly mind, as a father to his son,
285 and I won't forget them. But wait now—stay a moment, though
you wish to be on your way, so that you might have a chance to bathe
and to satisfy your heart to the fullest. Then I will give you a gift,
and you may be off on your ship, rejoicing in your heart—
a costly gift, very beautiful, which will be an heirloom to you
290 from me, such as guest-friends give to other guest-friends."

     Then the goddess, flashing-eyed Athena, answered him:
"No, don't hold me back, for I am eager to continue my journey.
As for the gift that your heart bids you give—give it to me
when I return, to carry to my home, and choose a very beautiful one.
295 I will bring you a similar one in return."

---

270 *to a husband*: It is not clear how this part of Mentes' advice accords with his earlier suggestion that
Telemachos send his mother back home to Sparta for her father Ikarios to marry her off, as many
commentators have complained. Probably Mentes/Athena is speaking casually, throwing out one idea after
another without thinking the whole plan through. Being a goddess in disguise, Mentes/Athena knows of
course that Odysseus is alive and will soon return, but being in disguise she cannot reveal this.

FIGURE 1.2 **Orestes kills Aigisthos.** With his right hand, a young, beardless Orestes (he is labeled), wearing armor, plunges a sword into Aigisthos' already wounded chest while with his left hand Orestes holds the bearded Aigisthos by his long hair. Aigisthos sits on a fancy chair and a cloth covers his lower body. To the left, Klytaimnestra tries to run away. Athenian red-figure, two-handled jug, c. 500 BC.

So speaking, flashing-eyed Athena

went off, flying upward as a bird. And she placed strength and daring
in Telemachos' heart. She made him think of his father more even
than he had been. In his mind he took account of her leave-taking
and he was amazed, realizing that she must be a god.

300 Immediately he went among the suitors, a man like a god.
A famous singer was performing before them, and they sat
in silence and listened. The singer sang of the miserable return
of the Achaeans that Pallas Athena imposed on them
as they headed home from Troy.° The clever Penelope, daughter
305 of Ikarios, heard the wonderful song from her chamber up above,
and she went down the high stairway from her room—not alone,
but two maids followed along behind. When the fair lady
came down to the suitors, she stood beside a pillar of the hall,
so well-constructed, holding a shining veil before her cheeks.
310 A faithful handmaid stood on either side.

Then in tears she spoke

to the divine singer: "Phemios, you know many other things
that are charming to mortals, the doings of men and gods
that singers make famous. So sing one of these as you sit there,
and let them drink their wine in silence. But cease from this
315 sad song, which ever tears at the heart in my breast. For a sorrow
never to be forgotten has come on me especially. I desire
and think upon the head of that dear man whose fame
is abroad throughout HELLAS and mid-ARGOS."°

Then the shrewd

Telemachos answered her: "My dear mother, why do you not let
320 the loyal singer bring pleasure in whatever way his mind
urges him to? Singers are not to blame, but I think it is
Zeus who is to blame! He gives to men who live
on grain just as he wishes. It is no cause for anger
if this man sings of the evil fate of the Danaäns.° Men praise
325 that song more which comes freshest to the audience.
Let your heart and spirit dare to listen. Not only

---

304 *from Troy*: Athena sponsored the Achaeans forces at Troy but she was outraged by Oïlean Ajax's rape of
Kassandra as she clung to the idol of Athena, according to later tradition. The *Odyssey* seems to refer to this
incident here.

318 *Hellas and mid-Argos: Hellas* is a territory near Achilles' realm in southern THESSALY, hence "northern Greece";
mid-Argos would be southern Greece, or the PELOPONNESUS: The whole phrase means "all of Greece."

324 *Danaäns*: Used interchangeably with *Achaeans* and *Argives*.

Odysseus lost in Troy the day of his homecoming,
but many other men perished. So go to your chamber
and busy yourself with your own tasks, your loom and distaff,°
and order your handmaids to do their own work.   330
Speech is man's concern, for every one of us, and especially
for me, because the authority in this house is mine!"

Amazed, Penelope went back to her room, for she took
to heart her son's wise speech. Going then into her upper chamber
with her slaves, she bewailed Odysseus, her dear husband,   335
until flashing-eyed Athena cast sweet sleep upon her eyes.

The suitors broke into an uproar throughout the shady halls,
and every one of them prayed that he might lie by her side.
Then shrewd Telemachos began to address them: "Suitors
of my mother, though you are insolent, let us now take pleasure   340
in the feast. But let there be no brawling. It is a good thing
to hear a singer such as this one, whose voice is like that
of the gods. But in the morning let us take our seats in the assembly,
all of us, so that I may declare my views to you outright—
that you depart from these halls! Make up other feasts, devour   345
your own possessions, changing from house to house.
If you think it is better and preferable to destroy the substance
of one man with impunity—go ahead and do it! But I will call
upon the gods who live forever, in case Zeus may grant
that you be punished for your acts. Then you would all perish here   350
without remedy!"

So he spoke, and all the suitors bit their lips in astonishment,
for he had spoken boldly. Then Antinoös,° the son of Eupeithes, spoke
to him: "Telemachos, surely the gods themselves are teaching you
to be a man of boastful tongue and to speak boldly! May the son
of Kronos never make you the chief in Ithaca surrounded by the sea,   355
though it is your right by birth."

Then shrewd Telemachos answered him:
"Antinoös, will you be angry at what I am saying? I would be willing
to accept even this chieftainship from the hand of Zeus. Do you think
that is the worst thing that can happen to a man? It is not a bad thing

---

329   *distaff*: The distaff was a stick held between the chest and upper arm at the end of which the wool was
       bunched for spinning.

352   *Antinoös*: "hostile," the ringleader among the suitors. His father is Eupeithes, "very persuasive," the last
       man to die in the poem (Book 24).

360 to be chief. Your house becomes rich right away and you are held
in highest honor. But there are many other chiefs of the Achaeans
in Ithaca, surrounded by the sea, young and old. One of these may have
this position, for godlike Odysseus is dead. But I will be the chief
of my own house and of the slaves that godlike Odysseus won in his raids!"

365   Then Eurymachos,° the son of Polybos, answered him: "Telemachos,
well, these things lie on the knees of the gods, who will be chief
of the Achaeans on Ithaca surrounded by the sea. As for your possessions,
you may have them and rule over your own house! May that man
never come who takes away your possessions by violence so long
370 as men still live on Ithaca! But, my excellent fellow, I would like
to ask about this stranger—whence does he come? From what land
is he? Where are his kinsmen and his ancestral fields?
Does he bring some news of your father's return, or does he come here
with his own purpose in mind? How he leaped up and was gone!
375 He did not wait for us to become acquainted with him. And yet
he did not seem in any way to be a base man to look upon."

        The shrewd Telemachos answered him: "Eurymachos, the homecoming
of my father is no more. I no longer believe in any news, no matter
where it comes from, nor do I put any faith in some prophecy
380 that my mother may learn from a seer when she has called him into the hall.
This stranger is a guest-friend of my father, from Taphos. He says
that he is Mentes, the son of wise Anchialos, and that he is lord
of the Taphians who love to row." So spoke Telemachos,
though in his heart he had recognized the deathless goddess.

385   Now the suitors turned to the dance and to pleasant song,
and they made merry, and they partied until the evening should come.
As they made merry, the dark night fell upon them. Then
each man went to his own house to take his rest. Telemachos
went to his chamber built in the very beautiful court,
390 lofty, in a place of broad outlook. He went up to bed there,
turning over many things in his head.

                    Wise and faithful
Eurykleia went with him, the daughter of Ops, son of Peisenor,
carrying blazing torches. Once Laërtes had purchased
her with his wealth, though he was still very young.

---

365 *Eurymachos*: Also a leader among the suitors.

He gave the price of twenty cattle,° and he honored Eurykleia   395
in his halls as he honored his faithful wife. But Laërtes never slept
with her, avoiding the anger of his wife.

                                    It was she who carried
the blazing torches for Telemachos. Of all the female slaves
she loved him the best, and she had nursed him when he was
a child. He opened the doors of the well-built chamber   400
and sat down on the bed. He took off his soft shirt and placed it
in the hands of the wise old woman. She folded the shirt
and smoothed it out, then hung it on a peg beside the corded bed.
Then she left the chamber, shutting the door by its silver
handle. She drove the bolt home with its strap. There,   405
all night long, wrapped in a woolen blanket, he pondered
in his mind the journey that Athena had shown him.

[Books 2 and 3 are omitted. Telemachos calls an assembly of all the Ithacans. He announces that he is fed up with the suitors' depredations and that somebody should do something about it. Telemachos requests a ship to sail in quest of his father. After taking stores from the palace, he escapes that night with the help of Athena, who takes on the form of a certain Mentor.

As in a flash, the boat with Athena/Mentor, Telemachos, and followers appears on the shore of Pylos where King Nestor is performing a great sacrifice to the god Poseidon. Telemachos asks Nestor if he knows anything about his father. He does not, but sends Telemachos inland to visit Menelaos, in case he may know something. Telemachos and Peisistratos, the son of Nestor, travel by chariot to Sparta, where Menelaos resides.]

---

395   *cattle*: A high price. Eurykleia's father and grandfather are named because she is evidently of high birth, no
        doubt captured by pirates.

BOOK 4. *Telemachos in Sparta*

[Lines 1–107 are omitted. Telemachos and Peisistratus come to Sparta on the very day that Hermionê, Helen's only child, and a bastard son of Menelaos are to marry in a double wedding ceremony. Telemachos is at first unrecognized in Sparta, but he sheds tears at the mention of Odysseus.]

While Menelaos was pondering these tears in his heart and in his spirit,
　　Helen came out from her fragrant high-roofed chamber,
110　like Artemis of the golden distaff.° Adrastê set up a well-made
chair for her, and Alkippê carried a rug of soft wool,
and Phylo carried a silver basket, which Alkandrê, the wife
of Polybos, had given her. She lived in Egyptian THEBES°
where the most wealth lies in men's houses. Polybos
115　gave to Menelaos two silver bathtubs, two tripods, and ten talents
of gold.° In addition his wife gave Helen very beautiful gifts:
a golden distaff and a wheeled basket made of silver,
its rim finished with gold. This the female slave Phylo now
brought, stuffed with finely spun yarn, and sat down beside her.
120　Across it a distaff was laid, loaded with dark violet wool.

　　Helen sat down in the chair, and below was a footstool
for her feet. At once she questioned her husband on every matter:
"Do we know, Menelaos nourished of Zeus, who these men
say that they are who have come to our home? Shall I make up
125　a story or speak the truth? My heart urges me to speak. I have
never seen anyone so like another, neither man nor woman—

110　*distaff*: It is not clear why Artemis should be associated with weaving because she is a goddess of the
　　fecundity of the wild.

113　*Thebes*: The splendid capital of New Kingdom EGYPT about 400 miles south of modern Cairo. The name
　　is a puzzle: none of the Egyptian names for this city sounds like "Thebes." Apparently it was so called in
　　Greek by analogy with the seven gates of Boeotian THEBES in Greek myth; the pylons—ceremonial temple
　　gateways in Egyptian Thebes—are to this day astounding for their size and magnificence. Homer's knowl-
　　edge of Egypt is vague, based on rumor. All the names of Egyptians given in this and following passages
　　(except Thôn) are Greek.

116　*...talents of gold*: None of these gifts is typically Egyptian. Tripods were highly valuable Greek artifacts
　　made usually of bronze; important examples from the eighth century BC have been found dedicated at the
　　sanctuary to Zeus at Olympia. *Talent* means "balance," that is the scale that measured out a certain portion.
　　In Homer only gold was measured in talents, but the weight of a Homeric talent is unknown. In classical
　　times, a talent was an enormous amount of money.

FIGURE 4.1 Helen and Menelaos. Menelaos (the figures are labeled off the picture) wears a helmet and breast-guard. His right hand is poised on top of a shield while his left, holding a spear, embraces Helen. She wears a cloth cap and a necklace with three pendants and a bangle around her arm. Her cloak slips down beneath her genital area, emphasizing her sexual attractiveness. Decoration on the back of an Etruscan mirror, c. 4th century BC.

amazement holds me as I look! Why this man looks *just like*
the son of great-hearted Odysseus, Telemachos, whom that man
left as a newborn child in his house when on my account—
130 bitch that I am!—the Achaeans went up under the walls
of Troy, laying down ferocious war..."

                        Light-haired Menelaos
answered her: "Yes, now I see the resemblance, wife,
as you point out the likeness. Why his feet and hands are just the same
as that man's, and the cast of his eyes, and his head and his hair above!
135 And just now when I was talking about Odysseus, and was telling
about all the pain and suffering that he endured for my sake—
why, he let a bitter tear fall from beneath his brows, holding up
his purple cloak before his eyes."

                        Peisistratos, the son of Nestor,
answered him: "Menelaos, son of Atreus, nourished by Zeus,
140 leader of the people, truly this *is* the son of that man,
just as you say. But he is a prudent man, and feels in his heart
that it is wrong to come before you and to make a show
of uninvited speech, in whose voice we take delight as in a god's.
But the horseman Gerenian Nestor sent me forth to come
145 with him as a guide. Telemachos wanted to see you
so that you could tell him of some word or deed. For a son
has many sorrows in his halls when his father is away,
when there are no others to help him, even as now Telemachos'
father is gone, and there are no others among the people
150 who might ward off ruin."

                        In reply to him light-haired Menelaos said:
"Well, wonderful! The son of a man much-beloved has come
to my house, a man who suffered many trials on my account.
I always thought that if he returned I would treat him best
among all the Argives, if Zeus whose voice is borne afar
155 gave us two a homecoming in our swift ships over the salt sea.
And in Argos I would have given him a city to live in, and built
him a house, leading him out of Ithaca with all his possessions,
and his son, and all his people—cleaning out one city
among those that lie nearby and obey me as their chief.
160 Then living here we would often have got together,
and nothing would have kept us apart, entertaining one another
and taking delight, until the black cloud of death engulfed us.
But I suppose that some god was jealous of this, who to that
wretched man alone gave no day of return."

So he spoke,
and he stirred all to a desire for lament. Argive Helen, daughter   165
of Zeus, wept. Telemachos wept, and Menelaos, the son
of Atreus, too. Nor was the son of Nestor able to keep
from weeping. In his heart Peisistratos thought of his handsome
brother Antilochos, whom the brilliant son of Dawn° had killed.

Thinking of him, Peisistratos spoke words that went   170
like arrows: "Son of Atreus, old man Nestor always said
that you were wise above all men, whenever you were mentioned
in our halls as we questioned one another. And now, if it is
in any way possible, listen to me, for I take no joy
in weeping during mealtime, and soon early dawn will be here.   175
I see no wrong in weeping for a mortal who has died
and met his fate. In fact, this is the only prize we give
to miserable mortals—to cut our hair and let a tear fall
from our cheeks. For my brother has died, and in no way was he
the worst of the Argives. You must know about him. I never met him   180
nor saw him, but they say that Antilochos was better than all
the rest, superior in both speed of foot and in battle."

Light-haired
Menelaos then answered him: "My friend, you have spoken such
as a wise man would say and do, even one that was older than you.
You are your father's son, and so you speak with wisdom.   185
It is easy to recognize the offspring of a man to whom
the son of Kronos spins out the thread of good fortune, both
when he is born and when he marries. Even so he has given
to Nestor throughout all his days that he reach a fine old age
in his halls, and that his sons should be clever and valiant with the spear. 190

"But we will give up this weeping that we have indulged in.
Let us think again of dinner, and let them pour water over our hands.
At dawn there will be stories for Telemachos and me to tell one
another at length!"

So he spoke, and Asphalion, the busy follower
of glorious Menelaos, poured out water over their hands.   195
They put forth their hands to the delightful refreshment lying
before them. Then Helen, the daughter of Zeus, had another idea.
At once she cast a drug into the wine they were drinking,

---

169   *son of Dawn*: Memnon, important in postHomeric stories about the Trojan War. Achilles' killing of
    Memnon is often represented on Greek pots.

to quiet all pain and anger and bring forgetfulness of evils.
200 Whoever would drink this down once it was mixed in the bowl
would not in the course of that day shed a tear from his cheeks—
not if his mother and father should fall down dead, nor if
before his eyes a brother or a beloved son should be stabbed
to death and he should see it with his own eyes. The daughter of Zeus
205 had such cunning drugs, healing drugs, which Polydamna had given her,
the wife of Thôn,° an Egyptian woman. In Egypt the bountiful
earth grows the best drugs, many that are healing when mixed,
and many that are deadly. For there every man is a doctor,
learned above all men: They are of the race of Paieön.°

210   After she had cast in the drug, and urged them to pour forth
the wine, at once she answered and said: "Menelaos, son Atreus,
nourished of Zeus, and you who are here, children of noble men—
now the god Zeus gives good and now evil, for he can do
all things—well, sit in our halls and feast and take delight
215 in telling tales. I will myself tell a story suited to the occasion.

    "I could tell all the labors of Odysseus of the steadfast heart,
and what a thing that mighty man dared to do in the land of the Trojans,
where the Achaeans suffered such pains. Raking his body
with cruel blows and throwing a cloth about his shoulders,
220 looking like a slave, he entered the broad-wayed city
of the enemy. He hid himself, looking like another man,
a beggar, such as there were none in the Greek camp.

    "In this likeness he entered the city of the Trojans, and no one
recognized him. I alone saw through his disguise, and I questioned him.
225 In his cleverness he avoided me. But when I was bathing him
and rubbing him with olive oil,° and putting clothes on him, and swearing
a great oath not to expose him as Odysseus among the Trojans
before he returned to the swift ships and the huts—then he told me
all the plans of the Achaeans. After he had killed many Trojans
230 with his long sword, he returned to the Argives, bringing back
much information.

---

206 ... *Thôn*: The only name that appears to be Egyptian: Thôn was a place in the delta. *Polydamna* means
     "much-conquering." The drug is often thought to be opium, but there is no evidence that opium was ever
     added to wine.

209 *Paieön*: A healing god, later identified with Apollo (but Apollo has limited healing functions in Homer).

226 *olive oil*: A function usually reserved for the female slaves of a house, here surprisingly performed by
     Helen herself. Helen of course tries in her story to show herself as a fifth column, working secretly for the
     Achaean cause.

"Then the other Trojan women shrilly wailed,
but my spirit rejoiced. Already my heart was turned to go
back home! I groaned or the blindness that Aphrodite gave me
when she led me there, far from the beloved land of my fathers,
abandoning my child and my wedding chamber and my husband,   235
a man who lacked nothing, either in wisdom or looks."

                              Light-haired
Menelaos then said in reply: "Yes, wife, surely you have spoken
rightly! Before this I have come to know the council and mind
of many fighting men, and I have traveled the wide earth, but not ever
did my eyes behold a man such as was Odysseus of the steadfast heart.   240
Why, what a thing that powerful man daringly performed
in the wooden horse, where all the best men of the Argives were seated,
bringing death and fate to the Trojans! Then you came out there.
I suppose some spirit urged you, who wished to give the Trojans glory—
and handsome Deïphobos° followed along with you. Three times   245
you went around the hollow ambush, feeling it with your hands,
and you called by name the chieftains of the Danaäns, making your
voice like that of the wives of all the Argives. Now Diomedes, the son
of Tydeus, and I, and Odysseus, were sitting in the middle of the men
and heard how you called out. Diomedes and I were eager   250
to rise up and come out, or else to answer right away from inside.
But Odysseus held us back, he prevented us, although we were eager
to go. All of the other sons of the Achaeans kept silent, but Antiklos°
alone wanted to answer your call. Odysseus continually
squeezed his jaws tight with his powerful hands, and so saved   255
all the Achaeans. He held him in this fashion until Pallas
Athena led you away."

                    The shrewd Telemachos
said in reply: "Menelaos, son of Atreus, nourished of Zeus,
leader of the people—it is really all the sadder! For in no way
did any of this deflect grievous destruction from him,   260
not even if the heart within him had been of iron. But come,
send us off to bed, because it is through sweet sleep that
we can take our pleasure in rest."

                    So he spoke, and Argive Helen
ordered the female slaves to set out beds in the portico

---

245 *Deïphobos*: A brother of Hector with whom Helen took up after the death of Paris, according to
     postHomeric tradition.

253 *Antiklos*: Not mentioned in the *Iliad*.

FIGURE 4.2 The Trojan Horse and Greek soldiers.   One of the earliest certain representations of Greek myth. The Greeks look out from little windows in the body of the wheeled horse, one holding out his shield, another a scabbard with sword. Some Greeks have climbed out of the horse. A warrior with two spears and shield walks on top of the horse and three other warriors walk on the ground. Other scenes on the pot show the rape of women, the killing of children, and general mayhem. Relief from the neck of an earthenware amphora, c. 640 BC, from Mykonos.

and to lay on beautiful purple blankets, and to spread covers 265
on top, and on these to place woolen cloaks to wear.
The slaves went out of the hall carrying torches in their hands,
and they set up the beds, and a herald led out the guests. And so
they slept there in the fore-hall of the house, the prince Telemachos
and the glorious son of Nestor. The son of Atreus slept in an inner 270
chamber of the high house. Beside him Helen with the long gown
took her rest, matchless among women.

When early born Dawn
spread out her fingers of rose, Menelaos, good at the war cry,
rose from his bed. He put on his clothes and around his shoulders
he cast his sharp sword. He bound his beautiful sandals beneath 275
his shining feet and went forth from the chamber like a god.
He sat down beside Telemachos, and he spoke, calling his name:
"What need brings you here, Prince Telemachos, to shining Lacedaemon
over the broad back of the sea? Is it a public matter, or private?
Tell me the truth." 280

The shrewd Telemachos then answered him:
"Menelaos, son of Atreus, nourished of Zeus, leader of the people,
I come here in the hope that you might give me some news
of my father. My home is being eaten up, my rich farm lands
are going to ruin, and my house is filled with men who devour
my herds of sheep and cattle with shambling walk—the suitors 285
of my mother—powerful, insolent men. I come now to your knees
on this account, to see if you might be willing to relate to me
his miserable death. Perhaps you saw it with your own eyes
or heard from another the story of his wanderings. For his mother
bore him to be wretched above all others. Please, don't sweeten 290
your words out of respect or pity for me, but tell me straight
how you came to behold him. I beg you, if ever my father, the noble
Odysseus, promised you anything in word or deed and fulfilled
it in the land of the Trojans, where the Achaeans suffered pains—
be mindful of these things, and tell me the truth." 295

Greatly grieved,
light-haired Menelaos then answered him: "Well, they want
to sleep in the bed of a man valiant of heart, they who are
themselves base cowards! As when a deer has lain down
her newborn suckling fawns to sleep in the lair of a mighty lion,
then gone to explore the mountain slopes and the grassy valleys 300
seeking pasture, and then the lion comes to his lair and on the two
fawns lets loose a cruel doom—even so Odysseus

will loose cruel doom on these men. I wish, O father Zeus,
and Athena and Apollo, that with such strength that he had
when he rose up in rivalry in well-settled Lesbos and wrestled
Philomeleïdes° and threw him powerfully, and all the Achaeans
rejoiced—I wish that in such strength Odysseus might deal
with the suitors! Then would they all be destroyed, and bitterly
married! But as for this matter that you ask and inquire about,
I will not shade the true story to speak of other things, nor will
I deceive you. Of all that the unerring Old Man of the Sea
told me, I will not hide or conceal one word.

                          "The gods
had held me in Egypt, though I was eager to return here,
because I did not perform the sacrifices that guarantee fulfillment.
The gods require that we be always mindful of their commands.
Now there is an island in the surging sea outside of Egypt,
and they call it Pharos,° as far as a hollow ship runs
in a full day's sail when a stout wind blows behind her.
There is a harbor there, a good place to put into land,
from where men launch well-balanced ships into the sea
once they have drawn a supply of black water. The gods
held me there for twenty days. No breezes arose that
blow over the deep, that speed men over the broad back
of the sea. And all the stores and the strength of my men
would have been spent then, except some god took pity on me
and saved me—Eidothea,° the daughter of the powerful Old Man
of the Sea. I had moved her heart above all others.

   "She met me as I wandered alone, apart from my companions
who were sauntering about the island fishing with bent hooks
as hunger tore at their stomachs.° Standing next to me
she spoke and addressed me: 'Are you such a fool, O stranger,
and poor in understanding? Or are you deliberately so neglectful?
Do you take pleasure in suffering pain? You are penned-up
in this island for a long time, and you cannot find a sign
of your deliverance. And the hearts of your companions grow faint.'

---

306 *Philomeleïdes*: This story is otherwise unknown, as is Philomeleïdes.

317 *Pharos*: An Egyptian name, *pr-hr*, "the house of Horus." It is the name of an island just a few hundred yards from the coast, the site of the famous lighthouse of Alexandria, not a full day's sail.

326 *Eidothea*: Probably "the knowing goddess," unattested elsewhere and no doubt Homer's invention.

330 *stomachs*: Normally Homeric warriors ate roasted flesh, not fish (in reality, the Greeks always ate a lot of fish).

"So she spoke, but I said in reply: 'I will speak out
and tell you, whoever you are among goddesses, that I am not
held here willingly. I must have offended the deathless ones
who live in the broad sky. So tell me—for you gods
know all things—who of the immortals ties me up here   340
and hinders my journey? Tell me of my homecoming,
how I might go over the fishy deep.'

                "So I spoke,
and the beautiful goddess immediately replied: 'Well
stranger, I will tell you everything straight out.
The Old Man of the Sea used to come here, the deathless   345
Proteus° of Egypt, the servant of Poseidon who knows
all the depths of the sea. They say that he is my father,
they say he begot me. If somehow you could lie in ambush
and capture him, he might tell you of your way, the measure
of your path, and of your homecoming—how you might   350
cross the fishy sea. And surely he will tell you, O Zeus-nourished
one, if you want to know, what evil and what good
has been done in your halls while you have been away
on your cruel long journey.'

             "So she spoke, and I said
in reply: 'Can you yourself think of a way I might ambush   355
the divine old man so that he will not see me in advance
and, seeing my purpose, avoid me? That is a tough project,
for a mortal to overcome a god!'

              "So I spoke, and the beautiful
goddess answered at once: 'Well, stranger, I will tell you exactly.
When the sun comes into the middle of the sky, then the unerring   360
Old Man of the Sea comes forth from the salt sea beneath
the breath of West Wind, hidden in a black ripple. He comes
out and takes his rest in a hollow cave and, around him,
seals, the offspring of the beautiful daughter of the sea,
sleep in a bunch, coming forth from the gray water,   365
exhaling the bitter smell of the deep salt sea. I will take
you there at the break of dawn and lay you down in a row—
you select three of your companions who are the best
in your well-benched ships.

            " 'I will tell you all the tricks
of this old man. First he will count the seals, going over them all.   370

---

346 *Proteus*: Probably "prophetic god."

Then, when he has counted them off by fives and seen them,
he will lie down in their midst like a shepherd among his flocks
of sheep. As soon as you see that he is asleep, then
may you be filled with strength and courage. Hold him
375 down there, though he will be vigorous, striving to escape.
He will try everything, taking on the form of all creeping things
on the earth, and of water, and wondrous blazing fire.
But hang on!—be unshaken and grip him still more tightly.

     " 'When at last in his own form—in the shape he had when you
380 saw him lie down to sleep—he will speak and question you.
Then, my warrior, give up your violence and let the old man go.
Ask him who of the gods is oppressing you so much,
and ask him about your homecoming, how you might cross
over the fishy sea.'

                    "So speaking, Eidothea plunged beneath
385 the surging sea. Then I went off to the ships, where they stood
in the sand, and many things my heart pondered darkly
as I went. But when I came to the ship and the sea,
we made ready a meal, and the refreshing night came on.
Then we lay down to sleep on the shore of the sea.

390   "When early-born Dawn spread out her fingers of rose,
I went along the shore of the sea with its broad ways,
praying mightily to the gods, and I took with me three companions
whom I trusted most in any circumstance. In the meanwhile,
the goddess had plunged beneath the broad bosom of the sea
395 and brought forth four skins of seals from the deep. All were newly
flayed, for she devised a trick against her father. She had scooped
out beds in the sea sand and sat there, waiting. We came very near her,
and she had us lie down in a row. Then she covered each one
of us with a skin. Our ambush would have been most terrible,
400 for the horrible stench of the sea-bred seals afflicted us
awfully—for who would lie down with a monster of the deep?—
But she saved us and devised a great relief: She brought
ambrosia and placed it beneath the nose of every man.
The ambrosia had a very sweet fragrance and stifled the smell
405 of the seals.

          "So throughout the entire morning we waited
with resolute hearts, and, finally, the seals came out
of the sea. They lay down in a row along the shore. At midday
the old man came out of the sea and saw the fat seals.

He went over all of them and counted their number.
Among the number of the beasts he counted us first, and he never   410
suspected in his heart that there was trickery in the works.

"Then he himself lay down, and we rushed on him
with a shout and threw our arms around him. But the old man
did not forget his clever wiles. First he became a lion with
a splendid mane, then a snake and a leopard, then a huge sow.   415
He became a stream of cold water, then a tree—high and leafy.
However, we hung on with steady heart, never flinching.

"The old man grew tired, though skilled in his destructive arts.
Then he spoke and questioned me: 'Who of the gods, O son
of Atreus, has concocted this plan—that you seized me against   420
my will while I was asleep? And what do you want?'

"So he spoke, but I said in answer: 'You know, old man!
Why do you try to put me off with this question?
How long am I stuck on this island? I can find no sign
of deliverance and my heart grows faint within me.   425
But please tell me—for the gods know all things—who
of the deathless ones ties me up here and delays my journey
and my homecoming, that I might travel over the fishy deep?'

"So I spoke, and right away he answered me:
'Well now, you should have made appropriate sacrifice   430
to Zeus and to the other gods before setting out,
so that you might have arrived as quickly as possible to the land
of your fathers, sailing over the wine-dark sea. It is not
your fate to see your friends and to arrive at your finely built
house and to the land of your fathers before you return   435
to the Zeus-nourished waters of Egypt,° and there perform
appropriate sacrifice to the deathless gods who inhabit
the broad sky. And then the gods will give you the journey
that you desire.'

"So he spoke, but my heart was shaken
within me because he commanded me again to go   440
over the misty deep to Egypt, a long and hard road.
Nonetheless, I answered him: 'I will do these things, old man,
just as you say. But come, tell me this and tell it straight:
Did all the Achaeans whom Nestor and I left when

---

436 *Egypt:* Homer does not know the name of the Nile river, but calls the river Egypt.

445　we set out from Troy come home safe in their ships?
　　Or did any perish by a cruel death on his ship
　　or in the arms of his friends, once he had rolled up
　　the thread of war?'

　　　　　　　　"So I spoke, and right away he answered me:
　　'Son of Atreus, why do you ask me these things?
450　There is no need to know, or to learn my mind. I don't
　　think you will be without tears long when you have
　　heard it all. Many of them were killed, and many survived.
　　Of the captains, two alone of the Achaeans who wear shirts
　　of bronze perished on their way home—as for what happened
455　on the field of battle, you were there yourself. And one,
　　I think, is still alive, held back on the broad sea. Ajax, son
　　of Oïleus, was overcome in his ships with their long oars.
　　Poseidon first drove him on the great Gyraean Rocks,
　　but saved him from the sea. Although Athena hated him,
460　he would have escaped his doom if he had not spoken an insolent
　　word in his great blindness of heart.° He said that he had escaped
　　the great gulf of the sea in spite of the gods. Poseidon
　　heard his boastful speech, and right away he took his trident
　　in his powerful hands and struck the Gyraean Rocks,
465　splitting them in half. One half stayed in place, but the other half
　　on which Ajax was then sitting dropped into the sea, for
　　he fell into blindness. It carried him down into the boundless
　　restless deep, and so he died, when he had drunk the briny water.

　　　"'As for your brother Agamemnon, he fled the fates
470　and escaped in his hollow ships. The revered Hera saved him.
　　But when he was about to reach the steep height of CAPE MALEA,
　　a storm wind caught him and drove him, moaning deeply,
　　over the fishy deep to the border of the land where Thyestes
　　used to live in earlier times, but where now Aigisthos,
475　Thyestes' son, lived. But when a safe return from there was showed
　　Agamemnon, and the gods changed the course of the winds,
　　and he reached home, then he stepped out on the land of his fathers

---

461　… *blindness of heart*: Ajax, the son of Oïleus, or Little Ajax, was a Locrian and unrelated to Big Ajax, the
　　son of Telamon, who ruled over Salamis, though they often fought together. After the sack of Troy, Oïlean
　　Ajax raped Kassandra as she clung to a statue of Athena, so incurring the goddess's wrath (see Figure 4.3).
　　The Gyraean ("round") Rocks were usually placed in the CYCLADES north of MYKONOS, but later tradition
　　places them at Kaphareus at the southeast promontory of EUBOEA. The word translated "blindness" here
　　and in line 467 is *atê* (a-tā) a word of unknown etymology that means the force that leads one to act in ways
　　that prove disastrous, or sometimes it refers to the disaster itself.

FIGURE 4.3 **Oïlean Ajax rapes Kassandra.** Kassandra clings to an idol of Athena. The idol holds a shield and spear and wears a helmet. Kassandra has on only a flimsy gown, exposing her nakedness. The helmeted Oïlean Ajax is "heroically nude" but carries a spear and shield with the blazon of the forepart of a horse. His left foot stands outside the frame of the picture. Because of this outrage, Oïlean Ajax is destroyed on his homeward journey. Athenian red-figure wine cup, by the Kodros Painter, c. 440 BC.

with joy.° Laying hands on the land, he kissed it, and many
hot tears poured from him, so welcome the land appeared.

480   "'But a lookout whom crafty Aigisthos had placed there,
promising him a reward of two talents of gold—that lookout
saw Agamemnon. So that he would not pass by unseen
and invoke his furious valor, the watchman went straight
to the house, to the shepherd of the people, to tell what
485 he had seen. Right away Aigisthos worked out a treacherous plan.
Choosing twenty of the best men throughout the land,
he set up an ambush. On the other side of the hall he ordered
that a feast be prepared. Then he went with chariot and horses
to summon Agamemnon, the shepherd of the people, intending
490 a foul deed. Thus he brought him up unaware of his doom.
He killed him after he had dined, as one kills an ox
in its stall. Not one of the comrades who followed the son
of Atreus survived, and not one of Aigisthos' men,
but they were all killed in his halls.'

               "So he spoke, and my heart
495 was crushed within me. I sat down on the sand and wept.
I no longer wanted to live and see the light of the sun.
But when I was sated with weeping and writhing around,
then the unerring Old Man of the Sea said to me:
'Do not, O son of Atreus, weep for a long time without end.
500 We achieve nothing by it. But strive as quickly as is possible
to return to the land of your fathers. You may find Aigisthos
alive, or perhaps Orestes will have already killed him,
and you may come upon his funeral feast.'

               "So he spoke,
and my heart and manly spirit were again warmed in my breast,
505 in spite of my anguish. I spoke and said words that went
like arrows: 'Of these men now I know. But what is the name
of the third man who is held back alive on the broad sea,
or else is dead? I would like to know, even though I am distressed.'

     "So I spoke, and right away he answered: 'The son
510 of Laërtes, who lives in Ithaca. I saw him on an island, pouring
down hot tears in the halls of the nymph Kalypso, who holds
him by force. He cannot come to the land of his fathers, for he

---

478   ...*with joy*: It is hard to sort out the topography of this passage. If Agamemnon was making for the Argolid,
it is strange that he should come near Cape Malea, the southernmost tip of the Peloponnesus (although that
is where storm winds regularly blow ships off course, including Odysseus'). Usually storm winds blow ships
to the south, but in this case they would have to blow north. The passage also seems to imply that Thyestes
lived somewhere in the south, perhaps in Sparta, but at this time he was living in Mycenae, in the north.

has no oared ships and companions who might send him
on his way across the broad back of the sea.

                      " 'But for you,
O Menelaos, it is not ordained that you die and meet your fate   515
in horse-pasturing Argos, but the deathless ones will send you
to the Elysian fields at the ends of the earth, where
light-haired Rhadamanthys° lives, where life is easiest for men.
No snow, nor heavy storm, nor rain, but always does Ocean°
send up breezes of the shrill-blowing West Wind to refresh men.   520
For you have Helen to wife and you are the son-in-law of Zeus.'

   "So saying, Proteus plunged beneath the surging sea,
and I went off to the ships and my godlike companions, and my heart
darkly pondered many things as I went. When I came to the ship
and the sea, we prepared our meal. Refreshing night came on   525
and we lay down to sleep on the shore of the sea.

                   "When early born
Dawn appeared and spread out her fingers of rose,
we dragged our ships into the shining sea. We set up the masts
and the sails in the well-balanced ships. We got in the ships
and sat down on the benches. Sitting in a row, we struck   530
the gray sea with our oars. I sailed back to the waters of Egypt,
the river fed by Zeus, and moored my ships there. Then we
performed sacrifices sure to bring fulfillment. When we had put
an end to the anger of the gods who live forever, I heaped up
a mound to Agamemnon so that his fame might be everlasting.   535
Having done this, I sailed away. The deathless ones
gave me a good wind. They sent me quickly to the land
of my fathers.

    "But come, stay awhile in my halls, until the eleventh
or twelfth day. Then I will send you on your way with honor, . . .

*[Lines 540–784 are omitted. Menelaos gives Telemachos a beautiful bowl as a gift-token.
Meanwhile, back on Ithaca, the suitors plot to murder Telemachos when he returns. They
arrange an ambush.]*

---

518 . . . *Rhadamanthys*: Probably a preGreek Cretan name. The notion of the Elysian Fields, so contrary to the
     Greek dark and cheerless House of Hades, is also probably Cretan, though it may derive ultimately from
     Egypt. *Elysian*, if it is Greek, might mean "struck by lightning," because any place or person struck by
     lightning was considered to be blessed. Menelaos is promised entrance to this paradise not because he has
     led a good life, but because of his family connections.

519 *Ocean*: Ocean is a river that runs around the world. The word is probably not Greek but Semitic. Ocean is
     the husband of Tethys, probably a Greek form of the Mesopotamian Tiamat, the primordial waters from
     which the world has sprung. Likewise Ocean is the "origin of gods" (*Il.* Book 14), and also the origins of all
     "rivers, springs, the sea, and wells" (*Il.* Book 21).

BOOK 5. *Odysseus and Kalypso*

Dawn arose from her bed beside the noble Tithonos°
in order to bring light to the deathless ones and to mortals.
The gods were sitting in council, and among them was Zeus
who thunders on high and whose strength is greatest.°

5   Athena was speaking to them of the many sufferings
of Odysseus, as she called them to mind. It was troubling to her
that he was in the house of the nymph: "Father Zeus and you other
blessed gods who live forever, let no other scepter-bearing
chieftain ever be kind and gentle and with a ready heart,
10 but always harsh. May he perform unjust deeds! For no one
of the people that he ruled remembers godlike Odysseus,
how he was gentle like a father. And now he lies on an island
suffering terrible pains in the halls of great Kalypso,°
who holds him against his will. He is not able to come to the land
15 of his fathers. For he has no oared ships, nor companions
who might send him over the broad back of the sea. And now
men scheme to kill his beloved son as the son returns
home, for he has gone to holy Pylos and to shining
Lacedaemon to see if he can learn news of his father."

20   Zeus the cloud-gatherer said in reply to her: "My child,
what a word has escaped from the barrier of your teeth!
Did you yourself not devise this plan so that Odysseus
could take vengeance on these men when he returned?
As for Telemachos, guide him in your wisdom.
25 You can do it! That way he will return to his native land
unscathed, and the suitors will return in their ship, thwarted
in their purpose."

---

1 *Tithonos*: A son of Laomedon, hence a brother of King Priam. Dawn snatched him away to be her husband
and gave him eternal life, but not eternal youth, according to the usual story.

4 *. . . greatest*: The narrative now returns to the council at the beginning of Book 1: As Athena went off to
Ithaca, Hermes goes off to the island of Kalypso. The action of Books 1–4 takes place at the same time as the
action of Book 5. A council of the gods often begins a new narrative element.

13 *Kalypso*: "concealer," no doubt Homer's own creation. She is like a goddess of death, concealing Odysseus
from human eyes, as Odysseus' return is like a rebirth. "Hades" means "the unseen."

Thus Zeus spoke, then said to Hermes,
his dear son: "Hermes, you are our messenger in many
matters—do go and tell the fair-haired nymph our fixed
resolve, the homecoming of long-suffering Odysseus: 30
that he might return without the guidance of gods or mortal men,
on a tightly bound raft, suffering many pains, and come
to rich Scheria on the twentieth day, to the land
of the Phaeacians, who are born near to the gods.
They will honor him like a god and send him forth   35
on a ship to the beloved land of his fathers. And they will give
him much bronze and gold and abundant woven things,
much more than Odysseus would ever have taken from Troy
if he had escaped without trouble with his due share of booty.
For it is his fate to see his friends and arrive to his high-roofed   40
home and to the land of his fathers."

       So Zeus spoke, and the messenger
Hermes Argeïphontes did not disobey. Immediately
he bound his beautiful sandals beneath his feet—immortal,
golden!—that carried him over the watery deep
and the boundless land with the blasts of the wind.   45
He took up his wand with which he enchants the eyes
of those he wishes, while he awakes others from their sleep.
Holding it in his hands, the powerful Argeïphontes
flew away. Stepping from the upper air onto Pieria°
he swooped onto the sea, and he sped over the wave   50
like a bird—a seagull that in search of fish over the dread
gulfs of the unresting sea wets its thick plumage in the brine.
Hermes rode like that on the numberless waves.

         But when
he came to the island far away, then he raced forth
from the violet sea onto the land. He came to the great cave   55
in which the nymph with her plaited hair dwelled.
He found her there inside. A great fire was burning
on the hearth, and the scent of split cedar and juniper wafted
over the island as they burned. Within she was singing
in her beautiful voice, going back and forth before her loom   60
with a golden shuttle. A luxuriant wood grew near the cave,
birch and poplar and sweet-smelling cypress. Long-winged birds
nested in them, owls and falcons and chattering cormorants

---

49 *Pieria*: The mountain range north of OLYMPOS.

FIGURE 5.1 Hermes weighing souls (*psychostasis*).   Hermes is the god of boundaries, and as such he is Psychopompos, or "soul-guide": he leads the souls of the dead to the house of Hades. In a sense Odysseus is dead, imprisoned on an island in the middle of the sea by Kalypso, the "concealer." Hence it is appropriate that Hermes deliver the message that he be released. Here the god is shown with winged shoes (in Homer they are "immortal, golden") and a traveler's broad-brimmed hat, hanging behind his head from a cord. In his left hand he carries the caduceus, a rod entwined by two copulating snakes, his magic wand. In his right hand he holds a scale with two pans in each of which is a *psychê*, a "breath-soul," represented as a miniature man (scarcely visible in the picture). Usually such weighing is given to Zeus, as when he weighs the fates of Hector and Achilles (*Iliad*, Book 22), but here Hermes weighs the *psychai* of Achilles and Memnon, to see which will die. Memnon is the famous warrior, the son of Dawn, who killed Nestor's son Antilochos, whom Achilles killed after the action described in the *Iliad*, according to postHomeric tradition. Athenian red-figure vase, c. 460 BC, by the Nikon painter.

whose business is upon the sea. A vigorous vine was stretched
there around the hollow cave, blooming with clusters   65
of grapes. Four fountains all in a row, close by one another,
ran with white water, turned in four different directions.
All around soft meadows of violets and parsley bloomed.
There even a deathless one might come and wonder and be amazed
and take delight in his heart.   70

     Just so the messenger Argeïphontes
stood and was amazed. But when in his spirit he had marveled
at everything, he went right into the wide cave.
Kalypso, the beautiful goddess, seeing him face
to face, recognized him, for the deathless gods are not unknown
to one another, not even if one lives a long ways away.   75
But he did not find great-hearted Odysseus inside,
for he sat on the shore weeping, as had become his custom,
racking his heart with tears and moans and agony.
He would look over the restless sea and pour down tears.

 Kalypso, the beautiful goddess, questioned Hermes, having him   80
sit down on a bright shining chair: "Why have you come,
O Hermes with the golden wand, an honored guest,
a welcome guest? In the past you have not come at all often.
Tell me what you have in mind. My heart bids me to fulfill it,
if I am able and it is possible. But follow me, so that I may place   85
entertainment before you."

     So speaking the goddess set before him
a table filled with ambrosia, and she mixed the red nectar.°
Then the messenger, Argeïphontes, drank and ate.
When he had dined and satisfied his heart with food,
then he answered and said: "You, a goddess, ask me about   90
my coming—I who am a god. I will speak my words truthfully,
because you ask. It was Zeus who ordered me to come,
although I did not want to. Who would willingly cross over
so great an expanse of endless salt water? Nor is there any city
of mortals nearby who sacrifice to the gods and make choice   95
offerings. But there is no way that a god may get past or avoid
the plan of Zeus who carries the goatskin fetish. He says
there is a man here, most wretched of all those men

---

87 *ambrosia ... nectar*: "ambrosia" seems to mean "undying" and is the food of the gods, though it has other
  functions; "nectar" has no known etymology: It is the drink of the gods.

who fought around the city of Priam for nine years—
100 then they sacked the city in the tenth year and went home.
But on the homeward journey they transgressed against Athena,°
who sent an evil wind and high waves against them.
There all the other noble companions perished, but as for him—
the wind and waves brought him here. He it is whom Zeus
105 now urges you to send on his way as quickly as possible.
It is not his fate to perish here far from his friends, but it is
his portion to see his friends and to arrive to his high-roofed
home and the land of his fathers."

                    So he spoke, and Kalypso,
the beautiful goddess, shuddered, and she spoke to him
110 words that went like arrows: "You are cruel, you gods,
envious above all others! You have it in for any goddess
who sleeps openly with a mortal man, if any should take one
as her dear bed-fellow. Just so when Dawn with her fingers
of rose took Orion as a lover,° you gods who live at ease
115 envied her until chaste Artemis of the golden throne
killed him in Ortygia,° attacking him with her gentle arrows.
Or when Demeter of the plaited hair, giving into passion,
mixed in love with Iasion in the thrice-plowed fallow field,
Zeus was not long ignorant of it: He killed Iasion,
120 striking him with his flashing thunderbolt.° Even so
you are now envious, you gods, that a mortal man should be
with me. I saved him when he was riding the keel and all alone,
when Zeus struck his swift ship with his flashing thunderbolt
and shattered it in the midst of the wine-dark sea! There
125 all his noble companions perished, but the wind and the waves
drove him here. I held him dear and I nourished him, and I said
that I would make him deathless and ageless for all time.

"But because it is not possible for a god to get beyond or avoid
the plan of Zeus who carries the goatskin fetish—let him go back

---

101 ...*Athena*: By Oïlean Ajax's rape of Kassandra at Athena's altar. Hermes speaks generally, or loosely:
In fact Poseidon wrecked Oïlean Ajax's ship (*Od.* 4), and Zeus wrecked Odysseus on the request of Helios,
as we will see (*Od.* 12).

114 ...*a lover*: A son of Poseidon, Orion was a great hunter, famed for his beauty and beloved by Dawn.

116 *Ortygia*: "quail island," usually said to be DELOS in the center of the CYCLADES. The reasons for Artemis'
killing Orion are variously given elsewhere, but never because of his affair with Dawn.

120 *thunderbolt*: The offspring of the union of Iasion and Demeter was said to be Ploutos, god of "wealth"
(of the land). The reference is to a fertility rite whereby sexual intercourse in a thrice-plowed field
increased the yield.

over the restless sea, if Zeus so urges and commands!   130
But it is not I who will send him, for I have at hand neither
oared ships nor companions who might conduct him over
the broad back of the sea. But I will gladly give him counsel,
and I will conceal nothing, so that he might arrive unscathed
at the land of his fathers."   135

        Then the messenger Argeïphontes
answered her: "So release him now, and avoid the wrath
of Zeus, so that he does not grow angry with you
and in time to come do you harm."

        So speaking, the powerful
Argeïphontes went off. And the revered nymph
went to great-hearted Odysseus, because she had heard   140
the message of Zeus. She found him sitting on the shore.
His eyes were never dry of tears. His sweet life
ebbed away as he longed in sorrow for his return,
for the nymph no longer pleased him. At night he slept
beside her in the hollow cave, under duress, unwilling   145
beside the willful nymph, but during the day he sat
on the rocks and the sand racking his heart with tears,
with moans and agonies, looking out over the restless
sea, pouring down tears.

        Coming close to him, the beautiful
goddess spoke: "Sad man, I wish that you would sorrow here   150
no more, wearing away your life. Now I shall send you
forth with a ready heart. Come now, cut long beams
with an ax and build a broad raft. Fasten on it cross-planks
above so that it might carry you over the misty sea. In it
I will put bread and water and red wine that satisfies the heart,   155
that will stave off hunger. I will put clothes on your back
and send a breeze behind you, so that you might arrive unscathed
in the land of your fathers, if the gods who live in the broad sky
are willing—those who are more powerful than I, and have such
a desire to fulfill their intent."   160

        So she spoke, and the much-enduring
Odysseus shuddered. He said to her words that went like arrows:
"You have some other purpose in mind, goddess! It is not
to send me away, seeing that you urge me to cross the great
gulf of the sea—in a raft! That is a dread and grave thing!
Not even shapely swift-traveling ships that enjoy a breeze   165

from Zeus can cross it. I would never set foot on a raft
against your will° . . . unless you, O goddess, will undertake
to swear a great oath not to devise any other further
evil against me."

　　　　　So he spoke, and Kalypso,
170　the beautiful goddess, smiled, and she stroked him with
her hand and spoke and addressed him: "You're a rascal.
And no fool, that you have thought to say this word! Well, let
earth and the wide heaven above be witness, and the cascading
waters of the Styx,° which is the greatest and most dread
175　oath of the blessed gods: *I will not plot any further evil*
against you. My thoughts and contemplations are such as I
would devise for myself, if I were in your position.
For my mind is just. This heart of mine is not made of iron.
I am compassionate."

　　　　　So saying the beautiful goddess quickly
180　led the way, and Odysseus followed in the footsteps
of the goddess. They came to the hollow cave. Odysseus
sat down on the chair from which Hermes had just arisen,
and the nymph placed before him every kind of food and drink,
such as mortal men eat. She herself sat down opposite
185　godlike Odysseus, and female servants set out for her
ambrosia and nectar.

　　　　　They opened their hands to the good board
lying before them, but when they had put the desire for
food and drink from them, Kalypso, the beautiful goddess,
began to speak: "Son of Laërtes, sprung from Zeus,
190　most clever Odysseus, so you want to go home to the land
of your fathers, right away? Well then, farewell. If you only knew
how many more sorrows that fate requires you to endure
before you come to your homeland—you would stay here
with me in this house and be immortal, although you desire
195　to see your wife, whom you long for all your days. I don't
think that I am worse than she in looks or beauty! Well,
it is really not fitting that mortals compete with the immortals
with respect to comeliness."

167　*against your will*: That is, he will not go if she does not *really* want him to go: Odysseus thinks that Kalypso's
　　　suggestion is ironic, that she does not mean it.

174　*Styx*: An oath sworn by the gods on the underworld river of the Styx can never be broken.

Then the resourceful Odysseus said
to her in reply: "Revered goddess, don't be angry about this.
I myself well know that the clever Penelope is less   200
to look upon than you in attractiveness and physique.
For she is a mortal, and you are an immortal and will never
grow old. Nonetheless, I wish and I want every day
to go home—to see the day of my homecoming. And if
some god shall strike me on the wine-dark sea, I will endure it.   205
I am a stout-hearted man. I can stand every affliction.
I have already suffered many things. I have labored much
on the waves, and in war. Let this, then, be added to all that."

So Odysseus spoke, and the sun went down and the darkness
came on. The two went into an inner recess of the hollow cave   210
and took their pleasure in love-making, lying side by side.

When early born Dawn appeared with her fingers of rose,
Odysseus quickly put on his cloak and shirt, and the nymph
clothed herself in a long white robe—finely woven, charming—
and around her waist she tied a beautiful golden belt,   215
and placed a veil on her head. And then she set out
to plan the return of great-hearted Odysseus.

                                        She gave him
a large ax made of bronze, fitted to his hands, sharp
on both sides. It had a very beautiful well-fitted handle
of olive wood. Then she gave him a well polished adze.   220
She led the way to the edge of the island where the trees
grew tall—birch and poplar and fir, reaching to the sky.
The trees were long dried-out and well-seasoned and would float
lightly on the water.

                        When she had shown him where the tall trees
grew, the beautiful goddess Kalypso went back to her house.   225
Odysseus cut the timbers, and his work proceeded swiftly.°
He cut down twenty trees in all, trimming them with the ax.
He smoothed them out—he knew just what he was doing,
making them true to the line. Meanwhile Kalypso,
the beautiful goddess, brought him drills. He drilled all the pieces   230

---

226 *proceeded swiftly*: This is one of the most difficult passages in Homer, filled with words that occur a single
time, and their meaning is unclear. Odysseus appears, however, not to be constructing a raft, but a boat,
though many of the details elude us.

and fitted them to one another. He hammered them together
with pegs and fastenings. As wide as a highly skilled man makes
the floor of a broad merchantman, even so wide did Odysseus
make his raft. He set up the deck-beams, fitting them to the close-set ribs.
235 Then he continued his labor, finishing the raft with long gunwales.°
He set up a mast and yardarm° fitted to it. He also made
a steering oar so that he might guide the craft. He closed-in
the whole craft with wickerwork, from stem to stern, as a defense
against the waves, and he strewed much brush upon it.°

240   In the meanwhile Kalypso, the beautiful goddess, brought
cloth to make a sail, and Odysseus made that too with skill.
He made fast the upper lines attached to the yardarm, and the lines
for raising and lowering the sails and for changing the sail's position,
and then used levers to lower the craft into the shining sea.
245 The fourth day came, and all the work was done.
On the fifth day Kalypso the beautiful goddess sent him
away from the island after she had bathed him and clothed him
in a scented garment. The goddess placed a skin of dark wine
on the raft and another, larger one of water, and provisions
250 in a knapsack. She put in it many delicacies sure to satisfy his heart,
and she sent forth a warm and gentle wind.

                                        Gladly godlike
Odysseus spread his sail to the breeze. Sitting down,
he skillfully guided the craft with the steering oar. Sleep
did not fall upon his eyelids as he watched the Pleiades
255 and the late-setting Boötes and Arktos, which men also call
the Wagon, which turns in place, ever on the lookout for Orion,
and alone has no part in the baths of Ocean.° This star Kalypso,
the beautiful goddess, had told him to keep on the left
as he traveled over the sea.

---

235 *gunwales*: The upper edges of the sides of a vessel, if that is what the Greek word means.

236 *yardarm*: A horizontal support for the sail.

239 *upon it*: Apparently the wickerwork and brush are to support cargo, but their function is obscure.

257 *... Ocean*: The Pleiades, probably "doves," are tightly grouped, the most obvious star cluster in the heavens,
     consisting of seven stars (only six are usually visible). Boötes, the "plowman," sets late in the month of
     October, perhaps giving a time for Odysseus' journey, a warning of stormy weather to come. Arktos, the
     "bear" (*Ursa Major*), is the Big Dipper that never sets, perhaps a corruption of a Near Eastern word for
     "wagon," an alternative name that Homer also gives; the bear is appropriately in proximity to the hunter
     Orion, a constellation bearing the same name today, as the name "Wagon" is suitable to the nearness of the
     Big Dipper to Boötes, the "plowman." These stars may have suggested specific navigational directions to
     Odysseus, but we cannot untangle the details.

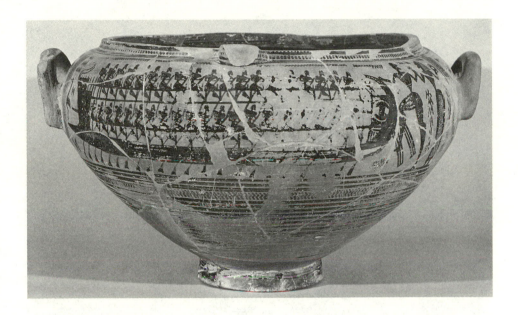

FIGURE 5.2   A ship from the days of Homer.   On the right a man seizes a woman by the wrist, evidently to abduct her. She holds a wreath in her left hand (barely visible). The ship he is about to board has 40 (or 39) rowers. Mostly in Homer the ships have 20 rowers, but some have 50. The rowers are shown above one another, but really they would sit on either side of the ship. The prow, on the right, is curved and a shield and sword hang from it. The stern, on the left, would have had a kind of half deck for the helmsman to sit on. Not shown is the mast, which stood in the center and was hinged so it could be folded down into the body of the ship. The mast had a single sail that allowed the boat to run before the wind, but it had no jib and so could not tack into the wind: Hence much travel by ship was powered by rowers. Geometric wine-mixing bowl from Thebes, 8th century BC.

FIGURE 5.3   Odysseus and Kalypso.   The goddess presents a box of provisions for the hero's voyage. The box is tied with a sash. The bearded Odysseus sits on a rock on the shore holding a sword and looking pensive. Athenian red-figure vase, c. 450 BC.

For seventeen days he sailed,

but on the eighteenth appeared the shadowy mountains of the nearest　　　　260
part of the land of the Phaeacians. It looked like a shield on the misty sea.°
But the lord, the earth-shaker, coming back from the Aethiopians,
saw him from afar, from the mountains of the Solymi.° He saw
Odysseus sailing over the sea, and he grew more angry in his heart,
and he shook his head and spoke to his spirit: "Well, I see that　　　　265
the gods have changed their minds concerning Odysseus
while I was among the Aethiopians! And now he is near the land
of the Phaeacians, where it is his fate to escape the trial
of misery which has come upon him. But even yet, I think,
I will give him his fill of evil!"　　　　270

So saying he gathered together

great clouds. Taking his trident in his hands, he stirred up the sea
and he roused all the blasts of every kind of wind, and he hid
the earth together with the sea in clouds. Night rushed down
from heaven. East Wind and South Wind dashed together,
and the wild-blowing West Wind and North Wind, born in a clear sky,　　　　275
rolled out a gigantic wave.

And then Odysseus' limbs were

loosened and his heart shivered, and, groaning, he spoke
to his great-hearted spirit: "Alas, wretched me, what is going
to happen to me at last? I am afraid all that the goddess said is true
when she said that I would suffer terribly before I came　　　　280
to the land of my fathers. And now all this is coming to pass!
Zeus overcasts the broad heaven with such mighty clouds,
and he has stirred up the sea, and the blasts of all kinds of winds
drive on. Now dire destruction is near. Three-times blessed,
and four times, are the Danaäns, who died in broad Troy, bringing　　　　285
pleasure to the sons of Atreus.° Would that I had died and followed
my fate on that day when gangs of Trojans hurled their bronze
spears at me as I fought over Achilles, the dead son of Peleus.
Then I would have received proper funeral rites, and the Achaeans
would have spread my fame. As it is, I am doomed to be taken　　　　290
by an unhappy death."

261　*misty sea*: That is, a shield lying on its inner side, because Homeric shields were concave and bossed.

263　*... Solymi*: Poseidon had gone to the land of the Aethiopians before the action of the *Odyssey* begins. The
　　　Solymi lived in LYCIA in southwest ASIA MINOR, an odd location from which to see Odysseus, who seems
　　　to be sailing in western seas.

286　*sons of Atreus*: Bringing pleasure by defending their honor, violated when Helen ran off with Paris.

As he spoke, a great wave drove upon him,
coming down from on high. It rushed on him with terrible strength,
whirling his raft round and around. He was thrown far from the raft,
and he let go the steering oar from his hands. The mast was broken
295 in two by a ferocious blast that came on the mingled winds.
The sail and the yardarm fell far out in the sea. For a long time
he was held underwater, and he could not rise at once from beneath
the onrush of the great wave. His clothes that Kalypso, the beautiful
goddess, had given him weighed him down.

                                                    At last he came up
300 and he spit up the bitter brine that gurgled in torrents from his mouth.
But even though he was worn down, he did not forget about the raft
but he sprang after it in the waves—he grabbed on to it, and he sat down
in the middle, avoiding the finality of death. A great wave shunted
the raft here and there along its course, as when in late summer
305 North Wind carries thistles across the plain and closely they cling
to one another—even so did the winds carry the raft here and there
over the sea. Now South Wind would throw it to North Wind
to carry along, now East Wind would yield it to West Wind to pursue.

    The daughter of Kadmos saw him, Ino with the pretty ankles,
310 who became Leukothea—earlier she had been a mortal of human speech,
but now in the depths of the sea she won a portion of honor among the gods.°
She took pity on Odysseus as he wandered, suffering agonies. She rose up
from the deep like a seabird on the wing. She sat down on the strongly
bound raft and said: "Poor man, why is Poseidon the earth-shaker
315 so terribly angry with you that he devises so many evils against you?
Even so he shall not destroy you, though he would very much like to.
    "But do this, for you seem to me a man of understanding:
Take off your clothes and leave the raft. Let it be carried by the winds.
Swim with your hands and try to reach the land of the Phaeacians—
320 for it is your fate to escape there. Here, take this immortal veil
and tie it beneath your breast. You need not fear you will suffer
anything. And when you get hold of the dry land with your hands,
untie the veil and throw it into the wine-dark sea, far from land.
Then turn away."

---

311 *among the gods*: Leukothea, the "white goddess," was the name that Ino took, a daughter of Kadmos of
Thebes, after she leapt into the sea with her baby Melikertes in her arms. He became a sea-god too. Ino is
otherwise known as the malignant stepmother of Phrixus and Hellê in the saga of the Argonauts, and she
was the nurse of Dionysos.

So speaking, the goddess gave him the veil
while she dove into the swelling sea like a seabird and was hidden   325
by the dark wave. But godlike, much-enduring Odysseus
pondered, and in grief he spoke to his great-hearted spirit:
"O no, I hope that one of the deathless ones is not again
preparing a deception, because she encourages me to leave the raft.
But I will not yet obey. I saw with my eyes the land far off   330
where she said there was a chance of escape. I will do this,
which seems to me to be the best: So long as the beams
hold together in their fastenings, I will stay and endure my affliction.
But when the wave shatters my raft, I will swim. There is
no better plan."   335

       While he was pondering these things in his heart
and spirit, the earth-shaker Poseidon caused a great wave to rise—
awesome and savage and overhanging!—and Poseidon drove the wave
on him. As when a powerful wind scatters a heap of dried straw,
and some of it blows here, some there, even so the wave scattered
the long beams of the raft. But Odysseus rode on a single plank,   340
driving it as though it was a race horse, and he discarded the clothes
that the divine Kalypso had given him. Immediately he tied the veil
beneath his breast and threw himself headlong into the sea.
He spread out his arms, eager to swim.

              The lord, the earth-shaker,
saw him, and shaking his head he spoke to his own heart: 345
"Go now, wanderer over the seas, having suffered many trials,
go until you come among men who are nourished by Zeus.
Even so, I don't think you will make light of your suffering!"
So speaking, he lashed his horses with beautiful manes and he came
to Aigai,° where his glorious house is.   350

          But Athena, the daughter
of Zeus, had another idea. She bound the paths of the other winds
and ordered them all to stop and to take their rest. Then she roused
the swift North Wind, and broke the wave before it until Zeus-born
Odysseus could come among the Phaeacians who love the oar,
and so avoid death and ruin.   355

         And so for two nights and two days
he was driven over the heavy waves, and often his heart

---

350 *Aigai*: Various places had this name, and its location is unclear.

looked death in the face. But when Dawn with her fine tresses
brought the third day to birth, then the wind stopped and there
came a windless calm. He caught sight of the nearby land,
360 and he cast a quick glance forward as he was lifted up
by a broad heaving swell. As when the life of a father appears
very welcome to his children when he has lain in sickness,
suffering terrible pains, wasting away for a long time
because a malevolent spirit has assailed him, but then
365 to their joy the gods release him from evil—so welcome
did the earth and the woods appear to Odysseus.

He swam on, eager to set his foot on the dry land. But when
he was as near a distance as a man can make himself heard
when he shouts, and he heard the thud of the waves against the reef
370 of the sea—for the great wave roared against the dry land,
belching terribly, as everything was wrapped in the foam
of the salt sea, and there were no harbors, no anchoring places
for ships, nor places of shelter, but only projecting headlands
and reefs and cliffs—then the knees of Odysseus were loosened
375 and his heart shivered, and, groaning, he spoke to his own
great-hearted spirit: "Alas, now that Zeus has allowed me
to see the land, beyond all hope, and I have cleaved my way across
this gulf, I can see no way out of the gray sea. There are steep cliffs
on the shore side, and around them the waves break roaring,
380 and the rock runs up sheer, and the water is deep in close,
and there seems no way to take a stand on both feet and escape ruin.
I fear that if I try to escape the water a great wave may seize
me and dash me against a jagged rock, and my trouble
will be for nothing. But if I swim on farther in hopes of finding
385 a sloping beach and harbors of the sea, I fear that a storm wind
will snatch me up again and carry me groaning heavily
over the fishy sea. Or some spirit may set a sea-monster on me
from the deep, such as glorious Amphitritê breeds in great number.
For I know that the famous shaker of the earth is angry with me."

390 While he pondered these things in his heart and spirit, a great wave
bore him toward the rugged shore. His skin would have been ripped
off there, and his bones smashed, if the goddess, flashing-eyed Athena,
had not put a thought in his mind. Rushing on, he seized the rock
with both hands and held on to it, groaning, until the great wave
395 went past. And so he escaped it in that fashion, until flowing backward
the wave broke on him again and carried him far off into the sea.

As when an octopus is dragged from its lair, many pebbles stick to its
suckers, even so the skin was ripped from his powerful hands
against the rocks, and the great wave covered him over.

Then wretched Odysseus would have died, contrary to what   400
was fated, if flashing-eyed Athena had not given him a plan.
Making his way forth from the wave where it belched against the land,
he swam outside it, looking landward, to see if maybe he could find
a sloping beach and a harbor of the sea. And then as he swam
he came to the mouth of a beautifully flowing river. That seemed   405
to him the best place, smooth of stones and also there was shelter
from the wind.

He recognized the river as it flowed forth
and he prayed in his heart: "Hear me, O king, whoever you are!
I come to you as to one most welcome, fleeing from out of the sea
from the threats of Poseidon. Respected is a man, even to the immortal   410
gods, who comes as a wanderer—as now I come to your stream
and to your knees, having suffered greatly. Take pity on me,
O king. I am your suppliant."

So he spoke, and promptly the river
stopped its flow, and held back the wave, and the river
made a calm before it and it brought Odysseus safely   415
to its mouth. Odysseus bent his two knees and his powerful
hands. For his heart had been overcome by the sea. His flesh
was swollen and torn. The sea water flowed from his mouth
and nostrils. He lay breathless and speechless, with barely the strength
to move, and a terrible weariness came over him. But when   420
he had caught his breath and his spirit was gathered in his breast,
then he untied the veil of the goddess from him, and threw it
into the river that murmured toward the sea. The great wave
carried it down the stream, and Ino quickly took it in her hands.

Odysseus, having turned away from the river, sank down   425
in the reeds and kissed the rich earth. Groaning, he spoke
to his great-hearted spirit: "Alas, what has happened to me?
What will happen to me in the end? If I pass a miserable night
in this river bed, I fear that the chilling frost and the soaking dew
together will overcome me, and from weakness I will have breathed forth   430
my spirit. For the breeze from the river blows cold in early morning.
But if I go up the slope into the shady wood and lie down

to rest in the thick brush, in hopes that the cold and weariness
will leave me, and if sweet sleep comes upon me, I fear
435 that I might become prey and sweet booty to wild animals."

As he pondered, this plan seemed to him to be best: He went up
into the woods and found a clear space near the water. He crept beneath
two bushes that grew from the same spot. The one was a thorn bush,
and the other olive. The cold strength of the damp winds could never
440 blow through these, nor could the bright sun strike with its rays,
nor could the rain come through, so closely did they grow
to one another, intertwined together. Odysseus crept beneath them,
and with his hands he put together a broad bed. There were many
fallen leaves there, as many as could shelter two or three men
445 in the winter season, no matter how bad the weather.

Seeing them, the much-enduring godlike Odysseus rejoiced,
and he lay down in the middle of the leaves, and he heaped
over himself a mass of them. As when a man hides a brand
beneath the dark embers in an outlying farm, where there are
450 no neighbors, preserving the seed of fire so that he won't have to
kindle it from someplace else—just so, Odysseus hid himself
in the leaves. Athena shed sleep on his eyes, enfolding his lids, so that
sleep might make an end to his awful fatigue as quickly as possible.

BOOK 6. *Odysseus and Nausicaä*

And so the much-enduring godlike Odysseus lay there,
overcome by sleep and weariness. But Athena went to the land
and the city of the Phaeacians, who earlier had lived in Hypereia°
with its broad places for dancing—near the arrogant Cyclopes°
who were greater in strength and constantly plundered them.   5
From there Nausithoös, who was like a god, had removed them
and settled them in Scheria,° far from men who labor
to raise barley. He built houses and he built a wall around the city.
He made temples for the gods and divided the farm lands.
But after this time, Nausithoös was overcome by death   10
and went to the house of Hades. After that Alkinoös° ruled,
made wise in his counsel by the gods.

                    Now the goddess,
flashing-eyed Athena, went to his house, to devise a homecoming
for great-hearted Odysseus. She went to the brightly decorated
chamber in which the daughter of great-hearted Alkinoös slept—   15
Nausicaä,° like to the deathless ones in beauty and form.
Two handmaidens, made beautiful by the Graces, slept close by,
one on either side of the doorway, and the shining doors were shut.

    Like a breath of air, Athena hastened to the couch
of the young girl. She stood over her head and she spoke,   20
taking on the appearance of the daughter of Dymas, famed
for his ships and of a like age to Nausicaä, dear to Athena's heart.

---

3 *Hypereia*: The "land beyond far beyond," a fanciful name emphasizing the Phaeacians' distance from human habitation.

4 *Cyclopes*: The "round-eyes," presumably the same as the beastly Cyclopes in *Od.* 9.

7 *... Scheria*: *Nausithoös* mean "swift in ships" and most of the Phaeacians have ship names. *Scheria* is of unknown etymology. By the fifth century BC, however, it was identified with the island of CORCYRA (modern Corfu) north of the IONIAN ISLANDS.

11 *Alkinoös*: Perhaps "strong in his mind."

16 *Nausicaä*: "excelling in ships."

In her form flashing-eyed Athena spoke: "Nausicaä, how is it
that your mother bore you to be such a careless girl? Your bright
25   clothes are lying there all uncared for, yet your marriage
time is nearing, when you really ought to be wearing nice clothes,
and to give similar garments to those who will accompany you.
It's from things like this that your good reputation goes up
among men, and your father and revered mother will rejoice.
30   So let us do some washing as soon as the sun rises. I'll go along
as your helper, so you should get ready as soon as possible.
You will not be a virgin much longer! Already all the best men
in the land of the Phaeacians court you, from whom comes your
own lineage. So come, ask your famous father to fit out mules
35   at dawn, and a wagon that can carry the shirts and robes
and shining clothes. It is much better for you, too, to go in this fashion,
for the washing tanks are far from the city."

So speaking, flashing-eyed
Athena went off to Olympos, where they say is the eternal seat
of the gods. Neither is it shaken by the winds, nor is it ever wet
40   with rain, nor does it snow there, but it is spread out clear
and cloudless, and over it hovers a brilliant whiteness.
There the blessed gods take their pleasure for all their days.
That is where the flashing-eyed one went, after she had spoken
to the young girl.

At once Dawn came along on her lovely throne.
45   She woke up Nausicaä with her beautiful robes. Nausicaä marveled
at her dream and went off through the house to tell her parents,
her dear father and mother. She came upon them inside the house.
Her mother sat at the hearth with her handmaids, spinning
purple yarn, the color taken from the sea, and she met her father
50   as he was going outside to join the glorious chieftains in the place
of council, to where the noble Phaeacians had called him.

Standing close to her father, she spoke to him: "Papa dear,
do you think you could fit out a wagon—a high one with good wheels—
so that I may take my fine clothes to the river to wash them?
55   They are very dirty! You too should have clean clothes when
you are at council with the leading men. And you have five sons
in your halls, two of them married, but three are sturdy bachelors.
They ought to put on clean clothes when they go to the dance.
I've been thinking about these things—"

So she spoke, too embarrassed
to mention her blooming marriage to her dear father.   60

But he understood everything and answered her: "You can
have the mules, my child, and anything else you want. Go then!
The slaves will fit out a wagon for you—a high one, with good wheels,
fitted with a box above."

So speaking, he called to his slaves,
who obeyed him. Outside the palace they fitted out a light-running   65
mule wagon. They led up the mules and yoked them to the wagon.
The girl brought the shining clothes out of her chamber and placed
them in the well-polished wagon. Her mother loaded a chest
with all kinds of food adequate to satisfy the heart. She loaded
it up with dainties and poured wine in a goatskin, and the girl   70
mounted the wagon. Her mother also gave her gentle olive oil
in a golden oil-flask so that she and her handmaidens might
anoint themselves with it after a bath.

Nausicaä took up
the lash and the shining reins, and she lashed the mules
to get them going. The mules clattered as they eagerly sped   75
along, carrying the clothing and the girl. She was not alone,
for her ladies went with her. When they came to the very
beautiful flow of the river, where the washing basins were
that never failed—much beautiful water flowed out from beneath
them to wash clothes no matter how soiled—there they freed   80
the mules from the wagon and drove them along the swirling
river to feed on grass sweet as honey. They removed
the clothes from the wagon by hand and carried them
to the black water. They trampled them in the trenches,
busily vying with one another.   85

When they had washed the garments
and cleansed them of all stains, they spread them out in a row
along the shore of the sea, where the sea washed against the land
and cleaned most of the pebbles. After bathing and richly anointing
themselves with olive oil, they prepared a meal on the river's banks
while waiting for the clothes to dry in the rays of the sun.   90

When Nausicaä and her ladies had had their pleasure of food,
they cast aside their veils and began to play ball. White-armed

Nausicaä was their leader in the song. Even as Artemis,
who takes joy in arrows, runs over the mountains, either
95   high Taygetos or Erymanthos,° delighting in the chase
after boars and swift deer, and with her play the woodland
nymphs, the daughters of Zeus who carries the goatskin fetish,
and Leto° rejoices in her heart, and high above them all
Artemis holds her head and brow, easy to recognize,
100   though they all are beautiful—even so Nausicaä, the young virgin,
untamed by marriage, stood out among her handmaidens.

But when she was about to fold the beautiful clothes
and yoke the mules to return home, the goddess, flashing-eyed
Athena, had another idea—that Odysseus might awake
105   and see the young girl with the fair face, and she might lead him
to the city of the Phaeacians.

The princess Nausicaä tossed
the ball to her ladies, but she missed the handmaiden and the ball
fell into the deep eddying water. The girls all screamed aloud
and godlike Odysseus awoke. He sat up and pondered
110   in his heart and spirit: "Alas, to the land of what mortals
have I now come? Are they violent and savage? Unjust?
Or are they hospitable, fearing the gods in their minds? I thought
I heard the voices of young girls, of nymphs who haunt the tall
peaks of the mountains and the springs that feed the rivers
115   and the grassy meadows. Could I be among folk of human speech?
But come, let me check out the situation, to see what's what."

So speaking, the godlike Odysseus emerged from the bushes.
With his powerful hand he broke off a leafy branch from
the thick woods to cover his flesh, to hide his male parts.
120   He came out like a lion reared in the mountains, trusting
in its strength, who goes forth beaten with rain and wind-tossed,
and with eyes ablaze he goes into the midst of the cattle
or the sheep or after the wild deer, and his belly orders him
to go even into a closely built farmstead to attack the flocks.
125   Just so, Odysseus was about to mingle with the young girls
with fine hair, even though he was naked, for necessity drove him.

---

95   *Taygetos or Erymanthos*: Taygetos is the high range of mountains between MESSENIA, where PYLOS is,
and LACEDAEMON, where SPARTA is. Erymanthos is a mountain range in the northwest PELOPONNESUS
between ARCADIA and ELIS, site of Herakles' famous pursuit of the Erymanthian Boar.

98   *Leto*: Artemis' mother.

But he appeared hideous to them, all besmirched with brine!
They ran every which way—one here, one there—across
the jutting spits of the beach. Only the daughter of Alkinoös
held her ground, for Athena placed courage in her breast   130
and took fear from her limbs. She stood and faced him. Odysseus
wondered whether he should clasp the knees of the young girl
with the fair face and beseech her, or stand apart just as he was
and implore her with honeyed words to give him some clothing
and show him her city. As he was pondering in this manner,   135
it seemed to him to be best to stand apart and implore her
with simple words. If he seized her knees, the young girl
might grow angry!

       Immediately he spoke a honeyed, cunning
word: "I entreat you, O queen—are you a goddess, or a mortal?
If you are a goddess, one of those who inhabit the broad heaven,   140
I would compare you in beauty and stature and form
to Artemis, the great daughter of Zeus. If you are a mortal,
one of those who live upon the earth, then your father and
revered mother are three-times blessed, and three-times blessed
are your brothers. Their hearts must always be warmed with joy   145
on account of you, when they see you entering the dance—
a plant so fair. But that man is blessed in his heart
above all others who prevails with his bridal gifts and
leads you to his house. For I have never yet beheld
with my eyes such a mortal as you, neither man nor woman.   150
I am amazed, looking at you!
           "In DELOS once I saw such
a sight—the young shoot of a palm springing up beside
the altar of Apollo. There I went, and many people followed
me on that journey when evil pains were my lot.° Just so,
when I saw that palm, I marveled long in my heart,   155
for never yet did such a shaft emerge from the earth.
In like manner, O lady, I do wonder at you and am amazed,
and I fear awfully to touch your knees. But painful anguish
has come upon me. Yesterday, after twenty grim days,
I escaped from the wine-dark sea. Until then waves   160
and the swift winds bore me far from the island of Ogygia.°

---

154   *my lot*: Apparently on the voyage to Troy, but nothing is known otherwise about a stop on Delos, the
      small central island of the CYCLADES. In classical times Delos was a center of the cult of Artemis and
      Apollo, and a palm tree grew there that Leto supposedly held onto when she gave birth to the twins
      Artemis and Apollo.

161   *Ogygia*: Kalypso's island.

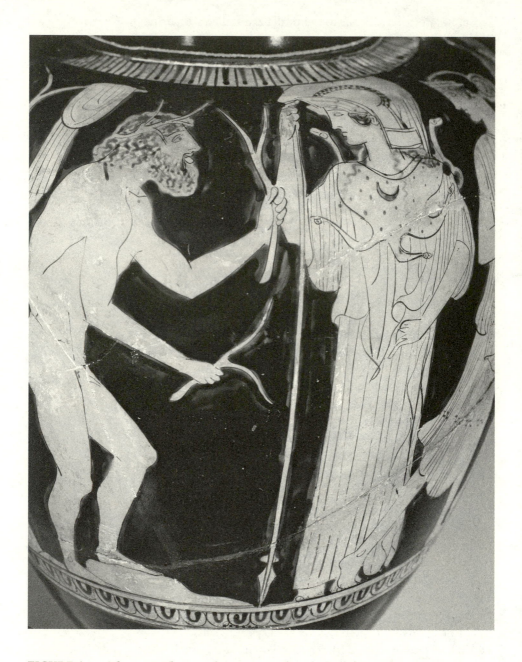

FIGURE 6.1 **Odysseus, Athena, and Nausicaä.** The naked Odysseus holds a branch in front of his genitals so as not to startle Nausicaä and her attendants. On the right near the edge of the picture, Nausicaä half turns but holds her ground. Athena, Odysseus' protectress, stands between the two figures, her spear pointed to the ground. She wears a helmet and the goatskin fetish (aegis) fringed with snakes as a kind of cape. A crescent moon decorates it. Clothes hang out to dry on a tree branch (upper left). Athenian red-figure water-jar from Vulci, Italy, c. 460 BC.

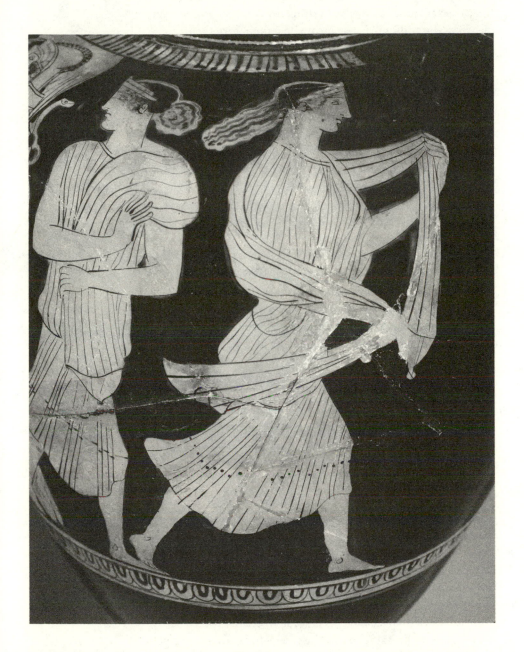

FIGURE 6.2 Nausicaä and a frightened attendant. Nausicaä on the left holds her ground while one of her ladies runs away with laundry draped about her shoulders (this is the other side of the vase shown in Figure *Od*. 6.1). Athenian red-figure water-jar from Vulci, Italy, c. 460 BC.

And now some spirit has cast me forth here, that here too
I may suffer some sorrow. For I think my troubles will not yet
be over. The gods will cause me much pain before then.
165   "But O Queen, take pity! I have come to you first
of all after suffering many evils. I know no one of the other men
who inhabit this city and this land—no one! Show me the city,
give me a rag to cast about my body if perhaps you
brought some wrapper for the clothes, when you came here.
170   As for yourself, may the gods grant all that you desire
in your heart—a husband and a house, and harmony of mind,
a noble gift! For there is nothing greater or better than this,
when a husband and wife live in a house with like minds,
thinking like thoughts, a great annoyance to their enemies
175   and a joy to those who wish them well—and they themselves
are aware of their happy situation."

                     Then white-armed Nausicaä
answered him: "Stranger, you do not seem like an evil or stupid
man. But Zeus the Olympian gives good fortune to men,
both to the good and the bad, to every man as he wishes.
180   So he has given this lot to you, as I see it, and you have no choice
but to endure it. But now, because you have come to our land
and city, you shall not lack clothing nor anything else appropriate
to a suppliant who has suffered a long time and then come our way.
I will show you the city, and I will tell you the name of the people:
185   The Phaeacians occupy this city and land. I am the daughter
of great-hearted Alkinoös, on whom the strength and power
of the Phaeacians depend."

                     Thus she spoke, then ordered her handmaids
who have lovely tresses: "Stop where you are, my ladies! Why are
you running at the sight of this man? Surely you do not think
190   that he is an enemy? No such man lives or exists who will
come to the land of the Phaeacians with hostile intentions,
for we are dear to the deathless ones. We live far away
in the stormy sea at the ends of the earth, and no other mortals
have dealings with us. But this is some wretched wanderer
195   who has come here. We must take care of him, for all strangers
and beggars are from Zeus, and a small gift is a dear one.
So come then, my ladies, give this stranger food and drink
and wash him in the river, where there is shelter from the wind."

So she spoke, and the girls stopped and called to one another.
Then Odysseus sat down in a sheltered place, as Nausicaä, the daughter   200
of great-hearted Alkinoös, had said. Beside him they placed
a cloak and a shirt to wear, and they gave him gentle olive oil
in a golden oil-flask, and they urged him to bathe himself in the river.

Then godlike Odysseus spoke among the young ladies:
"Ladies, stand apart over there so that I can myself   205
wash away the brine from my shoulders and anoint myself
with olive oil. It has been a long time since my flesh has felt oil.
But I won't bathe in front of you. I would be ashamed to be naked
in the midst of young girls with lovely tresses."°

So he spoke,
and the maidens moved away, and told Nausicaä. And godlike   210
Odysseus washed the brine that covered his back and broad
shoulders from his flesh, and he wiped off the foam
of the restless sea from his head. And when he had washed himself
and anointed himself with oil, he quickly put on the clothes
that the unmarried virgin had given him. Then Athena the daughter   215
of Zeus made him taller to look upon, and stronger,
and she made the locks from his head to fall in curls,
like the hyacinth flower. As when a man overlays silver
with gold, a skilled worker whom Hephaistos and Pallas
Athena have trained in every kind of craft, and he produces   220
work filled with grace—even so she poured out grace
on his head and shoulders.

Then he sat apart, going a little along
the shore of the sea, where he shone with handsome grace.
And Nausicaä marveled at him. Then she spoke to her ladies
with the fine tresses: "Listen to me, my white-armed ladies,   225
attend what I say. This man has not come to the godlike
Phaeacians without the will of all the gods who live on Olympos.
He seemed to be rather coarse before, but now he seems
like the gods who live in the broad heavens. Would that
such a man, living here, might be called my husband,   230

---

209 *lovely tresses*: Odysseus' modesty is remarkable, because it was the custom for the young ladies of
the house to bathe guests (Telemachos and Peisistratos are bathed by Nestor's daughters in Book 3).
Perhaps Odysseus is ashamed because of his filthy condition.

and that it might please him to remain here! But my ladies,
give food and drink to this stranger."

So she spoke, and they listened
and happily obeyed. They placed food and drink beside Odysseus,
and that much-enduring godlike man avidly drank and ate.
235 It had been a long time since he had anything to eat.

But white-armed Nausicaä had another thought. She folded
the clothes and placed them in the beautiful wagon. She yoked
the mules with their powerful hooves and mounted the wagon.
Then she called to Odysseus and spoke and addressed him:
240 "Now get up, stranger, and come to the city, so that I may escort you
to the house of my wise father. There, I say, you may come
to know all the best of the Phaeacians. Only do this—for you seem
to me to be a man of sense: So long as we go through the fields
and farms of men, keep up quickly with the ladies behind the mules
245 and the wagon. I will lead the way. But when we come into the city,
around which a high wall runs, a beautiful harbor lies
on either side of the city, and the entrance is narrow,
and ships with curved prows are drawn up along the way,
for each man has a station for his ship—there, too, is the place
250 of assembly around the beautiful temple to Poseidon.
The place is fitted with huge stones set down into the earth.
There the men are busy with the tackle of their black ships,
the ropes and sails, and they shape oars there. For the Phaeacians
are not concerned with bow or quiver, but with masts and oars
255 and with shapely ships. Rejoicing in them, they travel the gray sea.

"But it is their unkind speech that I want to avoid, in case
someone should hereafter taunt me. For there are unpleasant
people in the land. And thus some scoundrel might say,
if he were to meet us: 'Who is this tall handsome stranger
260 who follows Nausicaä? Where did she find him? I suppose
he will be her husband now! No doubt she has brought some
wanderer from his ship—from men who live far away, because
nobody lives nearby! Or maybe it is some god for whom
she has long prayed, come down from the sky, and he will have
265 her forever. Well that is better, if she has gone forth to find
a husband from somewhere else. For she scorns those Phaeacians
in the land, the many noble men who pursue her!'

"So some
might say, and this would be a reproach to me. And I myself

would reproach another girl who acted in this way, one
who should associate with men against the wishes of her own   270
father and mother, while they were still living, before
she should be openly married.

                 "So, stranger, please quickly heed
my words, so that with every speed you might obtain an escort
from my father for your homecoming. You will find a splendid
grove of Athena near the road, a grove of poplars. In it a spring   275
wells up, and around it is a meadow. There is my father's park,
and a blooming vineyard, as far from the city as a man's voice
carries when he shouts. Sit down there and wait awhile,
until we come into the city and arrive at the palace of my father.
Then when you think that we have reached my father's house,   280
go into the city of the Phaeacians and ask the way to my father's
house, the great-hearted Alkinoös. It is easy to recognize—even
a little child, a baby, could lead you there. For the houses
of the Phaeacians are not built like the palace of Lord Alkinoös.
    "Then when you reach the courtyard and the house itself,   285
go rapidly through the great hall until you come to my mother.
She will be seated on the hearth near the blaze of the fire,
spinning purple yarn, a color taken from the sea. She'll be leaning
against a column, and female slaves will be seated behind her.
My father's great throne rests against this same column.   290
There he sits and drinks his wine, like a god. Pass him by
and throw your arms around the knees of my mother, so that
you might with rejoicing quickly see the day of your homecoming—
even if you come from very far. If you receive favor in her sight,
then there is hope that you will see your friends and arrive   295
at your well-built house and the land of your fathers."°

                          So speaking
she struck the mules with the shining whip, and they moved
smartly, leaving the streams of the river. They moved along
nimbly, placing their hooves with speed and care. Nausicaä
drove carefully so that her ladies and Odysseus might follow   300
closely on foot, and she applied the lash judiciously.

                        The sun went
down and they came to the glorious grove sacred to Athena
where godlike Odysseus took a seat. He immediately prayed

---

296 *your fathers*: No one has ever convincingly explained why Odysseus should approach Nausicaä's mother
rather than her father to request his return.

to the daughter of great Zeus: "Hear me, child of Zeus
305 who carries the goatskin fetish—hear me, unwearied one!
Hearken to me now, for earlier when I was shipwrecked
you never did attend to me—when the glorious earth-shaker
wrecked me! But grant that I may come to the Phaeacians
as one to be welcomed and pitied."

                       So he spoke in prayer, and Pallas
310 Athena heard him. But she did not yet appear face to face,
for she feared her father's brother:° Furiously he raged
against godlike Odysseus until he reached his own land.

---

311 *father's brother*: Poseidon, angry because Odysseus blinded the Cyclops Polyphemos, his son (*Od.*
Book 10). But Athena abandoned Odysseus before this encounter. She does not appear in her own person
before Odysseus reaches Ithaca (Book 13), though she intervenes constantly from the moment of the
shipwreck.

BOOK 8. *The Stranger in Town*

[Book 7 and Lines 1–245 of Book 8 are omitted. Queen Aretê and King Alkinoös welcome Odysseus and entertain him with a banquet and athletic competitions. A Phaeacian noble insults Odysseus' athletic prowess. Odysseus then throws a discus farther than anyone else. The singer Demodokos entertains the crowd with a rowdy song about infidelity among the gods:]

Then Demodokos struck up the beautiful song on
  his lyre, the love song of Ares and fair-crowned Aphrodite,
how they first mingled in love, in secret,° in the house
of Hephaistos: "Ares gave her many gifts, and he shamed
the bed and couch of King Hephaistos. But Helios came to him   250
as a messenger, and he saw them as they made love. When Hephaistos
was told the dire tale, he went into his forge, pondering evil
thoughts in his heart. He placed his huge anvil on the anvil-block,
and he forged bonds that could not be broken or loosed,
that the lovers might remain fixed just where they were.   255
And when he had fashioned his trick, in his anger at Ares,
he went into the chamber where his bed lay, and everywhere
he spread around the bedposts the bonds, and many he hung
from the roof-beams above, as fine as spider webs so that no one
could see them, not even one of the blessed gods, so cunningly   260
were they made. And when he had suspended his snares all
around the couch, he pretended that he was going to Lemnos,
a well-founded city, which to him was much the dearest
of all lands.°

      Nor did Ares, whose reins are of gold, fail
to notice when he saw the marvelous craftsman Hephaistos   265
going away. He want straight to the house of glorious
Hephaistos, craving the love of beautifully crowned Kythereia.°
She had just come from the house of the mighty son of Kronos.

---

248 *in secret*: The marriage of Hephaistos and Aphrodite is scarcely attested outside the present passage: In the *Iliad* Hephaistos is married to Charis ("grace"). Nonetheless this famous story has inspired artistic representations even to the present day.

264 *all lands*: The island of Lemnos had a cult to Hephaistos and its principal town was called Hephaistia.

267 *Kythereia*: "she of CYTHERA," the island off the southernmost tip of the Peloponnessus, where Aphrodite was born according to some traditions.

She sat down. "Ares came into the house and he took her
270   by the hand and spoke and addressed her: 'Come here, my dear,
let us go to bed and take our pleasure, lying together, for Hephaistos
is no longer in the land, but has gone off to Lemnos, to the Sintians°
of wild speech.

          "So he spoke, and she liked the thought
of going to bed with him. So they went to the bed and lay down,
275   and around them the cunning bonds of the wise Hephaistos
fell. They could not move—could not lift their limbs—
and then they saw there was no escape. The famous god
with two powerful arms came up near them, for he had turned
back before he reached the land of Lemnos. Helios had been
280   his lookout and had brought word to him.

                              "He went off
to his house, troubled in heart, and he stood in the doorway
as a savage anger seized him. He cried out terribly, and he called
to all the gods: 'Father Zeus, and you other blessed gods
who last forever, come here!—to see a laughable business,
285   a matter not to be endured! Aphrodite the daughter of Zeus
always scorns me because I am lame. She loves this pestilent
Ares because he is handsome and strong of foot,
whereas I was born a weakling. But who is to blame?
My two parents,° who ought never to have begotten me!
290   But you will see where these two have gone up to my bed
to make love, and I am troubled to see it. But I doubt that they
will lie in this fashion for long, no, not for a minute, even though
they enjoy the sex. Soon they will both lose the desire
to sleep! The snare and the bonds will hold them until her father
295   gives back all the wedding gifts that I gave him for his bitch
daughter. She may be good-looking, but she can't contain her lust!'

          "So he spoke, and the gods gathered at the house
with the bronze floor. Poseidon the earth-shaker came,
and Hermes the helper, and King Apollo came, who works
300   from a long ways off. (But the lady goddesses stayed at home
for shame, each in her own house!) The gods, givers of good
things, stood in the forecourt, and an unquenchable laughter
arose among the blessed gods when they saw the art
of wise Hephaistos.

---

272   *Sintians*: Early inhabitants of Lemnos, probably from THRACE.

289   *two parents*: Here Hera and Zeus; in other traditions, Hephaistos was the child of Hera alone.

FIGURE 8.1 Ares and Aphrodite. Clad only in a gown that comes just above her pubic area, Aphrodite holds a mirror while her half-naked lover Ares, sitting on a nearby bench, embraces her and touches her breast. The device that imprisoned them is visible as a cloth stretched above their heads. Such paintings were especially popular in Roman brothels in Pompeii, where this fresco appears. Roman fresco from Pompeii, c. AD 70.

"Thus would one say, glancing at his neighbor:
305 'Evil deeds never prosper! The slow catches the swift! as even
now Hephaistos, though slow, has caught Ares, the swiftest
of the gods who live on Olympos. Though he is lame, Hephaistos
has caught him by guile, and Ares owes an adulterer's fine!'

"They said things like this to one another. Then King Apollo,
310 the son of Zeus, said this to Hermes: 'Hermes, son of Zeus,
messenger, the giver of good things, wouldn't you like to share
a couch with golden Aphrodite even though bound
in powerful chains?'

"The messenger Argeïphontes answered him:
'Would that this might come about, O King Apollo who shoots
315 from afar, that three times as many endless bonds might bind me,
and all you gods look on and all the goddesses too, if only
I might lay beside golden Aphrodite.'

"So he spoke
and laughter arose among the deathless gods. But Poseidon
did not laugh. He begged Hephaistos, the famous craftsman,
320 to let Ares go. And he spoke to him words that went like
arrows: 'Release him! And I promise this to you, just as
you bid, that he will pay all that is right in the presence
of the immortal gods.'

"The famous god, strong in both arms,
then said: 'Do not ask this, O Poseidon, shaker of the earth.
325 Pledges given on behalf of a worthless fellow are worthless!
How could I put you in bonds among the deathless gods
if Ares should avoid the debt and the bonds and escape?'°

"Poseidon the holder of the earth then said to him:
'Hephaistos, even if Ares avoids the debt and runs off,
330 I will pay it for him.'

"The famous god of two strong arms then replied:
'All right, I cannot refuse you.'

---

327 *and escape*: Hephaistos' point is that Ares would be sure to default on the pledge, but Hephaistos could not
very well move against Poseidon, the older god who stands up for respectability and due process while the
younger gods, Hermes and Apollo, find the same situation a cause for laughter.

"So speaking, the mighty Hephaistos
loosed the bonds, and the two lovers, when the strong bonds
were relaxed, leaped up. Ares went off to THRACE
and laughter-loving Aphrodite went off to CYPRUS,
to PAPHOS,° where her estate and her fragrant altar are.   335
There the Graces bathed her and anointed her flesh with
immortal oil such as gleams on the gods who are forever,
and around her they placed lovely clothing, a wonder to see."

This song the famous singer sang, and Odysseus was delighted
to hear it, and so were all of the oar-loving Phaeacians, men   340
famous for their ships.

*[Lines 342–420 are omitted. Odysseus is offered many gift-tokens, then given a bath. He
still has not revealed his identity.]*

When the female slaves had washed him
and anointed his flesh with olive oil, they put a beautiful cloak
and shirt around him. When he came out of the bathtub,
he went forth to the men who were drinking wine. Nausicaä,
gifted with beauty by the gods, stood beside the doorpost   425
of the well-built hall, and she marveled at Odysseus when she
saw him. She spoke to him words that went like arrows:
"Dear stranger, remember me when you return to your native land,
and thereafter, because to me first of all you owe the price
of your life."   430

The resourceful Odysseus then answered her:
"Nausicaä, daughter of great-hearted Alkinoös, even so may Zeus,
the loud-thundering husband of Hera, bring it to pass that I return
home and see the day of my homecoming. There I will pray to you
as to a goddess always, for all my days. For you, young girl,
gave me life."°   435

So he spoke and sat down on a chair beside
the chieftain Alkinoös. They were serving out portions and mixing
the wine. The herald came near, leading the fine singer Demodokos,
honored by the people. Demodokos sat down in the middle
of the diners, leaning his chair against a tall pillar. Then

---

335 *Paphos:* Where Aphrodite had a famous shrine.

435 *me life:* But in the summary of his wanderings told to Penelope in Book 23 he does not even mention
     Nausicaä.

440 the resourceful Odysseus spoke to the herald, cutting off
a piece of the backbone of the white-tusked boar°—there was still
plenty left—and there was rich fat on either side: "Herald,
here, give this meat to Demodokos, so that he might eat of it,
and I will greet him, though I am sad at heart. For to all men
445 upon the earth singers are endowed with honor and reverence
because the Muse has taught them the pathway of song.
She loves the tribe of singers."

                      Thus he spoke, and the herald
carried the lyre and placed it in the hands of the good man
Demodokos. He took it, glad in his heart. Then they put out their
450 hands toward the refreshment that lay before them. But when they
had put aside all desire for food and drink, then the resourceful
Odysseus asked Demodokos: "Demodokos, I praise you above all men,
whether the Muse, Zeus's child, has instructed you, or Apollo.
For you sing well and accurately the fate of the Achaeans—
455 all that they did and suffered, and all the pains that the Achaeans
endured, as if you yourself were present or had heard the story
from someone who was. But come now, change your theme
and sing of the building of the wooden horse that Epeios° made
with Athena's help, that godlike Odysseus once dragged up
460 to the acropolis as a deception, having filled it with men who sacked
Ilion. If you can tell me this tale truly, I will at once tell all men
that the god has readily given you the gift of divine song."

   So he spoke, and Demodokos began with an appeal to the god,
then let his song be heard. He took up the story where the Argives
465 had embarked on their well-benched ships and were sailing off,
having cast fire into their huts. In the meanwhile, a remaining band,
led by famous Odysseus, sat in the place of assembly of the Trojans,
hidden in the horse. For the Trojans themselves had dragged the horse
up to the acropolis. And there it stood, while the Trojans talked long
470 as they sat about it, but could reach no firm conclusion. There were
three opinions: that they should smash the hollow wood with
the pitiless bronze, or that they should drag it to the rampart and throw
it down on the rocks below, or that they should leave it alone
as a great offering to the gods. The third view was the one brought to pass,
475 for it was the Trojans' fate to perish when the city should enclose

---

441 *white-tusked boar*: The backbone (chine) was the cut of honor.

458 *Epeios*: He appears otherwise in Homer only as a boxer and weight-thrower in the funeral games for
Patroklos (*Il.* 23).

the great horse of wood. In it were the best of the Argives,
bringing death and doom to the Trojans.

          So Demodokos sang of how
the sons of the Achaeans poured out of the horse and, leaving
their hollow ambush, sacked the city. Some went this way,
some that, to waste the steep city, but Odysseus went to the house   480
of Deïphobos° together with godlike Menelaos. There, he said,
Odysseus braved his most bitter battle, but was victorious
with the help of great-hearted Athena. These things the famous
singer sang, and Odysseus was melted— he wet the cheeks
beneath his eyelids with tears.   485

          As a woman falls on her dear husband
and wails, a man who has fallen before his city and his people,
warding off the pitiless day from the city and from his children—
as she sees him dying and breathing his last, she shrieks
aloud and throws herself about him while the enemy
behind her strike the middle of her back and shoulders   490
with their spears, and lead her away into slavery to bear pain
and calamity, while her cheeks are wasted with the most
pitiful grief—even so Odysseus poured a torrent of tears
from beneath his brows. Only one noticed him weeping—
Alkinoös alone saw it and marked it, because he sat   495
next to him, and he heard him groaning deeply.

    Quickly he spoke to the oar-loving Phaeacians: "Listen
to me, O leaders and counselors of the Phaeacians—let Demodokos
leave off the clear-voiced lyre. For his singing is not pleasing
to everyone here! Ever since we began to dine and the divine   500
singer began to sing, the stranger here has not ceased
from sad lament. Surely grief has encompassed
his heart. But come, let Demodokos cease his singing
so that we might all take delight alike, both hosts and guest,
for it is better this way. On the honored stranger's account   505
all these things are made ready, his sending forth and the gifts
of friendship that, lovingly, we have given him. A stranger
and a suppliant is like a brother to a man who has some little
grasp of wisdom.

---

481 *Deïphobos*: A son of Priam and Hekabê and brother of Hector, who took up with Helen after the death
    of Paris, according to postHomeric accounts.

"Therefore do not hide with crafty thoughts
510 what I shall now ask you. The better course is to speak plainly.
Tell me the name by which your mother and father called you,
and the people of the town and those who live round about.
For no one of all mankind is altogether without a name,
neither base man nor noble, when he is first born, but parents
515 give a name to everyone when they are born. And tell me
your country, your people, and your city, so that our ships
may send you there, telling the course by their wits.
For the Phaeacians have no pilots, nor steering oars such as other
ships have, but their ships know the thoughts and minds
520 of men, and they know the cities and rich fields of all peoples,
and they quickly travel over the gulf of the sea covered
in a mist and a cloud. They do not fear harm or destruction.
    "But this story I once heard my father Nausithoös say—
he said that Poseidon is indignant with us because we give
525 safe transport to all men. He said that once, as a well-made ship
of the Phaeacians returns from an escort over the misty sea,
that Poseidon would strike here and heap-up a great mountain
around our city.° So spoke the old man. Either these things
the gods will bring to pass or will leave unfulfilled, as is pleasing
530 to the heart of the god.
                    "But come, tell me this and say it truly.
Where have you wandered? To what countries of men have you come?
Tell me of the thickly populated cites themselves, both of those
who are cruel and savage and unjust, and of those who love strangers
and are god-fearing in their minds. Tell me why you weep
535 and wail in your spirit when you hear the fate of the Argives
and the Danaäns at Ilion. This the gods brought about.
They spun the thread of destruction for men so that there might
be song for those yet to come. Did some family member die
before Ilion—a good man, your daughter's husband, or your wife's father,
540 who are nearest to one after his own flesh and blood? Or was it
some revered comrade, a man most dear, a good man? For a comrade
with an understanding heart is in no way less than a brother."

---

528   *around our city*: Apparently so they could no longer offer safe transport to strangers.

BOOK 9. *Odysseus in the Cave of Cyclops*

Then resourceful Odysseus spoke to him in reply:
"Lord Alkinoös, renowned above all men, truly
it is a lovely thing to listen to a singer such as this man is,
like to the gods in his voice. I don't think that there is
a greater fulfillment of delight than when joy holds   5
all the people, and while dining seated side by side
in the house they listen to a singer, and beside them
the tables are filled with bread and meat and the cupbearer
draws wine from the mixing bowl and carries it around
and pours it into the cups. This seems to my mind   10
to be the fairest thing of all. But your heart is turned
to ask about my grievous pains, that I might
weep and groan still more.

            "What then should I say first of all,
what last? For the gods in heaven have given me many
afflictions. Now I shall tell you my name so that you too   15
may know it and I, once I have escaped the pitiless day
of doom, may be a guest-friend to you, although I live far away.
I am Odysseus, the son of Laërtes, known among men
for my many deceits, and my fame reaches to the sky.
I live in clear-seen ITHACA. There is a mountain there, Neriton,   20
covered with forest, conspicuous. Round about are many other
islands close to one another—DOULICHION and SAMÊ
and wooded ZAKYNTHOS. Ithaca itself is low-lying
in the sea and is the furthest toward the west.° The others
lie apart toward Dawn, and the sun. It is a rugged island,   25
but a good nurse for young men. As for me, I can see nothing
sweeter than one's own land.

            "Truly Kalypso, the beautiful goddess,
tried to keep me there in her hollow caves, desiring
that I be her husband. Likewise did Kirkê, the crafty lady
of Aiaia,° tried to hold me back in her halls, desiring that I be   30

---

24 *the west*: Evidently Doulichion is modern Leucas; Samê is Kephallenia; Zakynthos is Zakynthos; Ithaca is Ithaca,
     but it is not the furthest "toward the west" (see MAP VI). As usual, Homer is somewhat cavalier about geography.

30 *Aiaia*: "earth," the name of Kirkê's mythical island.

her husband. But they could not persuade me in my heart.
For there is nothing sweeter than one's homeland and one's parents,
even if he lives far away in a rich house in a foreign country,
apart from his parents.° But come, let me tell you of my painful
35   homecoming that Zeus set upon me as I returned from Troy.
     "Coming out of Ilion, a wind drove us to the KIKONES,
to Ismaros. There I sacked the city and destroyed the men.
We took the women and much wealth from that city
and divided it up that no one might be cheated of an equal share.
40   I urged that we flee on swift foot, but the others would not
be persuaded—the great fools! There we drank much wine,
and we slaughtered many sheep beside the shore and cattle
with shambling walk. In the meanwhile the Kikones went
and called to other Kikones in the neighborhood, more numerous
45   and braver ones. They lived inland, experienced in fighting
the enemy from chariots and, where necessary, on foot.
They came in the morning, as many as there are leaves and flowers
in their season. And then an evil fate from Zeus fell upon us
ill-fated men, that we might suffer many sorrows. The Kikones
50   took their stand and fought beside the swift ships, and each side
threw spears of bronze at the other. So long as it was morning
and the sacred day progressed, for so long we held out
and fought them off, although they were more. And when
the sun turned to the time of the unyoking of oxen, then
55   the Kikones turned the tide of battle and overcame the Achaeans.
Six companions with fancy shin guards perished from each ship,°
but the others fled from death and fate.
                             "Then we sailed farther,
grieving in our hearts, saved from death, though we lost
our dear comrades. Nor did I allow the curved ships to travel
60   on farther before we had called out three times to each
of our wretched companions, those who died on the plain,
overcome by the Kikones.° But Zeus the cloud-gatherer
roused North Wind in an astounding tempest against
our ships, and North Wind hid the land and sea alike in cloud.
65   "Night rushed down from the heaven. Our ships were borne
sidelong—the strength of the wind tore the sails to shreds,
so we let down the sails into the ships, fearing death,

---

34 *parents*: Odysseus does not mention his wife, whose loyalty is in fact the focus of the story.

56 *from each ship*: Odysseus commands 12 ships, so he lost 72 men to the Kikones. The usual complement of
rowers to each ship was 20, though sometimes this could reach 50, as with the ship of the Phaeacians. It is
never clear how many men Odysseus has in each ship.

62 *by the Kikones*: A reference to the religious practice of calling out the names of the dead three times to assist
their transition into the other world.

and we hastily rowed the boats toward the land.
There we lay continuously for two night and two days,
eating our hearts out from exhaustion and torment. But when
fair-tressed Dawn brought the third day to birth, we raised
the white sails on the masts and took our seats. The wind
and the helmsmen steered the ships.

       "And then I would have
reached unscathed the land of my fathers, but as we
rounded MALEA° the wave and the current of North Wind
beat me back and drove me off course past CYTHERA.

 "Then we were carried by deadly winds over the fish-rich
sea for nine days, but on the tenth we came to the land
of the Lotus-eaters, who feed on a flowery food.° There we went
ashore and drew water, and quickly we took our meal
beside the swift ships. But when we had tasted food and drink,
I sent forth some of my companions to find out who were
the men who ate bread in this land. I picked out two men,
and sent with them a herald as the third. Quickly they went
and mingled with the Lotus-eaters, who did not plan death
for my men, but gave them to eat of the lotus. Whoever ate
of the honey-sweet fruit of the lotus no longer wished
to bring back word or to return home, but wanted to remain
there with the Lotus-eaters, feeding on the lotus, forgetful
of their return home.

    "I drove them, weeping, to the ships,
by force, and I dragged them beneath the benches
and bound them in the hollow ships. I ordered my other
trusty companions to depart with speed on the swift ships
so that none of them could eat of the lotus and forget his homeward
journey. Quickly they went on board and sat at the thole-pins,
and seated in a row they struck the gray sea with their oars.

 "From there we sailed on, grieving in our hearts. We came
to the land of the arrogant and lawless Cyclopes.° Trusting
in the deathless gods they neither plant with their hands nor

70

75

80

85

90

95

---

75 *Malea:* The winds and powerful currents off Malea, on the southeast coast of the PELOPONNESUS, are still a
  problem for seafarers. Menelaos, too, was driven off course here (Book 4).

79 *flowery food:* Beginning in the ancient world, and continuing today, commentators have attempted to trace
  Odysseus' wanderings on a map, but he is no longer in the real world and all such efforts are fruitless. "We're
  not in Kansas anymore," as Dorothy says in the movie *The Wizard of Oz.* Similarly, attempts to identify the
  lotus plant are misconceived. The plant is like that magical food in the other world that, once consumed,
  prevents one from returning to this world (in the myth of Persephone it is the seed of the pomegranate).

98 *Cyclopes:* Probably originally meant "with round face" or "with round eyes," but in Homer Cyclops is taken to
  mean "round-eye," that is, having only one eye. Homer never says that Cyclops has only one eye, but the story
  depends on it. In art he is often shown with three eyes. The relationship between Homer's Cyclopes and the
  Cyclopes (in Hesiod), who were the smiths of Zeus, forgers of the thunderbolt, has never been clarified.

100 do they plow, but all these things spring up for them unsown
and unplowed—wheat and barley and vines that bear grapes
for a fine wine. And the rain of Zeus makes them grow.
They do not have assemblies where they discuss policy, nor do
they establish rules, but they live on the peaks of high mountains
105 in hollow caves, each man laying down the law to his own
children and wives—nor do they care about one another.
    "There is a fertile island that stretches outside the harbor,
not close, not far from the land of the Cyclopes, wooded.
Countless goats live there, wild goats. The comings
110 and goings of men do not drive them away, nor do hunters
go there, men who suffer jeopardy in the woods as they tramp
upon the peaks of the mountains. The island is not occupied
by flocks, nor covered by plowland, but unsown and unplowed.
The island is every day empty of men, and it feeds
115 the bleating goats. For the Cyclopes have no red-cheeked ships,°
nor do builders of ships live among them who might build
ships with fine benches to provide them everything
they want, journeying to the cities of men, as men often
cross the sea in ships to visit one another. Such men would
120 have made of this island a pleasant place. It is by no means
a poor place, but would bear every fruit in season. There are
meadows in it, watered and soft, beside the shores of the gray sea.
Vines will never fail there. The land is level and suitable
for plowing. One could harvest a bumper crop every season,
125 for the soil is rich.
                "There is a secure harbor where there is
no need of mooring ropes, nor need of throwing out
anchor stones, nor of making fast the sterns of ships.
You need only draw the ships up on the shore, then wait
for the time that your spirit urges you again to put to sea,
130 when the winds blow fair.
                "At the head of the harbor
a spring of shining water flows from beneath a cave.
Poplars grow around it. There we sailed—some god
guided us through the dark night, for there was no light
by which to see. A thick mist covered the island all around,
135 and the cloud-hidden moon did not appear in the night sky.
No one had seen the island, nor the long waves rolling
onto the dry land until we ran our ships with fine benches
up onto the shore. When we had beached the ships,
we took down the sails and ourselves went ashore

---

115 *red-cheeked ships*: Because their sterns are painted red.

on the edge of the sea. There we fell asleep and awaited   140
the bright dawn.
          "When early-born dawn appeared, who has
fingers like roses, we wandered over the island, wondering
at it. Nymphs, the daughters of Zeus who carries the goatskin
fetish, roused up the mountain goats so that my companions
could have something to eat. Immediately we took out our bent   145
bows and javelins with long sockets from the ships. We split up
into three groups and set to throwing our missiles. Soon
the god had given us enough game to satisfy our hearts.
Twelve ships followed me,° and to each nine goats fell
by lot. For me alone they chose out ten.   150
                    "Then we spent
the whole day dining on endless flesh and sweet wine
until the sun went down. The red wine from our ships had not
yet run out. Some was still left, for we had taken a lot of it
in jars for each crew member when we sacked the sacred
city of the Kikones. We looked across to the land   155
of the Cyclopes, who lived nearby. We saw smoke and heard
voices and the sound of sheep and goats. When the sun went down
and darkness came on, we lay down to rest on the edge of the sea.
     "When early-born dawn appeared, whose fingers
were like roses, I called an assembly and spoke thus to all: 160
"The rest of you stay here, my trusty companions, while
I take a ship and some comrades and appraise these men,
to see who they are, whether they are violent and savage
and unjust, or whether they are friendly to strangers and have
minds that fear the gods."   165
                    "So speaking I got in my ship
and commanded my men to embark, to release the stern-cables.
They quickly got in and sat down on the benches.
Sitting in order, they struck the gray sea with their oars.
And when we had reached the place nearby, there,
at the edge of the land, we espied a cave close to the sea,   170
high up, overgrown by laurels. Many flocks were
accustomed to sleep there. A high wall surrounded
the cave, made of stones set deep in the earth, and tall
pines grew there, and high-crowned oaks. A huge man
slept alone in that place and herded his animals there,   175
all alone. He had no doings with others, but lived
in solitude, without laws. For truly he was an unearthly
monster, not like a man who lives by bread, more like

---

149 *followed me*: The first time we learn in the *Odyssey* how many ships were in Odysseus' contingent.

a wooded peak of a high mountain range that stands
180 out alone above all others.
                              "I ordered the remainder
of my trusty companions to stay by the ship and to guard it
while I went off, having selected twelve of my best men.
I had with me a goatskin of dark sweet wine that Maron
had given me, the son of Euanthes, a priest of Apollo
185 who used to watch over Ismaros.° He gave it because
out of respect we protected him, along with his wife and child.
He lived in a wood of Phoibos Apollo, and he gave me
splendid gifts. Of finely worked gold he gave me
seven talents, and he gave me a silver wine-mixing
190 bowl, and beside these he filled twelve jars with wine,
a divine drink—sweet, unmixed. No one in his household
knew about this wine, neither slave nor servant,
only his wife and the housekeeper. Whenever they drank
honeyed red wine, he would pour one cup of the wine
195 into twenty of water, and a wondrous odor would come up
from the mixing bowl. Then one could hardly resist
drinking it.
            "With this wine I filled a large skin and took
it along, also provisions in a leather sack. For my proud
spirit imagined confronting a man clothed in mighty strength,
200 a savage, not subjecting himself to laws or regulations.
We quickly arrived at the cave, but did not find him inside,
for he was shepherding his fat flocks in the fields.
Coming into the cave we marveled at everything—there
were crates filled with cheeses, and pens groaned with sheep
205 and kids. Each kind were penned separately—the older
by themselves, the younger by themselves, the newborn
by themselves as well. Vast jars were brimful of whey,
and the milk pails and bowls, finely made, into which he milked.
            "Then my comrades begged me to grab the cheeses and to leave
210 that place—to drive the kids and lambs quickly out of the pens
to our swift ship, and to sail away across the salt water.
But I was not persuaded—it were better if I had been!—
because I wanted to see him, in case he might give me gift-tokens.°
As it happened, his appearance was not to be a pleasing one
215 to my companions!

---

185   ...*Ismaros:* Maron is named after Maroneia, a wine-growing district in southern THRACE. His father is
        aptly named "blooming" (Euanthes). This is the only time in the *Odyssey* that a priest is referred to.

213   *gift-tokens:* To establish *xenia,* "guest-friendship." As we have seen with Odysseus' experience on Scheria,
        the aristocratic traveler could expect to be entertained and given a gift, often precious, that would ever
        thereafter bind the traveler and his descendants to the host.

FIGURE 9.1   Maron gives the sack of potent wine to Odysseus.   Wearing a Phrygian cap (though he lives in Thrace), net leggings, crossed belts on his chest, and a cape, the beardless Kikonian priest Maron gives the sack of wine by which Odysseus overcomes Cyclops. In his left hand he holds a spear pointed downwards. His crowned wife stands behind him with a horn drinking cup. The very long-haired Odysseus wears high boots and a traveler's cap (*pilos*), and he holds a spear over his shoulder with his right hand. To the far left stands a Kikonian woman. South Italian red-figure wine-mixing bowl by the Maron Painter, 340–330 BC.

"We made a fire and offered
sacrifice. We took some of the cheeses and ate them.
We sat inside and waited until he should return from
herding his flocks.
                    "He finally arrived with a large load
of dried wood, useful at dinner time.° He threw the wood inside
220 the cave with a crash. In terror we shrank back into a deep recess
of the cave. He drove his fat flock of sheep, all those
he needed to milk, deep into the wide cavern, leaving
the males outside—the rams and the billys—in the deep
courtyard. Then he placed a huge boulder in the opening
225 of the cavern, lifting it on high, gigantic. Twenty-two
fine four-wheeled carts could not have dislodged it from
the ground, such a towering mass of rock he placed
before the door.
                    "Then he sat down and milked his sheep
and the bleating goats, all in turn, and he placed
230 a suckling beneath each. And he smartly curdled half
the white milk,° gathered it and stored it in woven baskets,
and the other half he put in vessels so that he could use it
for drink, so that it might serve him for dinner.
                                        "When he had
finished his tasks, he built a fire and, finally, he saw us—
235 and he asked: 'Strangers, who are you? From where do you sail
the watery paths?°Are you on some mission, or do you cross
the sea at random, like pirates who wander around endangering
their lives while doing evil to men of other lands?'
"So he spoke—and our hearts were frozen in fear of his
240 rumbling voice and his immense size. Nonetheless I answered
in this way: 'We are Achaeans returning from Troy.
We have been buffeted by winds from every direction across
the great depth of the sea. Longing to go home, we have travelled
on a false course, by many stages. For so Zeus devised.
245 We are followers of Agamemnon, the son of Atreus,
whose fame is now the greatest under the heaven.
He has sacked a city of great size and destroyed its many
people. We come to you on our knees, as suppliants,
in the hope you might give us a gift-token or some other

---

219 *dinner time*: But for heating and light. He does not use the fire for cooking.

231 *white milk*: Presumably by adding a fermenting agent, such as fig juice.

236 *watery paths*: Cyclops inverts all the rules of *xenia*. In polite society the host entertains and feeds the guest
before asking the stranger's identity. Cyclops immediately wants to know who these men are, then instead
of feeding them, he eats them!

present, as is the custom among strangers. Respect the gods, 250
O mighty man! We are your suppliants, and Zeus
is the avenger of suppliants and strangers—Zeus the god
of strangers, who always stands by respectable voyagers.'

    "So I spoke, and he answered me immediately with a pitiless
heart: 'You are a fool, stranger, or you must come from faraway, 255
inviting me to fear or shun your gods. The Cyclopes have no care
for Zeus who carries the goatskin fetish, nor for any other
of your gods, because we are more powerful than they!
Not to avoid the hatred of Zeus would I spare you
or your companions, if my spirit did not so urge me. 260
But tell me, so that I may know—where did you anchor
your well-made ship, far away, or nearby?'

    "Thus he spoke, testing me, but he did not fool
my great cunning. I answered him with crafty words:
'Poseidon, the rocker of the earth, shattered my ship, 265
throwing it against the cliffs at the edge of your land,
driving it onto a headland. For a wind arose
from the sea, but I, along with my men, escaped
dread destruction.'

            "So I spoke. He did not answer from his
pitiless heart, but leaping up he seized two of my companions, 270
raised them high, then dashed them to the ground as if
they were puppies. Their brains ran out onto the ground,
wetting the earth. Cutting them limb from limb, he readied
his meal. He ate them like a lion raised in the mountains,
not leaving anything—not the guts nor the flesh nor the bones 275
rich with marrow.

            "Wailing, we held up our hands to Zeus,
seeing this vile deed and helpless to do anything about it.
But when Cyclops had filled his great belly by eating the flesh
of two of our men, and then drinking pure milk, he lay stretched
out among the sheep in the cave. I contemplated in my great 280
heart going up close to him, drawing my sharp sword
from my thigh, and stabbing him in the chest where the belly
shields the liver, feeling along with my hand to find
the right place. But a second thought came to me—
we would die then a grisly death! For our hands would be 285
incapable of budging the heavy stone he had set in place
against those high doors. So, groaning miserably, we awaited
the bright dawn.

            "When early-born dawn appeared
and spread her fingers of rose, Cyclops stirred up
the fire and milked his glorious herds, all in order, 290

again setting the young to each dam. When he had
finished his tasks, he again seized two of my men
for his meal. After he had made his meal, he drove out
the fat herds, easily lifting away the huge stone.
295 Then he put it back again, as if shutting the lid
on a quiver. With a loud whistle Cyclops turned
his flocks toward the mountains.
      "I was left there devising evil
in the depths of my heart, wondering how I could take
revenge, if Athena would grant me glory. Thinking on it,
300 I devised the following plan: A great club of Cyclops lay
beside a sheep pen, green, made of olive wood.
He had cut it to carry, once it dried out. Looking at it,
we considered it to be as big as a mast of a black
ship with twenty oars—a big merchantman that
305 crosses over the great gulf, so great it was to look at
in length and in breadth.
      "I went up to it and cut off
about six feet and gave the length to my companions.
I told them to strip off the bark and make it smooth,
while I stood by it and sharpened the point. Then I at once
310 placed the stake in the blazing fire to harden it.
Then I laid it away, hiding it beneath some dung
that was spread in big heaps all over the cave.° I ordered
the others to select by lot who would dare to assist me
in hoisting the stake and grinding it into his eye,
315 when sweet sleep overcame him. They selected the very
ones I myself would have chosen, four solid men,
and I the fifth among them.
      "At dusk Cyclops returned
from the fields, leading his herds with their beautiful fleece.
He drove the fat sheep into the broad cave, all of them
320 this time, leaving none of them outside in the deep court,
either because he had a foreboding, or some god urged him to.
Then he lifted high the huge rock and set it back in place.
He sat down and milked his ewes and bleating goats,
all in order, again placing each young beneath the teat
325 of every mother. When he had finished his tasks, he snatched
two of my men and prepared his meal.

---

312 *the cave*: Odysseus has forgotten all about his sword, which could have served as a lethal weapon, but the
   folktale hero needs a special weapon by which to overcome his adversary. In this case the weapon is the
   olive stake. Just such primitive fire-hardened spears were used in primordial times to separate man from
   nature, so the stake is a fitting symbol of civilization triumphant over barbarism.

"Then I spoke
to Cyclops, standing near him, holding in my hands
a bowl of ivy wood filled with black wine: 'Cyclops,
take this wine, drink it after your meal of human flesh,
so that you might know what manner of drink our ship   330
contained. I was bringing it to you as a drink offering,
in hopes you would take pity on me and send me homeward.
   " 'But as it is you are mad past bearing! Vile monster!
How will anyone else from all the multitudes of men
ever come here again when you have behaved so badly?'   335
   "So I spoke. He took the wine and drank it.
He was tremendously pleased, quaffing the sweet drink,
and again he asked me: 'Give me some more, be a good
fellow. And tell me your name right away so that I may give
you a gift-token that will make you happy. Surely the rich   340
plowland bears a fine grape for the Cyclopes, and the rain
of Zeus makes the grape grow. But this is equal to the food
of the gods!'
   "So he spoke, and again I poured for him
the flaming wine. Three times I brought it and gave it to him,
three times he drank it in his mindless folly.   345
                            "When the wine
had gone to his head, I spoke to him with honeyed words:
'Cyclops, you ask about my famous name, so I will tell
you and then you will give me a gift-token, just as you
promised. *Nbdy* is my name. My mother and my father
and everyone else calls me *Nbdy*.'   350
                            "So I spoke, and he at once
answered me from his pitiless heart: "Nbdy, I will eat you
last among your comrades, and the others first. *That* will be
your gift-token!'
                            "He spoke and then, reeling over, fell on
his back. He lay there, bending his thick neck, and sleep,
which overcomes all, took hold of him. From his throat   355
dribbled wine and bits of human flesh. Drunk, he vomited.°
   "I then pushed the stake I'd made into the hot ashes
until it glowed hot. I encouraged my companions, so that no man
would hold back from fear. Then, as soon as the stake was nearly
afire—although it was green, and glowed terribly—then   360
I went up close and took it from the fire, my comrades
attending me. A god breathed into us strong courage.

---

356   *vomited:* The demonic being in a folktale is often killed when drunk or at a banquet.

"They took the stake of olive wood, sharp on
its point, and thrust it into his eye. I threw my weight
365 on it from above and spun it around, as when
a man drills a ship's timber with a drill, and those
beneath keep the drill spinning with a thong, holding
the thong from either end, and the drill runs around
unceasingly—just so we took hold of that fiery stake
370 and spun it around in his eye, and his blood streamed
all around the heated thing.° The flame singed his
eyelid and eyebrow and the eyeball popped and its roots
crackled in the fire.
                    "As when a bronze-worker dips
a great ax or an adze in the cold water and the metal hisses
375 as he tempers it—from there comes the strength of iron—
so did Cyclops' eye hiss around the olive stake.°
He screamed horribly, and the rock echoed his cry.
    "In terror we drew back as he ripped out the stake
from his eye, mixed with a huge amount of blood. He wrenched
380 it from his eye and threw it away, throwing his hands about wildly.
    "Cyclops called aloud to the Cyclopes who lived
nearby in caves in the windy heights. Hearing his cry,
they assembled from here and there, and standing
outside his cave they asked him what was the matter:
385 'What is so bothering you, Polyphemos, that you cry out
through the immortal night and wake us all up? Can it be
that some man is driving off your flocks against your will?
Or is someone killing you by trickery or by might?'
    "The powerful Polyphemos answered them from the cave:
390 'My friends, Nbdy is killing me by trickery, not by might!'
    "And they answered with words that went like arrows:
'If nobody is assaulting you in your loneliness—well,
you cannot escape a sickness sent by great Zeus. Pray
to our father Poseidon, the king.'

---

371 *heated thing*: The stake is like a bow drill digging a hole. The forward thrust comes from the weight
of the user as he leans against it, while the twist of the drill comes from a thong wrapped in a single
turn around the drill. Men at each end of the bow push and pull so the drill turns, now clockwise, now
counterclockwise, like the drill of someone starting a fire by friction. Still, it is hard to see how Odysseus
could both put pressure on the stake and twist it, especially if its weight was carried by four other men.

376 *olive stake*: At the time that Homer was composing, iron was replacing bronze, so the bronze-smith is said
to quench an ax, and "from there comes the strength of iron." In Homer weapons are always of bronze,
but everyday implements can be iron. For centuries the effectiveness of tempering iron (immersion does
nothing for bronze) was thought to come from substances dissolved in the water into which the hot metal
was plunged, not from the sudden cooling of the metal: The word translated "tempers" really means "to
treat with a drug," that is, with something dissolved in the water.

"So they spoke and went away.
My heart laughed! My made-up name and my cunning   395
device had deceived him. Cyclops, groaning, in terrible pain,
fumbled around with his hands, then took away the stone
blocking his door. He sat down in the doorway with arms
outstretched, to catch anyone who might try to get out
of the door along with the sheep—so much did he hope   400
in his heart to find me a fool!
                    "But I considered what
would be the best plan to devise a sure escape
for my companions and for myself. I considered
every kind of trick and device, as is usual in matters
of life and death. A great evil was near . . . Now this   405
seemed to me to be the best plan: Here are his well-fed
rams with thick wool, handsome and large, with fleece
dark as violet. In silence I bound these together,
taking up three at a time, with twisted stems
on which the huge Cyclops, who knows no laws,   410
used to sleep.° The sheep in the middle would carry a man,
the two on the outside would go along, saving
my comrades. Thus each three sheep bore a man.
"As for me—there was a ram, by far the best of the flock,
and I climbed up on his back and then squirreled around   415
to his shaggy belly, where I lay, my hands clinging
constantly, with a steady heart, to the wonderful fleece.
    "Thus we waited, wailing, until the bright dawn.
When early-born dawn appeared and stretched forth her fingers
of rose, the rams hastened out to pasture. But the ewes,   420
unmilked, bleated in the pens, for their udders were full
to bursting. Their master, worn down by savage pain,
felt along the backs of all the sheep as they stood before
him—the fool! He did not realize that my men were bound
beneath the breasts of the wooly sheep.   425
                    "Last of all
the ram went out the door, burdened by the weight
of its fleece and my own devious self. Feeling along
his back, the mighty Polyphemos said: 'My dear ram,
why do you go out of the cave last of the entire flock?
In the past you would never lag behind the sheep,   430
but you always went out the very first to graze on
the tender bloom of the grass, taking long strides.
You always came first to the flowing rivers, and you were

---

411 *used to sleep*: Threaded in a bed-frame, the twisted stems would make a kind of mattress.

FIGURE 9.2 **The blinding of Polyphemos.** Odysseus and two of his men thrust the stake into the bearded giant's eye. In his right hand Polyphemos holds the cup of wine by which Odysseus had made him drunk. Odysseus is shown in white to distinguish him from his companions. This is the earliest representation of Cyclops' blinding, a popular subject in Greek art. Athenian black-figure two-handled jug, c. 660 BC.

always the most eager to return to the fold at evening.
But now you are the last of all. Perhaps you regret
the eye of your master that an evil man blinded,
along with his miserable companions, overcoming
my brain with wine! Nbdy, who has not yet, I think,
escaped destruction! If you could think as I do,
and you had the power of speech to tell me where
that man flees from my wrath, then would his brains
be smeared all over the ground of this cave when I hit him,
and my heart could take rest from the agony that this
good-for-nothing Nbdy has brought!'
                              "So saying
he sent the ram forth from the door. When we had gone
a short distance from the cave and the fold, I was first
to loose myself from the ram, and then I cut free my
companions. Quickly, turning constantly around, we drove
off the long-legged sheep, rich with fat, until we came to the ship.
Our friends who had escaped death were glad to see us, but they
bewailed those who were lost. I would not let them weep.
I nodded at each, ordering them to load aboard the herds
with beautiful fleece so we might sail away over the salt sea.
Then they boarded and sat down on their benches, and sitting
all in a row they struck the gray sea with their oars.
    "But when we were so far away you can barely hear
a man when he shouts, then I called to Cyclops with these
contemptuous words: 'Cyclops, it turns out that you did not eat
the companions of a man without strength in your hollow cave,
taking them by might and by violence. Surely your evil
deeds were bound to come back to you, wretch! You did not
shrink from devouring strangers in your own house.
For this Zeus and the other gods have punished you.'
    "So I spoke, and more anger boiled from his heart. He ripped
off the peak of a high mountain, and he threw it. The peak landed
just forward of our ship with its dark prow. The sea surged
beneath the rock as it came down and the wave carried
our ship back toward the shore on that flood from the deep—
driving it onto the dry land. But I seized a long pole
in my hands and thrust the ship off land again. I nodded
to my comrades, directing them to fall to their oars
so that we might escape this evil. They set to their oars
and rowed.
            "When we were twice as far away,
traveling over the sea, then I wanted to speak
to Cyclops again, but my comrades, one after the other,

tried to stop me with gentle words: 'Reckless man!
Why do you want to stir up this savage? Just now
he has thrown a rock into the sea and brought our ship
back to the dry land, and, truly, we thought we were
480 done for. If he had heard just one of us uttering
even one sound, he would have thrown a jagged rock
and smashed our heads and all the timbers of our ship!
He's a mighty thrower!'
                "So they cowered, but they did not
persuade my great-hearted spirit. I shouted back
485 at him with an angry heart: 'Cyclops, if any mortal man
ever asks about the disgraceful blinding of your eye,
you can say that *Odysseus*, sacker of cities, did it,
the son of Laërtes, whose home is in Ithaca.'°
                    "So I spoke,
and groaning he gave me this answer: 'Yes, yes—!
490 Now I remember an ancient prophecy. A prophet once
came here, a good man, a tall man, Telemos, the son of Eurymos,
who was better at prophecy than anyone. He grew old
among the Cyclopes. He told me that all this would happen
sometime in the future, that I would lose my sight at the hands
495 of Odysseus. I always thought that some big man, and handsome,
would come here, dressed in mighty power. As it is,
a little man, a man of no consequence, a feeble little guy—
he has blinded my eye after he got me drunk on wine!
  " 'But do return, O Odysseus, so that I can give you some
500 gift-tokens. And I can ask Poseidon, the famous shaker
of the earth, to give you a good trip home. I am his son,
you know, and he is my father. He himself will heal me, if he
wishes it: None of the blessed gods, nor mortal human can.'
  "So he spoke, and I said in reply: 'Would that I might
505 rob you of your breath-soul and your life and send you
to the house of Hades, as surely as the earth-shaker
shall never heal your eye!'

                  "So I spoke. He then raised
his hands into the starry heaven and prayed to Poseidon
the king: 'Hear me, Poseidon, holder of the earth,
510 you with the dark locks—if truly I am your son
and you are my father, grant that Odysseus, the son of Laërtes,

---

488   ... *Ithaca*: Homer is following a threefold narrative pattern, which repeats many times in the poem, of
      danger/defeat-of-an-enemy/recognition, and following this pattern Odysseus here gives his name. But
      knowledge of Odysseus' name gives Cyclops power over Odysseus, as in the curse Cyclops is about to give.

the sacker of cities, never reach his home, which he says
is in Ithaca. But if it is fated that he see his friends
again, and arrive to his well-built house, returning to the land
of his fathers—may he come after a long time, and after many   515
troubles, having lost all his companions, on someone
else's ship, and may he find grief in his own house!'
    "So he spoke in prayer, and the dark-haired one
heard him. Right away Cyclops picked up a much bigger
stone, twirled it around, and put all his strength   520
into the throw. The rock this time fell behind the ship
with its dark prows just a little bit, missing the blade
of the steering-oar. The sea surged as the stone submerged,
and its wake drove the ship forward and onto dry land.
    "But when we came back to the island,° the other ships   525
with fine benches were waiting, grouped together. Around
sat our comrades, wailing, awaiting us constantly.
We dragged the ship up onto the sand. We ourselves
got out of the ship and onto the shore of the sea. Then
we took the sheep out of the hollow boat and divided   530
them up so that no man, as far as I was able, would go
deprived of an equal share. My companions, who wear fancy
shin guards, gave the ram to me alone as a special gift
when the division took place. I sacrificed the ram
on the shore to Zeus of the dark thundercloud, the son   535
of Kronos, who rules over all, and I burned the thigh pieces.
He did not heed the offering but pondered how all
the ships with their fine benches might be destroyed,
along with my trusty companions.
                                        "So we spent the whole day
until the sunset, dining on endless flesh and sweet wine.   540
When the sun went down and darkness came on, then we went
to bed on the shore of the sea. When early-born dawn
came and spread her fingers of rose, I roused up my companions
and ordered them to embark, to loosen the stern-ropes.
Quickly they boarded the goats and sat down on the benches,   545
and all in a row they struck the gray sea with their oars.
From there we sailed farther, grieving at heart—glad to have
escaped death, but sorry for our dear companions who did not."

---

525   *the island*: Goat-island opposite the Cyclops' cave, from where Odysseus set out.

BOOK 10. *Odysseus and Kirkê*

"We arrived at the island of Aiolos, where Aiolos lives,
    the son of Hippotas,° dear to the deathless gods—
a floating island, and all around it is an unbreakable wall
of bronze, and the cliff runs up sheer. He has twelve children
5 in his halls, six daughters and six sons in their prime,
and he gave his daughters as wives to his sons.
These feast continually at the side of their dear father
and diligent mother, and endless refreshment lies beside them.
The house, full of steam from cooking, resounds all day long
10 even in the outer court, and at night they sleep beside
their chaste wives on blankets and corded beds.
    "Well, we came to their city and their beautiful palace,
and for a full month he entertained me and asked me about everything—
about Ilion and the ships of the Argives and the homecoming
15 of the Achaeans. And I told him everything in proper order. But when
I asked that I might leave and I pressed him to be sent on my way,
he did not deny me anything, and he arranged my sailing.
He gave me a skin made from a nine-year-old ox that
he had flayed and in it he bound the paths of the howling winds,
20 for the son of Kronos had made him the keeper of the winds,
both to stop and to rouse them, whichever he wished.°
    "He bound the bag in my hollow ship with a shining silver cord
so that not even the slightest bit of wind might escape. Then he sent
forth the breath of West Wind to blow so that it might carry the ships
25 and my men.° But West Wind was not to bring this to pass,
for we were ruined through our own foolishness.
                        "We sailed on
for nine days without stopping either night or day,
and on the tenth day we caught sight of our native land.

---

2 *son of Hippotas*: Unrelated to the hero Aiolos, founder of the house of the Aiolids, in which Jason and Nestor
    were to appear.

21 *he wished*: Aiolos acts as the proper host, in contrast to Cyclops: first a friendly welcome; the host's
    questions; the guest's replies; the request for a sending forth; the bestowal of a gift-token.

25 *my men*: We cannot, of course, say where the island of Aiolos is because it is a floating island, but it must be
    somewhere in the west if West Wind will blow them homeward.

We were so close that we saw men tending the watch fires
when, being exhausted, sweet sleep came over me. I had
constantly kept the rope for tightening the sail in my hand,
and had not given it to another of my comrades, so that
we might arrive more quickly to the land of our fathers.

   "Now my companions began to speak to one another,
saying that I was carrying home gold and silver,
a gift from great-hearted Aiolos, the son of Hippotas.
Thus one would say, glancing to someone sitting nearby:
'Think about it—this man is *so* dear and honored
by all men whose city and land he comes to!
And he is loaded with fancy treasure that he has taken
as booty from Troy, while we go home with empty hands,
though we have made the same journey. And now Aiolos
has given him this, showing kindness from friendship's
sake. But come, let us quickly see what this is here,
how much gold and silver this bag contains.'
                                 "So they spoke,
and the wicked counsel of my comrades prevailed. They opened
the bag and the winds escaped. The storm wind instantly
took hold and carried them, wailing, out to sea away from
the land of our fathers. I woke up and wondered in my heart
whether I should throw myself from the ship and perish
in the sea, or whether I should endure in silence and remain
among the living. But I endured and held on, and covering
my head lay down in the ship.
                                 "The ships were blown back
by the evil blast of wind again to the island of Aiolos,
and my comrades groaned. We went ashore to draw water,
and my companions quickly made ready a meal beside
the swift ships. But when we had tasted food and drink,
then I took a herald and a companion and went to the famous
palace of Aiolos. We found him feasting side by side with his
wife and children. Coming into his house we sat down beside
the doorposts on the threshold.
                                 "They were amazed in their hearts
and questioned us: 'How have you come here, Odysseus?
What evil spirit has assailed you? I believe we sent you forth
with kindly care so that you might arrive at the land
of your fathers, and your house, and whatever place you wanted.'
   "So they said, but with a sorry heart I spoke among them:
'With blind folly my evil companions injured me, and in addition
to that, accursed sleep. But make us well, my friends. For you
have the power.'

30

35

40

45

50

55

60

65

          "So I spoke, addressing them with gentle

70   words, but they fell silent. Then their father answered:
       'Quickly get off this island, you most vile of living men!
       It is not right that I help or send that man on his way
       who is hated by the blessed gods. Go, for you come here
       as one hated by the gods!'
                          "So saying he sent me out

75   of his house, as I deeply groaned. We sailed away from there,
       grieving in our hearts. The spirits of the men were worn out
       by the harsh rowing, all because of our own foolishness.
       No longer did any breeze come up to bear us on our way.
       "We sailed for six days, night and day without stopping,

80   and on the seventh we came to the steep city of Lamos,
       to Telepylos of the Laestrygonians, where herdsman calls
       to herdsman as he drives in his flocks, and the other answers
       as he drives his out. There a man who never slept could earn
       a double wage, one by herding cattle, the other by pasturing

85   white sheep, for the paths of night and day are close.°
       "When we had come into the famous harbor, around which
       steep cliffs ran continuously on both sides, and projecting headlands
       opposite each other reach out at the mouth, and the entrance
       is narrow—there all the others steered their curved ships inside.

90   They moored them within the hollow harbor close together.
       There no wave ever swelled, neither great nor small,
       but a white calm prevailed all around. I alone moored
       my black ship outside the harbor, on the border of the land,
       tying the ship to a rock. Then I climbed up to a rugged

95   place of outlook and I took my stand. I could see neither
       the works of men nor oxen. We saw only smoke rising
       from the land. Then I sent forth some of my comrades
       to find out who these men were who ate bread here on this land.
       I selected two men, and a third as herald. When they had gone

100   ashore they went along a smooth road over which wagons
       brought wood to the city from the high mountains. They met
       a young girl in front of the city, drawing water, the excellent
       daughter of the Laestrygonian Antiphates. She had come down

---

85   ... *are close*: Apparently Lamos ("gluttonous") founded the city of which, as we learn, Antiphates ("killing in
     return") is king. The etymology of *Laestrygonian* is quite obscure. *Telepylos*, the name of the Laestrygonian
     settlement, means "far-gated," associating it with the underworld. Because the Laestrygonians seem to live
     in a land of perpetual light, perhaps we are to think of this land as lying in the far East where Dawn arises;
     certainly Odysseus' next landfall on Kirkê's island is set in the East. Or it is like the far North with its bright
     summer nights, and the harbor is like a northern fiord. But this is a fairytale realm where directions are
     topsy-turvy, confused, and normal rules of existence do not apply.

to the lovely flowing spring of Artakia, from where they carried
water into the city.   105
     "My men stood around her and spoke to her
and asked who was the king of this people and who they were
over whom he ruled. And she at once showed them the high-roofed
house of her father. When they entered the glorious palace, they found
his wife, as big as the peak of a mountain, and they were aghast
at the sight of her. She quickly called the famous Antiphates   110
from the place of assembly, her husband, who devised a hateful
death for one of my men. At once he seized a companion of ours
and prepared his meal, but the other two leaped up and came
fleeing to the ships. Then Antiphates raised a cry in the city,
and the brutish Laestrygonians, hearing it, came running from   115
all sides, ten thousand of them, not like men but Giants.
From the cliffs they hurled rocks at us, as huge as a man can lift.
 "At once an evil din arose throughout the company of dying men
and smashed ships. Spearing my men like fishes, they carried
them off—a disgusting meal. While they were destroying my men   120
inside the deep harbor, I drew my sharp sword from my thigh
and cut the cables of the blue-prowed ship with it. Calling quickly
to my crew, I ordered them to fall to their oars so that we might flee
from this evil. They tossed the sea with their oars, fearing destruction.
Joyfully my ship fled the overhanging cliffs into the sea,   125
but the others were destroyed there, every one.
     "From there
we sailed on further, grieving in our hearts, saved from death
but bemoaning our dear companions. We came to the island of Aiaia,
where Kirkê° with the fine tresses lived, a dread goddess
of human speech,° the sister of Aietes of a destructive mind.   130
Both were the children of Helios who brings light to mortals,
and Persê was their mother, whom Ocean begot.° Here we put into
shore in silence, into a harbor safe for ships—some god led us.
There we disembarked and lay low for two days and two nights,
eating out our hearts from weariness and sorrow. But when Dawn   135
with her lovely tresses brought the third day to birth, then I took
my spear and sharp sword and quickly went up from the ship
to a place of wide outlook, in the hopes I might see the works
of men and hear their voices. I climbed up to a rugged place

---

129 *Kirkê*: "hawk," for some reason.

130 *human speech*: The meaning of this mysterious phrase is unclear.

132 *Ocean begot*: The story seems to owe a lot to the tradition of an *Argonautica*, in which Jason travels to the far
   east to Aia, "earth," and there seduces Medea. Aietes (ē-ē-tēz), Medea's father, Kirkê's brother, was Jason's
   enemy who subjects him to various trials.

140   of outlook and there took my stand. And I saw smoke rising
from the wide-wandered earth, from Kirkê in her halls, through
the thicket of oaks and the woods. I pondered then in my heart
and spirit whether I should go to investigate, because I saw
the fiery smoke. And as I pondered, this course seemed to me
145   to be the better: first to go to the swift ship and the shore of the sea
and give my companions a meal, then to send them out
to make a search.

                  "But when I came near to the curved ship,
some god took pity on me, being all alone, and sent a great
high-horned stag into my path. He was coming down
150   to the river from his pasture beside the wood, to get a drink,
for the power of the sun oppressed him. I hit him
with my spear in the middle of the back as he came out
of the wood, and my bronze spear pierced straight through.
Down he fell in the dust with a moan. His spirit fled
155   from him. I put my foot on him and pulled the bronze spear
out of the wound and left it there lying on the ground.
I plucked out sticks and willow-twigs. Weaving a rope
about five feet in length, I bound the feet of the monstrous
beast and went off to the black ship, carrying him on my back
160   and supporting myself with my spear. In no way could I carry him
on my shoulder with one hand, for he was a very huge beast.

    "I threw him down in front of the ship, and I cheered up
my companions with honeyed words, coming to each man in turn:
'My friends, we shall not yet go down into the house of Hades
165   before the fated day shall arrive, although we grieve. But come,
so long as there is still food and drink in our swift ship,
let us think of them, so that we do not waste away with hunger.'

    "So I spoke, and they hastily obeyed my words. Drawing
their cloaks from their faces, they wondered at the stag beside
170   the shore of the unwearied sea, for it was a huge beast. When they had
gladdened their eyes with looking, they washed their hands and made
ready a glorious meal. So until the sun went down we sat there dining
on the endless flesh and sweet wine. But when the sun went down
and the darkness came on, we went to take our rest on the shore
175   of the sea.

          "When Dawn appeared with her fingers of rose,
then I called my men together and spoke among all:
'Listen to my words, comrades, although we are suffering.
My friends, we do not know where the darkness is, nor where
the light, nor where the sun that brings light to mortals
180   goes beneath the earth, nor where it rises. But let us

quickly consider whether there is still any plan left to us.
I don't think there is. For I climbed up to a rugged place
of outlook and looked over the island, about which the endless
sea is set as a crown. The island itself is low-lying, and my eyes
saw smoke in the middle of it, through the oak thickets   185
and the woods.'
       "So I spoke, and their hearts were crushed, thinking
of the deeds of the Laestrygonian Antiphates and of the violence
of great-hearted Cyclops, the eater of men. They wept shrilly,
pouring down hot tears. But no good came of their wailing.
I divided up all my companions with fancy shin guards into two   190
groups, and I appointed a leader to each. Of one I was the leader,
of the other godlike Eurylochos. Quickly we cast lots in a bronze
helmet, and out leapt the lot of great-hearted Eurylochus.
He went off, and with him, weeping, went twenty-two companions.
They left us behind, groaning.   195
       "In a low place they found
the house of Kirkê, made of polished stone, in an open meadow.
There were wolves around it from the mountains, and lions
whom Kirkê had herself enchanted by giving them potions.
They did not rush up to the men, but waving their
long tails fawned about them. It was just as when   200
hounds will fawn about their master when he returns
from feasting, knowing he will bring them tidbits
to appease their hunger—so did these lions and wolves
of mighty paws cringe around them.
       "The men were terrified
beholding what seemed terrible monsters. They stood   205
outside the doors of Kirkê, a goddess with beautiful
hair. They heard Kirkê sing within in a lovely
voice as she went back and forth before a great loom,
immortal, weaving a delightful, shining design
to please the gods.   210
       "Polites spoke first, a natural
leader, whom I loved before all others, and trusted most.
'My friends, someone sings as she goes back and forth before
a wondrous loom, making the floor echo all around.
It is either some goddess or a woman. But let us make
ourselves known.'   215
       "So he spoke, and they all called out
to her. Promptly she came forth and flung open the shining
doors. She invited them in. In their ignorance they all
obeyed, except for Eurylochos, who suspected a trap.

"She gave them seats on couches and chairs.
220 She mixed up a drink of Pramnian wine° and cheese
and barley and bright honey, pouring in dangerous potions
so that they might forget their native land. When she
had served them, and they had drunk, she struck them
with her wand, then penned them up in her sties.
225 They now had the heads of swine, and a pig's snort
and bristles and shape, but their minds remained the same
as before. They wailed as they were penned up, but Kirkê
threw them acorns, both sweet and bitter, and the fruit
of the dogwood, the food that pigs, slithering in slime,
230 so love to eat.
          "Eurylochos came back quickly
to the swift black ship, to tell what happened
to his companions and what was their intolerable fate.
But at first he could not speak a word, though he wished to,
so overcome with grief was he in his great heart.
235 His eyes filled with tears and he gave forth
a deep sigh. Then when all of us questioned him,
amazed, at last he told of the doom of his comrades:
'We went through the forest, noble Odysseus, just
as you ordered. We found the house of Kirkê,
240 in a low place made of polished stone, in an open
meadow. There, someone was going back and forth before
a great loom, singing sweetly, either goddess or woman.
They all called out to her. Promptly she came forth
and flung open the shining doors. She invited them in.
245 In their ignorance all of them agreed, but I alone
remained outside, suspecting a trap. Then they
vanished all together, and not one of them appeared
again, though I sat there for a long time and watched.'
          "So he spoke, and I cast my silver-studded sword
250 around my shoulders, huge, made of bronze, and I shouldered
my bow too. I urged him to lead the way.
But he seized my knees and begged me, wailing, and spoke
words that went like arrows: 'Don't make me go there again,
you who are nurtured by Zeus, but leave me here!
255 For I doubt that you yourself will return, nor will
you bring back any of our comrades. But let us who
remain, swiftly flee. There is still chance for escape!'

---

220 *Pramnian wine*: A wine of high quality, evidently named after an unknown place.

FIGURE 10.1   Kirkê enchants the companions of Odysseus.   A seductive Kirkê stands naked in the center, stirring a magic drink and offering it to Odysseus' companions, already turning into animals—the man in front of Kirkê into a boar, the next to the right into a ram, and the third into a wolf. A dog crouches beneath Kirkê's bowl. The figure behind Kirkê has the head of a boar. On the far left is a lion-man beside whom Odysseus comes with sword drawn (but in the Odyssey they turn only into pigs). On the far right, Eurylochos escapes. Athenian black-figure wine-mixing bowl, c. 550 BC.

"So he spoke, but I answered him: 'Eurylochos,
you stay here beside the hollow black ship, eating and drinking.
260 I shall go alone, for go I must.'
                    "So speaking
I went up from the ship and away from the sea. But as
I journeyed through the sacred forest to the great house
of Kirkê, a connoisseur of drugs, Hermes of the golden
staff met me in the form of a youth who is just getting
265 his beard, in the comeliest time of life. He took
my hand and he said to me: 'Where are you going,
unhappy man, traveling alone through the hills,
knowing nothing of the country? For Kirkê has
penned-up your companions behind thick bars,
270 and turned them all into pigs! Do you plan on letting
them go? I'm telling you that you yourself will not return,
but will remain there in their company. But come,
I will free you from danger—I will save you. Here, take
this powerful herb and go to Kirkê's house. It will ward
275 off the evil day from you.
                          " 'Now let me tell you
the deceptions that the goddess Kirkê has in store.
She will make a potion for you, and mix drugs
with your food. But she will not be able to enchant
you because of the herb that I will give you. I will
280 tell you the whole story. When Kirkê strikes you
with her long wand, then you must draw your sword
from your thigh and rush at Kirkê as if you wished
to kill her. She, in fear, will then urge that you sleep
together. Don't refuse the goddess's bed, if you wish
285 to free your companions and entertain yourself. But first
force her to swear a great oath to the blessed gods
that she will plot no further evil against you. Otherwise,
when your clothes are off, she will unman you.'
"So speaking, Argeïphontes drew the herb from the ground
290 and gave it to me, showing me what it looked like.
At the root it was black, but its flower was like milk. 'The gods
call this *moly*. It is difficult for mortals to dig,
but there is nothing the gods cannot do.' Then Hermes
went off to high Olympos through the wooded island,
295 and I went on to the house of Kirkê, my brain boiling
with thoughts.
                    "I stood before the doors of the goddess
with beautiful hair. Standing there, I cried out, and the goddess
heard my voice. Promptly she opened the shining doors

and invited me in, and I followed, disturbed in my mind.
She suggested I sit on a lovely chair with silver rivets,   300
finely made, with a footstool attached. She prepared
a potion for me in a golden goblet, bidding me drink it.
But she placed drugs within it, wishing me ill.
    "She gave it, and I drank it, but was still not enchanted,
so she struck me with her wand and said, 'Go now to the sty!   305
Lie with your companions!'
                    "So she spoke. I drew
my sword from my thigh and rushed on Kirkê as if
I wished to kill her. But she with a loud cry
she ducked beneath the sword and seized my knees,
and wailing spoke words that flew like arrows: 310
'Who are you? Where is your city? Who are your parents?
I can't believe that you drank my potion and yet
were not entranced. No other has withstood this drug,
once he has drunk it and it has passed the barrier of his teeth.
The mind in your breast cannot be enchanted! Surely   315
you are the trickster Odysseus. Argeïphontes of the golden
staff always said you would come, returning from Troy
in your swift, black ship. But come, put away your sword
in your scabbard. Let us go to my bed, there to mingle
in love. Let us learn, lying together, to trust one another.'   320
    "So she spoke, and I answered her in turn.
'Kirkê, how can you think that I would be gentle
with you, who in your halls have turned my men
into pigs? You would keep me here, bidding me
with deceitful thoughts to go to your room and there   325
to have sex with you. But when I am naked you would
unman me! I don't think I want to bed with you until
you swear, goddess, a great oath that you will not plan
further evil against me.' That's what I said, and right away
she swore as I asked. And when she had sworn,   330
then we went to her bed and I mingled with the very
lovely Kirkê.
            "Meanwhile the four servants busied
themselves in the house, where they did all the housework.
They were children of the springs and the forests
and holy rivers that flow to the sea. One of them   335
spread purple cloth on the chairs, and beneath the cloth
white linen. Another set up tables of silver in front
of the chairs and placed golden baskets upon them. A third
mixed honeyed wine in a silver bowl, and set out
golden cups. The fourth drew water and lit a   340

FIGURE 10.2 **Odysseus threatens Kirkê with his sword.** He wears a broad-brimmed traveler's hat (different from the pilos or skullcap that he commonly wears). Kirkê has dropped the cup containing the magic potion and flees in terror before the armed Odysseus who has leapt from his chair. Athenian red-figure vase, c. 440 BC.

fire beneath a large tripod, and warmed the water.
When the water had boiled in the brilliant bronze, she sat
me in a tub and bathed me from the great tripod,
mixing the water so that it was just right. She poured
it over my head and shoulders until she had taken   345
all the dispiriting weariness from my limbs. And when
she had bathed me, and rubbed rich oil in my skin,
she cast a shirt and a beautiful cloak over my shoulders.
She brought me into the hall and sat me down in a chair
with silver studs, wonderfully made, and a footstool   350
was fixed beneath it. A servant brought in a beautiful,
golden vase, and poured water over my hands into
a silver basin for me to wash. Beside the basin
she set up a shining table, and on it, the bashful
servant placed bread and all kinds of meats, making   355
free use of what she had on hand. She urged me to eat,
but I was not at ease in my mind. I sat with other thoughts,
as I considered the evil that might come.
                                 "When Kirkê saw me
sitting but not eating, in deep sorrow, she stood beside me
and spoke words that flew like arrows: 'Why do you sit,   360
Odysseus, as if you were dumb, eating out your heart?
Nor do you touch your food or drink. Do you suspect
some other deceit? But you should not be afraid,
for I have sworn to you a mighty oath.'
                                 "So she spoke,
and I answered: 'Kirkê, what sort of man, if he did   365
his duty, would dare to partake of food or drink before
he had freed his companions and beheld them before
his eyes? But come, if you urge me with true good will
to drink and eat, let them go, let me see my trusty
companions with my own eyes.'   370
                                 "So I spoke, and Kirkê stalked
from the chamber, holding her wand in her hand. She opened
the door to the sty and drove them out. They were like
nine-year-old porkers. As they stood around her, she went
among them and anointed each with another charm.
The bristles fell from their limbs that earlier a harmful   375
charm of Queen Kirkê had caused to grow. They were men
again, but younger than before, and more handsome, and taller.
They recognized me, and clung each one to my hands.
A passionate sobbing took hold of them, and a tremendous
sound reverberated throughout the hall. Even the goddess took pity.   380

"She came near to me and spoke: 'Son of Laërtes, nurtured
by Zeus, much-devising Odysseus, go now to your swift ship
and the shore of the sea. First of all, drag your ship onto the shore,
and conceal your possessions and your weapons in a cave.
385 Then come back, and bring all your trusty companions.'
"So she spoke. I was content with her advice. I went
to the ship and the shore of the sea. I found my trusty
companions ailing piteously around the swift ship, warm
tears poring down their cheeks. Even as calves, lying in a field,
390 jump up and prance around their mothers as they come
in a herd into the yard, having grazed their fill—for the pens
no longer hold the calves, but mooing constantly
they run about their mothers—even so did those men
crowd around me when they saw me, weeping copiously.
395 It seemed as if we had reached our native land, and the city
itself of rugged Ithaca where we were born and raised.
"With a hearty cry they spoke to me words that went like
arrows: 'Seeing you return, you who are nurtured by Zeus, we are glad
as if we had returned to Ithaca, our native land. But come,
400 tell us of the fate of our other companions.' So they spoke.
"I answered with gentle words: 'First of all, drag the ship
up onto the land, and place our possessions, and our armor,
in a cave. Then let us all hurry up to Kirkê's holy house
where you may see your companions both eating and drinking.
405 They have everlasting store!'
                                "So I spoke. At once they obeyed
my words. Eurylochos alone held back my companions and spoke
to them words that went like arrows: 'What? Are you crazy?
Where are you going? Are you in love with death? You would go
to the house of Kirkê, who will change you to pigs or wolves
410 or lions that you might be forced to guard her house? Just what
Cyclops did when our companions went to his fold,
and this *brave* Odysseus followed with them! He killed them
with his reckless behavior.'
                                "So he spoke. I weighed in my mind
whether I should draw my sword from my strong thigh
415 and cut off his head, rolling it on the ground, though he was
a close relation, my brother-in-law.° But my companions
held me back with sweet words, saying: 'You who are
nurtured by Zeus, we will leave him behind, if you order it,
to remain beside the ship and guard it. Lead us to the holy halls
420 of Kirkê.'

---

416 *brother-in-law*: But we never learn to whom Eurylochos is married.

"So saying, they went up from the ship and the sea.
Nor did Eurylochos remain beside the hollow ship,
but he followed along, unnerved by my savage rebuke.
    "In the meanwhile, Kirkê kindly had bathed my other
companions and anointed them with rich oil, and cast shirts
and fleecy cloaks about their shoulders. We found them feasting   425
away in Kirkê's halls. When they saw and recognized one
another, face to face, the men burst out crying, and the hall
rang with their sobs.
                    "Standing near me, the beautiful goddess
said: 'No need for all this weeping any longer I know
the great sorrows you have suffered on the briny deep, and how   430
many pains cruel men have shown you on land. But come,
eat and drink! Let your spirits rise, as they were when
you first left your native land, rugged Ithaca. As it is,
you are feckless, discouraged, thinking always of the hardship
of travel. It's hard to be happy, when you have endured so much.'   435
    "So she spoke, and we did as she suggested.
Then we remained there all of our days for a full year eating
the abundant meats and drinking the delicious wine.
But when a year had passed, and the seasons turned
as the months passed along, and the long days came to an end,   440
then my trusty companions called me out, and they said:
Odysseus, you are behaving strangely! We must think
of our native land, and whether destiny grants that we be
saved, and whether we will return to our high-roofed homes
in the land of our fathers.'   445
                    "So they spoke, and my proud
heart agreed. We sat all day long until the sun went down,
dining on endless flesh and sweet wine. And when the sun went
down and the darkness came on, they took their rest throughout
the shadowy halls.
                    "But I went up to Kirkê's very beautiful bed
and beseeched her, clinging to her knees, and the goddess   450
heard my voice. I spoke words that went like arrows:
'O Kirkê, complete the promise that you made for me,
to send me home. My spirit is anxious to be gone,
and the spirit of my companions too, whose grief breaks
my heart as they surround me, mourning whenever   455
you are somewhere else.'
                    "So I spoke, and the beautiful goddess
answered me: 'Zeus-nourished son of Laërtes, resourceful
Odysseus, don't remain longer in my house if you are unwilling.
But first you must complete another journey—to go

460 to the house of Hades and dread Persephone, to ask
for a prophecy from the breath-soul of Theban Tiresias,
the blind prophet, whose mind remains unimpaired.
To him even in death Persephone has granted reason,
that he alone maintains his understanding. But the others
465 flit about like shadows.'
       "So she spoke, and my heart was shattered.
I wept, sitting on the bed, and my heart no longer wished
to live and see the light of the sun. But when I was surfeited
with weeping and flailing about, I answered her then with
the following words: 'O Kirkê, who will guide us on this journey?
470 No one has ever gone to the house of Hades in a black ship.'
 "So I spoke, and the beautiful goddess at once answered:
'Zeus-nourished son of Laërtes, resourceful Odysseus,
don't be concerned with your desire for a pilot to guide
your ship. Set up your mast and spread your white sails
475 and take a seat. The breath of North Wind will carry you there.
When you have passed over the river Ocean in your ship,
where there is a level beach and the grove of Persephone—
tall poplars and willows that shed their fruit before fully ripe—
beach your ship there by the deep-swirling river Ocean
480 and go yourself into the fetid house of Hades. There into Acheron
flow Pyriphlegethon and Kokytos, a branch of the water of the Styx.
There is a rock there, the meeting place of the two roaring rivers.°
There, my prince, approaching very near as I command you,
dig a pit an arm's length this way and that, and around it
485 pour a drink-offering to all the dead, first with milk and honey,
then with sweet wine, and finally with water. Sprinkle white
barley on top of it. Vow on the strengthless heads of the dead
that when you come to Ithaca you will sacrifice a barren cow
in your halls, the best you have, and will sacrifice on your altar
490 many good things, and that to Tiresias alone you will separately
sacrifice a ram, entirely black, that stands out in your flocks.
And when you have supplicated the glorious tribes of the dead
with prayers, then sacrifice a ram and a black ewe,
turning them toward Erebos°—but yourself, turn your face
495 backward toward the streams of Ocean. The many breath-souls
of the dead will come forth. Call to your companions. Order

---

482 ... *roaring rivers*: Acheron ("affliction") may be a lake; Pyriphlegethon ("burning with fire") and Kokytos
("wailing") flow into it; Kokytos is a branch of the Styx ("hateful"). An oath sworn by the gods on the Styx
can never be broken. The two "roaring rivers" are Pyriphlegethon and Kokytos.

494 *Erebos*: "darkness," a general term for the land of the dead. In Hesiod's *Theogony*, Erebos is the fifth
primordial element mentioned, which came out of Chaos. Conjoined with Nyx (Night), Erebos fathered
Aither (upper air) and Hemera (Day).

them to flay and burn the sheep that lie there, killed
by the pitiless bronze. Pray to the gods, to mighty Hades
and dread Persephone. Draw your sharp sword
from beside your thigh. Take a seat, and do not allow   500
the strengthless heads of the dead to come near the blood
before you have made inquiry of Tiresias. Right away
the prophet will come, the leader of the people, who knows
the road you will take and the measures of your journey
and your homecoming—how you may cross the fish-rich sea.'   505
        "So she spoke, and immediately Dawn sat on her
golden throne. She cast a cloak and a shirt around me
as clothing. The nymph herself put on a great silvery robe,
finely woven and filled with charm, and around her waist
she placed a beautiful golden belt, and on her head   510
she put a veil.
        "And I went through the halls rousing up
my companions. I stood beside each man and spoke with honeyed
words: 'Sleep no longer! Awake from your sweet slumber!
Let us go—the revered Kirkê has told me all.'
                        "So I spoke,
and their proud hearts were persuaded. But even so I was unable   515
to lead my men from there unscathed. There was a man,
the youngest of all, not especially distinguished in war
nor endowed with good understanding—he had lain down
apart from his companions in the sacred halls of Kirkê, heavy
with wine, desiring the cool air. He heard the noise and the bustle   520
of his companions as they moved about, and he suddenly
jumped up. He forgot to go to the tall ladder to climb back down
and fell headlong from the roof. His neck was broken away
from the spine, and his breath-soul went off to the house of Hades.
        "As my men were getting ready to go, I spoke   525
to them: 'You think that you are going home to the beloved
land of your fathers, but Kirkê has devised another road
for us: to go the house of Hades and dread Persephone
to seek a prophecy from Theban Tiresias.'
                        "So I spoke—
and their hearts were shattered. They sat down where they   530
were and moaned and tore at their hair. But no good came
of their lamenting. When we were on our way to the swift ship
and shore of the sea, grieving and pouring down hot tears,
and in the meanwhile Kirkê had gone to the black ship
and bound a ram and a black ewe there. She had gone   535
on ahead, easily. For who with his eyes could see
a goddess against her will, either going or coming?"

BOOK 11. *Odysseus in the Underworld*

"When we came down to the ship and the sea, we dragged
the ship first of all into the shining sea, and we set up
the mast and the sail on the black ship. We took on
the flocks and embarked. We went off mourning
5   and shedding warm tears. Kirkê, with the lovely tresses,
dread goddess of human speech, sent a wind that came
behind the ship with its dark prow and filled the sails,
a noble companion. Once we made all the tackle
on the ship secure, we took our seats. Wind favored us
10   and the helmsman kept her on a straight course.
   "All day long the ship's sail was stretched
as she sped across the sea. The sun went down
and the ways grew dark. We came to the limits
of deep-flowing Ocean. We came to the people and the city
15   of the Cimmerians,° hidden in mist and cloud, nor does
the shining sun look down upon them with its rays,
not when he mounts toward the starry heaven, nor when
he turns again to the earth from the heaven, but total
night is stretched over wretched mortals.
                                    "We came there
20   and dragged up our ship on the shore and off-loaded the sheep.
We walked along the stream of Ocean until we came to the place
that Kirkê had described. There Perimedes and Eurylochos° held
the sacrificial animals. I drew my sharp sword from my thigh
and dug a trench an arm's length wide in both directions.
25   Around it I poured an offering to all the dead, first
with milk and honey, then with sweet wine, and then
with water. I sprinkled white barley. Powerfully I entreated
the strengthless heads of the dead, saying that when
I came to Ithaca I would sacrifice in my halls a barren cow

---

15   *Cimmerians:* A historical people who descended over the Caucasus Mountains in the eighth century BC and
   for a hundred years terrorized Asia Minor. Either Homer's Cimmerians are a translation into myth of this
   people, or the historical Cimmerians were named in Greek after Homer's mythical Cimmerians, a word that
   might in Greek mean "those living in misty darkness."

22   *Perimedes and Eurylochos:* Perimedes is mentioned only here and once later but we have already seen
   Eurylochos as a rival to Odysseus' power, and he is important in later episodes.

to them the best I had, and that I would pile the altar
with excellent gifts, and that to Tiresias—to him alone—
I would sacrifice a ram, all black, an outstanding
one from our flocks.

    "When with vows and prayers
I had supplicated the tribes of the dead, I took the sheep
and slit their throats over the pit, and the black blood
flowed. Then the breath-souls of the dead who had passed
away gathered from Erebos—brides, and unwed youths
and miserable old men, and tender virgins with hearts
new to sorrow, and many others wounded by bronze spears,
men killed by Ares° wearing armor spattered with blood.
These came thronging around the pit, coming from here
and there, making a wondrous cry.

      "A sickly fear gripped me.°
I ordered my companions to flay and burn the sheep that lay
there, their throats cut with the pitiless bronze, and that
they pray to the gods, and to mighty Hades and dread
Persephone. I myself drew my sharp sword from my thigh
and took a seat, not allowing the strengthless heads of the dead
to come close to the blood before I had made inquiry of Tiresias.

  "First came the breath-soul of my companion Elpenor,
for we did not bury him beneath the earth with its broad
ways but left his corpse in the hall of Kirkê unwept
and unburied because another task drove us on.° I wept
when I saw him and took pity in my heart, and spoke to him
words that went like arrows: 'Elpenor, how did you come
beneath the misty darkness? You've gotten here faster
on foot than I in my black ship!'

      "So I spoke, and he answered me
with a groan: 'Son of Laërtes, from the line of Zeus, resourceful
Odysseus, the evil decree of some spirit, plus endless wine
has killed me. When I lay down to sleep in the halls
of Kirkê I did not think to go back down the long ladder
but fell headlong from the roof, and my neck was torn
away from the spine—my breath-soul went down to the house
of Hades. Now I beg you by those we left behind,

30

35

40

45

50

55

60

---

40 *by Ares:* That is, killed in war.

43 *gripped me:* Odysseus is at the edge of the world, standing beside the primordial waters where the sun never
  shines. Now he acts as a necromancer, a magician who summons the spirits of the dead so he can learn from them.

52 *us on:* That is, the need to go to the underworld to consult Tiresias. Elpenor can talk without drinking the
  blood because he is still unburied. Once his ghost is "laid"—when he is properly lamented and buried—
  then his breath-soul will lose its memory of past events and its reason.

those not present, by your wife and father who reared you
65 when you were little, and by Telemachos, whom you left
as an only son in your halls! For I know that when
you leave the house of Hades and go back, you will
put-in to the island of Aiaia in your well-built ship.
There—I beg of you, O captain!—I urge you to remember me.
70 Do not go off home and leave me unwept and unburied.
Do not turn away from me, or I may become a cause
of the gods' anger!° Burn me together with my armor,
all that is mine, and heap up a tomb on the shore
of the gray sea, in memory of a wretched man, so that
75 men yet to be born may learn of me. Do these things
for me and fix on the tomb the oar that I rowed
when I was alive among my companions.'°

                           "So he spoke,
and I answered: 'I shall accomplish these things for you,
my wretched friend, and bring them to pass.' Then the two
80 of us sat, exchanging melancholy words, I on one side holding
the sword over the blood, the phantom of my companion
on the other, who spoke at length.

                                "Then there came the breath-soul
of my dead mother, Antikleia, the daughter of great-hearted
Autolykos,° whom I left alive when I went to sacred Ilion.
85 I wept when I saw her and took pity in my heart, but I would
not let her come close to the blood, though I was deeply
sorrowful, before I had made inquiry of Tiresias.

    "Then the breath-soul of Theban Tiresias came to the pit,
holding a golden scepter. He recognized me and spoke:°
90 'Son of Laërtes, from the line of Zeus, resourceful Odysseus,
why, poor thing, have you left the light of the sun and come
down here? So that you could see the dead and this
joyless land? But stand back from the pit. Put up your sharp
sword so that I may drink of the blood and speak the truth.'
95   "So he spoke, and I drew back and thrust my
silver-studded sword into its scabbard. When he had drunk

---

72 *gods' anger:* He will become a malevolent spirit if his corpse is not treated with respect and his ghost is not "laid."

77 *companions:* Elpenor wants a hero's burial, although he is only a rower!

84 *...Autolykos: Antikleia* means "opposed to glory," perhaps because she had little enthusiasm for Odysseus'
exploits. *Autolykos* means "true-wolf," a thief and a trickster who gave Odysseus his name and entertained
him as a youth on Mount Parnassos (*Od.* Book 19). There in a boar hunt Odysseus received the scar by
which he is later identified.

89 *spoke:* Only Tiresias, because of his prophetic powers, can speak without first drinking from the blood
(except for the unburied Elpenor).

FIGURE 11.1 **Odysseus summons the spirits of the dead.** Odysseus sits on a rock, sword in hand. Beneath his booted feet lie the skins of the flayed sheep whose blood fills the pit. Elpenor stands to his right, in "heroic nudity" except for his cloak, boots, and traveler's cap. He holds a spear. Up from the ground (lower left) comes the head of Tiresias. Athenian red-figure vase, c. 460 BC.

the black blood, then the faultless seer said: 'You seek
to know about your honey-sweet homecoming, O glorious
Odysseus? Well, the god will make it harsh for you.
100 For I do not think you will escape Poseidon, the earth-shaker,
who has laid up anger in his heart, enraged because you blinded
his son. Still, you might arrive home after suffering many evils,
if you are willing to restrain your spirit and that of your
companions when you put your well-built ship ashore
105 on the island of Thrinakia,° escaping the violet-colored sea.
There you will find the cattle and good flocks of Helios,
who sees all things and hears all things, grazing. If you leave them
unharmed and remember your return journey, then you might
arrive at Ithaca, though suffering many evils. But if you harm them,
110 I predict the destruction of your ship and your companions.
  "'If you yourself escape, you will arrive home tardy,
on someone else's ship, in a bad way, having lost all your
companions. You will suffer trouble in your house from arrogant
men who consume your substance and try to seduce your godlike
115 wife with gifts. Surely you will take revenge for their violence
when you arrive! But when you have killed the suitors
in your halls either by trickery or openly with the sharp bronze,
then take a well-fitted oar in your hand and travel until
you come to where they know nothing of the sea, nor do
120 they eat food mixed with salt. They do not know
about ships with purple cheeks or well-shaped oars,
which are the wings of a boat. I will tell you a sign
that is very clear and cannot escape you: When another
wayfarer who meets you says that is a winnowing-fan°
125 on your strong shoulder, right there fix your well-shaped oar
in the ground. Make a generous sacrifice to Poseidon the king—
a lamb and a bull and a pig and a boar that mates with sows—
then go home and offer great sacrifice to the deathless
gods who hold the broad sky, to each of them in turn.
130   "'For you a very gentle death will come from the sea.
It will kill you when you are overcome with spruce old age.
Your people shall live in happiness around you. Now I have
told you the truth.'
         "So he spoke, and I answered: 'Tiresias, the gods
themselves have spun the thread of all this. But come,

---

105 *Thrinakia:* Of unknown meaning, the mythical island of Helios was at an early time identified with "Trinakria,"
or "three-cornered island," another name for Sicily. Even today Sicily is called the Island of the Sun.

124 *winnowing-fan:* A wooden implement used to throw the harvested grain into the air so that the wind blows
away the chaff (inedible seed casings) from the heavier edible grain, which falls to the ground.

tell me, and tell me truly—I see the breath-soul of my dead
mother. She sits there in silence near the blood in the pit,
nor does she dare to look on her son just opposite,
or to speak to him. Tell me, O master, how can she
recognize who I am?'

                "So I spoke, and he at once
answered: 'I shall tell you an easy word. Do fix it
in your mind. Whomever of the dead and gone you allow
to come close to the black blood, that one will speak
and tell you the truth. Whomever you refuse, he will
surely withdraw from the pit.'

                   "So saying, the breath-soul
of lord Tiresias went to the house of Hades. He had spoken
his prophecies, but I remained steadfast where I was until
my mother came and drank the dark blood. Immediately
she knew who I was, and moaning she spoke words that went
like arrows: 'My child, how have you come beneath the shadowy
dark, being still alive? It is hard for the living to see these things.
For there are great rivers between the living and dead, and mighty
floods—first of all Ocean, which no one can cross on foot
but only with a well-built ship. Have you come here after long
wanderings from Troy with your ship and companions? Have you
not yet come to Ithaca, nor seen your wife in your halls?'

   "So she spoke, and I said in reply: 'O mother,
my urgent need has been to go down to the house of Hades
to seek an oracle from the breath-soul of Theban Tiresias.
So I have not yet come close to Achaea,° nor have I walked
on my own land, but always I wander in misery, ever since
I first followed the good Agamemnon to Troy with its fine
horses, that I might help fight the Trojans. But come,
tell me and report it truly—what fate of grievous death
overcame you? Was it a long illness, or did Artemis, the shooter
of arrows, come and with her gentle shafts bring you down?
Tell me too of my father and my son that I left behind.
Do they still hold power, or does some other man have it,
and do they say that I shall never return? Tell me of the plans
and intentions of my wedded wife—does she stay beside
her child and keep all things steady? Or has someone already
married her, whoever is best of the Achaeans?'

                       "Thus I spoke,
and at once my revered mother answered: 'Yes, yes,
your wife remains with a steady heart in your halls. Miserable

135

140

145

150

155

160

165

170

---

159 *Achaea*: Probably he means the PELOPONNESUS.

do the nights and days wane for her, weeping tears. No one else
yet holds your power, but Telemachos rules over your
domains without harassment, and he hosts the equal feast
as is fitting for one who gives judgments. And all men
invite him.° Your father lives in the country and does not
come to the city. For bedding he has no bed, no cloaks nor bright
covers, and in the winter he sleeps with the slaves in the house,
in the dust near the fire, and the clothes on his flesh are filthy.
But when summer comes and the rich autumn, then everywhere
across the slope of his vineyard leaves are scattered on the ground
as a bed. There he lies, sorrowing, nursing great anguish
in his heart and longing for your return. A harsh old age
has come upon him. Even so did I perish and follow my fate,
for Artemis, who sees from a long way off, who showers
arrows, did not strike me down in my halls with her gentle
shafts. Nor did a sickness come upon me, which often
takes away the spirit from the limbs with grievous wasting.
It was my longing for you and your counsels and gentleness,
glorious Odysseus, that took away my honey-sweet life.'
    "So she spoke, but I pondered in my heart and wanted
to take in my arms my mother's breath-soul, which had passed
away. Three times I leaped toward her, for my heart
urged me to hold her. Three times she flew away, out
of my arms, like a shadow or a dream.
                              "A still sharper pain
came to my heart, and I spoke to her words that went
like arrows: 'My mother, why do you not await me?
I am eager to hold you, so that even in the house of Hades
we may delight in icy wailing, throwing our arms about one another.
Or are you just a phantom that the illustrious Persephone
has sent up so that I may groan and lament all the more?'
    "So I spoke, and at once my revered mother answered:
'Ah me, my child, most ill-fated of all mortals—Persephone
the daughter of Zeus does not deceive you, but this
is the way of mortals when someone dies. The tendons

---

178 *men invite him*: To host an "equal feast," where everyone receives the same portion, is a sign of social power.
Telemachos is also welcome at feasts given by others. Antikleia seems to be speaking of the present, when
Odysseus has been away from home, say, eleven or twelve years (ten years at the war; one year on Kirkē's island,
plus time for other adventures). Odysseus does not return home until the twentieth year. We learn elsewhere that
the suitors arrived in the house only three or four years before Odysseus' return, which is why Antikleia does not
mention them (though Tiresias does). If Telemachos was an infant when Odysseus went to Troy, he should be
very young now, only eleven or twelve, not even a teenager. It is remarkable that at this age he attends the "equal
feast" and "gives judgments." Sometimes Homer is as casual about chronology as he is about geography.

no longer hold together the flesh and the bones, but the mighty
force of fire destroys all that, when the spirit first leaves
the white bones and the breath-soul flies off like a dream,   210
hovering here and there.° But hasten to the light as quickly
as you can. Remember all these things so that hereafter
you might tell them to your wife.'

               "So we conversed
with one other, but other women came to the blood.
Illustrious Persephone sent them, whoever were the wives   215
and daughters of the chiefs. They gathered in a crowd around
the dark blood, and now I took thought how I might question
each one. This seemed the best plan to my mind. Drawing
my long sword from my strong thigh, I did not permit
all of them to drink together from the dark blood. One after   220
another they came, and each told me of her lineage.
I questioned them all.°

*[Lines 223–311 are omitted. Homer gives a long catalog of the famous women of olden
times, whose breath-souls Odysseus sees gathered around the pit of blood. Then he inter-
rupts his narrative:]*

   "But it is time that
we slept, either with the crew of your swift ship or here
in your own house. My voyage home will rest with the gods,
and with you."

            So he spoke. All were hushed in silence,
and were held enchanted throughout the shadowy halls.   315
Then white-armed Aretê° began to speak: "Phaeacians,
how does this man seem to you in comeliness
and stature and in his well-balanced mind? Moreover
he is my guest, though each of you has a share
in this honor. So don't be in a hurry to send him off,   320
and don't cut short your gifts to one in such need.
For you have much treasure in your houses, thanks to
the favor of the gods."

---

211   *here and there*: Homer knows only cremation as a way to treat the dead, never inhumation.

222   *them all*: By drinking the blood the ghosts temporarily regain the power of speech. The Catalog of Women
      that now follows (omitted here) was a genre of oral poetry in the days of Homer. Book 11 is a series of cata-
      logs: first of women; then of heroes; then of the denizens of the underworld.

316   *Aretê*: Aretê is apparently the only woman in the room.

The old warrior Echeneos,
one of the Phaeacian elders, then spoke to them:
325 "My friends, not wide of the mark or of our own thought
are the words of wise Aretê! Do act on them, though
it is on Alkinoös that the word and deed depend."°

Alkinoös answered and said: "This word shall come
to pass as surely as I am alive and rule over the oar-loving
330 Phaeacians. Let our guest, who longs so for his return,
remain until tomorrow, so that we may make our gift-giving
complete. His safe passage will be the concern of all men,
but especially mine, for I hold the power among the people here."

Resourceful Odysseus answered him: "King Alkinoös,
335 most excellent of all people, even if you encouraged me
to stay here a whole year, and would arrange my escort,
and would give wonderful gifts—why, I would do it! Much
better to return to the land of one's fathers with a full hand.
I will receive more respect from men and be dearer to all
340 of them when they see me returning to Ithaca."

Alkinoös
answered and spoke to him: "O Odysseus, when we look
upon you, we would never liken you to an imposter or a cheat,
such men as the black earth nourishes in great numbers,
scattered far and wide, making up lies from things that no man
345 can even see. But you understand the charm of words,
and your mind is noble. You speak as when a singer
speaks with knowledge, telling the sorrows of all the Argives
and of you yourself.
              "But come, tell me this
and do so truly—whether you saw any of your godlike
350 companions, who followed you to Ilion and there met
their fate? The night is very long, endless really. It is not
time for you to go to sleep in the hall. Tell me, please,
more of your wondrous deeds! I could hold out until
the bright dawn, if you were willing to sit here in our hall
355 and tell of your many woes."

Resourceful Odysseus said in reply:
"King Alkinoös, renowned among all people, there is a time

---

327 *word and deed depend*: Alkinoös, who holds the highest power, must bring to fulfillment Aretê's suggestion.
The addition of more gifts to Odysseus will necessitate the postponing of his departure by one more day.

for talk and a time for sleep. If you want to hear still more,
I will not hold back from telling you things still more pitiful
than these—the sorrow of my companions, who perished
after we escaped from the shrill war cry of the Trojans,   360
and those who were destroyed on their return through
the will of an evil woman.°
                        "When the holy Persephone
had scattered the breath-souls of the women here and there,
up came that of Agamemnon, the son of Atreus, groaning.
The breath-souls of all those who died and met their fate   365
in the house of Aigisthos were gathered around him.
Agamemnon right away knew who I was, after
he had drunk the black blood. He complained shrilly,
pouring down hot tears, throwing out his hands toward me,
longing to embrace me. But there was no lasting strength   370
or vitality, such as once dwelled in his supple limbs.
    "I wept when I saw him and took pity in my heart,
and spoke to him words that went like arrows: 'Most glorious
son of Atreus, king of men, Agamemnon, what fate
of grievous death overcame you? Did Poseidon overcome you,   375
raising up the dreadful blast of savage winds among
your ships? Or did enemy men do you harm on the dry
land as you cut out their cattle or their beautiful
flocks of sheep, or fought for a city, or for women?'
    "So I spoke, and he answered me at once: 'O son   380
of Laërtes, of the line of Zeus, resourceful Odysseus—
it was not Poseidon who overcame me, raising up the dreadful
blast of savage winds among my ships, nor enemy
men who harmed me on the dry land, but Aigisthos°
contrived my death and fate and killed me with the help   385
of my accursed wife. He invited me to his house and gave
me a meal, as you kill an ox at the manger. So I died
a wretched death, and my companions died in numbers
around me, like pigs with white teeth who are slaughtered
in the house of a rich and powerful man at a wedding feast,   390
or a potluck, or a thriving symposium. You've witnessed the death
of many men, either in single combat or in the strong press of battle,
but in your heart you would have pitied the sight of those things—

---

362   *evil woman*: Klytaimnestra, who murdered her husband Agamemnon when he returned home.

384   *Aigisthos*: Agamemnon's cousin and the lover of Klytaimnestra. He is the son of Thyestes, the brother
     of Atreus, Agamemnon's father. In other versions (most famously Aeschylus' play *Agamemnon*, 458 BC),
     Agamemnon is killed in the bathtub, not during a banquet.

how we lay in the hall across the mixing-bowl and the tables
395 filled with food, and the whole floor was drenched in blood.
      "'But the most pitiful cry I heard came from Kassandra,
the daughter of Priam, whom the treacherous Klytaimnestra killed
next to me. I raised my hands, then beat them on the ground,
dying with a sword through my chest. But the bitch turned away,
400 and although I was headed to the house of Hades, she would
not stoop to close my eyes nor to close my mouth! There
is nothing more shameless, more bitchlike, than a woman
who takes into her heart acts such as that woman devised—
a monstrous deed, she who murdered her wedded husband.
405 I thought I'd return welcomed by my children and slaves,
but she, knowing extraordinary wickedness, poured shame
on herself and on all women who shall come later, even on those
who do good deeds!'
                  "So he spoke, but I answered: 'Yes, yes,
certainly Zeus with the loud voice has cursed the seed of Atreus
410 from the beginning through the plots of women. Many of us
perished for Helen's sake, and Klytaimnestra fashioned
a plot against you when you were away.'
                              "So I spoke,
and he answered at once: 'And for this reason, be not
too trusting of even *your* wife! Don't tell her everything
415 that you know! Tell her some things and leave the rest unsaid.
But I don't think you will be murdered by your wife—
she is too discreet and carries only good thoughts in her heart,
this daughter of Ikarios, the wise Penelope. We left
her just a young bride when we went to war. She had
420 a babe at her breasts, just a little tyke, who now must be
counted among the number of men. How happy he will be
when his father, coming home, sees him, and he will greet
his father as is the custom! My own wife did not
allow me to feast my eyes on my son. She killed me
425 before that.
            "'And I will tell you something else,
and please consider it: Secretly, and not in the open, put your
boat ashore in the land of your fathers! For you can no longer
trust any woman. But come, tell me this and report it
accurately, whether you have heard that my son Orestes is alive
430 in Orchomenos or in sandy Pylos, or even with Menelaos
in broad SPARTA. For Orestes has not yet died on the earth.'
      "So he spoke, but I answered: 'Son of Atreus,
why do you ask me these things? I don't know the truth of it,

whether he is alive or dead. It is an ill thing to speak words
as empty as the wind.'   435
                    "And so the two of us stood there exchanging
lamentations and pouring down warm tears. Then came
the breath-soul of Achilles, the son of Peleus, and of the good
Patroklos, and of Antilochos, and of Ajax,° the best in form
and stature of all the Danaäns after Achilles, the good son of Peleus.
    "The breath-soul of Achilles, the fast runner, recognized me,   440
and, groaning, he spoke words that went like arrows: 'Son of Laërtes,
of the line of Zeus, resourceful Odysseus—poor thing! How will
you top this plan for audacity? How have you dared to come
down to the house of Hades where the speechless dead live,
phantoms of men whose labors are done?'°   445
                    "So he spoke,
but I answered him: 'O Achilles, son of Peleus, by far
the mightiest of the Achaeans, I came here out of need
for Tiresias, to see if he had advice about how I might come
home again to craggy Ithaca. I have not yet come to Achaea,
nor walked on my own land—always I'm surrounded   450
by misfortune. But Achilles, no man in earlier times or in those
that came later is more fortunate than you. When you were alive
we honored you like the gods, and now that you are here, you rule
among the dead. Therefore do not be sad that you are dead,
O Achilles.'   455
    "So I spoke, and he answered me at once:
'Don't sing praise to me about death, my fine Odysseus!
If I could live on the earth, I would be happy to serve as a hired
hand to some other, even to some man without a plot of land,
one who has little to live on, than to be king among all the dead
who have perished. But come, tell me of my good son,   460
whether he followed me to the war and became a leader or not.
Tell me of my father Peleus, if you know anything,
whether he still holds honor among the many Myrmidons,
or whether men deprive him of honor throughout Hellas
and PHTHIA° because old age has taken possession   465

---

438 ...*Ajax*: Patroklos was Achilles' friend; Antilochos was a son of Nestor; this Ajax was the son of Telamon
     (not the unrelated Ajax, son of Oïleus). In the *Iliad* Patroklos died trying to help the Achaeans; in the post-
     Iliadic tradition, Antilochos fell to Memnon, a Trojan ally from the East; in the *Odyssey*, Telamonian Ajax
     killed himself for shame (see just below), as dramatized famously in Sophocles' play *Ajax* (c. 450–430 BC).

445 *labors are done*: Although Odysseus is standing beside a pit of blood on the shore of Ocean in the land of
     the Cimmerians, the ghosts speak as if he were actually in the underworld; and soon this will be Odysseus'
     own point of view.

465 ...*Phthia*: The Myrmidons ("ants," for unknown reasons) are the followers of the house of Peleus. HELLAS
     is a territory in southern Thessaly near Phthia, Achilles' homeland. By the Classical Period, *Hellas* had
     come to designate all of Greece, but no one is sure why.

of his hands and feet. For I am not there to bear him aid
beneath the rays of the sun in such strength as I had
when at broad Troy I killed the best of their people,
defending the Argives. If in such strength I might come
even for a short time to the house of my father, I would
give pain to those who do him violence and deny him honor—
reason to hate my strength and my invincible hands!'

   "So he spoke, and I answered: 'Yes, I know nothing of Peleus,
but I'll tell you everything I know about Neoptolemos, your son,
just as you ask. I brought him in a hollow well-balanced
ship from SKYROS to the Achaeans who wear fancy shin guards.
Whenever we took council about the city of Troy, he always
spoke first. His words were on the mark. Only godlike Nestor
and I surpassed him. But when we fought with bronze
on the plain of the Trojans, he did not remain in the mass
of men, not in the throng, but he ran forth to the front,
yielding to none in his power. He killed many men
in dread battle. I could never tell them all nor give their
names, so many people did he kill defending the Argives.
But what a warrior was that son of Telephos whom he slew
with the bronze, I mean Eurypylos! And many of that man's
companions, the Keteians, were killed because of gifts desired
by a woman!° Eurypylos was the best-looking man I ever saw,
after the good Memnon.°

                           "'When we, the captains of the Argives,
were about to go down into the horse that Epeios made,°
and I was given command over all, both to open and close the door
of our strongly built ambush, then the other leaders and rulers
of the Danaäns wiped away their tears and their limbs trembled
beneath them. I never saw your son with my own eyes
either turning pale in his beautiful skin nor wiping
away a tear from his cheeks. He constantly begged
me to let him go out of the horse. He kept handling the hilt

---

488 ...*desired by a woman*: Eurypylos was the son of King Telephos in the territory near Troy called MYSIA.
     Achilles had previously wounded Telephos. After Achilles' death, King Priam bribed Telephos' wife,
     Eurypylos' mother, with a golden vine made by Hephaistos ("gifts desired by a woman") to get Eurypylos
     to join the Trojan side. The Keteians, mentioned only here, are plausibly the *Hittites* of central Asia Minor, a
     great power in the Aegean Bronze Age.

489 *Memnon*: A son of the Dawn goddess and Tithonos, brother of Priam. He was king of the Aethiopians, who
     lived someplace in the East. Achilles killed Memnon after he entered the fight as a Trojan ally in the time
     after that covered in the *Iliad* (where Memnon is not mentioned).

490 *Epeios made*: The carpenter Epeios built the Trojan Horse at Athena's instruction (though Odysseus takes
     credit for the plan). Epeios does not figure in the fighting in the *Iliad*, but participates in the funeral games
     for Patroklos.

of his sword and his spear heavy with bronze. He wanted
to lay waste the Trojans. And when we sacked the steep city
of Priam, after taking his share, a noble reward, he went up   500
into his ship unharmed, not struck with the sharp spear
nor wounded in the hand-to-hand, such as often happens in war.
For Ares rages in confusion.
     "So I spoke, and the breath-soul
of Achilles, grandson of Aiakos the fast runner, went off,
taking long strides across the field of asphodel, thrilled   505
because I said his son was preeminent. Other breath-souls
of the dead and gone now stood in a crowd. Each asked
about what was important to them. Only the breath-soul of Ajax,
son of Telamon, stood apart, angry on account of the victory
that I won over him in the contest for the armor of Achilles.   510
Thetis, Achilles' revered mother, had set them as a prize.°
The sons of the Trojans were the judges, also Pallas
Athena. I wish that I had never won in that contest
for such a prize! On account of this armor the earth
covered over so great a head, Ajax, who in comeliness   515
and in the deeds of war was superior to the other Danaäns,
except for Achilles.°
     "I spoke to him with honeyed words:
'Ajax, son of excellent Telamon, even in death you
won't give up your anger on account of those accursed
arms? The gods placed them as a calamity to the Argives.   520
We lost such a tower of strength in you. The Achaeans
lament your death ceaselessly, like that of Achilles,
son of Peleus. There is no other cause but Zeus, who thoroughly
hated the army of the Danaän spearmen, who set your doom
on you. But come now, King, so that you might hear   525
my honest speech. Conquer your anger and your proud spirit!'
  "So I spoke, but he did not answer me. He went
his way to Erebos among the other breath-souls of men
who are dead and gone. He might have spoken to me
even though he was angry, or I to him, but the spirit   530

---

511 *as a prize*: The prize was awarded to whoever helped the most in recovering the body of Achilles. That is
   why Trojans serve as judges—they knew best.

517 *for Achilles*: Although Ajax deserved the armor—he carried the body of Achilles from the battleground—
   Odysseus somehow won the contest and received Achilles' armor. Ajax went mad for shame and attacked a
   herd of sheep, thinking they were the Trojan captains. When he recovered his senses and saw what he had
   done, he threw himself on his sword, the only example in Greek myth of a practice common in the Roman
   period (see *Od.* Figure 11.2).

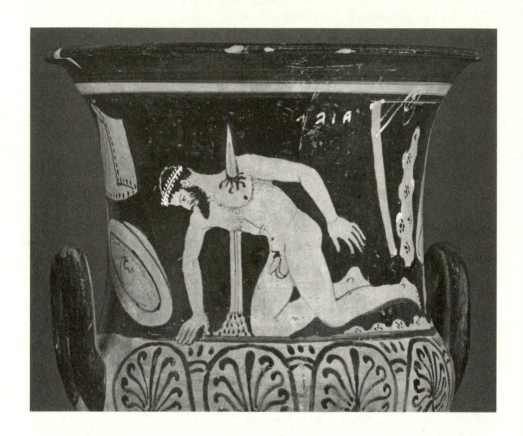

FIGURE 11.2   The suicide of Telamonian Ajax.   The naked hero has fixed his sword in a pile of sand and thrown himself on it. His shield and breastplate are stacked on the left, his club and the scabbard to his sword on the right. His name is written above him as AIWA. Athenian red-figure two-handled jug, from Vulci, Italy.

in my breast wanted to see the breath-souls of others
who had died.
        "I saw Minos, the glorious son of Zeus,
holding his golden scepter, giving laws to the dead
from his seat, while they sat and stood around the king throughout
the house of Hades with its wide gates, asking for his judgments.°   535
        "I saw huge Orion driving wild animals together
across the plain of asphodel, ones that he had himself
killed on the lonely mountains. He held in his hands
a club all of bronze, forever unbreakable.°
                                "And I saw
Tityos, the son of Gaia, lying on the ground, sprawled   540
over nine acres. Two vultures sitting on either side
gnawed at his liver, plunging their heads into his intestines,
for he could not ward them off with his hands. For Tityos
tried to carry off Leto, the glorious wife of Zeus, as she
went toward Pytho through Panopeus with its beautiful places.°   545
        "And I saw powerful Tantalos, suffering agony,
standing in a pool. The water came up to his chin. He stood
as if thirsty, but he could not take a drink. Every time
the old man stooped over, eager to drink, the water would
be guzzled up and disappear, and the dark earth would appear   550
all dry around his feet, as if as some god had made
it so. High leafy trees poured down fruit above his head—
pear trees and berry trees and apple trees with their shining
fruit, and sweet figs and luxuriant olive trees. But whenever
the old man would reach out to snare them with his hands,   555
a wind would hurl them to the shadowy clouds.°
                                "And I saw
Sisyphos suffering terrible agonies, trying to raise a huge
stone with both his hands. Propping himself with hands

---

535 *for judgments*: At this point Odysseus seems no longer to be standing by the pit of blood, but to be in the
     underworld itself. Homer makes this transition without explanation as he launches into a new catalog, the
     Denizens of the Underworld. Minos, son of Zeus and Europa, was a legendary king of Crete and a judge in
     the underworld. He continues in death doing what he did in life: issuing fair judgments to supplicants.

539 *unbreakable*: Orion too is portrayed as doing in death what he did in life, even hunting the same animals,
     or presumably their ghosts.

545 *beautiful places*: Tityos, a giant son of Gaia (Earth), was killed by Apollo and Artemis after he attempted
     to rape their mother Leto—Leto was not the "wedded wife" of Zeus, who is Hera, but his mistress. Pytho
     (DELPHI) and Panopeus are in PHOCIS, on the mainland.

556 *shadowy clouds*: According to later tradition, Tantalos, from PHRYGIA or LYDIA near Troy in Asia Minor,
     chopped up his son Pelops and served the cannibal stew to the gods to test their omniscience. Pelops was
     reassembled and fled to southern Greece where he gave his name to the Peloponnesus ("island of Pelops").

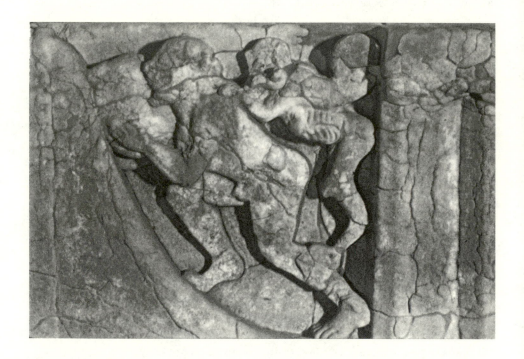

FIGURE 11.3 **Punishment of Sisyphos.** Sisyphos pushes the rock up a hill while a winged demon with a bird's head clings to his back. From a metope (sculptured relief) from the Temple of Hera at Foce del Sele in southern Italy, near Paestum, c. 510–500 BC.

and feet, he tried to thrust the stone toward the crest
of a hill. But when he was about to push it over the top,   560
its mighty weight would turn it back, and the brutish
stone would roll down again to the plain. Then straining
he would thrust it back, as sweat flowed down from his
limbs and dust rose from his head.°

                  "Afterward I saw
the mighty Herakles, or maybe a phantom of him—he who takes   565
his pleasure with the deathless gods at the banquet and has Hebê
to wife, the child of great Zeus and Hera, she whose ankles
are beautiful in her golden sandals.° A clanging of the dead
arose about him, like birds driven everywhere in terror.
Herakles was like the dark night, holding his bare bow   570
and an arrow on the string, glaring dreadfully, a man
about to shoot. The baldric around his chest was awesome—
a golden strap in which were worked wondrous things,
bears and wild boars and lions with flashing eyes, and combats
and battles and the murders of men. I would wish that the   575
artist did not make another one like it!°

                     "He knew who I was,
and weeping he spoke words that went like arrows:
'Son of Laërtes, of the line of Zeus, resourceful
Odysseus—Ah wretch, do you too lead an evil life such as
I bore beneath the rays of the sun? Though I was the son   580
of Zeus, I had pain without limit. For I was bound to a man
far worse than I, who lay upon me difficult tasks.
Once he sent me to bring back the hound of Hades,
for he could think of no contest mightier than this. I carried
off the hound and led him out of the house of Hades.   585
Hermes was my guide, and Athena with the flashing eyes.'

   "So speaking, Herakles went again to the house of Hades,
but I held my ground where I was, to see if another
of the warriors who had died in the days of old might come.

---

564 *from his head*: It is not clear why dust should rise from Sisyphos' head. As with Tantalos, Homer does not
     give the crime of Sisyphos, a son of Aiolos of Thessaly and a king of Corinth, known as the wiliest man who
     ever lived. Sisyphos was the real father of Odysseus (not Laërtes) according to a postHomeric tradition,
     having seduced Odysseus' mother on her wedding night. Later writers gave a variety of reasons for
     Sisyphos' punishment, one being that he bound Death himself so that (for awhile) no one died.

568 *golden sandals*: Homer wants to show Herakles in the underworld, but must deal with a strong religious
     tradition that Herakles became a god after death, hence lives on Olympos where he married Hebê,
     "youth"—that is, he never got old. Homer reconciles the two traditions by saying that the Herakles in the
     underworld was only a "phantom."

576 *like it*: That is, so lifelike are the terrible images on the belt that a second example would be unendurable—
     but the Greek is extremely obscure here.

590 I would have seen men of earlier times—and I wanted
to see them, Theseus and Peirithoös, the glorious offspring
of the gods, but before that the tribes of ten thousand dead
gathered around with a wondrous cry. Pale fear seized me—
perhaps the illustrious Persephone would send the Gorgon's
595 head upon me, that great monster out of the house of Hades!°
    "I went at once to the ship and I ordered my companions
to embark, to loosen the stern cables. Quickly they
got on board and sat down on the benches. The wave
of the stream bore the ship down the river Ocean. At first
600 we rowed, then we ran before a fair breeze."

---

595 *house of Hades*: According to the familiar legend, there were three Gorgons but only Medusa was mortal.
The hero Perseus cut off Medusa's head, and anyone who looked at it was turned to stone. But Homer does
not seem to connect the Gorgon with the legend of Perseus.

BOOK 12. *Odysseus on the Island of the Sun*

"When the ship had left the stream of the river Ocean
and had come to the wave of the broad sea and the island
of Aiaia, where is the house of early-born Dawn,
and her dancing ground and her risings of the sun°—
coming there we beached our ship on the sand.   5
We got out on the shore of the sea, then fell asleep
and awaited the shining Dawn.
                              "When early-born Dawn
appeared with her fingers of rose, then I sent my
companions off to the house of Kirkê to retrieve
the corpse of the dead Elpenor. We at once cut logs   10
and, mourning, pouring down hot tears, buried him
where the headland projects furthest into the sea.
When the corpse and the armor of the corpse were burned,
we heaped up a barrow and set up a memorial column.
On top of the mound we planted his finely shaped oar.   15
    While we busied ourselves with these various tasks,
Kirkê was aware that we had returned from the house
of Hades. She spruced herself up and quickly came along,
and her servants brought bread and abundant meat
and flaming red wine with her. Standing in our midst,   20
the beautiful goddess said: 'Poor things, who have gone
down alive to the house of Hades—men who will die
twice, while other men die but a single time. But come,
eat of this bread and drink this wine, staying here all day
long. At the coming of dawn you shall sail away. I shall   25
show you the way and make clear each matter so that
you do not suffer pain and misfortune through the wicked
and terrible designs of either sea or land.'
                              "So she spoke,
and our proud spirits agreed. So all the day until the sun
went down we sat dining on endless meat and sweet wine.   30
When the sun went down and the darkness came on,
my men lay down to take their rest beside the stern cable
of the ship. But Kirkê took me by the hand and led me apart

---

4 *of the sun*: Aiaia is therefore in the extreme East, although Odysseus has evidently been traveling in the far West.

from my dear companions. She made me sit down
and herself lay down beside me and asked me about
everything.
       "I told her all in proper order, and then
the revered Kirkê spoke to me and said: 'Thus have all
these matters been brought to completion. Now listen
to what I shall say. A god himself will remind you.
First you will come to the Sirens° who enchant all men
who come near them. Whoever comes close to them
in ignorance and hears the Sirens' voice, he will never
return to his home for his wife and little children
to stand by his side and rejoice. For the Sirens, sitting
in a meadow, enchant all with their clear song.
Around them there is a great heap of the bones
of rotting men, and the skin shrivels up around
those bones. But go on past them, and then seal
the ears of your companions by kneading sweet wax
so that none of them may hear. If you yourself want
to hear, let them bind your hands and feet in the swift
ship, upright in the hole for the mast, and let the ropes
be fixed to the mast itself° so that you might take delight
in hearing the voice of the two Sirens. If you beseech
and order your companions to release you, they must
bind you with still more bonds.
                          "'Now when your companions
shall have rowed past these beings, then I won't exactly
say which course you should take, but you must
consider it yourself in your own mind. I will describe both.
   "'On the one side are overhanging cliffs, and against them
a great wave of blue-eyed Amphitritê roars. The blessed
gods call them the Planktai.° Not even winged things,
nor timid doves that carry ambrosia to father Zeus,
can pass them, but the smooth rock always snatches
away one, and the father sends out another to make up
the full number. So no ship of men that ever came here
has escaped intact, but the waves of the sea and the blasts
of ruinous fire whirl the planks of ships and the bodies
of men in confusion. Only one seafaring ship has
ever sailed through the Planktai—the Argo, an object

---

40   Sirens: The origin and meaning of the name are unknown.

53   mast itself: It is not clear how Odysseus is to be tied in the "hole for the mast," but probably Od. Figure 12.1
     gives a good image of what Homer has in mind.

62   Planktai: The "clashing (rocks)."

of everyone's interest, sailing back from Aietes.
And even her the wave would have quickly dashed
against the great rocks, but Hera sent her on through
because she loved Jason.°

        " 'On the other path are two cliffs,
one of which reaches to the broad heaven with its cragged   75
peak, and a dark cloud surrounds it that never ebbs away.
Nor is the clear sky ever seen around that peak, neither
in summer nor harvest time. No mortal man could ever
climb it or set his foot on top, not if he had twenty hands
and feet. For the rock is smooth, as if it were polished.   80
And in the middle of the cliff is a shadowy cave turned
toward the west, toward Erebos—it is likely that you should
steer your hollow ship past it, glorious Odysseus.
Not even a strong man could shoot an arrow from his
hollow ship so that it reached into the hollow cave.   85
Skylla° lives there, barking terribly. Her voice is like
that of a new-born puppy, but she herself is an evil
monster. No one would ever take pleasure in seeing her,
not even if it was a god who met her. She has twelve feet,
all of them twisted, and six long necks, and on each one   90
a horrific head, and in each three rows of teeth, set close
together in great numbers, full of black death. She hides
up to her middle in the hollow cave, but she holds out her heads
from the terrible cavern and fishes there, greedily groping
around the cliff for dolphins and seals, or, if she can, catch   95
any other beast of those that deep-moaning Amphitritê
rears in great multitudes. No sailors can boast that they
have fled unscathed past her in their ships. With each head
she carries off a man, snatching him from the ship with its
prow painted blue.   100
        " 'Odysseus, you will notice that the other cliff
is lower—they are so close to one another, you could shoot
an arrow across. A large fig tree with many leaves is on it.
Beneath it the divine Charybdis° sucks down the black
water. Three times a day she vomits it forth, three times
she sucks it down—terrible! Don't be there when she sucks   105

---

74   *loved Jason*: The clearest proof that the *Odyssey*'s account of Odysseus' adventures owes something to a
traditional poem about Jason's wanderings, but we cannot be sure of the details. Aietes, the son of Helios
and Persê the daughter of Ocean, was the father of Medea and the brother of Kirkê, but Homer never mentions Aietes' position as king of Kolchis, land of the Golden Fleece, or the role of evil opponent that Aietes
played in the story of Jason.

86   *Skylla*: "puppy," hence the dogs' heads and the barking.

103   *Charybdis*: Looks like it might mean "swallower," but is probably not Greek.

it down! No one could save you from that evil, not even
the earth-shaker. Rather, go close to the cliff of Skylla
and drive your ship past. It is better by far to mourn
for six comrades than for all together!'
                              "So she spoke, and I said
110   in reply: 'But goddess, tell me this truly—is there someway
I can escape the foul Charybdis and ward off that other, too,
when she plunders my companions?'
                              "So I spoke, and the beautiful
goddess right away answered me: 'Poor man, all you think
about are the acts and the grind of war! Will you never yield
115   to the deathless gods? She is not mortal, but an immortal
evil—a dread terror, savage and unmanageable!
There is no defense. It is best to flee from her. If you take
the time to arm yourself beside the cliff, I fear that she will
leap out again and attack you with her many heads and seize
120   as many men as before. Drive past her aggressively
and call out to Krataiïs,° the mother of Skylla, who bore
her as a curse to mortals. Krataiïs will stop her from
leaping forth again.
                              " 'Next you will come to the island
of Thrinakia. The many herds of Helios' cattle graze there,
125   and the good flocks of sheep—seven herds of cattle
and as many beautiful flocks of sheep, fifty animals
to each. They have no offspring, nor do they ever die.
Goddesses are their shepherds, nymphs with fine tresses—
Phaëthousa and Lampetiê° —whom the beautiful Neaira
130   bore to Helios Hyperion. Their revered mother bore
and raised them, then sent them off far away to live,
to Thrinakia, where they look over their father's flocks
and the sleek cattle. If you leave these unharmed
and remember your homecoming, you may all arrive
135   still to Ithaca, though suffering terribly. But if you harm them,
then I foretell ruin for your ship and your companions.
Even if you alone escape, you will come to your home
late and in evil plight, having lost all your comrades.'
       "So she spoke, and promptly then golden-throned Dawn
140   arose. The beautiful goddess took her way up through
the island, while I went to the ship and roused my
companions, ready to set sail, to loosen the stern cables
and leave. Speedily they climbed aboard and sat

---

121   *Krataiïs:* "powerful one," otherwise unknown.

129   *Phaethousa and Lampetiê*: Significant names, "shining" and "radiant," appropriate to their father's nature.

down at the thole pins. They sat all in a row
and struck the gray sea with their oars. Fair-tressed   145
Kirkê, the dread goddess of human speech, sent a fair
wind that filled the sail behind the ship with painted
blue prow, our fine companion. When we had stowed all
the tackle in the ship, we took our seats. Wind arose
and the helmsman steered her along.   150
        "Then, sad at heart,
I spoke to my companions: 'My friends, it is not right
that one or two alone know the oracles that Kirkê
the beautiful goddess delivered. I will tell you all,
so that either in full knowledge we may die, or avoiding
death and fate we may escape. First of all she urged   155
that we avoid the voice of the wondrous Sirens from their
flowery meadow. She advised me alone to hear their
voice. But you must first bind me in tight bonds so that
I remain fast where I am, upright in the hole for the mast,
and let the cables be made fast to the mast. If I beg you   160
to let me go and order you to do it, then you must bind
me with more bonds.'
      "And so I went over everything and told
all to my companions. Meanwhile the well-built ship
came quickly to the island of the two Sirens, for a fair
wind bore her along. Then the wind stopped and there   165
was a windless calm—some spirit lulled the waves to sleep.
My companions arose and furled the sail and stowed it
in the hollow ship. Sitting at the tholes, they made the sea
white with their polished oars of pine. And with my sharp
sword I cut a great round cake of wax into small pieces,   170
then kneaded it in my powerful hands. The wax
quickly grew warm from the great strength of my hands
and the rays of King Helios Hyperion. I anointed the ears
of all my comrades in turn with it. They bound my hands
and feet alike in the ship, upright in the hole for the mast,   175
and they fastened the cables to the mast. Then they sat
down and struck the gray sea with their oars.
        "But when
we were as far away as a man can be heard when shouting,
driving swiftly on our way, the Sirens noticed the fast ship
as it came near, and they began to intone their clear song: 180
'Come here, O storied Odysseus, great glory of the Achaeans,
bring your ship over here so that you can hear the voices
of the two of us. For no man yet has passed
this island in his black ship before hearing the sweet

185 voice from our lips, but he takes pleasure in it and goes
on his way, knowing more. For we know all that the Argives
and the Trojans suffered through the will of the gods
in broad Troy, and we know all things that take place
on the much-nourishing earth.'

                                "So they sang, sending
190 out their beautiful voices. My heart wanted to hear them,
and I ordered my companions to set me free, nodding
with my brows. But they fell to their oars and rowed on.
Right away, Perimedes and Eurylochos stood up and bound me
in more ropes and pulled them tighter. When they had rowed
195 past the Sirens and could no longer hear their voices nor song,
my trusty companions quickly removed the wax with which
I had stuffed their ears, and they released me from my bonds.
When we had left the island, I immediately espied smoke
and a great wave and heard a roar. The oars flew from the hands
200 of my frightened men and fell in the water with a splash,
and the ship stood still where it was when they stopped
driving it on with their hands on the sharp blades.

                                       "I went
through the ship and encouraged my companions with
honeyed words, standing by each man in turn: 'My friends,
205 we have not been ignorant of evils before this, and surely this evil
is no worse than when Cyclops trapped us in his hollow cave
by brute strength! But even then we escaped, thanks to my
courage, counsel, and intelligence. I think that one day
we will remember this sorrow too. But come now, let us all
210 obey what I say. Keep your seats on the benches and strike
the deep surf of the sea with your oars in the hope that Zeus
may somehow grant us to escape and to avoid destruction.
To you, helmsman, I make this command, and do take it
to heart, because you control the helm of the hollow ship:
215 Keep the ship far away from this smoke and these waves.
Hug the cliff so that the ship does not swerve off to the other
side and cast us into destruction.'

                              "So I spoke, and swiftly they
obeyed my words. I did not mention Skylla—an incurable curse!—
so that my companions would not take fear, cease from their
220 rowing, and huddle together in the bottom of the ship. And I
forgot all about the hard warning of Kirkê—that she ordered
me not to arm myself—for I put on my famous armor and took
up two long spears in my hands and went onto the fore-deck
of the ship. Thought that Skylla of the rock, who was about to
225 bring catastrophe on my companions, would first appear here.

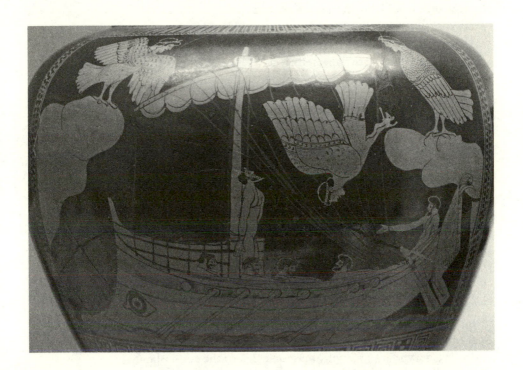

FIGURE 12.1 Odysseus and the Sirens.   In Homer, there are only two Sirens, but here there are three. They are represented as Egyptian ba-birds, the Egyptian souls of the dead. One Siren seems to fall to her death from the right-hand cliff in accord with a postHomeric tradition that the Sirens committed suicide from chagrin when Odysseus withstood their enchantments. Odysseus is tied to the mast while his men row on. Notice the helmsman to the right with his two steering oars, and the apotropaic ("turning away evil") eye painted on the ship's prow. Athenian red-figure vase, c. 460 BC.

But I could glimpse her nowhere, and my eyes grew tired
looking everywhere across the foggy rock. We sailed on up
through the narrow passage, lamenting as we went. On the one
side was Skylla, on the other the divine Charybdis sucked
230 down the salty water of the sea. And when she vomited it forth,
like a cauldron on a huge fire, she would foam right up
to the top, seething, in chaotic confusion, and high overhead
the sea-spray would fall on the tops of both cliffs. As often
as she sucked down the salty water of the sea, all within
235 was seen seething, and all around the rock was a terrible roar,
and down deep the earth appeared black with sand.
    "Pale fear seized my men. We looked towards her, terrified
of destruction. In the meanwhile Skylla seized six of my men,
the best in strength and power, from the hollow ship.
240 Looking across the swift ship and toward my companions,
I saw their feet and hands above me as they were lifted
into the air. They cried aloud to me and called me by name
for the last time, in anguish of heart. As a fisherman sits
on a jutting rock and throws in his bait as a snare to the little
245 fishes and with his long pole lets down into the sea the horn
of an ox of the field,° and then as he catches a fish and
pulls it out as it writhes for air—even so they were pulled
toward the rocks gasping for air, and there at her doors
she ate them as they screamed and held out their hands
250 toward me in the dread death-struggle. It was the most pitiful
thing that my eyes ever saw of all that I experienced while
exploring the paths of the sea. "When we had fled from the cliffs
of dread Charybdis and Skylla, we soon came to the good island
of the god where were the beautiful broad-browed cattle
255 and the many fat flocks of Helios Hyperion. While I was still in my
black ship out to sea, I heard the lowing of the cattle being penned
in stalls, and the bleating of sheep, and on my heart fell the words
of the blind seer Theban Tiresias and of Aiaian Kirkê, who strongly
encouraged me to avoid the island of Helios, who gives joy to mortals.
260   "Grieving at heart, I spoke to my companions: 'Hear my words,
though you are suffering, my companions, so that I may tell you
the oracles of Tiresias and of Aiaian Kirkê, who most strongly urged
me to avoid the island of Helios who gives joy to mortals.
She said that there is the grimmest affliction for us here. So drive
265 the black ship beyond the island.'
                      "So I spoke, and the hearts
within them were crushed. Right away Eurylochos spoke

---

246   *ox of the field*: A tube of horn was set above the hook to prevent the line from being bitten.

with loathsome words: 'You are a hard man, Odysseus.
Your strength is superior and your limbs never tire. You are
made entirely of iron—you will not let your companions,
worn out with labor and lack of sleep, set foot on the land,   270
where we might make a delicious meal on this island surrounded
by the sea. Instead you ask us, even as we are, to wander on
throughout the night on the misty sea. But rough winds, the wrecker
of ships, come from the night. How might anyone avoid
total destruction if somehow, suddenly, the blast of the wind   275
should come—either South Wind or blustering West Wind—
which most often ruins ships in spite of the will of the ruling gods?
Let us yield to black night and prepare a meal, remaining
at the side of the swift ship, and in the morning we will
embark again on the broad sea.'   280
          "So spoke Eurylochos, and my
other companions assented. I realized that some spirit was
designing evil, and I spoke words that went like arrows:
'Eurylochos, you force my hand, for I stand alone. But come now,
may everybody swear a powerful oath: If we come across a herd
of cattle or a great flock of sheep, let no one in evil folly   285
kill either cow or sheep, but be happy to eat the food
that deathless Kirkê has provided.'
          "So I spoke, and they
all promptly swore, just as I urged. And when they had sworn
and accomplished the oath, we moored our well-built ship
in the hollow harbor close by the sweet water, and my companions   290
climbed out of the ship. Skillfully they prepared a meal,
and when they had put the desire for food and drink from
themselves, they fell to weeping, remembering their companions
whom Skylla snatched from the hollow ship and devoured.
Sweet sleep came upon them as they wept. But then,   295
in the last third of the night, as the stars had passed to the other
side of the sky, Zeus the gatherer of clouds sent forth
a savage wind in an astounding tempest, and it hid the earth
and the sea alike in clouds, and night rushed down
from the heaven.°   300
          "When early-born dawn appeared with her
fingers of rose, we dragged our ship out and made her fast
in a hollow cave, where were the beautiful dancing places
and seats of the nymphs. Then I called my men to an
assembly and I said to them: 'My friends, there is food

---

300   *heaven:* That is, the clouds covered the stars so that there was total darkness.

305 and drink in our swift ship, so let us stay away from these
cattle so that we do not come to harm. These are the cattle
and fat sheep of a dread god, Helios, who oversees all things
and hears everything.'
                         "So I spoke, and their proud hearts
agreed. Then for a full month South Wind blew incessantly,
310 nor was there any other wind except for East Wind
and South Wind.° So long as my companions had food
and red wine, they kept their hands off the cattle,
being anxious to save their lives. But when all the provisions
from the ship were exhausted, and they were compelled
315 to wander around in search of game—of fish and birds
and whatever might come to their hands, fishing with
bent hooks. Meanwhile, hunger gnawed their bellies.°
     "Then I went up the island so that I might pray to the gods,
to see if they would show a way to go. When I had come
320 away from my companions as I went through the island,
I washed my hands in a place where there was protection
from the wind, and I prayed to all the gods who live
on Olympos. They poured out sweet sleep over my eyelids.
     "In the meanwhile, Eurylochos began to give wicked
325 counsel to my crew: 'Hear me, my companions, while we
are all in an evil plight. All death is hateful to wretched mortals,
but most pitiful is to die of hunger and so meet one's doom.
So come, let us drive off the best of the cattle of Helios
and sacrifice them to the deathless ones who hold the broad
330 heaven. And if we ever arrive to Ithaca, the land of our fathers,
we will build a rich temple to Helios Hyperion, and place many
fine offerings in it. And if he is angry because of his
straight-horned cattle and wishes to destroy our ship,
and the other gods agree, I would rather die of a sudden,
335 gulping down a wave, than to waste away slowly
on a desert island.'
                         "So Eurylochos spoke, and all the other
companions agreed. Immediately they drove off the best
of the cattle of Helios, who were nearby. The beautiful
sleek broad-browed cattle were grazing not far from
340 our blue-prowed ship. My men stood by these and prayed
to the gods, plucking the tender leaves of a high oak,
for there was no white barley in our well-benched ship.

---

311 *South Wind*: That is, the wind blowing incessantly is south-easterly.

317 *their bellies*: Epic heroes eat only beef, mutton, and pork, except in extreme circumstances.

"When they had prayed and had cut the throats of the cattle
and stripped off their skin, they cut out the thigh bones
and covered them with a double layer of fat and placed   345
raw flesh on them. They had no wine to pour over the blazing
sacrifice, but they poured drink-offerings of water and roasted
the guts. When they had burned the thigh bones and eaten
the entrails, they cut up the rest and put it on spits. It was
then that sweet sleep fled from my eyes, and I went down   350
to the swift ship and the shore of the sea.
                              "When I came near
to the beaked ship, then the sweet smell of the fat surrounded
me. Groaning, I cried out to the deathless gods: 'Zeus Father,
and you other blessed gods who live forever, you have
ruined me by lulling me with pitiless sleep. And now my   355
companions have devised a great wickedness in my absence.'
    "Quickly Lampetiê, who wore a long robe, came as a messenger
to Helios Hyperion, saying that we had killed his cattle.
Then quickly Helios spoke in anger to the deathless ones:
'Zeus, father, and you other blessed gods who live forever,   360
take vengeance on the companions of Odysseus son of Laërtes!
Arrogantly they have killed my cattle in which I rejoiced as I
journeyed into the starry heaven, and when I turned back again
to the earth from the heaven. If they do not pay me a suitable
recompense for the cattle, I will descend into the house of Hades   365
and shine among the dead!'
                              "Zeus the cloud-gatherer said to him
in answer: 'Helios, please, continue shining among the deathless
ones and among mortal men who live on the earth, the giver of grain.
As for his men, I will soon hit their swift ship with a shining
thunderbolt and shatter it into small pieces in the middle   370
of the wine-dark sea.' I heard about all this from Kalypso
with the lovely tresses, who herself heard it from Hermes
the messenger.
                              "When I came down to the ship and the sea,
I reproached all my men, standing in front of each one individually,
but we were unable to find a remedy. The cattle were already dead.   375
The gods then showed forth omens for my men. The skins crawled
along the ground and flesh, roast and raw, lowed on the spits,
and there was a mooing as of cattle. For six days my trusty
companions dined on the best of the cattle of Helios that
they had driven off. But when Zeus the son of Kronos brought   380
the seventh day on us, then the wind stopped blowing like a tempest.
    "We immediately went aboard and put out into the broad sea,
setting up the mast and spreading out the white sail. When

we had left the island, and no other land appeared, but only sky
385 and sea, then the son of Kronos set up a dark cloud over the hollow
ship, and the sea grew black beneath the cloud. She did not run
on for long, for quickly the shrill West Wind came on, blowing
with a great blast, and the storm wind snapped the front ropes
that held the mast so the mast fell backwards and all the rigging
390 was scattered in the bilge. In the stern of the ship the mast hit
the head of the helmsman and smashed together the bones
of his head. Like a diver he fell from the foredeck and his proud
spirit left his bones.
        "Then Zeus thundered and hit the ship
with lightning. The whole ship shook when struck by the lightning,
395 and it was filled with sulfur. My companions fell from the ship.
They were borne like sea-crows on the black waves around
the ship—the god had taken from them their day of return.
But I kept going up and down the ship until the surge tore
the sides from the keel, and the wave bore her on bare, and snapped
400 off the mast at the keel. But one of the ropes holding the mast,
made of the hide of an ox, was flung over the mast. I bound the two
together with this, keel and mast, and sitting on these was carried
along by the ferocious winds. Then West Wind ceased
to blow her tempest, and South Wind came up swiftly,
405 bringing sorrow to my heart.
                        "I feared that I might once
again cross destroying Charybdis. All night long I drifted,
and when the sun came up I came to the cliff of Skylla
and dread Charybdis, who still sucked down the salty
water of the sea. But I sprang up high, to the tall fig tree.
410 I clung to it like a bat. But there was no way to plant my feet
firmly, nor to climb it. Its roots were far away, its branches
out of reach, long and great, and they cast a shadow over
Charybdis. I clung to the tree steadfastly until she should
vomit forth the mast and the keel, and to reward my longing
415 they did come up again. At the time when a man rises up
from the market-place, where the many quarrels of contending
young men are judged—at that time those timbers reappeared
from Charybdis.
                        "I let go hands and feet from above and plunged
downward and fell with a thud into the middle of the water
420 beyond the long timbers. Sitting on these I rowed forward
with my hands. As for Skylla, the father of men and gods
did not allow her to see me. Otherwise I would not have
escaped sure destruction!

"Then I was carried for nine days,
but on the tenth night the gods brought me to the island
of Ogygia, where fair-tressed Kalypso lives, the dread goddess
of human speech. She welcomed and took care of me.
  "But why should I tell you these things? 'I told it
only yesterday in your home, to you and to your noble wife.
It is an unpleasant thing to repeat a tale plainly told."

BOOK 13. *Home at Last*

So spoke Odysseus, and they all fell into silence,
held in a spell throughout the shadowy halls.
Then Alkinoös answered him and said: "O Odysseus,
because you have come to my house with its high-roofed
5   floor of bronze, I do not think that you will return home
with further misfortune, even though you have suffered much.
And to every man of you who always likes to drink
the flaming wine of the elders in my halls while listening
to the singer—I lay on you this charge: There is
10 clothing for the stranger in the polished chest along with
gold, finely worked, and all other kinds of gifts that
the counselors of the Phaeacians have brought here.
So come, let us give him a great tripod and a cauldron too—
every man of you!° We will recoup the cost from among
15 the people. It is hard for one man to give generously
without recompense."

                    So spoke Alkinoös, and what he said
pleased them. Each man went to his house to lie down
to sleep. When Dawn with her fingers of rose appeared,
they hurried to the ships and they brought the bronze,
20 giver of strength to men. The powerful Alkinoös
himself carefully stowed the treasure beneath the benches
in the ship, so that it might not get in the way
of the crew while they were rowing, when they hurried
to ply to oars. Then they went to the house of Alkinoös
25 and prepared a feast. The powerful Alkinoös
sacrificed a bull for them, to Zeus the son of Kronos,
god of the dark cloud who rules over everything.
They burned the thigh pieces, then took high pleasure
in a fine feast. The divine singer, Demodokos, sang to them,
30 honored by the people.

---

14 *of you:* He seems to be referring to the twelve chieftains of the Phaeacians, each of whom would
    donate a tripod and cauldron, and presumably the thirteenth would be the gift of Alkinoös. These are
    valuable gifts.

But Odysseus turned his head
toward the bright sun, eager that it set, for he longed so
for his return. As a man wants his dinner, for whom
two wine-dark oxen have drawn the jointed plow through
the fallow land all day long, and the setting of the sun
is a welcome sight so that he may prepare his dinner,   35
and his knees grow weary as he goes—even so welcome
to Odysseus was the sight of the setting sun.

                Quickly
he spoke to the oar-loving Phaeacians, and he especially
addressed Alkinoös: "King Alkinoös, renowned above
all people, pour out drink offerings and send me safely   40
on my way—Farewell! All that my heart desired has been
brought to fulfillment, an escort and gift-tokens of friendship.
May the gods in heaven bless these gifts! And when I return,
may I find my excellent wife in my house and those
I love safe and sound. And you, staying here, may you   45
make your wedded wives and your children joyous.
May the gods give you every kind of prosperity, and may
no evil come to your people."

              So Odysseus spoke, and they all
agreed and urged that the stranger be sent off, for he had
spoken in accordance with what is right. And then   50
the mighty Alkinoös spoke to his herald: "Pontonoös,
mix the sweet wine in the wine-mixing bowl and give it
out to everyone in the hall so that, praying to father Zeus,
we might send the stranger on his way to the land
of his fathers."   55

            So Alkinoös spoke, and Pantonoös mixed
the honey-hearted wine. Coming up to each in turn he poured
it out. From where they sat, they poured drink offerings
to the gods—the blessed gods who hold up the broad sky.
Then godlike Odysseus stood up, and he placed
the twin-handled cup in Aretê's hands. He spoke and addressed   60
her with words that went like arrows: "May you fare well,
O queen—throughout the years until old age and death
that hangs over every mortal comes. As for me—I go my way,
but you must take pleasure in your house and your children
and your people and in chief Alkinoös."   65

So speaking, godlike
Odysseus crossed the threshold. With him the mighty Alkinoös
sent a herald to lead him to the swift ship and the shore
of the sea. Aretê sent her women slaves with him, one
carrying a newly washed cloak and a shirt, another carrying
70 the strong chest, and another carried bread and red wine.
When they came down to the ship and the sea, all the brave
young men who were his escort took these things and stowed them
in the hollow ship—all the drink and food. They laid out
a rug and a linen cloth for Odysseus on the deck of the hollow
75 ship, at the stern where he could get a good night's sleep.
Odysseus went on board and lay down in silence. The crew
sat down, every one at his thole pins, all in order, and they
loosed the mooring rope from the pierced stone. As soon
as they leaned back and tossed the brine with their oar blades,
80 then sweet sleep fell on Odysseus' eyebrows, a deep sleep,
most sweet, like unto death.

                              As when on a plain four yoked
stallions all leap forward under the strokes of the lash,
and leaping up high they quickly traverse their path,
even so the stern of the ship was lifted, and a great purple
85 wave of the loud-resounding sea ranged behind it, and she sped
safe and steady on her way. Not even the circling hawk,
the fastest of winged birds, could have kept pace with it.

And so she sped on swiftly and cut the waves of the sea,
bearing a man like the gods in giving advice, a man who
90 in earlier times had suffered many pains in his heart
and in the wars of men, and on the terrible waves. But now
he slept soundly, having forgotten all that he suffered.

When that brightest of stars arose, which comes to announce
the light of early-born Dawn,° finally the sea-faring ship
95 came close to the island. There is a harbor of Phorkys,°
the Old Man of the Sea, in the land of ITHACA. Two projecting
headlands strike the sea and slope downwards on the side
toward the harbor. These headlands keep back the great
waves raised by unfriendly winds outside, but, inside,
100 the well-benched ships lay calm without mooring ropes,

---

94 *early-born Dawn*: Probably Venus.

95 *Phorkys*: Probably a preGreek sea god, comparable to Proteus or Nereus, said to be the grandfather of
Polyphemos.

once they have reached the place of anchorage. At the head
of the harbor there is an olive tree with long leaves,
and near to it a lovely cave where vapors linger. The cave
is sacred to the nymphs, who are called Naiads.° In the cave
are mixing bowls and stone jars with two handles.   105
The bees store their honey there. There are stone looms,
very tall, where the nymphs weave cloaks dyed with the purple
of the sea, a marvel to behold, and ever-flowing water
within. There are two doors to the cave, one to the north
where men go down. The entrance to the south is for the gods.   110
Men would never come in there, for that is the path
of the deathless ones.°

        They drove in to the harbor, knowing it
from before. They were going so fast that they ran the boat
up on the beach to half the boat's length, for the arms
of the rowers were driving her that hard. They disembarked   115
from the finely benched ship onto the land. First of all
they raised up Odysseus from the hollow ship together
with his linen cover and shining rug. They set him down
on the sand, overcome by sleep. They lifted out the goods
that the noble Phaeacians gave him for his journey home,   120
thanks to the efforts of great-hearted Athena. These they set
all together beside the trunk of the olive tree, out of the path,
so that some passerby might not come upon them and do them
harm before Odysseus awoke.

        Then the Phaeacians returned home.   125

*[Lines 126–182 are omitted. When the Phaeacian ship gets back to Scheria, Poseidon
turns it to stone and throws up a mountain around the island, as was predicted.]*

---

104 *Naiads*: From a verb means "to flow." The Naiad nymphs are spirits of the fresh water—springs, rivers, lakes.

112 *deathless ones*: Sometimes Homer seems to speak from personal knowledge of Ithaca; sometimes he
     gets things wrong. Ithaca (MAP VI) is entirely mountainous and in the rough shape of an hourglass.
     Commentators imagine that Odysseus landed in the GULF OF MOLO on the east side of the island, enclosed
     by two steep headlands, and that he stored his loot in a nearby cave (CAVE OF THE NAIADS) that in fact has
     two entrances. He then proceeded to the northern portion of the island and his house. Parts of thirteen tri-
     pods dated to the late ninth century BC, possibly the time of Homer's activity, were found in modern times
     in the so-called CAVE OF THE TRIPODS near a harbor on the west side of the island. In Hellenistic times
     this cave was associated with Odysseus and it seems to correspond with the Homeric mention of tripods as
     gift-tokens to Odysseus, but the connection is controversial. Tourists to present-day Ithaca will be told that
     the pig herder EUMAIOS' HUT was at the southern tip of the island near a cliff where crows gather, but little
     evidence supports this conclusion.

In the meanwhile Odysseus
awoke from sleep in the land of his fathers. He recognized nothing,
185 for he had been gone a long time. The goddess Pallas Athena,
daughter of Zeus, had poured a mist around him so that she might
make him unrecognizable and then tell him everything,
and so that his wife and townspeople and friends would not
recognize him before he had taken full punishment on the suitors
190 for their transgressions. And so everything seemed strange
to the king—the unbroken paths and the harbors suitable for anchorage
and the steep cliffs and the blooming trees.

He sprang up
and beheld the land of his fathers. Then he groaned and struck
his thighs with the flat of his hands, and gloomily he said:
195 "Oh no! To the land of what men have I come? I wonder if they are
violent and savage, unjust, or are they a friend to strangers?
Do they respect the gods? Where shall I put all these things?
Where will I go now? I wish that I had stayed there with the Phaeacians.
Then I would have come to some other of the mighty chieftains.
200 He would have entertained me and sent me on my way home.

"But now I do not know where I should put these things.
I can't leave them here or they will become the spoil of others.
Yes, the leaders and counselors of the Phaeacians were not
altogether wise—nor just! They have left me off in a strange land
205 when they said they would take me to clear-seen Ithaca!
But they have not done it. May Zeus the god of suppliants
take vengeance on them! He watches over all men and exacts
punishment from the man who misses the mark.
                              "But come,
let me look closely and inventory my goods, to see if these
210 men have taken away anything in their hollow ship . . ."

So speaking, he counted the very beautiful tripods and cauldrons
and gold and beautiful woven cloth. Nothing of these was missing.
Then, pacing beside the shore of the loud-resounding sea,
he mourned for the land of his fathers and complained bitterly.

215   But Athena came close to him in the form of a young man,
a shepherd, young and handsome, such as are the children of kings.
Around her shoulders she had doubled a finely made cloak.
Beneath her shining feet were sandals, and she held a spear.

Odysseus was glad to see her and came up close and spoke
words that went like arrows: "My friend, you are the first man   220
I have come to in this land. Greetings to you! I hope that you
will be friendly to me. Help me save my goods—and me!
I pray to you as if to a god, and I beg you by your knees.
Tell me this truly so that I may know—What land? What people?
What men live here? Is this some island, clearly seen, or a headland   225
of the mainland with its rich soil that rests upon the sea?"

The goddess flashing-eyed Athena answered him: "You are
a fool, sir stranger, or you come from far off if you ask about
this land. It is not *so* without a name—very many know it,
both those who live toward the dawn and the rising of the sun   230
and those who live behind, toward the misty darkness.
It is a rugged island not fit for raising horses, but not so poor,
though it is narrow. It grows prodigious quantities of wheat,
and there is wine. The rain never fails, nor the blooming dew.
It is a good land for pasturing goats and cattle. There is forest   235
everywhere and watering holes that last all year round.
For this reason, stranger, the name of Ithaca has reached even Troy,
which they say is a land far from Achaea."°

So she spoke,
and much-enduring godlike Odysseus was glad, and he rejoiced
in the land of his fathers as he heard the words of Pallas Athena,   240
the daughter of Zeus who carries the goatskin fetish. And he spoke
to her words that went like arrows, but he did not speak the truth—
he took back the words he was about to speak, always storing up
cunning thoughts in his breast: "I have heard of Ithaca,
even in broad CRETE,° far over the sea. Now I have come here   245
with my goods. And I left just as much with my children when I fled,
because I killed the dear son of Idomeneus,° Orsilochos
swift of foot, who surpassed in fleetness of foot all men who live
by labor.° For he wanted to take away all the loot from Troy

---

238 *Achaea*: That is, the Peloponnessus.

245 *Crete*: For some reason Odysseus always claims to be from Crete in the series of false tales that begin here.
     Perhaps the philosophical paradox was already current in a folk saying: "All Cretans are liars," spoken by
     a Cretan: The statement refutes itself (first credited to the Cretan Epimenides, sixth century BC). If all
     Cretans are liars, then so is Odysseus, as in fact he is.

247 *Idomeneus*: Leader of the Cretan contingent at Troy.

249 *labor*: The theme of the homicide forced to go on the run is common in Homer. The same happened to an
     anonymous Aetolian (*Od.* 14); to Theoklymenos (*Od.* 15); to Medon (*Il.* 13); to Lykophron (*Il.* 15); and to
     Patroklos (*Il.* 23).

250 on account of which I had suffered so many pains in my heart,
passing through the wars of men over the savage waves.
I was unwilling to show favor to his father and be his father's
aide in the land of the Trojans but, well, I commanded other men
of my own!
　　　　"Yes, lying in ambush near the road with my companions,
255 I hit Orsilochos with my bronze spear when he came from the fields.
A very dark night covered the sky, and no man saw us. I took
away his life in secret. When I had killed him with my sharp bronze,
I went immediately to a ship and begged passage from some brave
Phoenicians, and I gave them booty enough to satisfy their hearts.
260 I urged them to take me aboard and let me off at Pylos or in shining
ELIS, where the Epeians are strong. But the power of the wind
drove them away, much against their will. They did not intend
to deceive me. Driven from there, we arrived here during the night.
We eagerly rowed into the harbor. There was no thought of a meal,
265 although we badly needed food. All of us went forth
from the ship just as we were and lay down. Exhausted,
sweet sleep came upon me. They took my things from
the hollow ship and placed them down where I lay on the sand.
Then they boarded their ship and went off to SIDON° with its
270 dense population. And I was left here, sorrowing in my heart."

　　　So Odysseus spoke, and flashing-eyed Athena, the goddess,
smiled, and she stroked him with her hand and changed her shape
to that of a woman, beautiful and tall and skilled in glorious
handiwork. And she said to him words that went like arrows:
275 "He would have to be clever and thievish in fact if he was going
to surpass you in every sort of trickery, even if a god encountered you!
Rascal! Fancy-thinker! Insatiate for deception!—you were *not* about
to leave off your deceiving tales and thievish lies even in your own country,
which you love from the bottom of your heart. But come, let us not
280 speak further of these things. We are, the two of us, masters of deception.
Of mortals, you are by far the best in counsel and in telling tales,
and I among all the gods am famous for my wisdom and devices.
　　　"And yet you did not recognize Pallas Athena, daughter of Zeus—
me!—who stands beside you in all your troubles, and watches over you!°
285 I made you welcome to all the Phaeacians. And now I have come
here so that we can weave a plan. We need to hide the treasure
that the noble Phaeacians gave you on your way home—this also

---

269　*Sidon*: A city in Phoenicia often mentioned in Homer. Oddly he never mentions Tyre, in Homer's day the
　　　preeminent Phoenician town. Homer may reflect a Bronze Age tradition, when Sidon was great.

284　*watches over you*: But this is the first time that Athena has appeared in her own person to Odysseus.

FIGURE 13.1 **Odysseus and Athena.** The goddess meets Odysseus wearing a cloak and carrying a spear. Athena wears the goatskin fetish (*aegis*) which has a Gorgon's head in the middle. She points to the ground as if to say, "This is Ithaca." Athenian red-figure vase, c. 440 BC.

thanks to my design and will. I also want to tell you about the trials
you are fated to endure in your own well-built house. But you must
290 bear it, I'm afraid, and not tell anyone, neither man nor woman, that
you have returned from your wanderings. You must suffer your trials
in silence and submit yourself to the abuse of men."

                                                            In answer
to her the resourceful Odysseus said: "It is a hard thing, goddess,
for a mortal just coming along to recognize you, even if he knows
295 a lot—why, you take on whatever shape you wish! I know this well,
that you were friendly to me when we sons of the Achaeans
fought at Troy. But once we sacked the high city of Priam
and went off in our ships, and some god scattered the Achaeans,
I never saw you a single time, O daughter of Zeus. Nor did I notice
300 you coming onto my ship so that you might fend off danger
from me. No, but always I wandered with a heart torn by misery,
until the gods released me from evil! At least until you cheered me
in the rich land of the Phaeacians with your words and personally
led me into the city.° But now I beg of you, by your father—
305 I don't think I have arrived in clear-seen Ithaca! I have been diverted
to some other land. I think you speak with mocking words to trick
my mind. Tell me if truly I have come to the land of my fathers?"

     The goddess flashing-eyed Athena then answered him:
"Always the same, that is the mind within you! And so I cannot
310 leave you in misery, because you are courteous and have a keen
intelligence, and you are shrewd. Another man, returning from
a long journey, would want to go to see his children and his wife
in his halls, but you are not yet minded to know and discover
anything until you have made trial of your wife, who sits as of old
315 in her halls and, ever sad, pours down tears as the nights and days
wear on. *I* never doubted this, but knew in my heart that you
would return home after losing all your companions. But I was
not willing to quarrel with my father's brother Poseidon, who
bore wrath in his heart, angry that you blinded his beloved son.°

320   "But come, I will show you the land of Ithaca, so that you may
become familiar with it. This is the harbor of Phorkys, the Old Man
of the Sea. Here is the long-leafed olive at the head of the harbor.
Near it is the lovely misty cave, sacred to the nymphs, who are

---

304 *into the city*: In fact Odysseus did not recognize her.

319 *son*: The Cyclops Polyphemos.

called Naiads. This is a high-roofed cave where you were accustomed
to make abundant sacrifice of perfect victims to the nymphs. Over there   325
is MOUNT NERITON, clothed in forest."

                             So speaking the goddess scattered
the mist, and the land appeared. Then much-enduring godlike Odysseus
was glad, and he rejoiced in his land, and he kissed the earth,
the giver of grain. Immediately he prayed to the nymphs, raising
high his hands: "O Naiad nymphs, daughters of Zeus, I never thought   330
I would behold you again, but now—hail, with loving prayers!
And I will give gifts as in earlier times, if the daughter of Zeus,
the gatherer of loot, allows with a good will that I continue to live
and that my son grow to be a man."

                            Then flashing-eyed Athena
spoke to him: "Take courage! Don't worry about any of this.   335
But let us put the treasures in a nook in the wondrous cave
right away, so that they may remain safe for you. Then let us
take thought for what will be our best course of action."

   So speaking, the goddess went into the misty cave
and searched out hiding places in the cave, while Odysseus   340
brought all of his loot nearby, the gold and the unwearying
bronze and the finely made woven things that the Phaeacians
had given him. All these things he carefully laid away,
and Pallas Athena, the daughter of the god who carries
the goatskin fetish, placed a stone over the door. Then the two   345
of them sat down near the trunk of the sacred olive tree
and took thought for how they would kill the insolent suitors.

   The goddess flashing-eyed Athena was first to speak:
"Son of Laërtes, of the line of Zeus, resourceful Odysseus,
consider how you will place your hands on the shameless   350
suitors who for three years have been lording it in your halls,
wooing your godlike wife and giving bridal-gifts. She, ever
mourning for your homecoming in her heart, gives hope
to all and promises to each man, sending them messages.
But her mind dwells elsewhere."   355

                         The resourceful Odysseus spoke
in reply to her: "Yes, I might have perished in my halls
by the same fate as Agamemnon, the son of Atreus! If you,
O goddess, had not told me all this! But come, let us weave
a plan so that I might take vengeance on them. Now, you yourself

360 stand by my side and infuse me with a bold power, such as
when we loosed the shining veil of Troy.° If you were to stand
beside me with a similar enthusiasm, O flashing-eyed one,
I would fight against even three hundred men—with you,
revered goddess, if you would come to my aid with an eager heart."

365   Then the goddess flashing-eyed Athena answered:
"I will be very much with you when we are busy with
this work. And I think that many of the suitors who devour
your substance will spatter the vast earth with their blood
and their brains. But come, I will make you unrecognizable
370 to all mortals. I will shrivel the beautiful flesh on your
supple limbs, I will destroy the blond hair on your head
and cover you in a rag so disgusting that seeing a man
wearing it would make you shudder. I will dim your two
eyes that before were so beautiful, so that they appear
375 a disgrace to the suitors, and to your wife and child
whom you left behind in your halls.

                        "But first of all you must go
to the pig herder who watches over your pigs and who
is kindly disposed toward you, who loves your child
and the prudent Penelope. You will find him tending
380 the swine who are grazing beside the rock of Korax
and the fountain of Arethousa,° eating acorns that satisfy
the heart and drinking black water, which cause the rich
fat on pigs to increase. Stay there and sit by his side
and question him about all matters while I go to Sparta,
385 land of beautiful women, to summon Telemachos,
your beloved son, O Odysseus. For he went to the house
of Menelaos in Lacedaemon with its broad dancing places
in order to learn news of you, and if you were still alive."

       The resourceful Odysseus answered her: "Why didn't
390 you just *tell* him? You know everything! I suppose you wanted
Telemachos to suffer sorrow, wandering over the restless sea,
while others devoured his substance . . ."

                        Then the goddess
flashing-eyed Athena said: "Don't worry over much

---

361 *veil of Troy*: To "loose the veil" is to rape a woman, hence "sacked the city."

381 . . . *Arethousa*: Korax means "Raven's Rock," perhaps a common name; there were eight springs named
Arethousa in ancient Greece, the name of a nymph.

about him. I myself guided him so that he might achieve
a noble reputation by going there. He does not labor,   395
but he sits at his leisure in the house of the son of Atreus,
and immeasurable good cheer is set before him. It is true
that young men lie in wait for him in their black ship,
hoping to kill him before he reaches the land of his fathers.
But I don't think it will happen. The earth will cover many   400
of the suitors who devour your substance before that happens!"

So speaking to him, Athena touched Odysseus
with her wand. She shriveled his beautiful skin on his supple
limbs, and she transformed his blond hair, and around all
his limbs she put the skin of an aged old man. She dimmed   405
his two eyes that before were so beautiful, and around him
she put other clothes—a disgusting cloak and shirt,
ragged and filthy, befouled with dirty smoke. She put
the large skin of a swift deer with all its hair removed
around him. She gave him a staff and a wretched pouch,   410
riddled by holes, hung by a twisted cord.

Having taken
counsel together in this fashion, they parted. And the goddess
went to shining Lacedaemon to find the son of Odysseus.

[Books 14 and 15 are omitted. Odysseus goes to the hut of the faithful swineherd Eumaios,
who entertains him and tells him about the suitors ravaging the palace. The disguised
Odysseus tells a lying tale, then predicts that Odysseus will soon be home. Meanwhile
Telemachos, returning from Pylos, avoids the suitors' ambush. He disembarks alone near
the swineherd's hut and sends his ship on to the harbor.]

BOOK 16. *Father and Son*

Meanwhile in the hut, Odysseus and the good pig herder
had started a fire and at dawn were making ready their
breakfast. They had sent forth the herdsmen with the droves
of swine, but the baying hounds fawned around Telemachos
5   and did not bark as he drew near. Godlike Odysseus noticed
this, the groveling of the dogs, and he heard the sound
of footsteps.

      He at once spoke to Eumaios words that
went like arrows: "Eumaios, I think that one of your
companions has arrived here, or somebody you know,
10 because the hounds are not barking. But they grovel around
the man. I hear the sound of his footsteps."

                          But he said no more,
because his own dear son stood in the doorway. Stunned,
the pig herder sprang up, and the jugs in which he was
busy mixing the flaming wine fell from his hands. He came
15 up to his king, he kissed his head and both his beautiful
eyes and his two hands, and a hot tear fell from Eumaios.
As when a father is overjoyed to welcome back his son
in the tenth year who has gone to a far land, an only son
and well beloved for whom he has cried again and again, even
20 so did the good pig herder clasp godlike Telemachos in his arms
and kiss him all over, as if he had escaped from death.

     Complaining, Eumaios spoke words that went like arrows:
"You have come, Telemachos, my sweet light! I thought
I would never see you again after you had gone to Pylos
25 in your ship. But come inside my house now, my dear child,
so that I might delight my heart in looking at you, recently
arrived from foreign lands. For you do not often come
to the fields to visit the herdsmen, but you remain in town.
I suppose that is pleasing to your heart, to watch over
30 the ruinous crowd of the suitors!"

The shrewd Telemachos
answered him: "That's right, old friend. But I have come
here on account of *you*, so that I might see you with
my own eyes and find out whether my mother is still
in the house, or has some other man married her while
the couch of Odysseus lies open without bedding, covered   35
with foul spider webs."

The pig herder, a leader
of men, answered him: "Yes, she remains in your house
with an enduring heart. The nights and days wear away
with agonizing pain as she weeps."

So speaking, Eumaios
took his bronze spear from Telemachos, and Telemachos   40
went inside, crossing over the stone threshold. As he
drew near his father, Odysseus rose from his seat to give
him a place, but Telemachos stopped him from his side
and said: "Sit, stranger, and I will find someplace else
to sit in our farmstead. There is a man here who will   45
set up a chair."

So he spoke, and Odysseus went back
and sat down. And for Telemachos the pig herder strewed
green brush beneath and a fleece above, and there the dear
son of Odysseus sat down. The pig herder set out platters
of roast meats left over from the meal the day before,   50
and quickly he piled bread in baskets, and mixed honey-sweet
wine in an ivy-wood bowl. Then he himself sat down
opposite godlike Odysseus. They reached forth their hands
to the good things that lay before them.

And when they
had put all desire for drink and food from themselves, then   55
Telemachos addressed the good pig herder: "My friend,
where does this stranger come from? How did sailors
bring him to Ithaca? Who did they say they were?
For I don't think that he came here on foot!"

Then you said
in reply, O Eumaios my pig herder: "Well, child, I will tell   60
you the whole truth. He says that he comes from a family
on broad Crete. He says that he has wandered through

many cities of mortals in his travels, for some spirit
decreed that such be his fate. Now he has run away from
65 a ship of the Thresprotians and come to my farmstead.
I hand him over to you. Do what you want. He declares
himself to be your suppliant!"

                          Then the shrewd Telemachos
said in reply: "Eumaios, what you have said greatly
troubles me. How shall I receive this stranger in *my* house?
70 I am young and I cannot rely on my power to defend myself
against a man if he becomes angry without any reason.
My mother is of two minds—whether she should stay
with me and take care of the house, respecting the bed
of her husband and the voice of the people, or whether
75 she should follow whoever is the best of the Achaeans
who courts her in her halls, and offers the most gifts.

    "But as for the stranger, because he has come to your
house, I will give him fine clothes, a cloak and a shirt,
and I will give him a sword sharp on both sides,
80 and sandals for his feet. And I will send him wherever
his heart and spirit desires to go.
                          "And if you are willing,
keep him here in your steading and take care of him.
I will send the clothing here, and plenty of bread to eat
so that he doesn't ruin you and your companions. I would
85 not let him go up to the house to mix with the suitors!
They are consumed by a wicked insolence. I fear that they
would mock him, which would pain me greatly. It is so hard
for one man to achieve anything against many, no matter
how strong he is, for they are much stronger."

90   Then the much-enduring good Odysseus answered:
"My friend, I think it is right that I make an answer.
My heart is torn when I hear you say these things—
that these suitors devise mad deeds in the hall in spite
of you, who are so good a man. Do you allow yourself
95 to be so abused? Or do the people throughout the land
hate you, following the voice of some god? Or do you
blame your brothers, on whom you can depend as helpers
in a fight even if a great quarrel should arise? In my
present state of mind, I wish I were as young as the son
100 of blameless Odysseus—or that I were Odysseus himself!

Then some foreigner might cut the head from my shoulders
if I did not become a fearsome scourge to those men
once I entered the hall of Odysseus, the son of Laërtes.
And if they should defeat me by their numbers, I being all
alone, I would still prefer to die cut down in my own halls   105
than to see these filthy deeds every day—strangers mistreated,
and the female slaves rudely dragged through the beautiful
rooms, and wine spilled all around, and men recklessly eating
my bread without limit—a bad business that will never end."

    The shrewd Telemachos answered: "Well, stranger,   110
I will tell you straight out. By no means do all the people
hate me, nor are they angry with me. Nor do I blame
my brothers, on whom you can depend as helpers in a fight,
even if a great clash should arise. You see, the son
of Kronos has made this house to run in a single line: 115
Arkeisios fathered a single son, Laërtes, and he fathered
Odysseus as his only son, and I was Odysseus' only child.
He left me behind in his halls and had no joy in me.
Now countless evil men inhabit the house. Many are among
the most powerful men in the islands of DOULICHION,   120
SAMÊ, and wooded ZAKYNTHOS—and as many as lord it
over rocky Ithaca—just this many court my mother and they
devour our store! And she won't refuse the hateful marriage,
nor is she able to bring it to fulfillment. Meanwhile
they eat up all my substance. Soon they will bring me to ruin!   125
    "But all this lies on the knees of the gods. Now, my dear
Eumaios, go up quickly and tell the prudent Penelope that I am
safe and that I have returned from Pylos. I will stay here.
Then come back. Only tell *her*! I don't want any other
of the Achaeans to find out, for many of them wish me ill."   130

    In reply you said, O Eumaios my pig herder: "I know,
I have the same thoughts. You are giving orders to one
who already understands. But come, tell me this and tell it
straight out—shall I go with the same news to the wretched
Laërtes, who in the past, though greatly mourning Odysseus,   135
still watched over his own fields and ate and drank with
the slaves in the house whenever the spirit moved him?
But now, ever since you went off in your ship to Pylos,
they say that he has not eaten nor drunk as before, nor does
he watch over the fields, but in agony and complaint   140
he sits weeping, and the flesh shrivels around his bones."

Then shrewd Telemachos answered him: "It is bitter,
but we must let it go, though we feel bad about it. If anything
could be had for the wishing, we would first of all choose
the day of my father's homecoming! No, after giving
your message, come back here, and do not go over the fields
looking for Laërtes. Tell my mother to send out the slave who
is the housemaid as soon as possible, in secret. *She* can tell
the old man."

Thus he spoke and roused the pig herder.
Eumaios took his sandals in his hands, and binding them
beneath his feet he went off to the city. Athena was aware that
Eumaios the pig herder had left the farmstead, and she
came near in the form of a beautiful, tall woman, learned
in glorious handiwork. She stood outside the door of the hut,
revealing herself to Odysseus alone. Telemachos did not
see her or notice her standing before him, for the gods
are not visible to everyone. But Odysseus and the dogs
saw her, and the dogs did not bark but, whining, they slunk
to the other side of the farmstead. The goddess nodded
with her brows, and godlike Odysseus saw it. He came
out of the house, past the large wall of the court,
and he stood before her.

Athena spoke to him, saying:
"Zeus-nourished son of Laërtes, resourceful Odysseus,
reveal your scheme to your son *now*, and don't hold back.
When you have planned how you will bring death
and fate to the suitors, you can go up to the famous city.
I myself will not be apart from you for long. I am eager
for the fight!"

She spoke, and then Athena touched him
with her golden wand. First she put a well-washed cloak
and a shirt around his chest, and she made him tall
and youthful. Once again he grew suntanned, and his cheeks
filled out, and the beard around his chin grew dark.
After doing this, she went away, and Odysseus went
into the hut. His son was astonished to see him!

In fear he turned his eyes aside, thinking he was some god.
He spoke to Odysseus words that went like arrows: "You seem
different, stranger, than a while ago . . . And you have different

clothing on, and your skin is no longer the same. You must
be some god who lives in the broad heaven! Be kind, so that
we might give you welcome sacrifices and golden gifts,   180
nicely made. But please spare us!"

                    Then the much-enduring good
Odysseus answered him: "I am no god. Why do you think I am
like the deathless ones? I am your father, on whose account
you have groaned and suffered many pains—a victim
of the violence of men."   185

              Having so spoken, he kissed his son,
and tears flowed down his cheeks to the ground, tears
Odysseus had steadfastly held back.

                  But Telemachos
did not yet believe that he was his father, and he again
answered and said: "You are not Odysseus, my father,
but a spirit enchants me so that I might groan in agony   190
still more. For no mortal man has devised these things
in his own mind. Only the gods themselves can do this
easily—can make an old man young again if they wish.
For just now you were an old man dressed in rags, but now
you seem like the gods who hold up the broad sky . . ."   195

  Much-enduring resourceful Odysseus answered him:
"Telemachos, you ought not to wonder too much that your father
is here in this house, nor be so amazed. Be sure that no other
Odysseus will ever come here. I am that man, such as you see me!
I have suffered evils and I have wandered far, and now   200
in the twentieth year I have arrived in the land of my fathers.
You should know this is all the doing of Athena, who gathers booty,
who makes me just as she wants. She has the power! First like
a beggar, then like a young man wearing nice clothes upon
his body. It is easy for the gods who live in the broad heaven   205
either to glorify a mortal man or to debase him."

                Having so spoken,
he sat down. Then Telemachos threw his arms around his noble
father and wept, pouring down tears, and the desire for lament
arose in the two of them. They wailed shrilly, more vehemently
than the wail of birds—of ospreys or vultures with crooked   210
talons whose young the country people have taken

from their nest before they could fly. Even so they poured
forth pitiful tears from beneath their brows.

And the light
of the sun would have gone down as they wept if Telemachos
215 did not suddenly say to his father: "On what kind of ship,
my dear father, did sailors transport you to Ithaca? Who did
they say they were? For I don't think you came here on foot!"

The much-enduring good Odysseus then said: "Well, my son,
I will tell you the truth. Phaeacians, famed for their ships,
220 brought me here. They give safe convoy to other men too,
whoever comes to them. They brought me, asleep,
in their swift ship over the sea, and set me down on Ithaca.
They gave me glorious gifts, bronze and gold and a pile
of woven cloth, which now lie in caves, thanks to the favor
225 of the gods. I have come here at Athena's instruction so that
we can plan the destruction of our enemies. But tell me,
what is the number of the suitors? I need to know how
many they are and what kind of men they are. Then I can
ponder in my faultless mind to decide whether we two will be
230 able to take them alone without help, or whether we should
recruit others."

Then the shrewd Telemachos answered him:
"Father, surely I have always heard of your great fame,
that you are a warrior in the strength of your hands and that
your counsel is excellent. But what you say is too much for me!
235 I am overwhelmed! Two men cannot fight against men who are
many and strong. There are not just ten suitors, nor twice
that, but many more. Here, learn their number: From
Doulichion there are fifty-two choice youths, and six servants
in attendance. From Samê there are twenty-four men, from Zakynthos
240 there are twenty youths of the Achaeans, and from Ithaca
itself there are twelve, all best men, and there is the herald Medon,
and the divine singer, and two aides° skilled at cutting
meats. If we were to take on all of them inside, I fear
that your coming to take revenge for their outrages

---

242   ... *aides*: the *servants* (*drêstêres*) are probably slaves; a *herald* (*kêrux*) was a gofer, a runner, a messenger, an
      assistant not of the same social class as the "best men" (*aristoi*) but free and of high rank. The *aides* (*thera-
      pontes*) were also free, but also of a lower social rank than the "best men."

FIGURE 16.1 Odysseus and his son Telemachos. A bearded Odysseus wears his typical felt traveler's cap. The young Telemachos is unbearded. The third figure in the lower right may be Eumaios, the pig herder. Roman mosaic, AD 1st century.

245 will be bitter, dread. But think, if you can find some helper—
one who will help us with an eager heart . . ."

                                           Then much-enduring
good Odysseus answered him: "Well, I will tell you, and you
take it to heart, and hear what I say. Tell me whether Athena
with the help of father Zeus will be sufficient for us two, or should
250 I take thought of another helper?"

                                The shrewd Telemachos
spoke to him: "These *are* fine helpers that you speak of,
though they take their seats high in the clouds. Surely
the two of them have power over all men and the other
deathless gods."

                            Then much-enduring good Odysseus
255 spoke to him: "And those gods will not be absent from
the terrible contendings for long, once the might of Ares
is put to the test between ourselves and the suitors
in my halls. But for the present, go to the house at the break
of dawn and mix with the arrogant suitors. Later on,
260 the pig herder will lead me to the city in the likeness
of an old man, a wretched beggar. If they disrespect me
in the house, let the heart in your breast endure to see me
suffering vile things, even if they drag me by the feet
through the house to the door, or strike me with missiles.
265 If you see this, bear up! Urge them to give up their foolish
behavior. Speak with gentle words. But you will not persuade
them, for the fated day stands near.
                              "I will tell you
something else, and you reflect on it in your breast.
When the counselor Athena puts it in my mind, I will
270 nod to you with my head. When you see this, then pick
up the warrior gear that lies in the hall and put it
in a secret place of the uppermost chamber—absolutely
all of it. As for the suitors, when they miss the armor
and ask you about it, then trick them with gentle words
275 and say: 'I have put the armor out of the way of the smoke,
for they no longer look as they did when Odysseus left them
and went to Troy. They are corroded by the breath of the fire
that has reached them. And furthermore, the son of Zeus
has placed this greater fear in my head, that when you get
280 drunk a quarrel may break out among you so that you wound

one another and put shame on the banquet and your courtship.
For iron draws a man to itself.'°
                          "But for us alone, leave two
swords and two spears and two shields to take up in our hands,
so that we can rush on these weapons and seize them.° As for
the suitors, Pallas Athena and Zeus the counselor will cast a spell   285
over them. And I will tell you something else, and please turn
this over in your mind. If you are truly my son and of my blood,
let no one know that Odysseus is in the house. May Laërtes
not know it, nor the pig herder, nor any of the household
slaves—not Penelope herself! By ourselves you and I   290
will learn the way it is with these women. And let us put
your male slaves to the test too, to see which ones fear us
and honor us at heart, and which ones do not care for us
and dishonor you, excellent as you are."

                          The glorious son
said in reply: "O father, you will come to know my spirit soon,   295
I think, for I am bound by no slackness of will. But I don't
think that this plan will be to our advantage, so I urge you
to think about it. It will take a long time for you to go about
the fields, vainly putting every man to the test while
in your halls these other men arrogantly and at their ease   300
devour your wealth, sparing nothing. As for the women,
I urge you to find out who among them disrespects you,
and who is without guilt As for the men in the farmsteads,
I would not want to put these men to the test, but to work
on that later, if truly you know of some sign from Zeus   305
who carries the goatskin fetish—"°

*[Lines 306 to the end of the book are omitted. Penelope learns of Telemachos' safe return.
The suitors realize that Telemachos has escaped the ambush, but they still plan to murder
him. Penelope angrily accuses the lead suitor, Antinoōs, and he does his best to calm her
down.]*

---

282 *to itself*: This proverb must have come into being after iron became standard for weapons, c. 900 BC.
     Ordinarily in the stylized world of epic battle, weapons are made of bronze.

284 *seize them*: In fact this never happens, as we will see.

306 ... *goatskin fetish*: If Athena and Zeus will help against the suitors, Odysseus and Telemachos will not need
     helpers from the farms.

BOOK 17. *The Faithful Dog Argos*

[Lines 1–179 are omitted. Telemachos goes up to the house and tells Penelope about his adventures. Meanwhile Odysseus and Eumaios get ready to go to the house.]

180 Odysseus spoke and he cast about his shoulders his wretched
pouch, riven with holes, suspended from a twisted cord.
Eumaios gave him a staff that pleased him, and the two set out.
The dogs and the herdsmen stayed behind to protect the farmyard.
Eumaios led King Odysseus to the city, looking just like
185 a beggar and an old man, hobbling on his crutch. Miserable
clothing hung about his skin. They went along the rugged path
and came close to the city. They arrived at the spring—
nicely worked, beautifully flowing—from which the inhabitants
of the city drew their water. Ithakos and Neritos and Polyktor
190 had boxed it in.° Around the spring was a wood of water-nourished
aspen, wrapping all the way around, and cold water flowed down
from high on the rock above. On top was built an altar
to the nymphs, where all passersby made sacrifice.

                                            At the spring
Melanthios, the son of Dolios,° met them, driving his she-goats,
195 by far the best of all the herds, as a meal for the suitors.
And two herdsmen followed him. When he saw Odysseus
and Eumaios, he spoke to them with violent and abusive insults,
and he greatly riled Odysseus' heart: "Now, surely a stinking
man leads another stinking man! As always, the gods bring like
200 and like together! Where are you leading this glutton,
you miserable pig herder? his annoying beggar, this wrecker
of banquets? He is just the man to stand at many doorposts,
rubbing his shoulders against them, begging for scraps,
not swords or cauldrons. If you were to give me this man
205 to protect my farmsteads, to clean out the pens and to carry
young shoots to the kids, then by drinking whey he *might*

---

190 ... *had boxed it in*: Ithakos, Neritos, and Polyktor ("much-possessing") are said in the scholia to be the
    founders first of Kephallenia, then of Ithaca, who gave their names to the island and to Mount Neriton on
    Ithaca. Polyktor is the name of the suitor Peisander's father (Book 18), but it is probably not the same man.
    The *Odyssey* itself gives us no more information about Ithakos, Neritos, and Polyktor.

194   *Melanthios, the son of Dolios*: "Blackie" son of "Tricky."

grow himself a strong thigh. But because he has learned
only evil deeds, he will not wish to busy himself with real work,
but skulks through the land thinking only to fill his insatiate
belly by begging. But I will tell you something, and I think   210
it will come to pass: If he comes to the house of good Odysseus,
many a footstool hurled around his head from the hands
of real men will break his ribs as he is pelted through the house!"

So Melanthios spoke, and as he passed, in his madness,
he kicked Odysseus on the hip with his heel. Yet he did not drive   215
him from the path. Odysseus held his ground and pondered
whether he should leap on Melanthios and club him to death,
or whether he should seize him around the waist, raise him up
and dash his brains on the ground. But he endured, holding back
from such intention.   220

The pig herder, looking Melanthios in the face,
rebuked him and he prayed aloud, holding up his hands: "Nymphs
of the spring, daughters of Zeus, if ever Odysseus burned
thigh-bones in your honor, wrapping them in rich fat of sheep
or goats, then fulfill for me this prayer—that that man might
come back! May some spirit guide him! Then he would   225
dispel the hollow show that you insolently now put on,
wandering always through the city while the wicked herdsmen
destroy the flocks."

Melanthios answered the goatherd: "Well, well,
what a word this sly dog has said . . . Some day I will take you
on a well-benched black ship far from Ithaca, so that you might   230
bring me much wealth. I wish that Apollo of the silver bow might
strike Telemachos in the halls, today! or that the suitors might kill
him—just as I hope that the day of Odysseus' homecoming has been
lost in some far land!"

So speaking, Melanthios left them there
as they slowly walked along. But Melanthios himself went quickly   235
forward and soon arrived at the house of the king. He went in at once
and sat down among the suitors, opposite Eurymachos, who liked
him especially. The attendants served Melanthios a portion of meat,
and the revered housekeeper brought in some bread and put it down
before him to eat.   240

Odysseus and the good pig herder stopped when
they came close to the palace, and around them came the sound

of the hollow lyre—it was Phemios striking the chords
to sing before the suitors. Then Odysseus took Eumaios by the hand
and said: "Eumaios, surely this is the beautiful palace
245 of Odysseus, easy to recognize and to pick out from among many.
There is building upon building, and the courtyard is built with wall
and coping, and the double doors are well fenced. No man could
equip it better. I notice that inside the house many men are feasting,
for the savor of flesh rises above it, and from inside the lyre sounds,
250 which the gods have made as companion to the feast."

                                            Then you said
in reply, O Eumaios, my pig herder: "You recognize it easily,
because you are not a stupid man. But come, let us consider
how things will be. Either you go in to the busy household first
and join the company of the suitors, and I will remain here—
255 or if you want, you stay here and I will go in first. But don't
stay long, or someone may see you out here and throw something
at you, to drive you off. I urge you to consider these things."

    Then the much-enduring good Odysseus answered him:
"I know, I do see. You are giving advice to one who knows.
260 But you go ahead, and I will stay behind. I am no stranger
to beatings or to being knocked about. My spirit is a daring one
because I have suffered so many evils on the waves and in war.
Let this be added to what has gone before. There is no way
to hide a greedy belly—so destructive!—which brings so many
265 evils to men, on account of which benched ships are fitted
out to sail across the restless sea, bringing misery to the enemy."

    They spoke to one another in this fashion, when the hound
dog Argos,° lying there, raised his head and pricked up his ears.
Odysseus, of enduring heart, had reared him long ago, but had
270 little joy of him before he went to sacred Ilion. In earlier
times the young men used him to chase wild goats and deer
and hares, but now, his king gone, he lay neglected on a pile
of excrement poured out by mules and cattle and piled up
in front of the gates, until Odysseus' slaves could take it away
275 to dung the master's wide fields. There the dog Argos lay,
a mess of fleas, but still, when he saw Odysseus standing near,
he wagged his tale and pricked up his two ears. Yet he did not
have the strength to move closer to his master.

---

268 *Argos*: "Speedy."

Looking aside,
Odysseus wiped away a tear, hiding it from Eumaios,
and right away he asked him: "Eumaios, it is odd that this dog   280
lies here in excrement! He has a good shape, but I cannot
know this clearly, whether he has speed of foot to match
his beauty, or whether he is like all those table-dogs that their
masters keep for show."

Then you answered, O Eumaios my
pig herder: "This is the dog of a man that has died in a far land.   285
If he were in form and action as when Odysseus left him
and went to Troy, you would quickly be astonished at his
speed and strength. No creature that he startled in the depths
of the thick woods could escape him, and he was a superior
tracker. But now he is in wretched way. His master has perished   290
in a foreign land, and the careless women do not take care
of him. Slaves, when their masters are not about, no longer
want to do what they are supposed to. For Zeus, whose voice
is heard afar, takes away half the worth of a man when
the day of slavery takes him."°   295

Then he went straight into
the house and among the proud suitors, but the fate of black death
took Argos when he had seen Odysseus in the twentieth year.

Godlike Telemachos was by far the first to see
the pig herder coming into the house, and swiftly he nodded,
calling him to come to his side. Eumaios looked around him   300
and took a nearby stool on which the carver sat when he cut
the many pieces of meat for the suitors as they feasted
in the hall. He placed it on the other side of Telemachos'
table and sat down himself. A herald took a portion of meat
and set it before him and some bread from the basket.   305

Coming right after him, Odysseus entered the palace
in the likeness of a wretched beggar, an old man leaning
on his staff, his repulsive clothes hanging from his flesh.
He sat down on the threshold of ashwood° just inside the doors,
leaning against a pillar made of cypress wood that once   310
a carpenter had expertly planed and trued to the measuring-line.

---

295   *takes him*: That is, slavery ruins one's moral fiber so that carelessness and treachery come easy.

309   *ashwood*: Earlier in this book it is made of stone.

FIGURE 17.1 Argos recognizes Odysseus.   Odysseus squats on a rock, his staff at his side, while Argos grovels before him. The doors of Odysseus' palace stand closed behind him. The face of Odysseus seems deliberately mutilated, no doubt from fear of the image's power. Relief on a Roman sarcophagus, AD 3rd century.

Telemachos spoke to the pig herder, calling him over,
and he took a whole loaf from the very beautiful basket,
and all the meats that his hands could hold in their grasp:
"Take these things to the stranger and give them to him.   315
Tell him to beg among the suitors, going among them
one and all. Shame is no good thing for a man in need."

So he spoke, and the pig herder went when he heard
Telemachos' command. He stood beside Odysseus and spoke
to him words that went like arrows: "Telemachos, O stranger,   320
gives you these things, and he says that you should go
through the suitors and beg, one and all. He says that shame
is no good thing for a beggar."

                          The resourceful Odysseus replied:
"King Zeus, I pray that Telemachos be blessed among men.
May he have all that his heart desires!"   325

                          He spoke and took
the food in both his hands and set it down there before his feet
on top of his disgusting pouch. He ate while the singer sang
in the halls.

                          When he had eaten, the divine singer stopped,
and the suitors broke into an uproar throughout the halls.
But Athena, standing close to Odysseus, the son of Laërtes,   330
urged him to beg for bread from the suitors so that he might
see which were righteous and which were lawless. Yet even
so she was not minded to save a single one of them from
destruction.

                          Odysseus began to beg of each man singly,
working from the right, extending to each his hands   335
as if he had long been a beggar. Some took pity and gave
him something, and they marveled at him. They asked
one another who he was and where he came from.

Then Melanthios the goatherd spoke to them: "Listen
to me, suitors of a glorious queen—I have something to say   340
about this stranger. I have seen him before. The pig herder
has brought him here. I am not sure where he claims to come from."

So he spoke, and Antinoös reproached the pig herder, saying:
"O you most distinguished *swine* herder, why have you brought

345 this man to the city? Don't we have enough homeless wretches
coming by as it is—annoying beggars, wreckers of the feast?
Don't you think it is bad enough that they gather here and consume
the wealth of the king? and now you bring in *this* man?"

And you answered, O my pig herder Eumaios: "Antinoös,
350 though you may be noble, you have not spoken properly.
Who of himself goes out and summons a stranger to come
from somewhere else, unless it is one of those who benefit
the people—a prophet or a healer of ills or a builder with wood,
or even a divine singer who might delight with his song.°
355 These men are called all over the boundless earth, but you would
never summon a beggar who would only wear you down.
You above all the other suitors are always hard toward Odysseus'
slaves, and especially to me. But I don't care, so long as the judicious
Penelope lives in these halls—and godlike Telemachos."

360   The shrewd Telemachos answered him: "Be quiet! Don't answer
that man with a long speech. It is always the habit of Antinoös
to provoke to anger in an evil way, and always with his harsh words.
And he eggs-on others to do the same!"

Telemachos spoke,
and he said to Antinoös words that went like arrows:
365 "Antinoös, truly you take care of me, as a father does his son.
And now you propose that I drive the stranger from this hall
with a dismissive word. May no god bring this to pass!
No! Take something and give it to him. I do not begrudge it,
for I myself ask you to give it. Don't worry about my mother,
370 nor any other of the slaves who are in the house of the divine
Odysseus. But I don't think this is what bothers you—you would
rather eat than give to another!"

Then Antinoös said in reply:
"Telemachos, you fat mouth, without restraint in daring—such
words you have spoken! If all the suitors should hand him as much
375 as I have, this house would be free of him for three months!"

So he spoke, and he took the footstool on which
he was accustomed to rest his shining feet while feasting,

---

354 *his song*: Our earliest evidence that such singers as Homer himself and craftsmen were itinerant workers in
    Greek society.

and he showed it beneath the table.° But all the others gave
the beggar something, filling his pouch with bread and meat.

Soon Odysseus was about to go back to the threshold and eat   380
what the Achaeans had given him, but first he stood beside Antinoös
and said: "Give me something, my friend. You don't seem
to me to be the worst of the Achaeans, but the best. You have
the air of a chieftain. Therefore you ought to give me a better
portion of bread than all the others. I will celebrate you over   385
the broad earth.
              "You know once I lived in a house among men,
a rich man in a rich house. And I often gave to a wanderer,
no matter who he was or with whatever need he came. I had
countless slaves and many other things by which men live well
and are called rich. But Zeus, the son of Kronos, ruined it all—   390
I suppose he wanted to. He forced me to go with far-traveled
pirates into Egypt, a long journey, so that I might perish.
Stationing my beaked ships near the river Egypt, I then ordered
my trusty companions to stay beside the ships and guard them.
I ordered scouts to go to places of outlook. But giving in to   395
insolence, confident in their strength, they quickly plundered
the very beautiful fields of the men of Egypt. They carried off
the women and little children, and they killed the men. Soon
a cry came to the city. Hearing the cry, the Egyptians came
at the crack of dawn. The whole plain was filled with foot soldiers   400
and horses, and the shining bronze.
              "Then Zeus who delights
in the thunderbolt cast a panic among my companions, and no one
dared to stand his ground. There was evil all around. The Egyptians
killed many with their sharp bronze, and others they captured
alive, to work for them by force. But they gave me to a guest-friend   405
who happened to come by, to take me to Cyprus, to Dmetor
the son of Iasos° who ruled with power in Cyprus. Having suffered
greatly, I have now come here from there."

                              Antinoös answered
him and said: "What spirit has brought this anguish here,
this sorrow to the feast? Stand off over there in the middle,   410
away from my table!—or you may quickly come to a *bitter*
Egypt and Cyprus! You are a bold and shameless beggar!

---

378   *the table*: That is, his generous gift to the beggar would be to throw a stool at him.

407   *son of Iasos*: Dmetor means "subduer"; nothing else is known about him.

You come up to everyone in a row, and they give recklessly,
because there is no restraint or pity in giving freely of another's
415 wealth, because each man has plenty beside him!"

Then the resourceful
Odysseus drew back and said: "My, my—I see that your wits
do not match your excellent looks. You would not give even
a grain of salt from your own house to one who asked—you who
sit at another's table would not dare to take a piece of bread
420 and give it to me, though you have plenty at hand?"

So Odysseus spoke,
and Antinoös grew still more angry in his heart. Looking beneath
his brows he spoke words that went like arrows: "I don't think
that you will leave this hall in such good shape, for you speak
insulting words."

So he spoke, and picking up the footstool
425 he threw it, hitting Odysseus at the base of his right shoulder,
where it joins the back. But Odysseus stood firm like a rock,
Antinoös' cowardly blow did not stagger him. Odysseus shook
his head in silence, pondering evil deep in his heart. Then he went
back to the threshold and took his seat. He put down his well-filled pouch.

430 Then he spoke to the suitors: "Listen to me, you suitors
of a glorious lady, so that I may say what my heart urges.
There is no pain of heart, nor sorrow, when a man is struck
fighting for his possessions, either for his cattle or his white sheep.
But Antinoös has struck me on account of my wretched belly,
435 that ruinous thing that gives so many evils to men. And if there
are gods and Erinyes° for beggars, may death's black end come
to Antinoös before his marriage."

Then Antinoös, the son of Eupeithes,
said: "Sit still and eat, O stranger, or go someplace else.
Else the young men will drag you through this house for the things
440 you say, taking hold of your foot or hand, and they will strip
off all your skin!"

---

436 *Erinyes*: Originally punishers of crimes against one's mother or father, and the guarantors of oaths, but here
simply the spirits of revenge.

So he spoke. But all the other suitors were exceedingly
indignant, so that one of the many young men would say: "Antinoös,
you did wrong to strike this miserable beggar, and a danger
if perhaps he turns out to be a god from heaven. For the gods wander
the cities in the likeness of strangers from abroad, taking on every   445
kind of shape, witnessing the violence and righteousness of men."

So spoke the suitors, but Antinoös paid no mind
to their words, while in Telemachos' heart the pain grew great
at the blow. Yet he shed no tear to the ground from his lids.
He shook his head in silence, contemplating the evil he would do.   450

*[Lines 451 to the end of the book and Book 18 are omitted. Penelope informs Eumaios
that she wants to speak to the stranger, and Odysseus says that he will speak with her later
on. A real beggar now appears who challenges Odysseus, but Odysseus knock him out with
one blow. Suddenly Penelope presents herself before the suitors and uses their lustful
admiration to extort gifts. Melantho, a female slave, insults Odysseus, and the suitor
Eurymachos throws a stool at him. Telemachos rebukes the suitors, and they go off to bed.]*

BOOK 19. *Odysseus' Scar*

The good Odysseus was left in the hall, pondering death for the suitors
with the help of Athena. At once he spoke to Telemachos words
that went like arrows: "Telemachos, you must store away the weapons
of war inside, absolutely all of them. Trick the suitors with soft
5   words when they notice that the armor is gone and ask you about it.°
Say: 'I have taken them down out of the smoke, because they
no longer have the same appearance as when Odysseus left them
and went off to Troy, but they are corroded, to the extent that the breath
of the fire reached them. Also, and even more, a spirit has put this
10   in my breast, the thought that when you are drunk a fight might
break out among you. You might wound one another and bring
shame to the feast and the suit for my mother's hand! For the iron
draws a man to it.' "

So he spoke, and Telemachos obeyed his father.
He called over the nurse Eurykleia and said to her: "Nurse, shut up
15   the women in their rooms while I put away my father's weapons
in the storeroom, the beautiful weapons which the smoke
is corroding as they lay uncared for throughout the house since
my father went away. I was just a little kid then. But now I want
to put these things away so that the breath of fire won't get to them."

20   The nurse Eurykleia answered him: "I only wish, child,
that you would take thought for the running of the house, and guard
all your possessions. But come, who will get a light and carry it
for you? For you do not allow the female slaves to precede you,
who might have given you light."

The shrewd Telemachos answered her:
25   "This stranger will do it. I will not allow a man to be idle who
eats my bread, even though he comes from a long way off."

So Telemachos spoke, for her words had gone like arrows.
Eurykleia shut the doors of the stately hall. Odysseus and his brilliant
son, the two of them, sprang up and carried off the helmets and bossed

---

5   *about it*: In fact the suitors never ask about the armor.

shields and the sharp-pointed spears. Pallas Athena went before them, 30
carrying a golden lamp° that made a very beautiful light.

Then suddenly Telemachos spoke to his father: "O Father,
truly this is a great wonder that my eyes behold! Surely the walls
of the house and the beautiful beams and the cross-beams of fir,
and the pillars that reach up high, seem as if they blaze with fire. 35
Surely, there is some god within, of those who hold the broad sky."

The resourceful Odysseus said in reply: "Be quiet! and check
your thought. Don't ask questions. This is the way of the gods
who hold Olympos. But you go on to bed, and I will stay here
behind so that I may challenge the slave women and your mother, 40
who will weep and ask me about everything."

So he spoke,
and Telemachos went through the hall, lit by the light of blazing
torches, to go to his chamber and lie down, where he was accustomed
to rest. Sweet sleep came over him as he lay down and awaited
the shining Dawn. But the good Odysseus was left behind in the hall, 45
pondering death for the suitors with the help of Athena.

The judicious
Penelope then came out of her chamber, looking like Artemis or golden
Aphrodite. Servants set down a chair for her near the fire, where
she liked to sit, worked with coils of ivory and silver. The craftsman
Ikmalios° once had made it, and he fitted beneath it a built-in 50
footstool for the feet. A fleece was thrown over the chair.
There the judicious Penelope sat. Her white-armed female
slaves came from the women's hall. They began to take away
the abundant food, the tables, and the cups, from which the too-bold
men had been drinking. They cast the embers from the braziers 55
down onto the floor, and they piled lots of dried wood
on the braziers, for illumination and heat.

Then Melantho for a second
time scolded Odysseus: "Stranger, will you continue to be a nuisance
to us through the night, roaming about the house? Will you spy on

---

31 *lamp*: This is the only time that a lamp (a wick in a vessel) is referred to in all of Homer. Otherwise lighting is
always provided by torches. Lamps disappear from the archaeological record after the end of the Bronze Age
(c. 1100 BC) and do not reappear until the 7th century BC, but perhaps their use continued in a cultic context:
This is the lamp of Athena.

50 *Ikmalios*: Probably "beater," as of one working metal; occurs only here.

60 the women? Why, get outside, you rogue, and enjoy your dinner
    there! Either that or be smashed with a torch and go out that way!"

       But the resourceful Odysseus looked from beneath his brows
    and said: "Good woman, why do you come on so against me with
    an angry heart? Is it because I am filthy, and I wear ragged clothes
65 around my skin, and I go around the country begging? But I cannot
    help it. Beggars and wanderers are like that. You know, once
    I lived in a house among men, a rich man in a rich house,
    and I often gave to a wanderer, no matter who he was or with
    whatever need he came. I had countless slaves and many other things
70 by which men live well and are called rich. But Zeus, the son
    of Kronos, ruined it all—I suppose he wanted to. Beware that
    you too, woman, do not lose all the glory through which you stand
    out among the slaves—if your mistress became angry with you,
    or if Odysseus returned. There is still room for hope. And already
75 his son is such as *he* was, by the favor of Apollo—Telemachos.
    He will be aware of any sexual play among you women.
    He is no longer the child he was."

                   So he spoke, and judicious Penelope
    overheard him. She rebuked Melantho and addressed her, saying:
    "Don't think, you hussy—you shameless bitch!—that your
80 outrageous behavior is unknown to me! With your *own* head you will
    wipe away its stain!° You knew full well—because you heard it
    from me myself, that I wanted to ask the stranger in my halls
    about my husband. I suffer *so* . . ."

                   She spoke, and then she addressed
    Eurynomê: "Eurynomê, bring a chair and put a fleece on it so that
85 the stranger can sit down with me and tell me his tale, and listen to me.
    I want to question him closely."

                   So she spoke, and Eurynomê quickly
    brought in a well-polished chair and set it down, and she threw
    a fleece over it. That is where the much-enduring good Odysseus sat
    as judicious Penelope began to speak: "Stranger, I would like
90 myself to ask you something first. Who are you among men,
    and where do you come from? Where is your city and your parents?"

---

81 *away its stain:* The expression comes from the custom of wiping the blood off the sacrificial knife onto the
    sacrificial victim, as if to divert the guilt for killing onto the victim itself. As used by Penelope here, the
    figure means that Melantho will *not* succeed in transferring guilt, but the guilt will fall on the head of the
    doer of the deed—herself.

The resourceful Odysseus then said in reply: "My lady, no
mortal on the boundless earth could find fault with you. Truly your
fame reaches the broad heaven, as does the fame of some excellent
chieftain who like a god rules amidst many powerful men, upholds   95
justice, and the black earth bears wheat and barley, and the trees
bristle with fruit, the flocks multiply unceasingly, and the sea
provides fish—all from his fine leadership as the people prosper
under his rule. For which reason ask me about anything—I am
in your house—but do not ask about my family and the land   100
of my fathers. You will fill my heart more with pain as I think
on such things. I am a man of many sorrows. Nor is it right
that I sit in another's house moaning and wailing, for it is a poor
thing to grieve continuously. Don't let any of your slaves be angry
with me, or you yourself, because you say that I swim in tears   105
because my heart is made heavy by wine."

                    The judicious Penelope
then answered him: "Stranger, I think that the deathless ones
destroyed all my excellence, both of beauty and of form, when
the Argives went to Ilion, and with them went my husband, Odysseus.
If that man were to return and take control of my life, my fame   110
would be greater and fairer. But as it is, I suffer. Some spirit
has set in motion many evils against me. Whoever are strong
in the islands DOULICHION and SAMĒ and wooded ZAKYNTHOS,
and those who live in clear-seen ITHACA itself—these men court me,
though I am unwilling, and lay waste to the house. For this reason   115
I pay no attention to strangers, nor to suppliants, nor to heralds,
who are workers for the public good. In longing for my dear
Odysseus I waste away my heart.

                    "But these suitors hasten
on the marriage, though I have woven a bundle of tricks. A spirit
suggested to me first of all that I set up a great loom in my halls   120
to weave a robe, fine and very wide. I right away spoke among the suitors:
'Young men, my suitors, because the good Odysseus has died,
be patient, though you are eager for my marriage, until I finish
this robe—I would not want my spinning to come to nothing!
It is a burial shroud for Lord Laërtes, for the day when the ruinous   125
fate of dreadful death will take him. In this way no one of the Achaean
women will be angry with me, saying that he lay without a shroud
who once was rich.'

                    "So I spoke, and their proud hearts agreed.
I wove at that great loom all day long, but at night, with torches

FIGURE 19.1   Odysseus and Penelope, a "Melian relief."   A curious series of small shallow relief sculptures with flat backs were produced on the island of Melos from about 470 to 416 BC. Details were once painted in, but the paint is now mostly gone. They usually show narrative subjects from Greek myth. They were perhaps made for wooden boxes, an inexpensive imitation for reliefs made in more expensive materials, such as ivory, and many have holes for an attachment. But their true purpose is unknown. In this relief Odysseus wears his typical felt traveler's cap. He is "hero-ically nude" from the waist down, but carries a pouch and a staff, just as Homer describes. He speaks to the demure Penelope, who typically casts her eyes to the ground. In 416 BC Melos was taken by Athens in the Peloponnesian War. The men were killed and the women and children sold into slavery, bringing to an end the production of Melian reliefs. Painted terracotta, c. 450 BC.

beside me, I unraveled it. And so for three years I deceived   130
and beguiled the Achaeans. But when the fourth year came on
as the seasons advanced, as the months raced away, as the many
days came to completion, then, thanks to my women slaves—
those uncaring bitches!—they came in and caught me. They loudly
reproached me.   135

      "And so I finished the robe, although I didn't want to—
but because I was forced to. And now I cannot escape the marriage.
I cannot find a way out. Furthermore, my parents want me to marry,
and my son is impatient as he sees the suitors devouring his livelihood.
By now he is a man and fully capable of taking care of a household
to which Zeus grants glory.   140

      "So tell me of your family, where you
are from. For I don't think you sprang from an oak, as the old story
tells it, nor from a stone!"°

      The resourceful Odysseus said in reply:
"Revered lady, wife of Odysseus son of Laërtes, will you *never*
stop asking me about my family? But I will tell you—and you will
cause me to suffer more pain than I already do. For that is the way   145
things are, when a man is gone for so long from his country
as I have been now, wandering through the many cities of men,
suffering always. Even so I will tell you what you ask and inquire about.

      "There is a land called CRETE in the middle of the wine-dark sea,
beautiful and rich, surrounded by water. Many men live there,   150
numberless, and ninety cities. One tongue is mixed with another.
There dwell the Achaeans, the great-hearted True-Cretans,
the Kydonians, and the Dorians divided into three tribes,
and the good Pelasgians.° The greatest city is KNOSSOS,
where Minos ruled in nine-year cycles,° he who conversed with   155

---

142   ...*a stone*: A proverbial expression apparently referring to myths of the origin of humans from oak trees or from stones. Penelope means that the beggar has real life-blood ancestors and now has come the time to reveal them.

154   ...*Pelasgians*: The Achaeans are the Mycenaean Greeks, under the leadership of Idomeneus; the True-Cretans are the aboriginal inhabitants, the descendants of the Minoans; the Kydonians live near the river Iardanos in the northwest of the island; the Dorians are, strangely, mentioned only here in all of Homer, the inhabitants of the Peloponnesus during the Classical Period (Sparta was a Dorian state) and the predominant group in Crete during the eighth century BC. The Pelasgians are a mysterious unidentified aboriginal people.

155   *nine-year cycles*: Perhaps to correspond with a ritual festival cycle; or the phrase could mean "when he was nine years old."

great Zeus. Minos was the father of my father, great-hearted Deukalion.
Deukalion bore me and King Idomeneus.°

                                 "Now Idomeneus went off
to Troy in his beaked ships together with the sons of Atreus.
My famous name is Aithon,° the younger by birth—Idomeneus
160 was older and a better man. There in Crete I saw Odysseus. I gave
him the gifts of guest-friendship. The strength of the wind drove
him to Crete as he made for Troy, knocking him off course
near CAPE MALEA. He docked his boats in AMNISOS, where there is
a cave of Eileithyia,° in a harbor where the water was rough,
165 and he barely escaped the storm. Odysseus went straight to the city
and asked for Idomeneus. He said that he was his guest-friend,
beloved and respected. But it was now the tenth or the eleventh
day that Idomeneus had gone off to Ilion in his beaked ships.
So I took him to my house and entertained him well, with kindly
170 welcome, and I drew from the abundance in my house. To the rest
of his companions, who followed with him, I gathered up
and gave out barley from the public store and flaming wine
and cattle to sacrifice, so that they might satisfy their hearts.
The good Achaeans remained there for twelve days, for the great
175 North Wind held them back. You could not even stand on the land!
Some hard spirit had aroused it. But on the thirteenth day
the wind subsided, and they put to sea."

                                He spoke on, knowing how
to make the many falsehoods in his tale seem like truth,
and Penelope's tears ran when she heard him, and her skin melted
180 from her tears, as when snow melts on the peaks of the high
mountains that East Wind has melted, when West Wind has scattered it.
The rivers fill with running water as the snow melts—even so her
beautiful cheeks melted as she poured down tears, lamenting
her husband, who even then sat there beside her.

                                 But Odysseus took
185 pity in his heart for his own weeping wife, though his eyes stood

---

157 *Idomeneus*: In his earlier false tale to Eumaios (Book 14) Odysseus claimed to be the illegitimate son of a
      Cretan nobleman by a concubine; now he has gone up the social scale and is brother to the king himself.

159 *Aithon*: "with-a-dark-complexion."

164 *of Eileithyia*: There is in fact a cave of the birth-goddess Eileithyia in the harbor of Amnisos on Crete, where
      there was cultic activity between the third millennium and the fifth century BC (c. 3000–450 BC). The
      name Eileithyia is sometimes explained as Greek "she-who-makes-one-come," that is, the child, but it may
      be a nonGreek name for the Great Mother goddess of nature and fertility. Her cult is testified by primitive
      figurines found all over the Near East from a very early time.

like horn or iron, unmovable between his lids, and cunningly,
he hid his tears. When she had had her fill of tearful wailing,
she answered him right away and said: "Now, stranger, I think
I will put you to the test to see if you truly entertained my husband
with his godlike companions in your halls, as you say. So tell me,   190
what kind of clothes was he wearing? And what kind of man was he,
and tell me of the companions who followed him."

                                Then the resourceful
Odysseus answered her: "Woman, it is hard for one who has been
so long gone to speak of this. It is already the twentieth year since
he went off and left my country, but I will tell you as I remember it.   195
The good Odysseus wore a purple cloak, woolen, doubled.
It had a brooch made of gold with twin sheaths,° and it was delicately
worked on the front. A dog held a spotted fawn with his forepaws,
staring at the fawn as he strangled it. Everyone who saw it was
amazed, how although made of gold the dog held down the fawn   200
and throttled it. The fawn writhed with its feet, striving to escape.
I noted the shirt around his skin that shone like the skin of a dried
onion, so soft it was, and it glistened like the sun. I can tell you,
the women marveled at him!

                        "But I will tell you something else,
and you take it to heart. I do not know whether Odysseus wore   205
this garment about his skin when he was at home, or whether
one of his comrades gave it to him as he went on the swift ship,
or whether perhaps a guest-friend gave it to him—for Odysseus
was guest-friend to many. There were few of the Achaeans
who were his equal. I gave him a bronze sword and a fringed   210
shirt of double fold—beautiful, purple-dyed—and I respectfully
sent him on his way in his well-benched ship.

                            "And his herald,
who was a little older than Odysseus, followed behind. And I will
tell you about this herald, what kind of man he was. He had round
shoulders, and a dark complexion, and he was curly-haired.   215
His name was Eurybates.° Odysseus honored him above all his
companions, because they were of a like mind."

                            So Odysseus spoke,
and he stirred in Penelope the desire to weep still more, because

---

197   *twin sheaths*: Into which two pins fit, to close the brooch.
216   *Eurybates*: He figures in the *Iliad* as Odysseus' herald.

she recognized the sure token that Odysseus had described.
220 When she had had her fill of tearful wailing, then she answered him
with these words: "Now, stranger, though before you were pitiable,
now you are a friend in my halls and we respect you. For it was
I who gave him these clothes that you describe, folding them
and removing them from the storage chamber, and I added
225 the shining brooch as a treasure. But I will never again receive
that man coming home to the land of his fathers. Truly Odysseus
went forth with an evil fate when he journeyed in a hollow ship
to see that cursed Ilion, not to be named!"

                        Then the resourceful
Odysseus said to her in reply: "O woman, honored wife
230 of Odysseus, son of Laërtes, don't stain your beautiful skin
any more with tears, and do not despair at heart, wailing for your
husband. I do not blame you at all. Any woman weeps when she
has lost her wedded husband, to whom she has borne children after
mingling in love, though her husband was different from Odysseus,
235 who they say was like the gods.

                   "But give up your weeping, and listen
to what I have to say. I will tell you truly and I will not conceal it.
I have heard that Odysseus will return home soon, that he is now
in the rich land of the Thresprotians—that he is alive! He has
acquired many fine treasures, begging through the land, but he lost
240 his entire crew and his hollow ship on the wine-dark sea when he left
the island of Thrinakia. Zeus and Helios were angered with him,
for his companions had killed the cattle of Helios. And so they
were all destroyed on the foamy sea, but a wave tossed
Odysseus, riding the keel of the ship, onto the dry land, the land
245 of the Phaeacians, who are close kin with the gods.°

                    "The Phaeacians
heartily honored him, like a god, and they gave him many gifts
and wanted themselves to send him home unharmed. And Odysseus
would long since have been here, except that it seemed better
in his heart to gather riches wandering over the broad earth.
250 Odysseus knows beyond all other mortal men the pathway
to riches, nor could any other compete with him.

---

245 *the gods*: Odysseus conflates the wreck off Thrinakia with the wrecked raft off Phaeacia and so avoids
having to talk about Kalypso!

                                "So Pheidon,
chief of the Thesprotians, told me the tale. And he swore to me,
pouring drink-offerings, that the ship was launched and the men
ready who would take Odysseus to the land of his fathers.
But he sent me off first, for there happened to be a ship   255
of Thesprotians that was going to Doulichion, rich in wheat.
And Pheidon showed the riches that Odysseus had gathered.
They would support a man's children up to the tenth generation,
so many treasures lay in the house of the king. But Odysseus,
Pheidon said, had gone to Dodona to hear the advice of Zeus   260
from the god's high oak, whether being gone so long he should
return openly or in secret.

                        "And so he is safe and will return soon—
very soon. He will not long be far from his friends and the land
of his fathers. All the same, I will swear you an oath. May Zeus
be my witness first of all, the highest and best of the gods,   265
and the hearth of noble Odysseus to which I have come:
All these things shall come to pass that I say. In the course
of this very month Odysseus will come home, as the old moon
wanes and the new one appears."°

                        The judicious Penelope answered
him: "I *wish* that what you say would come to pass. Then you   270
would quickly come to know of our friendship, and receive so many
gifts from me that someone, meeting you, would say you were blessed.

   "But this seems to me how things will turn out: Odysseus
will never return to his home, nor will you obtain a convoy
from here, because there are not such masters in the house as   275
Odysseus was among men—if he ever lived!—who can send away
and receive respectable guest-friends. Still—slaves, will you
wash this man and prepare a bed for him? And spread on a bedstead
robes and shining blankets so that he may arrive nice and warm
to Dawn on her golden throne. At dawn, bathe him and oil him,   280
so that he may take thought for dinner inside, with Telemachos,
sitting in the hall. And all the worse for any man who commits
any abuse against this stranger! That man will accomplish nothing
more here, though he is exceedingly angry.

                        "For how, O stranger,
will you know if I excel other women in wit and in a discreet mind   285

---

269   *appears*: When the new moon festival of Apollo will be held, the day of doom for the suitors.

if all unkempt and dressed in rags you sit in our halls to dine?
Humans don't live long. And everyone calls down pain in times
to come on him who is mean-spirited and hard-hearted,
and when he is dead everyone makes fun of him. But if one
290 is blameless and has a blameless heart, then strangers
spread his fame far and wide among all humans, and many call
him a real man."

      The resourceful Odysseus then said in reply:
"Lady, wife of Odysseus, the son of Laërtes, truly cloaks and shining
blankets became hateful to me on the day when first we turned
295 our back on the snowy mountains of Crete, sailing in a long-oared ship.
No, I will lie as I have been used to rest through sleepless nights.
Many are the nights I have slept on a foul bed awaiting shining Dawn
on her beautiful throne. Nor do baths for the feet give me pleasure.
And no woman will take hold of my foot of those who are servants
300 in this house—unless you have some ancient old lady, wise in her
years who has suffered as many pains in her heart as have I.
One such as that could touch my feet."

      Then the judicious Penelope said:
"Dear stranger, never has a wanderer from far away come into
my house whose words are more sensible. You are welcome here,
305 so wise and prudent is everything that you say. I have an old woman,
wise from her years, of good sense, who nourished and suckled
that wretched man—Odysseus—whom she took into her arms
when her mother first bore him. She will wash your feet, though
she is weak with age.

      "So get up now, wise Eurykleia, and wash
310 the feet of one of like age to your king! Even such as his are this
man's feet, and even such are his hands. For mortals quickly
grow old when their fortune is ill."

      So she spoke, and the old woman
hid her face in her hands, and she poured down hot tears, and she spoke
a word of lamentation: "O Odysseus, my child, I am in despair
315 about you. Surely Zeus has hated you above all humans, although
you are god-fearing. Never before has any mortal burned so many
fat thigh pieces to Zeus who delights in the thunderbolt, nor killed
so many perfect beasts as you killed in his honor, praying that you
might reach a sleek old age and raise your glorious son. But now
320 he has altogether taken away from you alone the day of your
homecoming. I suppose that the women of these strange and distant

lands mocked him when he came to their glorious houses, just as
these sluts mock you here, all of them. Is it to avoid their insult
and shameless words that you won't allow them to wash your feet?
Well, the daughter of Ikarios, prudent Penelope, asks me to do it, 325
and I am not unwilling. I'll wash your feet, for our Penelope's sake
and for your own. The heart within me is moved with sorrow.
But come now, listen to the word that I say—Many long-suffering
strangers have come here, but not ever do I think I have seen a man
so like another as you are like Odysseus in your stature, in your voice, 330
and in the shape of your feet."

Then the resourceful Odysseus said
in reply: "Old lady, that's what everybody says who has seen
the two of us with his own eyes, that we are remarkably like
one another, as you shrewdly observe."

So he spoke and the old
woman took the shining cauldron in which she was going to wash 335
his feet, and she poured in a quantity of cold water, then hot on top,
while Odysseus sat far away from the hearth. But quickly he turned
toward the shadows, suddenly realizing that, as she touched him,
she might notice his scar, that everything would come out into the open.

She washed him, coming in close to her king, and immediately 340
she recognized the scar, which once a boar had driven in with
his white tusks when he went to Parnassos, to Autolykos°
and his sons, the noble father of his mother, who surpassed all
men in thievery and in the swearing of false oaths. For the god
Hermes himself had given him this gift, to whom Autolykos burned 345
the pleasing thigh-bones of sheep and goats, and the god befriended
him with a ready heart.

Autolykos happened to come to the rich land
of Ithaca and found that his daughter had recently borne a son.
Eurykleia placed the child on his knees just after he had finished
dinner, and she said to him: "Now come up with a name that you can 350
give the dear child of your child, who has long been prayed for."

Autolykos replied and answered: "My son-in-law and daughter,
give this boy the name that I say. I come as a man *who has been*

---

342 *Autolykos*: "the wolf himself," a "speaking name" reflecting his character, similar to Odysseus' in all its
negative aspects. In *Iliad* 10, Autolykos is said to have stolen a boar's tusk helmet from a certain Amyntor.
Parnassos is a high snow-capped mountain in PHOCIS; DELPHI is built on the southern slopes of Parnassos.

angered [*odyssamenos*]° with many, both with men and women over
355 the much-nourishing earth. Therefore let the name of the child
be *Odysseus*, a signifying name. And when he comes of age let him
come to the great house of his mother's family at Parnassos, where my
possessions are. I'll give him some and will send him home in joy."

For this reason Odysseus came, so that Autolykos could
360 give him glorious gifts. Autolykos and the sons of Autolykos clasped
his hands in welcome and spoke honeyed words. Amphithea,
my mother's mother, took Odysseus in her arms and kissed his head
and both his beautiful eyes. Autolykos called out to his noble sons
to prepare a meal, and they heard his command. Right away they
365 brought in a five-year-old ox. They skinned and dressed the animal
and cut it into quarters. They cut these up skillfully and pierced them
on spits. They roasted and divided up the pieces. Thus they feasted
all day long until the sun went down, nor did the spirit of any lack
in the equal feast. When the sun set and the shadows came on,
370 then they lay down to rest and took the gift of sleep.

                                              When early-born
Dawn appeared with her fingers of rose, they went off on a hunt,
the hounds and the sons of Autolykos too, and with them went
the good Odysseus. They went up the steep mountain of Parnassos,
covered in forest, and soon they came into its windy valleys.
375 Helios was just then striking the fields as he rose from softly
gliding, deep-flowing Ocean when the beaters came into a gorge.
Before them went the hounds, tracking the scent, and behind
them came the sons of Autolykos, and with them the good Odysseus,
close on the hounds, brandishing his long-shadowed spear.
380 Now nearby in a dense thicket lay a huge boar. The strength
of the wet winds did not penetrate this thicket, nor did shining
Helios strike it with his rays, nor could the rains pierce through—
so thick it was!—and there was a huge mass of fallen leaves.

Then around the boar came the noise of the feet of men and dogs
385 as they pressed on in the chase. He charged from his hiding place,
his hair bristling and standing up, and he glanced fire from his eyes
as he stood right before them. Odysseus was first to rush up, holding
his long spear in a powerful hand, eager to hit him, but the boar
got in first and struck him above the knee, charging on him sideways,

---

354 *who has been angered*: The Greek is *odyssamenos*, punning on the name of *Odysseus*, but we are unsure of the
meaning of *odyssamenos*: Either it means "the man who has been angered" or it means "the man who makes
others angry." In reality the name of Odysseus is probably not Greek.

and with his white tusk he tore away much of the flesh. But he did   390
not reach the man's bone. Odysseus with his sure aim hit the boar
on the right shoulder, and straight through went the tip of the shining
spear. The boar fell in the dust with a cry, and his spirit fled away.

The sons of Autolykos busied themselves with the boar,
and they skillfully bound up the wound of handsome Odysseus,   395
like a god, and they stopped the black blood by a spell. Quickly
they returned to the house of their dear father. Autolykos and the sons
of Autolykos doctored him well and gave him glorious gifts
and soon sent him rejoicing to the lovely land of his fathers,
to Ithaca. Odysseus' father and revered mother were very happy   400
to see him return and they asked him about everything and how
he got the scar. He told them all the truth, how when he was hunting
a boar wounded him with its white tusk, when he went into Parnassos
with the sons of Autolykos.

     Touching this scar with the flat of her hands,
feeling over it, Eurykleia knew what it was, and she dropped his foot.   405
His leg fell into the basin and the bronze resounded. The bowl
tipped on its side and all the water ran out on the ground.
Joy and terror overcame her mind at the same time, and her two eyes
filled with tears, and her voice grew full.

     Taking hold of Odysseus' chin
she said: "Truly you are Odysseus, my child! And I did not   410
recognize you before I had handled my king all over." So she spoke
and glanced over at Penelope, wanting to tell her that her dear
husband was in the house. But Penelope could not see her,
nor understand, because Athena had turned her thoughts aside.

Odysseus, feeling for the old woman's throat, seized it   415
with his right hand and with his other pulled her in close to him
and said: "Old lady, why do you want to destroy me? You yourself
nursed me at your tit. Now after suffering many pains I have returned
in the twentieth year to the land of my fathers. But because you
have found out and a god has placed this in your heart—keep quiet!   420
Let no one else in these halls take notice. For I will tell you this,
and I think it will come to pass: If some god allows me to take
the bold suitors, I will not spare you, though you were my nurse,
when I kill the other slave women in the my halls!"

     The thoughtful Eurykleia
then said: "My child, what a word has come from your lips!   425

FIGURE 19.2   Eurykleia washing Odysseus' feet.   The old woman, wearing the short hair of
a slave, is about to discover the scar on Odysseus' leg. The bearded Odysseus, dressed in rags, holds
a staff in his right hand and a stick from which are suspended his pouch and a basket in his left. He
wears an odd traveler's hat with a bill to shade his eyes. Attic red-figure drinking cup by the Penelope
Painter, from Chiusi, c. 440 BC.

You know how my strength is steadfast and unyielding. I will be
as steady as hard stone or iron. I will tell you something else,
and you best take account of it. If some god allows you to overcome
the bold suitors, then I will tell you in detail which women
in the halls dishonor you, and which are guiltless."   430

                                               Then the resourceful
Odysseus said in reply: "Old lady, why will you tell me who they are?
There is no need. I can see for myself and I will come to know
about each. So keep your tale to yourself. Turn it over to the gods."

    So he spoke, and the old woman went through the hall to get
water for his feet, because all the first had spilled. When she had washed   435
him and anointed him richly with oil, Odysseus again moved
his chair over closer to the fire, to warm himself, and he concealed
the scar beneath his rags.

                                           Then the judicious Penelope was first
to speak: "Stranger, this little further thing will I ask you. Then soon
it will be the hour for pleasant rest, for him at least on whom   440
sleep can come, though one is troubled at heart. But for me some
spirit has given measureless sorrow. All day long I come to the end
of grieving, mourning, looking to my household tasks and those
of my attendants in the house. When night comes, and sleep
takes all, I lie on the bed. Then sharp anxiety, crowding around   445
my crowded heart, disquiets me as I mourn. As when the daughter
of Pandareos, nightingale of the green wood, sings beautifully
at the beginning of spring as she sits among the thick leafage
of the trees, and in thickly trilling notes pours out her many-toned
voice in mourning for her dear son Itylos, whom once she carelessly   450
killed with the bronze, the son of King Zethos—even so my heart
is pushed this way and that, whether I should stay with my son
and see that everything is safe—my property, the slaves, and the great
high-roofed house—respecting the bed of my husband and my reputation
among the people, or whether I should follow whoever is best   455
of the Achaeans in his suit, and has offered countless wedding-gifts.°

    "So long as my son was a child and of empty mind, he would
not let me marry and leave the house of my husband. But now that

---

456   ... *wedding-gifts*: The story of Pandareos and his daughter, who unintentionally killed her own child, the son of
      Zethus, king of Thebes, is unknown from other sources. A rather different story is known from the Athenian
      tradition. The obscure point of comparison seems to be that, as Pandareos' daughter bewailed her unintentional
      homicide, so Penelope may have to bewail her own son if the suitors kill him because she refused to marry.

he is big and has reached the measure of maturity, he begs me
460 to retreat from the hall, impatient over his wealth that the Achaeans
consume. But come, listen to this dream of mine, tell me what you
think. Twenty geese were out of the water and eating wheat
in my house, and I warmed with joy looking at them. Then a great eagle
with bent beak came from the mountains, and he broke the necks
465 of all of them and put them to death. They were scattered in piles
throughout the halls. Then he arose into the bright sky. But I wept
and was sorry, although it was a dream, and the Achaean women
with their fine hairdos gathered around me as I piteously complained
that the eagle had killed my geese.

              "Then the eagle returned
470 and sat down on a projecting roof beam, and with the voice
of a mortal man he restrained my weeping, and he said: 'Courage,
daughter of far-famed Ikarios! This is not a dream, but true reality,
a vision of what will come to pass. The geese are the suitors,
and I who once was the eagle, a bird, am now your husband
475 returned, who will impose a bitter doom on all the suitors.'
So he spoke, and then sweet sleep released me. I looked about,
and I saw the geese in the halls eating wheat beside the trough,
just as they usually do."

          Replying to her the resourceful Odysseus said:
"Lady, there is no way to turn aside the meaning of this dream,
480 for Odysseus himself indicates how he will bring this about—
destruction for the suitors, for all of them, is plain to see. Not one
of them will escape death and the fates!"

              Then the judicious Penelope
said: "Stranger, surely dreams are baffling and hard to interpret,
and they do not fulfill all things for all men. For there are two
485 gates of strengthless dreams. The one is made of horn, and other
of *ivory* [*elephanti*]. Those dreams that pass through sawn ivory, they *cause
harm* [*elephairontai*], bringing things that do not come to pass. Those that
pass outside through the gates of *horn* [*keraôn*], they *are accomplished* [*krainousi*]
as true, when some mortal sees them.° But I don't think that this

---

489   *...sees them*: The symbolism of the gates of horn, through which true dreams pass, and the gates of ivory,
     through which false dreams pass, has never been explained. In the Greek, however, Homer is punning on
     similar sounding words, as he punned on the name of Odysseus.

dread dream came from there—though it would have been welcome
to me and to my son.

          "But I will tell you something, and you take
it to heart. The dawn already comes on of an evil name, which
will cut me off from the house of Odysseus. For now I will set up
a contest of the axes, which Odysseus used to set up in a row
in his halls, like the props of a ship when you are building it,   495
twelve in all. He would stand a good distance away and shoot
an arrow through them.° Now I will set up this contest for the suitors.
Whoever shall string the bow in his hands most easily and shall
shoot through all twelve axes, I will follow him, leaving this house
of my wedded life, this very beautiful house, filled with livelihood.   500
I think I will remember it in my dreams."°

                    The resourceful Odysseus
said in reply: "Lady, revered wife of Odysseus, son of Laërtes,
no longer put off this contest in your halls. The resourceful Odysseus
will be here before these men, handling the well-polished bow,
shall have strung it and shot an arrow through the iron."   505

                    The judicious
Penelope then said: "Oh, if you could but wish to sit beside me,
in my halls, stranger, and delight me, then sleep would never be poured
over my eyes! But there is no way that human beings can go forever
without sleep. The deathless ones have appointed a proper time
for each thing upon the fruitful earth. I will go to my upper   510
chamber and lie down on my bed, which has become a bed
of wailing, mixed always with my tears, ever since Odysseus
went off to see that evil Ilion—not to be named! There I shall
lie down. You too lie down in the house, either spreading your
bedding on the floor, or have the slaves set up a bed for you."   515

---

497 *through them*: We cannot reconstruct how this contest worked from the information Homer gives us, and
     perhaps he did not understand it himself. What does he mean by "shoot an arrow through them"? In line
     505 he says that the shot will pass "through the iron." Some think that this means that the socket holes of
     the ax heads are lined up to make a kind of tunnel, but the bow shot would then be very close to the ground,
     if the blades of the ax heads are embedded in the ground. Another explanation is that these are votive axes
     with handles that terminated in a ring of iron to hang them from (but real votive axes were always small).
     Perhaps the ax heads, then, are set into the earth, forming at their upper end a tunnel of iron rings through
     which Odysseus shoots.

501 *. . . in my dreams*: Why Penelope should decide at just this moment to hold a suitor-contest and marry the
     winner has never been explained. Some interpreters have thought that Homer has used a version of the
     story in which Odysseus and Penelope plotted together to kill the suitors. In any event, Homer needed to
     move his story along and for that Penelope needed to set the contest.

So speaking she went up to her shining upper chamber,
not alone, but with her went the other female attendants. When
she came to the upper chamber with her women attendants,
she wept then for Odysseus, her dear husband, until
520 flashing-eyed Athena sent sweet sleep onto her lids.

[Book 20 is omitted. Odysseus lies in the great court, wondering whether to murder the
maids as they whore with the suitors, or to wait and kill them later. Athena appears to him
and promises the support he needs. Upstairs, Penelope wakes, having dreamed that her
husband lay beside her. Odysseus wakes as dawn breaks on another day of feasting.
Philoitios, a cowherd, brings animals to slaughter for the feast day in honor of Apollo. A
suitor throws an ox-hoof at Odysseus. Theoklymenos, a wandering seer being entertained
by Telemachos, gives a prophecy of doom. Penelope goes ahead with the contest of the
ax-heads.]

The goddess flashing-eyed Athena put it into the mind
of the daughter of Ikarios, the judicious Penelope, to set up
the bow and the gray iron in the feast-hall of Odysseus,
to be a contest and the beginning of death.°

She went up the steep
stairs of her house, and she took the bent key in her strong hand—   5
beautiful, made of bronze, and the handle was of ivory.
Then she descended from her chamber with her attendant
women to a storeroom at the far end the house.° The treasures
of her king lay there, bronze and gold and well-worked iron.
There was the back-bent bow° and the quiver that held   10
the arrows. Within were many arrows, the bearers of pain, a gift
that his guest-friend Iphitos, the son of Eurytos, had made him,
a man like the deathless ones.

They met in Lacedaemon.
The two of them came on one another in Messenê,° in the house
of the war-minded Ortilochos.° Odysseus had come after a debt   15
that the whole people owed him, for the men of Messenê
had stolen three hundred sheep from Ithaca in their ships
with many benches, and the herders along with them. On their
account Odysseus had come a long distance on an embassy
while still a youth, for his father and the other elders had sent   20
him forth. Iphitos, for his part, had come in search of twelve mares
that he had lost, with mules at the teat. They were about to become
death and fate for Iphitos, when he came to the proud-spirited
son of Zeus, the great Herakles, experienced in many deeds.
Herakles killed Iphitos in his own house—in cold blood!—   25

---

4   *beginning of death*: For the nature of this contest, see note on line 494, Book 19.

8   *the house*: For a possible reconstruction of the layout of the house, see MAP VII.

10   *back-bent bow*: A very powerful type of bow invented on the plains of central Asia consisting of a stave faced
with horn on the front and backed with sinew.

14   *Messenê*: Here evidently a town in LACEDAEMON.

15   *Ortilochos*: The name of the father of Diokles at whose house, in the southern PELOPONNESSUS, Telemachos
stayed when he journeyed to Sparta, perhaps the same man.

although Iphitos was a guest-friend, and he had no respect
for the will of the gods, nor for the table that Herakles set before him.
He killed Iphitos and kept the single-hoofed horses in his halls.°

    It was while asking for these mares that Iphitos met Odysseus
30 and gave him the bow that earlier great Eurytos had carried.
When Eurytos died he had left it to his son in the high-roofed
halls. And Odysseus gave Iphitos a sharp sword and a powerful
spear, the beginning of affectionate relations of guest-friendship,
though they never sat at the same table. Before that the son
35 of Zeus° killed Iphitos, the son of Eurytos, a man like the deathless
ones, who gave the bow to Odysseus. Odysseus never took it
when he went to war in the black ships, but he kept it in his halls
as a reminder of a beloved guest-friend, and he used it on his own land.

    The beautiful woman arrived at the chamber and stepped
40 on the oak threshold that a carpenter had once skillfully planed
and made true to the line, and fitted in doorposts and set
in them shining doors. She promptly loosened the strap
on the door-knob. She put in the key and with sure aim she shot
back the bolt.° As a bull bellows when grazing in the meadow,
45 even so the beautiful door panels bellowed, struck by the key,
and they swiftly opened wide before her. Then she stepped out
onto the high floor° where the chests lay in which the fragrant
clothing was stored.

              Standing up tall, she took down from a peg
the bow and the bright bow-case that surrounded it. She sat down
50 there and placed it on her knees, and she wept shrilly. She took
out the bow of her king. When she had had her fill of tearful
moaning, she went off to the feast hall and the bold suitors,
with the back-bent bow in her hands and the quiver for arrows.
There were many sorrowful arrows within it. Beside her,

---

28 *in his halls*: According to the story reconstructed from later sources, Autolykos, the maternal grandfather
    of Odysseus, had stolen the mares from Eurytos, a famous bowman from Oichalia (perhaps somewhere in
    the Peloponnesus), and entrusted them to Herakles for safe-keeping. Iphitos came to Herakles for help in
    finding the mares, not knowing that they were in Herakles' possession. Herakles lured him to the rooftop,
    pushed him off, and kept the horses.

35 *son of Zeus*: Herakles.

44 *bolt*: The double door is double-locked. First Penelope must untie a thong attached through a hole in the
    door to a bolt on the inside. This thong is tied to a knob or handle on the outside. Untying the thong releases
    the bolt inside. The key is not like a modern key, but is a large device with an ivory handle. By now inserting
    the key into a second hole in the door, Penelope shoots back the bolt that holds the door locked.

47 *high floor*: Apparently the storeroom has a built-in raised floor.

assistants carried a chest in which was a quantity of iron   55
and bronze, the armor of her king. When the beautiful woman
came to the suitors, she stood beside the doorpost of the well-made
house, and she held her shining veil before her cheeks.
A faithful assistant stood at either side.

                        Immediately she spoke
to the suitors and said: "Listen to me, you noble suitors who afflict   60
this house with your constant eating and drinking, while the man
of the house has been a long time gone. You have not found
any better excuse to plead than that you wanted to marry me
and make me your wife. Well, then—come on suitors, since this
appears to be your prize!   65

                 "I will place before you the great bow
of godlike Odysseus. Whoever strings the bow most easily
in his hands and shoots through all the twelve axes—I will
follow him, leaving this house of my wedded life behind,
this very beautiful house, filled with livelihood that I now will
see only in my dreams."   70

                So she spoke, and she urged Eumaios,
the good pig herder, to set out the bow and the gray iron°
for the suitors. Bursting into tears, Eumaios took them and set
them down. In another part of the room the cow herder wept too
when he saw the bow of his king.

                   Then Antinoös reproached them
and spoke, calling out: "You fools! Bunglers! Thinking only of today!   75
You wretches—why do you *now* pour down tears and get this
woman all excited? She already has enough troubles, for she
has lost her dear husband. Sit down and eat in silence, or go
outside and wail. But leave the bow here—a decisive contest
for the suitors. But I do not think it will be easy to string this bow.   80
For there is no man among all those here such as Odysseus was.
I myself saw him, and I remember him well, although I was
just a little boy."

             So he spoke, but his heart in his breast hoped
that he could string the bow and shoot through the iron. Yet he
was to be the first to taste an arrow from the hands of the noble   85

---

71   ...*iron*: The axes, evidently also in the storeroom and carried in the chest along with the "armor of her king."

Odysseus, whom even then, sitting in the hall, he disrespected,
and Antinoös urged on his companions too.

Then the strong, mighty
Telemachos spoke to them: "Well, Zeus the son of Kronos
has just knocked the senses from me. For my dear mother,
90 although she is a woman of understanding, says that she will follow
along with another and leave this house! That makes me laugh,
and I am glad in my senseless mind. Come, suitors, since *this* is
the prize, a woman unique in all Achaea, and in holy Pylos,
and Argos, and in Mycenae, and in Ithaca itself, and on the dark
95 mainland . . . But you know this yourselves! Why do I need
to praise my mother?

"Come, do not put the matter off with excuses.
Let us no longer turn away from the drawing of the bow, so that
we may see the outcome of this matter. I myself will first try the bow.
If I succeed in stringing and shooting through the iron, then it won't
100 bother me at all if my revered mother leaves this house,
going with another—and I will be left behind alone to wield
the beautiful battle-gear of my father."

He spoke and he flung down
the purple cloak from his shoulders. He stood up tall. He took
off the sharp sword from his shoulders. First of all he set up the axes,
105 digging a single deep trench for them all, and he made the trench
true to the line. Then he tamped down dirt around the axes. All were
amazed when they saw it, how expertly he set up the axes,
though he had never before seen them. Then Telemachos went
and stood on the threshold and began to try the bow. Three times
110 he made it quiver in his eagerness to string it, and three times
his strength gave out—although he wanted in his heart to string
the bow and shoot through the iron. And now for the fourth time,
when he tried, he *would* have strung it, but Odysseus nodded
his head and held him back in his eagerness.

The strong, mighty
115 Telemachos then said: "Sure, in days to come I will no doubt
be said to be a coward and a weakling, or I am still too young
and I do not trust in the power of my hands to defend myself
from some man's attack, if he is the first to take offense.
But come, you who are greater in strength than I—have a try
120 at the bow, and let us finish this contest."

So speaking, he placed
the bow on the ground, leaning it against the jointed polished
door, and nearby he leaned the sharp arrow against the curved
tip of the bow. Then he went and sat down on the chair from
which he had arisen.

Antinoös, the son of Eupeithes, spoke to them:
"Get up, all you of our company! In a row, from left to right,   125
beginning with the place where the cupbearer pours the wine."

So spoke Antinoös, and his word was pleasing to them.
Leiodes stood up first, the son of Oinops,° who inspected the entrails
of victims for them. He always sat next to the beautiful wine-mixing
bowl in the innermost part of the hall.° He alone hated the foolish   130
shenanigans of the suitors and was indignant at their antics.
It was he who first took up the bow and the sharp arrow. He went
and stood on the threshold and tried the bow, but he could not
string it. His arms grew tired as he pulled the string with his soft,
delicate hands.   135

Leiodes spoke to the suitors: "My friends,
I can't string it. Let someone else try it. This bow will rob the spirit
and breath of many of the best men, because it is much better
to die than to live on, ever missing the mark on account of which
we always gather together here, waiting, day after day. Many
a man hopes in his heart and is eager to marry Penelope,   140
the wife of Odysseus. But when he has tried his hand at the bow
and has seen the outcome, then let him pursue some other
of the Achaean women with their fine gowns, showering them
with wedding gifts and hoping to win one. Then Penelope should
marry him who offers the most presents and comes as her man   145
of destiny."

So he spoke, and he put down the bow, leaning it up
against the jointed well-polished door, and he leaned the sharp arrow
up against the curved bow-tip. Leiodes sat back down in the seat
from which he arisen.

---

128   *Leiodes ... Oinops:* "smooth" the son of "wine-face," that is, the weakling son of a weakling father, first heard
       of here.

130   *of the hall:* He inspects the entrails of sacrificed animals looking for "signs" of good and bad luck in their
       shape. The wine-mixing bowl (*krater*) that Leiodes sits beside was ordinarily kept on the floor.

But Antinoös reproached him and spoke
150 and called out: "Leiodes, what a word has escaped the barrier
of your teeth! Fearful, horrid—I am angry to hear it. You say this bow
will 'deprive many of the best men of spirit and life'—just because
you can't string it! But your revered mother did not beget you
to be strong enough to draw a bow and shoot arrows. Others
155 of the noble suitors will quickly string it."

So he spoke and he called
to Melanthios, the goat herder: "Look sharp, Melanthios,
light a fire in the halls,° and put a great stool beside it, and throw
a fleece on the stool, and bring in a big cake of lard that they keep
in the house. Then we young fellows may warm the bow, and rub
160 it with fat, and so make trial of the bow, and bring this contest
to an end."

So he spoke, and Melanthios quickly built the restless
fire. He brought in a stool and set it down, and he spread
a fleece over it. Then he brought in a large cake of lard that was
in the house. The young men warmed and tried their hand at the bow,
165 but they could not string it, for they were much too weak.

Antinoös and godlike Eurymachos remained to try to string the bow,
but meanwhile Odysseus' cow herder, Philoitios, and his pig herder,
Eumaios, went together at the same time out of the hall.

The good Odysseus himself went forth from the house after them.
170 When they got outside the gates and the court,° Odysseus spoke
to them with honeyed words: "Cow herder, and you, O pig herder,
shall I tell you something, or should I keep it to myself? My spirit
urges me to say it. Are you such men as would defend Odysseus
if he should suddenly come from somewhere and some god should
175 bring him in? Would you help the suitors or Odysseus? Speak how
your heart and spirit commands."

The cow herder then said: "Father
Zeus, if this hope should ever come to pass, that this man should
come, and some spirit should lead him—then you would know what
my power is and how my hands obey!" In a like manner Eumaios

---

157   *in the halls*: Not on the hearth, which is already burning to keep the house warm, but in a brazier.
170   *the court*: That is, they are in the street.

prayed to all the gods that the resourceful Odysseus would return   180
to his home.

　　　　　When Odysseus knew with certainty their minds,
he immediately spoke to them in reply: "I am here at home then!
After suffering much I have returned in the twentieth year
to the land of my fathers. I see that I have arrived in answer
to your desires, alone of the slaves. For I have heard of not one   185
other praying that I return home again.

　　　　　　　　　"But to you two I will
tell the truth, how it will be if a god grants that I take down
the proud suitors. I will give you both a wife and give you
property and a house built close to mine. You two will be
the companions and brothers to Telemachos. But come, I will   190
show you a clear sign so that you may know for certain
and have trust in your hearts—the scar that a boar once
gave me with his white tusk when I went with the sons
of Autolykos to the slopes of Parnassos."°

　　　　　　　　So speaking he parted
the rags to show the huge scar. When the two men saw it   195
and realized what it meant, they wept and threw their arms
around war-minded Odysseus. Rejoicing, they began to kiss
his head and shoulders, and in the same way Odysseus kissed
their heads and hands.

　　　　　　　　　And the sun would have gone down
as they wailed, if Odysseus himself had not put a stop to it   200
and said: "Cease from your weeping and wailing, or someone
may come out of the feast-hall and see, and tell those inside.
Go in one by one, not both together. I'll go in first, and you after.
And let this be the sign: All the other noble suitors will not
allow that the bow or the quiver be given to me, but you, good   205
Eumaios, when you are carrying the bow through the house,
place it in my hands, and tell the women to close the tightly fitting
doors of their hall. If one of them should hear the groaning
and the fighting of men going on inside our walls, let them
not rush outdoors, but remain in silence at their labor where   210
they are. And you, good Philoitios, I'm asking to shut up the doors
of the court with a bolt and swiftly throw a cord upon it."

194　...*Parnassos*: It is not obvious how Philoitios and Eumaios would have known about the scar.

So speaking he went into the stately house. He went over
to the stool from which he had arisen and took his seat.
215 The slaves of Odysseus went in as well. Eurymachos was holding
the bow in his hands, warming it on this side and that in front of
the flame of the fire. But even so he was unable to string it,
and his bold heart groaned mightily within.

                                        With a burst of anger
Eurymachos spoke and said: "Well! There is grief here for me
220 and grief for all of us! It is not so much the marriage that I regret,
though that does make me sad. There are many other Achaean
women, both here in Ithaca itself, surrounded by the sea, and in other
cities. But if we fall so far short of godlike Odysseus, seeing
that we cannot string his bow—this will be a reproach for men
225 to learn about in times to come!"

                                   Antinoös, the son of Eupeithes,
then answered him: "Eurymachos, it will not be so, and you yourself
know it. For today is a festival throughout the land of the god,
the sacred feast. Who then would bend a bow? So put it down
quietly, in peace. As for the axes—what if we let them all
230 stand as they are? For I don't think that anyone is going to come
into the house of Odysseus, son of Laërtes, and steal them!

    "But come, let the cupbearer pour wine in the cups for a drink-offering,
and let us put aside the bent bow. In the morning tell Melanthios,
the goatherd, to bring in she-goats, those that are the best
235 in the herds, so that we may lay thigh pieces on the altar
to Apollo, famous for his bow. Then we may try our hands
at the bow and put an end to this contest."

                                      So spoke Antinoös,
and his word was pleasing to them. The heralds poured out
water over their hands, and the young men topped-up the bowls
240 brim full of drink. They served out wine to all, first pouring
out wine for the drink-offering into the cups.

                                      When they had
made the drink-offerings and drunk as much as they wanted,
then the resourceful Odysseus spoke to them with a crafty mind:
"Hear me, suitors of a famous lady, so that I may say what
245 my heart urges me to say. I ask Eurymachos especially
and godlike Antinoös, for he has spoken in accordance
with what is right—yes, put down the bow for now, turn it

over to the gods. At dawn the god will give strength to whomever
he wishes. But come, give *me* the well-polished bow so that
among you I can try the strength of my hands, to see if I still   250
have strength such as once I had in my supple limbs. But the sea
and bad food have brought me low."

          So he spoke, and all of them burst
out angrily, fearing that he might string the well-polished bow.
Antinoös reproached him and called out: "Ah, you wretched
wanderer, you've lost your mind completely! Are you not   255
content that you dine at your ease among this proud crowd,
and you lack nothing of the feast, and you hear our words
and our speech? There is no other stranger or beggar who hears
our words! Sweet wine has wounded you, which has done
harm to others too, whoever takes it in gulps and drinks more   260
than he should.

    "Wine drove the Centaur, the famous Eurytion,
mad in the hall of great-hearted Peirithoös, when Eurytion went
to the Lapith land. When his mind was driven mad by wine,
in his madness he did an evil act in the house of Peirithoös.°
Distress took hold of the heroes, and they leaped up and dragged   265
Eurytion outdoors through the gateway, and they cut off his ears
and nose. He went off driven mad in his mind, bearing his madness
in the madness of his heart. From that arose the quarrel between
the Centaurs and men,° but it was for himself, heavy with wine,
that he first discovered evil.   270

      "And thus do I predict a *big* pain for you,
if you string the bow! For you will not meet anyone with kindness
in our land, but we will send you right away in a black ship—
to the chief Echetos, the most cruel of all men. There you will
never save yourself. So drink up at ease, and do not contend
with men who are younger than you!"   275

         Then the judicious Penelope
answered him: "Antinoös, it is not a pretty sight, nor is it just,
when you mistreat Telemachos' guests who come to the house.

---

264 *Peirithoös:* Peirithoös was king of the Lapiths. The Centaurs came to his wedding party, got drunk, and
     attacked the bride and her attendants, beginning the war between the Lapiths and the Centaurs.

269 *and men:* Homer may not have thought of Centaurs as half-horse, half-man, but his "Centaurs and men"
     suggests that the Centaurs were something other than men.

Why, do you think that if the stranger should string the great bow
of Odysseus, trusting in his strength and power—that he will
280 take me to his house and make me his wife? I don't think *that* is
what he has in mind. So let no one of you from fear of this sit
here at table grieving at heart—it is really not fit and proper."

Eurymachos, the son of Polybos, then said in reply: "Daughter
of Ikarios, judicious Penelope, it's not that we think that the man
285 will lead you to his house—that would hardly be right!—but we
fear the talk among men and women. At some time one
base Achaean may say, 'Weaker men by far are courting the wife
of a noble man, and they can not string the well-polished bow.
Then some *beggar* came wandering along and easily strung
290 the bow, and he shot through the iron!' So they will say—
and this will be a disgrace for us."

Then the judicious Penelope said:
"Eurymachos, there can never be a good reputation among the people
for those who dishonor and consume the house of a great man.
How do you rate *that* disgrace? This stranger is tall and well built,
295 and he says he is the son of a noble father. But come, give him
the well-polished bow so that we may see. I will say this,
and I think it will come to pass—if he strings the bow, and Apollo
grants him glory, I will give him a cloak and a shirt, fine clothes,
and I will give him a sharp spear to ward off dogs and men
300 and a two-edged sword. I will give him sandals for his feet,
and I will send him wherever his heart and spirit urges."

Then the shrewd Telemachos answered her: "My mother,
as for the bow, there is no one of the Achaeans who has more
right than I to give it or refuse it to whomever I wish—not anyone
305 who claims rule in rocky Ithaca, nor anyone in the islands toward
horse-pasturing ELIS. Of those, not *anyone* will force me against
my will, not even if I want, say, to give the bow to the stranger to carry
off with him—

"But go now into the house and attend to your affairs,
your loom and your distaff, and command your attendants to join
310 in the labor. The bow is a matter of concern for men, and especially
for me. For I have the power in this house."

In astonishment Penelope
went back into the house, for she had much taken to heart the wise
words of her son. She went into her upper chamber with her

attendant women, and she wept then for Odysseus, her dear husband,
until flashing-eyed Athena cast sweet sleep on her eyelids. 315

    Now the good pig herder had picked up the bent bow
and was carrying it, and all the suitors were crying out in the halls.
And one of the arrogant young men would say: "Where are you
taking the bent bow, you loathsome pig herder, you madman?
Soon the swift dogs will devour you near your swine, alone and apart 320
from men, the dogs that you yourself raised!—if Apollo will
be gracious to us and the other deathless gods!"

                        So they would say,
and the pig herder put the bow back where he got it, being afraid,
because many were shouting in the feast-hall. Then Telemachos
from the other side shouted out in a threatening manner: 325
"Old man, bear the bow onward! You will not do well to obey
everyone here. Though I am younger I will chase you to the field,
pelting you with stones! I am greater in strength. I only wish I had
as much power in the strength of my hands over the suitors who
are in my house—then I would soon send many a one in hatred 330
from our house! They are the devisers of evil." So he spoke,
and all the suitors laughed sweetly at him, and they relaxed their
harsh anger toward Telemachos.

                But Eumaios carried the bow
through the hall and, coming up to war-minded Odysseus,
he placed the bow in his hands. Then Eumaios called out 335
to the nurse Eurykleia: "Telemachos calls you, good Eurykleia,
to bar the closely fitting doors of the feast-hall. And if any
of the women hears a groaning or racket from the men who are
within our walls, don't let them run outside. They should stay
in silence at their work." 340

             So Eumaios spoke, and Eurykleia knew
what he meant. She closed the doors of the stately feast-hall.
Philoitios leaped up and went outside in silence. He barred
the gates of the court with its thick walls. Now there was a cable
for a beaked ship in the portico, made of papyrus, with which
he tied up the gates. Then he himself went inside. He went over 345
to the stool from which he had arisen, and he sat down. He looked
over to Odysseus, who was handling the bow, turning it round
and round, trying it this way, then that, in case worms had eaten
the horns while the king was away.

And thus would one say, looking
350   to his neighbor: "Say there, he is a connoisseur and a sly rogue with
a bow! Perhaps he has a similar one lying back in his home?
Or maybe he is thinking of making one. See how he handles it
in his hands, turning it this way and that—this bum, learned in evil!"

And another of the arrogant young men would say:
355   "May this fellow be as successful in other matters as he is about
to be in stringing the bow—"°

So spoke the suitors. But the resourceful
Odysseus hefted the great bow and looked it over carefully—
even as when a man skilled in the lyre and in song easily
stretches the string around a new peg, making the twisted
360   sheep gut fast from both ends, so Odysseus without trouble
strung the great bow. Holding it in his right hand, he tried
the string. It sang sweetly beneath his touch, like the sound
of a nightingale.°

But a great anger took hold of the suitors, and they
lost color in their skin. Zeus thundered aloud, showing forth a sign.
365   The much-enduring good Odysseus rejoiced then, because
the son of crooked-counseling Kronos° had sent him a sign.
He took up the swift arrow, which lay beside him on the table,
all by itself. The others lay inside the hollow quiver, which
the Achaeans were soon to taste.

Taking the arrow, he laid it on
370   the thick part of the bow and drew back the bow-string
and the notched arrow, still sitting on his stool, and he fired
the arrow, aiming carefully. He did not miss a single hole,°
but the arrow, heavy with bronze, went straight out through
the doorway.

---

356 *stringing the bow*: That is, may he be *un*successful in other affairs, as I hope he will be unsuccessful in stringing the bow.

363 *nightingale*: Many commentators have suggested that the singer must at this moment have twanged the
string on his lyre.

366 *crooked-counseling Kronos*: Kronos led the revolt of the older gods against Ouranos (Sky), waiting for his
father in ambush, then castrating him. For his deviousness he was called "crooked-counseling."

372 *a single hole*: The Greek here is highly obscure, but the fact that Odysseus fired while sitting on a stool might
agree with the theory that the ax-heads were buried by the blades in a trench with the haft-holes lined up so
that the shooter could shoot the arrow "through the iron."

Odysseus spoke to Telemachos: "Telemachos,
the stranger who sits in your halls brings no shame upon you.   375
I did not miss the mark, nor did I have to work a long time to string
the bow. My strength within is still steadfast, not as the suitors
contemptuously mock me. But now it is time to make dinner
ready for the Achaeans, while there is still light, and after that
we must make sport in a different way, with song and lyre.   380
For those are the companions of a feast."

                              He spoke and nodded
with his brows. Telemachos put on his sharp sword, the dear son
of godlike Odysseus, and in his hand he took up his spear. He stood
beside the chair at his father's side, armed in gleaming bronze.

BOOK 22. *The Slaughter of the Suitors*

And then the resourceful Odysseus stripped off his rags,
and he leaped up onto the great threshold, holding his bow
and his quiver filled with arrows, and he poured out the swift
arrows before his feet, and he spoke to the suitors: "Now at last
5 this mad contest comes to an end. And now for another
target, which no man has yet struck—I will know if I can
hit it and Apollo give me glory!"

             He spoke, and he aimed
a bitter arrow at Antinoös, who was about to raise up a beautiful
two-eared cup, made of gold. Antinoös held it in his hands
10 so that he could drink the wine. Death was not in his thoughts,
for who among many diners could think that one man, even if
he were strong, would fashion for himself evil death and black
fate by taking on so many?

             Taking aim, Odysseus hit him
in the throat with his arrow, and the point went straight through
15 the tender neck. Antinoös sank to one side, and the cup fell
from his hand when he was struck. Immediately a thick jet
of the blood of this man came through his nostrils. He quickly
kicked the table away from him, hitting it with his foot, and he
spilled his food on the ground, and the bread and roast meat
20 were befouled.

             The suitors fell into an uproar throughout the house
when they saw that man fall. They leaped from their chairs,
driven in fear through the house, looking around everywhere
along the well-built walls. But there was no shield or strong spear
to be had. They railed at Odysseus with angry words: "Stranger,
25 you shoot at men at *your* cost! You will never engage in a contest
again! Your destruction is certain now! You have killed a man
who is by far the best of the young men in Ithaca. Therefore
the vultures will devour your flesh!"

             So spoke each man, because
they did not think that the beggar had killed Antinoös on purpose.

The fools! They did not see that the cords of doom were fixed   30
upon them.

       The resourceful Odysseus spoke to them,
looking from beneath his brows: "You dogs, you did not think
that I would ever return home from the land of the Trojans,
so you wasted my house. You sleep with the women slaves
by force, and you court my wife while I am still alive, having   35
no respect for the gods who dwell in the broad sky. Nor do you
think there will be blame among men in time to come. The cords
of doom are fastened over you now—one and all!"

                So he spoke,
and a green fear fell on all of them, and each man looked about
to see how he might flee dread destruction. Eurymachos alone   40
dared answer: "If you really are Odysseus of Ithaca returned,
then this is just, what you say that the Achaeans did—many
acts of out-and-out folly in your halls, and many in the field.
But that man who was the cause of it all—Antinoös—is already dead.
It was *he* who encouraged these acts, not so much through desire   45
or need for the wedding, but having other things in mind,
which the son of Zeus was not about to bring to pass—that
throughout the land of well-settled Ithaca *he* be the boss
and that we might lie in wait for your son and kill him. Now he
lies dead, as was his fate.   50

       "But you should spare your own people!
And after this we will go through the land and gather recompense
for all the wine that has been drunk, and all the food that
has been eaten in your halls. And each man of us will pay
in compensation the worth of twenty oxen. We will repay in bronze
and gold until your heart is warmed! It is hardly surprising   55
that, until then, you are angry."

       The resourceful Odysseus looked
at him from beneath his brows and said: "Eurymachos,
not if you were to give me all the wealth of your fathers—
as much as you now have, and if you were to add more to it
from someplace else—not even then would I hold back   60
my hands from slaughter, before I have avenged every
arrogance of you suitors. Now you have two choices: to fight
or to flee, if anyone wants to avoid death and fate. But I don't
think that any of you will escape utter destruction."

So he spoke,
65 and their knees were loosened where they stood, and their hearts
dissolved. Eurymachos spoke for a second time, to the suitors:
"My friends, this man will not restrain his invincible hands,
but because he has taken the well-polished bow and the quiver,
he will continue to shoot from the polished threshold until he kills
70 every last one of us! Let us remember our courage! Draw your
swords and turn over the tables against the deadly arrows.
Let us mass against him in hopes that we can get him away
from the threshold and the door. Then let us go through the city
and quickly raise the alarm. Then this man will soon have fired
75 his last arrow!"

So speaking, Eurymachos drew his sharp bronze sword,
edged on both sides, and he leaped on Odysseus, screaming terribly.
But at the same time the good Odysseus loosed an arrow
and hit Eurymachos in the breast beside the nipple, and the swift
missile was fixed in his liver. The sword fell from his hand
80 to the ground, and tumbling across the table he doubled over
and fell. He knocked the food to the ground, and his two-handled cup.
He hit the ground with his forehead, in agony of spirit, and with both
feet kicked the chair and overturned it. A mist poured over his eyes.

Then Amphinomos rushed on the bold Odysseus,
85 coming straight at him, and he drew his sharp sword in hopes
he might drive Odysseus from the doorway. But Telemachos got
Amphinomos first, throwing from behind and hitting him with
the bronze spear right between the shoulders. Telemachos drove
the spear through his chest, and Amphinomos dropped with a thud,
90 striking the ground with his full forehead. Telemachos leaped back,
leaving the long-shadowed spear still in Amphinomos, for he feared
that one of the Achaeans might rush on him and stab him
with his sword, or deal him a blow as he stooped over the body.

Telemachos moved at a run and came quickly to his dear father.
95 Standing beside him, he spoke words that went like arrows:
"Father, I will bring you a shield and two spears and a bronze helmet
well-fitted to your temples, and when I come back I will arm myself.
I will likewise arm the pig herder and the cow herder. It is better
to be in armor."

In reply the shrewd Odysseus said to him: "Run,
100 bring it, so long as my arrows hold out. I am afraid that they will
push me from the door, because I am just one."

So he spoke,
and Telemachos obeyed his dear father. He went off to the storeroom
where the famous weapons° lay. From there he took up four shields,
eight spears, and four helmets made of bronze with thick horse-hair
crests. He carried them out, and quickly he came to his dear father.   105
He first of all cloaked his own flesh in bronze. Likewise
the two slaves put on the handsome armor, and they stood beside
war-minded Odysseus, the man of many devices.

And Odysseus,
so long as there were arrows, took aim and fired at the suitors
in his house, one by one, and they fell one on top of the other.   110
But when the king ran out of arrows to fire, he leaned the
bow to stand up against the shining side-walls of the vestibule near
the doorpost.° He himself put the shield with four layers around
his shoulders, and on his powerful head he placed the well-made
helmet with horse-hair crest, and the crest nodded terribly   115
from above. Now there was a rear-door in the well-made wall
of the feast-hall, and hard by the threshold of the well-built feast-hall
was a passage into the hall, closed by well-fitting doors. Odysseus
ordered the good pig herder to watch this, taking his stand
nearby, for there was but a single approach.   120

Then Agelaos spoke
to the suitors, making his words clear to all: "My friends,
won't somebody go out by the rear door and inform the people
so that the alarm can be quickly sounded? Then this man would
soon be done with his bowmanship!"

Melanthios the goat herder
then answered him: "That's not possible, god-nourished Agelaos.   125
For it is fearfully close to the beautiful doors of the court,
and the opening to the hall is dangerous. One man could hold off
all of us there, if he is strong. But come, I will bring armor
out of the storeroom for you to arm yourselves. For it is within,
and no place else I think, that Odysseus and his glorious son have   130
put the armor."°

---

103 *weapons*: This seems to be a separate storeroom from that where the bow was kept, because Telemachos
     does not use a key to open it. Later he regrets not locking the door. See MAP VII.

113 *doorpost*: This vestibule would be located at D in MAP VII, which helps to clarify the following description.

131 *the armor*: That Telemachos and Odysseus earlier removed from the walls. But we are not told how
     Melanthios knows where this armor is.

FIGURE 22.1 Odysseus shoots the suitors. Dressed in rags, his pouch at his side, he pulls back the powerful back-bent bow. Behind him stand two of the slave girls, one anxiously holding her chin in her hand, the other anxiously holding her hands before her. Athenian red-figure cup, c. 450–430 BC.

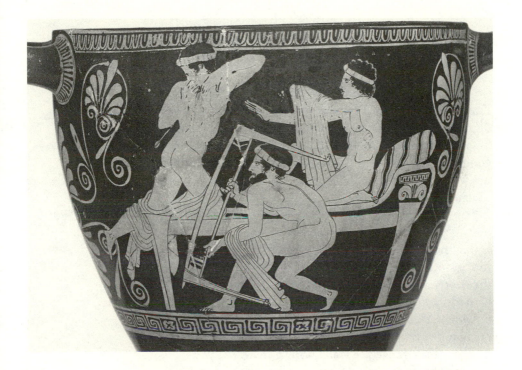

FIGURE 22.2 **Death of the suitors.** This is the other side of the cup from Figure 22.1. All the suitors, situated around a dining couch, are in "heroic nudity" but carry cloaks. On the left a suitor tugs at an arrow in his back. In the middle a suitor tries to defend himself with an overturned table. On the right a debonair suitor, with trim mustache, holds up his hands to stop the inevitable. Athenian red-figure cup, c. 450–440 BC.

So saying, Melanthios went out by the rear door
and down the side-hall to the storerooms of Odysseus. There
he took up twelve shields and as many spears and bronze helmets
with thick horsehair crests. He went off with these and quickly
135 brought them and gave them to the suitors. And then Odysseus'
knees were loosened, and his heart melted, when he saw the suitors
putting on armor and wielding long spears. Now the task appeared
immense to him.

But he quickly called to Telemachos words
that went like arrows: "Telemachos, truly some woman
140 in the halls is rousing up evil battle, or it is Melanthios!"

Then the shrewd Telemachos answered him: "O father, it is
I myself who made this mistake—there is no one else to blame.
I left the tightly fitting door of the storeroom ajar. Someone
has made better sense of the situation than we have. But come,
145 good Eumaios, close the door of the storeroom and find
out who of the women has done this, or is it the son of Dolios,
Melanthios? as I think."

Thus they conversed with one another,
and in the meanwhile Melanthios, the goat herder, went again
to the storeroom, to get some beautiful armor, but this time
150 the good pig herder saw him. Being near to Odysseus,
he said: "Zeus-nurtured son of Laërtes, much-resourceful
Odysseus, there is that vile man whom we already suspect,
going to the storeroom. Tell me truly—should I kill him,
if I prove the stronger, or shall I bring him here to you
155 so you might take payment for the many crimes that he has
planned against this house?"

The resourceful Odysseus then
answered him: "Telemachos and I will hold the proud suitors
inside the feast-hall, no matter how fierce they become.
You two bind Melanthios' feet behind him and his hands above,
160 and throw him into the storeroom. Tie boards to his back, then
bind a woven rope to his body, and hoist him up a high pillar—
bring him up near the rafters. Let him stay alive a long time.
That way he will suffer the more."

So he spoke, and they heard him
and obeyed. They went to the storeroom and, inside, Melanthios
165 did not notice them. He was looking for armor in the deepest

recesses of the chamber. Philoitios and Eumaios stood on either
side of the doorposts, waiting. When Melanthios the goat herder
came over the threshold, he carried in one hand a beautiful helmet
and in the other a broad ancient shield sprinkled with rust
that had belonged to the fighting man Laërtes, who wore it 170
when he was young. Then it lay in the storeroom, and the seams
of its leather straps were loosened.

           Philoitios and Eumaios leaped on
Melanthios. They seized and dragged him by the hair inside
the storeroom. They threw him, terrified, on the ground, and they
bound his feet and hands with dread bonds, mean and tight. Bending 175
his legs behind his back—as the son of Laërtes, the much-enduring
good Odysseus, had advised—they then bound a woven rope
to his body and hoisted him up a high pillar, near the rafters.
And Eumaios said in mocking tones: "Now, I think Melanthios,
you will watch the whole night through, lying in as soft a bed 180
as befits you. Nor will you fail to see the early-born Dawn,
the golden-throned, rising from the streams of Ocean, at a time
when you are accustomed to bring in your she-goats to the dandies
to make their feast in the house."

           And so they left him there,
stretched in tight bonds. Then the two slaves put on armor 185
and closed the shining door. They went back to war-minded
Odysseus, the man of many devices.

           There they stood, breathing
fury. There were but four of them on the threshold, and within
the hall were very many men—brave men! But Athena, the daughter
of Zeus, came close to them in the likeness of Mentor, in appearance 190
and in voice.

           Odysseus saw and was glad, and he said:
"Mentor, ward off ruin! Remember me, your dear comrade,
and all the good things I have done for you. Furthermore, you are
the same age as I." So he spoke, knowing that it was really
Athena, the rouser of the people. 195

           On the other side of the room
the suitors were raising an uproar in the halls. First Agelaos,
the son of Damastor, rebuked Athena: "Mentor, don't let Odysseus
wheedle you with fancy words to fight against the suitors
and defend himself. For I think that this plan of ours will come

200 to pass in just this way—once we have killed these men, father and son,
then you too will perish along with them. For such deeds as you
think you can pull off in these halls. You will pay with your head!
And when we shall have stripped you of all your power through
the bronze, all the possessions that you have both inside
205 and outside we will add to those of Odysseus. Nor will we
allow your sons to live in their halls, nor your daughters,
nor your faithful wife to live openly in the city of Ithaca!"

So he spoke, and Athena grew still more angry in her heart,
and she reproached Odysseus with angry words: "Apparently,
210 Odysseus, your steady strength and your bravery are no longer
the same as when you fought without end for nine years against
the Trojans for the sake of high-born Helen of the white arms.
You killed many men, then, in the dread contendings, and it was
through a plan of yours that the broad-wayed city of Priam
215 was taken.° How then can you come back to your house and your
possessions and grumble that you must be brave against
the suitors? But come, friend, stand beside me and behold
the deed, so that you might see what sort of man is Mentor,
the son of Alkimos, to repay kindness in the midst of the enemy."

220 She spoke, but by no means gave him a completely decisive victory.
She continued to make trial of the strength and valor of Odysseus,
and of his noble son. She herself flew up to the roof-beam of the smoky
feast-hall and sat there in the form of a swallow.

But the suitors were
pressed on by Agelaos, the son of Damastor, and by Eurynomos—
225 and Amphimedon, and Demoptolemos, and Peisander the son
of Polyktor, and war-minded Polybos. These were by far the best
of the suitors in valor of those still alive and fighting for the sake
of their breath-souls. The bow and the thick-falling arrows had already
cut down the others.

Agelaos spoke then, addressing his words
230 to everyone: "Friends, now this man will hold back his invincible
hands! Mentor has gone off after mouthing his empty boasts,
and they are left alone at the outer doors. Let us not all throw
our long spears at the same time, but—you six—throw first
in the hopes that Zeus will grant that Odysseus be struck

---

215 *was taken*: The Trojan Horse was Odysseus' idea.

and that we win glory. Don't worry about the others once   235
this man falls!"

        So he spoke, and the others eagerly threw their
spears, just as he said. But Athena made most of them
fly in vain. One man hit only the doorpost of the well-built
feast-hall, another hit the close-fitting door. The ash-spear
of another, heavy with bronze, struck the wall.   240

        When they had
dodged the spears of the suitors, then the resourceful good
Odysseus began to speak to his companions: "My friends,
now I give the word—cast your spears into the crowd of suitors,
who are anxious to kill us, in addition to their earlier crimes!"

        So he spoke, and they all threw their sharp spears, taking   245
careful aim. Odysseus killed Demoptolemos, Telemachos
killed Euryades, the pig herder killed Elatos, and the cow herder
killed Peisander—all those four bit the vast floor with their teeth,
and the surviving suitors fled into the innermost part of the feast-hall.

        Odysseus and his men rushed forward and snatched the spears   250
from the corpses while the suitors eagerly threw their sharp spears,
but Athena made them fly mostly in vain. One man hit the doorpost
of the well-built feast-hall, another hit the close-fitting door.
The ash-spear of another, heavy with bronze, struck the wall.
But Amphimedon hit Telemachos on the hand by the wrist,   255
a glancing blow, and the bronze broke the surface of the skin.

        Ktesippos grazed Eumaios on the shoulder, throwing over
his shield with a long spear, but the spear flew on and fell
to the ground. Then the crafty war-minded Odysseus and his men
threw their sharp spears right into the crowd of the suitors.   260
City-sacking Odysseus hit Eurydamas, Telemachos got Amphimedon,
and the pig herder hit Polybos.

        Then Philoitios struck Ktesippos
in the chest, and the cow herder said, boasting over him:
"Son of Polytherses, you lover of insult, I don't think you will again
give into foolishness and talk your big words. We'll let the gods   265
have the last say—they are stronger by far. This is *your* gift of guest-
friendship, to match the hoof that once you gave to godlike Odysseus,
when he begged through the house."

So spoke the herdsman
of the bent-horned cattle. Then Odysseus wounded the son of
270 Damastor, taking him on in the hand-to-hand with his long spear.
Telemachos wounded Leiokritos, the son of Euenor, getting him
in the soft underbelly and driving the bronze straight through.
Leiokritos fell forward onto the ground and hit the earth with full face.

Then Athena spread out her man-destroying goatskin
275 fetish high from the rafters, and the hearts of the suitors were
aghast. Some ran off through the feast-hall like a herd
of cattle that the nimble stinging black fly falls upon and drives
along in the season of spring when the days are long.
Even as vultures with their crooked talons and their curved
280 beaks come from the mountains and dart upon smaller birds
who fly low over the plain beneath the clouds, and the vultures
pounce on them and kill them, and valor or flight is useless,
and the men in the field rejoice watching the chase—even so
did Odysseus and his men set upon the suitors throughout the house,
285 striking them from the left and from the right. A repulsive groaning
arose from them as their heads were smashed, and all the floor
ran with blood.

But Leiodes° ran up to Odysseus and took hold
of his knees, and, begging, he spoke words that went like arrows:
"By your knees I beg you, Odysseus! Respect me and take pity!
290 I say that I have never done any harm to the women in the house,
neither in word nor in deed. I tried to hold back the other suitors
whenever any one would do such things. But they would not
listen to me and keep their hands away from foul deeds. And so
they have met an unpleasant fate for their loutish behavior.
295 But I, who am just a soothsayer, will lie low along with them
although I have done nothing—so true it is that there is never
any ultimate thanks for deeds well done . . ."

The resourceful
Odysseus looked from beneath his brows and said: "If you are
the soothsayer among these men, you must often have prayed
300 in the halls that my sweet homecoming be a long ways off,
and that my wife might follow you and give you children.
For this reason, you will not escape sorrowful death!"

---

288 *Leiodes:* He was the first to try to string Odysseus' bow (Book 21).

                    So speaking
he took up in his powerful hand a sword lying there that Agelaos
had thrown to the ground when he was killed. He drove the sword
through the middle of Leiodes' neck, and the seer's head was mixed   305
with the dust even as he still spoke.

                    But Phemios, the singer,
the son of Terpes, avoided black fate because he sang for the suitors
from compulsion. He stood holding the clear-toned lyre
in his hands close beside the rear door. His mind pondered two
courses—either to slip out of the feast-hall and take a seat on   310
the well-built altar of great Zeus, the god of the court,° where
Odysseus, the son of Laërtes, had burned the thigh-bones of many
cattle—or whether he should rush upon Odysseus and entreat him.
This seemed to be the better course: to take hold of the knees
of Odysseus, the son of Laërtes.°   315

                    So he put down the hollow lyre
on the ground, in between the wine-mixing bowl and the chair with
its silver rivets, and he rushed to Odysseus and clasped his knees,
and, begging, he spoke words that went like arrows: "By your knees
I beg of you, O Odysseus—respect me and take pity! It will
be trouble for you in times to come if you kill a singer—I who   320
sing to gods and humans. I am self-taught, but a god has breathed
into my heart the many pathways of song. And I seem to sing
by your side as by the side of a god. So don't be eager to cut
my throat! And Telemachos, your own son, will confirm these things—
that I never came willingly or through desire to your house   325
to sing to the suitors after their feasting. But they were many,
and strong, and they forced me to come here."

                    So Phemios spoke,
and the strong and mighty Telemachos heard him and quickly
he spoke to his father, standing near him: "Don't do it! Don't
slice him with the bronze, for he did nothing wrong. And let   330
us spare the herald Medon too, who always took care of me
in the house when I was little—unless Philoitios or the pig herder
has already killed him. Or perhaps he went up against you
as you raged through the house."

---

311   *of the court*: Still in classical times Greek houses usually had an altar in the open courtyard dedicated to
      Zeus of the Court (*Herkeios*), a protective spirit that defended the household.

315   *of Laërtes*: To clasp the enemy's knees was a sign of abject submission all over the ancient world.

So he spoke, and the intelligent
335 Medon heard him. For he lay crouching beneath a chair. He had
clothed himself in the skin of a newly flayed ox, trying to avoid
black death. Quickly he arose from beneath his chair and swiftly
he threw off the ox-hide. Then he rushed forward and clasped
the knees of Telemachos, and, begging, he spoke words that went
340 like arrows: "My friend, this is me—do not strike! And tell your father
not to cut me down with the sharp bronze in the greatness of his power,
being angry with the suitors who consumed the possessions in his halls.
And—the fools!—they did not honor you."

Then the resourceful
Odysseus said with an encouraging look: "Take courage, for Telemachos
345 has protected and saved you, so that you might know in your heart,
and that you might tell others, that good deeds are better than bad ones.
But go outside the halls and sit outside in the court away from
the slaughter—you and the renowned singer—so that I can go
through the house and do what is required."

So he spoke and the two
350 men went outside the feast-hall, and they sat down on the altar of great
Zeus, looking around, expecting death at every instant. And then Odysseus
looked around his house to see if anyone of the men were hiding,
still alive, trying to avoid black death. He saw them all fallen
in the blood and the dust, the great mass of them, like fish
355 that the fishermen has dragged out of the gray sea up on the curving
shore in the mesh of their nets, and they all lie in piles longing
for the waves of the sea, and the burning sun takes away their
breath—even so, the suitors lay in piles on top of one another.

Then the resourceful Odysseus spoke: "Telemachos, come:
360 call out the nurse Eurykleia, so that I can say the word that is
in my mind."

So he spoke, and Telemachos obeyed his father.
Shaking the door,° he spoke to the nurse: "Come out here, old lady,
you who are in charge of the female slaves throughout our halls.
Come! My father calls you, because he wants to say something."

365 So he spoke, but she did not reply. Then she opened the doors
of the stately feast-hall and came forth. Telemachos led the way
before her. She found Odysseus with the corpses of the dead,

---

362 *shaking the door*: By the knob to which the thong was attached.

splattered with blood and filth like a lion that comes from feeding
on a cow in the field, and all its chest and its cheeks on both sides
are covered in blood, and he is terrible to look upon—even so   370
Odysseus was splattered with blood on his feet and hands.

When Eurykleia saw the corpses and the endless blood,
she began to exult for joy, for she saw what great deeds had
been done. But Odysseus restrained her and held her back
in her eagerness, and he spoke to her words that went like arrows: 375
"In your *heart*, old woman, take joy, but restrain yourself
and do not cry out for joy. It is not holy to boast over the corpses
of the dead. It is the fate of the gods that has overcome them,
and their own evil deeds. They honored no one of the men
who walk on the earth, neither wicked nor good, whoever   380
would come to them. And so through their folly they have come
to a shameful end. But come, tell me about the women in the halls—
which ones disrespect me and which ones are innocent."

                                 The dear nurse
Eurykleia then answered him: "Well, child, I will tell you the truth.
There are fifty slave women in your house, whom we have taught   385
to do their work, to card wool and to bear the lot of slaves.
Of those, twelve are utterly without shame, honoring neither me
nor Penelope. Telemachos has only recently grown up, and his mother
would not allow him to rule over these slave women. But come,
I will go upstairs to the shining chamber to tell your wife,   390
on whom some god has cast sleep."

                            The resourceful Odysseus then
answered her: "Don't awaken her yet, but order the women to come
here, those who have committed these indecencies."

                                So he spoke,
and the old woman went through the feast-hall to make her
announcement to the women, and to order them to come. Odysseus   395
called Telemachos and the cow herder and the pig herder to himself,
and he spoke words that went like arrows: "Start to carry
out the corpses, and have the women help you. Then clean
the beautiful chairs and the tables with water and porous sponges.
When you have set the whole house in order, lead out the women   400
slaves from the well-built feast-hall to a place between the round-house°

---

401   *round-house*: We cannot say what the purpose or nature of this building was.

and the handsome wall of the court. There, cut them down
with your long swords until you have released the breath-souls
of all of them, and they have forgotten all about the sex that they
405 enjoyed with the suitors—sleeping with them in secret."

So he spoke,
and the women came all in a group, weeping gruesomely, pouring
down hot tears. First they carried out the corpses of the dead
and set them down beneath the portico° of the well-walled court,
leaning them up against one another. Odysseus himself gave
410 the orders, hastening on the work, and the women were compelled
to carry out the bodies. And they cleaned the very beautiful chairs
and the tables with water and porous sponges. Then Telemachos
and the cow herder and the pig herder scraped the floor of the tightly
built house with hoes. The slave women carried out the scrapings
415 and placed them outdoors. When they had set all the feast-hall
in order, they led the women forth from the well-built chamber
to the place between the round-house and the handsome enclosure
of the court, and there they confined them in a narrow space from which
they could not escape.

The shrewd Telemachos was the first to speak
420 to them: "Let me not impose a clean death on those women
who have heaped insults on me and my mother and slept with
the suitors."

So he spoke, and he tied one end of the cable of
a blue-prowed ship to a great pillar of the portico and the other
to the round-house, stretching it up high so that no one could reach
425 the ground with her feet. As when long-winged thrushes or doves fall
into a snare set in a thicket as they launch themselves toward their
resting place, but hateful is the bed that gives them welcome—even so
the women held their heads in a row, and around the necks of all
of them were placed nooses so that they might die most piteously.
430 They writhed a little with their feet, but not for long.°

Then they brought
out Melanthios into the forehall and the court, and they cut off
his nose and ears with the cruel bronze. They ripped out
his groin and fed it raw to the dogs, and they cut off his hands

---

408 *portico*: Evidently this is the same as the forehall.

430 *for long*: We cannot reconstruct the details of this execution, or see how in practical terms it was carried out.

and feet in their furious anger.° They then washed their hands
and feet and went into the house, to Odysseus. The deed was done. 435

Odysseus spoke to the dear nurse Eurykleia: "Bring in
sulfur, the driver-away of evils, old lady, and bring fire to me
so that I may purify the feast-hall. You tell Penelope to come
here with her attendant women. Order that the remaining female slaves
come into the house." 440

The dear nurse Eurykleia then spoke: "You have said
everything, my child, that is right. But come, I will bring you clothes,
a cloak and shirt so that you don't have to stand in the feast-hall
with your broad shoulders wrapped in rags. This is hardly appropriate."

Then the resourceful Odysseus said in reply: "First make a fire
in the halls." So he spoke, and the dear nurse Eurykleia did not 445
disobey. She brought fire and sulfur, and Odysseus purified
the feast-hall and the house and the court.° The old lady went
through the beautiful house of Odysseus to make her announcement
to the women, to command them to come. They came forth from their hall
carrying torches in their hands. They swarmed around Odysseus 450
and embraced him, and they kissed his head and shoulders and hands
in loving welcome. Then sweet desire for weeping and wailing took
hold of him, for he recognized each one of them in his heart.

---

434 *furious anger*: We do not learn who exactly performs these mutilations.

447 *and the court*: Ghosts do not like the smell of sulfur, and the feast-hall is at the moment filled with ghosts.

BOOK 23. *Husband and Wife*

The old woman went into the upper chamber, laughing loudly,
to tell her mistress that her dear husband was within the house.
Her knees were nimble, and her feet were swift beneath her.

She stood over the head of Penelope and said: "Wake up,
5 Penelope, my child, so that you might see with your own eyes
that which you have hoped for every day! Odysseus has come
and reached his home, though returning late. He has killed
the proud suitors who plundered his house and ate his animals
and threatened his child with violence."

                              Then the judicious Penelope
10 answered her: "My dear nurse, the gods have made you *mad*,
for they can easily remove one's wits even if you are highly sensible,
even as they can put the simple-minded on the road to understanding.
It is they who have harmed your wits, although you were of sound
mind before. They have struck you. Before you were temperate
15 in your heart. And why do you mock me, who have a heart full
of sorrow, by telling me this wild tale and rousing me from a sweet
sleep that has covered over and bound my eyes? For I have never
slept better than this, ever since Odysseus went off to see that
cursed Ilion, a place not to be named.

                         "But come, go back downstairs
20 to the women's quarters. If any other of the women who attend
me had come to me and told me this story and waked me up
from sleep, I would quickly have sent her back with much
ill-feeling to the women's quarters. But in this you shall profit
from your old age."

               Then the dear nurse Eurykleia answered her:
25 "I do not mock you, my child, but truly Odysseus has come
and arrived at his home just as I say—the stranger whom everyone
despised in his halls. Telemachos knew long ago that he was
in the house, but in his wisdom he hid his father's purpose until
Odysseus could take revenge on the violence of the haughty men."

So Eurykleia spoke, and Penelope was thrilled, and she leaped   30
from the bed and embraced the old lady, and she poured down tears
from her eyelids and spoke words that went like arrows: "But come,
tell me truly, dear nurse, if he has really come home, as you say, how
he was able to put his hands on the shameless suitors, being alone
when they were always inside in a crowd?"   35

                              The dear nurse Eurykleia
then answered: "I didn't see it, and I do not know—only I heard
a groaning of them as they died. We women were sitting
in the innermost part of our well-built chambers, terrified,
and the well-fitting doors shut us in until your son Telemachos
called me to come forth from the women's quarters. For his father   40
had ordered him to summon me. Then I found Odysseus standing
in the midst of the corpses of the dead. They lay around him,
covering the hard-packed ground, and they lay on top of one another.
It would warm your heart to see it! Now they are all gathered
together near the gates to the court, and your husband is cleansing   45
the beautiful house with sulfur, and he has kindled a great fire.
Odysseus ordered me to fetch you. Do follow along, so that the two
of you can enter into joy, for you have suffered many evils.
Now at last has your longtime hope come to pass. Your husband
has come home alive, he has found you and his son in the halls.   50
As for the suitors who did him dirt, he has taken vengeance
on them, one and all, in his house."

                            The judicious Penelope answered her:
"Dear nurse, do not boast loudly over them, laughing. You know
how welcome Odysseus would appear to everyone in the halls,
and especially to me and my son, whom the two of us bore.   55
But this story cannot be true as you tell it. Perhaps one of the gods
killed the bold suitors, paying them back for their infuriating
violence and their evil deeds. They would not respect *anyone*
of men who walk on the earth, neither good nor bad, whoever
should come to them. Therefore they have suffered evil for their   60
folly . . . but Odysseus has lost his homecoming, far away from
the land of Achaea, and he himself has perished."

                            The dear nurse
Eurykleia then answered her: "My child, what a word has escaped
the barrier of your teeth! That your husband, who is inside the house
beside the hearth, would never come home! Your mind is always   65
unbelieving! But come and I will tell you another clear sign—

FIGURE 23.1   Penelope and Eurykleia.   The mourning Penelope is in a traditional pose with
her hand to her forehead and her legs crossed. Her head is veiled. Here she stares gloomily downward,
seated on a padded stool beneath which is a basket for yarn, while the ancient Eurykleia,
her head veiled, her fist clenched, tries to persuade her that her husband has returned. The purpose
of these terracotta reliefs, found in different parts of the Roman world, is unclear. Roman Relief,
AD 1st century.

the scar that once a boar etched in with his white tusk—I recognized
it when I was washing him. I wanted to tell you, but he laid
his hands on my mouth and in the great wisdom of his heart
would not let me speak. But come! I will put my life at stake   70
if I am deceiving you, so that you can kill me with a pitiable death!"

Then the judicious Penelope answered her: "Dear nurse, it is
hard for you to understand the counsel of the gods who last forever,
no matter how wise you may be. But all the same, let us go to
my son, so that I can see the dead suitors, and see who killed them."   75

So speaking, she descended from the upper chamber. And her mind
rushed this way and that, whether she should interrogate her husband
from a distance, or whether she should stand beside him and kiss
his head and take hold of his hands. And when Penelope went into
the chamber and crossed the stone threshold, she took her seat   80
opposite Odysseus in the glare of the fire against the further wall.
He sat down against a tall pillar, looking down, waiting to see
if his excellent wife would say something when she saw him with
her own eyes.

She sat in silence for a long time, and amazement came
upon her heart. Now she would look in full gaze at his face, now she   85
would fail to recognize him because of the foul clothing that he wore.

Telemachos reproached his mother and spoke and called her out:
"Mother of mine—*cruel* mother! With an unfeeling heart! Why do
you stay apart from my father and not sit by his side and exchange
words with him and converse? No other woman would so harden   90
her heart and stand apart from her husband who after suffering many
pains came on the twentieth year again to the land of his fathers.
Your heart is always harder than a stone!"

Then the judicious Penelope
answered him: "My child, the heart in my breast is amazed,
and I cannot say a word, neither to ask a question nor to look him   95
in the face. If this truly is Odysseus, and he has come home,
surely we will know each other even better. For we have special
signs that we two alone know, kept secret from others."

So he spoke, and the much-enduring good Odysseus smiled,°
and quickly he spoke to Telemachos words that went like arrows: 100

99   *smiled:* The only time in the *Odyssey* where Odysseus smiles.

"Well, Telemachos, let your mother put me to the test in the halls.
Then she will soon know all the better. For now, she scorns me
because I am filthy. I have evil clothes about my flesh, and she does
not think that I am he. But as far as we ourselves are concerned,
105 let us consider what will be the best course. If someone kills
one man in the land, even one who has few supporters left behind,
he still flees, leaving his family and the land of his fathers.
But we have killed the cream of the city, those who were the best
young men in Ithaca. I think we should think about this."

110   The shrewd Telemachos said in reply: "You yourself should
look to this, dear father. For they say that your counsel is the best
among men and that not any other of mortal men could contend with you.
As for ourselves, we will follow you eagerly, and I don't think
that we will be lacking in bravery, as far as our strength permits."

115   Then the resourceful Odysseus said in reply: "I will tell you
what seems to me to be the best plan. First of all, wash yourselves
off and put on clean shirts, and order the female slaves in the halls
to put on clean clothes too. Then have the divine singer with his
clear-toned lyre lead a merry dance for us, so that someone coming
120 along and hearing the sound will think that a wedding feast
is going on, either someone going along the road or someone
who lives nearby. I don't want news of the death of the suitors
to get out through the broad city before we ourselves can go out
to our well-wooded farm.° There we can take thought about
125 what advantage the Olympian places in our hands."

                                                  So he spoke,
and they heard and obeyed him. First they washed themselves
and put on clean shirts that the women provided. Then the divine
singer took up his hollow lyre and roused in them the desire
for sweet song and the noble dance. The great hall resounded
130 all about the feet of the men and women with beautiful waists
as they danced. And thus someone who heard the hoopla from
outside the house would say: "Looks like someone has married
the much-courted lady—cruel woman! She did not have the daring
to preserve the great house of her wedded husband to the end,
135 until he returned."

---

124   *well-wooded farm*: He means the farm of his father Laërtes, mentioned several times before, where in fact
        Odysseus goes.

Thus would one say when they did not know what
had happened. Then Eurynomê, the housekeeper, bathed great-hearted
Odysseus in his house and anointed him with olive oil, and she threw
around him a cloak and a shirt. Then Athena poured out abundant
beauty, making him taller to see and more robust. And from
his head she made locks to curl down like the hyacinth flower.   140
As when a man overlays silver with gold, a man whom Hephaistos
and Pallas Athena have taught every kind of craft, and he fashions
lovely works—even so did Athena pour out grace on Odysseus' head
and shoulders.

He emerged from the bath like in appearance to
the deathless ones. He sat back down in the chair from which he had   145
arisen, directly opposite his wife, and he said to her: "You are
a strange woman! To you beyond all women those who live
in Olympos have given a heart that cannot be softened. For no other
woman would dare to stand apart from her husband, who after
suffering many sorrows came to her in the twentieth year in the land   150
of his fathers. But come, nurse, prepare a bed for me so that I can get
some rest. Her heart—it is like iron!"

The judicious Penelope then spoke
to him: "Well, *you* are a strange man. I am not acting proudly,
nor do I make light of you, nor am I so amazed,° but I know well
that you looked the same then, when you left Ithaca, traveling in your   155
long-oared ship. But come, make up the stout bedstead for him,
Eurykleia, and put it outside the well-built chamber that Odysseus
himself built. Set up the stout bedstead there and put bedding on it,
fleeces and cloaks and bright blankets."

So she spoke, putting her husband
to the test. But Odysseus, bursting with anger, spoke to his sensible   160
wife: "Woman—truly you have uttered a grievous word! *Who* has
moved my bed elsewhere? That would be hard to do even for one
highly skilled, unless some god should come down himself
and easily will it to be in another place. But no living man, no matter
how young and strong, could easily have moved it, for a great   165
sign is built into the decorated bed. *I* made it, and no one else.

"There was a bush of long-leafed olive growing inside my
compound, flourishing and vigorous. It had the thickness of a column.

---

154 *so amazed*: Amazed, perhaps, at his transformation, meaning that she *should* recognize him now that he
     looks like he did when he left her, but still, she holds back. But her reply is obscure.

I built my chamber around the olive, working on it until it was done,
170 making the walls of close-set stones, and I fitted a roof overhead,
and I installed joined doors, close-fitting. Then I cut off the leafy
branches of the long-leafed olive and, trimming the trunk up
from the root, I skillfully polished it with a bronze adze.
I made it straight to the line, thus making the bedpost.
175 I bored it all with the augur.° Beginning from this I worked
everything smooth until it was done, inlaying it with gold
and silver and ivory. And I stretched ox-hide cords, stained red.

"Thus I tell to you a sign. But I do not know at all, woman,
whether my bedstead is still in place, or whether someone
180 has cut from beneath the trunk of the olive and set the bedstead
someplace else."

So he spoke, and he loosened her knees
and melted her heart, for she recognized the sure signs that
Odysseus had told her. Weeping, she ran straight toward him
and threw her arms around the neck of Odysseus and she kissed
185 his head and said: "Don't be angry with me, O Odysseus,
for in all other things you were the wisest of men. It is the gods
who gave us this sorrow, who didn't want us to enjoy our youth
together and come to the threshold of old age. So do not be angry
with me for this, nor resent me, because I did not welcome you
190 when I first saw you. Always the heart in my breast was filled
with shivering that someone should come and deceive me
with his words. For there are many who devise evil things.

"No, not even Argive Helen, the daughter of Zeus, would have
lain in love with a man from another people if she had known
195 that the warlike sons of the Achaeans would bring her home again
to the dear land of her fathers. It must be some god that prompted her
to that shameful act. For she did realize in her mind the dread
blindness° from which, at the first, the sorrow came to us too.

"But now, because you have told the clear signs of our bed,
200 which no other mortal but one has seen—you and I and our
attendant, the daughter of Aktor,° whom my father gave me

---

175 *with the augur:* To drill holes for the oxhide thongs that create the mattress, that he mentions in line 177.

198 *dread blindness:* The Greek word is the untranslatable *atê* which refers to the act of divine intervention; the delusion thus caused; and the disaster that follows.

201 *daughter of Aktor:* Not mentioned elsewhere; perhaps Eurynomê is meant.

at the time I came here, who guarded the doors of our strong bridal
chamber. So you have persuaded me, though I am hard of heart."

So she spoke, and she stirred in Odysseus still more
the urge to weep, and he cried, holding his beloved wife in his arms,   205
she who was true of heart. As welcome as the land appears
to swimmers, whose well-built ship Poseidon has smashed on the sea
as it was driven on by wind and rough waves—few escape
the gray sea by swimming to the mainland, and a thick crust of brine
has formed around their flesh, and gladly have they gone forth   210
onto the land, fleeing evil—even so was her husband welcome
to Penelope as she looked upon him, and she would not let loose
her white arms from his neck.

And Dawn with her fingers of rose
would have appeared as they still lamented if flashing-eyed Athena
did not have another thought. She held back the night at the end   215
of its course so that it was long, and she stayed golden-throned
Dawn at the streams of Ocean, and she would not allow Dawn
to yoke her swift horses Lampos and Phaëthon,° which are the colts
that draw her car, that bring light to men.

And then the resourceful
Odysseus addressed his wife: "Wife, we have not yet come   220
to the end of our trials. There is still measureless labor ahead of us,
long and hard, that I must see through to the end. For thus did
the breath-soul of Tiresias prophesy to me on that day when
I went down into the house of Hades to learn of the homecoming
for my companions and myself. But come, let us go to our bed,   225
woman, so we might take pleasure in sweet sleep."

The judicious
Penelope then answered him: "We can go to bed any time you
want, for the gods have brought it about that you have come back
to your well-built house and the land of your fathers. But because
you have thought of this, and a god has put it into your heart—   230
come, tell me what *is* this trial. In time to come, as I think,
I will learn of it. To know it at once is not a worse thing."

The resourceful Odysseus then said in reply: "Strange woman!
Why do you insist that I talk of such things? Alright, I will tell you,

---

218   *Lampos and Phaëthon:* "light" and "shining," "speaking names" reminiscent of the nymphs who looked after
      Helios' cattle on Thrinakia (Book 12), *Phaëthousa* and *Lampetiē.*

235 and I will hide nothing. You won't be happy about it, nor am I
myself happy about it.

"Tiresias advised me to go forth through
the many cities of men, holding in my hands a well-fitted oar,
until I come to people who do not know what the sea is,
nor do they eat food mixed with salt, nor do they know of ships
240 with painted red cheeks, nor of well-fitted oars that are the wings
of ships. He gave this very clear sign to me, and I will not
conceal it. When another traveler, coming upon me, should say
that I have a winnowing-fan on my strong shoulder, then
he ordered that I fix the oar in the earth and perform holy sacrifices
245 to King Poseidon—a ram and a bull and a boar that mates
with sows—then go home and perform holy sacrifices
to the deathless gods who inhabit the broad sky, to all of them,
one after the other.

"And Tiresias said that a gentle death would
come to me from the sea,° which will kill me when I am
250 overcome in a vigorous old age. And around me all the people
will be prosperous. Tiresias said that all this would come to pass."

The judicious Penelope then answered him: "If the gods
are going to bring about a better old age, there is hope that
you will find an escape from evil."

Thus they spoke such things
255 to one another. In the meanwhile Eurynomê and Eurykleia
prepared the bed of soft covers by the light of blazing torches.
When they had busily made the stout bed, the old nurse went
back to her chamber to lie down, and Eurynomê, the lady
of the bedchamber, led Odysseus and Penelope on their way
260 to the bed, holding a torch in her hands. After she had led them
to the bedchamber, she withdrew. The couple gladly came to the place
of their ancient marriage bed.

In the meanwhile, Telemachos
and the cow herder and the pig herder stopped their feet

---

249 *from the sea*: It is not clear whether this means "away from the sea," inland, or whether it means as the
result of something "coming from the sea." Taking the second interpretation, later tradition reported that
Odysseus' son Telegonos (by Kirkê, of whom Homer has no knowledge) mistakenly killed him with a spear
tipped with a stingray barb "from the sea," but this is hardly a "gentle" death.

from the dance, and they stopped the women, and they themselves
went to bed in the shadowy halls.   265

                                   But when Odysseus and Penelope
had had their fill of the joy of love-making, they entertained
one another by telling tales to one another. She, a goddess
among women, told of all the things she endured in the halls,
beholding the destructive crowd of the suitors who on her account
butchered many animals, both cattle and fat sheep, and a huge   270
amount of wine was drawn from the jars. And Odysseus recounted
all the agonies that he had brought on men, and all the labor that
he himself in sorrow had to endure. She took pleasure in hearing him,
nor did sleep fall on her eyelids before he had told her all.

[Lines 275–299 are omitted. Odysseus recounts his adventures, summarizing the
highpoints]

   Then he came   300
to the Phaeacians, as he suffered terribly, who heartily honored him
as if he were a god, and sent him on his way in a black ship
to the land of his fathers, after giving him a mass of bronze
and gold and fine cloth.

                                This was the last thing he said before
sweet sleep, the looser of care, settled upon him, loosening   305
the cares of his heart. But flashing-eyed Athena had another thought.
When she judged that Odysseus had taken sufficient pleasure
from mingling with his wife, and from sleep itself, she immediately
roused from Ocean early-born golden-throned Dawn, who brings
light to men.   310

                    Odysseus arose from his soft bed and he gave a command
to his wife: "Woman, surely we have had our fill of trials, both of us,
you here and me crying about my troublesome homecoming. But Zeus
and the other gods bound me with sorrows far away from the land
of my fathers, although I was eager to return. Because we have
both come to the marriage bed that we both wanted so much,   315
I want you now to take care of the possessions that are in the house.
As for the flocks that the proud suitors have wasted, I shall restore
them through raids, and the Achaeans will give some,° until they
fill up all my pens. But now I must go to my well-wooded farm,

---

318 *give some*: He means those peoples under his direct control: Responsibility for allowing the suitors to
    behave as they did implies responsibility for making good the damage.

320 to see my noble father, who grieves bitterly for me. To you, woman,
I give this charge, though you are in any event a sensible woman.
Right away, at the time of the rising sun, a report about the suitors
I killed will get out. You go up to your upper chamber with your
attendants and wait there. Look on no man and ask no questions."

325   He spoke and put on his beautiful armor around his
shoulder, and he roused Telemachos and the cow herder and
the pig herder, and he pressed them all to take up war gear
in their hands. They obeyed him and armed themselves
in bronze. And they opened the gates and went out. Odysseus
330 was in the lead. Already the sun shone on the earth, but Athena
covered them in night and led them swiftly forth from the city.

BOOK 24. *Father and Son*

In the meanwhile Kyllenian Hermes° called forth the breath-souls
of the suitors. He had a wand in his hands—beautiful, golden—
with which he enchants the eyes of those he wishes, while
he awakes others from their sleep, whomever he wishes.
He drove them on with it, and gibbering they followed.   5
As when bats in the depths of a wondrous cave fly around gibbering,
and then one falls from the rock in the chain in which they cling
to one another, even so the breath-souls went off gibbering.
And Hermes the Deliverer led them over the mildewy ways.

And they came to the streams of Ocean and the White Rock,   10
and they went past the Gates of Helios and the Land of Dreams.
Quickly they came to the meadow of asphodel, where the breath-souls
were, the images of men who are done with their labor.°
They found the breath-soul of Achilles, son of Peleus, and of Patroklos
and of noble Antilochos and Ajax,° who was the best in form   15
and muscle of all the Danaäns, after the noble son of Peleus.

So these were swarming around Achilles when the breath-soul
of Agamemnon, son of Atreus, filled with sorrow, came up close.
Around him were gathered all those who had died and met their fate
together with Agamemnon in the house of Aigisthos. The breath-soul   20
of the son of Peleus first addressed him: "Son of Atreus, we thought
that you above all fighting men were dear to Zeus who delights
in the thunder, and for all your days, because you ruled over many
powerful men around the land of the Trojans, where the Achaeans

---

1 *Kyllenian Hermes*: Because he was born on Mount Kyllenê, in the Peloponnesus, according to later accounts.
  Only here in Homer is Hermes called Kyllenian and only here does he appear as the *psychopompos*, or "soul-
  guide," who leads the breath-souls to the other world. He does, however, serve an analogous function in the
  Iliad, when he leads Priam through the night into the camp of the Achaeans (Book 24), and in the *Odyssey*
  when he meets Odysseus on the otherworldly island of Kirkê.

13 . . . *labor*: Asphodel, a pretty blooming herb, is often associated with the underworld and was planted on
  graves. The White Rock, not mentioned elsewhere, is somewhere in the other world, as are the Gates of
  Helios and the Land of Dreams.

15 . . . *Ajax*: Heroes of the Trojan War, all killed in battle. Patroklos is Achilles' friend. Antilochos is the son
  of Nestor. (Big) Ajax is the son of Telamon and the best fighter after Achilles, whose breath-soul turned
  away in anger from Odysseus in the underworld because Odysseus had cheated Ajax of the arms of Achilles
  (Book 11).

25 suffered so horribly. But it was your fate that death would claim you
prematurely, before your time, the fate that no one born can escape.
I wish that, still enjoying the honor that was yours, you had met
death and found your fate in the land of the Trojans. Then all
the Achaeans would have made you a tomb, and for your son
30 you would have won great glory in the times to come. But as it is,
fate has decreed that you be taken in a most pathetic death."°

The breath-soul of the son of Atreus answered the breath-soul
of Achilles in this fashion: "Most fortunate son of Peleus! Achilles,
like to the gods, who died in Troy far from Argos—around you
35 others were killed, the best of sons of the Trojans and the Achaeans,
fighting over your corpse.° You lay in a whirl of dust, mighty in your
power, forgetful of your horsemanship. But we fought all day long
and would never have left off the fight if Zeus had not stopped it
with a storm. Then, when we had carried you from the war to the ships,
40 we lay you down on a bier and cleansed your beautiful flesh
with warm water and anointing oil. The Danaäns poured
out abundant hot tears, and they cut their hair. Your mother came
from the sea, along with the immortal nymphs of the sea, when
she heard the news. A wondrous cry arose over the sea,
45 and a trembling took hold of all the Achaeans. Then would they
have sprung up and rushed to the hollow ships had not a man
with vast experience of olden days held them back—Nestor,
whose counsel always seemed best in earlier times. With good
intentions he spoke and addressed them: 'Stay now, Argives—
50 don't flee, young men of the Achaeans! His mother has come
from the waters with her deathless nymphs of the sea in order
to see the face of her dead son.'

"So Nestor spoke, and the great-hearted
Achaeans held back from their flight. Then around you the daughters
of the Old Man of the Sea stood, weeping piteously,
55 and they clothed you with their deathless garments. The Muses,
all nine of them, singing in antiphony with their beautiful voices,
sang the threnody. Then you could scarcely have seen a dry eye
among the Argives, so deeply did the clear-toned Muse stir
them. For seventeen days and nights we lamented you—
60 both deathless gods and mortal men. And on the eighteenth
we gave you to the fire. We killed many well-fatted sheep

---

31 ... *death*: The breath-soul of Achilles seems only now for the first time to encounter the breath-soul of
Agamemnon, although ten years have passed.

36 *your corpse*: Seemingly Achilles has not heard the story of his death before.

FIGURE 24.1 **Ajax carries the body of Achilles from battle.** The figures are labeled. Big Ajax was usually credited with saving Achilles' corpse from the battle, although the *Odyssey* does not say so. Ajax here wears a helmet, breastplate, and shin guards, but his genitals are exposed. He carries a spear. A naked Achilles, killed by an arrow fired by Paris, is suspended over his shoulder. From the handle of the famous François Vase, signed by the potter Ergotimos and the painter Kleitias. Athenian black-figure wine-mixing bowl, c. 570 BC.

around you, and cattle with crumpled horns. You were burned
in the clothing of the gods, and with rich unguent and sweet
honey. Many of the Achaean fighting men danced an armed
65 dance around the fire as you burned, both foot soldiers and drivers
of cars. And a great cry arose.

        "But when the flame of Hephaistos
had put an end to you, in the morning we gathered together
your white bones, O Achilles, and placed them in unmixed
wine and oil. Your mother gave you a golden two-handled
70 vase. She said it was a gift of Dionysos, the work of the justly
renowned Hephaistos. Your white bones lie within it, glorious
Achilles, mixed with those of the dead Patroklos, son of
Menoitios. But in another jar lie the bones of Antilochos,°
whom you honored above all your other companions, once
75 Patroklos was dead.

        "And around them the holy army of spear-bearing
Argives heaped up a great and handsome tomb on a projecting
headland on the broad HELLESPONT, so that it could be seen
by men from far over the sea, both those who live now
and those who are to come after.°

        "Your mother asked the gods
80 for beautiful prizes, and she set them out in the middle
of the contestants' arena for the best of the Achaeans.
Before now you have been at the burials of many fighting men,
when, at the death of some king, young men tie a belt around
their middles and prepare for the competition. Still, had you
85 seen that sight, you would most have marveled in your heart,
such beautiful prizes did Thetis, the goddess whose feet are
of silver, set out on your behalf. For you were very dear
to the gods. And so, though you have died, your name lives on,
and your fame will always be great on the lips of men, Achilles.

90   "But to me!—what was the sweetness in having survived
the war? For Zeus had in mind a wretched death for me
on my return at the hands of Aigisthos and my ruinous wife!"

---

73 *Antilochos*: The son of Nestor, killed by Memnon, an Ethiopian king, in the postHomeric tradition. It is odd
that Homer mentions him here. Perhaps in some other version of the poem Antilochos had a close relationship with Achilles, or Patroklos has even replaced him in this tale.

79 *come after*: There was in fact a barrow near the Hellespont called the "tomb of Achilles," but we cannot be
sure that Homer refers to that here. The barrow may have been so called after this passage.

They spoke to one another in this fashion, then Argeïphontes
the guide came up close to them, leading down the breath-souls
of the dead suitors. The two—the souls of Achilles   95
and Agamemnon—marveled when they saw them, and they
went straight toward them. The breath-soul of Agamemnon,
son of Atreus, recognized the dear son of Melaneos, the famous
Amphimedon, for Amphimedon was a guest-friend, having his
house on Ithaca.   100

          The breath-soul of the son of Atreus spoke first:
"Amphimedon, what has happened to you that you come
down here beneath the black earth—all of you picked men,
all of the same age? If one were to pick the best men in the city,
one would not choose otherwise. Perhaps Poseidon overwhelmed
you in your boats, arousing savage winds and high waves?   105
Or did enemy men harm you on the land while you were
rustling some cattle, or beautiful flocks of sheep, while they
fought for their city and their women? Tell me, because I am asking!

    "I tell you that I am a guest-friend to your house. Don't you
remember when I came there to your house along with godlike   110
Menelaos to recruit Odysseus, to get him to follow us to Ilion
in ships with fine benches? It took us a full month to cross
over all the wide sea, for we could hardly persuade Odysseus,
sacker of cities."

          Then the breath-soul of Amphimedon answered:
"Most glorious son of Atreus, king of men, Agamemnon,   115
I remember all of these things, Zeus-nourished one, just
as you say. And I will tell you all this exactly, how my evil
death came to be.

          "We courted the wife of Odysseus, who was gone
for so long a time. She would neither refuse the hated marriage,
nor accept it, but instead contemplated death and black   120
fate for us. She contrived this trick in her mind: She set up
a great loom in her halls and wove before it, work very fine
and large. And she said to us: 'Young men, my suitors, though
godlike Odysseus has died, be patient in your eagerness
for my marriage. Wait until I finish this robe. I don't want   125
my spinning to go for nothing! It is a shroud for Lord Laërtes,
for that day when the dread fate of woeful death will take him—
so that none of the Achaean women in the land reproach me if he
were to lie without a shroud, this man who once had much in life.'

130   "So she spoke, and our trusting spirit was persuaded.
By day she would weave at the great loom, but at night
she set up torches and unwove. Thus for three years she beguiled
us by a trick, she deceived the Achaeans. But when the fourth
year came and the seasons rolled around as the months passed by,
135   and many days came to completion, then one of the women,
who knew well, told us, and we caught her unweaving
the glorious robe. And so she finished it by compulsion,
all unwilling.

            "When Penelope showed us the robe that she had
woven on the great loom, like to the sun or to the moon
140   after washing it, even then some evil spirit brought Odysseus
to the outskirts of the land, to where the pig herder lived.
There too came the son of godlike Odysseus, returning from
sandy Pylos in his black ship. The two of them, planning black
death for the suitors, came to the famous city—Telemachos first
145   and then Odysseus came along after. The pig herder brought him
dressed in vile clothes, like a miserable beggar, an old man
leaning on a staff. He wore wretched clothes about his flesh,
and not any one of us knew who he was, so suddenly returned.
We attacked him with evil words and threw things at him.
150   But he endured in his own house with a steadfast heart, although
he was struck and insulted.

                "But when the mind of Zeus who carries
the goatskin fetish roused him, he with the help of Telemachos
took up all the beautiful armor and laid them away in the storeroom,
and he locked the bolts.° Then in his great cunning he urged
155   his wife to set up his bow and the gray iron to be a contest
for us ill-fated men, the beginning of our destruction.°

    "No one of us was able to string the powerful bow—we didn't
even come close! But when the great bow came into Odysseus'
hands, then we all cried out that the bow not be given
160   to him, no matter what he should say. Telemachos alone urged
him on and told him to take it. When much-enduring godlike
Odysseus had received it in his hand, he easily strung the bow
and shot it through the iron. Then he went to the threshold

---

154   *locked the bolts*: In fact this is not mentioned in Book 19.

156   ...*destruction*: Odysseus did not really conspire with Penelope to set up the contest of the bow, but this is
the way it seems to Amphimedon. Also, there was a lapse of time between the finishing of the shroud and
the return of Odysseus, but to Amphimedon they seemed to happen at the same time.

FIGURE 24.2 **Penelope at her loom with Telemachos.** Telemachos stands to the left holding two spears, reproaching his mother. She sits mournfully on a chair, head bowed and legs crossed in a pose canonical for Penelope. The partially completed weaving shows a border of two winged horses (Pegasos?), a winged god (Hermes?), and a winged sphinx. Athenian red-figure cup, by the Penelope Painter, c. 440 BC.

and stood there, and he broadcast the swift arrows before him,
165 looking around with a terrible stare. Then he hit chief
Antinoös, and he shot his arrows, rife with groaning, at the others,
taking careful aim. And they fell thick and fast. Then it was clear
that some god was their helper, for right away rushing through
the house they killed men left and right in their rage. And an awful
170 moaning arose as heads were smashed, and all the floor ran
with blood.

      "And so, Agamemnon, we died, and even now
our bodies lie uncared for in the halls of Odysseus. For our friends
in every man's home know nothing of this, those who might wash
the black blood from our wounds and lay out our bodies with wailing.
175 For that is the gift due the dead."

                  Then the breath-soul of the son
of Atreus spoke: "O happy son of Laërtes, much-devising
Odysseus! Truly, *you* got a wife of great goodness! How good
were the brains in blameless Penelope, the daughter of Ikarios,
that she never forgot Odysseus, her wedded husband! The fame
180 of her virtue will never die. The deathless ones will fashion for men
on earth a pleasing song about the faithful Penelope.° Not like
that did the daughter of Tyndareus° fashion her own evil deeds—
killing her wedded husband! The song about *her* will be hateful
among men! Why, she brings a bad reputation to all womankind,
185 even on her who does the right thing."

             And so they spoke to one
another in this fashion, standing in the house of Hades
beneath the depths of earth.

           As for Odysseus and his men, when
they went down from the city, they came quickly to the beautiful
farm worked by Laërtes, which once Laërtes had won for himself,
190 and much had he labored upon it. There was his house.
Huts ran all the around it in which the slaves ate and sat
and slept, those who did his bidding. Among them was an old
Sicilian woman who took kindly care of the old man there
at the farm, far from the city.

---

181 *Penelope*: Like the *Odyssey*.
182 *Tyndareus*: Klytaimnestra.

Odysseus spoke to the slaves,
and his son: "You now, go inside the well-built house. Quickly   195
butcher the best of the pigs for dinner. In the meanwhile I will
put my father to the test, to see if he recognizes me and knows
me by sight, or whether he does not recognize me because I have
been gone such a long time."

So saying he gave his battle armor
to the slaves. They went swiftly into the house, and Odysseus   200
went near the fruitful orchard in his search. He did not find Dolios
as he went down into the great orchard, nor did he find
any of Dolios' slaves, nor his children. They had gone off
to gather stones for a wall around the vineyard, and Dolios
was their leader.   205

Then Odysseus found Laërtes in the well-tended
garden, digging around a plant. He was dressed in a rotten
shirt—patched, unsuitable!—and around his shins he had tied
stitched oxhide shin guards to ward against scratches.
He had put gloves on his hands to protect him from brambles,
and he wore a goatskin cap on his head, nourishing his sorrow.   210

When the much-enduring godlike Odysseus saw Laërtes, worn
out with old age, he stood beneath a tall pear tree and with great
sorrow in his heart poured down tears. Then he debated
in his mind and heart whether he should kiss and embrace his father,
and tell him everything—how he came back to his native land—   215
or whether he should first question him and put him to the test
on every matter. As he thought about this, this seemed to him
to be the better course—first to test his father with mocking words.°

With this in mind, the godlike Odysseus went straight to his father.
Laërtes kept his head down—he was working the soil around   220
a plant. His glorious son stood beside him and said: "Old man,
I don't think that you lack skill in tending a garden. Your care
is good, nor does any plant—not a fig, a vine, an olive, a pear tree,
nor any garden-plot in all the field—lack for care. But I will
tell you something else, and do not become angry—you yourself   225
receive no good care! Why, you bear a gloomy old age and you

---

218   *mocking words*: It is not clear what Homer means by this and many have complained about what appears
     needless cruelty toward Laërtes. But Homer's narrative is driven by a deep pattern: Odysseus always "tests"
     the principal figure of the episode, then reveals his true identity, whether this be Cyclops, Kirkê, the suit-
     ors, Penelope, or Laërtes.

live in this wretched squalor, and you dress in foul clothes!
Not because of your idleness does your master not take care
of you, nor do you look like a slave in stature or form—
230   you look like a king! Like one who, when he has bathed
and eaten, sleeps in a soft bed. For this is the way of old men.

"But come, tell me this, and tell it straight out: Whose slave
are you? Whose orchard do you care for? Tell me this truly
so that I may know full well, if truly we have come to Ithaca,
235   as a man I just met told me as I came here. But he didn't
show himself very obliging. He did not condescend to tell
me of each thing, nor did he listen to me when I questioned
him about a guest-friend of mine, whether he was still alive,
or whether he had died and gone to the house of Hades.

240   "I will tell you right out, so please pay attention and listen:
I once befriended a man in my own native land who came
to our house, and never did any man of strangers from a far
country come as a more welcome guest-friend. He said he was
an Ithacan, that Laërtes the son of Arkeisios was his father.

245   "Well, I took him to my house, and I entertained him
with kindly welcome from the rich store within the house,
and I gave him gift-tokens, as is appropriate. I gave him seven
talents of gold and a wine-mixing bowl made all of silver,
embossed with flowers, and twelve cloaks with a single fold,
250   and as many coverlets, and as many beautiful cloaks, and as many
shirts on top of those, and four very fine-looking women skilled
in fine handiwork, whom he himself chose."

                                                    Then his father
answered him, pouring down tears: "Stranger, truly you
have come to the land that you ask about. Violent and reckless
255   men are in control of it. I'm afraid that you gave all those gifts
for nothing, the countless gifts that you gave. But if you had
found Odysseus alive in the land of Ithaca, he would have sent
you on your way after reciprocating with many gifts and fine
entertainment. That is only right for him who began the kindness!

260   "But come tell me this, and tell it truly—how many years
has it been since you entertained that man, your unfortunate
guest-friend, my own son—if in fact he ever existed!—
Fated to bad luck! Either fish ate him on the sea, far from his friends

and the land of his fathers, or he became prey to wild animals
and birds on the land. Nor did his mother weep over him   265
after preparing him for burial, nor his father—those who gave
birth to him. Nor did his wife, who was courted with many gifts—
the judicious Penelope—bewail her husband on his bier, closing
his eyes, as is appropriate. For that is the gift due the dead.

   "And now tell me this truly, so that I may know: 270
Who are you among men? Where is your city and your parents?
Where have you moored your swift ship, the one that brought
you and your godlike companions here? Or did you come
as a passenger on someone else's ship, who put you out
and then went on?"   275

       The cunning Odysseus then answered him:
"I will tell you everything exactly. I am from Alybas,
where I live in a glorious house. I am the son of Apheidas,
son of king Polypemon. But my own name is Eperitos.
Some spirit drove me here from Sikania against my will.°
I moored my ship in the fields far from the city. But as for Odysseus,   280
this is the fifth year since he left from there and departed the land
of my fathers. Luckless man! But the birds were of good omen
for him on the right hand as he left, so I was glad to send him on,
and he was glad to go. Our hearts hoped to meet again
in guest-friendship and to exchange glorious gifts."   285

             So he spoke,
and a dark cloud of anguish descended on Laërtes. Taking black
dust in both his hands, he poured it out over his gray hair,
groaning deeply. But Odysseus' heart was stirred, and a bitter pain
shot up through his nostrils as he looked on his father.

   Then Odysseus sprang forward and embraced him and kissed   290
him and said: "That man, about whom you ask, dear father, is me—
come in the twentieth year of absence to my native land!
But restrain your wailing and your tears. I will tell you something,
though haste is of the essence: I have killed the suitors in our house,
taking revenge for their insolence and their evil deeds!"   295

---

279 ... *my will*: The improvised names in this false story suggest riches, though Laërtes does not pick up on the
    meaning of the names: *Alybas* is probably the same as Alybê, a source of silver (*Il.* Book 2); *Apheidas*, is
    "unsparing" (that is, generous); *Polypemon*, "one who has suffered much" (to obtain his riches); *Eperitos*,
    "the chosen one." *Sikania* is Sicily.

FIGURE 24.3 Odysseus and his father Laërtes. Odysseus, wearing his felt traveler's cap, lovingly embraces his father. Fragment from a marble sarcophagus, 2nd century AD.

Laërtes answered him and said: "If surely you have come
as Odysseus, my son—give me a clear sign now so that I can
be persuaded."

And the cunning Odysseus said in reply: "Well, first
take a look at this scar, which a boar gave me with his white tusk
on PARNASSOS when I went there. You and my honored mother   300
sent me there to Autolykos, my mother's father, so that I could
claim gifts that he had promised and agreed to give me when
he came here. And come, I will tell you the trees which once you
gave to me in the well-ordered garden, and I while just a child
was asking you about every single thing as I followed you through   305
the garden. We came past these very trees, and you named every
one of them and told me about each one. You gave me thirteen
pear trees and ten apple trees and forty fig trees. And you promised
to give me fifty rows of vines that ripen at different times.
And on them are clusters of all kinds, whenever the seasons   310
of Zeus weigh them down from above."

So he spoke, and Laërtes'
knees were loosened beneath him and his heart melted
when he recognized the sure signs that Odysseus told him.
He threw his powerful arms around his dear son, and godlike,
much-enduring Odysseus caught him as he fainted.   315

But when he revived and his spirit was gathered again into
his breast, immediately Laërtes spoke in reply: "Father Zeus,
truly the gods are at home in high Olympos, if in reality the suitors
have paid the price for their crass insolence. But now I fear terribly
in my heart that soon all the Ithacans will assemble here against   320
us and that they will send messengers everywhere to the cities
of the Kephallenians."

The resourceful Odysseus said to him in reply:
"Courage! Don't worry about any of this. But let us go to the house,
which lies close to the orchard. I sent Telemachos ahead,
and the cow herder and the pig herder, to prepare a dinner   325
as soon as possible."

When they had spoken to one another,
they went to the beautiful house. When they came to that good
house, they found Telemachos and the cow herder and the pig
herder cutting up the abundant meat and mixing the flaming wine.
Meanwhile the Sicilian attendant washed great-hearted Laërtes   330

in his house and anointed him with olive oil, and around him
they cast a beautiful cloak. And Athena, standing nearby, filled out
the limbs of the shepherd of the people, and she made him taller
and stouter to look upon.

He got out of the bath. His son stared
335   with amazement when he saw him up close—like the deathless gods!—
and he spoke words that went like arrows: "Father, surely someone
of the gods that live forever have made you greater in size
and stature to look upon."

The sensible Laërtes spoke to him:
"I only wish, O father Zeus and Athena and Apollo, that I were
340   such as I was when I captured Nerikos,° the well built citadel,
on a promontory of the mainland, when I was king of the Kephallenians!
And I wish that I had stood yesterday in our house, wearing armor
on my shoulders—stood with you as you beat back the suitors.
Then I would have loosened the knees of many in the halls, and you
345   would have rejoiced in your heart."

So they spoke to one another
in this fashion. When everyone had ceased from his labor and made
ready the meal, they all sat down in a row in the seats and chairs.
They were about to set their hands to the food when the old man
Dolios drew near, and with him were the sons of that old man,
350   tired from their work in the fields. Their mother, the old Sicilian
woman, had gone out and called them in, she who nourished them
and took care of the old man in a kindly fashion, now that old age
had taken hold of him.

When Dolios and his sons saw Odysseus,
and appreciated what this meant, they stood amazed in the halls,
355   and Odysseus, speaking gentle words, said: "Old man, sit down
and eat. Give up your wonder. Long have we waited in the halls,
eager to set our hands to the food, expecting you to come at any time."

So he spoke, and Dolios went straight to Odysseus with both hands
outstretched, and he took Odysseus' hand and kissed it on the wrist,
360   and he spoke words that went like arrows: "My beloved master—
at last you have returned to us who longed greatly for you,
but thought that we would never see you again! And now the gods

---

340 *Nerikos*: It is not clear where this is.

themselves have brought you here. Hail to you, and greetings!
May the gods grant you happiness! But tell me this truly so that
I may know—does the judicious Penelope know that you have   365
returned, or shall we send a messenger?"

                                  The resourceful Odysseus
then answered him: "Old man, she knows already. Why be busy
with this?"

       So he spoke, and Dolios sat down immediately
on a polished stool. In a similar way the sons of Dolios gathered
around great Odysseus, and they greeted him with words   370
and clasped his hands. Then they sat down in a row beside Dolios,
their father. So they were busy with the meal in the halls.

       Meanwhile, Rumor, the messenger, went swiftly everywhere
through the city, telling of the awful death and fate of the suitors.
The people heard it all at once and gathered from every corner,   375
with moaning and groans, in front of Odysseus' house. Each carried
his own dead from the house, and they buried the corpses. Those
who had come from other cities, they sent to their homes, placing
them on swift ships for seamen to carry. They themselves then
gathered into the place of assembly, sad at heart.   380

                                  And when they
were gathered and assembled into a group, Eupeithes° stood up
and spoke to them. For a violent grief lay upon his heart for Antinoös,
the first man that godlike Odysseus had killed. Weeping for him,
he spoke and addressed the assembly: "My friends, truly this man
has contrived a monstrous deed against the Achaeans. Some he led   385
forth in his ships, many men and noble, but he has lost his hollow
ships and he has destroyed his people, and others he has killed—
by far the best of the Kephallenians—when he came back. So come,
before this man gets quickly to PYLOS, or to shining ELIS where
the Epeians are strong. Let us go, or in times to come we will   390
be covered in shame! For this is a disgrace for men to learn
who are yet to be—if we do not take revenge for the deaths
of our children and brothers. At least for me life would no longer
be a sweet thing, for I would rather die at once and be among
the dead. Let us go then, before Odysseus and his men get away   395
from us and cross over the sea!"

---

381   *Eupeithes*: "easily persuading," aptly named, the father of Antinoös, who appears here for the first time.

So he spoke, pouring down tears.
And pity seized all the Achaeans. Then Medon the herald came up
in their midst, and the godlike singer from the house of Odysseus,
when sleep had released them.° They took their stand in their midst,
400 and those around were astounded to see them. Medon, a wise
man, spoke to them: "Now listen to me, Ithacans—Odysseus did not
perform these deeds without the help of the gods! I myself saw
an immortal god, who stood next to Odysseus in the likeness
of Mentor. First he would appear as an immortal god, egging
405 him on, and then he would charge through the hall striking terror
into the hearts of the suitors. They fell thick and fast!"°

So he spoke,
and a green fear took hold of everyone. Then among them spoke
Lord Halitherses,° the old man, the son of Mastor. He alone saw
before and behind. With the best of intentions he spoke and addressed
410 them: "Through *your own* wickedness, my friends, these things have
come to pass! You would not believe me! Nor would you believe
Mentor, shepherd of the people, that you should stop your sons
from their craziness.° Instead they performed a monstrous deed
in the viciousness of their folly, wasting away someone's possessions
415 and disrespecting the wife of an excellent man. They said he would
never return! And now it has happened. Believe what I say: Let us
not go off, so that no one find an evil that he has brought on himself."°

So he spoke. But they leapt up with loud cries, more than half
of them. The others remained seated together. For Halitherses'
420 word was not pleasing to their hearts—and so they followed
Eupeithes. Quickly then they put on their armor. When they had
placed the gleaming bronze about their flesh, they gathered
in a group in front of the city with wide dancing-places. Eupeithes
in his foolishness was their leader. He thought that he would avenge

---

399   *released them*: The herald and the singer seem to have taken a nap after the slaughter!

406   *thick and fast*: The differences between Medon's descriptions of Athena's intervention and the poet's are small, arising from Medon's desire to show that divine interference was decisive in Odysseus' victory.

408   *Halitherses*: Perhaps "sea-bold," he was introduced in Book 2 when he predicted that Odysseus would soon return. At first the gathering in the place of assembly has appeared to consist of the families of the dead suitors, but now it seems to include the Ithacan populace.

413   *...craziness*: Mentor, whose form Athena takes to accompany Telemachos on his journey and to aid Odysseus in the slaughter of the suitors, appears only once in the *Odyssey* in his own person: in Book 2 when he advises the suitors to give up their depredations.

417   *on himself*: A central Odyssean theme, that some of the misfortunes that befall a man are fated, but some he brings on himself. Zeus makes this point in Book 1.

the death of his son, yet he himself would not return home—   425
for he would meet his fate now.

But Athena spoke to Zeus the son
of Kronos: "Father of us all, son of Kronos, highest of rulers,
tell me when I ask: What purpose do you hide within? Will you
rather make evil war and the dread din of battle, or will you
establish friendship between the two parties?"   430

Cloud-gathering Zeus
then said in reply: "My child, why do you ask and inquire about
these matters? Was this not your plan all along? that Odysseus
should return and take vengeance on these men? Do what you
want, but I will speak as seems right to me. Now that godlike
Odysseus has taken his revenge on the suitors, let them swear   435
a solemn oath, and let him be chieftain for all his days.
And let us for our part bring about a forgetting of the death of their sons
and brothers. Let them love one another as before, and let there
be wealth, and let peace abound."

So speaking he roused up Athena,
who was already eager, and she went down in a rush from the peaks   440
of Olympos.

Now when Odysseus and his companions had put
aside the desire for honey-sweet food, the much-enduring godlike
Odysseus began to speak: "Let somebody go out and see
if they are coming near." So he spoke, and a son of Dolios went out,
just as he commanded. He went to the threshold and stood,   445
and he saw the suitors' kin coming near.

Quickly he spoke words
to Odysseus that went like arrows: "They are close by. Let us arm
quickly!" So he spoke, and they rose up and put on their armor.
Odysseus and his men were four,° and there were the six sons
of Dolios. Among them, too, Laërtes and Dolios, although advanced   450
in age, also put on armor, forced now to fight. And when they
put the shining armor about their flesh, they opened the doors
and went forth. Odysseus was in the lead. And Athena, the daughter
of Zeus, came near to them in the likeness of Mentor, both
in form and voice.   455

---

449 *four*: Odysseus, Telemachos, and the two herders.

The much-enduring godlike Odysseus rejoiced
when he saw her, and right away he spoke to Telemachos, his dear
son: "Telemachos, now you will learn, when you have come
to where the best men are tested in battle, how not to bring
disgrace on the race of your fathers who in earlier times were
460   superior in strength and courage over the entire earth."

                                           The sensible
Telemachos then replied: "You will see, if you want, dear father,
that in my present state of mind I will bring no disgrace on your house,
just as you say!"

      So he spoke, and Laërtes was glad and he said:
"What a day this is for me. Dear gods! I am so glad! My son
465   and my son's son compete with one another in valor!"

      Standing beside him the flashing-eyed Athena said:
"Son of Arkeisios, by far the dearest of all my companions,
make a prayer to the flashing-eyed virgin and to Zeus the father,
then brandish your long-shadowed spear right away, and hurl it."

470   So spoke Pallas Athena and breathed great strength into him.
Then Laërtes made the prayer to the daughter of great Zeus,
and right away he brandished his long-shadowed spear, then hurled it.
He struck Eupeithes on his helmet with bronze cheek pieces.
The helmet did not stop the spear, but the bronze went straight
475   through. Eupeithes made a thud when he hit the ground
and his armor clanged about him.

                       Then Odysseus and his glorious
troop fell on the foremost fighters. They stabbed with their swords
and their spears, sharp at both ends. And surely now they would
have destroyed all of them and taken away their day of return,
480   if Athena, the daughter of Zeus who carries the goatskin fetish,
had not shouted out and put a stop to the people: "Hold off
from savage war, O Ithacans, so that you may be separated
as quickly as possible without bloodshed!"

                    So spoke Athena,
and a green fear took hold of them. When the goddess spoke,
485   then all of their arms flew from their hands and fell to the ground.
They turned toward the city, longing for life. Then much-enduring
godlike Odysseus cried out terribly as he gathered himself
together and swept on them like a high-flying eagle.

And then the son of Kronos threw down his flaming bolt
of thunder, and it fell at the feet of the flashing-eyed daughter   490
with the mighty father. The flashing-eyed Athena said to Odysseus:
"Son of Laërtes, nourished by Zeus, resourceful Odysseus—cease!
Stop this quarrel of leveling war, or Zeus, the son of Kronos,
whose voice is heard from a long ways off, will grow angry."

So spoke Athena, and he believed her, and he rejoiced   495
in his heart. Pallas Athena, the daughter of Zeus who carries
the goatskin fetish, appearing in the likeness of Mentor in form
and voice, drew solemn oaths for all time from both parties.

Bibliography

GENERAL WORKS ON HOMER

F. A. Wolf, *Prolegomena ad Homerum* (Halle, 1795; English translation, Princeton, NJ, 1985)

A. J. B. Wace and F. H. Stubbings, *A Companion to Homer* (London, 1962)

G. S. Kirk, *The Songs of Homer* (Cambridge, UK, 1962)

A. Heubeck, *Die homerische Frage* (Darmstadt, 1974)

I. Morris and B. B. Powell, *A New Companion to Homer* (Leiden, 1997)

J. Latacz, *Troy and Homer: Towards a Solution of an Old Mystery* (Oxford, 2004)

R. Fowler (ed.), *The Cambridge Companion to Homer* (Cambridge, UK, 2004)

B. B. Powell, *Homer* (2d ed., Malden/Oxford, 2007)

M. Finkelberg, *The Homer Encyclopedia* (Malden/Oxford, 2011)

TEXT AND TRANSMISSION

T. W. Allen, *Homer: The Origins and Transmission* (Oxford, 1924)

J. A. Davison, "The Transmission of the Text," in A. J. B. Wace and F. H. Stubbings, *A Companion to Homer* (London, 1962), pp. 215–233

M. L. West, *Studies in the Text and Transmission of the Iliad* (Munich, 2001)

HOMER AND ORAL TRADITION

A. B. Lord, *The Singer of Tales* (1960; 2d edition, Cambridge, MA, 2000)

M. Parry (intro. by A. Parry), *The Making of Homeric Verse* (Oxford, 1971)

G. S. Kirk, *Homer and the Oral Tradition* (Cambridge, UK, 1976)

E. Bakker, *Poetry in Speech: Orality and Homeric Discourse* (Ithaca, NY, 1997)

J. M. Foley, *Homer's Traditional Art* (University Park, PA, 1999)

W. Ong, *Orality and Literacy: The Technologizing of the Word* (2d edition, New York, 2001)

B. B. Powell, *Writing and the Origins of Greek Literature* (Cambridge, UK, 2003)

HOMER AND THE NEAR EAST

M. L. West, *The East Face of Helicon* (Oxford, 1997)

B. Louden, *The Iliad: Structure, Myth, and Meaning* (Baltimore, 2006)

———, *Homer's Odyssey and the Near East* (Cambridge, 2011)

DATING THE HOMERIC POEMS

R. Janko, *Homer, Hesiod and the Hymns* (Cambridge, 1982)

B. B. Powell, *Homer and the Origin of the Greek Alphabet* (Cambridge, UK, 1991)

The *Iliad*

EDITIONS (*TEXTS IN HOMERIC GREEK*)

Demetrius Chalcondyles, *editio princeps*, Florence, 1488

W. Leaf, *Iliad* (London, 1886–1888; 2d ed. 1900–1902)

D. B. Monro and T. W. Allen, *Homeri Opera* (5 volumes, 2d ed., Oxford, 1912)

H. van Thiel, *Homeri Ilias* (Hildesheim, 1996)

M. L. West, *Homeri Ilias*, 2 volumes (Munich/Leipzig, 1998–2000)

COMMENTARIES

G. S. Kirk (gen. ed.), *The Iliad: A Commentary* (6 vols., Cambridge, 1985–1993)

J. Latacz (gen. ed.), *Homers Ilias. Gesamtkommentar. Auf der Grundlage der Ausgabe von Ameis-Hentze-Cauer* (1868–1913) (6 volumes published so far of an estimated 15, Munich/Leipzig, 2002–)

SELECTED ENGLISH TRANSLATIONS

A. Lang, W. Leaf, E. Myers, *The Iliad* (London, 1883)

S. Butler, *The Iliad* (London, 1898)

A. T. Murray, *Homer: Iliad*, 2 volumes (London, 1924); revised by William F. Wyatt (Cambridge, MA, 1999)

R. Lattimore, *The Iliad* (Chicago, 1951)

R. Fitzgerald, *The Iliad* (New York, 1974)

R. Fagles, *The Iliad* (New York, 1990)

S. Lombardo, *The Iliad* (Indianapolis, 1997)

B. B. Powell, *The Iliad* (New York, 2013)

INFLUENTIAL READINGS AND INTERPRETATIONS

U. von Wilamowitz-Möllendorff, *Die Ilias und Homer* (Berlin, 1916)

J. T. Kakridis, *Homeric Researches* (London, 1949)

J. Griffin, *Homer on Life and Death* (Oxford, 1980)

S. Schein, *The Mortal Hero: An Introduction to Homer's* Iliad (Berkeley, 1984)

M. W. Edwards, *Homer, Poet of the* Iliad (Baltimore, 1987)

The *Odyssey*

EDITIONS (*TEXTS IN HOMERIC GREEK*)

Demetrius Chalcondyles, *editio princeps*, Florence, 1488

William Walter Merry and James Riddell, *Odyssey I–XII* (2nd edition, Oxford, 1886)

D. B. Monro and T. W. Allen, *Homeri Opera* (*Odyssey*, 2nd edition, five volumes, Oxford, 1917–1920: the basis for this translation)

H. van Thiel, *Homeri Odyssey* (Hildesheim, 1991)

P. von der Mühll, *Homeri Odyssea* (Munich/Leipzig, 1993)

COMMENTARY

Heubeck, A., et al. *A Commentary on Homer's* Odyssey, 3 vols. (Oxford, 1988–1992)

SOME ENGLISH TRANSLATIONS

S. Butler, *The Odyssey* (London, 1900)

A. T. Murray, *Homer: Odyssey* (Cambridge, MA/London, 1919); revised by G. Dimock (Cambridge, MA, 1995)

R. Lattimore, *The Odyssey* (Chicago, 1968)

R. Fagles, *The Odyssey* (New York, 1997)

R. Fitzgerald, *The Odyssey* (New York, 1998)

S. Lombardo, *The Odyssey* (Indianapolis, 2000)

B. B. Powell, *The Odyssey* (New York, 2014)

INFLUENTIAL READINGS AND INTERPRETATIONS

U. von Wilamowitz-Möllendorff, *Die Heimkehr Des Odysseus: Neue Homerische Untersuchungen* (Berlin, 1927)

W. J. Woodhouse, *The Composition of Homer's* Odyssey (Oxford, 1930)

E. Auerbach, *Mimesis: The Representation of Reality in Western Literature* (Princeton, NJ, 1953; orig. pub. in German, Bern, 1946), Chapter 1, "Odysseus scar"

A. Thornton, *People and Themes in the* Odyssey (London, 1970)

M. I. Finley, *The World of Odysseus* (New York, 1978)

D. L., Page, *Folktales in Homer's* Odyssey (Cambridge, MA, 1973)

J. S. Clay, *The Wrath of Athena: Gods and Men in the* Odyssey (Princeton, 1983)

W. B. Stanford, *The Ulysses Theme: A Study in Adaptability of the Homeric Hero* (Oxford, 1983)

G. Dimock, *The Unity of the* Odyssey (Amherst, 1989)

H. Bloom, ed., *Homer's* Odyssey (New York, 1996)

Egbert J. Bakker, *The Meaning of Meat and the Structure of the Odyssey* (Cambridge, 2013)

Credits

diameter: 21.7 cm (8 9/16 in.). Henry Lillie Pierce Fund, 99.518. Photograph ©2014 Museum of Fine Arts, Boston.

10.2 SuperStock / SuperStock

11.1 Bibliotheque Nationale de France, Paris; Erich Lessing / Art Resource, NY

11.2 British Museum, London, Great Britain; © The Trustees of the British Museum / Art Resource, NY

11.3 Museo Archeologico Nazionale, Paestum, Italy; Art Resource, NY

12.1 Photographer: Marie-Lan Nguyen / Wikimedia Commons

13.1 Galanis Donation, 1891

16.1 Kunsthistorisches Museum, Vienna, Austria; Erich Lessing / Art Resource, NY

17.1 Museo di S. Martino, Naples, Italy; Erich Lessing / Art Resource, NY

19.1 DeAgostini / DeAgostini

19.2 Museo Archeologico, Chiusi, Italy; Erich Lessing /Art Resource, NY

22.1 bpk, Berlin / Staatliche Museen / Johannes Laurentius / Art Resource, NY

22.2 bpk, Berlin / Staatliche Museen / Johannes Laurentius / Art Resource, NY

23.1 Museo Nazionale Romano (Terme di Diocleziano), Rome; Erich Lessing / Art Resource, NY

24.1 DeAgostini / DeAgostini

24.2 Museo Archeologico, Chiusi, Italy / Erich Lessing / Art Resource, NY

24.3 Museo Barracco, Rome, Italy; Universal Images Group / Art Resource, NY

Index, with Pronounciation Guide and Glossary

I have included names in the text together with a pronunciation guide, except for names where the pronunciation is obvious. I give the meaning of the names, where this is clear; many of the names in Homer are "speaking names," that is, they reveal the role of the character in the narrative and, in many cases, appear to be made up for the occasion. The meaning of many other names is opaque or unknown. I give the number of the Book in which the name appears, together with the page numbers, except for common names such as "Apollo" or "Agamemnon."

A

Abioi (**a**-bi-oi), "devoid of violence;" a nomadic Scythian tribe, (*Il.* 13) 141

Achaeans (a-**kē**-ans), a division of the Greek people; Homer's word for the Greeks at Troy, *passim*

Acheloös (ak-e-**lō**-us), a river in Sipylos south of Troy, (*Il.* 21, 24) 208, 242

Acheron (**ak**-er-on), "sorrowful," river of the underworld, (*Od.* 10) 350

aegis (**ē**-jis), "goat skin," a shield with serpent border used by Athena and Zeus, 18, 304, 391

Aeneas (ē-**nē**-as), son of Aphrodite and Anchises, greatest Trojan fighter after Hector, descended from Tros, ancestor of the Roman people, (*Il.* 5, 11, 16, 20) 63–72, 121, 175, 202

Aetolia (e-**tō**-li-a), district north of the Corinthian Gulf, containing cities of Pleuron and Kalydon, (*Il.* 5, 9, 24) 76, 112, 114, 242

Agamemnon (a-ga-**mem**-non), son of Atreus, brother of Menelaos, leader of Greek forces at Troy, *passim*

Agelaos (a-ge-**lā**-os), son of Damastor, one of the suitors of Penelope, (*Od.* 22) 451, 455, 456, 459

Agenor (a-**jē**-nor), Trojan leader, son of Theano and Antenor, (*Il.* 11, 21) 121, 209–211

Aiaia (ē-**ē**-a), "earthland," island home of Kirkê, (*Od.* 9–12) 319, 339, 354, 371

Aiakos (ē-**a**-kos), son of Zeus, father of Peleus, king of Aegina, (*Il.* 9, 11, 16, 18, 21) 102, 129, 161, 166, 167, 183, 191, 208; (*Od.* 11) 365

Aietes (ē-**ē**-tēz), "man of earth," king of Kolchis in Aia, brother of Kirkê, father of Medea, (*Od.* 10, 12) 339, 373

Aigai (**ē**-jē), where Poseidon had his palace, probably in Achaea in the northwestern Peloponnesus, (*Il.* 13) 141; (*Od.* 5) 295

Aigisthos (ē-**jis**-thos), son of Thyestes, lover of Klytaimnestra, murderer of Agamemnon, killed by Orestes, 5; (*Od.* 1, 4, 11, 24) 252, 253, 260, 261, 278, 280, 361, 475, 478

Aisepos (**ē**-se-pos), a river in the Troad, (*Il.* 4, 12) 53, 132

Aithon (**ē**-thon), name assumed by Odysseus when in disguise on Ithaca, (*Od.* 19) 422

Aithra (**ē**-thra), daughter of Pittheus, king of Troezen, handmaiden to Helen, mother of Theseus, who had sex with Poseidon and her husband on the same night; she became Helen's slave when Helen was abducted from Athens by the Dioscuri, (*Il.* 3) 41

Akamas (**a**-ka-mas), Trojan, son of Agenor, leader of the Dardanians with Aeneas, (*Il.* 11, 16) 121, 172

Akrisios (a-**kris**-i-us), father of Danaë, killed accidentally by Perseus, (*Il.* 14) 152

Alkinoös (al-**kin**-o-us), "strong of mind," king of the Phaeacians, father of Nausicaä, who entertains Odysseus, (*Od.* 6, 8, 9, 11, 13) 299, 303, 306, 307, 309, 315, 317, 319, 360, 384–386

Alkmaon (alk-**mā**-on), an Achaean, son of Thestor, killed by Sarpedon, (*Il.* 12) 138

Alkmenê (alk-**mēn**-ē), daughter of Elektryon, wife of Amphitryon, mother of Herakles, (*Il.* 14) 152

Altes (**al**-tēz), king of the Leleges, lived in Pedasos near Mount Ida, (*Il.* 21, 22) 205, 213

Althaia (al-**thē**-a), daughter of Thestios, wife of King Oineus of Kalydon, mother of Meleager, (*Il.* 9) 114, 115

Amphidamas (am-fi-**dā**-mas), father of the playmate killed by Patroklos, (*Il.* 23) 230

Amphimedon (am-**fim**-i-don), the suitor of Penelope who was a guest-friend to Agamemnon, (*Od.* 22, 24) 456, 457, 479, 480

Amphinomos (am-**fin**-o-mos), the "good" suitor of Penelope, from Doulichion, killed by Telemachos, (*Od.* 22) 450

Amphitritê (am-fi-**trī**-tē), a Nereid, wife of Poseidon, (*Od.* 5, 12) 296, 372, 373

Amphitryon (am-**fit**-ri-on), descendant of Perseus, husband of Alcmena, (*Il.* 5) 70

Anchises (an-**kī**-sēz), prince of Troy, lover of Aphrodite, father of Aeneas, (*Il.* 5) 65–67

Andromachê (an-**drom**-a-kē), wife of Hector, mother of Astyanax, taken captive by Neoptolemos at end of the Trojan War, (*Il.* 6, 21, 22, 24) 79, 88, 89, 91, 93, 204, 224–227, 245

Anteia (an-**tē**-a), daughter of the king of Lycia, wife of Proitos, fell in love with Bellerophon, (*Il.* 6) 81, 83

Antenor (an-**tē**-nor), a Trojan elder (*Il.* 3, 4, 6, 11, 16, 19, 21) 40, 41, 44, 53, 86, 121, 172, 194, 209, 210

Antikleia (an-ti-**klē**-a), daughter of Autolykos, wife of Laërtes, mother of Odysseus, (*Od.* 11) 354, 358

Antilochos (an-**til**-o-kos), son of Nestor of Pylos, a suitor to Helen, (*Il.* 16, 18) 171, 172, 183–185; (*Od.* 4, 5, 11, 24) 269, 284, 363, 475, 478

Antinoös (an-**tin**-o-os), "wrong-thinker," leader of the suitors in Odysseus palace, (*Od.* 1, 17, 21, 22, 24) 263, 411–415, 437–440, 442, 443, 448, 449, 482, 489

aoidos (a-**oi**-dos, pl. *aoidoi*), Greek word for such oral poets as Homer and Hesiod 102

Arcadia (ar-**kād**-i-a), mountainous region in the central Peloponnesus, (*Od.* 6) 302

Aretê (ar-**ē**-tē), queen of the Phaeacians, mother of Nausicaä, (*Od.* 8, 11, 13) 311, 359, 360, 385, 386

Ares (**air**-ēz), Greek god of war, *passim*

Argeïphontes (ar-jē-i-**fon**-tēz), "Argus-killer," epithet of Hermes, (*Il.* 16) 167; (*Od.* 1, 5, 8, 10, 24) 252, 254, 283, 285, 287, 314, 344, 345, 479

Argive (**ar**-jīv), a word to designate the Greeks at Troy (in addition to Achaean and Danaân), *passim*

Argonauts (**arg**-o-notz), Jason and his companions on the *Argo*, (*Od.* 5) 294

Askalaphos (as-kal-**ā**-fos), "owl," a son of Ares and one of the leaders of the Orchomenos contingent, killed by Deïphobos (*Il.* 13, 16) 144, 175

Astyanax (as-**tī**-a-naks), "king of the city," son of Hector and Andromachê, known as Skamandrios to his parents, (*Il.* 6, 22, 24) 89, 92, 227, 245

atê (**ā**-tā), "madness, delusion, blindness," which clouds the minds of gods and men, 112, 278, 470

Atreus (**ā**-trūs), king of Mycenae, son of Pelops, brother of Thyestes, father of Agamemnon and Menelaos, *passim*

Attica (**at**-ti-ka), region in central Greece where Athens is located, (*Il.* 3) 41

Autolykos (ow-**tol**-i-kos), "true wolf," rogue and thief, son of Hermes, father of Antiklea, grandfather of Odysseus, (*Od.* 11, 19, 21, 24) 354, 427–429, 436, 441, 487

Automedon (ow-**tom**-i-don), "self-ruler," the charioteer of Patroklos and Achilles, (*Il.* 9, 16, 19, 24) 103, 166, 168, 170, 176, 179, 183, 198, 237, 241, 242

B

Bellerophon (bel-**ler**-o-fon), Corinthian hero, grandson of Sisyphos, tamed Pegasus and killed the Chimaira, (*Il.* 6, 16) 81–84, 172; (*Od.* 1) 259

Boeotia (bē-**ō**-sha), "cow-land," region north of Attica, where Thebes was situated, (*Il.* 9, 16) 108, 172

Boötes (bo-**ō**-tēz), "plowman," a constellation, (*Od.* 5) 290

Briareos (bri-**ar**-e-os), one of the Hecatonchires, the "Hundredhanders," who came to Zeus's aid when other gods wished to bind him, (*Il.* 1) 24

Briseis (brī-**sē**-is), Achilles' war-captive, taken by Agamemnon, (*Il.* 1, 6, 9, 20, 24) 15, 16, 21, 22, 24, 89, 112, 195, 201, 244

C

caduceus (ka-**dū**-se-us), a wand with two intertwined snakes, carried by Hermes, (*Il.* 16) 178; (*Od.* 5) 284

Centaurs (**sen**-towrs), savage creatures of the mountains, (*Il.* 1, 4, 6, 11, 14, 21) 19, 58, 83, 131, 152; (*Od.* 1, 4, 6, 11, 14, 21) 443

Charites (**kar**-i-tes), the Graces, imparters of feminine charm, (*Il.* 14) 149

Charybdis (ka-**rib**-dis), dangerous whirlpool, opposite Skylla, said to be in the Straits of Messina, 6; (*Od.* 12) 373, 374, 378, 382

Cheiron (**kī**-ron), "hand," the wise Centaur, the most just of the Centaurs, (*Il.* 4, 9, 11, 16) 58, 110, 130, 131, 166

Chimaira (ki-**mēr**-a), "she-goat," offspring of Typhoeus and Echidna, with a lion's body, snake's tail, and goat's head protruding from the back, killed by Bellerophon, (*Il.* 6, 16) 82, 83, 172

Chryseïs (krī-**sē**-is), daughter of Chryses, given as booty to Agamemnon, (*Il.* 1, 6, 9, 16) 15, 16, 20, 23–25, 89, 102, 166

Chryses (**krī**-sēz), father of Chryseïs, a priest of Apollo whom Agamemnon insulted, (*Il.* 1) 11, 12, 14, 15, 23, 25

Chrysothemis (kri-**so**-the-mis), a daughter of Agamemnon and Klytaimnestra, (*Il.* 9) 106

Cimmerians (si-**mer**-i-anz), live across the river Ocean, where Odysseus summons the spirits of the dead, (*Od.* 11) 352, 363

Corcyra (kor-**sīr**-a), modern Corfu, an island off the northwest coast of Greece, identified with Phaeacia in the *Odyssey*, (*Od.* 6) 299

Corinth (**kor**-inth), city on isthmus between central Greece and the Peloponnesus, (*Il.* 6, 9, 14) 81, 109, 152; (*Od.* 1, 11) 259, 369

Cyclades (**sik**-la-dēz), "circle islands," around Delos in the Aegean Sea, (*Od.* 4–6) 278, 286, 303

Cyclops (**sī**-klops), "round-eyed," rude one-eyed giant Polyphemos whom Odysseus blinded, (*Od.* 1, 6, 9, 10, 12, 13, 24) *passim*

Cythera (**sith**-e-ra), island south of the Peloponnesus, sometimes said to be the birthplace of Aphrodite, (*Il.* 14) 152; (*Od.* 8, 9) 311, 321

D

Danaäns (**dān**-a-anz), descendants of Danaös, one of Homer's name for the Greeks, *passim*

Danaë (**dān**-a-ē), daughter of Akrisios, mother of Perseus, whom Zeus possessed, (*Il.* 14) 152

Dardanelles (= Hellespont), straits between the Aegean Sea and the Propontis (= Sea of Marmora), 2

Dardanos (**dar**-da-nos), early king of Troy, son of Zeus, father of Erichthonios, grandfather of Tros, after whom the Trojans were called Dardanians, (*Il.* 11, 24) 124, 242

Deïphobos (dē-**if**-o-bos), brother of Hector and Paris (who took up with Helen after Paris' death), (*Il.* 22) 218, 220; (*Od.* 4, 8) 271, 317

Delos (**dē**-los), "clear," tiny island in the center of the Cyclades, where there was a cult of Apollo and Artemis, who were born there, (*Il.* 14) 152; (*Od.* 5, 6) 286, 303

Delphi (**del**-fī), sanctuary of Apollo at foot of Mount Parnassus, (*Il.* 6, 9) 91, 109; (*Od.* 11, 19) 367, 427

Demeter (de-**mēt**-er), daughter of Kronos and Rhea, mother of Persephone, goddess of the grain harvest, (*Il.* 14, 21) 152, 205; (*Od.* 5) 286

Deukalion (dū-**kāl**-i-on), son of Minos, father of Idomeneus, king of Crete, and of Odysseus in one of his false tales, (*Od.* 19) 422

Diokles (**dī**-o-klēz), rich king of Messenian Pherai, whose sons Ortilochos and Krethos were killed by Aeneas in the *Iliad*, (*Od.* 21) 435

Diomedê (dī-o-**mē**-dē), a daughter of the king of Lesbos, a war-captive and concubine of Achilles, (*Il.* 9) 117

Diomedes (dī-ō-**mēd**-ēz), son of Tydeus (who fought in the Seven Against Thebes), a principal Greek warrior at Troy, (*Il.* 4–6, 8, 9, 11, 14, 16, 19) *passim*; (*Od.* 4) 271

Dionê (dī-**ō**-nē), feminine form of "Zeus," a consort of Zeus, mother of Aphrodite, (*Il.* 5) 70–72

Dioscuri (dī-os-**kūr**-ī), "sons of Zeus" and Leda, Kastor and Polydeukes, brothers of Helen, (*Il.* 3) 41, 45

Dmetor (d-**mē**-tor), "subduer," a king of Cyprus mentioned by Odysseus in a lying tale (*Od.* 17) 413

Dodona (do-**dōn**-a), site of oracular shrine of Zeus in northwestern Greece, 70; (*Il.* 16) 169; (*Od.* 19) 425

E

Eëtion (ē-**et**-i-on), (1) father of Andromachê (*Il.* 1, 6, 9, 16) 23, 89, 90, 102, 166, 225, 227; (2) of Imbros, guest-friend of Priam, ransomed Lykaon, (*Il.* 21, 22) 204, 205

Eidothea (ē-**do**-the-a), "the knowing goddess," daughter of Proteus, the Old Man of the Sea, (*Od.* 4) 274, 276

Eileithyia (ē-lē-**thī**-ya), "she who makes one come," goddess of childbirth, (*Il.* 16) 167; (*Od.* 19) 422

Elatos (**el**-a-tos), one of the suitors, (*Od.* 22) 457

Elpenor (el-**pēn**-or), companion of Odysseus who died after falling from Kirkê's roof, (*Od.* 11, 12) 353–355, 371

Emathia (e-**math**-i-a), "sandy," the same as Macedonia, (*Il.* 14) 148

Enopê (**en**-o-pē), one of the seven towns that Agamemnon offers Achilles if he will return to the fight, (*Il.* 9) 106

Enyalios (en-**yal**-i-os), a name for Ares (*Il.* 5, 22) 67, 215

Epeios (e-**pē**-os), builder of the Trojan Horse, (*Od.* 8, 11) 316, 364

Ephialtes (ef-i-**al**-tēz), a giant who stormed heaven, one of the Aloads; with his brother Otos he imprisoned Ares in a jar, (*Il.* 5) 70

Ephyra (**e**-fir-a), (1) another name for Corinth (*Il.* 6) 81, 84; (2) a city on the Selleïs River in Thresprotia, (*Od.* 1) 259

Erinys (**er**-i-nis), or plural, Erinyes (er-**in**-u-es), the underworld punisher(s) of broken oaths; the fulfillers of a curse, (*Il.* 9) 115

Euboea (yū-**bē**-a), long island east of Attica, site of vigorous Iron Age community where the alphabet seems to have been invented, (*Il.* 9, 14) 117, 151; (*Od.* 4) 278

Eudoros (yū-**dō**-ros), one of the five captains of the Myrmidons led into battle by Patroklos, a son of Hermes, (*Il.* 16) 167, 175

Euenos (yū-**ē**-nos), an Aetolian, father of Marpessa, wooed by Apollo and Idas (*Il.* 9) 114

Eumaios (yū-**mē**-os), "seeker after good," Odysseus' loyal swineherd, (*Od.* 4, 13, 16, 17, 19, 21, 22) *passim*

Euneos (yū-**nē**-os), "good with ships," a king of Lemnos, son of Jason and Hypsipylê, (*Il.* 9, 14, 21) 117, 148, 204

Eupeithes (yū-**pē**-thēz), "good at persuasion," father of the suitor Antinoös, he led an attack against Odysseus and was killed by Laërtes, (*Od.* 1, 17, 21, 24) 263, 414, 439, 442, 489, 490, 492

Euphorbos (yu-**for**-bos), a Trojan, first man to wound Patroklos, (*Il.* 16) 181–183

Europa (yū-**rōp**-a), daughter of Agenor, brother of Kadmos, seduced by Zeus in the form of a bull, mother to Minos, (*Il.* 14) 152; (*Od.* 11) 367

Euryades (yū-ri-**a**-dēz), one of Penelope's suitors, (*Od.* 22) 457

Eurybates (yū-**ri**-ba-tēz), Odysseus' herald, (*Il.* 1, 19) 21; (*Od.* 1, 19) 423

Eurydamas (yū-ri-**dā**-mas), one of Penelope's suitors (*Od.* 22) 457

Eurykleia (yū-ri-**klē**-a), "wide-fame," Odysseus' nurse, who recognized his scar, (*Od.* 1, 19, 21–23) 264, 265, 416, 426, 427, 429, 430, 445, 460, 461–466, 469, 472

Eurylochos (yū-**ril**-o-kos), a comrade and relative of Odysseus, the instigator of disobedience, (*Od.* 10–12) 341–344, 348, 349, 352, 376, 378–380

Eurymachos (yū-**rim**-a-kos), a leading suitor of Penelope, (*Il.* 5) 70; (*Od.* 1, 17, 21, 22) 264, 407, 440, 442, 444, 449, 450

Eurymedon (yū-**rim**-e-don), "wide ruling," (1) Agamemnon's charioteer, (*Il.* 4) 59; (2) Nestor's charioteer, (*Il.* 11) 126

Eurynomos (yū-**rin**-o-mos), suitor of Penelope, (*Od.* 22) 456

Eurypylos (yū-**rip**-i-los), (1) a Thessalian leader, whom Patroklos attended to when wounded (*Il.* 11, 12, 16) 127, 129–132, 161, 164; (2) Eurypylos, a king of Mysia, son of Telephos, (*Od.* 11) 364

Eurytion (yū-**rit**-i-on), a Centaur who drank too much and was mutilated, (*Od.* 21) 443

Eurytos (**yū**-ri-tos), a king of Oichalia, father of Iphitos, a famous bowman, (*Od.* 21) 435, 436

G

Gaia (**ghī**-a), "Earth," sprung from Chaos, consort of Ouranos, mother of the Titans, (*Od.* 11) 367

Ganymede (**gan**-i-mēd), son of Tros, beloved of Zeus, cupbearer of the gods, (*Il.* 5) 64, 65

Glaukos (**glow**-kos), a co-leader of the Lycians, with Sarpedon, (*Il.* 6, 12, 16) 79–84, 134–138, 177

H

Hades (**hā**-dēz), "unseen," lord of the underworld, son of Kronos and Rhea, husband of Persephonê, *passim*

Hebê (**hēb**-ê), "youth," married to Herakles on Olympos, (*Il.* 4, 5) 51, 73, 78; (*Od.* 11) 369

Hekabê (**hek**-a-bē), wife of Priam, queen of Troy, mother of Hector, (*Il.* 6, 15, 22, 24) 86, 91, 156, 214, 218, 224, 246; (*Od.* 8) 317

Hekamedê (hek-a-**mē**-dē), Nestor's maid-servant, (*Il.* 11) 126

Helenos (**hel**-e-nos), Trojan prophet, brother of Hector, 91; (*Il.* 6) 79

Hellê (**hel**-lē), daughter of Athamas and Nephelê, sister of Phrixus, fell from the golden ram into the Hellespont, (*Od.* 5) 294

Hellenes (**hel**-ēnz), at first the inhabitants of Hellas in Thessaly, later all the Greeks, (*Il.* 16) 169

Hemera (**hēm**-er-a), "day," one of the first beings, daughter of Erebus and Nyx, (*Od.* 10) 350

Hephaistos (he-**fēs**-tos), Greek god of smiths, son of Zeus and Hera or Hera alone, *passim*

Hera (**her**-a), "mistress(?)," daughter of Kronos and Rhea, wife and sister of Zeus, *passim*

Hermionê (her-**mī**-o-nē), only daughter of Helen and Menelaos, whose marriage coincided with Telemachos' visit to Sparta, (*Od.* 4) 266

Hesiod (**hēs**-i-od), Greek poet, eighth century BC, composer of *Works and Days* and *Theogony*, 70, 78, 147, 149, 185, 230, 321, 350

Hiketaon (hik-e-**tā**-on), Trojan elder, brother of Priam, (*Il.* 3) 41

Hippolochos (hip-**pol**-o-kos), (1) a Lycian son of Bellerophon, father of Glaukos, (*Il.* 6), 79, 80, 83, 124, 134, 137; (2) a Trojan killed by Agamemnon, (*Il.* 11) 124

Hirê (**hir**-ē), a town in Messenia promised to Achilles if he will return to the fight, (*Il.* 9) 106

Hittites (**hit**-ītz), Indo-European Bronze Age warrior people in central Anatolia, their capital was Hattusas near modern Ankara, 82

Hypereia (hi-per-**ē**-a), "land beyond the horizon," a fanciful name designating a faraway place or the Phaeacians' original home, (*Il.* 6) 91; (*Od.* 6) 299

Hyperion (hī-**per**-ion), "he who travels above," epithet and synonym of Helios, (*Il.* 8, 19) 99, 198; (*Od.* 1, 12) 251, 374, 375, 378, 380, 381

Hypsipylê (hip-**sip**-i-lē), queen of Lemnos, mother of Euneos by Jason, (*Il.* 14, 21) 148, 204

I

Iapetos (i-**ap**-e-tos), a Titan, father of Prometheus, Epimetheus, and Atlas, (*Il.* 8) 99

Iasion (i-**as**-i-on), consort of Demeter, father of Ploutos, (*Od.* 5) 286

Iasos (i-**ā**-sos), father of Dmetor, king of Cyprus, in a lying tale of Odysseus, (*Od.* 17) 413

ichor (**i**-kor), the fluid in the veins of the gods, (*Il.* 5) 69, 71

Ida (**ī**-da), Mount, a mountain near Troy, *passim*

Idaios (i-**dē**-os), Priam's herald, (*Il.* 24) 237

Idas (**ī**-das), brother of Lynceus, an Argonaut who competed with Apollo for Marpessa, (*Il.* 9) 114

Idomeneus (ī-**dom**-i-nūs), grandson of Minos, leader of the Cretan contingent at Troy, (*Il.* 1, 3, 6, 13, 16, 22, 23) 15, 44, 90, 144, 172, 218, 231; (*Od.* 13, 19) 389, 421, 422

Ilos (**ī**-los), (1) early king of Troy, son of Tros, grandfather of Priam; his tomb was a landmark on the plain, (*Il.* 5, 11, 21) 65, 124, 210; (2) of Ephyra, from whom Odysseus tried to obtain poison for his arrows, (*Od.* 1) 259

Ino (**ī**-nō), daughter of Kadmos and Harmonia, sister of Semelê, nurse of Dionysus, wife of Athamas, became Leukothea, (*Od.* 1, 4, 5) 264, 280, 294, 297

Iphianassa (if-i-a-**nas**-a), "powerful queen," one of Agamemnon's three daughters, offered in marriage to Achilles, (*Il.* 9) 106

Iphimedeia (if-i-me-**dē**-a), "mighty mistress," mother by Poseidon of Otos and Ephialtes, (*Il.* 5) 70

Iphis (**ī**-fis), Patroklos' concubine captured by Achilles on Skyros, (*Il.* 9) 117

Iris (**ī**-ris), "rainbow," messenger of Zeus (*Il.* 3, 5, 18, 22–24) 40, 41, 69, 189, 190, 226, 234, 237

Ismaros (**is**-ma-ros), city in Thrace, sacked by Odysseus, (*Od.* 9) 320, 324

Ixion (ik-**sī**-on), a Lapith king, father of the Centaurs, tried to rape Hera, married to the woman (Dia) on whom Zeus fathered Peirithoös, (*Il.* 14) 152

K

Kadmos (**kad**-mos), "man of the East," founder of Thebes, eponym of the Kadmeians, the inhabitants of Thebes, father of Ino (Leukothea), (*Od.* 5) 294

Kalchas (**kal**-kas), prophet of the Greek forces at Troy, (*Il.* 1, 13) 13, 14, 143

Kallikolonê (kal-i-ko-**lō**-nê), "pleasant hill," a landmark on the Trojan plain, (*Il.* 20) 202

Kalydon (**kal**-i-don), main city in Aetolia in southwestern mainland Greece, home of Meleager, site of the Kalydonian Boar Hunt, (*Il.* 9) 112–115

Kalypso (ka-**lip**-so), "concealer," nymph, daughter of Atlas, who kept Odysseus for seven years on her island Ogygia at the navel of the sea, 6; (*Od.* 1, 5) 251, 282, 292

Kapaneus (**kap**-a-nūs), one of the Seven Against Thebes, struck down by Zeus as he climbed its walls, father of Sthenelos, (*Il.* 5) 61

Kastor, "beaver," son of Tyndareos and Leda, brother of Polydeukes, one of the Dioscuri (*Il.* 3, 9) 41, 45, 113

Kaystrios (ka-**is**-tri-os), a river in Asia Minor, (*Il.* 2) 35

Kebriones (keb-ri-**ō**-nēz), half-brother of Hector, one of his charioteers, (*Il.* 16) 180, 181

Kephallenians (kef-al-**ēn**-i-ans), the followers of Odysseus from the Ionian Islands, (*Od.* 24) 487–489

Kinyras (**kin**-i-ras), "lyre-man(?)," a ruler on Cyprus who gave a corselet to Agamemnon as a guest-gift when he heard that the Greeks were planning to sail to Troy, (*Il.* 11) 118

Kirkê (**kir**-kê), daughter of Helios, enchantress who entertained Odysseus for a year on her island, 6; (*Od.* 10) 336, 339, 343, 346

Klymenê (**klī**-me-nê), "famous," (1) one of Helen's lady slaves, (*Il.* 3) 41; (2) one of the thirty-three Nereids who lament Patroklos, (*Il.* 18) 185

Klytaimnestra (klī-tem-**nest**-tra), "famed for her suitors," or "famed for her cunning," daughter of Tyndareos and Leda, sister of Helen, wife of Agamemnon, whom she killed, then was herself killed by Orestes, 5; (*Il.* 1, 11, 24) 14; (*Od.* 1, 11, 24) 253, 261, 361, 362, 482

Knossos (**knos**-sos), principal Bronze Age settlement in Crete, where labyrinthine ruins have been found, where Daidalos built a dancing place for Ariadnê, (*Od.* 19) 421

Kos (kōs), Greek island near Asia Minor, whose contingent was led by grandsons of Herakles, (*Il.* 14, 15, 16) 149, 154, 161

Ktesippos (ktēs-**i**-pos), "horse-acquiring," one of the suitors of Penelope, (*Od.* 22) 457

Kuretes (kur-ē-tēz), "young men," an Aetolian tribe inhabiting Pleuron ten miles west of Kalydon, (*Il.* 9) 112–115

Kyllenê (ki-**lēn**-ê), mountain in Arcadia, where Hermes was born, (*Od.* 24) 475

Kythereia (ki-ther-ē-a), "she of the island of Kythera," another name for Aphrodite, (*Od.* 8) 311

L

Lacedaemon (las-e-**dēm**-on), a valley in the southern Peloponnesus, bounded by Mt. Taygetos in the west and Mt. Parnes in the east, (*Il.* 3–6, 13, 21) 45, 48, 49; (*Od.* 3–6, 13, 21) 273, 282, 302, 394, 395, 435

Laërtes (lā-**er**-tēz), father of Odysseus, husband of Antikleia, (*Od.* 1, 5, 9–13, 16, 17, 19, 21–24)
    passim

Laestrygonians (les-tri-**gōn**-i-anz), cannibal-giants who destroy all Odysseus' ships save one, 6;
    (*Od.* 10) 338, 339

Lamos (**lā**-mos), probably the founder of the Laestrygonian city Telypylos (*Od.* 10) 338

Laodameia (lā-o-da-**mē**-a), daughter of Bellerophon, mother of Sarpedon by Zeus, (*Il.* 6) 83

Laodikê (lā-**o**-di-kē), (1) daughter of Priam and Hekabê, sister of Hector and Paris (*Il.* 3, 6), 40, 85;
    (2) one of the daughters of Agamemnon offered to Achilles in marriage, (*Il.* 9) 106

Laodokos (lā-**o**-do-kos), a Trojan son of Antenor, (*Il.* 4) 53

Laomedon (lā-**om**-e-don), early king of Troy, father of Priam, 100, 118, 282; (*Il.* 5) 65

Laothoê (lā-**oth**-o-ê), a secondary wife of Priam, mother of Polydoros and Lykaon, (*Il.* 21, 22)
    205, 213

Lapiths (**lap**-iths), Thessalian tribe, led by Peirithoös, that defeated the Centaurs, 41, 443

Leiodes (lē-**ō**-dēz), a soothsayer suitor of Penelope, (*Od.* 21, 22) 439, 440, 458, 459

Leiokritos (lē-o-**kri**-tos), an Ithacan suitor of Penelope, killed by Telemachos, (*Od.* 22) 458

Leleges (**le**-le-jēz), allies of the Trojans who lived in Lyrnessos and Pedasos, (*Il.* 21) 205

Leto (**lē**-tō), mother of Apollo and Artemis, supporter of Troy, (*Il.* 1, 5, 14, 16, 19, 20, 24) 11, 12, 72,
    152, 183, 198, 202, 242; (*Od.* 6, 11) 302, 303, 367

Leukothea (lu-**koth**-e-a), "white goddess," a sea-goddess, formerly the mortal Ino, who gave
    Odysseus a magic sash, (*Od.* 5) 294

Lycia (**lish**-a), region in southwest Anatolia, home to the Trojan hero Glaukos, (*Il.* 4–6, 12, 16)
    54, 61, 63, 81–84, 134–138, 172, 175, 176, 179; (*Od.* 5) 293

Lykaon (li-**kā**-on), (1) a son of Priam killed by Achilles in the river, (*Il.* 3, 21, 22) 45, 204–206, 213;
    (2) the father of the Trojan Pandaros, (*Il.* 4, 5) 53, 54, 61, 63–66

Lykomedes (li-ko-**mē**-dēz), a Boeotian warrior, (*Il.* 12) 137

Lykourgos (lī-**kur**-gos), "who keeps wolves at bay," Thracian king, opposed Dionysus, (*Il.* 6) 80

M

Machaon (ma-**kā**-on), son of Asclepius, physician at Troy, wounded by Paris, (*Il.* 4, 5, 11, 16) 58,
    68, 125–127, 131, 161, 175

Maira (**mē**-ra), a Nereid, (*Il.* 18) 185

Marpessa (mar-**pes**-a), beloved of Apollo and Idas, she chose Idas, (*Il.* 9) 114, 117

Medea (me-**dē**-a), witch from Colchis, daughter of Aeëtes, wife of Jason, (*Od.* 1, 10, 12) 259,
    339, 373

Medon (**mē**-dōn), a herald loyal to Odysseus, (*Od.* 13, 16, 22, 24) 389, 402, 459, 460, 490

Medusa (me-**dūs**-a), "[wide]-ruling," one of the three Gorgons, beheaded by Perseus, (*Od.* 11) 370

Meges (**mē**-jēz), leader of the contingent from Doulichion and a leader of the mainland Epeians,
    (*Il.* 16) 171; (*Od.* 1) 259

Melanthios (mel-**an**-thi-os), "blackie," treacherous supporter of the suitors of Penelope, (*Od.* 17, 21,
    22) 406, 407, 411, 440, 442, 451, 454, 455, 462

Meleager (mel-ē-**ā**-jer), "he who cares for the hunt," Aetolian hero, brother of Deaneira, killed
    Kalydonian Boar, (*Il.* 9) 114, 115

Melos (**mē**-los), one of the Cycladic islands, whose population the Athenians destroyed
    in 416 BC, 420

Menelaos (men-e-lā-os), king of Sparta, son of Atreus, husband of Helen, brother of Agamemnon, 5; (*Il.* 1, 3–6, 11, 16, 18) *passim*; (*Od.* 1, 4, 8, 9, 11, 13, 24) 260, 265–271, 273, 281, 317, 321, 362, 394, 479

Menestheus (men-**es**-thūs), leader of Athenians at Troy, (*Il.* 12) 135, 137

Menoitios (men-**ē**-ti-os), son of Aktor, father of Patroklos, (*Il.* 1, 9, 11, 12, 16, 18, 19, 21, 23, 24) *passim*; (*Od.* 24) 478

Meriones (mer-i-**ō**-nēz), an archer, aide to Idomeneus, second in command of the Cretan contingent, (*Il.* 16, 18, 22, 23) 172, 189, 218, 231

Messenia (mes-**sēn**-i-a), territory in the southwest Peloponnesus, (*Od.* 6) 302

Minos (**mī**-nos), Cretan king of Knossos, son of Zeus and Europa, husband of Pasiphaë, judge in the underworld, (*Il.* 14) 152; (*Od.* 11, 19) 367, 421, 422

moly (**mo**-lē), magic herb that protects Odysseus from Kirkê, 6; (*Od.* 10) 344

Mycenae (mī-**sēn**-ē), largest Bronze Age settlement in the Argive plain, home of the house of Atreus, (*Il.* 4, 6, 11) 52, 55, 87, 119, 126; (*Od.* 4, 21) 280, 438

Mynes (**mī**-nēz), king of Lyrnessos, killed by Achilles, (*Il.* 19) 195

Myrmidons (**mir**-mi-dons), "ants," followers of Achilles (*Il.* 1, 9, 11, 16, 18, 19, 21, 23, 24) *passim*; (*Od.* 11) 363

N

Naiads (**nī**-adz), water nymphs, (*Od.* 13) 387, 393

Nausicaä (now-**sik**-a-a), "ship-girl," Phaeacian princess, daughter of Alkinoös and Aretê, who helped Odysseus, (*Od.* 6, 8) 299–302, 304–309, 315

Nausithoös (now-**sith**-o-os), "swift in ships," king of the Phaeacians who ruled before his son Alkinoös, (*Od.* 6, 8) 299, 318

Neaira (ne-**ē**-ra), mother by Helios of two nymphs who cared for the cattle of Helios on Thrinakia, (*Od.* 12) 374

Neleus (**nē**-lūs), son of Poseidon and Tyro, father of Nestor, founder of royal house of Pylos, (*Il.* 2, 11) 31, 125, 127

Neoptolemos (nē-op-**tol**-e-mos), "new-fighter," son of Achilles, also called Pyrrhos, "red," (*Il.* 6, 19, 24) 91, 196, 245; (*Od.* 11) 364

Nereids (**nē**-re-idz), "daughters of Nereus," nymphs of the sea, (*Il.* 18) 185–187, 189

Nereus (**nē**-rūs), son of Pontos and Gaia, wise Old Man of the Sea, (*Il.* 18) 185; (*Od.* 1, 13) 254, 386

Nerikos (**nēr**-i-kos), a city sacked by Laërtes when he was young, (*Od.* 24) 488

Niobê (**nī**-o-bē), daughter of Tantalos, wife of Amphion, whose sons and daughters were killed by Artemis and Apollo, (*Il.* 24) 241, 242

Nysa (**nī**-sa), mythical land that received the infant Dionysus, (*Il.* 6) 80

Nyx (nux), "night," sprung from Chaos, (*Od.* 10) 350

O

Ogygia (ō-**gij**-ya), Kalypso's island, (*Od.* 1, 6, 12) 254, 303, 383

Oichalia (ē-**kāl**-i-a), a city variously located, over which Eurytos ruled, (*Od.* 21) 436

Oïleus (o-ī-lūs) (1) father of Little Ajax, king of Locris, 278, 363; (*Il.* 6, 12, 16) 122, 137, 172; (2) a Trojan killed by Agamemnon, (*Il.* 11) 90

Opoeis (**op**-o-ēs), principal city in Locris, birthplace of Patroklos, (*Il.* 23) 230

Orchomenos (or-**kom**-en-os), major Bronze Age site in northern Boeotia, (*Il.* 9) 108; (*Od.* 11) 362

Orestes (or-**es**-tēz), son of Agamemnon and Klytaimnestra, who killed his mother and her lover Aigisthos to avenge his father, (*Il.* 9) 106; (*Od.* 4, 11) 252, 260, 261, 280, 362

Orion (ō-**rī**-on), a hunter, lover of Dawn, turned into a constellation, (*Il.* 5, 22) 61, 213; (*Od.* 5, 11) 286, 290, 367

Orsilochos (or-**sil**-o-kos), "well-skilled in the ambush," Odysseus killed him in one of his fictitious tales, (*Od.* 13) 389, 390

Ortilochos (or-**til**-o-kos), king of Pherai in Messenia, (*Od.* 21) 435

Ortygia (or-**tij**-ya), "quail island," where the sun turns and Artemis killed Orion, equated in classical time with Delos, birthplace of Apollo and Artemis, (*Od.* 5) 286

Otos (ō-tos), gigantic brother of Ephialtes who attempted to pile Olympos and Pelion on Ossa in order to reach heaven, (*Il.* 5) 70

Oukalegon (ou-**ka**-le-gon), "not-caring," one of the Trojan elders, (*Il.* 3) 41

Ouranos (**ou**-ra-nos), "sky," consort of Gaia/Earth," castrated by his son Kronos, (*Il.* 1, 5) 24, 70, 78; (*Od.* 21) 446

P

Pallas (**pal**-as), an epithet for Athena, *passim*

Paphos (**pāf**-os), city in Cyprus, sacred to Aphrodite, (*Il.* 5) 67; (*Od.* 8) 315

Patroklos (pa-**trok**-los), son of Menoitios, Achilles' best friend, killed by Hector, 4; (*Il.* 1, 4, 6, 8, 9, 11, 12, 16, 18, 19, 21–24) *passim*; (*Od.* 8, 11, 13, 24) 316, 363, 364, 389, 475, 478

Pedasos (**pē**-da-sos), (1) a horse that Achilles stole from Thebes, killed in battle (*Il.* 6, 16) 89, 166; (2) a town near Mt. Ida (*Il.* 21) 205; (3) one of the towns that Agamemnon offers to Achilles, (*Il.* 9) 106

Peiraios (pē-**rē**-os), Achaean grandfather of Agamemnon's charioteer Eurymedon, (*Il.* 4) 59

Peirithoös (pē-**rith**-o-os), son of Zeus by Ixion's wife, king of the Lapiths, foe of the Centaurs, friend of Theseus, (*Il.* 1, 3, 14) 19, 41, 152; (*Od.* 11, 21) 370, 443

Peisenor (pē-**sē**-nor), grandfather of Eurykleia, (*Od.* 1) 264

Peleus (**pē**-lūs), grandson of Zeus, son of Aiakos, husband of Thetis, father of Achilles, (*Il.* 1, 4, 9, 11, 16, 18–24) *passim*; (*Od.* 5, 11, 24) 293, 363–365, 475, 476

Peloponnesus (pel-o-po-**nēs**-us), "island of Pelops," the southern portion of mainland Greece, linked to the north by the narrow Isthmus of Corinth, 12, 41, 57, 127, 152, 262, 280, 302, 321, 357, 367, 421, 436, 475

Pelops (**pē**-lops), son of Tantalus, father of Atreus and Thyestes, grandfather of Agamemnon and Menelaos, eponymous hero of the Peloponessus, (*Od.* 11) 367

Peneleos (pē-**nel**-e-os), an Achaean leader of the Boeotians, (*Il.* 16) 172

Perimedes (per-i-**mē**-dēz), one of Odysseus' companions, (*Od.* 11, 12) 352, 376

Periphas (**per**-i-fas), an Aetolian killed by Ares, (*Il.* 5) 76, 77

Persephonê (per-**sef**-o-nē), daughter of Demeter, wife of Hades, (*Il.* 9, 14) 110, 115, 152

Perseus (**per**-sūs), "destroyer (?)," son of Zeus and Danaë, beheaded Medusa, married Andromeda, founded Mycenae, (*Il.* 6, 14) 82, 152; (*Od.* 11) 370

Peteos (**pet**-e-os), father of the Athenian leader Menestheus, (*Il.* 12) 135

Phaeacia (fē-**āsh**-a), the island of Scheria, where Nausicaä lives, equated with Corcyra, (*Od.* 19) 424

Phaëthon (**fā**-e-thon), "shining," one of Dawn's two horses, (*Od.* 23) 471

Phaethousa (fā-e-**thu**-sa), "shining," one of the daughters of Helios put in charge of his cattle on
Thrinakia, (*Od.* 12) 374

Pheidon (**fē**-don), king of the Thresprotians who hosted Odysseus, (*Od.* 19) 425

Phemios (**fēm**-i-os), "the famous one," an oral poet who sang for the suitors, (*Od.* 1, 17, 22) 256,
262, 408, 459

Philoitios (fil-**oi**-ti-os), "desirable fate," cowherd who helps Odysseus kill the suitors, (*Od.* 19, 21, 22)
434, 440, 441, 445, 455, 457, 459

Phocis (**fō**-sis), region in central Greece where Delphi is located (*Od.* 11, 19) 367, 427

Phoinix (**fē**-niks), 187; (1) tutor to Achilles (*Il.* 9, 16, 18, 19), 102, 103, 110, 116, 117, 167, 168, 196;
(2) king of Tyre, father to Europa, (*Il.* 14) 152

Phorkys (**for**-kis), an ancient sea-god, son of Pontos and Gaia, father of the monster Skylla,
(*Od.* 1, 13) 254, 386, 392

Phrixus (**frik**-sus), son of Athamas and Nephelê, brother of Hellê, escaped on the back of a golden
ram, (*Od.* 5) 294

Phrygia (**frij**-a), region in Asia Minor east of the Troad, (*Il.* 3, 24) 43, 48, 240; (*Od.* 11) 367

Phthia (**thī**-a), region in southern Thessaly, home of Achilles (*Il.* 1, 9, 11, 16, 19, 23) 15, 16, 105,
108–111, 128, 161, 169, 195, 196, 230, 232; (*Od.* 11) 363

Phyleus (**fil**-ūs), father of Meges, the leader of the Epeians, (*Il.* 16) 171

Pieria (pi-**er**-i-a), "fat," region in Thessaly near Mt. Olympus, home of the Muses, where the gods
land when coming down from Olympos, (*Il.* 14) 148; (*Od.* 5) 283

Pittheus (**pit**-thūs), king of Troezen, host to Aegeus, father of Aithra, (*Il.* 3) 41

Plakos (**plā**-kos), a mountain in the Troad, (*Il.* 6, 22) 89, 90, 227

Pleuron (**plu**-rōn), a town in Aetolia, (*Il.* 9) 112

Podaleirios (pod-a-**lēr**-i-os), son of Asklepios, brother of the physician Machaon, (*Il.* 11, 16) 131, 175

Polites (pol-**ī**-tēz), a companion of Odysseus, (*Od.* 10) 341

Polyphemos (pol-i-**fēm**-os), "much famed," 6; (1) a Lapith prince (*Il.* 1) 19; (2) the Cyclops blinded
by Odysseus, (*Od.* 1, 6, 9, 13) 254, 310, 330–332, 386, 392

Pontonoös (pon-**ton**-o-os), Phaeacian herald, (*Od.* 13) 385

Poseidon (po-**sīd**-on), son of Kronos and Rhea, god of the sea, 6; (*Il.* 1, 2, 5, 8, 12–15, 20) 24, 35, 70,
100, 132, 141–144, 146, 154, 155, 202; (*Od.* 1, 4–6, 8, 9, 11, 13, 23, 24) *passim*

Poulydamas (po-li-**dā**-mas), prominent Trojan fighter who repeatedly warns Hector against rash
action, (*Il.* 22) 214

Priam (**prī**-am), king of Troy, son of Laomedon, husband of Hekabê, father of Hector and Paris, 5;
(*Il.* 1–6, 9, 11–13, 15, 16, 18, 19, 21–24) *passim*; (*Od.* 5, 8, 11, 13, 22, 24) 282, 286, 317, 362, 364,
365, 392, 456, 475

Proitos (**prē**-tos), king of Tiryns, father of the Proetids, whose wife attempted to seduce
Bellerophon, (*Il.* 6) 81, 83

Propontis (prō-**pon**-tis), sea between the Aegean and the Black Sea (= Sea of Marmara), 141

Protesilaos (pro-tes-i-**lā**-os), son of Iphiklos, first man to die at Troy, (*Il.* 15, 16) 159, 170

Proteus (**prō**-tūs), shapeshifting prophetic Old Man of the Sea, (*Od.* 1, 4, 13) 254, 275, 281, 386

Psychopompos (si-ko-**pom**-pos), "soul-guide" (see Hermes), (*Od.* 5) 284

Pylos (**pī**-los), Bronze Age settlement in the southwest Peloponnesus, kingdom of Nestor where
important archaeological remains have been found, 5; (*Il.* 1, 5, 9, 11) 19, 71, 106, 127; (*Od.* 1, 5, 6,
11, 13, 16, 21, 24) *passim*

Pyraichmes (pir-**ēk**-mēz), "fire-spear," Trojan ally, killed by Patroklos, (*Il.* 16) 170

Pyriphlegethon (pi-ri-**fleg**-e-thon), "river of fire," in the underworld, (*Od.* 10) 350

R

Rhadamanthys (rad-a-**man**-this), brother of Minos, judge in the underworld, (*Il.* 14) 152; (*Od.* 4) 281

Rhea (**rē**-a), a Titaness, wife of Kronos, (*Il.* 14) 147

Rhodes (rōdz), Aegean island near southwestern tip of Asia Minor, (*Il.* 11) 120

S

Salamis (**sal**-a-mis), island near the port of Athens, (*Od.* 4) 278

Samê (**sa**-mē), "hill," one of the Ionian islands, later called Kephallenia, (*Od.* 1, 9, 16, 19) 259, 319, 399, 402, 419

Sarpedon (sar-**pēd**-on), grandson of Bellerophon, Lycian prince, ally of Troy, killed by Patroklos, (*Il.* 5, 6, 12, 16) 61, 79, 83, 134–138, 172, 175–179

Satnioeis (sat-**ni**-o-ēs), a river in the Troad, (*Il.* 21) 205

Scaean (**skē**-an), "left" or "western" gates, the principal gate at Troy, (*Il.* 3, 6, 9, 11, 16, 22) 41, 84, 86, 89, 90, 108, 124, 182, 212, 222

Scheria (**sker**-i-a), island of the Phaeacians, equated with Corcyra, 6; (*Od.* 5, 6, 9, 13) 283, 299, 324, 387

Semelê (**sem**-e-lē), daughter of Kadmos and Harmonia, beloved by Zeus, mother to Dionysus, destroyed by lightning, (*Il.* 14) 152

Sidon (**sī**-don), Phoenician city in the Levant, (*Il.* 6) 86; (*Od.* 13) 390

Simoeis (**sim**-o-ēs), a river in the Troad, (*Il.* 5, 12, 20) 74, 75, 132, 202

Sipylos (**sip**-i-los), mountain in Asia Minor, where Niobê was turned to stone, (*Il.* 24) 242

Sisyphos (**sis**-i-fos), son of Aiolos, punished in the underworld, 368–369 (*Il.* 6) 81; (*Od.* 11) 367

Skylla (**skil**-la), "puppy," many-headed monster who attacked Odysseus, 6; (*Od.* 12) 373–379, 382

Skyros (**skir**-os), island west of Euboea where Neoptolemos was raised, (*Il.* 9, 19) 117, 196; (*Od.* 11) 364

Solymi (**sol**-i-mē), a tribe of warriors in Lycia defeated by Bellerophon, (*Il.* 6) 83; (*Od.* 5) 293

Spercheios (sper-**kē**-os), a river in Thessaly, (*Il.* 1, 16, 23) 15, 167, 231, 232

Styx (stiks), "hate," a river in the underworld, (*Il.* 14, 15) 149, 155; (*Od.* 5, 10) 288, 350

T

Talthybios (tal-**thib**-i-os), the herald of Agamemnon, (*Il.* 1, 3, 4) 21, 22, 40, 58

Tantalos (**tan**-ta-los), an early king of Lydia who fed his son Pelops to the gods, one of the damned in the underworld, (*Il.* 24) 242; (*Od.* 11) 367, 369, 372

Taygetos (tā-**ig**-e-tos), "big," a mountain range between Messenia and Lacedaemon, (*Od.* 6) 302

Telamon (**tel**-a-mon), son of Aiakos, half-brother or friend of Peleus, father of Big Ajax and Teucer, (*Il.* 3, 4, 6, 9, 11, 12, 16, 18) 46, 55, 79, 90, 116–118, 137, 165, 190; (*Od.* 4, 11, 24) 278, 363, 365, 475

Telemachos (tel-**em**-a-kos), "far-fighter," son of Odysseus and Penelope, 5; (*Od.* 1, 4–6, 11, 13, 16, 17, 19, 21–24) *passim*

Temesa (**tem**-es-a), a town in southern Italy, a source of copper, (*Od.* 1) 257

Tenedos (**ten**-e-dos), an Aegean island near Troy, (*Il.* 1, 11, 13) 12, 25, 126, 143

Tethys (**tē**-this), a Titan, wife of Ocean, mother of the Oceanids, (*Il.* 14) 147, 151; (*Od.* 4) 281

Teucer (**tū**-ser), half-brother to Big Ajax, a great bowman, (*Il.* 12) 135, 137, 138

Theano (the-**an**-o), wife of Antenor and priestess of Athena, (*Il.* 6) 86

Thebes (thēbz), (1) principal city in Boeotia, unsuccessfully attacked by seven heroes, destroyed by their sons, (*Il.* 1, 14) 23, 152; (2) city in the Troad destroyed by Achilles, (*Il.* 5, 6, 22), 75, 84, 89, 90, 227; (3) capital of New Kingdom Egypt, (*Il.* 9) 102; (*Od.* 4) 266

Themis (**them**-is), "what is laid down," "law," a Titan, sponsors assemblies, (*Il.* 20) 200

Thersites (ther-**sīt**-ēz), the ugliest man who went to Troy, opposes Agamemnon, (*Il.* 2) 32–34

Theseus (**thē**-sūs), son of Poseidon and Aithra, killer of the Minotaur, consort of Ariadnê, (*Od.* 11) 370

Thetis (**the**-tis), a daughter of Nereus, wife of Peleus, mother of Achilles, 5; (*Il.* 1, 6, 9, 16, 18, 19, 23, 24) *passim*; (*Od.* 11, 24) 365, 478

Thrasymedes (thras-i-**mē**-dēz), a son of Nestor, (*Il.* 16) 171, 176

Thrinakia (thrin-**āk**-i-a), island where Helios kept his cattle, equated with Sicily, (*Od.* 11, 12, 19, 23) 356, 374, 424, 471

Thyestes (thī-**es**-tēz), son of Pelops, father of Aigisthos (Klytaimnestra's lover), brother of Atreus, 280; (*Od.* 4), 278

Tiresias (ti-**rēs**-i-as), blind prophet of Thebes, (*Od.* 10–12, 23) 350, 358, 363, 378, 471, 472

Titans (**tī**-tans), offspring of Ouranos and Gaia, the generation of the gods before the Olympians, 78, 99, 147, 149, 155; (*Il.* 14) 151

Tithonos (ti-**thōn**-os), brother of Priam, beloved of Dawn, given eternal life without eternal youth, (*Il.* 11) 118; (*Od.* 5, 11) 282, 364

Tityos (**tit**-i-os), tortured in the underworld by vultures because he attacked Leto, (*Od.* 11) 367

Tlepolemos (tlē-**pol**-e-mos), a son of Herakles, leader of the Rhodian contingent, (*Il.* 16) 174

Tritogeneia (trit-o-ghen-**ē**-a), an obscure epithet of Athena, (*Il.* 8, 22) 96, 217

Tros (trōs), eponymous founder of the Trojan race, son of Erichthonios, king of Troy, father of Ilos and Ganymede, (*Il.* 5) 64, 65

Tydeus (**tī**-dūs), son of Oineus, father of Diomedes, fought at Thebes, (*Il.* 5, 6, 8, 11, 16, 19) *passim*; (*Od.* 4) 271

Tyndareos (tin-**dar**-e-os), Spartan king, husband of Leda, (*Od.* 24) 482

X

xenia (ksen-**ē**-a), "guest friendship," the conventions that govern relationships between host and guest, 81, 160, 324, 326

Z

Zeleia (zel-**ē**-a), a city in the Troad, homeland of Pandaros, (*Il.* 4) 54